I0522749

A BRAND NEW WORLD

A BRAND NEW WORLD

THE SIMULACRUM · BOOK 1

Egathentale

Podium

All rights reserved. No part of this publication may be reproduced, stored in a retrieval system, or transmitted in any form or by any means electronic, mechanical, photocopying, recording, or otherwise without prior written permission from Podium Publishing.

This is a work of fiction. Names, characters, places, and incidents are either products of the author's imagination or used fictitiously. Any resemblance to actual events, locales, or persons, living, dead, or undead, is entirely coincidental.

Copyright © 2022 by Gábor Horváth

Cover design by Podium Publishing

ISBN: 978-1-0394-0986-6

Published in 2022 by Podium Publishing, ULC
www.podiumaudio.com

A BRAND NEW WORLD

PROLOGUE

"Are you sure?"

The question came from a voice dancing on the very edge of my hearing. It was barely audible yet somehow awfully loud at the same time, and its strange cadence stirred me right out of unconsciousness.

"Of course I'm certain!" snapped a second voice. It was just as ethereal as the first one, yet for some reason I couldn't help but find it more masculine than the previous speaker's. "I tell you, he got through!"

"Then where is he?" the first voice spoke again with a hint of alarm.

"How the hell should I know?" the gruff voice of the second speaker lashed out once again.

Interesting, I thought. For some reason, I felt that I was supposed to feel sympathy towards the first voice being menaced by the second one, but I couldn't. Why feel sympathy, though? It wasn't as if I knew either of them. Weird thought.

"Now, now. No need to shout." A new voice entered the fray with all the self-assurance of an adult chiding unruly children. "Are you sure he didn't bounce off?"

Her voice, for I was quite sure she was a woman, hinted at bemusement.

"Yes," came the somewhat uncertain answer from the first voice of ambiguous gender. For the sake of simplicity, I decided to start labeling the speakers, so I mentally tagged him as The Boy. Anyways, he continued by saying, "Five layers were circumvented, three pierced, one completely shattered."

"That's just nine. What about that special bottom layer of yours?" the latecomer asked, and by now she sounded weirdly familiar. It was probably the tone—a mix of sultriness, arrogance, and assumed superiority that made the small of my back itch.

The small of my back? I wondered. Somehow, saying that felt subtly wrong. Maybe it had something to do with my head feeling all fuzzy and detached from my senses.

Well, whatever. I christened her The Woman until further information was available.

"It was... completely erased," the Boy answered meekly. Then quietly added, "Sorry."

"You better be," scoffed the abrasive voice of The Man. By the way, that was his label. Yeah, my naming sense was boring but practical. "We've been planning this for ages and you blew it!"

"Tch-tch," the Woman clicked her tongue, and I could totally picture her wagging her finger disapprovingly while doing so. "Last time I checked, it was your job to make sure we knew where he was in case he broke through, yet I don't see you looking for him."

"W-well..." The Man shrank back for a moment, but then he quickly regained his attitude. "Yeah, I lost him, but it would've never even happened if he'd done his job, and—"

"Hey there, guys!" came a sudden exclamation from a newcomer entering the scene, her voice carrying enough enthusiasm for a whole cheerleading squad.

This time I was 101 percent sure that it was a young girl. As for her temporary label, The Girl was fitting enough. I was nothing if not consistent.

Wait. Now that I think about it, what was I, anyway...?

"What did I miss?"

"He's in," The Man answered curtly.

"He got through all those defenses?" chirped The Girl with childlike glee, finally tearing me away from my moment of existential musing. "He's goooood!"

"Yes, he is," The Woman, whom I pinpointed as the de facto leader of the group, uttered bitterly.

"Where is he now? Let me see!" The Girl yelled, and I could also hear some pitter-patter, so... maybe she was running around the place? What place? Where was this all taking place, anyway? And where was I? While I pondered on these things, The Girl's excitement was only met with an awkward silence.

"We don't know where he is. Not yet," The Boy stated, dispelling the silence and my train of thought at the same time.

"Really?" The Girl exclaimed and let out a jaunty little whistle. "Damn, he is *sooo* good!"

"What are we going to do now?" The Boy asked in a mousy voice, and for a few long seconds, the entire group fell silent.

"There's not much we can do now, is there?" The Woman at the helm finally said, her question clearly rhetorical. "We'll just have to wait for him to make the first move."

With that, the presence of the group slowly dissolved and... wait, presence? Was I actually feeling their presence all this time? I felt incredibly confused. Then, since there was nothing to see, hear, smell, touch, or taste, my consciousness slowly folded in on itself, and I drifted into what felt like sleep, still confounded and confuddled over what I'd just witnessed.

CHAPTER 1

PART 1

As far as mornings are concerned, this particular one wasn't so bad... once you overlooked the splitting headache, the whirling nausea, and the loud screaming of my alarm clock apparently hell-bent on waking the entire neighbourhood. Aside from those things, everything was just peachy.

For a few seconds I only grumbled under the sheets, but then I actually woke up properly, and I hit the off button with a swipe of hand fueled by the righteous fury of the sleep-deprived. After a long yawn, I groggily sat up in bed. Then promptly fell back down with a soft thud.

"Goddammit, what the hell was I doing last night...?" I mumbled while cradling my aching skull. For a moment or two, I almost felt relieved that I couldn't remember a thing. At least it spared me from the unavoidable onslaught of shame I knew was coming the moment my memory decided to start working properly. I could make some educated guesses. The answer probably involved booze, and based on the white-hot axe of agony planted between my lobes, a lot of it.

In the end, I decided to just lay in my bed for the next five minutes or so. I buried my steadily pounding head deep into the wildflower-scented pillows and delighted in whatever momentary relief a stray cynical thought could offer. After a while, conscious thought finally reasserted itself into the driving seat of my grey matter, and my mind's eye was soon flashing warning lights like my brain was some misshapen Christmas tree.

From the sheer force of bafflement, I somehow managed to get myself back into a sitting position, and gently massaged my temples. Panic steadily rose in the pit of my stomach all the same.

I couldn't remember a thing. Not just last night. I couldn't remember yesterday, or the one before that. By this point, cold sweat was trickling down my back like I was an igloo in the Sahara.

"What the...?" I mumbled, and panic began worming its way into my head at once. Whatever happened to me had to be drastic, as for a split second, I had a hard time recognizing my own voice. That was a sensation I could definitely forgo for the rest of my life. It might not have been *the* creepiest thing ever, but it was definitely up there.

I shook my head and sprang to my feet.

"Right. I still must be half asleep or something. Let's wait half an hour. If it's still a problem, then I'll panic."

Following that rationale, I decided to get a cold shower. If that wouldn't wake me up, nothing would. I threw the door of my room open and rushed towards the bathroom. I quickly realized, to my considerable relief, that I could find my way around the spacious family home with easy familiarity. If nothing else, my functional memory seemed to be in order.

With that reassuring thought, I opened the bathroom door and looked at my surroundings. A modest shower, a sink, and a shiny white washing machine tucked away in the corner, surrounded by blue tiled walls and floor. It was a simple and fairly typical setup as far as bathrooms were concerned, but at the same time distinctly—odd.

But why?

I let my brain wrack itself over the source of the abnormality while I peeled off my fancy blue pajamas. And I do mean fancy. It seemed like they were made of silk or something, and they fit me like they were tailor-made. Hell, they might as well have been, as far as I knew—which wasn't particularly far. They seemed brand new, a tiny observation that finally jogged the rusted cogs of my brain, just as I was about to take off my briefs.

It just didn't feel lived-in. The bathroom, I mean, not my briefs. Everything was squeaky clean. No, what is even cleaner than *squeaky?* Whatever it was, the bathroom was it. Not a speck of dust on the floor. No hint of scaling on the sink. It was like a daily cleaned room of a high-class hotel suite. It simply didn't agree with the homey atmosphere of the rest of the house.

Or... did it?

I pulled my underpants back up and glanced back into the corridor from whence I came. It wasn't as readily apparent, but on closer inspection, it appeared to be just as disturbingly clean as the bathroom...

Oh well, there must be some kind of rational explanation for that, right? But back on track: I was supposed to get a cold shower. I could think all about the quality of the house service once I shook off my current confusion over the huge empty space where my memories were supposed to be.

So I stepped through the bathroom door again, turned right, and then promptly froze dead in my tracks. In the mirror over the sink was a face I didn't recognize, staring back at me. He was a teenager, a high school student at best. His face was reasonably attractive, though I'll be the first to admit I'm not a good judge of these things, and his short brown bed-hair was sticking out in so many different and altogether unlikely directions, it brought Escher art to mind.

I instinctively reached out towards my scalp to comb through it with my fingers, only to freeze mid-motion. The realization finally sank in: It was me. Me. I was looking at my own bloody reflection, and I couldn't even recognize it!

I stood there dumbfounded for the next couple of seconds.

"All right..." I muttered as I let my hand fall. "I am going to freak out now."

PART 2

"Leonard Dunning," I rolled the words around in my mouth as if tasting them. "Leonard... Dunning..."

It still felt strange even after several repetitions. The name was both familiar yet subtly wrong at the same time. Worst of all, it was my own. At least according to the student ID card in my hand, that is. I threw the piece of plastic onto the pile of related papers and documents and sighed as I wrung cold water out of my wet hair using the fluffy blue towel draped over my shoulders.

After encountering my new reflection, I'd allowed myself four and a half minutes of freaking out, most of which I spent running around in the house, screaming at the top of my lungs. It was a strangely liberating experience, I must admit. Maybe I should do it from time to time, just for kicks. But back to the point: after that initial existential crisis, I somehow forced myself under the cold shower, which did calm me down and give me a number of insights. First and foremost, never take a cold shower ever again. Second, especially never take a cold shower with your underwear on and without any spares on hand. And, finally, if I had the time to panic, I might as well use it more constructively.

So I did just that. First, I proceeded to explore the entire house (after getting a dry set of undergarments, of course) and made a number of discoveries.

Discovery number one: It was a relatively spacious family home with two floors, three bedrooms, a living room, a pretty big kitchen, and the already explored bathroom. There was also a garage, but I couldn't find the keys for it, so I couldn't say whether it contained any vehicles or not.

Discovery number two: I was completely alone. I didn't really need to check the rooms to conclude that, as there was no way anyone would have ignored my incoherent screaming, but I did so anyway, just to be thorough.

No signs of anyone living here aside from me. The other bedrooms were furnished and the beds were set, once again giving a certain high-class hotel vibe to the place, but there were no actual signs of habitation. I did find a couple of framed photographs in the living room, but none showed any actual people. In fact, they looked like stock photos someone found on the internet and slapped them into some fancy frames.

Discovery number three: The fridge was stocked. Wieners, beans, sliced ham, fruit, extra-pasteurized milk, et cetera. It was like the residents were preparing for a zombie invasion. Hmm. Maybe that's the reason no one else was around? They were eaten by zombies. Housemaid zombies that cleaned up afterwards. Elementary, my dear Watson.

Jokes aside, being reminded of the fridge made the soft grumbling of my stomach slightly more pronounced. I sighed wearily as I stood up, throwing the damp towel onto the arm of the sofa, and proceeded to grab some light snacks and a bottle of Coke before returning to the table with my papers.

Right, the papers. There were a few discoveries related to them as well, only one of which was my apparent name. Leonard Dunning. I repeated it in my head again, and I still couldn't shake the sense of a distinct oddness out of the back of my skull. But moving on: I also discovered that I'd just turned seventeen, my blood type was AB negative, my apparently missing mother's maiden name was Jane Doe, and I was just starting my second year in high school. Speaking of which, I was apparently enrolled into Blue Cherry High, which sounded just as silly on second reading as it did on the first.

I also found some bank papers, according to which I had an account with over two and a half million Jen on it, with a monthly income of eighty thousand more transferred from my missing father's account. I would have been pretty happy about this if I'd known anything about how much that money was worth. For now, I decided to pretend I was rich until proven otherwise. Woohoo.

My next target of interest was the calendar on the wall. According to it, today was the first of September in the year 20XX. I would have probably been more surprised about the whole "20XX" thing under normal circumstances, but for the time being I decided to just roll with it. I also glanced aside and saw a large grandfather clock ticking away one second after the other. Looking at the time gave me a strange feeling in the pit of my stomach.

It slowly sank in. It was 8:43... That meant... Holy shit, I was late!

I whirled around, my legs ready to carry me away. Then my higher brain functions reasserted themselves and I froze mid-stride. Wait just a minute... What was I late for, again?

I glanced between the calendar and the papers on the table and the answer quickly presented itself: school, of course. It was the first of September and that meant a new school year with all the studying, friendships, romances, and other assorted bothers it implied. Which, as it happened, also covered all the things I didn't feel like shouldering at the moment. I mean, I'd just lost all my memories. Didn't that warrant cutting me some slack? Maybe skip a day or two? With that thought in mind, I turned around and headed for the sofa. However, the moment my heel touched the floor, a sudden headache assaulted my senses, and my knees almost buckled.

I began to curse and take another step, but to my shock and horror, I found myself turning around against my will. I steeled myself and halted again, only for the headache to nail another spike of agony into my hindbrain. My legs took another step, and I could feel panic well up in the pit of my stomach. What the hell is going on?

A head-splitting anguish ravaged my senses, yet I managed to put two and two together: Somehow my body was trying to get me to school, whether I consented or not. For a moment, I felt defiant. Like hell would I obey some kind of disembodied urge, just like that!

As if in reaction to my thoughts, a new spike of searing torment flashed between my ears. I nearly fell to my knees. For what felt like an eternity, I was completely lost in the waves of pain. I grabbed hold of the wall to keep myself from collapsing. This kind of pain wasn't normal. It was in my head, but at the same time it felt like my entire body was hurting, as if my perception narrowed into a small ball that represented the entirety of me and it was set on fire while being pummeled by a sledgehammer.

Then, right as the pain was at its most intense, a brand-new idea elbowed its way to the forefront of my stunned mind: Why did I want to avoid school again? As much of a bother as it could prove to be, getting in contact with other people might be my best bet for figuring out what was going on. Not to mention, what's wrong with studying, friendships, romances, and other assorted bothers anyways?

Nothing, I supposed. I closed my eyes and took a step, and before I knew it, I was climbing the stairs. By the time I reached the room where I'd woken up (my room, I supposed), the headache had all but disappeared. In its place, an intoxicating fog covered my thoughts, masking any residual pain and even making me slightly giddy. Adrenaline, I surmised. Then I promptly swept it right under the proverbial rug in one of the dusty (and currently quite empty) recesses of my mind. I would think about it later, I decided. For now, I should focus on getting my stuff together.

Like clothes. I had already inspected my wardrobes when I was looking for dry underwear, so I knew exactly where to find the uniforms. Yes, Blue Cherry High apparently had a uniform code. I took out a set and laid them on my bed. It consisted of a white shirt, a dark grey vest with matching trousers, a khaki jacket, and a black tie. While the colour choices were fairly unorthodox, overall it looked like a perfectly ordinary Japanese school uniform.

Japanese uniform, Jen allowance money... Was I in Japan? The yen and Jen weren't exactly the same, but it was close, and school uniforms were a stereotypically Japanese thing, weren't they? Some small corner of my mind questioned how I knew about Japan but not my own father's name. I told it to hush up, and congratulated myself on my deduction. It wasn't perfect, though. I mean, if this was Japan, why did the new school year start in the autumn instead of the spring? Not to mention, I was fairly certain I wasn't Asian.

I shook my head and exhaled sharply. Later. I'll think about these things later. For now, I should focus on getting my bearings and hauling my ass to school. There I'd have the entire day to ponder.

With that in mind, I swiftly got dressed, though finding socks proved to be a bit of a challenge. I mean, who puts socks on the top shelf in a wardrobe, anyways? Bah.

Grabbing my school bag, I headed for the entrance, only stopping by the living room to get my student ID and wallet. I left the papers lying on the table. Unless my absent parents happened to get back before me (which I sincerely doubted considering the state of the house), I'd gather them up in the afternoon.

I got outside and locked the door behind me with practiced motions. Weird.

No idea how I knew the key was in my school bag's side pocket, but I did. Before I knew it, it was in my hand. I shook my head to chase away the fog dulling my thoughts. It didn't really help, so I just shrugged and made sure the door was locked before slipping the key away. With that, I turned around and took my first good look at the neighbourhood.

My house... or rather, the house where I woke up... was one of several cookie-cutter buildings lining the street near an intersection. All white-walled, red-roofed family homes, with small backyards and their entrances opening almost directly to the sidewalk.

Speaking of sidewalks, the hilly street was eerily silent. Aside from the distant and strangely repetitive sounds of traffic with some ambient birdcalls sprinkled on top, there was nothing else to hear. Or see, if we were at that. During my uneventful commute to Blue Cherry High, I didn't encounter a single soul. To be fair, it only took me about fifteen minutes on foot to reach the school gates, and most of that was spent on backstreets and the occasional shortcut through a narrow alley between buildings, but even then, I should've met someone. Right?

Not only were there no people, but there were no signs of life—no cars, no pets... No birds that were supposedly singing from somewhere. No trash or dirt on the roadside either. There weren't even weeds in the cracks, because there weren't cracks to be found in the pristine sidewalks. Normally I might not have noticed all this, but my prior experiences with the spotless house had already primed me. The city management must have been filled with neat freaks. Or... maybe my zombie maid hypothesis wasn't so implausible after all?

Anyways, since there was nothing to see and no one to talk to, and especially since I had no idea where I was going and instead just let my legs carry me (they sure knew the way better than I did), I decided to rummage through my school bag to pass the time. Not much to see there, either. A few notebooks. Pens and other assorted writing utensils. An overdue library book titled *Legends of the British Isles* with a bookmark at King Arthur and his round table. Nothing to write home about.

My final find, however, was quite surprising. In fact, it was so unusual that I didn't even recognize it for a moment. It was a phone. One of those "dumbphones," and an older model at that. The kind you could use to clobber someone over the head without even denting it. The phone, that is. I wouldn't guarantee the same about the person's skull. After some further fiddling, I figured out how to turn off the key lock (just who the hell thought pressing down asterisk for three seconds and then pressing the off button made any kind of sense?), I looked up my contact list. Sadly, it turned out to be a bit of a disappointment.

It only contained one name: Joshua Bernstein. I'd expected to find at least a few numbers, like my parents'. My call history wasn't helpful, either. Aside from this Joshua fellow, there was only one other call from some random number. Maybe that was one of my parents' numbers, after all? I decided to try giving it a call later. For now, I simply saved it in my phone book under the name *Mystery Number X*.

It was around this time that I reached the school gates. I slid the phone back into my bag and took a good look at Blue Cherry High. It was a fairly underwhelming sight, to be honest. A large blocky building painted in a fairly neutral shade of blue with large white windowsills. To no one's surprise, it also looked just as pristine as everything else I'd encountered since I'd woken up.

I was still observing its flat, fenced roof—no doubt one of those stereotypical ones where students would go during lunch breaks to engage in embarrassing romantic escapades—when I was startled by the clear ringing of a bell. Was the first period already over? While I mused on that question, I was startled once more as the metal gate in front of me soundlessly slid aside. I blinked at the now open gate and tentatively looked around the high white brick wall. My eyes met with those of a guy about my age. He wore the same uniform as I did, except for the bright red armband around his upper arm. While his build was fairly balanced, his face was gaunt and his small spectacles made his eyes look sunken.

Our eyes met, but he only gave me a blank look, so we just stared at each other for a while. Whatever he thought of my late arrival was beyond my ability to decipher. In fact, he seemed to be completely still, like a wax statue. Was he even breathing?

At last, I gave him a small nod and, to my relief, he returned the gesture, though with a small but noticeable delay. Whether it was because of consideration or confusion, I didn't know and didn't care. Instead, I muttered some half-hearted greeting under my breath and picked up the pace towards the main entrance.

On the other side of the wide glass doors, I found another staple of the Japanese education system: shoe lockers. Maybe I *was* in Japan after all. Perhaps as a transfer student. That would explain a few things, but not enough to make sense of my situation. While pondering that, my body took me to my locker, and I put on the dark grey indoor shoes without a hitch. And the shoes? Brand new, too.

I locked up my street shoes and headed for the classroom. I had no idea which one, so I just set my legs cruising and hoped for the best. Hey, it'd worked for me this far, hadn't it? And before you ask, yes, the interior of the school building was just as immaculate as, well, everything else. By the time I reached the third floor, the other students had begun to pour out of the classrooms, filling the hallways with dull steps.

Looking around pretty much torpedoed my idea of this being Japan. While some of the faces looking back at me were kinda-sorta Asian, the vast majority seemed to have an amalgamation of features that made it impossible to get any more specific than "light-skinned" when talking about them. Well, saying that they were "looking back at me" might be a bit of an overstatement. While everyone present acted like high-school students on break, there was something odd about them. Their eyes seemed to be glazed over, and even when talking to someone right beside them, usually pursuing some shallow topic, their gazes were distant and unfocused. The pinnacle of the oddness was how, if I looked at any one of them for too long, it felt like they weren't really there, just occupying space. It was crazy. Or maybe

I was the crazy one for even thinking something like that. Neither option thrilled me.

But back to the others... Another peculiar detail I quickly noticed was the lack of different body types. Boys generally had wide shoulders and were about a head taller than girls. The girls, on the other hand, were fairly short, slim, and moderately pretty. No, scratch the "moderately" part. There wasn't a single unattractive one among them.

On second thought, though, if you were to take any one of the students out of the context and looked at them on their own, everyone was quite attractive. Once you threw them back into the mix, however, they all looked like a single monotonous blob of pure indistinctiveness. I wasn't even sure I could tell them apart if I had to.

Furthermore, while they didn't look exactly the same, I couldn't help but feel that the variation was only superficial. Everyone was moderately handsome, as if cut from the same mold and then tweaked afterwards. If not for the different hair styles and colours (which included a number of technicolour shades as well), I would've sworn this was a school dedicated to the education of clones.

I wondered how I could fit this new pile of information into my zombie maid apocalypse hypothesis when my train of thought was interrupted by my legs abruptly halting in front of a classroom. "3-C," or at least that's what the sign said over the open sliding door. I'd finally arrived. I took a deep breath to steel myself and stepped through. The classroom was just like everything else: immaculate, bland, and filled with odd people. It triggered no memories either. I let out my breath in a disappointed sigh and took a closer look from the doorway.

There was not much to say about the classroom. Rows of desks, a blackboard, a pair of storage lockers at the back... the usual stuff. Not much to say about my apparent classmates either. They looked only slightly less uniform and vacant than everyone else, but that didn't say much. My eyes circled around the room and I honestly felt like I could see through them. That is, until my eyes met *his*.

He was sitting at his desk by the windows at the far end of the room, looking right at me. I gave him a quizzical look in response, and he suddenly smiled. The first overt human expression I'd witnessed since my memories began, aka since this morning. It made me shiver with what I thought was a mix of excitement and relief. Before I even knew it, my legs were taking me towards him, and this time, I didn't mind their independent action.

"Yo!" he raised a hand in a lazy wave and flashed a knowing grin. "You've got balls, skipping the entrance ceremony like that."

He had a carefree expression and his alert eyes struck me as alive compared to the dull gazes I'd encountered thus far. His short dark hair was in stark contrast to his pale white skin, yet he didn't seem sickly. If anything, he looked just the opposite, a human-shaped bundle of health and energy. He wasn't wearing his khaki jacket and the flaps of his shirt poked out under his grey vest in what seemed less like lazy dressing and more like a deliberate fashion choice.

"I... had some problems in the morning," I replied tentatively, and his face tensed visibly upon hearing my words. Did I know him? Judging by his tone, I probably did.

"Are you all right?" He sounded concerned.

Crap, that somehow made me feel guilty.

"Eh," I answered with forced nonchalance as I reflexively dropped my bag onto the desk next to his. Huh, so this was my seat. I suppose that explained how I knew him. After some consideration, I added, "Just a mild case of retrograde amnesia."

His face went blank, then he let out a tired sigh.

"And here you had me almost worried. You shouldn't joke about things like that," he grumbled.

"I'm not," I quickly protested. Now that I thought about it, broaching the subject like that really did sound like a joke. What was I thinking?

"Sure," he rolled his eyes. "Friendly advice, though—don't try that excuse with Angie. She's mad enough at you already for skipping, don't throw more fuel onto the fire."

"Angie?"

If I sounded confused, it's probably because I was. I really couldn't follow what he was saying. He sighed again.

"Do you really want to keep going at it? Fine, be my guest. Just let me get out of the crossfire when the time comes, okay? You already got me into hot water today, I don't want to get any deeper. How was I supposed to know where you were, anyway?" He kept grumbling until he noticed my expression, at which point he gave me an inquisitive look. I used the momentary silence to interject a simple question.

"Can I ask you just one thing?"

"Shoot." He shrugged.

"Who are you?"

His eyes opened wide as saucers, and he finally sat straight and looked me in the eye. "You *are* joking, right?" I shook my head as solemnly as I could manage under the circumstances and his face went even paler than it already was by default. "You cannot be serious... It's me, Joshua!" The moment the words left his mouth, his eyes narrowed and he sent me a suspicious squint. "Wait, this isn't one of your dumb pranks, is it?"

"What pranks?"

"The ones you are pulling all the time."

"I wouldn't know, I can't remember a thing."

He paused for a second and gave me another dubious look.

"You are really freaking me out right now. I swear to god, if you're just pulling my leg, I will punch you."

I rolled my eyes. "I'm not a... PC?" I paused and I could feel my brows knit. "Wait, what?"

That made no sense. What was the connection between him punching me and being a computer? Suddenly a small tugging sensation in a corner of my mind got the words stuck in my throat. There was an idea embedded in that tug, something about lost memories and RAM and computers and hitting them to fix them and... That made no bloody sense! That was not even a joke, just a complete non sequitur! Why the hell would I—?

I let out an involuntary hiss. The morning's headache was back with a vengeance. A searing spike of agony shot through my skull, and I had to grab my desk to stop myself from toppling over. I gritted my teeth and tried to straighten my posture, but it only made my legs shake even harder.

"Hey! Are you okay?" Joshua's voice sounded distant. My brain was too busy processing the pain to bother formulating an answer. I forcefully inhaled and exhaled, trying to focus on the cadence of my breath instead of the pain. It helped a little, but in the end, it was just a broom pushing back against an ocean. The headache, along with the urge to say something completely stupid, kept getting stronger and stronger, and with it, my field of vision slowly narrowed into a grey tunnel.

Then there was a new thought in my head, popping out of the pain-filled mist like a flash of lightning.

Just say it. Just go along with whatever compels you. Like in the morning. Going to school made the pain go away. Just say your piece and it will be all over.

Right, that'll work, I conceded. I could try to explain it later. Rationalize it. Later. I swallowed hard, and in a moment of weakness, I opened my mouth... But then another thought rose to the surface of my conscious mind like a giant bubble, and it popped with a thundering roar of indignation.

Like hell I was going to go along! No bleeding voice in my head was going to make me do something that dumb, even if that voice was mine! With a growl, I snapped my mouth shut and a sharp pain blew some of the haze over my mind away, leaving me with the taste of metal in my mouth.

Guess I'd bitten my tongue. I quickly relaxed my jaw and blinked. Joshua was still in his seat and looking concerned. Meeting his gaze made the headache surge again, so I just shook my head.

"I have to get out of here," I muttered.

He reached after me, but his words didn't register. I could feel a faint tug on my jacket, but I got loose and bolted out of the classroom, each step feeling like I was wading through deep water as I ran down the hallway. Students left and right turned hollow gazes in my direction, only to return to whatever they were doing beforehand the moment I was gone.

I ran and ran without direction. There was a wheezing sound in my ears, and it took me a while to realize it was my own breathing. My legs felt heavy and the pain in my head kept a beat with my frantically thumping heart. By this point, the initial compelling thoughts were gone, only to be replaced by an urge to return to the classroom before the next lesson started. "Screw that," I muttered half-deliriously as I ran down another hallway. I'd completely lost my sense of direction, just running for the sake of running.

I needed a place. Somewhere safe. Away from the classroom, the headache, and the crazy thoughts that were mine but somehow weren't. A place like... "The roof," I gasped for air as I stopped by the stairwell and leaned against the wall for a moment. Yes, the roof would do. There would be no one there until lunch. I could think there without being bothered. Maybe the fresh air would help.

I gathered my strength and began scaling the stairs, two steps at a time. My legs felt weak and the pain in my head made my stomach twist. I pushed the sensations away and continued climbing. The roof, I just had to get to the roof...

And that was when I slipped. In retrospect, running up the stairs while barely being able to stand was probably not the brightest idea. I could feel my center of gravity slowly shifting backwards, but my feverish mind was still too preoccupied with thoughts of getting to the roof to register the danger. Then, just as I finally realized the direness of the situation, my vision blurred and I felt like I was floating in the air.

I didn't even have time to be surprised. A blink of an eye later, my back hit the hard concrete tiles and drove the breath out of me, which I barely noticed as my head hit the floor right after that. For the first time in my life, I understood what people meant when they said they saw stars. The violent bursts of light dancing on my eyelids made me momentarily forget the pain and nausea. It didn't last, and soon pain flooded my senses again.

I groaned and instinctively cradled my head in my arms, which only made the nausea even worse. Now that I had a comparison, I had to conclude that my headache was unnaturally sharp, to the point it made the recent blunt force trauma feel positively diffused and manageable. For some time, I lay on the ground in a fetal position, holding my head, until the nausea subsided. Then I noticed something. There was a faint wind. Not only that, I could feel the sun on my skin.

It took some effort to get my eyes open. The sight before me was baffling. I was on the roof. The surprise and confusion probably amounted to a small adrenaline burst, as the pain momentarily abated and I could sit up with relative ease and gaze at the morning skyline. There was no question about it; I was indeed on the roof.

But how? Last I remembered, I was running up the stairs, and the next moment I was here. I shook my head, which in retrospect turned out to be a bad idea. The movement almost made me empty my stomach.

Great, it seemed like I not only had retrograde amnesia, but I also had empty spots in recent memories, as well. That, or the head trauma made me blank out.

After sitting still for a few more minutes, I carefully rose to my feet. I felt unsteady and weak and my legs were burning. I was more or less right in the middle of the roof, so I decided to move to one of the benches by the nearest corner, and plopped down with a weary sigh.

The headache wasn't going away, but at least it didn't worsen either. How's that for a silver lining? Thankfully whatever urge was tugging at my strings was mostly absent, though I couldn't help but find myself thinking about going back to the classroom at regular intervals. I sighed again and gazed at the clouds.

There wasn't much else I could do. I originally wanted to get to the roof to avoid the classroom and to give me some space to think. The former was accomplished all right, but I simply couldn't think straight with the pain pulsing in my brain and coating everything in a red haze. I rubbed my forehead and then the lump on the back of my head, which had swollen considerably. It didn't help.

But then again, why was I suffering like this? If only I went back to the classroom...

"No..."

Right. There is no point to this. I came out here think, but that's impossible to do right now. I should just go back to the classroom...

"No."

Classes are about to start, anyway. I shouldn't skip any more classes, or she will be mad at me...

"I don't even know who 'she' is!"

I should just get going and...

"I said NO!"

My legs were about to move on their own again, but in the last second, I hijacked their movement, grabbed hold of the fence with both hands, and smashed my forehead against the thick metal pole upholding it. There was a loud, echoing thud. I couldn't tell whether it came from the pole or from my head, but either way, it momentarily filled my vision with sparks again and cleared my mind of the involuntary thoughts. The pain receded like water being tossed aside by an impact, but then it came flooding back with a vengeance.

"No!" I yelled accompanied by another headbutt. "I am not going anywhere! I've had enough of this headache, enough of these thoughts, and especially enough of this entire amnesia bullshit!" I kept shouting, punctuating my words with headbutts over and over. It was strange. The more my forehead hurt and my eyes flared, the more the headache receded. It was as if it was being pushed back, one strike at a time.

Finally, on my last hit, something broke. I didn't know how, but I just knew it. At first, I was afraid it might have been my skull, but the crackling, screeching sound filling my ears was more like a trailer full of champagne glasses getting crushed by a bulldozer. The world shifted. Formless colours danced in my vision, and it took all my willpower to hold on to the fence. My fingers turned purple with the effort. I only distantly registered that I began emptying my stomach. Acid burned my throat.

At last, just as the pain and nausea and noise and lights reached a crescendo, it all stopped. So suddenly that I reeled back from the fence and fell on my butt. The urge and the headache were both gone, only to be replaced by a different headache and a welling nausea.

My forehead hurt like hell, and the back of my head was sore too, but it all felt quite pleasant compared to my previous experiences. My fingers, on the other hand, felt much more uncomfortable. The way I held on to the fence etched deep marks into them and they were turning purple, sending jolts of pain through my hands whenever I moved them.

"Well, that's going to get more uncomfortable later. Joy."

That said, I still fished out a handkerchief from my jacket's inner pocket (I think it came with the uniform) and wiped my mouth. Since I only had some snacks for breakfast, the puddle in the corner of the roof consisted entirely of stomach acid, and the concrete tiles already drank up most of it. That was one thing off my mind, at least.

I put the hankie away and tried to get up, but my legs felt like they were made of jelly. I strained for a while, but only managed to get myself queasy again. Guess I might've given myself a concussion with that little stunt with the fence post. Go figure.

I decided to lie down for a while, at least until the world stopped spinning. The concrete was surprisingly warm and, most importantly, solid. I never knew how reassuring firm ground can be. So, there I was, skipping classes on the roof under the warm autumn sun. And the best part of it? No pesky random thoughts trying to convince me to go anywhere. Pure bliss.

In the distance, the bell rang, signifying the start of the second period. I couldn't care less. I felt warm and giddy and my eyelids were made of lead... I closed them and the nausea receded. Ah. I think I should stay like this for a while. Just for a few more seconds...

CHAPTER 2

PART 1

I opened my eyes again and had to blink in surprise. Where did those clouds come from? I blinked again, and by then my brain had gathered enough momentum to realize that the sun had also wandered away from the horizon. Evidently I'd fallen asleep for a while. I tried to sit up to check the time and then had to brace myself to keep from falling back down.

My head was throbbing like crazy. If I had to give it a numeric value, it was a solid seven-point-eight on the just-kill-me-already scale. In other words—quite pleasant compared to what I'd already endured in the morning. I reached for my forehead and hissed in surprise as my fingers brushed against the big lump on it. Oh, right. I'd been hitting my head against a fence post.

"Why did I think that'd be a good idea?" I mumbled a tad wryly as I gently rubbed the bump. Actually, there were at least three of them, all so close to each other they might as well have been a single gigantic one. Oh well, at least this time I knew where the pain was coming from. That somehow made it more tolerable.

I couldn't say the same about the nausea, though. It generally just smoldered in the background when I didn't move, only to flare up with a vengeance whenever I tried to get up. Probably had something to do with the concussion and the inner ear canals and all that crap. I sighed and decided to lie back down, only to let out another hiss the moment I touched the ground. Right, I had a bump on the back, too. How careless of me.

I rested one arm under my head and the other over my eyes, and for the first time since I'd arrived at school, I felt like my thoughts were clear. As a matter of fact, my mind felt as sharp as a freshly edged knife, at least compared to how it operated before. Strange, I thought. I didn't notice it at the time, but I was on autopilot all morning ever since...

I frowned into my forearm. Right, it all started with that headache when I noticed I was late for school. Everything after that was covered in a fine mist of dull compliance. The more I thought about it, the more bizarre my earlier behaviour appeared. My body had moved on its own, and I'd just dismissed it as my legs remembering what I'd forgotten. How dumb.

Speaking of which, was I still missing my memories? In most stories, getting hit on the head again usually solved one's amnesia. If that is even remotely how it works, after my little stunt with the fence post, I should remember even my future by now.

… Nope. Still blank. I tried to recall my mother's face but the huge pile of nothing I got in return almost made me reconsider whether I even had a mother in the first place. Wow, I had it bad. Same deal with my father. Speaking of which, I couldn't even remember his name, though I think I'd spotted it when I was looking at my financial papers.

I should write it down somewhere once I get back home.

What else? Well, there's that guy… what was his name again?… It started with a J or G… Actually, now that I thought about it, I realized he was the only entry in my phone book. Too bad I couldn't check it, as I'd left my phone in my bag. And my bag in the classroom.

Gritting my teeth at the mere thought of the classroom, I waited for the headache to come. It didn't. I sighed in relief.

Good, that crap was getting old, anyway.

Then, "Joshua! That's his name!" I let out a contented little chuckle. At least my short-term memory was more or less still in working order, if a bit laggy.

There was another name though, someone he mentioned. I think I was supposed to know who he was talking about. A common acquaintance, maybe?

I think her name had something to do with angels. Or engines. Or maybe engineers? Angelica? Angela? Angelina? I couldn't recall, but to my surprise, there was another thing I couldn't recall either, namely her face.

Normally this would have been no surprise, with the amnesia and all, but it made me realize that I actually had a hazy picture of her in my mind. I couldn't really say anything specific about her, though. Her face was barely more than a blur, but I think her hair was brown… maybe auburn-ish? I wasn't even sure about that. What really surprised me was that, though I couldn't really describe her, I felt confident I'd recognize her if I came across her on the street. I couldn't help but wonder what it said about me that I could remember her but not my parents…

I stretched a little. My neck was getting sore from lying on the concrete for too long, so I carefully set both my arms under my head to put it into a more comfortable position. This of course meant that I had to uncover my eyes, which once again reminded me that the sun was up pretty high in the sky. I was just about to wonder about the time when my concerns were preemptively answered by the soft chime of the bell. It was a variation on the classic Big Ben theme and it ran for quite long.

To my surprise, this fact actually jogged a memory. I pursued it, grabbed hold of it, and finally recalled it: a long chime meant lunch break. I couldn't help but smile. There might be hope for me yet.

Before long, there was a quiet rattle from the direction of the stairwell and the door to the roof opened without a creak, letting the students pour outside. Well, "pour" might have been too strong of a word. It was more half-hearted meandering than anything else. They arrived mostly in ones and twos, with the occasional smaller group every now and then.

Though I wasn't exactly surprised by it after my mad dash through the school grounds, the way they completely ignored me still made me a bit uncomfortable. Maybe people lying on their backs on the roof with huge bumps on their heads were a common sight around these parts? No, I sincerely doubted that. They weren't just uninterested or ignoring me, they simply looked through me like I wasn't even there. Hell, one girl almost stepped on me until she twitched and swerved to the right in the last moment. She didn't look at me even then.

I wasn't in the mood to tempt fate and get trampled by accident, but all my attempts at getting up were vetoed hard by my viciously spinning vision. In the end, I reached a compromise by placing my arms under me and raising my torso a little. I probably looked pretty stupid, like a fully clothed sunbather, but I honestly couldn't care less even if I tried.

From my new vantage point of about... let's say, thirty centimeters off the ground, I took a better look at the steadily increasing number of students occupying the roof. Most did nothing even remotely interesting, or anything at all if we were at that. There was this one guy in particular who just stood by the fence and stared into the distance with unblinking eyes. He was so motionless, I wondered if he even had a pulse.

Not far from him, a girl sat, eating a sandwich. Or at the very least that's what it looked like. Sure, she kept raising it to her mouth from time to time with mechanical motions, but the sandwich didn't seem to get any smaller no matter how long I was looking.

"For Christ's sake, girl, take a proper bite!" I murmured under my breath, and to my shock, she looked over at me. For a few moments, we looked each other in the eye as I wondered whether she'd heard me, but then she blinked once and returned to her food as if nothing happened.

Well crap, that was unnecessarily intense.

Though... on a second look, maybe she *was* taking bigger bites.

Nah, probably just my imagination.

Moving on, my next objects of interest were two boys sitting on a nearby bench. What made them remarkable was not what they were talking about (it was something about the local soccer team), but how they were talking about it. Saying that their conversation went in circles was an understatement. They literally repeated the same ten or so lines over and over again. It really made me want to get up just to walk over and see if I could jog them out of the loop, but before I could even try, my attention was drawn by a loud voice.

"There you are!"

The new voice entering the fray made me twitch, cutting through the murmurs I was focusing on like a hot-knife-analog through the butter-analog. I followed it to the source, and I found Joshua standing by the stair-well door, looking quite disgruntled.

"Hey, Josh." My voice sounded more strained than I intended but better than I feared it would be. The dubious look on his face only got worse as he walked over to my sprawled body.

"What the hell happened to you?" He sounded half concerned and half outraged, especially after he took a good look at my face. His pale skin seemed to glow under the noon sunlight, making the furrows on his forehead even more prominent. "First you babble about amnesia, then you nearly collapse, and now I find you on the rooftop like this! Please tell me you really are sick, or I swear to god I'll kick you."

"Kinda," I answered weakly. "Could you help me up first? My legs are in a rebellious phase."

The look on his face was still critical, but he helped me to my feet, and I managed to stand on my own without collapsing again. Progress!

"What happened to your forehead?"

"I had a bit of a disagreement with myself and used one of the fence posts to accentuate my arguments."

Joshua's face twitched in a grimace.

"Let me guess. You won."

"Of course I did." I smiled as I plopped down onto a bench. Joshua followed my example.

"So, about your amnesia..." He suddenly sounded a bit less collected than before. I couldn't blame him; it wasn't a sentence anyone would have expected to say.

"Oh, that?" I waved a hand. "I still can't remember squat, but I'll manage."

"You are serious," he stated rather than asked.

That was good. It meant I had no more convincing to do. I looked him in the eye and nodded sharply.

"Damn, that's messed up."

"Tell me about it." I surprised even myself by how cynical I sounded. Standing up probably made the blood rush to my head.

"What did the nurse say?"

"What nurse?"

The critical look instantly returned to Josh's face.

"The school nurse, who else?"

"Oooooh, that nurse..." I nodded sagely. "I dunno. I didn't see her."

"It's him, and—what do you mean you didn't see him? Where've you been, then?"

I gave him a decently executed wry eyebrow raise and opened my arms.

"You can have three guesses."

Joshua's eyebrows rose in a perplexed arc. "The roof?"

"Ding-ding. That is correct."

"But... but the roof is only opened during lunchtime! How did you get up here?"

I was about to open my mouth for yet another snappy retort, but I froze midway.

"That is... actually a very good question," I told him while scratching my chin. "How the hell *did* I get up here?"

"You are kidding, right?" He gave me a deadpan look and, to my sincerest surprise, he managed to look even more dubious. "Is it your amnesia again?"

"No, no." I shook my head lightly, though it still made me a bit dizzy. "This is completely unrelated."

"Whatever." Josh leaned back on the bench and looked at the sky before returning his gaze to me. "So, what now? Are you going to the hospital?"

"I suppose I should," I replied uncertainly. That was without a doubt the logical thing to do. "Where is the closest hospital, anyways?"

"That is your first question today that's made any sense."

"Why?"

My query apparently threw him for a loop, just as he was about to sound more confident. "I suppose it's because you just transferred, so you probably don't know your way around yet."

"Wait, I'm a transfer student after all?!" I hastily toned down my unintentionally raised voice and looked around. No one seemed to mind, so I continued, "When did I transfer?"

"A few weeks before the end of the first year."

"Really? From where?"

"Overseas."

"Just... overseas?"

"Yes."

"I see..."

I nodded sharply, mostly to myself, though I quickly regretted it after the nausea kicked in. So, I *was* a transfer student in this Japanese-style school, after all. Maybe I should trust my instincts more. That said, Joshua was right about one thing: before anything else, I needed some professional help ASAP. "So again, where's the closest hospital?"

"Two blocks down the park, near the old shopping district. Big white building, hard to miss it."

I gave Joshua a sardonic glare and groaned.

"Dude, I can't remember anything! What am I supposed to do with landmarks?"

"Well, excuse me!" This time it was his turn to raise his voice. "If my directions are not good enough for you, look them up yourself."

"I..." I was just about to snap at him, but then his words registered, and I thought better of it. "Huh. I guess I will do that. Do we have a public net terminal around here?"

"A what?" Josh looked at me like I was speaking a foreign language.

"A PC I can use to access the internet," I clarified wearily.

"Oh, that... In the computer room, I suppose. But they can only be used during classes or by the computer club."

"Wi-Fi?"

"What?"

"Wireless network for... wait, scratch that. I don't have a smartphone." I shook my head and stood up. My legs wobbled only a bit. "That settles it then," I said, straightening my creased uniform. "I guess I head home first, get my directions plus maybe a new set of clothes, then go to the hospital."

"Wait, you mean now?" Joshua followed after me in a hurry as I took a beeline for the stairwell. "We still have afternoon classes!"

"Nope, *you* do," I told him with a wink. "Tell the homeroom teacher I came down with a sudden case of acute something or the other and had to go home. He will understand."

"It's a she..." Josh automatically corrected me and grabbed my arm just as I reached the door leading to the stairs. "Wait, at least give me a proper cover story or Angie will know something was up."

"Angie?"

"Angeline. Our friend. I guess you wouldn't remember her, either."

I clicked my tongue. So that's what her name was! I was so close... Anyways, I gave him a reassuring smile and carefully peeled his fingers from my arm.

"Just tell her the truth."

"But she won't believe that!" he protested with uncharacteristic vehemence. "Hell, I'm not even sure I buy your story."

"Sorry, but that's the best I can offer. Maybe start by telling her I was kidnapped by aliens. The amnesia explanation will sound much more credible after that."

"But you can't—" he started, but the end of the sentence was lost as he lunged towards me to grab my arm again, just as I was about to tumble down the stairs.

"Whoa!" I exclaimed louder than intended, my heart in my throat. "Damn, that was scary... Thanks."

Joshua still looked at me doubtfully, but there was a hint of acceptance on his face. He forcefully exhaled, and a moment later, he put on a determined expression.

"You know what? You are right, you really should leave."

I smiled at him. "You see, I knew you would come around."

"And I'm coming with you," he told me resolutely, and before I could respond, he pulled my arm over his shoulder and led me down the stairs. It was so sudden that I couldn't even muster a protest until we reached the first turn.

"Is this really necessary?"

Joshua gave me a sharp look and elbowed me lightly in the side. "If I wasn't here, you would've already broken your neck. If I let you out onto the street like this, you'd get run over before you cleared the first block. In fact, I think I'll just take you right to the hospital."

I wanted to retort, but my knees wobbled again and I decided to shut up. To my surprise, Josh didn't take me back to the classroom. Instead, we hobbled down to the ground floor and then he led me to an unassuming corner of the west wing. Strangely enough, I could tell exactly where we were. It wasn't like in the morning where I'd just gone everywhere on autopilot. Rather, I felt that the corridors were vaguely familiar, and once we walked down them, I could place them in a rudimentary floor plan in my head, as if I was tapping puzzle pieces into their spots.

At long last, we came to a halt in front of a door that didn't seem any different from the others down the hallway, yet I somehow knew it was the nurse's office. Josh lightly knocked, then reached for the doorknob without waiting for an answer. The moment he did so, the heavy odor of disinfectant slapped me in the face. Yep, it was the nurse's office all right.

"O-ho-ho! Come in, come in." The deep, jovial voice came from the belly of a cheery elderly man, or at least he looked a fair bit older than I expected. It was mostly due to his bushy white mustache and balding head. He was wearing a white coat over a brown suit and was sitting by a desk opposite the two white beds by the open window.

Josh hauled me in and put me down onto the closest bed. "I'll go get our bags. Get yourself looked at in the meantime."

"Sure," I replied half-heartedly, but by then he was already closing the door behind himself. I sighed and turned to the nurse. I knew it was shallow of me, but I was a little crestfallen when I looked at him. School nurses were supposed to be busty, mature twenty-something-year-old beauties, not mustachioed old men. Whatever. I suppose it was my fault for having weird expectations. I took a deep breath and addressed the man. "What's up, doc?"

At first he didn't answer, opting to just stare at me with a fixed smile. He was admittedly much more animate than the students, yet I couldn't shake the feeling there was something peculiar about him, too.

"O-ho-ho. Collapsing like that on the first day of school is very unseemly, young man. You should sleep properly."

"I did," I said in response while trying to find a comfortable spot on the bed. To think that these uncomfortable slabs of uncomfortableness are often considered one of the stereotypical means of high school romantic jaunts... Just how desperate were some kids?

"O-ho-ho," the nurse continued with the same jovial voice as he sorted through the bottles on his desk with his chubby fingers. "I suppose you need some cold medicine to get rid of that fever then."

"I don't have a fever."

"O-ho-ho, then I suppose you should lie down until your anemia gets better."

"I am not anemic, either." I was getting more exasperated by the second. "Also, stop that."

"O-ho-ho, what do you mean?"

"Your laughing. It's annoying."

"O-ho-ho, that's just the low blood sugar talking. Here, have a candy." He offered me a hard candy and, while I wasn't really in the mood, I took it. Doing otherwise would have been just rude.

"Say, doc?" I asked as I popped the candy into my mouth.

Ugh, grape of all things?

"Yes?" He looked at me with that wide, grandfatherly smile still plastered on his face.

"Do you have anything for amnesia?"

The nurse's face went slack and he looked at me with glazed eyes. "Pardon?"

"Amnesia. The retrograde kind. Do you have any advice?"

"I..." He suddenly went pale and I could swear his eyes went unfocused. "I don't understand."

"Amnesia. Retrograde. The kind where one loses their memories up to when they wake up," I repeated patiently.

He didn't respond, unless you count completely freezing up and refusing to even blink as a response. I was just about to get worried about the poor man when the door of the infirmary opened and Josh entered with two bags under his arms.

"That was quick."

"I had to run," he answered between heaves. "Angie caught me in the hallway."

Just how scary was this Angie girl? I wondered, though not for long, since he handed me my bag.

"Can you walk?"

Good question. As an answer, I stood up and, to everyone's surprise, I didn't even wobble. Yay.

Josh gave me a relieved nod and gestured towards the door with his head. "Good, let's go."

With that, he practically pulled me out of the infirmary, not even sparing a look at the still frozen man staring blankly at the place where I was sitting a moment before.

PART 2

"Wait, let me see if I get this straight..." I said as I gestured for Josh to stop. Well, technically he was standing still anyway since we were waiting for the streetlights to turn green, but who cares about semantics? Anyways, I continued, "So, she is your neighbour, you grew up together, you come to school together each morning, and your families hang out all the time. Don't tell me she also wakes you up every morning."

"Not *every* time..." he told me while avoiding eye contact. "She lives next door and she is an early riser. There is nothing weird about it."

"Right, totally normal childhood friend behaviour."

"I'm serious!"

In the meantime, the light switched and we began walking again. This time the streets actually had pedestrians, and the occasional car rolled by, though the people seemed just as substance-deficient as the students were.

"I'm not joking either," I responded as sincerely as I could. "That is totally normal childhood friend behaviour, no sarcasm here."

At least as long as you live in a cheap romance manga, I wanted to add, but decided against it.

He still looked at me critically but didn't continue the discussion. Instead, he rubbed his temple and changed the topic.

"Déjà vu." He tried to act as if he was only talking to himself, though it was obvious he was trying to change the subject. I decided I might as well oblige him.

"Which part?" I asked while trying to sound oblivious. In the meantime, we passed by a newsstand, and I had to stop and look at the newsboy shouting, "Extra, extra! Read all about it!" nearby. It was so horribly outdated, it was strangely adorable.

"Your questions," Joshua answered glumly, apparently not sharing my newfound admiration of anachronistic media-delivery personnel. "It's just like when you transferred."

"Really?" I caught up to him, only sparing one last glance at the paperboy. My goodness, he was even wearing britches and suspenders! Some people really go that extra mile for their job. I allowed myself one last smile, then returned to the discussion at hand. "Speaking of which, where did I live? Before I transferred, I mean."

Josh shot me a withering look. I have no idea how he did it, but he could somehow manage to increase the severity of his doubtful glares with each fresh glare. A truly impressive feat.

"How should I know?"

"What kind of friend doesn't know where the other came from?"

"I don't know. What kind of friend doesn't remember the other's name?"

"Touché, but I at least have amnesia for an excuse. What's yours?"

He paused for a few seconds just as we were walking across a pedestrian bridge. This part of town seemed to be less frequented than the previous streets. For a while, we barely met a soul.

"You know, you never really talked about yourself," Josh finally told me with a difficult expression. "Now that I think about it, I don't even know where you live right now. Whenever we hung out, it was either at my place or in town, and we mostly talked about school stuff. Actually, now that you mention it, you were always very evasive about to your old school. And friends. And family. And so on."

That was actually bad news. If I really didn't talk to him about such obvious things, chances were he'd know little to help me recover my memories. Dang it..

"I suppose that's it, then. How far is the hospital again?"

"Just over the next block, and then we should—" The words abruptly got caught in Josh's throat and he let out a short hiss. I had no idea what happened, so I glanced over at him and followed his fixed gaze to the three figures loitering by the roadside. They were also students, though they were wearing a full black uniform and...

"Oh my God, that guy actually has a pompadour!" I exclaimed as I pointed at the largest member of the trio. Josh immediately caught my arm and pulled me aside.

"What are you doing!?" His whispers were so loud, he might as well have said it normally.

"But look!" I pointed again and I could barely hold myself back from laughing. It wasn't even a simple pompadour, oh no! It was one of those cartoonish ones that jutted a good thirty centimeters forward like a tank turret. That thing probably required a sacrifice of a full box of hair gel to the elder gods of silly hairstyles every morning.

"Look what we have here!" the big delinquent exclaimed as he sauntered over, his two companions following right behind him. The ringleader was built like a tank: bottom-heavy and with a turret on top, and his voice rumbled like treads on asphalt. Joking aside, his build was just heavy instead of being particularly muscular, and he had fingers big enough to grip a basketball one-handed.

The other two guys were also of unusual body shapes. One was taller than their leader by about a head but razor-thin, with sunken eyes and buckteeth visible even with his mouth closed. The third one barely reached up to Tank Guy's chest and had a large, round face that seemed to be disproportionate compared to the rest of his body. These two also sported pompadours, though theirs were nowhere near as hilariously over the top as the leader's. The trio also seemed to remind me of something, but I couldn't really remember what, especially since I was so busy trying to keep myself from laughing.

"Skipping class, aren't we?"

The big guy stood in front of us. Beside me, Josh gulped. For some reason, even that felt funny.

"That's not a very nice thing to do," the tall one said in a high-pitched nasal voice that sounded like a scratched vinyl record compared to the leader's resounding bass. His eyes reminded me of a ferret's.

"Yea, yea!" The small one nodded eagerly. "Icz noc nice ac all!" If the big guy's voice was deep and rumbling, and the tall one's was high and nasal, this guy sounded like he had a parrot trapped in his throat. A parrot that smoked Winston Churchill's entire cigar stash in one go.

"Right, Baggins, bad boys like these two have to be—"

That was the point I couldn't hold it in any longer. Laughter burst through the hand clapped over my mouth, and it took all my willpower to keep me from slapping my knees. "You cannot be serious!" I exclaimed. "You actually nicknamed the short one Baggins? Ah, ah... My sides...! You are killing me!" The three glared at me in unison, but I couldn't stop. "What are you called then? Wait, don't tell me, it's—"

"I'm... I'm Ladder Jones," the tall one protested. He seemed to be defensive, even meek in his response.

"Aw, shucks! You totally ruined your theme-naming already."

"You... You...!" The big one glared at me ferociously, as if to draw my attention.

"Ah, right. And you are supposed to be...?"

"I am..." The guy faltered under my scrutiny. He cleared his throat and began anew. "I am... Heavy Tony..." He tried to give his name a grandiose spin, but he ran out of steam.

I rolled my eyes with extreme prejudice.

"Laaaaame."

"Why you little...!"

I cut off the outrage with a wave. "Seriously, the short guy had the right idea. You guys should follow up on that. If you really want to come up with nicknames, go for broke, don't settle for 'Ladder Jones' and 'Heavy Tony'!" I pursed my lips thoughtfully, then added, "Well, okay, the last one at least rhymed. Good work on that."

"T-thanks?" Heavy Tony shared confused glances between me and his cronies.

"You're welcome. Now, if you excuse me, I have to go to the hospital."

"But... we didn't even do anything to you..." the short one protested, albeit weakly.

"Long story, gotta go. Think about what I said. Bye."

I waved at the trio and began walking and, to my surprise, they waved back. Then their eyes kind of glazed over. Because of course they did.

"What the hell were you thinking!?"

"Whoa!" I almost toppled over as Josh yanked on my arm and pulled me into an alley. Damn, for a moment, I thought he'd dislocated my shoulder. "What the hell are you doing?"

"That's my line!"

Joshua's normally pale face was practically glowing red as he glared at me from a few centimeters away. I leaned away from him and managed to hit the back of my sore head against a wall.

"The mother-fluting son of a cow!" I mumbled while holding my brainbox. My alleged friend didn't even flinch at the display.

"Don't try to change the subject!"

"I'm not changing the subject, I'm in pain!" I retorted.

At this point, Josh threw his hands into the air and exclaimed, "Good riddance! You could have gotten us both killed."

Now it was my turn to give him a skeptical look. I lightly shook my head to check if the nausea was back, and since I was still standing on my own two feet at the end of it, I concluded that the previous impact had more bark than bite. With that, I turned my attention back to the guy still fuming in front of me.

"Don't be so dramatic. They were just delinquents."

"*Just* delinquents?"

"Hey, hey! Don't shout."

"Then don't say irresponsible stuff like that, you idiot! Those three have been preying on the neighbourhood for a while. They target the students of our school for their allowances and lunch money."

"Well, they didn't take ours..."

"Only because you were acting crazy!"

I raised a finger. "Not crazy. It's called 'Refuge in Audacity.'"

"Uh, what?"

I sighed. "Refuge in audacity. It's when you act completely self-assured while you are saying or doing something you shouldn't. Other people won't challenge you simply because they'll assume that you must have a good reason to do what you did and they'll be afraid they'll look silly in front of others if they involved themselves. It's how the *Mona Lisa* got stolen at one point. A guy just walked into the Louvre dressed as an employee, took the painting, hid it under his smock, and left. No one even stopped him. Con artists do this kind of thing all the time."

"I... see." It seemed like Joshua had calmed down, though his eyes were still jumping between me and the mouth of the alley like he expected the trio to show up any minute. "But what if it didn't work? We could've been in big trouble."

"Oh please! Those three are complete jokes." I laughed and began counting on my fingers. "I mean, they dressed and acted like stereotypes, they had silly nicknames, they were totally running with the old big-short-tall trio dynamic, and they were completely nonthreatening." I dropped my hand. "Seriously, if this were a game, those three would be the goldfish poop gang that did nothing more than annoy us and serve as occasional comic relief."

Josh's face was still grim. At last, he grimaced and dropped his shoulders in resignation.

"Maybe, but this is not a game. We could've been in real trouble back there."

"Sure, sure, this is not a game, but..."

And then it suddenly hit me. Like a lightning bolt out of the bright blue sky, illuminating the puzzle pieces in my head and making me see how they fit together all along.

"Oh my God."

Suddenly everything made sense. This whole world—everything was brand new and squeaky clean. People were samey and nondescript and they couldn't deal with being introduced to unexpected stimuli. Even the stereotypical bullies and...

"OH! MY! GOD!"

"What? What!"

Joshua, understandably distressed by my behaviour, was frantically scanning the premises to figure out what happened. I reached out, grabbed him by the shoulders, and looked him in the eye.

"Listen, Josh, I figured it out!" I began—but then faltered. Just how the hell was I supposed to tell him about this without sounding crazy? Hell, maybe I *was* crazy. No, I just needed more time, more data points.

"Yes?" Joshua squirmed between my hands. It took me a moment to collect my thoughts and answer.

"Sorry. I just remembered something." I let him go with a vague wave. "I've got to go."

"Wait!" He reached after me but missed and only grabbed thin air. "What's going on? What about the hospital?"

"Later. Sorry for dumping you here, but I really have to run! If you hurry, you might get back to school before the period ends. See you tomorrow!" I finished my rapid-fire response with a casual salute, and I didn't even bother waiting for his answer. I took off running and never looked back.

If I was right... Oh my God, if I was right...

CHAPTER 3

I let out a tired groan as I opened my bag and started rummaging through its pockets. I was hungry, parched, and the early afternoon twilight made finding my keys harder than strictly necessary. If that didn't make it abundantly clear, taking off like that turned out to be one of my less brilliant ideas.

For a start, after leaving Josh behind, it had taken me a good five minutes to realize I had no idea where I was. Since going back and asking for directions would have been awkward (not to mention, unlikely that he'd be standing around in that alley, waiting) I decided to ask some passersby. Another less-than-stellar idea. Most folks just locked up with thousand-yard stares the moment I tried to get any information out of them. If I hadn't stumbled upon a public park with information boards and a map, I probably would've still been wandering the streets.

But I was home. I finally found the key and unlocked the door with a satisfying click. I threw it open and rushed inside, not bothering to take off my outdoor shoes. The living room was in the exact same condition as I'd left it, down to the still lightly damp towel on the sofa. My alleged parents hadn't come home yet. If they even existed. I only spared a glance at the clock on the wall, which told me that it was a little after 5 p.m., and headed for the kitchen.

After concluding my raid on the fridge, I returned to the living room with the spoils: a carton of milk in one hand and a hastily thrown together ham sandwich in the other. I dropped my posterior onto the sofa and sighed in relief. It felt good to sit down. I took one last gulp from the milk box before I placed it onto the table, after which I stretched my limbs. My legs all but sighed with respite. After limbering back up a little, I leaned back and rested, staring at the ceiling in absentminded lethargy. It felt good to not think about anything in particular.

I allowed myself the luxury for only a couple of minutes, though. Unfortunately, I had things to think about. Weird, confusing, and downright terrifying things. In a twisted sense, it was lucky that I'd gotten lost in town. Wandering around allowed the revelation to sink in a little and blunted the worst of the existential crisis, though I'd be lying if I said it wasn't still lurking somewhere deep in my gut. I mean, it's not every day you realize you aren't real.

Okay, to be fair, it was also possible that it was the world that wasn't real. Not that said possibility made things any less complicated or scary.

It was at this point that I lurched forward to sit straight again. I was getting ahead of myself. I should start from the beginning and think things through properly before jumping to conclusions.

I stood up, grabbed hold of my discarded bag, fished a pen from a side pocket, then grabbed a spiral notebook. It didn't matter which one; they were all empty. I cleaned up the table, piling the documents I collected in the morning into a neat stack before sitting down again with my writing implements in front of me. It was fairly clear what I had to do.

First I needed to collect data. I inadvertently did a lot of that today, but tomorrow I would have to make a conscious effort and continue with this specific goal in mind. Then I had to collect and organize the information so that I could either prove or disprove my hypotheses. Finally, using the data and my research assembled in the first two points, I had to figure out just what the bloody hell was going on. Easy-peasy. But then I was getting ahead of myself again.

Let's see my current hypothesis first.

I hit up the notebook and wrote, *This isn't reality and/or I am part of some sort of constructed world*, onto the top of the page. I paused and rubbed my cheek. Yeah, thinking about it and actually putting it to paper are very different, but I wasn't considering something this crazy lightly.

Under the title, I wrote up a new heading: *Observations*.

First off, my own situation. As far as I could tell, I was a fairly tall but otherwise average male Caucasian high schooler living in a large house without any parental oversight. I was also a transfer student in a Japanese-style school, but not necessarily in Japan; I had a friend called Joshua; and I apparently knew a girl called Angeline, who was his childhood friend. I was probably on friendly terms with her, too.

I also had amnesia, which was another telltale sign. I think it's supposed to make me a... what's the word... audience-surrogate, I think? I decided I should look the term up later. I was fairly sure there was a site out there that cataloged these kinds of things...

But back to the topic at hand: These tidbits basically designated me as a protagonist. I was only missing three things: an annoying but sweet little sister, a female childhood friend, and a male idiot friend. I paused and, though he didn't seem to fit the bill exactly, I wrote *Joshua* over the idiot friend entry in my book. I frowned at my handiwork and, after some hesitation, added a large question mark after his name.

Moving on.

I wrote *Environment* on my list and paused again. I had already noted how everything was clean, but on second thought I had to change my description to "new." The longer I watched my surroundings, the more it felt like I was on the set of a sitcom or soap opera that was only supposed to convincingly mimic reality under stage lighting.

Speaking of genres made me think of another thing, and I wrote *Setting* on the top of the next page. I looked at the word and it somehow made me feel silly. Normally, people didn't consider their circumstances part of a setting. On the other hand, these were anything but normal circumstances.

Anyways, as far as I could tell, it was a stereotypical Japanese high school background with some anachronisms thrown into the mix. That would imply either comedy or romance. Well, the appearance of the delinquents certainly placed the ball in the court of the former, though given the fact that I largely took myself out of the proceedings of the day, it wasn't impossible that I'd missed some sort of designated romantic encounter. With my luck, it would have probably been a tsundere girl colliding with me on the street with a half-eaten slice of toast still hanging from her mouth, or something similarly stereotypical.

I paused to take a sip from the milk box and found myself frowning by the time I put it back down.

What did I just write here?

I scanned the page with my eyes and found the word close to the bottom. *Tsundere.*

The hell is that?

Somehow I had a hazy mental image of what the word should mean in the form of a short, blonde, ponytailed girl yelling at someone while blushing. Was that the name of someone? No, I think it was something along the lines of a... personality? An archetype? Concluding that I should look the word up later, I underlined it. I frowned at the page one last time and let out a soft groan.

"So now I'm using words I don't even know. Just bloody fantastic."

This incident, however, gave me a new idea.

I wrote up my next heading to the top of the following page: *Anomalies.* I cracked my fingers. Now, this was a meaty subject if I'd ever seen one.

First on the list was my amnesia. Thankfully my memories didn't seem to be completely wiped clean, at least if my hazy image of that Angeline girl was any indication, but that was good news in the same way as telling a quadriplegic that they should be happy they still had their head. But then again, it was a start. If nothing else, it showed that some memories could still lurk in my head somewhere... though, as I thought about it, maybe the using-words-I-don't-know anomaly that made me start this segment was actually related to my amnesia, as well. It was possible that I'd actually known these words, once. I decided to look into this later, along with the symptoms of retrograde amnesia. It was probably all related.

I nodded to myself. Right, I really should look into them later. What were they again...? Audience-surrogate, tsundere... Then there was that *refuge in audacity* thing with Josh. That must've come from somewhere... Oh, and there was that thing that had to do with goldfish, though I can't remember the exact line. It still felt like it made sense in context, but I couldn't remember the exact term, because why would anything be easy today?

Leaving that annoyance aside, here was another one: the issue of those sudden headaches and the strange urge I felt when they struck. They were gone for the moment, but couldn't they return? It would be best to figure out what they were about. At the very least, I had to be on guard against them in the future.

Next, I wrote up my arrival to the roof and the short blackout preceding it. According to Joshua, the door leading to the roof should have been closed until noon... So how did I get up there?

"I guess I'll investigate the stairs and the door to the roof tomorrow. There must be some traces there."

I scratched my head. This was probably the question I had the least clues about, so for now I underlined the question mark and moved on.

Then there were the people. This was arguably the biggest and most glaring anomaly of them all, though the general spotlessness of the world gave it a run for its money. The lack of variety at school, the lack of individual personalities, the glassy stares whenever they encountered something unexpected, and just the general haziness of their existence all pointed in the same direction: there was something seriously wrong with everyone. Well, almost everyone. The only people who actually felt real were Joshua and, to a degree, the three delinquents we met. Oh, and the nurse, but he was a borderline case at best.

In retrospect, Josh made sense if we went with the I'm-the-protagonist idea. He was supposed to be my friend and all, but the delinquents didn't really strike me as similarly important. Or maybe that's what made them even more important? For my research purposes, I mean.

I exhaled a sigh and began munching on my sandwich while I considered my points once again. I underlined a few important looking bits, fixed a few typos, decided to refer to any seemingly unimportant people as "placeholders" for simplicity's sake, and by the time I finished eating, I was reasonably sure I'd gotten the most important observations down. Now came the hard part: I had to figure out how everything fit together.

I stared at the open notebook, scanning the lines one last time. My first idea was fairly tame: This was all a dream. I could be sleeping in my bed right now and lucid dreaming this entire scenario. It would explain most, if not all, of the anomalies, except for a single serious flaw. Dreams don't tend to stay so consistent for so long. Not to mention I'd been awake, unconscious, in pain, hungry, thirsty, and a hundred other things since I'd gotten up this morning, all of which I could remember clearly. That's just not how dreams worked. They're more... volatile and, dare I redundantly say, dreamlike? Also, if I was aware this was a dream, why hadn't I woken up the moment I started writing this sentence? No matter how I looked at it, these facts pointed at me being in something much more stable than your average lucid dream.

The second possibility flowed from the first quite naturally: I could be in a coma, walking the thin line between life and death in some hospital ward somewhere. This experience could very well have been caused by head trauma, an adequate explanation for how my memories got screwed over, and it would also explain the stability of the dream... though not its consistency. No, the real problem wasn't even the consistency of the dream itself but its anomalies. When one's dreaming, the part of the brain that governs reality-testing is offline. That's why you can have a dream where you are riding tiny pink elephants on the wing of a jet plane while playing the balalaika and never even question the weirdness of it all. Oh, speaking of weirdness...

"The heck's a balalaika? I think it's a musical instrument or something, but..."

I groaned and leafed back a few pages to write *balalaika* under *Words to Look Up Later.*

Then, back on topic.

Your brain only has two settings. Reality-testing either works or it doesn't. Hence, if this were all just a dream, I shouldn't have been able to notice any anomalies, since my reality-testing suite would have been offline. I would have accepted everything at face value. It obviously wasn't the case, as the slowly filling notebook could testify.

While this was not enough to completely rule out the possibility of a dream, either coma-induced or garden-variety, I personally considered it unlikely.

Putting those aside, the next option was the one that first reared its head when I talked to Josh: I was in some kind of virtual reality. A game, maybe even an MMO. There were two lines of evidence pointing this way.

First off, the people. If this was a dream, there was no reason why they should be so flimsy and acting so weird, but if I presumed that they were literal placeholders, NPCs who were only supposed to fill the background, their behaviour made sense. Their AIs were not programmed to deal with unexpected stimuli. Just like in some games, you could throw a bucket on a shopkeeper's head and steal all their valuables. If they couldn't see you doing it, as far as they were concerned, it hadn't happened.

Note to self: Try the bucket thing if the opportunity presents itself. It sounds hilarious.

Now back on track. This hypothesis also provided an elegant explanation for the ever-present cleanness of the world. If this were a simulation, it would make sense that it didn't simulate absolutely everything, especially if it were a game world, as I suspected. You didn't find dusty windowsills or dirty floors in a game environment. Creating those consumed system resources that could be used elsewhere, so unless the area specifically needed those things, like a dusty cellar or a garbage-filled alleyway, the world would generally appear clean.

I tapped my pen against the notepad. After some thinking, I stood up and returned to the kitchen. I looked through the cupboards and quickly found what I was looking for, a couple of small packages of flour tucked away in a corner. I opened one of them and stuck my finger inside, stirring up the powder. It looked and felt just as it should.

I decided to go the whole distance. I reached in and took out a pinch, and then let the powder trickle out of my grasp and onto the kitchen table. I watched it for a while before I blew on it. The flour acted exactly how it was supposed to, billowing around the table in a fine white mist. It looked normal enough, which got me thinking.

Let's presume for a moment that this was indeed a simulation. Simulating an environment to this level of detail required a lot of processing power, so much processing power that I couldn't even fathom what kind of computer could manage it. For the moment, let's also grant the existence of such a machine, one that could crunch all the numbers necessary. However, a good simulation didn't really need to simulate *everything* to be convincing.

Take, for example, a car. If one wanted to create a simulation of a car in, say, a racing game, one didn't need to simulate every single aspect of the machine. In reality, the car's movements were the result of a thousand forces and counterforces working at the same time, transmitted from the explosion of the fuel in the engine to the traction between the tires and the asphalt. A perfect simulation of the car required taking all of these individual forces into account, how they affected the thousands of individual moving parts, and how those in return affected the movement of the whole. An enormous amount of data needing to be calculated.

But what if one wasn't looking for a perfect simulation? What if one only cared about the final product, the movement of the car being authentic, and didn't care about the intermediate steps? If one was to abstract all the tiny forces and only focus on the important ones, one could easily reduce the number of variables required to simulate a car to manageable levels. The energy of the explosions in the engine chambers transmitted through the pistons, the friction between the moving parts, the time needed to accelerate certain parts or even the whole car. All these things could be boiled down to numbers... At which point, you don't need to simulate all the intricacies of the engine block anymore. In fact, one could simply remove it altogether, like taking out a large chunk of an algebraic equation to replace it with that part's solution before moving on to solve the rest.

I watched in silence as the fine white powder stopped swirling in the air in front of me and slowly settled on the table. I clicked my tongue, made a mental note to clean up the mess later, and returned to the living room. My little experiment only raised more questions. If I were to presume that this was indeed a virtual world that lacked dirt in order to conserve processing power, then how come it was perfectly capable of simulating dust particles like that?

Maybe it was a question of time? Maybe it was a new simulation and there was simply no time for dust and dirt to pile up yet. Or maybe it was a question of scale? As in, it would be able to deal with a handful of flour particles from time to time but not an entire city's worth of dust. Hell, as far as I knew, it might've only simulated the flour because I was looking. In fact, that last one sounded decidedly possible. Hell, maybe the only part of the entire world that was simulated at any given time was the area I was actually observing at the moment.

But how could I test something like that?

I rubbed my face in frustration and slumped back on the sofa. I didn't have any illusions of solving my situation from my armchair just by writing up my guesses in a more organized manner, but the longer I was at it, the more daunting this whole mess felt. In the end, I gritted my teeth and grabbed hold of my pen again. I had to press on.

So, where was I? Right, the simulation. So, what are its limits? I mean, *if* this really is a simulation, that is... Anyways, it appeared it could emulate dust and fine particles. To see if it did so for smaller particles, like actual molecules and atoms, I would need professional equipment I didn't have access to. Now, what *could* I test? Maybe cells? Those would be in line with my car analogy. Why would a simulation bother to build a human up from the cellular level when abstracting the body and its functions would work just as well?

Thinking of humans reminded me of something else: if this simulation was sophisticated enough to emulate dust physics, why would it have place-holders that are barely more than automatons? I paused and underlined the question again. I had no answer at the moment, and my speculations about processing power and simulation resolution already sounded too specific for something I had no bloody idea about. I decided I should leave this line of inquiry for later, when I had more data points to work with.

Now it was time to get back to the original question: how did I fit into this simulation hypothesis? In the case of this being a dream, my role was obvious. Someone had to dream the dream after all. In the case of the simulation, there were two very distinct possibilities: I was either from the "outside," like a player trapped inside a virtual reality MMO, or I was from the inside to begin with, like an NPC that just gained sentience.

Both possibilities had data to bolster them. If I was a player, so to speak, it would explain my in-universe situation. The protagonist living alone in a house without parental oversight was a staple of most Japanese school life fiction, with which the setting showed the most similarity. My lack of memories could have come from several sources, such as a failed disconnection or my real body suffering some sort of injury while inside.

The NPC variant, on the other hand, had a number of lines of evidence as well. My lack of memories could come from the simple fact that I had none to begin with, my headache could have been the system freaking out when I went against my programming, and many of my anomalies could have been because I was a glitch in the system.

Both possibilities raised a couple of intriguing questions. Was this an independent simulation, like a scientific experiment, or was it a con-structed one for outside observers? Were there any other players in the system, and if there were, who were they? Alternatively, if there were none, why did I gain sentience, and how does that affect me and the world? Or maybe this was all just a dream of a narcoleptic elder god, and none of it could possibly make sense. I dream of being a squid who dreams of being me or something along those lines... I was never good with my zen metaphors.

I paused yet again and looked at the line I'd just written. My letters were all crooked and weird. It took me a moment to realize the reason: my hand was shaking. Not only that, my entire body was tense like I was an overstrung bow, ready to snap at any moment. I put down the pen and buried my head in my hands.

"I suppose you can only keep existential dread at bay for so long, huh?"

I reached for the milk box to cool my head, but the liquid inside was already at room temperature. I drank it all the same, but I still wanted something cold to fix my nerves. Maybe there was some booze in the fridge and...

"No, that won't do."

I stood with weary steps and threw the empty box into the trashcan in the kitchen's corner. I wanted to douse my anxiety, not pour more fuel onto it via alcohol. Not to mention I needed to think clearly. Also, I was a minor, though it wasn't like anyone cared. So I shrugged it off and walked back to the table. Well, and since I was already standing, I decided I might as well do something else. I just need something to take my mind off the immediate horror of the situation for a while. I wasn't burying my head in the sand, I was... reprioritizing. Yes.

I snatched up my notes and returned to my room. Just as I remembered, there was a PC in the corner, a sleek and powerful beast of a machine... by 1990s standards. After some fiddling and assorted headaches (bad news: my PC had a password on it; good news: it was *swordfish*, so I got in on the second try), I managed to get the internet working, though it was surprisingly sluggish.

Note to self: put that money in my account to good use and buy a better rig. Or better yet, a laptop for mobility.

Nevertheless, I put my notebook in my lap and clicked on the search bar. I wrote in *amnesia* and was about to click OK but I stopped and glanced back at the notes. I hesitated for a moment, then hit backspace instead and wiggled my fingers.

"I'll get to that, but first... let's find out what the heck a tsundere is."

CHAPTER 4

PART 1

"Ah, there it is! *Goldfish Poop Gang*!" I smiled triumphantly and began jotting down the description. "An ineffectual group of bad guys who keep showing up and are often played for laughs. Got it."

I put a period to the end of the line and my smile slowly turned into a frown. I had to cram the second half of the sentence into a corner and it still ran over to the next page. And this was one of the easier-to-read parts of my notes. Most pages were scribbled over with corrections and underlines while others were half-empty and the entire thing was a mess in general.

I snapped the notebook shut and clicked my tongue in irritation. I'd have to copy the entire thing over to the computer soon. It should make things easier to correct and organize in the long run.

"I guess I'll do it after school." Speaking of which, I moved the cursor over the taskbar and checked the time. "Damn, it's seven in the morning already?"

I glanced at the window and, surely enough, there were rays of light seeping through the shutters. I stood up and limbered up my neck. I felt surprisingly awake. I haven't slept a wink and yet I wasn't drowsy. Not even particularly tired. That was weird.

And if something was weird...

"No need for sleep?" I scratched the phrase into the cramped bottom of the Anomalies page and put an especially big question mark at the end. Maybe it was only the adrenaline that kept me running all night long, or possibly just the site I was browsing... who knows?

Speaking of which, I leaned over the computer and leafed through the twenty or so open tabs in my browser. For a moment I thought about sitting down again, but I decided against it. Whilst researching terminology, jumping from link to link, my primary objective was collecting more empirical data, and I could hardly do that while I was cooped up in my room. Thus I made sure my tabs were bookmarked and then put the machine into standby mode.

I straightened my back and stretched, enjoying the rush of blood while it lasted, then began my morning preparations. I still had more than enough time till school started, but I wanted to get some other things done before I went there, and as they say, there's no better time than the present.

PART 2

It was exactly 7:39 when I slipped through the school gate. I gave a quick nod to the guy with the armband, and while he returned the gesture, I couldn't help but feel that his blank face was somehow disapproving. But he didn't say anything, just grabbed hold of the sliding gate and began closing it after me.

Huh. So the gates closed twenty minutes before the first bell. Good to know.

I looked around the courtyard and found myself frowning. The school looked exactly like it had on the first day—ditto the people milling around—yet somehow, something felt different. For a while I couldn't really pinpoint what it was, but then I knew.

It was me.

As I walked, I made note of many things I'd missed the day before. Yesterday I was too preoccupied with my amnesia and staring at the unrealistic cleanliness of the environment to care about such minor things as aesthetics. After a day of acclimation, I found myself staring for other reasons. While I might've dismissed the school as stereotypical the first time around, a second look proved the building and its environs to be quite imposing.

The wide brick walkway leading to the entrance of the school was practically shining with morning dew. Light seeped through the trees on either side. It was early autumn, so they were not in full bloom as another stereotype would have demanded, yet the cherry trees still looked impressive in their fading green.

The building itself was remarkable, if not exactly breathtaking. The three rows of large windows, each one of them mirror-shined, reflected the morning light, and together with the white and light blue of the walls, they gave the illusion of a building made of ice and snow. Then I noticed the smaller details, such as the small leaf-motif embossments running around each window and especially the large relief of a single cherry tree on a hill placed right above the entrance. Speaking of the entrance, it was the first time I noticed the curved handrails around the steps leading up to it or the huge doors made entirely of safety glass, opening and closing on their own as people approached.

For a moment I felt really, really shallow. I shook off the feeling and I marched up to the entrance, promising myself to pay more attention to such details in the future. I walked up the steps and entered the building. The entry hall was large but unadorned, and it only housed the three rows of the large, dark-blue shoe lockers I was already familiar with. At least I wasn't missing any aesthetic details *there*...

With a self-derisive smirk, I rushed over to my own locker and opened the cabinet. I wasn't exactly sure whether I should hurry or not; although classes wouldn't start for a good fifteen minutes, I had little to no idea about where to find my classroom. Last time I'd gone on autopilot. So while I had a general idea of where it should be, I still wanted to have some leeway, especially in case there were complications on the way.

Just as I reached for my shoes, I heard a commotion from the direction of the stairs. For a moment I was tempted to put my shoes back on and check out what it was, but in the end, I figured I had better things to do. With that decided, I quickly slipped into my indoor shoes and closed the locker door.

I was ready to head towards the second floor (for I was pretty sure my classroom was in that vicinity) when my attention was directly drawn to the aforementioned commotion, whether I liked it or not. It was a word, something that sounded vaguely familiar...

"Leonard Dunning!"

There! That was it, the familiar words! It took me a few seconds to process them, but then the little bulb lit up over my head all the more vigorously.

"Ah, right. That's my name," I mused aloud as I turned around to face the source of the exclamation. To my sincerest surprise, my eyes met the fiery glare of a short girl. I involuntarily cocked my head to the side for a moment and squinted at her.

She had shining auburn hair in a tidy ponytail with a white hairpin holding her bangs to the side, large blue eyes, and a cute button nose in the middle of her face, right where it belonged. She didn't appear to wear any makeup, yet her face was spotless with a light complexion and full lips. If I had to rate her, I would have said she was really pretty in a natural, girl-next-door kind of way, but after being immersed in a world full of generally attractive people, I didn't feel confident in my sense of beauty anymore. More importantly, though, she seemed vaguely familiar.

It didn't take long to figure out who she was, considering that aside from Joshua, there was only one other person I could theoretically recognize. Unfortunately, the realization took too long to show up on my face. In fact, it was so long that by then her glare lost all its edge. Now she was cocking her head to the side too, with a confused look in her eyes.

Seeing that, I cleared my throat.

"Angie?"

"Yes?" she asked back, her brows knitting together once again.

"Errr..." For a few seconds, I floundered like a fish out of water. Sure, I could kind of recognize her, and I'd heard about her from Josh, but I didn't actually *know* her, per se. I had no idea why she was glaring at me or what I was supposed to say in this kind of situation. After some urgent brain-racking, I decided to play it safe with an innocent, "Good morning?"

Her face looked like it was carved marble, the visage of a Greek Fury in a high school uniform. I am not going to lie, the image was a little amusing, but I didn't dare to smile. At last, she got her face vertical again and sighed.

"Good morning? Is that all? That's all you have to say for yourself?"

I raised a hand to halt her. I had a nagging feeling that if I let her continue to rile herself up, I would soon end up as the unfortunate end of a slapstick comedy duo.

"Hold up. What exactly do you mean?"

"You know exactly what I mean." She tried to be deadpan. It might've worked if her brows weren't twitching.

"No, I don't. That's why I'm asking."

Her eyes narrowed before she raised an accusatory finger and poked my chest. I blinked in surprise. I was so caught up with the situation that I didn't even realize we were standing at arm's length. I instinctively took a step back. My heel hit the lockers with a loud clank. From the outside, it must have looked like she pushed me back with a finger, but thankfully none of the placeholders were looking or even acknowledged our dispute to begin with. As for her, my reaction appeared to momentarily break her glare, but then she redoubled her efforts to etch wrinkles into her forehead.

"Stop playing dumb."

She was tenacious, wasn't she? Also, her face was twitching again. At first, I thought it was because she was angry, but on closer inspection, it almost looked like she was undertaking some sort of physical effort. Then she noticed my scrutiny and she immediately tried her best to look furious again.

Suppressing the urge to roll my eyes, I flashed a smile instead.

"Let's talk while we walk. Classes should start soon," I told her while I threw my bag onto my back. She didn't answer but fell in line beside me while I headed for the stairwell. When I got there, I slowed down just enough to let her get a half step ahead of me. This way she'd hopefully lead me to the classroom without me having to ask her and reveal my amnesia.

As for why I didn't want to tell her about it... Well, it was both complicated and fairly straightforward. I wanted to figure out this place's deal, and to do that I had to make observations. Because of that, I had to interfere as little as possible to avoid contaminating the data, and letting everyone know about my amnesia was the surefire way to do just the opposite. No, for the time being, I decided I'd keep my condition and my suspicions about this "setting" to myself.

Speaking of suspicions, I glanced at Angie and almost got my legs tangled by the surprise. She was honest-to-goodness massaging her eyebrows as if she'd strained them. I laughed out loud. I couldn't help it.

"W-What?!" She glared at me again, her face red as a lobster.

"Nothing," I squeezed out between two snickers.

"Ah!" She exhaled sharply. "I know what you are doing! You are trying to change the subject! It won't work on me!"

That's actually what you are doing right now, I wanted to say, but I refrained. Instead, I gave her a rueful smile and staggered theatrically. "Oh no, my masterful rouse has been found out! Whatever shall I do?"

She didn't find it amusing. Tough crowd tonight. In the end, I straightened myself and looked her in the eye... which almost made me collide with another student. I settled for stepping a bit closer and dividing my attention between her and the corridor. "So, what exactly did you want to talk about again?"

"You know already!"

With my urge to roll my eyes intensifying, I gave her what I hoped to be an exasperated look.

"No, I have no idea. That's why I'm asking. For a second time."

"You made Joshua skip afternoon classes yesterday, didn't you?" She hissed at me with righteous indignation as we rounded a corner.

"Oh please. He was the one that offered to take me to the hospital."

Angie stumbled for a moment and then rushed forward to catch up with me, her glare breaking away in an instant.

"Wait, what? Hospital? Why did you have to go to the hospital? Did something happen? What happened? How come this is the first time I'm hearing about it? Why didn't you call me? Why—?"

I raised both hands in the air and somehow managed to stall her efforts to drown me in a torrent of questions. I sighed and let my hands down with a shrug. Now, how should I answer her?

"I hit my head yesterday," I told her at last. It wasn't the whole truth, but technically I wasn't lying, either. "Josh took me to the hospital, but then something else came up. I thought he told you. He said he met you when he took our bags."

"Well, he didn't!" she grumbled and puffed up her cheeks into an epic pout. I am not going it lie, it was kinda cute. It was hard to imagine that she was giving me a death-glare just a few moments before.

"He probably didn't want to worry you."

I didn't really know why I said that. I suppose I just wanted to help the poor guy out a little. He was in this mess because of me after all.

"But I was worried anyway!" Angie's outburst wasn't loud, but it was intense. She once again glared at me and let another torrent loose. "Why did you keep it a secret from me? Why didn't you call me in the first place? Do you have any idea how worried I got when you didn't show up during the assembly? Or when Joshua ran away from me? You are horrible! You never care about other people's feelings and—"

I raised a hand to rub my temple. On a whim, I stopped it midway and instead extended it towards her, poking the creases between her brows with my index finger. She fell silent as if I muted her and her mouth hung open with a difficult expression. I couldn't help but chuckle at the sight.

"You are going to get wrinkles if you scowl too much," I told her and removed my hand. Her facial expression froze, then slowly relaxed. "See? It's not that hard."

She was silent. By the time she spoke, we were almost at the classroom, which I only recognized by the 3-C sign over the door. She stopped and grabbed my sleeve, halting me as well.

"Listen, Leo..." Her voice was soft and slightly insecure, though I only recognized that after I finally figured out "Leo" was my name.

Damn, amnesia is annoying.

"Yes?"

"We're friends, right?"

"I am led to believe that, yes."

She pinched my arm.

"Ow! Okay, okay, we are friends. Geez..."

She smiled at me innocently and continued.

"Friends are supposed to help each other, right?"

I nodded.

"So if something like that happens, ever again, I want you to tell me about it and let me help, okay? I don't want to be the only one left in the dark."

It wasn't on purpose! I wanted to protest, but thought better of it. In the end, I just sighed and nodded.

"You two are really alike." Seeing her questioning eyes, I hastily added, "You and Josh. You are the nicest worrywarts I know."

Which was technically true, due to the fact that they were the only two people I knew. I was getting good at these half-truths, if I do say so myself.

"That's not an answer." She pouted again and I couldn't help but chuckle.

"Sure, if it's within your power to help, I will come to you." I nodded towards the classroom. "Come on, classes are about to start."

She didn't seem completely satisfied with my answer, but followed after me all the same. It was just a few minutes before eight when we entered, and the room was almost full. There were at most five or six empty seats, including mine next to Josh's and the one in front of mine. Speaking of Josh, he was looking at the entrance with wary eyes jumping between me and Angie like a frightened kid caught during a prank.

I casually walked over and dropped myself onto my chair. Angie seemed to want to come over with me, but then the bell rang, so she sat down by her desk in the first row. I was surprised. I'd expected the empty seat in front of mine to be hers, but apparently I was wrong. At last, I sighed and turned to Josh.

"Morning."

He eyed me for a while, his gaze occupying the emotional borderland somewhere between sympathetic and suspicious, before he whispered, "So. You got caught, huh?"

"Oh, you mean by Angie?" I involuntarily glanced in her direction and found her staring daggers at us. Well, maybe just Joshua. I gave her a timid wave and she returned it with a small smile before her attention returned to Josh and she did her best to get her brows to touch each other again. I chuckled.

"Man, she's really pissed at you..."

Josh didn't find my comment amusing and commenced to aim a scowl of his own at me.

"Why is she mad at me? You're the one who got me into trouble!"

"What trouble?"

"Oh, don't you try to act innocent now!" By this point, his whispers were getting a bit loud, so I gestured to him to calm down. To his credit, he actually did. "Seriously, you got me to take you to the hospital, skip classes, and then had the nerve to ditch me in an alley! If anyone should be angry here, that would be me!"

As much as I hated to admit it, he had a point. I took a deep breath and rubbed the bridge of my nose in embarrassment.

"Fine, you're right. That was a dick move. Sorry."

Josh opened his mouth and then stopped and left it hanging for a moment as if he only registered my words halfway through. He stayed like that for a beat, then snapped his jaw shut.

"Well, so long as we are clear on that, I suppose it's fine. Water under the bridge."

He sounded almost sulky. Thinking about it, he probably had a huge tirade prepared to chew me out on, and I'd just cut him short with a swift apology. I almost felt bad about it. Almost.

"So, what did you find out?"

"Huh?" I looked up at him uncomprehendingly, whiplashed by the sudden shift in the conversation. "That a balalaika is a Russian stringed musical instrument with a characteristic triangular body and three strings?" I said tentatively.

For a moment, I almost panicked as Josh slid into the thousand-yard stare I'd seen so often with placeholders, but then his eyes snapped back, and... he delivered a swift chop on the top of my head.

"Ow! Hey!"

Well, so much for my trying not to land in comedic slapstick situations...

"Stop messing around!" After a brief pause, no doubt caused by my confused looks, he added in a whisper, "I'm talking about your amnesia! Remember, the thing you were supposed to get looked at?"

"Oh, that!" I paused thoughtfully while rubbing the crown of my head. "Nothing new on that front."

"Then why did you run off like that yesterday? I thought you had a breakthrough or something."

"Nah, that was completely unrelated. By the way, I'd like to keep the whole amnesia-business low-profile for a while."

Josh narrowed his eyes suspiciously.

"Why?"

"It's... a long, complicated, and borderline crazy story, but let's just say that I found out that my missing memories are just the tip of the iceberg."

"What iceberg?"

"A long, complicated, and borderline crazy one?"

Joshua shook his head in defeat and leaned back in his chair with a tired exhalation.

"Fine. Don't tell me if you don't want to."

"Well, it's not that I don't *want* to, but that I have no concrete idea about what's going on, either. I will update you the moment I figure things out."

"Promise?"

I groaned.

"Yes, I promise." I waved my hand in dismissal and then something caught my interest. Well, the lack of something, at the very least. "Shouldn't the teacher be here already?"

"Now that you mention it..." Josh glanced at his phone. It was another brick phone like my own, though his machine seemed to be at least slightly newer. "It's past eight. She *should* be here."

As if on cue, the sliding door—By the way, did I even mention that the classrooms had sliding doors? Because they did, and they were *weird*. But, personal feelings aside—the door slid open with a hissing sound (see, that's what I'm talking about; doors aren't supposed to make that noise!), yet it wasn't the teacher who entered. All non-placeholder eyes focused on the newcomer, a fairly tall, bespectacled girl with a bubble haircut and a metal shield the size of my palm pinned on her rather generous chest.

"Oh. I didn't even notice Ammy was missing."

"Ammy?" I whispered back to Josh, and he gave me a dubious glance before he theatrically hit his own forehead.

"Riiiiight, you can't remember anything. Sorry, my bad."

I am not gonna lie, it took a lot of willpower to stop myself from flipping his desk on him. Maybe he realized the magnitude of my inner struggle, for Joshua forcefully cleared his throat and continued.

"That's Amelia. She is our prefect."

"You mean the class representative."

"No, I mean *prefect*. Anyways, listen, she probably has something to say."

True enough, by the time I returned my attention to her, the class rep was already standing behind the teacher's desk and was trying her hardest to get the attention of the placeholders, or at the very least get them to stop whispering about repetitive and completely random topics for a minute. I wondered if she even recognized the futility of it, or if she could even comprehend the difference between relatively normal people like Josh and the placeholders, but then I halted that train of thought as I took a closer look at her.

"Oooooh..."

I knew there was something that bothered me about her, and I just managed to put my finger on it: it was her hair! Not that I literally put my finger on it, of course—that wouldn't even make sense, but... anyway, her hair was unusual, but not in an unusual way. This requires some elaboration, doesn't it?

So, I already established that the vast majority of the placeholders looked alike, right? That, of course, included hairstyles as well, though hair was still the most varied thing about them. From the viewpoint of a stylist (which I admittedly wasn't, but never mind that), the boys and gals both wore simple, functional, yet overall nice hairdos.

And then there was her.

First off, while her chin-length bubble-cut appeared pure black at first glance, on a closer look, I realized it had a fairly distinct bluish shine to it. Also, while I called it bubble-cut, her hairdo was actually a little disheveled, but in the cute, fashionable way one might see on a Hollywood actress during an action sequence; the kind that needed several hours of work to appear somewhat natural. Not only that, but since I only saw her from profile at first, I didn't realize that she had a single thin, braided lock of hair hanging in front of her left ear, and it even had a purple ribbon weaved into it. All things considered, it was a hairdo that probably required way too much effort to maintain every day, yet here she was.

At this point, my train of thought switched rails.

Angie. She also had a fairly atypical haircut. While I'd already commented on the luster and the large hairpin she used to keep her bangs from interfering with her vision, she also had a big white ribbon on the back tying two long strands from the front together and holding the rest of her hair in a nice ponytail. That also didn't look like an everyday hairdo.

Considering all this, I had to wonder: was there a reason behind these two standing out like this? I glanced over to Josh, and soon my brows furrowed on their own accord.

"What?" He looked at me questioningly after glancing behind himself.

I had to wonder just how I never noticed it before, but Joshua also sported an unusually tidy and well-groomed hairdo, though he obviously lacked the girls' accessories.

"What!" Josh repeated impatiently.

I sighed and ran my fingers through my own mop.

"I'm just worried about my hair."

Josh's reaction was poetry in motion. First, he raised an eyebrow in surprise, then let it back down in incomprehension, and finally cocked his head to the side and gave me the most blatant *Dude, what the bloody hell are you talking about?* deadpan stare I'd ever seen. I tell you, the guy was a natural straight-man.

"That was totally random, even for you."

"My thoughts are complex. It's not my fault you can't follow them," I told him nonchalantly while I dived into my bag and retrieved my notebook.

I placed it in front of me and penned, *Hair: An indication of narrative importance?* I paused and tapped my pen against my chin in a decidedly thoughtful manner before I added, *Needs more data points,* and closed the notebook.

"What's that?" Joshua asked, craning his neck to get a better look.

"This?" I thumped the notes with my finger. He nodded. "My observation diary. I write things down to help me figure stuff out."

"That's... actually a pretty decent idea. By the way—" Apparently he'd remembered what we agreed upon before, since he leaned closer and took his whispers down a notch. "About your amnesia... Are you one hundred percent sure there is no change?"

After some face-rubbing, I decided to throw the guy a bone, if only so he'd stop looking at me like that.

"Well... I recognized Angie. Sorta."

Josh's eyes suddenly lit up with relief, like he was the one who'd made progress.

"That's good news, right?"

"I suppose."

If my answer sounded a wee bit ambivalent, it was because my attention was drawn back to the girl repeatedly clearing her throat in front of the inattentive class of placeholders.

"I have an announcement to make. Please pay attention."

Falling on deaf ears, the class rep's pleas kept going in a circle with no end. I think I could even see tears of frustration in the corners of her eyes.

"Shouldn't someone do something?"

"Hm?" Joshua followed my eyes and frowned in kind. "Yeah, you are right." To my sincerest surprise, he actually stood up and cleared his throat. "Guys! Please let Amelia talk!"

In response to his heartfelt plea, the class... showed exactly zilch reaction. There were a few glances in his direction, but overall the placeholders just kept at whatever they were doing before he spoke, which in the case of two guys at the back included playing cards.

Josh looked at me with crestfallen eyes and I had to roll mine in response. I stretched my fingers and gave him a *That's not how you do it* look. I limbered up my shoulders and then inhaled until my chest hurt before raising my hand high in the air.

I paused for a moment for the sake of dramatic tension, then I slapped my desk as hard as I could, which resulted in a surprisingly loud bang and an unsurprisingly painful stinging sensation in my palm. I waited for a moment for the echoes of the sound to die down and then let out all the air trapped in my lungs with a mighty bellow.

"SHUT THE BLOODY HELL UP ALREADY, YOU MISERABLE SIMPLETONS!"

The ordeal left me heaving for a while and for the next second or two, I felt lightheaded. But it worked. By the time the rushing blood retreated from my ears, the classroom was so silent, you could hear a queen of clubs being dropped, which incidentally was exactly what happened at the back.

I shifted in my seat to look back to Josh with a completely natural and in no way smug grin before I faced forwards again to wave to the class rep.

"Proceed."

She nodded with an awkward smile and cleared her throat.

"It seems like we will receive a transfer student today. It was sudden, so Mrs. Applebottom has to take care of the paperwork. Because of that, the first period is going to be free study. Please don't be rowdy and keep the noise to a minimum."

With her announcement finished, the class rep bowed and walked over to her desk in the front near Angie's.

"Mrs. Applebottom?" I inquired from Joshua after a few well-aimed elbow-pokes got his attention again.

"Our homeroom teacher. Young, thin, wears her hair in a bun. Ring any bells?"

I thought for a moment and shook my head. Josh clicked his tongue but didn't say anything else, so I took the initiative again.

"So, a new transfer student. On the second day of the school year."

"They probably had their reasons," Josh answered a smidgen absentmindedly.

"Sure. Any guesses?"

"About the early transfer?" he mused. "The sudden moving of the family. Late application. A bureaucratic error. My bet is on the last one—she had problems with her papers."

I nodded sagely, which he interpreted as agreement, though I had a feeling there was a more meta reason. Transfer students are a staple of any story featuring a high school. They are either used to kick off the plot or serve as some sort of catalyst. A female transfer student in particular usually means one of two things (and sometimes both): romantic interest and plot-hook. Taken that Josh already had a solid one in the form of Angie, and that I was the theoretical protagonist of this theoretical narrative, it was quite possible that this one was aimed at me. Theoretically.

We'll see.

As I was pondering the implication of a sudden love interest appearing out of the blue and how I would deal with it... suddenly a girl appeared in front of me!

Well, all right, maybe I'm being a wee bit dramatic here. What really happened was that the class rep walked over to Joshua's desk, which of course was right beside mine, so she kind of just popped into my peripheral vision while I was looking elsewhere.

She looked at each of us in turn and then gave a slight bow. Speaking of which, she bowed at the end of her announcement too. Was that a thing around these parts? I was tempted to write the question down into my notebook, but I decided I should do that later.

"I would like to thank you for your help. I truly appreciate it."

Well, I guess that's roughly what she said. The acoustics were pretty bad since she was talking to the floor, and by this point, the background noise also rose by a level.

"You're... welcome?"

Compared to my uncertain answer, Josh's words seemed to come naturally to him.

"It was only natural. If you need help in the future, you know you can always rely on me."

I was just about to roll my eyes at his overly verbose answer when the class rep straightened herself, smiled at him as she... she actually blushed? I mean, literally. I mean, sure, she was fairly pale-skinned, so it wasn't unthinkable, but this was the first time I'd seen someone with a cartoonishly blatant blush like that. And... she was blushing at *Josh*?

"The heck?"

I looked at her, then at Angie's back, then back at the class rep again. Did... did I just stumble upon a love triangle? That's unusual, unless... Was this some kind of romance narrative?

I put my elbows on the desk and began massaging my temples. If I was right, it validated some other things. If two of the named, unique-looking girls in class were pining for the only normal guy I knew, it meant that appearances really served as a good indicator of one's importance in this world.

On the other hand, it was one of the worst types of narratives to find myself in. For a start, I was bad with romance. I could tell this much even with the amnesia, due to the knot in my stomach I felt ever since the mere chance of the transfer student being *aimed* at me came up. And to make it even worse, since I already knew where things were heading, I'd never be able to act naturally without having doubts about the sincerity of anyone's affections. I mean, if this was really some sort of romantic fiction, people falling in love with me wouldn't be their choice, but just par for the course... But then again, that same logic applied to every other interaction under the sun, so...

No. Stop. Don't go down that alley; that way lies Paranoia Boulevard. Start doubting the feelings of one person and you'll soon start doubting the feelings of everyone and see shadows of narrative contrivance everywhere.

But then again, wouldn't that be the prudent thing to do? If I took my hypothesis about the world to its logical conclusion, wouldn't that mean that everyone, placeholders and normal people alike, were just actors playing out their designated roles?

I looked over at Josh, who was in the middle of receiving the appreciation of the class rep with a dopey smile, completely unaware of her sheepish glances and fidgeting hands. I couldn't help but chuckle and then subsequently shake my head.

No, they must have free will. I wanted to believe that, at least until I was certain of the contrary, so I promptly and firmly made it my policy from this point onwards.

"Are you all right?"

"Hm?" I glanced up and my eyes met with the bust of the class rep, so I blinked inconspicuously and glanced even higher to meet her eyes. For some reason, she was leaning over my desk and studying me. Then the actual question finally got processed by my cognitive machinery, so I answered.

"Sure, I'm fine. Why do you ask?"

"You were holding your head and shaking it. Does it hurt?"

I hadn't realized this before, but she did have a surprisingly soothing voice when not flustered.

"Nah, I'm fine," I answered with a smile I hoped was reassuring enough and leaned back on my chair. "Fit as a fiddle."

"Ah." Her face lit up like I'd just reminded her of something, and she leaned in closer. "Peabody was asking for you."

"Peabody?" I asked back reflexively, raising an eyebrow.

"The school nurse." Josh had come to my rescue in the nick of time.

"Ooooooh, *that* Peabody!" I parroted in fake realization as I turned back to the class rep. "Sorry, my mind was on something else. What did he want?"

"Something about amnesia."

"Ah, that..." Seeing the question marks in her eyes, I quickly added, "I asked him about it last time. It's for a paper. Extracurricular."

"On the second day of school?"

"Yup, I need the credits," I lied through my teeth like a pro, but I didn't want to press my luck, so I decided a sudden change of topic was in order. "So, can you tell us anything about the transfer student?"

"Yeah, I'm curious too."

I involuntarily blinked in surprise upon hearing the new voice entering the conversation. It came from behind our seats, so I glanced over my shoulder and found myself face-to-face with Angie.

"Whoa!" Joshua nearly jumped out of his chair. "Um... morning?"

Instead of returning the greeting, the girl averted her face with a pout and a small harrumph.

"Is there a problem?" the class rep asked tentatively, obviously taken off-balance by the unusual tension between the two.

"Nah, they just had a fight."

"Correction." Angie raised a finger. "We are only *going* to have a fight. Right now we are just not on speaking terms."

"So, you are not fighting?" the class rep asked again with a small frown that raised the glasses on her nose.

"Think of it this way," I spoke while gesturing with my hands. "They already have a casus belli. Right now they are having a cold war, and then there will be a war of total annihilation, which Josh will obviously lose. Right?"

"Right!" Angie nodded earnestly.

"Harsh," Josh whispered.

"I would like to warn you, I will not tolerate any fighting in the classroom. If you pick a fight with Joshua, I will have to report it to the teacher."

Angie took a step back like she was hit with a bucket of cold water.

"Hey, we are not fighting, right?"

"Then why are you here?"

Damn, the class rep might have looked meek, but her tongue was sharp. I saw Angie's brows furrow and I suddenly remembered that these two were the opposing prongs of a possible love triangle. After some reflection, I decided that preventing a possible fight was probably in my best interest as well.

"Wait, don't tell!" I exclaimed before Angie could answer and raised an open palm for emphasis. "I am going to use my newly developed psychic powers to predict exactly why she is here!"

With theatrical motions, I raised my left hand to my temple and extended my right hand towards Angie. She looked surprisingly amused by the display. I held the dramatic silence.

"I see..." I nodded sagely like I was receiving some great insight. "You were angry at Joshua for being a jerk, so you were sulking at your desk when you saw the class rep come over."

"Class rep?" "Jerk?" two-thirds of my audience mumbled. Angeline, on the other hand, was surprisingly attentive.

"You were jealous..." I paused and decided not to go the whole mile yet, so I hastily added, "... that we were having fun over here while leaving you out, but you thought that simply walking up to us would be awkward, so you snuck around and waited for the right moment to jump into the conversation."

Angie stayed silent. In the end, and to my sincerest surprise, she sighed and threw her hands into the air.

"Fine, you got me. Guilty as charged. But you know, it was really unfair to leave me out like that." Her mouth curled into an impish smile. "And if we're all being honest here, you, Leo, are a jerk too for not inviting me over! I was actually signaling you, you know?"

I couldn't help but burst out in laughter at her jab. In retrospect, I think this was the moment where I started to like her.

"I'm not a jerk," Josh sulked at my side, and it only made me laugh harder.

"What's a 'class rep'?" Amelia, now that she could find a lull in the conversation, inquired with a perplexed frown.

I pointed at her. "You are."

"I am?"

"Yup."

She needed some time to digest this, so I turned to the childhood friends on my other side. They seemed to be in the middle of figuring out the least awkward way to start a conversation. I sighed at the spectacle and raised a hand to pat Josh on the shoulder. If I went out of my way to stop one possible fight, I might as well go for broke and try to stop Angie's total war of annihilation as well.

"Just tell her you are sorry," I whispered to him matter-of-factly. He had the nerve to give me a withering look in return, the ungrateful toe-wriggler...

"Why?"

"Because you got her worried yesterday... which is not a hard feat, considering she is a giant worrywart, but still." He seemed unconvinced, so I patted him on the shoulder a bit harder this time. "Come on, we both know you two will make up in no time anyway, so please just get it over with so we can focus on more important things." I really hoped that my intended subtext of *I have too many things to worry about already and have no time for your crap* got across, loud and clear.

The guy groaned and dropped his shoulders in defeat.

"Fine, fine. I'm sorry. Are you happy now?"

"I dunno. Let's ask the recipient, shall we?"

I turned to Angie and, to my renewed surprise, she was looking at me with a strange mixture of suspicion and... respect? Or was it even awe? Either way, it made me uncomfortable.

"Wow, Leo. Wow. What happened to you over the summer?"

For a minute there, I thought she meant my amnesia, but then I replayed the previous conversation in my head and didn't find anything out of place, so I decided to play it safe.

"What exactly do you mean?"

"You... changed. Grew up, I suppose? Don't take me wrong, it was about time, but... it's still strange."

Now that was something I didn't consider before. Keeping my amnesia a secret for research purposes might be entirely pointless if people figured it out for themselves because I acted differently. But then again, I had no idea how I was supposed to act, though taken that they didn't bat an eye at my psychic performance, it must have been something they would've expected from the old me. Either way, I made a mental note about requesting Joshua to describe how I used to act in public. For now, it was best to play it safe.

"Nah, it's probably just your imagination." I waved my hand for emphasis, though she didn't seem all that convinced. I deemed it was time for another tactical switch in topics. "So, are you two going to make up or what?"

Angie puffed her cheek for a moment as she looked over at Joshua, who in turn looked decidedly awkward.

"He doesn't really mean it," she said at last.

"Oh, but he totally does. He is very sorry that he made you worry yesterday, but it was an emergency. Not to mention, it was ultimately because of me, and you have already forgiven me, so it's all good, anyway. Just sign that peace treaty and get this cold war over already."

"Hmmm..." Angie acted like it was a very hard decision to make (or at least I hoped she just acted the part), but at last she relented. "Oh, fine."

"Phew." Josh exhaled hard as if a weight had fallen off his chest.

"But we are still going to have a talk about this. In private," she added, much to Josh's chagrin.

"Fine. Whatever you do behind closed doors is none of our business, so long as it is soundproofed," I jested, and they both turned red. It took me a moment to realize that my joke could be read two different ways, so I decided to engage in my newfound hobby of tactical discussion re-railment. "Say, now that I think about it, I believe we didn't get our question about the transfer student answered, did we?"

I looked at the class rep and the others followed suit. Attention successfully averted. Yay.

I also couldn't help but notice that Angie was no longer frowning at either of us, so I suppose that was a step forward as well. Not that the class rep cared about that, as she was currently in the process of shrinking back from the sudden shift in attention.

"I... don't know much."

"You were at the teachers' office, right? Have you seen them?" Angie's inquiries seemed surprisingly eager. The class rep only nodded in response. "So?"

"She was a short-ish blonde girl... And she wore a dress."

"A dress? Really?" Now it was Josh's turn to interject. He also seemed surprisingly into it.

Huh, I guess everyone likes to gossip.

I, on the other hand, was reflecting that if my hypothesis about *uniqueness of appearance = importance* was correct, a girl wearing a dress in this high school setting would most definitely be an important addition. But what about her hair?

Should I ask about it? I pondered. Nah, they might mistake my purely academic inquiry as some kind of fetish.

"Yes. I think she didn't have her uniform delivered yet," the class rep continued without paying attention to me.

"But a dress?" Angie mused with a finger on her lips. "She must be rich."

"She had a butler, too," the class rep added, finally getting caught up in the gossip.

"Seriously?" Josh whistled.

"Let me guess..." I said as I stroked my chin in a manner most intellectual. "He is an elderly gentleman in a sharp suit, and his name is..."

Insert dramatic pause here.

"Sebastian."

The class rep's eyes opened wide and she sounded excited for the first time.

"Yes! How did you...?"

I theatrically raised a hand to my temple and stated, "Psychic powers."

"Really?" She looked like she was taking me seriously. I laughed and waved my raised hand with a grin.

"Nah, I'm just pulling your leg."

"Then how did you know?" Angie asked while leaning uncomfortably close. I've noticed this before as well, but she had problems recognizing personal space.

"I guessed." Since she didn't seem convinced at all, I decided to elaborate. "He is a butler to a girl wearing dresses when meeting with teachers, right? That means she and her family care a lot about appearances, so of course their butler would be wearing a suit. I guessed he would be an elderly gentleman because butlers generally come in two sizes: either older grandparent figures or young strapping lads doubling as bodyguards. So, it was fifty-fifty, but I figured you would've mentioned it if he was young, as it's more unusual. As for the name, I just picked the most stereotypical butler name that came to mind. Quite elementary, my dear Watson."

I did something like a half-bow with a flourish, though it probably looked silly considering I was still sitting at a desk. The childhood friend duo shared a glance, and then gave me three sarcastic claps in unison. The class rep, on the other hand, seemed to be completely lost in thought. I wasn't even sure she was listening, but then she suddenly hid her hands behind her back.

"How many fingers?"

"Pardon?"

"How many fingers am I showing?"

"Errr... None?"

"Behind my back. How many fingers, behind my back?"

She became so intense, I was caught off guard.

"Um... five?" I blurted out a random number that came to mind.

"Now?" she asked again after fidgeting.

"Seven?"

"And now?"

"One?"

"Fascinating!" The class rep seemed really impressed, even though I was just throwing random numbers at her.

"Say, by off chance, are you into parapsychology?" I asked tentatively, and she immediately stiffened.

"I... might be a... little interested..." she answered, her voice slowly reverting to her more reserved baseline, as if the previous excitement was bleeding out of her.

I shrugged and didn't pursue the question any further. Everyone had a hobby, even if it was a weird one, and considering my own hypotheses about the world, I really shouldn't be the one to cast the first stone.

PART 3

The rest of the free study period proved to be fairly uneventful. Since the class rep didn't know anything else about the new student, that line of discussion dried up quickly and the discourse soon shifted to more mundane topics, such as classes, teachers, recent episodes of shows I knew nothing about, after-school activities, and the occasional playful jab. All things considered, it was a laid-back and rather pleasant experience.

Not that it kept me from making notes, even if only the mental variety. I was mostly concerned with the group dynamic of these people.

First off, there was Josh. Somehow, he rarely seemed to be in the center of attention, yet he was always there to add a comment to any topic in question and the two girls seemed to pay him some heed whenever he opened his mouth. But then again, I suppose the last part was a given.

Angie, on the other hand, was the most active speaker in the group. She talked, joked, and teased nonstop, yet somehow she never really appeared to be trying to be in control. Even when it came to Josh, where she threw more proverbial punches than she took, their interactions felt more like the joshing (no pun intended) between close siblings rather than one side domineering the other. I suppose that's how childhood friend relationships are supposed to look, huh?

As for the class rep, she mostly stayed silent and listened, only nodding and speaking short sentences when asked about something. The only time she took the initiative was when we started to get too rowdy or when it looked like Angie was picking on Josh.

Overall, I had to conclude that these guys were nice and it was fun hanging out with them even if doing so didn't really further my overall goals. It just felt strangely relaxing.

At last, the first period ended with the ringing of the chime and our impromptu group broke into its constituents. Well, technically Josh and I were still sitting by each other, but I was too busy copying his homework to bother socializing.

My next class was math by the way, which was also taught by our homeroom teacher, Mrs. Applebottom. Now that I'm on the subject, am I the only one who thinks her name sounds really, really British? Just me? Anyways, just a quick glance at the homework problems showed that either my math skills were really, really rusty, or that they'd started teaching rocket science in high school while I wasn't looking. The problem wasn't with the operations; I could do most of them in my head without a calculator, but I just didn't know the right formulae for anything... which, taken that I had amnesia, shouldn't have been all that surprising.

"Man, I became dumb."

"*Became?*" Josh grinned at my side, but I brushed him off with a roll of the eye and continued copying.

The lesson started only a few seconds after I finished, and the teacher arrived almost the moment the bell rang. She was a slender young woman in a dark blue turtleneck sweater, and she wore her light brown hair in a tidy bun on the back of her head. She stood in front of the blackboard and the class fell silent.

"Good morning, children." Her soprano voice was quite pleasant, but also sounded a little off. "As you have probably already heard, our class received a new addition this morning. She is from the mainland, so please help her out if she doesn't know how to do something around here."

A particular word in that sentence hit me like a sledgehammer. Mainland. I'd never had the time to really wonder about this, but just where the hell was I, anyway? Geographically, I mean. I already knew that I was in a fairly big town—that much I could gather from the maps from the day before—but I had no idea where the town was in relation to, well, every-thing else. I decided to quickly scribble the question into my notebook and shelve it for the time being in favor of more pressing concerns.

"Her name is Eleanor Dracis. Please give her a warm welcome."

On the teacher's cue, the sliding door (still weird) opened wide to let in a blonde girl of average height but above average poise. To my, and pre-sumably some others' disappointment, she wasn't wearing a dress, but the standard female school uniform: a white shirt, a khaki jacket worn over a grey knitted vest, and a knee-length skirt of the same colour. Not that she needed a dress to stand out in the first place, mind you.

To put it bluntly, she was beautiful. Sure, Angie was cute and the class rep was also pretty, but she was just supermodel-tier. And not the starving, anorexic type, either. That much was made obvious by how well she filled out her clothes, front and back.

Then there was her sparkling blond hair adorned by a red metal hairband that I nearly mistook for a tiara at first glance. It was long (her hair, I mean, not the hairband), and she wore it in twin tails that seemed to naturally curl into drills as they cascaded down behind her shoulders. Actually, I think those are called *ringlets*, a hairstyle often denoting wealth and nobility. Huh. At this rate, I could safely update my hypothesis about the link between physical appearance and importance to an actual theory.

But back to the topic at hand: The girl strutted into the classroom with confident steps and stood by the teacher's desk for a moment before she did a small curtsy. After the stereotypical ooooh-aaaah-ing and squeeing finally died down (I had to give it to them, the placeholders were nothing if not predictable), she slowly looked over the class.

Her eyes seemed to pass over me, completely unaware of just how nervous I was getting by the whole ordeal. It was at this moment that I was at the highest risk of something incredibly embarrassing happening. Thankfully nothing of the sort came about, and instead she smiled and spoke up with a dignified voice.

"Please allow me to introduce myself. I am Eleanor Dracis. It is my pleasure to meet you." She curtsied again to another bout of applause and turned to the teacher. "Please take good care of me."

Mrs. Applebottom's lips widened into a warm yet stiff smile. "Naturally. Please take a seat over there."

She pointed at the empty desk right in front of mine. I barely managed to stifle a groan in response. Yup, just as expected. Furthermore, she seemed just as ambivalent about the idea of sitting next to me as I was, but then she looked over at Joshua and her face softened. That stopped me in my tracks again, but I had no time to realize the look's implications.

She walked over to the desk and sat down. The lesson began, robbing me of any opportunity to ponder for another forty-five minutes.

PART 4

The rest of the morning classes proved to be fairly uneventful. I studied the material as best I could under the circumstances during the lessons, and then I hung out with Josh and Angie during the breaks. It seemed like the class rep was either not part of our close circle or she was just too busy helping the new girl catch up with the curriculum to socialize with us. Angie and Josh also exchanged a few courtesies with her, but nothing more. All things considered, nothing really remarkable happened.

My observation diary gained a new entry, though, under Anomalies. Apparently, every single class was taught by Mrs. Applebottom. When I asked Joshua about this, he just scratched his head and said that there were other teachers as well, but I sure as hell never saw one.

As for our new transfer student, she caused quite a stir amongst the placeholders. No break passed by without a throng of them swarming her, making small talk with wooden smiles and asking inane questions. On the bright side, since she was sitting in front of me, I could learn a lot of small details about her.

She was apparently from the Abakazian Mountains (which I was 95 percent sure didn't exist), her parents were working overseas (which I still had no idea about), she was living in a renovated mansion in my own neighbourhood (which I didn't see during my wandering the day before, either) and she was single but didn't plan on staying that way for long (which sent shivers down my spine). There were also some trivia like her blood type and her three sizes, but those didn't even warrant recording in my notes.

Finally, lunch break rolled around, and I immediately waved for Josh to stick to me.

"We have a cafeteria, right?" I asked once he leaned over.

"Yeah?" he answered cautiously, as if it were a trick question.

"Should we check out today's menu?"

"It's the same as every other... Oh." At long last it finally dawned on him why I was asking for him to accompany me and he gave me a small nod. "Sure thing. You have the money?"

"Yup," I answered while shaking the stuffed leather wallet in my hand.

"Okay, follow my lead and—"

"Excuse me."

We both halted on our tracks as an unfamiliar voice called out to us. Josh and I turned in unison to find the new girl standing by his desk. She had a large, rectangular package wrapped in a plaid cloth in her hands and a pleasant smile plastered on her face.

"Yes?"

"You see..." She raised the package in her hands. "I'm afraid my cook got a little too eager about my first day in school this morning and she packed my lunch box to the brim. There is no way I can eat all this alone, so would you care to join me?"

I involuntarily frowned. What was this obviously transparent performance about? Inviting classmates like that on her first day would have been mildly odd already, but doing so to two boys she barely knew was definitely fishy. And then, on top of that, there was something odd about her bearing. It was like she was performing rehearsed lines in a play. It felt totally artificial. In other words, double-fishy.

I saw Josh was just about to answer, but considering the friendly smile on his face, I had a feeling he didn't pick up on any of the red flags. As such, I decided to cut him off by lightly elbowing him in the kidney. For friendship.

"Sorry, but we already had plans. Why don't you ask the class rep?"

"The who?" The girl's stage-smile flickered for a moment, but ultimately it held.

"Amelia," Josh answered through a smile of gritted teeth before he angrily stomped on my foot.

"Yeah, her." I hid my grimace with a nod.

"But..." She wavered for a moment. "But I'm afraid two girls wouldn't be able to finish it all." She turned her pleading eyes directly at Josh and continued the assault. "My cook used some really, really high quality ingredients and I would hate for them to go to waste."

"Sorry, I already decided on the cafeteria," I told her. She paused for a moment and turned back to Josh.

"Then how about just you?"

I clasped the guy on the shoulders before he could say anything.

"Nope, he's coming with me too."

"But why? I assure you, my lunch box is better than anything in your cafeteria."

"Doesn't matter, I already have my reservation."

"In the cafeteria?"

"On him."

"What does that even mean?" she exclaimed.

"Do I have any say in this?" Josh cried out in confusion.

"Nope," I answered his inquiry, accompanied by a thump on the back.

"But he obviously doesn't want to go with you! He should come with me!"

"First come, first served," I stated matter-of-factly and began pushing Joshua through the door. The girl suddenly lunged forward and latched onto his arm while brandishing her package with the other.

"These are made from very rare ingredients!"

I nodded.

"Yes, you already told us that."

"They are very, very valuable."

"I... think that logically follows, yes," Josh spoke, still a little bewildered by the scene. The new girl turned to me, her sapphire eyes all but crackling with frustration, looked me right in the eye, and hissed, "If they go to waste because of your flippant obstinacy, I *will* make you pay."

To her apparent surprise, I nodded with a weary sigh.

"Well, we can't have that, can we?" Before she could say anything in return, I let out a jaunty whistle and raised my free hand high over my head in a wave.

At the other end of the classroom, Angie looked up from her bag and cocked her head to the side in inquiry. I waved to her again and she trotted up to us with a curious expression.

"What's up?"

"Listen, Angie, you won't believe this!" I told her with mock enthusiasm, completely ignoring the confused stares of the other two.

"What? What?" she answered with her own brand of fake gusto.

"The new girl over here has an incredibly awesome lunch box she wants to share!"

"Really? How awesome is that awesome?"

"It's like a five-star menu made by a team of world-renowned French chefs, made exclusively from the body parts of creatures you find at the end of high-level side-quests!"

"Wow. That's almost thirty percent more awesome than I expected!"

"I know!" I answered and winked at her. She winked back. Good, for a moment I thought she'd stopped being sarcastic. "But there is too much of it for her alone, so she wants to share it so it won't go to waste."

"How nice of her."

"And she *especially* wants to share it with Josh over here."

"Oh?"

Finally recognizing what was going on, Angie's smile went from amused to appreciative and then downright impish.

"Sadly, however, Josh has already promised to accompany me, and you know him—he never, ever breaks a promise."

"I know, I know. He is really honest and forthcoming like that."

"I know, right? But leaving her behind and letting her precious food go to waste would also trouble him."

"He is such a nice guy!" Angie nodded with a voice all but dripping with sarcasm.

"So, to alleviate his worries, could I ask you to help the princess munch through all of her food?"

The new girl suddenly stiffened and looked at me with eyes wide as saucers. She obviously wanted to say something, but Angie grabbed hold of her arm before she could even utter a squeak and began dragging her.

"A great idea! I should get the usual suspects and have us all eat together."

I didn't know who these usual suspects were, but for the time being, I also grabbed hold of Josh and began pulling him in the opposite direction.

"See you later!"

"Wait!" the new girl protested. "Why did you—?"

I couldn't make out the last of her words, as by that time I was already dragging Josh out of the classroom and down the stairs. Once we were out of earshot, I stopped. My shoulders sagged in exhaustion.

"I guess you are going to tell me now just what the heck is going on, right?"

"Hm?" I glanced at Joshua and this time I quite deliberately shrugged my shoulders. "Nothing special. Why?"

"Nothing special? Nothing special! You hit me in the back and practically dragged me away from the transfer student!"

"Oh, that? It was for your own good." Josh gave me a deadpan look, so I sighed and decided to elaborate. "Listen, didn't you find it strange that she wanted to invite us to lunch?"

"No..." he answered hesitantly. "Thought she was just friendly."

"Oh come on, think about it for a moment." I gestured at his head, but he only frowned at me again. "Listen, it is not normal for girls to invite boys they don't even know to share lunch on their first day in school. It's just way too forward. Sure, maybe she is just friendly, but if I had to bet, I'd say she had some other motives. With hidden motives comes trouble, and right now we are already running on full capacity on that."

"We?" Josh wiggled an eyebrow at me in a surprisingly competent display of facial gymnastics. "Don't you mean *you*?"

"Don't fret the semantics." I waved a hand and took a step forwards, then stopped. "By the way, which way is the cafeteria?"

My friend pointed in the opposite direction I took a step in and I clicked my tongue. I'd had a fifty-fifty chance, and I still blew it. It would probably take weeks before I'd be able to navigate this damn school building. Anyways, I started striding in the indicated direction and Josh fell in line beside me.

"Just admit it, you put up that whole display because you'd be lost without me." He paused for a moment before adding, "By the way, did you really need to hit me on the back? That hurt."

"You nearly flattened my feet afterwards, so we're even. As for the first part... I honestly think getting involved with that girl right now will be too much trouble."

"Why?"

"It's... complicated. I'll tell you when I am certain."

"Now where did I hear that before..."

I ignored the barbs in his tone. I mean, technically I *was* imposing on him without telling him my real reasons, so he had all the right in the world to be indignant... but then again, I had no idea how he would react to me saying, *Well, that girl is part of the stereotypical romance narrative that is probably aimed at me, and I really don't have time to waste on stuff like that. Not to mention, it would be awkward.* Sharing my real motives was out of the question.

"Anyways, I have a question for you," I told him as we exited the main building through the back. It seemed that the cafeteria was in the large building on the other side of the sizable inner courtyard.

"Yes?"

"Am I acting weird?"

Josh gave me another of his perfect deadpan looks. "Yes."

"No, you don't get it," I emphasized by shaking my hands. "I mean, am I acting differently from how I used to be before the—" I paused to see if there was anyone around who could overhear and finished with, "... the whole amnesia business?"

This time it took a few seconds for Josh to formulate an answer, though it turned out the same.

"Yes."

"How so?"

My friend scratched his cheek in an awkward motion and finally let out a sharp breath.

"Well, you are mostly the same. I mean, your sense of humour is as terrible as ever."

"Ouch!" I clasped my hands over my heart. "Your words wound me most grievously!"

He suddenly raised a hand and pointed at me.

"See, that's what I am talking about! That's the kind of thing you used to pull all the time, acting all dramatic and weird." He waited for me to let my hands back down before continuing. "Now... now you are a different kind of weird."

"Please elaborate."

He pointed at me again.

"That, right there! Sometimes you just slip into this mannerism where you talk all sophisticated and act like you know everything! It's unnerving."

"My good sir, I assure you, I most certainly never do such a thing."

"There, you are doing it again!"

I laughed and patted him on the back.

"Nah, I'm just pulling your leg. But I can kind of see what you're getting at."

Sadly, it was not something I could easily change. I mean, if it was just a few verbal tics, I could easily fake that, but changing my entire mannerism? That might be a little bit beyond my acting abilities. Still, I had to be careful and keep a close eye on my outward attitudes from this point onwards.

It was around this point that we finally entered the cafeteria, and my jaw nearly dropped to the floor. For a moment I had to check behind me to see if we didn't accidentally exit the campus and end up in a French restaurant across the street.

First off, the dining hall was huge. It could easily hold about two hundred people at once, and didn't do so in your typical rows-upon-rows-of-tables setup. Oh no, this place looked like a proper restaurant, with scores of round tables arranged in a neat pattern under its vaulted ceiling. Not only that, but everything was covered in wooden paneling, including the brownstone columns holding up said vaulted ceiling. Combined with the ambient lighting provided by the huge glass panels serving as walls on two sides of the hall, the place had the distinct impression of a classy modern restaurant.

"What the hell is up with this place?" I asked Josh in the entrance between two bouts of gawking.

"Ah, yeah. It's been recently renovated, so the cafeteria became a bit gaudy. Don't worry, the standard menu is just as bland and boring as it used to be." He smiled at me and ushered me towards the food counter.

"Gaudy is a bit of an understatement," I murmured as I let myself be led through the constantly flowing stream of placeholders.

At last, we arrived in front of one of the three counters and got in line. Once we got our place reserved, Josh turned to me and began explaining the process.

"This is where you get in line first. You can either buy cold food, such as sandwiches or one of the premade lunch boxes, or you can get a meal ticket. You take the meal ticket to one of the other two counters, depending on which one is less crowded, and you get the meal you paid for there. You can see all the prices on the boards up there."

"I see..." I followed Josh's finger, only to freeze on my tracks mid-step and gape at the price tags. "Something isn't right here."

"Hm?" Joshua turned back to see why I stopped and followed my eyes to the price board for the premade stuff. "Which one?"

"All of them!" I answered with a bit more zeal than I originally planned and quickly toned back a little. I fixed my eyes on the prices again. There is this well-known, slightly tongue-in-cheek thing in economics known as a *burger index*. It is used to compare the prices of the same goods in different countries, but it is also a good indication of the value of a currency. In other words, telling you how many of the exact same burgers you can buy for the same amount of currency tells you about the strength of that currency and just how much purchasing power it has.

Now, if I were to transplant that idea into my current situation and turn it into a *chicken sandwich index*, it would mean...

"Oh my God..."

"What?" Josh looked at me funny.

"Oh. My. God!" I repeated, this time with even more passion.

"What?!"

I grabbed Josh by the shoulders and pointed at the menu.

"Are those prices accurate?"

My friend seemed to be utterly confused, but at last he nodded. I took a deep breath and looked him in the eye.

"Josh... I... I think I'm filthy rich."

"Huh?" He tilted his head to the side uncomprehendingly, so I quickly got my wallet out and opened it up for him to see its contents. His eyes opened as wide as if I'd just showed him the Ark of the Covenant. "What the...?! Where? How?"

At the moment, my wallet held ten thousand *Jen*. How much did a chicken sandwich cost? Oh, about *two*.

Josh clasped my hand over my wallet and leaned closer to whisper. His eyes were downright bewildered.

"Are you involved in some kind of shady business?"

"No!" I answered instinctively, only to then pause and add, "Well, at least I don't think so. This is just a fraction of my monthly allowance."

"Seriously?"

"Yeah. I wanted to buy some stuff, so I went to an ATM this morning to take out some money, but I had no idea how much a Jen is worth, so I decided to take ten-K."

In retrospect, I probably should have figured something was off when the machine gave me a pile of hundred Jen notes, but I was late for school, so I just stuffed them into my wallet and ran.

"That's crazy!"

"Tell me about it!"

We both sighed in unison.

"So, what now?" Josh asked wearily, unaware of the blockade we were causing in the waiting line.

"We buy some food?" I said with a shrug. "I mean, we might as well. Do you want anything in particular?"

"Your treat?"

"Well, I did get you into trouble yesterday, and I dragged you along just now, so... yeah, why not?"

Joshua nodded to himself and looked over the menu.

"You know," he turned back to me, with an ominous smile. "I've always wondered what lobsters taste like..."

CHAPTER 5

PART 1

"I still can't believe they had lobsters on the menu... Just what kind of school is this?!"

Of course my question was purely rhetorical, partially because I already knew that the place was completely artificial and thus unbound by common sense, but mostly because there was no one else around to answer. After he stuffed his face full of lobster meat (which he declared tasted like chicken, go figure), Josh left ahead of me while I finished up my own meal, a small serving of lasagna. He told me he wanted to check on Angie and the new girl, and since I didn't have any good reason to hold him back (not to mention, my mouth was too full to answer properly), I let him go without further ado.

There was still a good fifteen minutes left of the one-hour lunch break, which at first sounded excessive, but after seeing the scope of the cafeteria and its dishes, I could completely understand the need. Of course, a longer lunch break meant that afternoon classes ended later as well, so the school day would end just after 3 p.m., but it was only to be expected. Anyways, I finished up my plate and left the cafeteria just a few minutes earlier, and decided on a small detour prior to returning to the classroom.

I rounded another corner and breathed deep in relief as I found myself at the door of the nurse's office. For a second or two I was afraid I'd gotten lost again, but it seemed I'd at least grasped the basic layout of the school. As for why I was here, the class rep told me that the nurse was looking for me, so I decided to get ahead of any possible complications and see him as soon as possible, meaning right then and there.

I lightly knocked on the door and it opened to a crack. Evidently, it wasn't closed properly, so I opened it farther as I looked inside.

"Mr...?" Wait, what was his name again? Something about legumes. Ah, right. "Mr. Peabody?"

"O-ho-ho! Come in, come in!"

It was impossible to mistake that combination of jovial voice and annoying laughter. I stepped inside and found the old man... well, to be fair, he was probably only middle-aged, but either way, he was sitting by his desk and welcomed me with a smile half-hidden under his mustache.

"You were looking for me."

"O-ho-ho. Indeed I was." I sat down on the chair by his side without any prompting. He didn't seem to mind. "It is about your question from yesterday."

It took me a moment to realize what he was talking about, but when it did, to say that it piqued my interest was an understatement.

"You mean about the amnesia."

"O-ho-ho. Indeed."

"Stop that."

"O-ho-ho. What do you mean?"

"Your laughing. It's... wait, didn't we already have this conversation?"

"O-ho-ho. So you can remember that much. Good, very good."

By this point, my first rush of curiosity subsided and I started to feel quite uncomfortable, which turned into outright worry the moment I noticed the large rubber mallet on his desk.

"What's that for?"

"O-ho-ho. I sadly couldn't give you an answer yesterday, so I consulted my medical journals and picked the most effective treatment option."

"A hammer."

"Indeed! Apparently, all you need is a single good whack on the—"

I stood up and casually left the room before he got even halfway through his spiel, and for a moment I thought he would continue talking without even noticing, but then he called out to me just as I was about to close the door behind myself.

"Wait, where are you going?"

"Classes."

"But we haven't applied your treatment yet!"

I paused and tried to imitate one of Josh's deadpan glares. I presumably did an inadequate job, as the nurse kept doing practice swings with his hammer.

"Sorry, doc, but I already tried that."

His last swing wilted mid-motion and he gave me a disappointed "Oh." I decided not to stick around, lest he would try to hit me just to be sure, so I gave him a wave and scurried off posthaste. Once I was out of sight, I leaned against a wall and sighed. Hard. What a colossal waste of time...

Well, it wasn't like I had high expectations in the first place, but the guy was supposed to be a trained medical professional. I was expecting some questions, or maybe a boring info-dumping session about amnesia littered with Latin terms I would've had to look up later, but I certainly wasn't expecting a friggin' hammer! What is this, Looney Tunes?

I was just about to be on my way back to the classroom when I was caught off guard by a sharp "Ha!" coming from behind me. I glanced over my shoulder and found the new girl standing straddle-legged in the middle of the hallway, one hand curled into a fist and placed on her hip while the other extended towards me and ending in an accusatory finger. Needless to say, she was also glaring at me. People around me did that a lot lately. I wonder if that's normal?

Anyways, I suppressed my urge to say something along the lines of "Ha what?" and instead I just shook my head and walked up to her.

"Hello."

She blinked at me, her fierceness faltering, but then she forcefully set her mouth in a thin line and pointed at me again.

"Did you think you could hide from me?!"

I looked left, right, then behind myself and turned back at her with a wry smile.

"Oh no, I've been found out! I was certain no one would find me at my trusty hiding place, a well-populated and open corridor!" I exaggeratedly hit my forehead with the heel of my hand. "Oh, wait. No, that's the exact opposite of a hiding place. What was I thinking? Oh, the humanity."

I managed to say all that with one breath and without breaking my poker face. I'm not going to lie, I was actually a little proud of that. My accuser out of the blue, on the other hand, seemed more and more flustered by the second.

"Don't try to make a fool out of me!"

Why would I? You are doing an admirable job of it yourself! Well, that was what I wanted to say, but after my pointless meeting with the nurse, I really wasn't in the mood anymore.

"I don't. By the way, could you step to the side? You are holding everyone up."

She glanced around and it apparently just dawned on her that she was standing in the middle of a crowded corridor. Her face abruptly flushed red and she even let out an admittedly cute yelp as she scampered to the side to let the traffic flow again. I shook my head with a grimace and followed after her.

"So, what is this whole thing about?"

"Don't act innocent!" She hissed at me. While she regained some of her composure, she still seemed pretty flustered to me.

"About what?"

"Your actions!"

"Which one in particular? I do a lot of those."

She glared at me even more fiercely and I think I saw her clenched fists trembling.

"Why did you go out of your way to refuse my invitation? What is your agenda?"

"Agenda?"

"Your motive, your plan, your scheme, your—"

"I know what the word means, I just don't know what the hell you're talking about!"

She stomped her feet and leaned in to glower at me from even closer, though since she was almost a head shorter than me, it only worked if I looked down on her. Maybe that annoyed her too?

"You went out of your way to ruin my chance to invite him! Did you really think I wouldn't find it suspicious?!"

"Him?" I parroted after her, a touch uncomprehendingly, before I realized what she was talking about. "Oh, you mean Josh?"

"Yes!" she yelled so loud even some of the placeholders turned our way. Maybe they were more susceptible to her because she was a transfer student and was supposed to be interesting? Food for thought. Anyways, she looked around and asked, "Where is he anyway?"

"Oh, he actually wanted to check on you, so he left a few minutes ago."

All of a sudden, all the anger in her face fell away to reveal a dopey expression.

"What?"

"Josh. He said he wanted to see how you and Angie were doing, so he left the cafeteria ahead of me. Didn't you meet him on the way?" She shook her head. "Oh well, I guess you missed each other."

She stomped her feet with a growl reminiscent of a revving chainsaw and gave me her most fiery glare yet.

"Why didn't you stop him?!"

For a moment, all I could do is to stop myself from burying my face in my hands.

"First you were angry because I went away with him, now you are angry because he is not around anymore? Would you please make up your mind, princess?"

To my sincerest bafflement, she seemed to panic and jumped back a step. I cocked my head to the side and she nearly poked out my eye as her hand lashed out her accusatory finger again.

"I knew I heard it right the first time around!"

"You heard the what the when?"

If I sounded completely confused and worn down by the erratic pace of the conversation, it was only because I kept my cool. I was actually screaming in frustration on the inside.

"Why did you call me that? How did you know? Who sent you? Are you here to interfere with my...?"

She kept on asking questions, but I didn't really listen, as I was still trying to figure out the answer to the first one. What did I call her again? I replayed our conversation in my head and finally realized.

"Princess?"

She once again let out a weird sound (something along the lines of "Yafuu!") and jumped back, looking left and right like a frightened wild animal caught in a corner by a pack of wolves.

"Stop saying that!"

"Why?"

"Because I said so!"

"And that should matter to me because...?"

"Arggh!" She began shaking and her head started to go from beet red to a shade of purple.

That couldn't have been healthy, so I gently patted her on the shoulder and told her, "Hey, calm down, calm down. Everybody's looking."

In the span of three seconds, her face went from purple to red to normal to deathly pale as she glanced around and noticed the placeholders staring at us. She looked at my hand on her shoulder and squeaked again, jumping so far back, she was once more standing in the middle of the corridor.

"Y-y-youuu!"

"Me?"

"I hate you!" she declared, stomping her foot. She did that a lot. "I hated you from the first time I saw you! You keep getting in my way, you are annoying, and you smell bad!"

"Well, excuuuuse me, princess!" I answered with a frown of my own as I folded my arms.

She let out another yelp, and before I knew it, she was already sprinting down the corridor, pushing the placeholders aside like an angry bull on the streets of Pamplona. She rounded a corner... then a few seconds later, she poked back around the same corner, pointed at me angrily, and yelled, "This is not over yet! I will get you for this!"

In response to her declaration of war, I simply rolled my eyes, raised my hands to my mouth to form a funnel, and answered, "Whatever you say, princess!"

She nearly fell out of the corner with another squeal but caught herself at the last moment, glared at me one last time, and ran away. Again. Once I was sure she wasn't coming back for another bout, I dropped my shoulders in exasperation and groaned hard enough to make my throat hurt. Yep, *definitely* a tsundere.

My return to the classroom suffered no further setbacks, and I arrived a good five minutes before the next lesson started. Josh and Angie were already (or still?) talking by my desk, while the princess was nowhere to be found. That was odd, but I didn't really mind at the moment.

I waved to the guys, who were arguing about whether a lobster or some kind of rare beef tasted better, and plopped down onto my chair, ready to record my previous discoveries in my notebook. Then I remembered something and turned to Josh instead.

"Hey, guys, got a sec?"

"Hm?" He and Angie both looked at me curiously. "Yes?"

"Guys, give it to me straight. Do I smell weird?"

The two of them gave me sardonic looks that were mirror images of each other. If synchronized deadpan was an actual sport, these two would have had a head start towards the Olympic gold. At last, Angie leaned closer and took a whiff.

"Hmmm... No, not particularly." She took another whiff and suddenly she perked up. "Oh, wait... is that citrus? I actually kinda like that."

"Probably my shampoo," I answered a tad absentmindedly.

"Why do you ask?"

"Nah, just checking."

It was about this time that the princess entered the classroom with a huff and a puff. She sent me a glare when our eyes met, but then she averted her gaze, strutted over to her desk, and sat down without even acknowledging my existence.

I didn't really mind, but I couldn't help but wonder where she had been. She left before me but arrived later, and judging by her heaving, she must've been running for a while... Oh well, maybe she just got lost. She was as new to the place as I was, so it wouldn't have been unusual if she took a wrong turn somewhere and couldn't find her way back. I mean, it's not like *everything* had to have some deeper narrative meaning. Sometimes simple explanations can work too... Right?

PART 2

The afternoon classes were exactly the same as the morning classes in practically every regard. Once again all the lessons were taught by Mrs. Applebottom, I once again had to struggle to catch up to the curriculum, I once again spent all the breaks with the gang, and I generally had a fair amount of fun.

Well, okay, on second thought, there *was* a slight difference. In the morning, the girl sitting right in front of me didn't seem to be aware of me, while at this point, she was actively trying to deny my entire existence. At least, when she wasn't sending death-glares my way. There was little functional difference, though, so it didn't really change my school life experience.

It was exactly at three in the afternoon when the final lesson ended with the ring of the familiar Big Ben chime that the entire class erupted with noise, completely disregarding the teacher still in the room. Not that she minded. She only bothered to finish her last sentence about the geopolitical tensions that led to the First World War before she just snapped her book shut and marched out the door. It wasn't even a complete paragraph, for crying out loud! That's a placeholder for you, I guess.

I stretched in my chair and also began to pack my bag when Angie snuck up to my desk.

"Hey, Leo? Wanna go home together?"

I blinked at the directness of the question and sent a sneaky glance at Josh. My friend gave me an amicable smile, but then he finally realized the reason behind my hesitation and cut in with a cough.

"Just until the crossing, of course."

"Yeah, of course." Angie nodded twice.

"Then sure. Let me grab my stuff and I'll meet you at the lockers."

"Oh-kay!" Angie giggled and all but dragged Josh out through the door. She seemed to be in high spirits. It suited her.

It was only then that I realized that the two exiting the stage left me alone with the princess, but when I cautiously looked around, she was nowhere to be found. Where did she go? And when? She must've left while I was paying attention to Josh, but that was like, what? Three seconds? Did she jump out the window during that time or what?

I shook my head and stood up. Don't look the gift horse in the mouth, they say. If this way I could avoid another round of awkward and annoying comedy play, I was not complaining. I walked down the rows while dodging the other students when my eyes were caught by the class rep still sitting at her desk. It looked like her bag was already packed and she was just calmly staring ahead of herself without a word. I hesitated, but then I had an idea and decided to call out to her.

"Hey there, class rep."

She shuddered and looked up at me like I'd startled her even though I walked up to her right in her line of sight.

"Oh... Hello, Leo. Can I help you?"

"I really hope so."

Once she confirmed I had business with her, the tension visibly escaped from her shoulders. I had a niggling suspicion since this morning, and this moment only reinforced it: While it didn't really show when she was performing her duties, she was a bit socially awkward when it came to small talk. It wasn't to the degree where she would be considered shy, but she definitely looked uncomfortable whenever she had to talk with people about something other than schoolwork.

Anyways, she looked at me with expectant eyes, so I cleared my throat.

"Say, class rep?"

She puckered her brows and interrupted me.

"Why are you calling me that?"

"Because you are the class rep. Anyways," I continued before she could interject again, "I wanted to ask you if you could lend me your notes."

She blinked at me in surprise.

"Don't you have yours?"

"Sorry, I wasn't clear enough. I meant last year's notes."

She blinked twice this time and even frowned a little.

"I... I am not sure I still have them," she faltered. "Why do you need them?"

"Well..." I deliberately scratched the back of my head before I plied her with, "you see, last year I transferred fairly late, so I didn't have to worry about it too much, but I'm not sure we had the exact same curriculum in my old school. I want to make sure I don't miss anything that might be on future tests, so I wanted to borrow your notes so I could cross-reference things."

"That's... very diligent of you," she told me with an approving smile.

"Thanks," I answered with a chuckle. "Could I also ask you to give me some pointers? Only if it wouldn't be too much trouble, of course."

"Naturally. I will see if I can find my notebooks and I'll gladly help if you have any questions."

"Thank you very much." After this exchange, we stayed perfectly still in the empty classroom for several seconds. It was getting really awkward, so I lightly cleared my throat. "Say, aren't you going home yet?"

"In a minute," she told me with a small smile that didn't quite reach her eyes. Then it was silence again.

"Do you... want to go home together?"

Her eyes fluttered wide open for just a moment.

"You and me?"

"Um... who else? Plus Josh and Angie too, of course."

"Oh..." The class rep averted her gaze with an awkward smile. "I see. It's been a while, so I was caught off guard."

"So, are you coming?"

"Sure," she immediately declared with a nod and stood up.

I patiently waited for her to pack her bag and we left the classroom side by side. We quickly reached the stairs leading to the main hall and I couldn't help but smile all the way. I was bothered by my lagging behind the others academically all day, and while it was something of a whim, having the class rep's notes would surely help me catch up to the others. Originally I wanted to ask Josh, but this was obviously the smarter idea. No offense to the guy—he wasn't dumb by a long shot—but there was just no competition.

We reached the shoe lockers in no time. Josh and Angie were already by the entrance and waving, though the girl had a question mark written over her face when she noticed the class rep at my side.

"I'll be with you in a moment!" I yelled over to them, but they probably couldn't hear it properly over the noise the other departing placeholders made, and so they walked over to me instead. Oh well, it didn't make much of a difference in the long run.

"Is Ammy with you?" Josh asked once he was within earshot.

"Yeah. She looked a little lonely, so I decided to invite her along. Is there a problem?"

Josh grinned at the class rep, who was currently busy studying her own shoelaces like her life depended on it, and he shook his head.

"Nah, the more the merrier, right, Angie?"

"Yeah."

She didn't seem as enthusiastic about going home together as before, but she still managed to sound cheerful enough. In the meantime, the class rep broke off from the group to find her own shoe locker and so did I. I opened the cabinet and as I did, a small piece of paper flew out with the draft.

I was too surprised to react fast enough, and by the time I'd recovered it, Angie had already taken note.

"What do you have there?" she asked on her tiptoes, trying to get a better look.

"Nothing in particular. Just a piece of paper."

The girl's eyes glinted mischievously and she waved to the others.

"Guys, come quick! Leo's got a love letter!"

I aimed a barbed look at her, but she only gave me a toothy smile in return.

"A love letter?" Josh arrived first and he started to rise onto his toe-tips to get a better look. It didn't really occur to me before, but I was actually the tallest person in the group by far. Using my newly discovered physical superiority, I raised the paper high over my head and silently glared at the others to express my disapproval. After a few seconds, they got the message and stood down.

"Is everything all right?" The class rep looked around one of the large lockers with a quizzical expression.

"Leo just got a love letter," Angie repeated, and to my sincerest surprise, the class rep immediately walked over and grabbed hold of the two gawkers.

"Let's give him some privacy then."

She dragged them away, and I just had to wonder how great the difference was between her normal mode and her authority mode. Still, she didn't have to go that far.

"Wait, you really don't have to do that." She looked back at me questioningly and I waved the letter in my hand. "It obviously isn't for me."

"How can you be sure?" Josh asked.

"I can't but..."

"Then read it already!" Angie demanded with hungry eyes.

I took a deep breath, raised the piece of paper to eye level, and began scanning the lines. I nodded once or twice for good measure, and as soon as I finished, I let out the breath I was holding in as a shallow sigh.

"What?"

"Just as I said," I told them as I pocketed the piece of paper. "It is actually for a girl. The poor guy must've been really nervous and put the letter into the wrong shoebox."

"Oh..." Angie was deflated for a second, but then she perked up again. "What are you going to do?"

"What else? The letter said the girl should meet him behind the school, so I should go there and give back the letter. Otherwise, he might think he got rejected."

"Aww..." Angie cooed. "That's really nice of you." She skipped over to me and poked my side with a cattish grin. "You might look all tall and burly, but you are actually a big softie on the inside."

"No, I'm not," I told her in a voice I hoped was somewhat sulky. I probably succeeded, as she giggled in response.

"Should we wait for you?" Josh inquired.

"Nah, this could take a while. With my luck, I'll probably have to listen to the guy spilling his heart out about his unrequited feelings and all that jazz."

"A huuuuge softie!" Angie laughed. "Seriously, though, for a moment you were disappointed it wasn't for you, right?"

After a moment of hesitation, I decided to go with the brash solution, so I just brushed her off with what I supposed was a suitably embarrassed roll of the eyes and walked past her. She let out another giggle in return, so I hopefully succeeded.

"So... what about me now?" With her authority mode gone, the class rep's voice sounded more timid than usual. She shrank back a little when Josh turned to her with a curious expression.

"What do you mean?"

"I was invited by Leo, but since he is not coming anymore..." Her voice trailed off into mumbles, and after a second of hesitation, Josh smiled warmly at her and grabbed her arm.

"Don't worry about it."

"Yeah!" Angie agreed with a huge nod and grabbed hold of her other arm. "It's been ages since we last hung out together!"

"Back in middle school?" Josh turned to her and Angie nodded again. "Now that you mention it... Wow, it has really been a while."

"Let's make it count then!" Angie declared and began pulling the nervous class rep, who in turn had Josh trailing behind her. They waved to me one last time before they left the building, which I obviously returned with a smile, and off they went. I made a mental note about how the childhood friends and the class rep apparently went way back, but I shelved the thought in favor of the more pressing issue.

I took out the letter and read it one more time. It's probably obvious already, but it wasn't written by a guy. In fact, I pretty much lied through my teeth from beginning to end, though I had a good reason for that. This wasn't a letter of love, but one of challenge.

I hereby challenge you to an honourable duel with the purpose of settling our feud. I request your presence at the rooftop after school hours. Fail to show yourself, and you shall be forever known as a despicable coward.

Signed,

Eleanor Dracis

I tried, I really did, but there was just no way I could do this without actually facepalming, and thus I soon found my head buried in my hand. It was strangely relaxing. But alas, having my head buried in the proverbial sand wouldn't have solved much of my problems, so after I was sure that the trio was out of the gates, I took to the stairs and marched towards what promised to be a giant pain in the ass.

PART 3

A loud, metallic bang.

"Come on!"

A long, violent rattle.

"Open up!"

The sound of several kicks landing on a door.

"Argh! I can't believe this is happening!"

While all of this was going on, I stood quietly behind the bend of the stairs leading up to the roof access door and was massaging my temples in exasperation. I mean, I wasn't expecting much in the first place, but the sight before me was just sad.

I was well out of view, but I held my breath for a moment as the princess looked over in my direction. After she decided I wasn't coming, she began angrily stomping up and down in front of the door again like an enraged bull.

I suppose I'd better explain how the current situation came about, right? But then again, there isn't much to elaborate on. The situation speaks for itself.

"Open, open, open!"

The princess began kicking the door again, and for a moment I couldn't decide which to groan about—her display of uncalled violence upon inanimate objects or her strange need to vocalize all her thoughts? I decided to go with the former, as I realized I'd already been baffled by her monologue-ing when I first came to the stairs. At first, I'd even thought she might've noticed me and was putting up a show, but the longer I observed her, the less likely that seemed.

Still, at this rate something would get broken, either the door or her feet, and I was too tired to deal with either of those on top of all my problems. So I took a deep breath, steeled my nerves, stuck my hands into my pockets, and walked up the stairs as casually as I could manage.

Unexpectedly, I got no reaction. She just kept kicking the door like I wasn't even there. How rude. Anyhow, I loudly cleared my throat to get her attention, and she halted her first-degree battery and assault upon the poor entrance. She didn't say anything, though, just froze mid-motion.

The silence stretched until I got tired of waiting and cleared my throat again.

"I'm sorry to bring bad news, but you cannot go up there."

"And why is that?" she hissed back at me over her shoulder.

"Because... it's locked?" I stated the obvious.

"This is your doing, isn't it?"

"What's my doing?"

"The door!" she pointed at it, then me, then at the door again as if she couldn't decide who to accuse.

"So... let me see if I got this straight. You think I somehow not only found out that you wanted me to come here, even though I never had any chance to find your letter, but I somehow got here before you, even though you left the classroom before me, and that I rushed up here, somehow locked the door, and then ran away and hid for no reason whatsoever?"

"Well, when you put it like that..." She wavered for a moment, but then she whipped her hand to the back and pointed at the door. "But then how do you explain that!?"

"That's always locked."

"Don't take me for a fool! I've already been up here today with that pushy girl!"

"Pushy girl...? Ah, you mean Angie?" I was actually a little surprised by this. I thought she asked to meet me on the roof because that was the stereotypical thing to do, but apparently she did so because it was a place she already knew. "Yeah, they only open the door during lunch break."

"Oh." Colour me damned. She actually looked crestfallen for a second.

"Don't worry about it. You just transferred, you couldn't have known."

"H-h-how dare you!? I don't need your comforting!"

It was at this point that the princess, nostrils flaring and fist shaking, began teetering on the edge of the steps. If I had time to do so, I would have facepalmed. I wasn't surprised, though. I mean, what else was I supposed to expect in this situation? The whole *pretty girl falls onto the hapless guy on the stairs and he accidentally cups a feel for comedic effect* thing was old as dirt and so obviously telegraphed, it was almost painful.

However, since I was expecting it, I'd already made my preparations. By the time she began to lose her balance, I was already moving, dashing up the steps two at a time. Her eyes widened in shock and she flailed her hands defensively which, surprise-surprise, only made her tip over completely.

She didn't fall, though. With one last leap, I reached her, ducked under her arms, grabbed her by the waist, and raised her off her feet before she could gather momentum. She let out a surprisingly cute squeak and froze in what I presumed was shock, her feet ineffectually dangling in the air under her.

She was... well, I wouldn't say she was heavy per se, but she was heavier than I expected. Even more surprisingly, I had no problem holding her up. I saw myself in the mirror, I knew I had some muscles, but seeing them in action was something else.

Speaking of muscle, she was also harder than I expected. Girls were supposed to be soft, right? Not her, apparently. Maybe I just wasn't grabbing the right place (nor did I have any inclination to do so at the moment), but her side and stomach felt as hard as a pumped tire. Maybe she was working out?

Anyways, while I was pondering these things, she just kept staring at me. Pretty awkward. So I decided to set her down. First I needed better footing, though, so I stepped up to the top of the staircase and gently placed her onto her feet, making sure she wouldn't tumble down again.

"You..." Still looking like a mannequin set in an awkward pose, the princess gave me a look halfway between fury and wonder, so... furnder?

"Me?" I prodded her after she refused to continue for a minute.

"... caught me."

I nodded with a smile.

"I'm in awe of your astute skills of observation."

"Why?"

I made sure to give her a sour look long enough for her to realize how displeased I was with the absurdity of her question, but she just kept gazing at me furnderingly. Or was it furnderously? Coming up with new words is hard work.

The point is, I raised my hand and swiftly flicked her right in the middle of the forehead. She let out another cutesy sound and clasped her hands over the point of impact, finally breaking her out of the mannequin routine.

"Would you please start using proper sentences?"

"You hit me!" she yelled at me from only a couple dozen centimeters away.

"That's a start, though I expected something more elaborate. B minus."

"You. Hit. Me!" she yelled each word separately for emphasis.

"Aaaaand there you go, slipping back to sentence fragments. Bad form princess, bad form."

The word had the desired effect, as she immediately cringed and jumped away from me. Thankfully it was in the direction of the locked door, so I didn't have to dive after her for another rescue.

Once at a distance, her glare returned to its original, pure hostility, and she raised the familiar accusatory finger in my direction.

"Stop saying that!"

"Why? Should I call you *your highness* instead?"

"No! Stop trying to blow my cover!"

"Uh, your what?"

For a good five seconds, we both stared at each other.

"Argh!" The princess suddenly let out a barely stifled scream and held her head in her hands. "I wasn't supposed to say that! You! This was your plan all along!"

"Whoa, hold on a moment. I'm not following your logic."

"Who sent you? Why do you—!"

"Stop," I told her flatly as I raised a hand, fingers poised ready to flick. She shut up and slapped her hands over her forehead. "Good."

I groaned and tried to digest the information while also stopping the girl from flying off the handle. Despite my best efforts, I sighed again. I was doing that a lot these days.

"Okay, from the beginning. What are you accusing me of?"

She seemed uncertain but answered, nevertheless.

"You were sent here to provoke me and get in my way."

"By whom?"

"How should I know?"

"And you are a princess."

"You already know the answer to that."

"Oh-kay... Let me see if I got this straight." I rubbed the bridge of my nose and began. "So, you are accusing me of being sent here by someone to provoke you into revealing your identity, which would be bad for some reason, and the avenue I chose to do so was at the door leading to the roof, where we were all alone and you only revealed something to me that we are allegedly all aware of. Is that the gist of it?"

Her glare slowly dissolved as she began thinking, and after a few seconds, she shook her head.

"It sounds silly. You must be really bad at your job."

This time she had no chance to defend herself as I flicked her right between the brows.

"Awawa! You hit me again! You hit me twice now! No one hits me! Not even my dad hits me!"

"Do I look like I care?"

She honest-to-goodness growled at me and stomped. Twice.

"Fine, what do you want from me?"

That gave me a pause.

"What do *I* want from *you*? Weren't you the one who called me out here?"

"Then why do you keep getting in my way?!"

"When did I ever get in your way? All I was ever doing was trying *not* to get involved. *You* are the one who always came after me!"

"Because you were interfering! You didn't even let me talk to him!"

"Who? Wait, you are talking about Joshua again, aren't you? Just why would you—?"

I could hear my voice trail off as the waters of recognition slowly seeped into my conscious thoughts, followed by a veritable dam-breaking flood of implications. It staggered me. I literally had to place my hand against the wall to regain my balance.

"Oh my God..."

"What?" The princess looked slightly unnerved at my sudden outburst, but she kept glaring defiantly, anyway.

"OH. MY. GOD!"

This time the volume made her jump back with another "Gyafuuun!" or some similarly cutesy yelp. Either way, I wasn't listening, or caring. My latest revelation blew away so many of my preconceived notions that I couldn't spare the brainpower.

The princess was not *aimed* at me. From the very beginning, she was after Joshua... Which meant that the guy had three girls pining after him. That not only blew apart the initial love triangle I was expecting, but it also completely changed the genre of this setting!

This wasn't just a rom-com narrative... This was a harem comedy!

That might not sound like that big of a difference, but it suddenly put a ton of details into a different light. For the most obvious example, it meant that I wasn't the protagonist! It was Josh all along! That fact alone turned half of my observations on their heads!

"I should have noticed sooner. It should have been obvious the moment you insisted on inviting Josh in particular." I looked up from my musings and found the princess staring at me with wide eyes, her face pale but her ears bright red, an impressive feat of contrasting emotional responses. "So you are after him, huh?"

After a moment of hesitation, she nodded, her lips curling up to an almost vicious smile.

"The cat's out of the bag. I guess I have no choice but to—"

"Well, good luck, I guess," I told her, cutting her off as I began walking down the stairs. "I guess you are going to need it, with all the competition."

"What? What do you mean?"

I couldn't see her expression, but her voice sounded a little panicky.

"No time. You'll see it for yourself."

I turned back to wave over my shoulder at her, and in a moment I could practically feel the blood escaping my face.

"Wait!" she yelled as she reached after me... and magnificently managed to miss the top step in the process and began teetering on the edge.

"Oooh shit..."

PART 4

"Ow-ow!"

"O-ho-ho. Don't worry, it's just a little strain," The jovial man in the white coat told us with a smile and he patted the princess's ankle, eliciting another stifled "Owie!" from her. "You are lucky you got here before I went home."

"We know, doc, you've already said that," I grumbled while I gently massaged the bump on the back of my head, adding yet another landmark to the already hilly geography of my cranium.

Once again, the situation probably speaks for itself, but let me elaborate for clarity's sake:

So, the princess predictably fell down the stairs, and I, selfless gentleman that I am, jumped after her and tried to save her. In the end, the only thing that accomplished was that we both tumbled down, though thankfully without any comedic *landing in an awkward position* or *touching an inappropriate body-part* wackiness. But, given that we were both alive and only suffered minor injuries, I was going to shamelessly attribute that to my heroics. Yay me.

Anyways, after we landed and I confirmed that I hadn't broken anything, we discovered that the princess had strained an ankle, and after much protesting, she allowed me to carry her to the nurse's office, where the annoying old man was just getting ready to leave. And thus we reached the present, where he was inquisitively staring at me.

"O-ho-ho."

"Stop that. I told you, it's creepy."

"So you hit your head, young man?" He wiggled his brows, completely disregarding my words. "How are your memories?"

"Memories?" the princess echoed the word as she looked over at us in mild puzzlement.

"No change," I glared at the nurse and shooed him away. "Shouldn't you worry about her leg instead?"

"Fine, fine." He walked over to a cabinet and glanced inside. "O-ho-ho, it seems like we are out of pressure bandages. I'd better go and get some."

And with that, he slapped on a wide-brimmed brown felt hat and left the office. The door didn't even have the chance to close before the princess repeated her question.

"Memories?"

"He is... a bit weird in the head," I deflected, though I suppose I wasn't entirely off the mark, either. "He's obsessed with figuring out the link between head trauma and memory loss. Look, he even has a mallet he hits people with."

She glanced over at the rubber hammer on the desk and shuddered.

"I was wondering what that was for..." Suddenly she frowned at me as if she just remembered that she wasn't supposed to have friendly conversations with me. "And you took me to a place like this!? How irresponsible can you be?"

I sighed for the umpteenth time that day.

"You are aware that he is still our school nurse and the only medical expert around, right?"

She gave me a loud "Hmpf!" and looked aside. It was at this point when the awkward silence was supposed to settle down on us, but I cut it short with a question.

"So, why are you after Josh?"

As usual, the princess let out a cartoonish sound effect (like this was her character tic or something) and nearly fell off the bed.

"Ha... haha... W-what could you mean?"

"Oh please." I shook my head. "I saved you twice today. I think I deserve a little honesty."

The princess looked at me intently, then she averted her eyes in apparent embarrassment.

"You already know the reason," she mumbled sulkily at the wall. I could feel the corner of my mouth twitch in response.

Well, duh, of course I knew the reason. Josh was the protagonist in a harem narrative, therefore girls were attracted to him like moths to a flame. However, there had to be an in-universe reason for that attraction. Angie was a given; childhood friend romance is a staple of the genre. As for the class rep, I just discovered that they might've known each other since middle school, so their acquaintanceship was old enough to create some kind of romantic spark. But the princess? She'd just come out of nowhere (correction: "from the mainland," which for all intents and purposes was the same thing) and had no prior history with Joshua... or did she?

"Of course I know the reason," I stated, barely stopping myself from adding, *probably more than you do.* "What I really want to know is why *you in particular* are interested in him."

I must have hit a nerve, for she suddenly trembled and looked back at me with giant doe eyes before she turned away and began sulking again.

"I can't tell you."

I raised a hand and extended two fingers.

"Twice. That's two times. One plus one. The number with the hook top and the flat bottom. That's how many times I've stopped you from breaking your neck."

I could have continued, but the princess let out a defeated groan and threw up her hands.

"Fine, fine! I get it, stop harping on it!"

I waited for her to stop waving her hands, and then I prompted her with a curious, "So?"

For several long seconds she stared at me with a conflicted expression, but once her internal struggle saw a victor, she awkwardly gestured for me to come closer. I followed her request and sat by her side on the bed.

"I..."

"Yes?"

"You see..."

"Yes?"

"Well..." At last, she buried her face in her hands and shook it violently, then looked at me with determined eyes. "Listen. You have to promise you aren't going to tell this to anyone. Especially not him."

I thought about it and concluded that, unless what she was about to tell me posed a danger to him, which I sincerely doubted, I had no obligation to share it in the first place. As such, I gave her a firm nod. "Sure, I can promise that."

"Do you swear?"

"Sure, I can do that too, but I don't see—"

"Swear on the..." She paused. "Do you have a religion?"

"No, I don't think so."

"You don't *think so?*" she parroted after me, and I shrugged.

"It's complicated."

"Fine. Then swear on your family."

"I don't really have one."

"Oh..." For a moment her frown was overcome with a flash of sympathy, but an instant later it was back in its previous state. "Then any other symbol? Nationality?"

"Nah, I don't really have any attachments like that, either."

"You want to tell me you don't have anything?" She sounded more stunned than frustrated, though I guess I could only tell it because I was already so familiar with her annoyed tone.

"No." For a little while she kept blinking at me, and for some reason I couldn't help but feel she pitied me. It made me feel a bit awkward, so I let out a forced cough and made an offer. "How about we forget about the whole swearing business? You just have to trust the guy who saved you twice a third time."

"I told you to stop harping on that. Also, you didn't really save me the second time."

"Oh, do you want to say that embracing you while you were falling and putting my body between you and the cold, hard ground wasn't even the least bit helpful? That you would have been okay without me putting my body and life on the line for your safety without a second thought?"

"Well, no, but..." She shook her head and glared at me with crimson cheeks. "Fine, I get it! I will trust you, so stop embarrassing me!"

Wait, just when was I embarrassing her? I mean, yes, I was trying to embarrass her, but not "embarrass" her in that sense of the word and... Oh, whatever.

The princess took a deep breath and looked up at the ceiling, probably collecting her thoughts, before she spoke in a soft voice.

"He and I... we actually met. A long time ago."

"When you were kids?" That much I expected. I figured she had to be a forgotten childhood acquaintance or the like. It was a pretty common harem narrative element too.

She nodded. "My father was visiting a... business partner in the city, and he took me with him. One day I was bored and wanted to look around the neighbourhood, so I asked Sebastian..." She paused to clarify, "Sebastian is my butler."

"I know." The princess raised an eyebrow in response, so I quickly supplied the answer: "This is a high school. Gossip runs rampant around here and a butler stands out."

It seemed like my explanation satisfied her, as she nodded and went on.

"There was this public park near our mansion, and it had a playground."

"And that's where you met him?"

She nodded. "Yes. He was playing with some other kids from the neighbourhood, and when he saw me and Sebastian walking in the park, he just ran up to me and invited me to play." Without any warning, the princess's face bloomed into a smile that was both nostalgic and melancholic. "When I asked why he wanted to play with me, he just gave me this giant smile and told me that I looked lonely."

I chuckled. I could totally imagine a kindergarten-aged Josh doing that, and the image was somehow both hilarious and heartwarming.

"Over the next two weeks, we played in the park almost every day. I snuck out of the mansion once to do it. I was scolded for an hour that evening, but it was worth it."

The princess's pure smile seemed to be contagious, as I found myself grinning warmly at her. Over the next twenty or so minutes, she gave me a jumbled, hard-to-follow but overall adorable account of her play-sessions with Josh. It was like a highlight reel of all the laid-back, silly stuff every kid would do during summer vacation, yet from her mouth, it sounded like some kind of life-changing experience. Then, at last, we reached the crux of the story.

"One morning, my father told me he had finished with his visits and we would return home the next day. That day I went to the park again and told him we would never meet again, and... well..."

"Let me guess." I raised a hand. "He made you pinky-swear that you two would meet again one day..." I said, and based on her reaction I was spot on, so I decided to stretch my luck and added, "... and get married?"

Her reaction was more extreme than any of her previous freak-outs. If I didn't reach out to her at once, she probably would've fallen off the bed in a flailing mass of limbs.

"H-h-how did you? Did he tell you that? When?!"

"Calm down," I chided her. "I just guessed."

"How could you guess something like that?!"

"Well, it was pretty typical," I began, but decided to soften my words a little. "I mean, I don't want to undermine the weight of your promise or anything, but it is something that tends to happen between kids."

"So... it's not strange? You are not going to laugh at me?"

"Why would I? I think it's cute." At this point I was able to reflexively catch her as she began squeaking and flailing again. "I wish you'd stop that..."

Not a blink of an eye later, she stopped as abruptly as she began.

"Wait, you mean these kinds of promises are common?"

"Well..." For some reason, I felt my choice of words was very important, so I took a deep breath to collect my thoughts before I said, "I wouldn't call it common, but it's not unheard of."

"So, could it be that... he didn't mean it?"

I gave her a flat look.

"How should I know? You should ask him."

"I can't!"

"Why not?"

"Because it would be embarrassing! And what if he doesn't remember the promise? Or didn't think anything of it?" She suddenly gasped. "What if he doesn't even remember me? He didn't seem to recognize me! What if—?"

I placed a finger on her lips and she fell silent. Teenagers and their over-complication of romance. But then again, what did I know? According to my ID, I was a teenager too.

"So, if I may ask, what was your plan if you never wanted to directly confront him? Invite him to lunches, hang around him, and hope for the best?"

"Well..." For the first time since I'd known her (which admittedly was only a few hours, but still), she looked meek. "You think it won't work?"

"Oh, it would," I told her frankly and to her obvious surprise. "Sooner or later, I mean. But doing that would probably take a while, lead to a bunch of misunderstandings, and would only really happen when something needlessly dramatic comes around. You'd be better off by just telling him directly and be done with it."

"I... don't think I can."

"And why not?"

She gave me a flat look.

"You know all too well how complicated the situation is."

I wanted to tell her that I didn't, but our dear nurse chose this exact moment to barge into the room with a giant cardboard box in his hands.

"What the...?"

I reflexively stood up to help him carry the thing.

"O-ho-ho! Thank you, young man."

"What the heck is this?"

"Why, they are bandages, of course!"

"Do you want to turn her into a mummy?"

"O-ho-ho. Of course not. I just thought that I might as well get some spares while I was at it."

I put down the box and asked the question that had been silently plaguing me ever since he left.

"Just where did you go, anyway?"

"O-ho-ho, just over to the storage room."

"For half an hour?"

"I thought I would give you youngsters some privacy." After saying that, he leaned closer and whispered, "I hope you didn't forget to use contraception."

For a moment, all I could do was to blink at him.

"Pardon?"

"Contraception. It is the..."

The old man began a long-winded description about the usage and benefits of contraceptives, but I didn't really catch most of it as I was too busy fighting an inner battle deciding whether I should just brush him off or apply his own rubber hammer to his head. In the end, the calmer response won over, but only because I couldn't be sure that the rules of slapstick would apply if I did that, and I was in no mood to explain a hypothetical corpse with a mallet embedded in his forehead.

Once he finished his diatribe, he flashed us a mustachioed smile, reached for one of the rolls in the box, and began applying it to the princess's ankle. She squirmed a little but didn't seem to be in too much pain.

"O-ho-ho. That should do it. Try not to strain your leg for a few days and it'll heal in a jiffy!"

"Thank you." The princess nodded to him and then looked at me. I took it as my cue to help her onto her feet.

"Can you stand?"

She wobbled a little but managed to stand up straight.

"I think I will be okay."

"Are you sure? I could carry you again if you—"

"Out of the question!" she snapped. "Riding on you once was more than enough!"

"O-ho-ho! The vigor of youth is truly amazing!"

"She didn't mean it that way."

"What way?" the princess blurted out, followed by a series of confused blinks.

"The way you didn't mean," I answered before addressing the nurse again. "Is there anything else, doc?"

"O-ho-ho. Nothing I can think of."

"Good." I clapped and rubbed my palms together. "We should get going then. It's getting late."

Without further ado, I pulled the princess through the door (making sure she wasn't straining her feet, of course), and before I knew it, we were already in the main hall. I looked at her bandaged feet and asked, "Do you need any help?"

"No, I'm fine!"

"With the shoes, I mean? Wouldn't it be hard to get your feet into them?"

"I'll improvise," she huffed and limped across the hall to her shoe locker. I shrugged and went the other way to grab mine. Thankfully this time there were no letters attached to my shoes, so I swiftly slipped into my sneakers and skipped to the door to wait for her. I suppose we could have parted at this point, I wasn't really responsible for her or anything, but it would have just felt weird if I'd left an injured person behind like that. After several minutes of waiting, I found her peeking around the lockers and glaring at me resentfully. Once it became obvious she wouldn't come over, I silently grumbled and walked up to her instead.

"What's up?"

She didn't say anything, just turned her face away from me with a "Hmpf." I glanced down and found the reason why she didn't come out.

"So it didn't fit after all?"

She was wearing only one shoe while the other was only halfway on and had her walking on tiptoes.

"That won't do. You're only going to hurt your feet even worse if you try to walk like that."

"Then what should I do? Go home barefoot?"

"Well, I could carry you."

"Shut up, shut up, shut up!" She pouted and tried to stomp her feet, but the moment she raised one, she cringed and I had to catch her.

"Whoa, easy there. You're really going to hurt yourself at this rate." Before she could say or do anything, I reached down and snatched the shoe off her injured foot.

"Give it back!"

"I will. Once you're back at your place, safe and sound."

She gave me one of her most fiery glares yet, though it was slightly undermined by her pouting and the wet blotches in the corner of her eyes.

"You are infuriating! Why do you insist on getting in my way all the time?!"

I thought about the question a bit longer than I should have and at last, just shrugged.

"I suppose because, against my better judgment, I'm worried about you."

She made another "Gyafuu!" sound... or was it "Hawawa!"? One or the other.

Anyways, once she got over her first overreaction, she pointed her finger at my nose and yelled, "Stop it then! Stop worrying about me! Stop complicating things!"

"I... don't see how helping you complicates things. As for not worrying about you, that's something you should fix yourself."

"Me?"

"Yeah," I stressed with a vigorous nod. "You are just too over-the-top and clumsy, and it makes me want to look after you. I just keep getting worried that you're going to do something silly and injure yourself again."

Instead of the yelp I was expecting, the girl just slowly, very slowly, started getting redder and redder, and before I could even react, she rushed past me towards the door.

"Hey!" I yelled after her, raising the hand holding the shoe over my head. "You forgot this! And you are going to hurt your leg if you run like—"

"Shut up, shut up, shut up!" she shouted back from the entranceway while the automatic door behind her opened by itself. "I hate you! You are annoying, nosy, and you still smell weird!"

Before I could react to her declaration, she turned around, leaped forward... and hit the glass door with her forehead at full force. As it turns out automatic doors close after a few seconds if you don't go through them. Who would have thought?

"Hey! Are you all right?" I rushed up to her while she was still cradling her head on the carpet and crouched down next to her. "That sounded painful. Can you stand? We should go back to the nurse's office and—"

Before I could say anything else, she looked up at me, her face still red as a lobster and tears in the corners of her eyes. More importantly, even though she had a large lump growing on her forehead, she could only muster a blank look as she gazed at my face from up close. Then she let out another yelp, jumped back like a wet cat, and rushed out through the now-opened door.

"I will get you for this!" she shouted between stifled *ow-ow-ows* as she ran down the walkway and out through the school gates. In the end, I could only stare blankly after her dust trail.

"You will get me back for what?" I mumbled as I stood up again and hung my head. And here I thought we were actually starting to get along? That girl was about ten different flavours of weird.

I glanced at the shoe in my hand, and on a whim, I decided to stick it into my bag.

I'll give it back to her tomorrow, I thought to myself as I walked through the entrance as well.

At last, I sighed, even deeper and harder than usual.

"I was right. This entire rooftop-business really did turn out to be a pain in the ass."

PART 5

It was in the late afternoon when I got home. Originally, I'd planned on going on a shopping spree after school, but the princess's challenge and the aftermath torpedoed those plans. "Maybe on the weekend," I decided after throwing my bag into a corner in the living room before I paused and wondered for a moment. Just how much foodstuff *did* I have?

My brief inventory of the fridge and the cupboards revealed a new and baffling fact: The place was stocked. And I don't just mean I still had a lot of food left; the fridge was literally full of fresh milk and ingredients. Not only that, but the trash can was also emptied and the mess I'd made with flour the day before was completely gone too. It was as if someone had cleaned and replenished the place while I was away. Maybe my nonexistent parents weren't so nonexistent after all?

No, this was different, I concluded after returning to the living room. While the place was cleaned, the paperwork I'd gathered the first day was still stacked exactly the same way I'd left it. Not only that, but my room was also in the same condition as well, discarded clothes and all. And no message or signs of life left behind. That could only mean one thing...

"The zombie maids are also ninjas!"

For some reason, the idea didn't seem half as silly as it should have. But then again, there was another possibility.

"Maybe the world removes clutter after a while and resets when no one is looking. Could it be to reduce resource usage?" I pondered as I grabbed hold of my notes to make some new entries. While I was at it, I also noted some of the events with the princess. "Now that I think about it, I never really asked if she was an *actual* princess or only metaphorically. Like a yakuza-princess or the daughter of some CEO..."

After I made myself a reminder to ask her about it later, I finally rested my backside against the comfy sofa in the living room and let out a breath of delight. I allowed myself a brief break, during which I absently stared at the ceiling and let my thoughts run free. It only took a few minutes, but it felt reinvigorating. At long last, I stood back up, grabbed an industrial-sized cookie jar filled with chocolate chips from the kitchen counter, and returned to my room to begin my main task for the evening: transcribing my notes to the computer.

In retrospect, I suppose I should have written them there in the first place, but then I would've also needed a separate way to make quick notes on the fly during school.

Maybe I should buy a tablet? Or stay analog and just get one of those spiral notebooks old-timey journalists carried all the time? Decisions for another time.

Once I arrived in my room, I placed the cookie jar onto the left of my PC desk, my notebook on the right, and I limbered up my fingers in preparation for a lot of typing. Then I froze mid-motion and looked at the random page where my notebook opened. It was the one dealing with the observations I'd penned the first day, most of which today's revelation proved to be misinterpretations, but there was one entry in particular that made me stop in my tracks. It had a huge question mark at the end that made it jump out from the rest, and it read *Idiot Friend: Joshua?*

Now I knew that I was really off the mark with that one. Josh was obviously the hero of the story, which also meant I wasn't. Then the gears in my brain began creaking again, and I could feel my eyes open wider than I ever thought possible.

"Oh my God... Oh. My. God!"

For a moment I almost felt faint and had to grab hold of the desk for support, but there was no question about it.

Josh is the hero. The hero always has a male friend tagging along for comic relief. I am his only male friend. Q.E.D....

"I AM THE IDIOT FRIEND?!"

CHAPTER 6

PART 1

I yawned, more out of a sense of habit rather than actual fatigue, as I walked down the morning streets. In fact, I didn't feel drowsy at all even though I'd stayed up all night transcribing my notes, browsing the web for data, and watching funny cat videos, in that order. I supposed I might as well tick the *confirmed* box next to my *doesn't need any sleep* article, but I decided I should go for broke and wait another day.

With such thoughts on my mind, I rounded another corner and noticed a familiar back in the distance. I increased my pace and in a minute or so I managed to catch up to the guy and greeted him via a friendly pat on the back.

"Morning!"

"Ugh." Josh looked up at me with weary eyes. "Why do you have to be so unnecessarily energetic so early in the morning?"

"I don't know, but I'm working on it."

Josh didn't respond and just let out a melancholic sigh before he continued putting one leg after the other.

"Did something happen?"

As if he was only fishing for the question from the very beginning, the guy immediately perked up the moment I asked.

"You won't believe what happened to me yesterday!"

"Won't I? Careful, that sounded like a challenge."

"Okay, here it goes... So yesterday I was hanging out with the girls—"

"You mean Angie and the class rep?"

"Of course I mean them."

"Just checking."

"Anyways, we had a nice afternoon, kind of like old times."

"Oh, so you used to hang out before?"

"Yeah, in middle school. We were in the same class back then, and we were in the student council together. Can I continue?"

"Sure, sorry for interrupting."

"Anyways, we were having fun. Going to the joint to get some fast food, hanging out in the park, window-shopping, stuff like that. Then Angie decided to take Ammy to a place I couldn't go."

"Shopping for lingerie?"

"No!" My friend protested and gave me a disappointed squint. "Is that really the first thing that comes to your mind?"

"Well, yeah? That, and the toilet."

"Ew."

"What?" I protested in turn. "Girls go to the toilet together all the time!"

"Doesn't matter, they weren't going there." He paused, presumably for dramatic effect. "They went to the bookstore."

I gave him a shrug and said, "So what? Are you allergic to books or something?"

"You don't get it. Angie was taking her to the young adult aisle."

"Once again: so what?"

Josh sighed and began rubbing the base of his neck.

"Listen, have you ever read any of the books there?"

"Uh, did you just seriously ask that from the guy with the amnesia?"

"Fine, then let me explain! Nowadays, those books are all about a bunch of monsters falling for vapid teenage girls. Vampires, werewolves, aliens, chupacabras..."

"That sounds like a gross oversimplification, but whatever. So? How does that affect you?"

"I'm getting to it! You see, Angie had a... phase. Arguably she's still in it, but nowhere near as deep as she was a few years ago."

"She was reading those books?"

"Worse. She was *obsessed* with them. I mean, she was reading them, talking about them, watching the adaptations multiple times. At one point she even forced me to read her favourite series under threat of physical violence."

"I gather you didn't like it."

"It was horrible! The plot made no sense, the protagonist was a bland idiot, and it had a handsome teenaged werewolf for the male lead... who didn't turn into a wolf at full moon! The books didn't even mention the phase of the moon! I mean, who writes a book where werewolves don't respond to the moon?! There were also some vampires in there, but those only *seemed* like vampires, and in reality they were just Russian immigrants with a magic disease, so I could cut those some slack, but the werewolves?! I hated the entire thing from beginning to end."

"Did you actually tell all that to her?"

"I did, and then some more," he answered with his chest puffed up.

"And how did she take it?"

The second I uttered that question, his chest deflated at record speed.

"She refused to talk to me for a week."

"Ouch... But how does that relate to your story?"

"I told you, I'm getting to it! So, Angie wanted to go to the bookstore to look at new releases, and I refused to go on principle." At this point he hesitated for a moment, but then he ultimately continued with, "We... might have also had a little fight over it."

"Oooh... I was just about to ask where she was." I grinned at my friend and he scoffed in return. "Giving you the cold shoulder again? Are you feeling lonely?"

"Oh, shut up." He rolled his eyes and sullenly tucked his hands into his pockets. "And it's not the reason why she isn't here."

"Really? Then why?"

He looked at me, took a deep breath, and finally got to the meaty part of the explanation.

"You see, after that happened, Angie and Ammy went into the bookstore and left me outside. Of course, they left their bags with me, so I had no choice but to wait for them... and then this girl showed up."

Now *that* grabbed my interest. Another suitor appeared? So soon?

"What kind of girl?"

"Average height, a little curvy, long white hair."

"White?"

"Yeah, pure as snow. It was the thing that first caught my eye too."

I nodded in satisfaction. This new girl most certainly fit into my *unusual hair equals importance* theory.

"So, what happened? Did you hit on her?" Josh gave me a deadpan look in response, so I guessed, "You didn't."

"Of course I didn't! What kind of guy do you think I am?!"

"Okay, then what?"

He shook his head in frustration before he returned to the story.

"Here comes the really weird part. The girl just walked up to me, during the middle of the day, on a crowded pedestrian road, and she just kissed me!"

"She kissed you?" I repeated after him to make sure I'd heard that right, and he nodded.

"Yes! Right on the mouth too!"

"And she didn't say anything?"

"She told me I was cute and then she ran away and disappeared into the crowd before I could say anything!"

"Huh. You are right. That must've been pretty weird."

"I know, right?"

"Sooo, how does that relate to Angie not coming to school with you?"

"Well, she came out of the bookstore to get her purse right when this happened. She left it in her bag, I think, and she saw what happened. Then once the girl was gone, she started arguing with me about kissing random people on the street. Like it was my fault!"

"I hear you."

"Man, girls are weird!"

"No, I think it's just that you don't really get them," I told him furtively. He raised an eyebrow in return.

"What do you mean?"

"She was jealous, you idiot. That's why she flipped out."

My friend suddenly flushed red (people around these parts do that a lot) and vigorously shook his head.

"No-no-no! You are misunderstanding something—we aren't like that."

"Not like what?"

"I mean... it's not like we are in a relationship or anything..." His words became less sure as he went on.

"And so she can't be jealous? You see, this is what I mean when I say that you don't get girls."

"Oh really?" It seemed like I put too much pressure on the guy and so he became petulant. "Then can Mr. Casanova, the one true explorer of the female heart, give me any advice?"

"Sure!" I answered enthusiastically just to take him off guard. "Apologize."

"For what?"

"Doesn't matter. Telling her you're sorry is just the foot in the door. Once she calms down, you use the opportunity to explain what happened. If she still doesn't melt, just exaggerate how much it shocked you. Cook up a small speech about how violated you felt that some random girl on the street stole your first kiss that you were saving for *that special someone,* and that should let you sail through the roughest part. Oh, also make sure you reconcile with her about the whole refused-to-enter-the-bookstore-thing while you're at that. You can be a little more mundane there, just tell her your tastes might not align but you are not judging her. Ah, and before I forget it—did the class rep see the kiss too?"

"I don't know... why?"

"It doesn't matter. Make sure she is either there when you explain things to Angie, or pull her aside and tell her everything, as well."

"But why? She had nothing to do with it."

"Just trust me, okay? It'll help you a lot in the long run if you try to avoid misunderstandings."

"But why the class r... I mean, why Ammy?"

"Just do it and don't ask questions, okay?" I snapped and he immediately gave me a nod. "Good."

After that, we walked in silence until we could see the school gates, at which point Joshua tentatively spoke up again.

"Say, Leo?"

"Yeah?"

"Are you... experienced with girls?"

"Dude, for the umpteenth time—am-ne-sia!"

"Yeah, I know, but... you sounded so sure of yourself when you talked about dealing with them."

"Okay, Josh, here's a pro-tip then: Don't think of them as *girls.*"

"I... shouldn't?"

"No. Think of them as just people like you. Try to put yourself into their shoes and figure out what they are thinking about. For example, what would you think if you saw that some guy kissed Angie on the mouth in the middle of a street without her resisting?"

"I would be... I..." Obviously conflicted and lost for words, Josh hung his head in defeat. "I don't really know."

"You better think about it then." I grinned and patted the guy on the back.

"Yeah..." For a few seconds he stayed silent, and then he directed a suspicious glance at me and asked, "Are you *really* sure you are not experienced with girls?"

"I told you, I've no idea. If I had to guess, though, I'd say I'm not."

"Really? Why would you think that?"

"I dunno. I guess I am just not the kind of guy girls would be interested in."

Josh stopped for a moment to give me a flat look.

"Okay, you are just messing with me right now."

"Well, I'm not."

"But... you are the handsome athletic guy of our duo!"

I grinned at him.

"What does that make you then?"

He grinned back in kind and said, "I am the clever, charming one, obviously."

We looked each other in the eye for a second and burst out laughing.

PART 2

"Wish me luck," Josh implored a touch wearily as we stood in front of the classroom.

"An arm and a leg, man."

"Uh, what?"

"It's a variation on *'break a leg.'*"

"I thought it was about something costing a lot..."

"No, I'm pretty sure I meant the former."

My friend shrugged with a face that said, *Fine, I'll take whatever I can get,* and we entered the classroom. Following a diminutive nod, he headed for Angie's desk. I honestly wished the guy some luck, in my heart at least, and walked over to my own spot.

It was early, so there were still a lot of placeholders idling around the desks in small groups, repeating stock phrases to each other like broken machines. Sometimes I wondered why Josh and the others wouldn't notice this, but I didn't dare to point it out to them for fear of breaking the spell and irrevocably contaminating my future observations.

I practically fell into my chair and stretched my arms and back like a cat. I already did that a few times this morning, but my limbs still felt wooden. Probably because I'd spent the entire night sitting in front of my computer, organizing my notes. Maybe I should start exercising in the morning?

Being reminded, I reached into my bag and retrieved my new and improved notebook... Well, okay, maybe it was only new, but I liked to pretend that starting anew without all the messed up, cramped, and stricken out text was an improvement in and of itself.

While I entered all of my previous ideas and observations into a handy text file that I could freely edit in the future through the magic of the backspace key, I still needed a physical notebook, as carrying a PC on my back around school didn't exactly fit my definition of fun. Should I get a smartphone with a keyboard? I did some research the previous night, and it was apparent that while I and my immediate social circle might've used outdated bricks for telecommunication, the technology actually existed. I should really buy one this afternoon, I decided. Or better yet, maybe try one of those tablet machines. Preferably a tough one with a long battery life.

I was still considering my options when my ears caught a small creak coming from the desk in front of mine. I glanced up and, sure enough, the princess was hastily sitting down while overtly ignoring me. That reminded me: I still had her shoe in my bag, didn't I?

I grimaced as I recalled the previous day's events and began staring at the girl's back with a slowly swelling urge of mischief. At last, I quietly leaned forward, making sure I made no noise. Slowly, very slowly, I got close enough that my face was almost in line with her shoulders, and then I whispered right next to her ear.

"Good morning, princess."

"Gyaaaaa!"

As predictable as ever, the princess jumped in her seat with a strange noise. In fact, for a moment she was teetering on the edge of falling over, with only two legs of her chair touching the ground. I grabbed the backrest of her chair and set it back with a solid yank.

"Careful there." I tried to sound as friendly as possible. "You might hurt yourself if you fall over. Again."

"Youuu!" She glared at me with the kind of fiery disapproval usually reserved for door-to-door salesmen.

"Me?" I asked back innocently, and for a moment I felt a distinct sense of déjà vu.

She kept up her glare for a few seconds before averting her face with a *harrumph*.

"What are you doing?"

"I'm ignoring you," she answered with a pout, completely unaware of the irony of her words.

"Why?"

"For what you did yesterday."

"Saving you from breaking your neck?"

Her eyes snapped back to me.

"No, what you did after that!"

"Saving you from breaking your neck... again?" Seeing that her face was getting crimson with what I presumed to be blood-curdling rage, I wisely decided to change the subject. "Speaking of which, how's your ankle?"

"Oh, it's fine, I can barely feel it anym-HEY! Don't change the subject!"

I clicked my tongue. She was onto me.

"Fine. We apparently remember the events of yesterday differently. Would you enlighten me on which part are you angry about?"

She looked at me blankly for a moment before she turned around again.

"I can't."

"Why?"

"Because it's..."

Her voice trailed off, and while I could swear I saw her jaw moving, I couldn't hear the end of her sentence.

"Because of what?" I pressed on for clarification. Instead she just turned back to me and yelled at me again.

"Shut up, shut up, shut up!"

"Whoa!" I raised my hands, palms out, in a sign of surrender. "Easy there. We're in public."

As if the information just dawned on her, the princess looked around and turned pale at the sight of the placeholders looking at her. After a brief pause, she jumped to her feet, ready to bolt out of the room... at which point I promptly grabbed her again and pulled her back onto her seat. She landed with a soft puff and looked at me like she didn't understand what just happened.

"Don't make a scene," I scolded her gently, as you would do to a misbehaving puppy. "Classes are about to start."

"Sorry."

That's what she said, but if her expression was any indication, she wanted to murder me and my unborn children with a teaspoon. In retrospect, it was probably just a mixture of anger, surprise, and embarrassment. Angprizerassment?

... That was horrible. I apologize.

"Is there a problem?"

I turned and smiled at the new voice entering the conversation.

"Good morning, class rep."

She gave me a long, level look in return.

"You still haven't told me what that means."

"I'm pretty sure I did."

"That's beside the point," she said curtly and turned to the princess. "Why were you shouting?"

"I... er..."

"We are terribly sorry for causing a ruckus," I said, coming to the rescue. "We were just acting out a scene from an old show and it got out of hand. It won't happen again."

The class rep looked at me dubiously for a moment before she turned to the princess.

"Is that so?"

"Err... I mean... Yeah, I suppose?"

Amelia looked unconvinced, but in the end, she relented and turned back to me.

"Please be more careful in the future." With that said, her expression abruptly became less formal and she even smiled a little. "Oh, before I forget it. I found what you were asking for."

It took me an embarrassingly long moment to realize what she was talking about, but then I smiled back in kind.

"Ah, you mean the notes!"

She nodded.

"Thanks, I thought it would take longer."

"You are welcome," she said before she stepped back to her desk and handed me a huge stack of notebooks. And then went back to deliver an identical pile. I had no choice but to whistle in amazement.

"How did you even bring these to school?"

"I asked some... friends for help."

"Either way, thanks a lot. You are a lifesaver."

She smiled demurely at my repeated thanks and moved back to her seat. I took another look at the stacks and gulped.

Good thing I don't need to sleep, I thought.

I wanted to open one and take a peek, but something else drew my attention. The blonde girl in front of me was once again glaring at me (we were getting to the point where I should only note when she *wasn't* doing so, I guess) and also slightly shaking, her face a shade of crimson I thought belonged only to humanoid aliens in low-budget afternoon sci-fi series.

She reminded me of a boiling kettle on the brink of exploding. In fact, I felt tempted to poke her cheeks just to see if steam would come out of her ears in a whistle. However, before my mischievous impulses could take control again, a different person appeared at our side.

"Morning!" She beamed an infectious smile at me and I immediately returned it.

"Hi, Angie."

The princess only nodded at her before she resumed her attempts to burn my face off with the fierceness of her eyes.

"You didn't greet me when you came in," Angie stated with an exaggerated pout.

"Sorry, I didn't want to be a third wheel."

"A-ha!" She struck a triumphant finger in my direction and exclaimed, "I knew it was you! You sent Joshua over to make up!"

"Guilty as charged," I answered modestly.

"Too bad, though. For a moment I actually thought he might have gotten over his stubborn streak."

"Hey, I am right here, you know?" Josh protested, and true to his word, he was standing right behind Angie.

"I know." The girl grinned and stuck out her tongue, which elicited a weird grimace from my friend. They were both smiling, though, so I figured they'd buried the hatchet. "So, what was that all about?"

Angie's question shook me out of my momentary daze, and I responded with a vague, "What was what about?"

"The shouting."

"Oh, that... We were just talking about what happened yesterday."

Josh and Angie looked at each other questioningly.

"You mean, between you two?"

"No!" the princess protested right away. "There is absolutely nothing between the two of us."

"Except the desk and her chair, of course," I helpfully added before I remembered something. This might not have been the most appropriate moment, but I decided I might as well hand over her shoe right then and there. Just so I wouldn't forget, you know? Avoid further complications down the line, and in no way because I found her flustered reactions infinitely amusing. Not even the slightest. With that rationale in mind, I reached into my bag and presented the aforementioned footwear.

"Here, you forgot this yes..." It was at this point when she started making funny noises and tried to rise to her feet to run away, so I once again tugged on the back of her jacket and pulled her back onto her chair before she could cause any more of a ruckus. "... terday. Also, I would really appreciate it if you stopped that."

She once more looked at me like she had no idea what just happened or how I'd managed to restrain her. I sighed and forcefully handed the shoe over to her. She looked at it blankly for a moment, then at me.

"What are you supposed to say when someone returns your property?"

"Thank you?"

"Exactly. Good girl." I gave her a thumbs up, and she once again reddened in embarrassment. Well, at least she was still too dazed to glare at me, so that was a relief.

"Excuse me?" Angie interjected with a hand on my table. "Why exactly do you have Elly's shoe?"

"Elly?" I asked back in reflex until I remembered that the princess actually had a name. "Oh, you mean her?"

"Hey!" This time it was the princess's turn to interject, seemingly regaining her lost vigor. "I told you I have no need for nicknames!"

"But everyone has one!" Angie retorted as she began to point at each one of us in turn. "Angie, Josh, Leo, Ammy, and Elly."

One of those names caught my interest. Just when did the class rep come back? Nevertheless, I flashed my most innocent smile at her.

"Let me guess," I said with one hand on my temple. "You came over because we were making a ruckus, but then you didn't find a good opportunity to interrupt, so you were just standing there frowning and waiting for us to notice you."

The class rep looked astonished for a moment before she picked a pen from a pocket and began scribbling on her palm, then closed it and turned to me.

"What did I write?"

"Excuse me? I thought we were over this already."

"Come on, guess!" Her eyes were almost sparkling with expectation, so in the end I didn't have the heart to refuse her.

"Circle."

Her eyes opened wide again, but before she could continue her impromptu ESP research, I quickly pulled Josh over.

"Hey, have you talked to the class rep yet?"

"Who...? Oh, you mean Ammy? One of these days, you've really gotta tell me why you keep calling her that."

"Don't mind that. Quick, grab her and talk to her before classes start. Preferably in that corner."

"But why?"

"Just do it, soldier!" I grunted at him, and after a moment he gave me a sarcastic little salute accompanied by a wry look.

While Josh was doing his thing, I turned back to the other two girls. "So, I believe we were at the shoe, right?"

"Riiiiiight..." Angie glanced suspiciously between me and the retreating Josh and class rep. "What exactly are they supposed to talk about?"

"The weather, studies, your threesome date yesterday... the usual stuff."

"You don't have to put it like that," she mumbled with a cute pout. It was refreshing to see a non-over-the-top embarrassed reaction after dealing with the princess all morning. Speaking of which...

"Hey, Elly?"

"Hawawa?!"

I looked at her flatly and shook my head. "You really have to work on your overreactions. People are going to bully you if you keep making them."

"You do! You already do!" she retorted, and I naturally let her protest slide off me like water off a duck's back.

"My point exactly."

"A-ny-ways," Angie re-entered the conversation with her usual gusto, "what was this shoe business about again?"

"Oh, that? She lost it, I returned it."

Angie looked decidedly skeptical.

"How do you even lose a shoe?"

I was about to answer when I saw that the princess was vigorously shaking her head with an expression that said, *If you tell her anything about what happened yesterday, I will bury you neck-deep in an anthill and cover your face with rancid mayonnaise.* Well, maybe those weren't the exact words, but a close approximation.

"I'm curious too," Josh butted in upon his return from the discussion corner. Based on his smile, I supposed his discussion with the class rep was also successful.

"Stuff happened," I told them mysteriously, but it didn't seem to satisfy them, so I decided to make something up. "Remember how I had to stay behind yesterday? Well, on return from my business, I found the princess tumbling down some stairs. She injured her leg and couldn't wear her shoe, so I took it for safekeeping. Nothing spectacular."

I was expecting a torrent of questions when I finished my explanation, but instead the group was only looking at me a tad apprehensively.

"The *princess*?" Josh asked and it finally dawned on me. Crap, I'd accidentally called her that. I sighed. Oh well, it was going to happen sooner or later.

"Well, she is kind of a princess, don't you agree?" I said as pointed at the girl who was in the process of burying her face in the desk. Josh nodded to himself.

"Now that you mention it... it fits surprisingly well."

"Yeah," Angie agreed tentatively. "She does have a butler, after all."

"It's still a better nickname than *class rep*," the class rep brandished her occasionally sharp tongue at me, and I took it like a good sport.

"Hey, can we call you that?" Angie poked the princess's shoulder, who in turn looked like a dead fish spread out on the desk.

"Do whatever you want..." she answered in utter defeat. I am not going to lie, for a moment I felt a little bad about it, so I leaned forward to place my hand on her shoulder.

"Hey, would you like if only I called you that?"

She immediately perked up and yelled at me, "Who would want that?! That's even worse!"

I smiled in satisfaction as I leaned back on my chair.

"All right then. You almost had me worried there for a second, but it seems the princess we all know and love is back."

"L-l-l-l..."

Her face suddenly emptied of all emotion, and before I knew it, she jolted upright... only for me to grab her and sit her down again, for the third time. I sighed as she kept making embarrassingly cutesy noises while burying her face in her arms. The others just smirked around us. I looked up at them and tried to awkwardly return the gesture.

"I guess we still have to work on those reactions..."

PART 3

The morning classes were like a freight train: long, noisy, and altogether boring, but at least they went by pretty fast. To be perfectly honest, I didn't pay much attention to them. Once I had the deal with the princess explained (and she resumed her practice of ignoring me), I actually had a couple of other things to consider, such as the future of my observations.

I hated to admit it, but my point of view was biased. Case in point, I'd automatically assumed that I was the center of this... well, let's just call it a *narrative*. Whatever it was, the problem was the same. My perceptions coloured my interpretations of things.

I figured there was only one way I could combat this: I needed a different perspective, a fresh one without my biases. For example, if I'd've had a third, unspoiled observer to give input on the princess's behaviour, I would have realized her deal sooner and avoided a lot of awkward events.

Then there was the next set of questions: Who, how, and how deep?

First, the *who* part: I needed someone who wasn't involved in the larger narrative. While I was sure Josh and company would be happy to help, if only out of bile fascination, using the targets of my observations as observers was a bit counterproductive.

Next, how: Exactly how was I supposed to break this subject? *Hey there! I think we're living in a fake world. Would you like to help me uncover its mechanics?* I'd be lucky if they only thought I was crazy after saying something like that.

Finally, I had to decide ahead of time just how deeply I'd pull this person into this. I would get the best, most objective observations if I kept the person mostly in the dark, but doing so greatly reduced the usefulness of said observations, not to mention it meant they could provide me with little in-the-field support. It was a sliding scale of accuracy versus utility.

I spent my entire morning pondering these things and I came up with the following: I needed a placeholder, one of the featureless background guys. It was best if my future helper was male, as it reduced the chances of them being pulled in by Josh's harem protagonist magnetism. They also had to look as plain and unimportant as they come to make sure they weren't involved in the narrative some other way. Last, but not least, I needed to have them at arm's length, so a classmate was preferable.

With these criteria in mind, I made an account of all my classmates. There were twenty-seven of us in total. I didn't know if that was a lot or not around here, but, frankly, it didn't really matter. The gender ratios were twelve males and fifteen females. Once I subtracted our little group, that left me with ten guys (plus twelve girls, but they were beside the point for now).

To both my joy and dismay, I found that aside from one fat guy, the rest looked so similar to each other that I could hardly even tell them apart. On one hand, this meant I had a smorgasbord of generic sidekicks to choose from, but on the other, it also meant that the best I could do when picking one was random chance. I didn't like that.

It didn't seem like I had any other choice, though. I spent all my breaks straining my ears to try to listen in on their conversations, but no dice. They all kept talking about the exact same thing, sometimes using the exact same words. It was all *"Dude, did you watch the game last night?"* and *"This movie is awesome, it has explosions and stuff!"* Truly riveting.

By the way, doing this almost got me in trouble with Angie when I wasn't paying attention to what she was saying. Something about an animated show with giant robots and drills that tried to stay underground at all costs. It sounded silly.

But to get to the point, I was no closer to making a choice by the time lunch break rolled over. *Maybe I should just give up and pick one at random after all?* I thought. I was pondering my choices when Josh patted me on the back.

"Hey there. Wanna grab something?"

"Huh?" I looked up at him in a daze before I shook it away. "For lunch? In the cafeteria?"

"Duh, where else? Unless you brought a lunch box, that is."

The word involuntarily made me look at the princess, and she flinched as our eyes met.

"Th-that was a one-time thing, you hear me?"

"Oh well..." Josh shrugged. "The cafeteria it is, then. I've always been curious about caviar."

"Whoa, whoa!" I raised my palm to stop him. "Are you planning to mooch off me again?"

Josh didn't reply, just smiled with an expression that said, *Of course I'm going to! Buying me food is the meaning of your existence now! Bwahahaha!* Well, okay, maybe not so explicitly, but that was the gist of it. I glanced around to find an excuse, and when my eyes landed on the girl sitting in front of me, I suddenly got an idea. "Hey, princess?"

After the obligatory noises, she gave me a death-glare and hissed, "Stop calling me that in public!"

"Whatever," I brushed her off and continued to press my idea. "You wanted to invite us yesterday, right?"

"I... yes, but..."

"But we refused. That was rude."

"Yes, we can agree on that," she replied once she found her conversational sea legs.

"Is this another of your schemes?" Josh wearily asked.

I whispered, "Pst! Just wait a moment. This is going to be worth it."

My friend stealthily rolled his eyes as I turned back to the princess to continue.

"How about we have Josh invite you this time around?"

"What?" The two of them spoke in perfect unison.

"It's only fair," I told them with a smile that was in no way sly or smug. "It should also be a good opportunity for you to learn about the cafeteria. Joshua over here is an expert."

"But... but..." the princess protested with a hand raising a neatly wrapped box. "Look, I already have my lunch."

I leaned forward and with a frown of my own whispered, "I am trying to help you, idiot! Stop being contrary!"

"I don't need your help!" she hissed back. Then after a moment she added, "And I am not an idiot."

I sighed.

"Oh well, that's a problem," I told them while I stood up and snatched the lunch box out of the princess's hands.

"Hey, what are you...!" she protested. She flailed, trying to grab it, but she had no chance.

"As you so eloquently explained yesterday, we cannot have such a pricey lunch box go to waste, so I will sacrifice myself for the greater good. You two can go and try your caviar, knowing that your lunch box is in good hands."

"Wait a moment..." Josh tried to interrupt me, but by then I already had my wallet out and handed it to him.

"It's on me. Have fun." I winked at him and strode out of the classroom before the princess could shake off her stupor and lunge after me.

PART 4

"Bon appétit, I suppose," I said to myself as I took the lid off the lunch box. The fragrance of home-cooked food instantly filled my nostrils, and to my surprise, I found that the meal inside was still warm. The box must have been insulated.

Thankfully the stuff inside was chunky. Fried chicken breasts, fries, some kind of sauce plus a handful of sandwiches—all things I could eat with my bare hands. Sure, the lunch box came with a set of utensils, but eating with those would have felt like a major breach of privacy. Not that snatching away one's lunch box was much better, but in my defense, it seemed like a good idea at the time.

I sighed and the sound of my breath was carried away by a light breeze. The rooftop was unusually empty... though I couldn't even be sure of that, as I'd only been up there once during lunch break. Once I left the classroom, this seemed to be the obvious place to have lunch, but it wasn't the only reason why I'd decided to come here.

Following my previous ponderings about my choice of an independent observer, I decided to leave it up to fate, or rather random chance. I picked the bench facing the entrance to the roof and decided that the first guy from my class to come through that door would be my primary candidate. It sounded fine in principle; too bad it didn't bear fruit.

To put it bluntly, I was all alone. Not a soul had arrived to eat, and though lunch break was far from over, not seeing anyone was a little unnerving.

"Oh well." I reached inside the box and popped a chicken nugget into my mouth. It was... really good. Not on par with yesterday's lasagna, but still a very fine meal. The vivid red sauce that I had first mistaken for ketchup also turned out to be something much spicier, and tastier, than expected.

Immersed in eating, I almost didn't notice when the door opened. I put the fried potato wedge in my hand (which was also covered in some blend of spices that made it way more awesome than it had any right to be) back into the box and focused on the newcomer. Regrettably, it was a bit of a letdown. It was a girl.

With a weary sigh, I returned to my meal. I was just about to unwrap one of the sandwiches packed neatly in a smaller compartment to find out what kind of shockers those had in wait when a shadow fell over me. I glanced up and found the girl standing right in front of me and staring.

I blinked and was about to awkwardly greet her when I noticed her fixed stare wasn't really on me but the place where I was sitting. I tried shifting a little, and as I'd expected, she didn't follow me with her eyes.

"Do you... want to sit here?"

She didn't react for several seconds. But when I was just about to speak up again, she nodded. Without further ado, I slid to the other end of the bench and she immediately sat down, seemingly forgetting about my presence altogether. She was a placeholder so I didn't expect much, but still...

I watched her unpack her bag and take out a large ham sandwich. She was... well, like other placeholders. She was short, though at this point I was starting to feel that everyone was short compared to me. She was pretty in the same, generic way as all other placeholders—slim but well-proportioned, a symmetric face, a simple shoulder-length cut of straight black hair. No makeup, no accessories.

What really captivated me was her grace. She was mechanical. Efficient. She acted without wasted movement, yet she didn't seem rigid at all. She unpacked her sandwich, grabbed it with both hands like you'd see in a commercial... and took a gigantic chomp.

It took all my self-discipline not to laugh out loud at the sight, but some snickers still escaped and drew the girl's gaze. When she turned her face to me, her cheeks were so stuffed, she looked like a hamster. That was the last straw. I burst out in uncontrollable laughter and almost knocked over my half-eaten lunch box in the process.

I laughed for a good minute, but the girl didn't seem to mind. She kept chewing absently, totally unperturbed by my display. At last, she gulped loudly and her cheeks returned to their normal state. She kept looking at me, then faced forwards again, mechanically raised the sandwich to her mouth, and chomped. Again.

For some reason I couldn't look away. It felt like I was in some kind of nature documentary.

Here we find the wild placeholder in her natural habitat, quickly consuming her food before a predator discovers her.

The seconds turned into minutes, and before I knew it, she'd finished her sandwich. For some reason that made me disappointed. I was just about to leave it at that when I noticed that she was still staring at me. Furthermore, she seemed to be... questioning me?

I froze up. Oh, crap, I thought. I should've expected this. Placeholder or not, staring at a girl for that long was obviously weird.

"Um... hi?"

"Hello." Her voice was flat but somehow it still felt very nice, even if a little deeper than I would have expected.

There didn't seem to be any further development after this exchange, yet she kept looking at me like she was expecting something from me. For the first time since I woke up, I felt completely lost for words and awkward.

"So... um... how was your sandwich?"

She absently looked at the empty wrapper in her hands.

"It was okay, I think."

I couldn't help but be amazed. Not just because a placeholder actually gave me a proper answer without the expected blank stare, but I had to admit that her voice wasn't just nice, but downright pleasant. It had a sort of warm softness to it that I had a hard time describing without going into superlatives. Needless to say, making such observations only made me feel more awkward.

"Really? I thought so..."

We once again fell silent and I really wanted to pound myself on the forehead. That was a world-class conversation, idiot. And to make things even worse, she kept staring at me. For a moment I even thought it was her way of getting back at me for staring at her, but... could placeholders hold grudges?

I paused. The question hit me hard. I mean, could they? Exactly how independent are they? Can they develop? I was so focused on my circle and the setting that I completely forgot about these kinds of questions. *This right here* was the reason I needed another observer.

I should find these things out... and I had the perfect opportunity on my hands. Just to make sure, I glanced around the rooftop and couldn't see anyone else. I stopped and weighed my options.

On one hand, I had already decided to leave things up to chance, so grabbing this one (not literally, of course) was in a way appropriate. While she only hit one point of my criteria, being a placeholder, you weren't supposed to look gift horses in the mouth.

On the other hand... well, she only hit one point of my criteria. Not to mention, she was weird. By placeholder standards, I mean. Would that pose a problem to my observations?

After some further painful vacillations, I finally shrugged and decided to throw caution to the wind. Nothing ventured, nothing gained. If things didn't work out, I could still pick a guy after this. So, with that determination in mind, I met her eyes, took a breath, and made sure to ask her in a very natural—

"So, hey. I think we're living in a fake world. Would you like to help me uncover its mechanics?"

I paused for a second and then hit myself on the forehead. What the hell, brain? Just... what the bloody hell!

The girl, on the other hand, didn't seem to be fazed either by my question or by my actions afterward. In fact, she seemed to be seriously considering my question. The silence was very loud for a while before she finally nodded with the same, empty yet serious expression.

"Sure."

I couldn't believe my ears.

"Excuse me, could you repeat that?"

"Sure, I'll help."

"So I heard it right..." I mumbled. "How did that even...? Did I just hit a hidden flag or something?"

To my further surprise, the girl looked around attentively and told me, "No, I don't see any flags."

She sounded so serious, it almost made me laugh out loud.

"No, no. Not that kind of flag. It's a colloquialism." She was still giving me an uncomprehending look, so I explained, "How should I put this...? You see, in games where you have choices, sometimes you can change the flow of the scenario by picking certain ones. It is called *setting a flag* when you pick a choice that leads to a branch in the scenario."

"Why flags?"

"That... that's actually a very good question," I answered, somewhat impressed. "It has to do with programming. You see, variables in these games are called flags, so..."

And so on and so forth. She asked, I answered, and before I knew it, I was completely wrapped up in the conversation. We (or rather I) talked about event flags, arcs, branching story structures, mediums and genres that use them, and so on and so forth. What's more, my interest in the girl grew with every passing minute.

Sure, she didn't show much emotion (or any, to be honest), and she only asked short, concise questions, but they were always on the mark, and by the look in her eyes I could see that she really tried to understand everything I was telling her. Before long I found my inhibitions breaking down and began dropping hints towards my actual hypotheses.

"So, let's imagine that we were living in a world where such things applied," I began, and she obediently nodded. "So, in such a world, anything could be a flag."

"Anything?"

"Yup. Who you talk to, what you say to them, even what you ate for breakfast."

"Like real life."

"Not quite!" I raised a finger, and she followed it with her eyes. On a whim, I moved it around a bit and she still kept following it like a cat chasing the laser pointer, and with a deadly serious expression to boot. Once I got my share of amusement out of that, I continued. "So, as I was saying, the difference is that there are rules. Shorthands. Conventions. A world like that would follow things like that."

"Such as?"

"Lots of things. Personality archetypes, common events, entire scenarios, you name it. However—and herein lies the main difference from ordinary reality—these tropes wouldn't stand on their own. They come in different sets and shapes depending on the genre and situation. Once you grasp that, you can begin to unravel everything and figure out what makes the world tick."

"You want to do that?"

"Errr..." Well, here came the plunge. I steeled myself, and nodded. "Yes. I believe this is how this world works, and I would like to ask you to help me figure it out."

"Sure."

Her answer was so immediate that it took me a moment to register. "Okay... Welcome aboard... I think."

It was final then. It was both relieving and disappointing in a way. I expected it would take more convincing, or I would have to prove it to her somehow, yet this girl... this... girl...

Holy crap! I thought. I didn't even know her name. I asked her, dragged her in, and I didn't even ask her name! What the hell was wrong with me today?

Not only that, just then I realized that lunch break was almost over and that I still had half my lunch left.

"Oh, crap..." I murmured as I opened the box again.

"Is there a problem?"

"No, it's just that..." Just then I noticed that she was looking at the sandwiches and an idea came to me. "Want some?"

She looked at the sandwiches some more, then at me.

"Payment?"

"Erm... If you want to take it that way...?"

Before I'd even finished my line, she'd already reached into the box and taken a bundle. She unwrapped it, raised it to her mouth, and took a large bite. Then she noticed my inquisitive look and turned back to me.

"Mhmmhf fmmmfh."

"Please swallow before you speak," I reprimanded her. She chewed in a hurry and once again swallowed everything with one large, loud gulp.

"Delicious. Payment accepted."

"You're... welcome?"

We spent the rest of the lunch break finishing off the lunch box. The sandwiches, as it turned out, were only filled with a generous amount of chocolate cream, but somehow they still felt as high-quality as the rest. Once we were done, we wordlessly cleaned up and left the empty rooftop.

It was only when we separated at the foot of the stairs when I realized I still hadn't asked for her name. I silently cursed under my breath as I turned to dash after her, but by then she'd disappeared from the corridor. I clicked my tongue and checked the time. I hadn't even asked which class she attended! How was I supposed to find her? I groaned and headed back to my classroom with weary steps.

When I arrived, I found Angie and the class rep talking by the latter's desk, Josh lazing by mine, and the princess sprawled over her own with an exhausted expression.

"What happened?" I asked my only male friend as I sat down.

"You missed a huge show, that's what." Seeing the incomprehension on my face, Josh smiled wryly and handed me back my wallet. "You see, we went to the cafeteria, and when Elly learned that you would be paying, she went on a spree!"

"Go figure," I told him as I sat down and checked the content of my wallet. "Not that much is missing though?"

Josh gave me a withering look.

"Only you could say that three hundred Jen for a single meal is *not much*."

I ignored the comment and glanced over at the princess.

"Is that why she looks so worn out?"

"Yep. She ate a full course, an entire turkey, and a huge parfait just to dent your wallet."

"Really?"

"Yeah, she said so. Also that she hates you, that you are a meddler, and you smell bad."

"Yeah, she says that a lot," I told Josh absentmindedly as I poked her in the back. She looked up at me and twitched.

"You! When did you come back?!"

"I've been here for a good five minutes by now," I answered amicably, then paused. "You look really out of it."

"W-why do you care?"

"Binging like that is bad for your stomach and it can lead to a bunch of nasty problems. You really shouldn't do that." I paused again as I took a look at the rings under her eyes. "You really look bad. Are you all right?"

"S-shuddup!" She slurred while trying to dodge the hand I extended to check her temperature. "Leave me alone! I don't need your care!"

"Whatever you say." I relented and set the empty lunch box on the desk. "By the way, thank you for the food."

"Oh…" In a shocking display, the princess completely calmed down as she stared at the empty box. "How was it?"

"Hm?" I was momentarily perplexed by her sudden change of gears. "Delicious. I especially liked the sauce."

"Oh, that's an original recipe of mine," she stated with a proud and borderline charming smirk. In fact, forget about the borderline part. When she wasn't beet red from embarrassment or glaring at me, she was pretty cute.

More importantly, I noticed a small discrepancy and asked, "Wait, you made that?"

"Yes."

"I thought you had a cook."

"Yes…"

"So you have a cook, but you packed a homecooked meal because…?"

"It wasn't for you!" she protested loudly, at which I could only shake my head.

"Of course it wasn't for me, it was for him."

"Yes! I mean, no! I mean…" With a frustrated growl, the princess tried to stomp her bad foot, winced, and burst out an angry, "Argh! I hate you!"

And with that, she buried her head in her arms and fell over her desk again. I looked over at Josh. His face simply read, *Girls are weird.*

Mine answered, *They sure are.*

Just then the sliding door opened, but instead of the teacher, a girl entered. For a moment I could only gawk at her as she walked in and sat down at the other end of the classroom. It was her! The girl from the roof!

"Josh?"

"Yeah?" My friend looked up at me from rummaging through his bag.

"Who's that girl?"

He followed my eyes and apparently had to think for a few seconds.

"That's… Judy. Why? Did you remember her or something?"

"Nah, it's not that."

"Then what?"

I stared at the girl, and after a few short seconds, she looked my way and gave me a small nod. I couldn't help but grin as I looked over at my friend.

"Hey, Josh? Two out of three is pretty good, right?"

"I… don't follow. What do you mean?"

I paused, then shook my head.

"Nothing. It's complicated."

I sat back in my chair, still grinning, and from the corner of my eyes, I could see an expression on Josh's face that declared that girls weren't the only weird thing in the room…

CHAPTER 7

PART 1

"Finally!" The moment the last bell of the day sounded, Josh stretched his arms over his head and then jumped to his feet. I felt slightly less enthusiastic, to put it mildly, even when he turned to me. "Wanna hang out?"

"Sorry, but no. I have other obligations."

My choice of words made him raise a brow.

"Obligations? That sounds serious."

"Nah, it's just... well..."

"Complicated?"

I nodded, and after studying me for a while, he simply shrugged.

"Fine. Maybe tomorrow then."

As my friend began to pack his bag, he shifted and so I got a clear view of the source of my current discomfort. The girl from the roof, Judy, was still sitting stiffly at her desk and looking in my direction. She'd been doing that through all the classes and even during the breaks and it was, frankly, freaking unnerving.

When I looked her way, for some reason it felt like she was waiting for instructions, so on a whim, I tried to point her towards the door with a few subtle hand motions. There was no reaction at first, but then, just as I was about to give up, she abruptly stood up and left without any further ado. Was she really waiting for my input, or did her placeholder routine suddenly trigger? Either way, she was out of my hair for now. Hopefully, by the next time we met, I'd know how to interact with her.

While all of this was going on, Josh finished stuffing enough books and paraphernalia into his bag to fill two of them and he casually slung it over his shoulder.

"What about the others?" I asked him before he could leave.

He glanced back at me, obviously expecting me to explain myself.

"I mean, aren't you going home together today?"

"We didn't really make any plans... Why?"

I looked around and waved to Angie. True to form, she skipped over as if she had been waiting for me all along and came to a halt by my side.

"'Sup?"

"Hey there, aren't you going home with Josh today?"

She seemed a little surprised by the directness of the question, but once she got over that she shook her head so hard, for a moment I thought she wanted to shake off something caught in her hair.

"No, I was planning to go home with Ammy for a change..." She gave Josh a pointed look. "Not to mention, after yesterday's events, I'm not sure I *want* to go home with him."

"Hey! I already apologized!" Josh objected, but Angie only shook her head again.

"You didn't apologize on your own, so it was only a half-apology. You will need to buy me at least one ice cream to make it complete."

"Ice cream? In autumn?"

"An extra-large serving."

"This is extortion!"

"With lots of toppings!"

At last, Joshua turned his pleading eyes to me. "Don't just watch! Say something!"

"Josh..." I stood and placed a warm hand on his shoulder. "Stop digging yourself in deeper. Just roll with it and take her on the ice cream date she wants."

"It's not a date!" They both protested in perfect unison.

"Whatever you say..." I made sure I sounded very dismissive of their claim before I returned to my casual tone. "Still, someone should really stick close to Josh in case that drive-by-kisser shows up again."

"Drive-by-what?" The princess perked right up after having spent the whole afternoon sprawled out on her desk. Indeed, on closer look, the left side of her face had the flat imprint of the desk on it.

"Morning, princess. I hope you slept well." She stifled a squeak and I smiled in return. "Look at that! We are finally making progress!"

"Shut up and tell me about this kissing business!"

I looked at the others in turn, uncertain whether I should milk the situation for comedy, but the princess looked so fierce, I decided to drop the issue. I cleared my throat with a raspy cough and tried to make myself look and sound as innocent as I could.

"Just what it sounds like. Josh was kissed on the street by some girl."

"When? How? Why?"

"Yesterday. With her mouth. I dunno. Any further questions?"

The princess didn't answer but continued to fume instead, so I turned to Josh with the biggest friendly grin I could manage without splitting my face open.

"Hey, I have a great idea!"

"Uh-oh…" Josh backed away.

"Brace yourself, everyone," Angie followed up with a grin barely hidden behind her façade of fright.

"Ha. Ha. Ha. Seriously though, hear me out. Why don't you take the princess with you?"

"What?" The subject of the previous sentence uttered, positively confounded, while I continued to voice my idea.

"She's new around these parts, so you could show her around while you hang out." I turned to the girl and addressed her in turn. "Also, it would let you stand guard against any further affectionate assailants."

"Why would she want to…?" Josh started, but then stopped, let his head droop, and then finally sighed in defeat. "You know what? I don't care. What I *do* care about is what *I* get out of this arrangement."

"Aside from another pretty girl clinging to you?" Suddenly feeling the pressure of several glares focused on me, I hurried on with, "If you take her home afterward, she can show you her mansion. Think about it—when was the last time you made friends with a girl with a mansion?"

It was at this point that the princess tried to lunge at me while seated (needless to say, it didn't really work), with her hands extended, either to cover my mouth or to strangle me. I didn't want to leave the choice up to her, so I grabbed her wrists and kept her at a distance while trying to ignore the incoherent slew of stifled curses she hurled at me.

Josh groaned. "Ugh, fine."

"I'm okay with it," Angie added, "but only if we first show her around the local sweets shops."

"You were serious about that ice cream, weren't you?"

"I'm always serious about ice cream," Angie answered with an impish smile. "I'll go and get Ammy and we can all go."

"Actually…" I raised my voice while slowly releasing the princess (since she'd stopped trying to murder me). "I wanted to talk with her about something."

"Yes?"

"Whoa!" I almost jumped out of my chair when the class rep's voice came right behind me, out of the blue. Actually, as I thought about it, wasn't that how she always appeared during these conversations? Might be worth looking into later, I concluded.

Anyways, I turned to her in a very dignified manner and solemnly said, "Holy cow. You are a freaking ninja!"

"Errr… I don't really understand…" Her glances kept awkwardly circling around the entire group counterclockwise as if searching for someone to explain to her what I meant. In the end, she returned to me with an uncertain look. "Was... was that an insult or a compliment?"

I waved a hand and told her, "Neither. I was just thinking aloud. That said, do you happen to have a couple of minutes?"

She looked curious, but then she noticed how I was resting my left hand on one of the notebook stacks she'd handed me that morning and the uncertainty completely disappeared from her features.

"You mean what we talked about yesterday? Of course, I would be happy to help."

"Great! I won't take up much of your time." I turned to the rest and smiled. "Sorry, guys, it looks like I'll be stealing her for a while. Please go ahead and have fun with the princess."

"Hey! Don't I have any say in this?" the blonde tsundere complained, though she was already packing her things.

"You have spoken and the court overruled you. Now shoo, shoo." I waved her away and she finally joined with the others, though she was still glaring at me. I couldn't fathom why. She should've been happy I'd played matchmaker for her. But then again, my *put yourself in their shoes* advice I'd given Joshua that morning only worked if the other person was even remotely reasonable.

I turned back to the class rep, who was in the middle of picking up one of the stacks.

When she noticed my questioningly raised eyebrow, she set it back down. "We should go to the library. They have tables specifically for extra-curricular studies."

I didn't really see the reason why we couldn't study in the classroom just the same, but she was the class rep, so I presumed she knew what she was talking about. I threw my bag on my back and grabbed hold of the other stack. It was heavy, but nothing I couldn't manage. I hurried forward to hold open the door for the class rep, and I only realized how pointless that was when I got there.

"Argh, sliding door!" I muttered angrily to express my undying hatred towards the accursed contraption. I turned back to the class rep to let her through... except she wasn't behind me.

I looked over, and I found her still by my desk, barely managing to move with the stack in her hands. As I reflected on the scene, I realized that she seemed to have had problems with it earlier in the morning too. I clicked my tongue with minor irritation, mostly at myself for not noticing it sooner, and quickly walked back to her side.

In the end, I ended up carrying both stacks while the class rep led me through the school building. She did so quite literally, as I had a hard time seeing ahead of me with all the notes piled into a column reaching up to my forehead. Thus she walked a step ahead of me, making sure that no one was in the way and that I wouldn't fall off the stairs.

As we moved on, I couldn't help but notice how the longer we walked, the more fidgety she became. Her fingers restlessly ran over her uniform and hair, and every few seconds she sent me a self-conscious glance that I am sure she thought was sneaky. It was a little unnerving, to be honest, as I couldn't remember doing anything that would warrant such looks.

By the time we reached the ground floor, I just couldn't bear it any longer and decided to speak up... only to be beaten to the punch by her instead.

"Is... is everything all right?"

I looked at her in puzzlement for a second.

"Why are you asking *me* that?"

"Well... you seemed so quiet, so I thought..."

"You thought...?" I parroted her in an effort to help her continue, but it only made her clam up for a while before she spoke up again.

"Are you... angry because you have to carry everything?"

I blinked twice at her and nearly stopped in my tracks.

"No. Why would I be?"

"Oh, thank goodness!" She sighed in relief, and I would have awkwardly scratched my head at this point if my hands weren't already occupied. I knew that she was a little awkward, but this was a brand-new level of social anxiety.

"Nah, you shouldn't worry like that. Just because I am not talking to you all the time, it doesn't mean there is a problem."

"It doesn't?" She seemed genuinely surprised by the idea, which made me wonder just what kind of references she'd had before.

"No, staying quiet is fine. You are not obligated to hit up a conversation unless you really want to. For example, a good common topic helps."

"Oh. I see." For a few steps she seemed to be deep in thought, then suddenly commented, "T-the weather is nice, isn't it?"

"Yeah... Good try. Needs practice."

"Aw." She sounded disappointed, but at least she was no longer fidgeting. One had to value small victories, I supposed. Before I knew it, I found myself chuckling. She looked at me funny, so I hastily explained myself.

"To be honest, I am a little relieved. I thought *you* were the one who was mad at *me*."

"Me? Why?"

"Well... I did hijack you and stopped you from going home with Josh, for a start."

She averted her eyes and began fidgeting again. "I don't see how that is related to anything."

"Oh please... It's obvious you like him."

Her eyes snapped back to me and opened wide with shock. "W-why would you think that?" she muttered, looking as if her face couldn't decide whether to pale or blush.

"I just looked at you."

Her expression swiftly changed to a curious one, overriding her previous emotional states in an instant.

"Did you... read my mind?"

I sighed and rubbed the bridge of my nose with, for lack of a better implement, the edge of the stack.

"I told you, that was just a joke." I almost rolled my eyes, but I stopped as I realized something and looked back at her. "Wait, doesn't that mean you just admitted it?"

"A... Ahaha... Of course I like him as a *friend*. I very much do so. As a friend. I have no other attachments or hidden agendas. None at all," she sputtered and finished with an awkward smile.

"That was some *suspiciously* specific denial, but okay. If you don't want to talk about it, I can roll with it."

It was around this time we left the main school building through the back door, and with that, the previous conversation also came to an end. Across the sports field, I could see the empty building of the now-familiar cafeteria. It wasn't our destination this time, but the similarly sized square building behind it.

Its base area was slightly smaller than the cafeteria's, but it was three stories high, and while at first I thought the two buildings were just part of one huge structure, there was actually an alley separating the two. We entered through the same kind of automatic door the school's main entrance had, and my jaw dropped to the floor.

"Are you kidding me?" The class rep turned to me and I felt an urge to clarify myself. "Is this really a high school library?"

"Yes. Why?"

For lack of a better explanation, I just waved a hand to indicate the entirety of our surroundings, which in retrospect was a bad idea, as I nearly dropped the notebooks in the process.

But back to the library.

It was huge. The building already looked pretty big from the outside, but it was something entirely different to see it from within. The entrance opened to a counter where we had to flash our student ID, after which we entered an atrium surrounded by a forest of bookshelves. In the middle, there was a wide spiral staircase with suspended catwalks extending out towards the balconies of the next level. What's more, the entire place was built around the aesthetics of oak wood and polished bronze, giving the library a distinctly old and venerable feel, even though I rationally knew it was just as new and freakishly clean as everything else.

I tried my hardest not to gawk as the class rep led me to the back of the hall, where we found a couple of vintage wooden tables and chairs hidden behind a wall of book racks.

"I guess we arrived," I whispered absentmindedly as I set the stacks on the closest table and limbered up my arms. We were in a library so, knowing the class rep's personality, I decided to play it safe and be quiet lest I trigger her authority mode and be on the receiving end of a scolding. Speaking of her, she took a seat at the table as naturally as if she were at home.

"Let us begin then. Which subject did you want to start with?"

I sat down as well, and after a moment of thinking, I said, "Let's start with math, I guess. Only give me the pointers, please."

"Very well," She nodded and picked out a notebook from the middle of the stack, and when she opened it up and placed it in front of me, it was indeed a page full of equations. How did she know? Maybe they were colour coded?

Anyways, after I gathered my wits, we both immersed ourselves in our study session, and while I only asked for the outlines, the class rep was gracious enough to answer all my questions and sometimes elaborate on her own if she saw I didn't know what was going on. She was nice like that.

To my own sincere surprise, we blazed through the math notes and then continued on with the history, language, and finally the geology notes. To my shock, an hour had passed before I knew it, and we decided to have a short break.

"Thank you very much," I told her while stretching. "I already feel like I have a better grasp on these subjects."

It wasn't an exaggeration either; I really did feel like it. As it turned out, amnesia or no, most of the info was already in my head. I just didn't have the framework to connect the dots before. I would still need to study a lot to catch up, but with her notes and instructions, I no longer felt like it was a daunting task to undertake.

"You're welcome." She smiled timidly at me in return.

I wanted to say some more, but then I noticed something behind her. I could feel my eyes open wide against my will in shock. It was a curious sensation.

"Is... there a problem?"

The class rep sounded concerned, so I tried to relax and smile.

"Nah, I just remembered something. I'll be right back."

She only nodded as I stood up and walked past the table we'd been sitting by. Once I was sure she wasn't following me with her eyes anymore, I rounded one of the long bookcases and quietly walked up to the girl standing at the end of the row, at a place with a perfect view of the still sitting class rep. As I got closer, she casually turned to me, her face as inexplicably unreadable as ever.

"Hello," she greeted me soullessly, like she'd just met a distant acquaintance on the street. I held my forehead in my right hand and moved even closer so that she would hear my whispers.

"What are you doing here?"

She looked over at me, then glanced back at the place where I'd been sitting a few moments before. She lingered there for a short while and then looked back at me. Throughout all this, she kept a perfectly still, emotionless face. At last, after yet another dramatic pause, she pointed at herself and said, "My job."

"Excuse me?"

For the first time I could remember, I noticed a small sign of emotion on her face, something akin to disappointment, and I expected her to sigh in irritation. She didn't do so, but instead she pointed at me.

"You wanted observations. I looked for something you couldn't observe before: you. Therefore, I did that."

"That—" I was about to raise my voice but then I paused as the words sank in. "That's... actually pretty ingenious."

"I was complimented," she stated as monotonously as ever, and I inadvertently smirked at the incongruity of her display.

"Yeah, you were. It was a good idea, and I haven't even explained what you should be looking out for."

"Oh." If an expressionless syllable could sound crestfallen, this was it. I wiped the smile off my face and relaxed my shoulders.

"Don't worry about it. I'll explain exactly what you should be observing later. I like your out-of-the-box thinking, though."

She nodded, and for some reason I had a feeling that she wanted to say something.

"Is there something else?"

"My first report." She produced a single sheet of paper from her breast pocket and handed it over. On it were several lines written by a neat hand.

"Oh?" I cautiously took the page from her and ran my eyes over its contents. In the meantime, Judy was looking at me with what I presumed to be expectant eyes. It was hard to tell with her, so I cleared my throat to ease the tension.

"This says that I am a... *'nice guy'*? *'Quite handsome'*?" She nodded and I felt like it was also to urge me to continue. "Okay, I can live with that. It also says that I have a strange sense of humour and that—" I stopped at this point for a double-take before looking up at her and blurting out, "I'm a flirt?"

She nodded again.

"How?"

"Most of your friends are pretty girls. You also have no problem teasing them or asking them to do weird extracurricular activities with you without hesitation."

"Wait, you are including yourself?"

She nodded again.

"And what do you mean I asked you out without hesitation? That was completely different! That was on an impulse!"

"So you are talking, teasing, and involving girls with yourself on impulse. Understood."

"Are... are you teasing me right now?"

She shook her head, but I swear she was grinning underneath her expressionless exterior! She had to be! That said, she poked at the paper to urge me to read on.

Thankfully the rest of her descriptions of me were less outrageous, mostly pertaining to my connections with the guys in our group, and Josh in particular. There was also a comprehensive physical description of me (I didn't know I had wide, masculine shoulders and a distinct jawline. Good to know, I suppose...) and minor notes about my habits (though contrary to her notes, I didn't think I was sighing a lot... or was I?).

Best of all, the entire page was ordered in an easy-to-understand bullet-point-based layout and written in neat, pretty handwriting. I'd be lying if I said I wasn't impressed. I looked up and my eyes met with hers, and I still couldn't help but feel that she was expectant under the expressionless exterior. I handed her back the paper.

"Your dedication and methodology are very impressive."

"I got complimented again. Yay."

I nearly fell over. Just how could someone say such high-spirited words without any emotion? It sounded completely incongruous! It either had to be on purpose, or she was my natural nemesis, the unreadable emotionless character. Either way, I sighed (no, this one was on purpose, and that doesn't mean I do it a lot!) and massaged my forehead, trying to put the thoughts of just what kind of trouble I'd gotten myself into off my mind.

"Still, there is no need for more observations today," I told her and glanced over to the class rep. She was getting restless; it was about time I returned.

"I already got paid for it. I want to earn it."

"Nevertheless. I am going to study with the class rep for a while longer. You can go home for the day if you want to."

"Home?" Suddenly her eyes lost focus and her expression grew even slacker than usual. I almost panicked, as I recognized these symptoms as the onset of the thousand-yard-stare lockup other placeholders experienced when I asked them about something they were not equipped to answer. Then, just as I was about to lose hope, she snapped out of it.

"No, it's too early to go home. I'll stick around."

She didn't seem to notice her own slip, so after some consideration, I decided not to mention it to her just yet.

"Fine, but no more observations for the day. Pace yourself."

She nodded, and so I got out of the row of bookshelves and walked back to the class rep's side. I was practically standing right beside her by the time she noticed my approach and she frowned at me.

"Welcome back," she told me and then looked behind me. I froze and turned around with hunched shoulders to face Judy standing right in my shadow.

"A moment," I raised a finger towards the sitting girl and gently pulled my assistant aside. "What are you doing here?"

"I told you I'd stick around."

"I thought you meant in the library!"

She looked at me, then at the class rep, and finally at the stacks of notebooks. She pointed at them and said: "I'll help."

"With studying?"

"Hello, errr... Judy?" The question came from the class rep, who appeared behind me in her usual manner. At this point, I wasn't even startled anymore. What did draw my interest, however, was how unsure she sounded about her. It was as if she had to struggle to even remember her name. Intriguing. Maybe there was more to *"important characters"* not noticing placeholder behaviour than just simple inattentional blindness after all.

While I was chasing these thoughts around in my head, Judy returned the class rep's greeting in the form of a nod so deep it almost looked like a small bow.

"Class rep." Her tone was as flat as ever, yet I could see the other girl's fingers twitch as if she just mocked her.

"Why are you calling me that?"

Judy once again raised a hand and casually pointed at me.

"He called you that."

"Oh no. It's spreading." The class rep hung her head, devastated.

"Now, now. No need to worry about it. Let's just get back to studying, shall we?"

To my surprise, it was Judy who nodded in agreement first. She walked over to the table and sat down without even waiting for the class rep to collect herself. After a short moment of uncertainty, I sat beside her and the class rep soon followed, taking her previous seat in front of us.

In the meantime, Judy grabbed a notebook (the biology one) and began browsing through the pages... or at the very least that's how it looked, only spending a few seconds on each page. Yet her actions were too precise, her eye movements too mechanical for idle paging. Eventually I couldn't bear it any longer and had to ask.

"What exactly are you doing?"

She looked up from the notebook with the first clearly recognizable expression I had seen on her, and infuriatingly enough, it was one filled with pity, as if I'd just asked something extremely dumb.

"I'm reading."

I glanced over to the class rep, and she looked just as puzzled as I was.

"You can read that fast?"

"Yes."

"Hand that over, please?" I gestured towards the notebook in her hands, and she obediently turned it over. I opened it on one of the early pages she'd reportedly read and asked, "The main difference between a eukaryote and a prokaryote?"

"The presence of a nucleus."

"Photosynthesis?"

"The production of complex carbohydrates from water and carbon dioxide via an organism's chlorophyll by harnessing light."

"What does the ribosome do?"

"It is the structure in the cell where protein-synthesis takes place by linking amino-acids through mRNA instructions."

I nodded and closed the notebook.

"Correct, word by word. Are you a robot or something?"

Judy looked puzzled for a moment, or at least as puzzled as her stoic bearing allowed, then she reached into her bag. I curiously followed her hand as she took out a sharpened pencil from her case and, to my abject horror, she pressed it against her thumb. Without a blink of hesitation, I lashed out and grabbed her hands before she could do any damage.

"Whoa! What the hell are you doing?!" I scolded her as I took away her pencil.

She looked at me expressionlessly, then at her thumb, and then showed it to me. While she didn't break the skin, the spot where she had tried to stab herself still had an indentation on it.

"I was doing a test."

"Are you an idiot? It was just a joke! To ease the tension! Not to mention, if you really were a robot, we have better ways of finding that out!"

"CT scan?"

"Among other things. Like just check your pulse."

"But that doesn't tell us anything about my internal structure. I might still have a layer of tissue over a metal endoskeleton."

"Yeah, but you couldn't disprove that by stabbing your finger either, now, could you? Also, it would make you a cyborg instead of a robot."

"What is the difference?"

"In this case? Mostly semantics?"

"I see." She answered, then she tilted her head at an angle and added, "To be sure, I could always remove an eye to see if there is a red light underneath it."

"No! Absolutely no eye-removal under my watch! Understood?"

She nodded with what I hoped to be enthusiasm, and I could feel that the smile I gave her in return was just a tad forced. Just what kind of trouble did I unleash on myself by recruiting this weirdo? Incidentally, I could hear the class rep beside us mutter something under her breath about birds and feathers, but it didn't seem to match the topic, so I didn't pay much heed.

In the end I leaned back on my chair in relief and handed the pencil back to Judy.

"Here. No more hurting yourself." She nodded in response and I scratched my chin in contemplation. "But still, I can't believe you can read and memorize things so fast. It's pretty amazing." Not to mention, it should prove incredibly useful for the tasks I had in mind for her, but I should only discuss those in private.

"Photographic memory," the class rep supplied the term. "I'd never imagined there was someone like that in our school."

Seeing how enthusiastic she was made me immediately suspicious.

"Does it have anything to do with ESP?"

The class rep frowned and crossed her arms in front of her chest.

"I already told you, I am not particularly interested in that subject."

"Really? Too bad, I actually had a really interesting experience I might have shared with you...."

The class rep faltered.

"You... you did?"

"Yeah. Inexplicable, even."

"What... exactly happened?"

I smiled wryly and picked up the notebook in front of Judy with a show of disinterest.

"Nah, I don't want to bore you with it. You wouldn't be particularly interested in it, anyway."

"Awwww... Come on!"

If my ears weren't lying, she sounded a little desperate as she tried to tease the information out of me, and it made me a bit uncomfortable. Before I could clear things up, however, I noticed that Judy at my side was writing on a familiar piece of paper.

"What are you doing?" I tried to mask the alarm in my voice, but I wasn't sure it worked. She looked at me and turned the paper around while pointing at a certain line.

"I am expanding the observations."

"I told you, you don't have to do it today." I tried to object, but by then she'd moved on to the next line and spoke again.

"According to recent events, your flirting habits also extend to flattering and bribing girls."

"Flattering? Bribing?"

At this point I probably sounded like a frog trapped in a well. She pointed at herself first, then at the class rep and said:

"In that order."

"Flirting...?"

I hastily shook my hands in front of me when faced with the disapproving look on the class rep's face.

"She is just messing with you. She does this all the time."

"Really?" She sounded less than convinced. "I meant to ask this already, but since how long have you two known each other?"

"Errr..." I looked at Judy and I couldn't read her at all, so I decided to wing it. "Not... too long?"

"Then how can you say she does this all the time?"

"Psychic link," the girl on my left blurted with her usual, emotionless tone.

"A-ha!" The class rep suddenly perked up. "I knew it!"

"You knew *what?*" I tried to hold her back while scowling at Judy at the same time. "What do you mean by—?"

As I looked at her, I saw something that I have never expected in her eyes: mischief. It was well hidden behind her emotionless façade, but it was there. The little...! She did that on purpose! I once more cursed my stupid brain for even coming up with the idea of associating with her, and I cried bitter (if only imaginary) tears over the future hardships I would inevitably have to face.

PART 2

"Bye!"

"See you tomorrow!"

The class rep waved one last time before we separated by the front of the school gates. I only returned her gesture by wiggling my head, as my arms were still occupied.

The rest of the study session, once the whole ordeal spawned by Judy's comment was sorted out, concluded in a resounding success. It took a while, the sun was pretty low on the sky already, but we managed to chew our way through all of the notes. I felt confident that once I reviewed them a few more times, I'd be able to catch up to the current curriculum to the point where I wouldn't have to worry about repeating a year.

Not only that, but once we finished, the class rep even pulled some strings (she was apparently also on the library committee, go figure) to let me borrow a pair of large plastic bags so that I could carry the notes home with relative ease. All things considered, things worked out fine.

Then I remembered the girl standing by my side and an involuntary sigh escaped my lips. She looked at me in return, finally interrupting the mechanical waves she was giving to the class rep already out of sight.

"Forty-three."

"Pardon?"

"The number of sighs," she told me authoritatively. "Forty-three."

"No way. I do not sigh that much."

"The data doesn't lie." In response to her insistence, I promptly rolled my eyes and exhaled a shallow—"Forty-four."

I froze up for a second, and then *only* rolled my eyes before I began walking down the street.

"Let's agree to disagree. See you tomorrow." My voice was not irritated at all. Not one bit.

I walked down the low hill away from school. Speaking of which, how come high schools were always on hilltops? Was there a practical purpose, or was it just a random convention? Or maybe it was a trope? Anyhow, I was just about to get immersed in my thoughts when I noticed a second lanky afternoon shadow stretching beside mine on the pavement.

I looked over my shoulder and, just as I expected, I found Judy walking a couple of steps behind me and staring at my back with her usual unperturbed expression.

"Aren't you going home?"

There was a long pause, so long that for a while I was afraid she couldn't hear me, but she finally answered, "I am."

"So? Why are you following me?"

Another long pause later, she uttered a slightly uncertain, "We live in the same general area?"

"How should I know? Wait, why was that a question in the first place?"

There was another round of silence, and this time it didn't seem like she was about to answer at all. I was just about to shoo her away when I realized that I was just handed an opportunity.

I never really paid much attention to placeholders before, considering I had enough trouble with the important "characters" already, but now that I had one at my beck and call, I figured I might as well use the chance to do some preliminary data collection. Not to mention, going home alone would've been boring, anyway. With that in mind, I beckoned her closer, and after a few short seconds she caught up and fell in line beside me.

"Say, Judy?" She twitched and looked over at me with questioning yet at the same time conflicted eyes. I couldn't help but wonder what that was about. "What?"

"You just used my name for the first time," she stated matter-of-factly.

"Yes. So...?"

"I don't know whether I should record that under friendly interactions or flirting."

"Neither!" I protested loudly. "Stop recording for now! Also, this is a business interaction at most."

"Oh."

I wanted to yell *"Why are you looking at me with those disappointed eyes?!"* but I swallowed my urge and forced myself to start the actual topic.

"So, Judy? I wanted to ask you something." She looked attentive enough, so I took that as her being okay with it. "Do you have parents?"

The question might have sounded silly at first, but I had a solid rationale behind it. As far as my limited interactions with them had indicated, placeholders were fulfilling a very specific role, the same kind of role an NPC would hold in a video game or a background extra in a TV show. They were there to provide the appearance of people where you would expect them and thus enhance the realism of the environment. After all, just how unnatural would our school look if only our small group of seemingly important people attended it?

However, since they were just extras going through their routines for the sake of appearances, it raised the question of whether they had lives on their own after their roles were fulfilled. Did they have homes to return to? Did they eat or sleep? Would they disappear once no one was looking, to preserve system resources? So many questions, so few hours in a day.

Speaking of questions, Judy didn't seem to be about to answer mine. Instead, she slipped into the same kind of momentary daze as before. I waited for a bit longer, and she soon shuddered as life returned to her eyes.

"Yes. Why do you ask?"

Stating my reasons outright at this point might have contaminated the data, so I fell back to my handy helpers: half-truths!

"Because I don't have any, or at least I haven't met them yet. I was curious."

She acknowledged my words with a grunt, but then she remained silent, forcing me to prod her a little.

"So?" She tilted her head uncomprehendingly, so I clarified. "What are your parents like?"

"Normal?"

"Was that a question or an answer?"

Another long, nail-biting pause ensued, and I was just about to shake her, when she blinked at me.

"They are normal. My mother is... a housewife. My father is a salaryman."

"Yeah, that's fairly normal. Do you have any siblings?" She shook her head. "I see. Any other relatives?"

She shook her head once more.

"Are these questions for research?"

"Yup," I said, but honestly, I was also just really curious. "Next question: what do you usually do when you get home?"

This time I wasn't even bothered by the momentary lockup. I also noticed that they were getting shorter, a promising sign.

"Normal things."

I gave her a critical look and scoffed in disapproval.

"Come on, stop dodging."

"Do I have to answer?"

"Did you ask for permission when you were researching me?"

"You play dirty. I will have to add this to the observations."

"You can do that after you've answered."

There was yet another silence, but this time she didn't lock up. In fact, she looked like she was thinking really, really hard.

"I read?"

"That was a question again," I warned her.

"I read," she stated this time. I pushed back the urge to chew her out and just gestured for her to continue.

"What do you read?"

"Books."

I gave her another critical glance, but she looked entirely serious.

"I am really tempted to hit you right now, you know?"

This time she was the one who gave me an odd look.

"Does that mean that you are violent? I should add that to my observations as well."

"No, it doesn't! Also, I said I was *tempted* to do that! How is that violent?"

"You are right. It was just a threat, so psychologically abusive."

I raised my hands high in surrender, which was harder than it sounded due to the two bags in them.

"Fine, fine! I wasn't serious! Now, would you just tell me what kind of books you read? Pretty please?"

She hesitated for a moment, and at last she blurted out, "I read... historical books."

"You mean historical fiction? About famous people?" She nodded. "Anything else?"

"I sometimes listen to music."

"How about a PC? Do you have one?"

For a few seconds she just gazed at me intently, and it almost felt like she was trying to figure out what answer I would prefer.

"No, I don't."

"Really? Too bad."

"Then I do."

This time it was my turn to pause for a while, followed by a short sigh. So she really *was* trying to give me an answer she thought I'd like.

"Listen, Judy. I would really appreciate it if you were serious about this. Don't change your answers just to fit my preferences."

She looked as emotionless as ever, but when I looked her in the eye, she did seem at least a little embarrassed. Or maybe I was just hoping she was? Either way, she gave me a firm nod and an equally determined "Okay."

"All right then. Is there anything else you do? Do you have any hobbies?"

After some further consideration, she ultimately shook her head.

"No. I go home from school, eat dinner, do my homework, and then read a book or use the computer until bedtime."

I could have pointed out that people usually say, *"I do X on the computer"* instead of *"I use the computer,"* but she looked so serious I had no heart to heckle her any further.

"Very average."

"Very."

Look at that! Finally something we both agreed on! Progress!

"How about friends? Do you hang out with anyone?"

"I do."

"Really?"

She nodded and pointed at me. "I'm doing that right now."

"Errr... We are not really hanging out per se; we're just going home together." Speaking of which, I was only a few corners away from my place, so I brought up the question, "Hey, do you really live around here?"

"... Yes." There was a pause! There definitely was a pause again! "I live..." She looked over the streets and pointed in a seemingly random direction. "... over there."

"So you coincidentally live in my neighbourhood."

"It seems so."

I didn't have the energy to argue. If she said so, then I'd let her have it.

It was about this time we rounded the last corner leading to my street, and I noticed a group of familiar figures. I reflexively extended an arm to the side to block Judy's path and we both stepped back and out of sight.

"Is there a problem?" she asked with upturned eyes.

"Wait here a moment," I told her in lieu of an answer, put down the bags, and then silently crept forward. I peeked around the corner just to see if my eyes hadn't deceived me the first time around, and nope, they hadn't.

"Come on, boss, he is not coming!" cried a familiar nasal voice.

"Yeah, boss, it's way late. Let's go 'ome."

"Shut up!" the deep bass of the aforementioned boss exclaimed, his ridiculous hairdo swaying up and down like a half-finished suspension bridge in an earthquake. "He goes home this way every day, and we are going to get him today even if it's the last thing we do... before curfew!"

I returned behind the corner with a groan and rubbed my face. Great, this was just what I needed.

"Friends of yours?" Judy appeared to be more inquisitive than worried by the three delinquents arguing a couple of meters away.

"Acquaintances."

"Hm." She nodded sharply, and for some reason, I really didn't like the light in her eyes, so I quickly added: "We ran into them a few days ago with Josh. They're a goldfish poop gang."

"Say that again!" a nasal voice called out to me, and from a lot closer than before.

"Yeah, what did you just call us?"

I turned around with a weary sigh. Big pompadour and his little posse were standing by the corner and all three were glaring at us. I stepped forward, partially so that I was between them and Judy, and partially so that I wouldn't need to shout for them to hear me.

"Good evening."

My casual greeting caught them off guard for a second, but then they only glowering at me harder.

"Did you think we forgot about what you did to us?" the big guy growled with a sound reminiscent of gravel being sandpapered with a jackhammer.

"Did ya think? Did ya?" the small one parroted while trying to look threatening.

"Sorry, but what exactly are we talking about? My past few days have been kinda busy, so could you be more specific?"

"Don't mess with us!" the tall one shrieked at me and I involuntarily flinched.

"You have loud friends," Judy complained behind me with two fingers lodged in her ears.

"They are not my friends," I told her again over my shoulder, but she only looked uncomprehendingly at me.

"What did you say? I can't hear you."

"Then unplug your ears."

She was about to say something when the big guy let out a rumbling laugh.

"Look what we have here! He brought his girlfriend along!"

"What did he say?" Judy inquired with an elbow poking me in the side.

"Unplug. Your. Ears." I told her animatedly so that she could read my mouth. In the meantime, the short delinquent began cackling.

"Kihihihi... Pretty little thin', right, Treebe'rd?"

"She sure is, Bagg—"

"Whoa!" I exclaimed with a raised hand, interrupting him mid-word. "What did he just call you?"

Suddenly a lot less confident, the pompadour-fashionista set his jaw.

"Now I am called Treebeard. Do you have a problem with that, punk?!"

"Of course I do!" I replied, taking him off guard again. "That totally doesn't fit you! You don't even have a beard, for crying out loud!"

"But... I am big."

"So are trolls," I pointed out, and the guy practically flinched like I'd slapped him across the face.

"But there are no named trolls in the books..." the tall one muttered.

"There a'e in *The Hob*—"

"No!" the leader of the trio bellowed with a red face. "I don't care about no books about midgets!"

"Little people," the tall member interjected with a raised finger, and the big guy snapped at him.

"What?"

"Little people. You shouldn't call them midgets. It's insensitive."

"Like I care!"

"Awww..." The small guy put on a sad face and the boss backpedaled right away.

"I don't mean you, Baggins. You're okay." He patted the short delinquent on the back and then looked up with a confused expression. "Wait, where was I?"

"Something about not caring about little people?" I supplied the answer, and he promptly and vehemently shook his head, which incidentally made his pompadour shake in new and altogether hilarious ways.

"No, before that!"

"Being a troll?"

"Right!" He nodded, sending his hairdo into a series of further sways. "I don't want to be no stinking troll!"

"What about you?" I aimed the question at the tall one and he shrank back at once. "Come on, don't be shy. What is your new nickname?"

"Uh, it's Noldor." I must've looked baffled, as he quickly added, "Noldor. You know, because they were *high* elves and... well... you know... being tall and all..." His words trailed into a whispered mumble, and I could only hold my head in my palm.

"I'm disappointed, guys. I'm very disappointed." I looked each one of them in the eye before I continued. "You had this huge book series with a gigantic appendix, and you couldn't come up with anything?"

"We tried..." the boss sheepishly tried to object, an act which looked absolutely ridiculous on him.

"And yet here we are again. Shameful. Utterly shameful."

The three of them hung their heads in unison and then, out of nowhere, the boss let out a blood-curdling scream.

"Oooo! I won't take this abuse anymore!" He inflated himself like a toad trying to scare off a predator, stood tall… and then turned tail and ran away, followed by his cronies shortly after. He only stopped at the end of the street to turn around and add, "Don't think this is the last time you heard from us!"

And with that, they disappeared behind the corner, leaving me and Judy all alone on the quiet street.

"What did your friend say?"

I looked to the side and found Judy standing there with her fingers still firmly lodged in her ears. I reached out with the accompaniment of an exasperated roll of the eyes and pulled her hands apart.

"They are not my friends."

"Oh." She looked down the street where the trio disappeared. "I wonder what they wanted."

"You'd know if you didn't plug your ears."

"They were loud."

"True. To be honest, you didn't miss much."

For the next few seconds, we both just absentmindedly stared in the direction in which the three left. A strangely tranquil experience. But the sun was getting low in the sky and I had a lot of things to do, so I decided that wasting time like that was not really an option.

"So." I turned to the girl at my side. "Which is your house?"

She blinked at me and looked down the street again. At last, she raised a hand and pointed at a house way down the street.

"There?"

"And now we're back to answering questions with questions again." I sighed in resignation and pointed in the other direction. "I live in the fourth house on the left down that street."

"I see."

"I guess it's goodbye then," I told her as I turned around and headed for my bags on the ground. I wanted to do that thing where I walk away while waving back over my shoulder, but I was stopped dead in my tracks by Judy grabbing the back of my jacket and yanking me back.

"Ow-ow! Hey!"

She was looking just as expressionless as always, but the way she was holding on to my jacket conveyed a sense of desperation.

"Take me home."

"Eh?"

"Take me home," she repeated. "It's what boys are supposed to do."

"Uh. Were we on a date?"

"No, but there are suspicious people around. And by suspicious people, I mean your friends."

"I told you they are—" I stopped myself, took a deep breath, and then exhaled it hard. "You know what? Fine, I'll take you home. *But it's just down the street, for crying out loud...*" I grumbled under my breath as I unclenched her fist around my jacket and led her down said street.

"Some friendly advice, though?" I said as I turned to her, about halfway there. "In the future, don't just ask a guy to take you home out of the blue."

"Why?"

"Well, you see... Some guys might think that you mean they should take you to *their* home, if you know what I mean." She apparently didn't, so I spelled it out. "They might think you are soliciting them."

"Ah." She looked like she gasped with shock, but the act was ruined by her typical blank expression. "Are you one of these guys?"

I almost missed a step and fell flat on my face in surprise.

"No, of course not! What kind of question is that?"

"It's fine then." We reached our destination just as she said that. It was a fairly plain-looking house of the same design as mine, except for an added balcony on the first floor. Judy turned to me in front of the fence gate and looked me in the eye. "I am only ever going to ask you."

It took me a moment to digest her words, but by the time I was ready to object, she was already reaching for the front door knob.

"Wait a minute! You mean you want to make this into a regular thing?"

She didn't say anything, just looked over her shoulder, gave me a small, mechanical wave, and then disappeared through the door with what I swore was a smile in her eyes. For the next couple of seconds I just stood there, frozen to the spot, before I regained my senses with a soft groan and began walking again, this time towards my own place.

"Why did I think asking her to be my assistant was a good idea again? What was I thinking?"

CHAPTER 8

PART 1

"Sixty-eight... Sixty-nine... Seventy..."

I counted my push-ups aloud, and I couldn't help but be pleased with myself. I was following the idea I got yesterday, and I found that working out a little in the morning felt surprisingly good. I was also pleasantly surprised about just how fit I was. I was about to reach a hundred push-ups and I wasn't even short of breath yet. Maybe my body was used to this kind of thing?

With one final heave, I finished the last set and sat up on the floor. Basking in the rush of blood following the exertion, I leaned back, supporting my weight on my hands behind me, and let my thoughts wander.

I probably did work out in the past, I concluded. While I wasn't exactly a bodybuilder, some closer inspection in front of the mirror (which in no way or shape involved posing) revealed that I had an evenly balanced, toned body. You don't get one of those without putting work into it.

That made me wonder: just what kind of person was I before my amnesia? Did I train just for the sake of shaping my body, or was there some other reason? Athletics? Some other sport? And since we're asking, what were my hobbies? What kind of movies did I watch? Did I have a favourite band? Did I even listen to music?

I had no answers to any of these questions. During the breaks at school, I tried to interrogate Joshua about myself a few times, but his answers were inevitably the same as the first time: I never really talked about myself, so he didn't know for sure. I tried to covertly inquire from Angie as well, but she seemed to know me even less than Josh. From their point of view, I was always the goofy guy who got Josh into trouble, an image I wasn't entirely comfortable with.

But then again, the more I thought about it though, the less significant the problem seemed. After all, there was a distinct possibility that Leonard Dunning didn't even exist until I woke up on that confusing, headache-filled morning. Scary, but possible.

I rested, waiting for my heart rate to return to normal, then headed for the bathroom. I took a quick shower and returned to my room with a towel still draped over my head. On my computer screen, I saw that I still had my last observation document open, so I walked over and saved it.

This one was a separate file I had for keeping tabs on the people I knew. It was mostly about the circle of me, Josh, and his three love interests, though I also had a few short entries for the nurse and the three stooges. And then of course there was Judy.

Before I knew it, I let out a sigh. Even after a full night's reflection, I still couldn't decide where I stood with her. She turned out to be a lot less docile than I expected from a placeholder, and I had a hard time reading her through her perma-deadpan face, but she also seemed enthusiastic enough, and her notes and observations were up to notch... save for that whole flirting business, of course. That one was dead wrong.

I absently scrolled through the document without sitting down before I closed it, revealing a flood of browser tabs and windows of the same site hiding underneath it. Needless to say, I'd spent most of my night surrounded by those pages. I specifically focused on the genre I suspected I might've been trapped inside: the high school harem comedy. I mostly did so through the mountains of examples I could find online, as I suspected seeing those would give me more ideas than reading some generalized description.

Unfortunately, my research left me with about as many questions as I started with, though not necessarily the same ones.

First, there was the issue of Josh. Was he blissfully unaware of the girls' affections, or was he just keeping his distance for fear of complicating things and possibly hurting them? In other words, did he play the clueless archetype or the indecisive one? Or maybe a combination of the two? At least I didn't take him for a harem seeker, so the third archetype was out of the question. As for the girls themselves, my research had only reinforced my initial impressions of them.

Angie was the childhood friend. They had a Japanese term for it— osana... somethingsomething. I'd look it up again later. They were a staple of the genre, but at the same time, they weren't the most likely to end up with the protagonist. That spot belongs to the first newcomer, the one who shakes up the status quo. That would be the princess in our case, but I was afraid my early, misguided interventions might have derailed her role. In my defense, once I realized what I'd done, I'd gone out of my way to get her involved with the guy and repair the damage, but only time would tell whether I'd succeeded.

The class rep fulfilled the role of the third option, the character who would hopelessly pine after the protagonist without much of a chance and who mostly exists to round out the early love triangle.

Finally, the girl who kissed Josh. For now, I called her *Mystery Girl X*. She appeared sooner than I would've expected, and if I had to venture,

I'd say it was so that she would kick off the plot since the princess hadn't done it. If my hunch was correct, I would be hearing more about her in the near future. She probably won't amount to much in terms of the love-dodecahedron (or whatever this would end up as); late arrivals seldom win in the relationship-tug-of-war... unless Josh ended up with a harem in the truest sense, of course.

I took a deep breath and rubbed my face with my palms.

Remember, they are still people and not just characters in a story, I reminded myself. They make their own choices, and while they might embody certain tropes, it doesn't necessarily mean they are ruled by them.

With that thought in mind, I saved my tabs and put the computer into standby mode. I was a good twenty minutes early, but I decided to go to school anyway. I put on my freshly washed and ironed uniform (apparently the ninja zombie maids fixed my clothes up overnight if I put them into the wardrobe in the evening, or at least that was my currently preferred hypothesis), packed my bag, checked my wallet, and ultimately left the house a good ten minutes ahead of my usual schedule.

The morning streets were emptier than usual. By the looks of it, placeholders took their own schedules very seriously and wouldn't move around if they had no place to hold in the background. At least that's what I thought until I noticed someone standing by the crossroad. My suspicions about the identity of said person were soon proven to be correct once she noticed me and began walking towards me.

"Good morning," Judy greeted me in all her deadpan glory.

"Hi," I replied absently, as my attention was drawn to a certain odd detail. "Are those circles under your eyes?"

She rubbed her eyes with her wrist, and on closer look I also noticed she had bloodshot eyes.

"I didn't sleep well," she told me while conspicuously averting her eyes, an act that was already more animated than what most placeholders were capable of.

"That's an understatement if I've ever heard one. Are you going to be all right? Should I call in sick for you?"

She hesitated, but ultimately she shook her head.

"I'm fine."

I scrutinized her again, but in the end I simply shrugged, gave a curt, "If you say so," and started walking, at which point she practically rushed to catch up to me. She really didn't have to. I wasn't about to run away.

We walked in silence for a while before she yawned so widely, it startled me. I looked at her again and could only shake my head at the sight.

"I tell you, you look really bad." She didn't give me a reaction, and it made me wonder. "Just why couldn't you sleep, anyway? Did something happen?"

She didn't answer right away, but then just as I was getting impatient, she uttered the word, "Insomnia."

"Just insomnia? Out of nowhere?" This time she nodded. I was pretty sure there was more to it, but she didn't seem to want to talk about it and I didn't want her to clam up on me, so I decided to drop the issue. "All right, let's go with that, then. By the way, were you waiting for me at the crossroad?"

She hesitated for a while before she nodded. "I didn't know where you lived."

"Wait, you wanted to pick me up in the morning?"

She nodded once more.

"You really don't have to do that."

"I don't?"

"No, you don't."

"Then are you going to pick me up instead?"

I gave her a wry look, but she didn't seem to get the hint and just looked at me with a sincere interest.

"No. No one picks up anyone."

"I see," she stated as she nodded to herself. "So we will meet at the crossing like today."

"No, I meant... Uh. You know what? Fine. Let's do that."

She gave me another firm nod and I just had to wonder why she was so fixated on this. On second thought, though, the situation was actually quite handy. I wanted to discuss some things with her anyways, and having company on my way to school didn't sound that bad, all things considered.

"Say, I haven't actually told you what you should be looking out for, have I?"

She thought for a moment and then shook her head.

"Okay, here's the plan—"

"A moment." After interrupting me, she fished a small book out of her breast pocket. It was about the size of my palm and had a leathery pink cover with a small pen fastened to it on a short string. She took the pen tip off, poked a page a few times, and then directed her gaze at me again. "Go on."

"All right then..." I continued a tad tentatively. She was already taking this way more seriously than I expected. That was a good thing... right? "So, as I was hinting at yesterday, I have a certain hypothesis about the nature of this world." She continued to stare at me unblinkingly, so I decided to cut to the chase and drop her into the deep water in one go. "I believe this world is following the mechanics of a story. A harem comedy, to be precise."

"Harem comedy?"

"It's a genre where a bunch of girls are vying for the affection of a single guy, but it is mostly played for laughs and only gets serious at the end."

"I see," she whispered, and furiously jotted down something into her notepad, then paused and directed a critical look at me, or at least one as critical as her poker face allowed. "Is that why you are flirting with every girl?"

"No, and I told you I'm not flirting with anyone. I'm just being friendly."

"Uh-huh."

Why are you looking at me like that!? I wanted to yell at her incredulous eyes, but I swallowed it and moved on.

"Listen, the guy at the center of attention is not me but Josh."

"Josh?"

"Joshua... Umm... A moment..." I floundered for a second while looking for my phone. "It's... Ugh... Where is my contact list when I need it?"

"You don't know your friend's name?" she asked with the incredulity in her eyes swelling to epic proportions, which in her case meant *barely visible but present, under the right lighting conditions, if you squinted hard enough.*

I awkwardly cleared my throat and tried to smile.

"Oh, right. I guess I haven't mentioned it yet, but I seem to have an itsy-bitsy case of retrograde amnesia."

"I see." She wrote a few more lines into her little book.

That was a... slightly underwhelming reaction. I was about to move on when, just as the whole name-business was about to settle, a brand-new question popped up.

"Speaking of which, Judy, what's your name?" At first she only blinked at me in mild confusion, so I decided to reiterate. "I mean, your surname. You never told me."

I was expecting her to lock up, but instead she just blinked again, and her brows furrowed into deep crevices like she was thinking hard about a math problem.

"Sennoma," she told me at last.

"Sennoma?" I repeated after her, and she nodded in confirmation.

"Yes. What's yours?"

"Mine?"

She nodded again, and I couldn't help but raise a suspicious brow at her question. Shouldn't she already know that?

"Well, it's Leonard..." I began, only to then flounder again under her inscrutable gaze. "Erm... Give me a second, it's on the tip of my tongue."

"You don't know your own name?"

"Hey!" I protested a touch louder than I planned. "You had to think for a moment too! I have amnesia, what's your excuse?" In the meantime I had a sudden moment of revelation, and I snapped my fingers. "Wait, I remember now! It's Dunning. Leonard Dunning."

"I see." She nodded to herself for the umpteenth time while jotting down something. "What are the names of the others?"

"I... well, we kind of only call each other by nicknames, so I honestly don't know," I grudgingly confessed. "It never came up since I lost my memories."

"Nicknames?"

"Yes, like how I call the princess princess, or the class rep class rep."

She paused to ponder for a while, which in her case involved tapping the back of her pen to her lips... which frankly looked ridiculous, as she had to place her notebook right under her chin for the string to reach that far. Anyways, after a few seconds, she glanced up at me again.

"Can I have a nickname too?"

"Excuse me?" The question came out of the blue so hard it dazed me for a moment.

"A nickname. I think I should have one too."

I narrowed my eyes and scrutinized her face for any sign of a joke, but she looked entirely serious. Though again, she always looked completely serious, except when a few microscopic expressions broke to the surface, so maybe I shouldn't have even tried. I slowly shook my head and told her, "Normally you don't just up and demand a nickname, you know? It kind of has to come about naturally."

"I see."

Was she... was she actually disappointed? It was hard to tell from her expressionless face, but she definitely seemed crestfallen... which in turn made me feel guilty for some mysterious and thoroughly annoying reason. However, before I could say anything, she perked up and pointed her pen at me.

"I will call you Chief," she declared in her usual monotone, which was somehow still fired up. More importantly, though...

"Wait a moment! Wasn't this about *you* wanting a nickname?"

"Yes, but I decided I'd let it come about naturally, Chief."

I blinked once, twice, and then promptly buried my forehead in my palm.

"Please don't tell me you are going to stick *Chief* at the end of all your sentences."

"No. Only when the situation demands it." She paused a beat, then added, "Chief."

"You did that on purpose!" I borrowed a page from the princess's handbook and pointed an accusatory finger at my assistant, but she only looked blankly at me, though her eyes once again betrayed the wicked grin she was suppressing... Or maybe I was just seeing things. Either way, I dropped my finger in defeat. Time for a tactical retreat. Commencing the shift in topics in three, two, one...

"Anyways, we were talking about your part in my research before this whole conversation got hijacked by nicknames, right?" She let out a soft grunt in agreement, so I told her, "Okay, here's the deal: I already have a set of notes with the outlines of my initial observations." I reached into my bag and handed her a couple of bound pages I'd printed out the night before. "If you give me an e-mail address, I'll link you a few sites useful for gathering references and tropes to look out for."

She carefully took the notes from me and glanced over them.

"Fascinating."

I almost stumbled when I heard her. This might have been the first time I'd heard her express overt emotion, and being in awe over the rough outlines of my various hypotheses and their supporting evidence was the last place where I expected it to happen. She flipped over the pages, one after the other, and before I knew it she was handing it back to me. I only looked blankly at her extended hand before I remembered her crazy memory. I took my notes back and put them away, though at the same time I couldn't help but wonder why she was using her own notebook if she could remember everything anyway. Maybe it was for my benefit?

"That's the gist of it. What I really need is a second opinion, so I want you to be around me and observe the same things that I do, then at the end of the day, we compare notes and see if our interpretations match."

"So you are telling me that I should stand by your side for the whole day."

"Yes, as much as possible."

She nodded hard and gave me a look full of determination before stepping right into my personal space, followed by the words, "I can do that."

"Easy there," I said to her with a smile and a raised hand. "Just act natural."

"I can do that too."

"Okay then."

I took half a step away from my unusually fierce assistant, but she didn't get the hint and just closed the distance, anyway. I was about to ask her to for some space, but then all of a sudden something hit my back.

"Morning!" I was greeted via blunt force trauma by my best, by default, male friend.

"Same to you," I replied with a pointed look while theatrically stretching my back.

Josh let out a merry chuckle, but then abruptly fell silent when he noticed Judy. He gave me a look that said *Dude, what?* (Josh's expressions were rarely eloquent), at which point I felt obliged to introduce her.

"You remember Judy, right?"

"Of course I do," Josh sounded as if I just insulted him. "She's in our class. You asked me about her yesterday."

Now it was my assistant's turn to look at me, her expression saying, *What is he talking about?...* Or maybe *They have a sale on beef in the supermarket?* With her, it was a wee bit harder to tell.

"It was after we met on the roof," I told her, and she nodded in response, at which point I returned my attention to Josh. "So you see, we kind of had a chance meeting yesterday."

"I get that, but why are you two walking to school together?"

"We live close to each other," Judy supplied the answer, yet he seemed less than satisfied by it.

"Just like that?"

"Well, there are some other circumstances—" I answered tentatively, but then I was suddenly interrupted.

"What's your surname?" Judy interjected with her notes in hand.

"Excuse me?" Josh fixed her with an incredulous stare, but she didn't seem to care.

"What's your surname?" she dutifully repeated before pointing at me with her pen. "The Chief can't remember because of his amnesia."

"Whoa!" Josh raised his hands in a time-out sign and turned to me with a scowl. "Why does she know you have amnesia? Wasn't that supposed to be secret? And who the hell is this *chief*?"

"She's a special case. She's helping me with collecting info to recover my memories. She is an assistant of sorts." I paused to scratch the side of my jaw, then added, "As for the 'chief'... that's me..."

"I thought we were observing people to pffffpfh..." Judy sputtered through my hand hastily clasped over her mouth.

"A moment," I smiled at my friend before I dragged her a bit back, leaned closer to her, and then whispered directly into her ear.

"He doesn't know that part. In fact, I want to keep even my amnesia a secret from everyone else. If anyone asks, you are helping me with a school project. Got it?"

She nodded and I let go of her with a sigh.

That was way too close to my liking.

"What was that?" Josh asked with one of his highly skeptical expressions.

"Nothing, just a little tactical discussion."

"Don't you think that was a tiny bit suspicious?"

"Nah, nothing suspicious here, right, Judy?" I looked over my shoulder at her and found her rubbing her jaw with a grimace. For a moment I almost panicked. "Oh crap, did I hurt you?"

She shook her head and replied, "I just bit my tongue a little."

"Oh crap, I'm sorry. I didn't mean to... I mean... geez."

She looked at me floundering in front of her with her usual expressionless visage and then raised two fingers. I, in turn, looked at her with mild puzzlement.

"Two what? Or is that a victory sign?"

She shook her head again and moved her fingers closer to my face.

"I want two extra sandwiches and you are forgiven."

"Sandwiches? Since when did I agree to pay you in sandwiches? Not to mention, I have none. That lunch box from yesterday was an exception, not the rule."

"In that case, you are not forgiven," she stated as matter-of-factly as if we were talking about the weather. "Now I will hold a grudge and plan an elaborate and needlessly complicated revenge against you. It will probably involve sharks."

"Ugh... You know, it's hard to tell if you are joking when you are saying everything so seriously." Her usual poker face somehow seemed more intense than usual, so I had no choice but to give up. "Fine, fine! How about something from the cafeteria?"

She paused with a thoughtful gleam in her eyes and nodded after about five seconds.

"That should do. You are on probation until then."

"How gracious of you." I smiled a touch ruefully as I turned back to Josh. "Where were we?"

My friend remained silent for a while, and then simply uttered, "Nothing. I don't even want to know anymore." With that, and a small shrug, he started walking again. I rushed after him, and Judy stuck to me like my own shadow.

Once we were in line, I turned my head to the side and whispered to her, "You see what you've done? You totally put him on guard! I told you to act normal!"

"I was."

"You were? Then from now on, act like how it would be normal for someone else."

"I see." She jotted this down and then looked up to me again. "How do I do that?"

"Ugh." I grimaced at the question, and then with a defeated expression I told her, "Just follow my lead and improvise."

"Got it."

With that concluded, I took a deep breath, renewed the smile on my face, and addressed the grumpy guy walking beside me.

"So, how did yesterday's date go?" A single look at his rapidly darkening face was enough to tell the answer. "That bad?"

"Worse!" Josh exclaimed in righteous indignation. "First Angie ate my entire allowance for the month in the form of a giant parfait I'm pretty sure couldn't even fit in her frame. Then we went on window-shopping and Elly insisted on going into a jewelry store and gawk at wedding rings of all things! And *then*, on top of all that, *that* girl showed up again."

"Mystery Girl X?" My friend gave me a questioning look, so I hastily explained myself. "The white-haired one?"

"Who else? She tried to drag me away while the others weren't looking, but then Elly noticed her and tackled her out of the shop!"

"Wait, this was still in the jewelry store?"

"Nah, it happened later. It was a phone shop. They were looking at straps or something. Anyways, she did a flying tackle on the girl, and by the time Angie and I got out to help, she ran away."

"The princess?"

"No, the white-haired girl! Then on top of that, the prin... *Elly*, sprained an ankle..." I nearly exclaimed *Again?*, but held it down. "... so I had to take her home on my back, and of course Angie was nagging me all the way about inappropriate touching, like I had any time to even think about such things, and then once we arrived at Elly's mansion, her butler scolded *me*, like any of it was my fault!"

I waited a few seconds for Joshua to regain his wind.

"So, it was an unmitigated disaster?"

"Yes!" He yelled out so loud even some of the placeholders on the street looked at us.

"And do you feel better about it now that you got it off your chest?"

"I... Huh." With a puzzled look in his eyes, Josh raised a single eyebrow. "Actually, I do."

"Good." I patted him on the shoulder with a smile and he tentatively returned the gesture. The smile part, I mean. There was no reason for him to pat *me* on the back after all. "No more triple dates for a while, I suppose?"

"It wasn't a triple-date, we were just hanging out," he insisted sourly. "But no, no more of those for a while."

"And what if Mystery Girl X shows up again when you are on your way home?"

Josh gave me a wry look. "I think I'll be able to deal with a pretty girl chasing after me, thank you very much. I will ask her name, make small talk about the weather, school life... maybe invite her over to a coffee or something..."

I held his gaze for a while and it took me a lot of effort to keep my face still.

"You're going to run away, aren't you?"

Josh broke out into a grin and gestured with his hand as he exclaimed, "Like the wind!"

We held it in for a second or two before we both laughed out loud, but even while doing so there was something else on my mind. I waited for him to stop chuckling before I brought it up.

"Hey, Josh, maybe there is a third option."

"Oh?" He looked surprisingly intrigued, though also a little on guard. "I'm listening, but I warn you—if you tell me it's another triple-hangout with the other two girls, I will punch you."

"Nah, maybe tomorrow." He gave me a flat look, which I promptly disregarded. "I actually wanted to go out and buy a new phone. You mentioned you were at a phone shop yesterday..."

"And you want me to take you there?" he finished my thought.

I nodded. "Yup."

Josh didn't hesitate for long.

"Fine by me. We haven't hung out for nearly a week. I was just about to miss it."

I smiled at the comment and couldn't help but notice that my assistant was busy making notes by our side. I leaned in her direction and, using my height advantage, peeked over her head. To my surprise, there were barely any words on the page, though those were written in the same impeccable penmanship as her other notes. She looked up at me, and for a moment I swear I saw a tiny flush on her cheeks, but she averted her face so fast I couldn't be sure.

"It's hard to write while walking," she stated with a distinct sense of sulkiness to her voice.

"You shouldn't write while walking at all. It's dangerous. You are going to—"

Just then, as per the unwritten laws of ironic timing, we reached an intersection with a high curb, which she magnificently missed. With practiced girl-catching reflexes (it's weird that I even needed to have such a skill), I managed to grab her shoulders before she stumbled and fell flat on her face. In fact, I grabbed her so firmly that I left her feet dangling on the other side of the curb.

She blinked at me, then glanced down at her airborne feet before returning her eyes to me, and at last she muttered, "Point taken," in her customary monotone.

Hearing that, I carefully let her down. "You need to be more careful. It's important to make notes, but you can do them later. There is no sense in endangering yourself. What if a car was coming down the road just now?" While I scolded her, I proceeded to straighten her uniform on her shoulders where I'd crumpled it, and once I was satisfied with my handiwork, I concluded with an emphatic, "Safety first."

She nodded at my words, so I let her go and we followed after Josh. We didn't have to go far, as I found my friend standing still, scrutinizing me from under knit eyebrows.

"What?" I asked, and he cocked his head to the side, his gaze even more suspicious than before.

"What did you say was your relationship again?"

I raised a single brow before glancing over to Judy.

"I told you, she is my assistant."

"Aren't you a little too unreserved for just that?" Seeing my confused expression, Josh pointed at Judy. "People don't just casually touch each other like that in public. You didn't even hesitate."

"We do that too." I pointed at him in turn, but he only shook his head.

"That's guy stuff. She is a girl."

"How does that make a difference?" I wasn't trying to be confrontational there; I really didn't see the difference.

"It just does!" came the heated reply. "There are different rules for these kinds of things!"

Was Josh a bit of a prude? I wondered. Anyways, at the end of the day I simply shrugged.

"Well, it was an emergency. It wasn't anything inappropriate, so I don't see a problem with it. How about you?"

Judy shook her head and stated, "No. I get paid extra for it."

"Whoa there! Hold on a minute! You are not getting paid extra for that."

"I'm not?"

"Nope. You get the standard rate."

"What is the standard rate?"

I paused with my mouth half open, and then murmured, "Now that you mention it, we've never actually figured out the finances, have we?"

"I want three sandwiches," she proposed on the spot, and then amended, "plus dental."

"You seriously want to get paid in sandwiches?" She gave me a nod, so I had no choice but to play along. "Fine, but only normal ones. And no super-sizing. It's bad for your health."

Judy raised a hand. I nodded to indicate that she could speak.

"Chief, I want a raise."

"What!? You've been only working for a day!"

"But in that day, I was a model worker. I ought to be promoted, but I am willing to compromise."

"Absolutely not! We have rules at this business, young lady!"

Judy tried to fold her arms, but her notebook was in the way, so she put it away first before she crossed them in front of her chest.

"In that case, if our demands are not met, we will strike."

"We?"

She gave me an uncharacteristically enthusiastic nod. "I unionized."

"When?"

"Just now."

I stomped my foot in response, then a second later I melodramatically hung my head.

"Argh, fine. Three sandwiches and a soft drink, but not a french fry more!"

"Sir, you have a deal."

We theatrically shook hands and then I turned back to Josh.

"Oh, sorry. Business negotiations can creep up on you like that. What were we talking about?"

Josh looked at me with a slew of fourteen different flavours of bafflement sprinkled with a generous dose of flabbergastedness (I don't think that's a word, but it should be), and in the end he just threw his hands into the air.

"Fine, I give up! Sorry for asking! Geez!"

With that, and some stomping, he began walking up the hill leading to the school gate ahead of us. I fell back to Judy's side with a smile and whispered:

"Great improvisation."

"Thank you," she answered as stoically as ever. "I would prefer Coke."

That threw me for a loop for a moment, and I tentatively asked, "Wait, you were serious back there?"

Instead of answering she looked at me and... was that... Yes, I could actually see the corners of her mouth twitch upwards in a cute little smile. It was barely there, but from her, that might as well have been a giant, ear-to-ear grin. By the time I got out of my surprise-induced stupor, she'd skipped ahead to Josh's side and I could only sigh.

"I have to figure her out, and do it fast, or one day that girl is going to be the end of me..." I grumbled as I picked up the pace as well, ready to begin yet another decidedly non-average school day.

PART 2

The rest of my morning commute was fairly uneventful. Once we reached the classroom, Angie, after a cursory greeting that didn't even take note of Judy, grabbed hold of Josh and dragged him away before either of us could say a thing. It was probably related to yesterday's events, I surmised, so it had little to do with me. Hence, I headed for my desk, sat down, prepared my books... and finally turned to the motionless girl imitating a somewhat boringly positioned wax statue by my desk.

"Say, shouldn't you go to your seat?"

My assistant looked at me as dispassionately as ever and stated, "I'm supposed to observe you."

"Yes, but you can do that from over there, too, can't you?"

"... Yes."

Contrary to her words, she continued staring at me. I tried my best to hold back the urge, but I soon let out a long sigh anyway.

"So?"

Prompted by my question, she microscopically furrowed her brows. "I'm still thinking."

"About what?"

"A good excuse to stay."

"Don't just admit you are looking for excuses! Not to mention, you're bothering the others."

She looked around with an expression obviously asking, *What others?* She had a point, as much as I didn't want to admit it. We were fairly early, which meant only a few placeholders were idling around the classroom. Josh and Angie were missing due to already explained reasons, the class rep wasn't at her desk either (though I could see her bag on it, so maybe she was just on an errand), and as for the princess, she was fashionably late, as usual.

Just as I was thinking about her, I noticed a tuft of golden hair fluttering by the entrance. I focused my attention over there and, after a couple of seconds, the rest of the princess's head came into view as she peeked in. I pointed at her as I turned to my assistant.

"For example, her."

Judy's gaze followed my finger to the confused blonde (in fact she might as well have had a giant red question mark over her head at this point) and then looked back at me.

"She isn't here. I cannot bother her."

"She is over there because of you. She is shy and doesn't know what to make of you."

"Is that so?"

We looked over again, and by this point the princess had about three question marks, so I decided to end her self-imposed exile and waved for her to come over. She was hesitant at first, but then she glared at me (or maybe it was Judy?), straightened herself, and strutted into the classroom with the dignity of royalty. A peevish, sulky, and slightly awkward one, but royalty all the same.

"Good morning, princess!" I greeted her with an extra 50 percent of cheeriness to try to ease her up a little. It didn't quite work.

"Who is that?" she inquired as she pointed at my assistant, and this time it was my turn to frown.

"Don't be rude," I scolded her, and to my sincerest surprise, she immediately toned down the passive-aggressive scowling. It still wasn't perfect, though, so I proceeded to introduce them to each other to ease the situation a little. "She is my assistant, Judy-bot. She is the cutting edge in artificial note-taking technology. Isn't that right?"

A long beat of silence hung in the air for a few seconds, so I hastily sent a meaningful glance at Judy, and she responded to my prompt with a flat yet somehow uncertain, "Beep-beep?"

"Wait, no, that's wrong," I interjected right away. "That's something a forties robot would say! You are *cutting edge*! You're supposed to have a better voice modulator!"

She looked at me blankly for a few seconds, but then she puckered her lips and let out a series of dull, hissing sounds before she turned her disappointed eyes down.

"I can't whistle."

"Ah, my deepest condolences," I said in a low voice. "I'm sure it will get implemented in the next patch."

She didn't respond, so I peeked at the other girl, and she was befuddled to the point of hilarity. Once she noticed that I was looking at her, she let out a small, confused noise and then uttered, "Are you serious?"

"No," we answered in unison and the princess's face flushed crimson.

"Then what was that all about?!"

"You seemed down, so I thought I'd cheer you up with some levity?" I ventured a half-truth, and my words instantly stole some of the wind from the princess's sails and her outrage deflated like a faulty balloon. It was at this moment that Judy took the opportunity to close the gap.

"I am Judy Sennoma. We've already met."

"We have?"

"On the day you transferred."

The princess pondered for a moment, but ultimately shook her head with a complicated expression.

"Sorry, I cannot remember. So many people said hi, it all blends together." That comment actually raised my interest. Maybe she couldn't tell placeholders apart? Both Judy and I had the same idea, as we reached for our respective notes, then we both froze mid-motion as we noticed what the other was doing. The princess, on the other hand, didn't notice any of this. "At any rate, you still didn't answer my question!"

"Which one?

"About what she's doing here!"

"We already answered that," Judy informed her, and I confirmed her words with a nod.

"Yeah, I told you she is my assistant."

"But what does that even mean?"

"She is helping me with research," I answered calmly. "It's an extracurricular paper."

"Oh? The one you asked the nurse about?"

"One and the same," I replied with a reassuring smile, and all of a sudden her cloudy expression cleared.

"Why didn't you just say that in the first place? Idiot." With that, the princess sat down and entered pouting mode. As she did so, I couldn't help but notice that she was still favoring one of her legs.

"How's your ankle?"

She looked back at me with a startle and hurriedly declared, "It's perfectly fine!"

"Are you sure? I heard from Josh that you hurt it again yesterday."

The girl blushed, this time obviously not from anger. It was a welcome sight. I was just about to get bored with her being angry at me all the time.

"I thought it healed, but I guess it will need a few more days..."

"You should really take better care of yourself," I gently warned her, then for good measure I also added, "and maybe not tackle people on the street, especially when you are injured."

"W-why do you even care?!"

I sighed. Fury-free princess was nice while it lasted...

"Because you are clumsy and I'm worried that you'll hurt yourself again," I explained in my most harmlessly amiable voice, which only made her even more furious.

"Stop doing that!"

"Stop doing what?"

"Saying things like that!"

"Listen, princess, I told you this already, but you can't just tell your friends not to worry about you. That's not how friends work."

Her eyes opened wide and she let out one of her cutesy squeaks before she turned around and hid her head under her arms.

Great. Now we're back to this again. Two steps forwards, one step back.

"Chief, are you done flirting?" Judy demonstrated her horrible sense of timing at my side, earning her a barbed glance in the process.

"I told you, I am not flirting," I stated emphatically.

"It sure looked like that from where I was standing."

"Then you were standing at the wrong place. Why not try another vantage point, like that one?"

Judy looked over to the place I was pointing and answered, "That's my desk. I cannot hear what you are saying from that far away."

"Precisely."

She remained silent, then stated, "Very well. I will come up with my own dialog then."

"No, wait! That sounds worse!" It was at this point that I realized that our ribbing could be easily misunderstood, so I quickly leaned forward and poked the princess in the back to get her attention. "Listen, don't take what she says too seriously, she is just fixated on this for some reason. I really wasn't even trying to flirt."

Suddenly the princess snapped up and pointed a silent but incredibly cutting glare at me. For the next couple of seconds I tried to meet her gaze, and just when I was about to give up, she abruptly yelled out, "Shut up, shut up, shut up! I hate you, I hate you, I hate you!" And with that, she fell over her desk again and covered her head with her hands.

I blinked once, twice, and then gave a withering glance to my assistant.

"You see what you've done?" I grumbled and pointed at the still slightly trembling princess. She looked over, ever-so-slightly shrugged her shoulders, and promptly turned on her heel. "Hey, don't just walk away at your own leisure!"

She didn't listen to me, but wordlessly took a seat. I was still groaning in defeat and massaging my forehead when I heard the creaking of a chair beside me. I looked over and nearly fell out of mine when I saw Josh. The guy was not only disheveled, but he also had the print of a slender hand clearly outlined on his cheek in red. I almost had to get a double-take before I managed to speak.

"And just what happened to you?"

He looked at me with tired eyes and exhaled in a pained groan.

"Angie asked me for help. She and Ammy had to carry some handouts to the teacher's office, and they wanted a boy to do the heavy lifting."

"What does that have to do with the handprint?"

"I'm getting there. So, we were carrying these giant stacks of photocopying paper down the stairs when there was a breeze. It sent a few papers from the top flying, so Ammy tried to catch them, but she slipped and fell on me..."

"Oooh..." I nodded to myself sagely. "I can see where this is going..."

"So," Josh continued wearily. "I tried to break her fall and I might have... accidentally..."

"You cupped a feel."

"No! I mean, maybe I touched it a little, but it was a total accident!"

"I hear you. So, what happened next? Did the class rep slap you?"

"That's the weirdest part!" Josh exclaimed with an ocean of indignation. "Angie did! And then she ran away and I had to gather all the fallen papers!"

"That's cold."

"Yeah... Girls are weird, man."

I glanced over at the princess on the front and my assistant at the rear, and for the first time, I was inclined to wholeheartedly agree with my friend.

"They are, Josh. They sure are."

PART 3

"Why are you so excited?" Joshua low-key grumbled while looking at me sideways. The mark on his face had already faded considerably by the end of the first period and now was barely visible. I glanced back at him between two swings of my arms and smiled.

"Why shouldn't I be? I missed the last PE class and my body is full of excess energy to burn off."

"If you say so..." He sounded decidedly unconvinced. I didn't really care though; I was too busy limbering up my joints. Then he asked, "This isn't about the girls' uniforms, right?"

Now it was my turn to look at him sideways while doing the splits.

"Pardon?" For some reason Josh was only giving me a *How are you doing that?* look, so I repeated myself a bit louder. "I said, pardon? What was that about the girls?"

"Nothing." He dismissed me and began his own warm-up routine.

Now, that was just a dick move, piquing my interest like that.

I tried not to be bothered by it as I did a few one-handed push-ups, alternating between the arms after every fifth push, and I felt nice and limber in no time. Since the weather was still nice, we were having the physical education class outside, on the sports field behind the main building. The class was co-ed and, unsurprisingly enough, it was also taught by Mrs. Applebottom. Nevertheless, we were still separated into two groups. The guys, which of course included me, were preparing at one end of the field while the girls did so at the other, and Joshua's comment involuntarily drew my attention to them.

They were... nothing special, really. I mean, they were generally attractive teenage girls doing warm-up exercises, but it wasn't like it was a special sight. I took an even closer look, but it wasn't the clothes either. I was half-expecting them to wear those silly formfitting tight shorts they inexplicably called bloomers in certain corners of the internet, but they weren't. In fact, their getup was fairly sensible, with almost knee-long sports shorts and thick white T-shirts. There was nothing really titillating about them.

"A-ha!" Josh suddenly exclaimed at my side.

"Hm?" I looked over to him and he was smiling triumphantly.

"What?"

"You were looking at the girls!"

"Erm... Yes, I was. So? I wanted to figure out what you were talking about."

"Uh-huh." My friend patted me on the back with a smile in tow as he walked by, leaving me wondering just what the heck he was getting at.

The confusing start aside, the rest of the class went swimmingly. After some further warm-ups mandated by the teacher, the class continued their separated yet equal activities. We were playing basketball, which was a ton of fun. I had a natural height advantage over practically everyone, and since I was brimming with energy, I kept dashing around the court and scoring points left and right.

The only guy in the class who could keep up with me was Josh. We were on opposing teams, and over time the game slowly devolved into a duel just between the two of us. I was bigger and stronger, plus I proved to be pretty nimble on my feet, but Josh was just a little faster and had better control over the ball. Not only that, he was better at pacing himself, and while I soon lost the initial rush I felt over being able to move freely, he was able to give an even performance from beginning to end. It was a tough game, but in the end my team, and by that I mean me in particular, came out victorious, though only by two points. Most importantly, it was a blast.

As for the girls, most of them were gawkers, cheering for one side or the other. Angie in particular was constantly shouting advice to Josh. Most of her suggestions were actually good, so they must've made up during one of the breaks when I wasn't looking. The class rep seemed to prefer the underdog, always cheering for the side that didn't have the ball, though in her case "cheering" might have been too strong a word. Let's go with "reserved encouragement" instead. Now the princess, on the other hand, was loud enough to make up for two and then some. Unfortunately for me, though, she wasn't as much cheering for Joshua as rooting against me. In a sense, I had to admire the way she managed to come up with insults that somehow didn't sound insulting. Although how "handsome lecher" even relates to my basketball skills, I still don't know. That said, she was distracting enough that I missed a couple of shots because of her.

As for my assistant, she mostly stayed silent, kept writing her notes, and whenever I looked at her, she made it a policy to limp-wristedly wave a tiny *Go, Team _______!* flag. (Don't ask me where she got it. I have no idea either.)

As for why the girls had time to cheer, it was mostly due to the fact that they were playing tennis, and there were only two courts for that. Some amused themselves by playing with the rackets and spare balls, but whenever it wasn't their turn, they generally just idled around the basketball court. On the other hand, when it *was* their turn, they immediately stopped cheering, even the core girls, and rushed to play.

As far as I could gather from the snippets of placeholder dialog I overheard during the game, girls' tennis was actually getting popular in the country, which I had no idea about, but it made me stop and think for a moment: What country? Not only that, I kept forgetting to check the geography of this world, so I still had no idea where the hell I actually was!

Then I had an idea: Why not ask Judy? She should be able to tell me, and then some other details too, stuff that asking Josh about would have been awkward and possibly data-contaminating. In the worst-case scenario, where she had no idea either, I could still ask her to remind me to look into it so that I wouldn't keep forgetting about it.

With that in mind, I stood up from the bench where I had dropped myself after the game was over just as Josh was returning from a quick errand, carrying a pair of soft drinks (for which I had to pay, of course). He tossed me one of the cans and it felt almost icy against my sweaty palm.

"Thanks."

"You are welcome."

He raised his can and we toasted before drinking them in one go. Once emptied, I handed the can back to him.

"Could you throw this away for me? I have something to take care of before I forget it again."

"Sure." He took the can, but his eyes were fixed on me.

"Have you seen my assistant?"

"Judy?" His eyes suddenly narrowed in suspicion. "Last time I saw her she was sitting on the grass by the tennis court. Why?"

"Because what I need to take care of involves her."

"Oooo..." Josh smiled knowingly and I rolled my eyes.

"Get your brain out of the gutter, please."

"Hey there, pot. This is kettle. He says you're black."

"Ha. Ha. I would love to listen to more of your stellar wit, but I have to run."

I walked past him and he kept waving after me with the same smile. Seriously, why was he convinced that I was some sort of pervert?

"Hm... Maybe I used to be...?" I contemplated as I headed for the tennis court. It took me about half a second to find Judy in the crowd, which surprised even me. It was probably because of how much I'd interacted with her recently, but to me, she stuck out of the uniformity of the other place-holders almost as much as any one of Joshua's girls.

I found her leaning on the ball-catching fence around the court in the company of a few other girls. I walked up to her without hesitation, and somehow my presence seemed to scatter the other students. I didn't mind it, though; the fewer people around, the lower the chance they might overhear something.

She didn't notice me right away. In fact, she was so wrapped up in watching the match that I had to poke her shoulder a bit for her to look my way.

"Hi. Whatcha watching?"

With a "duh" in her eyes, she wordlessly pointed to the court, and I had to whistle in amazement. It was Angie and the princess playing, and they gave one heck of a performance. Now, I'll be the first to admit that I know as much about tennis as I do quantum mechanics, but even I could see they were pretty damn impressive. There were times I could barely see more than a yellow blur of the ball.

Just as I looked over, the princess returned a high ball with a sharp smack that landed just a hair's breadth outside Angie's reach. My assistant raised her little triangular flag in the familiar unenthusiastic wave. So she was doing that for everyone, huh? In a way, that was both a relief and a little disappointing.

"Where did you get that?" I asked, pointing at her hand.

"From the storage room," she answered matter-of-factly while pointing at the small white building at the other end of the field with her flag. "They have a lot of them, though most of them already had sports teams written on them. It's either 'Team Eduard' or 'Team Jackson.'"

"Huh. Those are weird names for a team."

"Maybe they are for individuals? Probably a team's star player."

"That's really rude to the rest of the team."

"Agreed."

We both concurred and then fell silent, watching the match between Angie and Elly unfold. The princess was in the lead, and she looked like she was in her element on the court, but Angie wasn't half bad. In fact, she looked really fired up and was dishing out fastballs as hard as she got them.

I was just thinking about whether they might have been actual professionals when I noticed the princess stumbling. It was only for a moment, but after that I paid closer attention to her and noticed that she indeed was still favoring one of her legs. I formed my hands around my mouth in a funnel as she was about to serve and called out to her.

"Take it easy, princess! You are going to hurt your ankle again!"

She twitched and looked around frantically. She finally found me and waved her racket in my direction in a show of almost comical outrage.

"I don't need your warnings! I hate you!"

"Those two things are in no way related! Just be careful, okay?"

"Shut up, shut up, shut up!"

I lowered my hands and shrugged. "She sure is an irritable girl," I muttered, and Judy nodded. In the meantime, the princess served and it prompted another heated duel on the court. "They are pretty good."

"Angeline is on the tennis team. Eleanor was apparently playing in tournaments on the mainland," Judy explained to me, though she didn't actually take her eyes off the match.

"Really? That explains a lot..." As I was saying that, her last word finally sunk in and I remembered why I came over in the first place. I clicked my tongue over the near-miss and turned to her to hit the iron while it was hot. "Hey, Judy? Can I ask you a quick question?"

She turned away from the match to face me, but all of a sudden, her legs buckled and she fell backward, away from the fence.

"Whoa!" I immediately reached out and caught her by the waist before she could completely topple over. Her legs were still slack, so I lowered her and had her sit down. I also realized that she was warm. She wasn't burning up or anything, but she definitely had a high temperature, and as I took a closer look, I quickly realized that she was pale even beyond her usual complexion.

"I'm all right..." she told me between pained breaths, and somehow her words managed to remain impassive even in this situation.

"Like hell you are!" I completely ignored her protests and put my hand on her forehead. "Just as I thought, you do have a fever. Why didn't you say anything?"

"I'm not sick, just drowsy."

"No, you are both."

It was around this time that Angie came to the fence and began tiptoeing around like she could see more that way.

"What happened?" Her voice sounded more curious than worried, but then she noticed the girl lying in front of me and her face tensed up.

I looked up at her and gestured towards my assistant. "According to her, it's just a lack of sleep. I'll take her to the infirmary, just to be safe." Saying so, I turned back to Judy. "Can you walk?"

She feebly nodded and tried to rise to her feet, but she was so wobbly it was painful to watch. I lent her a shoulder, though she had some difficulty holding on due to the height difference. Just then I noticed that there was a disturbance in the loose ring of placeholders idling around us, and a moment later a familiar face elbowed his way to our side.

"Is there a problem?" Joshua asked as he finally arrived by our side. "I saw her collapse, did something happen?"

"Hopefully nothing serious. I'm taking her to the nurse. Where's the teacher?"

Josh looked around and gave me an unknowing shrug.

"Fine, it's not like they would be a lot of help. Please tell her what happened once she actually shows up."

I didn't even wait for him to nod before I began all but dragging Judy along.

PART 4

"O-ho-ho. Kids these days just don't know their own limits."

I tapped my feet against the floor in irritation and responded with, "Hey, doc, could we skip the pleasantries and the annoying laugh and get to the point where you actually examine her?"

"I'm all right," Judy insisted, but I vetoed her protest by keeping her sitting on the examination table with just one finger on her shoulder.

"O-ho-ho. If what the young lady says is true, then it's just a case of mild exhaustion due to lack of sleep triggered by sudden exertion during your physical education class. Some sleep and drinking lots of fluids should take care of that in a jiffy! O-ho-ho."

"Now you're only doing the laugh to annoy me, aren't you?"

"O-ho-ho. Kids these days are so short-tempered."

I rolled my eyes and faced my sick assistant. She'd already recovered some of her colour, much to my relief, though the rings under her eyes were still as dark as before. I didn't like that, so I turned back to the nurse.

"Can she sleep here?"

"O-ho-ho. Most certainly! That is why we have beds, contrary to what some might believe."

"Why are you looking at me like that?"

The old man continued to smile mysteriously.

"I told you, I am not taking girls here for that."

"For what?" Judy asked, her eyes betraying just a hint of suspicion.

"Long story, I'll tell you once you get better. It involved the princess's injured ankle."

"Okay then." Thankfully, she seemed satisfied with my answer and didn't press the issue. I suppressed an irritated sigh and was just about to continue with my previous line of thought when the door to the nurse's office opened with a loud bang.

Startled, I looked up to find myself face-to-face with Angie, still wearing her PE uniform and heaving like a furnace.

"How is she?!"

I could only blink for a moment at the loud question, and it took me an embarrassingly long time to regain my composure.

"She's fine, I think."

She immediately eased up upon hearing my words.

"Thank goodness, I was worried sick for poor what's-her-name!"

I gave the girl in the doorway a critical look. "You don't even know her name."

"Details!" She smiled as she walked in. "She is your friend, and a friend's friend is a friend!"

"That... haaahh... right... haaahh..." Josh heaved as he stumbled into the office as well.

Great, now the entire worrywart squad was here.

"You really didn't need to run here without changing, you know..." I told them a touch wearily, to little effect.

"Nonsense. A friend's friend's friend was sick. Of course we would hurry!"

"That was one friend too many," Judy stated in her typical deadpan manner, but Angie only waved a dismissive hand in her direction.

"Semantics!"

"So..." Josh started speaking between heaves. "What was... the... problem...?"

I looked at him and couldn't help but skeptically furrow my brows at the sight of him leaning against the doorframe like he'd just run a marathon. Anyways, I answered: "She just needs sleep, something your presence isn't helping."

"Oh, don't be rude!" Angie scolded me with a thin-lipped smile. "Showing camaraderie to our friends' friends is really important when they're ill."

This time I directed the same skeptical eye at her and asked, "You still don't know her name, do you?"

"Why are you so fixated on such small details?!"

All of a sudden Judy tugged on my shirt, drawing my attention away from the angry pout of the childhood friend before me.

"Yes?"

"It's lunch break," she stated dryly, and it took me a moment to gather what she was getting at.

"Right. I owe you some sandwiches, don't I?" She nodded, so I told her, "Later. You have to sleep first."

"I cannot sleep on an empty stomach."

I gave up with a sharp sigh and dropped my shoulders.

"Fine, I'll get you something, but you are staying here. What would you like?"

She pondered that for a moment, and even cocked her head to the side a little before answering. "Something with lots of meat."

"I recommend the meat-lover's double-decker! It has fried chicken breast and slices of bacon between two beef patties. You cannot get any meatier than that!" came the unwanted recommendation from Josh, and when he belatedly noticed the look I was giving him, he hastily added, "What? You're loaded. You can afford it."

"It's not about that!" I started to object, but then Angie inserted herself between the two of us.

"Nah-ah! That's the wrong attitude! You are supposed to follow a sick friend's wishes if you can, no matter the cost!"

"I tell you, something like that is—"

"Are you saying that you do not care about the well-being of our poor, sick friend enough to get her the food she desires? And to say so in front of poor what's-her-face. For shame!"

"Just ask her name, will you?" At this point I let out a shallow groan and turned to Judy, only to find Joshua confidentially whispering to her. Just when did he get behind me, anyways? I could only hear the last words of their conversation, but my fears were confirmed when she turned to me with a hungry gleam in her eyes.

"I want a Wagyu-beef sandwich," she stated about as empathically as her monotone allowed. I glared at Joshua, then directed a slightly less pointed look at her before I crossed my arms in front of my chest.

"What the heck is that?"

"Wagyu-beef?" my friend grinned at me with an enthusiasm that showed that he had been fishing for the question. "It is a kind of cow meat from Japan. It is well known for its exquisite taste, beautifully marbled appearance, and high unsaturated fat content. They make it by massaging the cows and feeding them sake and beer and it's—"

"Wait, stop!" I raised my hands to hold off the torrent of trivia. "Did you actually do research on this?!" He nodded enthusiastically. "Let me guess—it was so that you can mooch off me." He nodded again, this time a bit more hesitantly. I rolled my eyes at him in disapproval, then focused my attention on Judy, who was almost drooling at the description. It was a sight especially unusual on her face, but I had to stand my ground on this, so I took a deep breath and told her, "No. You are exhausted, so you need something light and easy to digest. You are not getting any of these hyper-fancy sandwiches, and that's final."

"Stingy," Angie grumbled at my side.

"Yes, stingy," Judy echoed, completing the united front of accusing eyes arrayed against me.

I tried to object, but their faces told me it would be a waste of time, so instead I grabbed hold of the two culinary corrupters and quickly drove them out of the infirmary. They protested as hard as one would expect them in this situation, but Angie was what, half my size? As for Josh, he was still heaving for some reason and felt as weak as a kitten, so I managed to push them back to the door without much effort.

"Stop interfering and let her rest," I told them firmly between two pushes. "Not to mention, you need to get changed or nobody will eat anything!"

With that, I ever-so-gently threw them out of the premises and then dusted my hands with flair to affirm my superior people-pushing skills. I was ready to return to Judy when I noticed that there was another person in the corridor.

"And what about you?" I inquired just a touch wryly as I turned to the blonde girl sticking to the wall next to the door. She was red as a tomato and refused to meet my eyes.

"I-i-it's not like I came here to check on you two or anything!" she sputtered at me in a feeble display of accusative outrage, and I couldn't stop myself from chuckling at her.

"No, I'm sure you didn't."

"I'm serious!"

"Sure you are."

"I didn't say anything funny—stop laughing!"

"Actually, you did."

The princess stomped her foot (the uninjured one, so she was at least learning) and growled at me with eyes more at home on a Viking warrior than a teenage girl.

"I hate you!" she declared from the top of her lungs and took off, nearly toppling Josh and Angie in the process. My friend watched her go and then faced me, one eyebrow arched.

"Do you have a problem with her or something?"

It took me a moment to formulate an answer to such a blatantly off-key question.

"No. What gave you that idea?"

"Well, you *are* always messing with her, and she apparently hates you."

"Nah, that's just the tsundere talking. I bet she is prickly with you, too."

Josh pondered for a moment before giving me a weak nod. "She has a bit of a temper, yes, but if you know about it, then why do you always provoke her?"

"You've got it all wrong," Angie interjected. "Leo only does that because he secretly likes her."

I gave Angie a flat look, but since it apparently failed to get the message, I had to voice it as well.

"That is just as wrong in the opposite direction," I firmly told her. "True, I don't dislike her. I mostly just find her hilarious, that's all."

"Uh-huh." Angie nodded knowingly, though her mischievous smile said she either didn't believe me or that she found her own interpretation more amusing.

So I gave up trying to reason with those two and instead shooed them away once more. "Just go already, will you? I want to check on my assistant one more time and then I'll meet you at the cafeteria."

Following my insistent pushing, the two finally gave in and walked away. I made sure they were out of sight before I rubbed my face and returned to the infirmary, only to find the nurse jovially stoking his mustache by the door.

"O-ho-ho. Oh, to be young again!"

"What?"

"O-ho-ho. Watching the affairs of youngsters like yourself just makes me so nostalgic." He leaned closer to me and whispered, "If you ever need advice on the matters of the heart, you can always ask me. You might not think so, but I was quite popular at your age." He paused to wink and added, "I can also help with the other kind of problems of the heart too. I know a good cardiologist."

After a few flat blinks, I proceeded to rub my face and completely deny the existence of the annoying old man in front of me. I wordlessly walked around him and only stopped in my tracks when I noticed Judy was already lying down on one of the beds, covered under a blanket, with her back to me.

"Oh..." I whispered as I drew a little closer to check on her.

"I'm already asleep. Go away," she stated flatly, though she did sound at least a little sulky.

"Then how are you talking to me?"

"This is a pre-recorded message."

"Okay then. If you are asleep, then I suppose you don't need your food after all."

My assistant visibly twitched under the blanket.

"This pre-recorded message also predicts that I will only nap for a few minutes, so I will have time to eat lunch."

I silently rolled my eyes, just for myself, and turned on my heel, circled around the still chuckling nurse, and left the office. Once outside, I allowed myself a few more sighs before I headed for the dressing room, just in time for the long chime of the lunch break to sound.

That meant I had to hurry up. I had to change, get my wallet, head for the cafeteria to buy food both for myself and Judy, and then get back to the nurse's in time so we could actually eat. As I counted all that, I shook my head in discontent. I hoped my life would start making more sense as my research progressed, but instead each day was more of a pain in the neck than the last. I knew getting involved with Judy was a bad idea, and

I couldn't help but wonder how much easier my life could have been if I'd stuck to the original plan and chosen a generic male classmate for an assistant. I also wondered if the cafeteria even had those fancy beef sandwiches, and whether she would like them.

"Maybe I should buy a couple of different kinds and let her choose?"

And with that final whisper, I quickened my pace and rounded a corner with a small smile on my face that I didn't even notice at the time.

CHAPTER 9

PART 1

"How about that one?" Josh pointed at a device sitting in its own little transparent plastic case on one of the myriad shelves in the phone shop. It was relatively big, flat, and looked incredibly fragile. In other words, it was just like any other modern smartphone.

"I don't know... I want one that can take some punishment."

My friend looked at me curiously as he turned away from the display case.

"Why exactly? Do you want to clobber people with it?"

"No," I answered calmly, in no way petulant or irritated. "I am just going to store some important information on it, and I want it to be secure."

"Important information, huh?" Josh looked like there was a question on the tip of his tongue, but in the end he didn't ask and just shrugged. "Fine then. Why don't we ask the clerk for recommendations?"

"Yeah, maybe we should've done that in the first—" It was about this time that I became aware of someone insistently tugging at my sleeve. I turned around and found my assistant pointing at a different display case. After the quick nap in the infirmary, and eating the ridiculously overpriced sandwich she made me buy for her, she was in much better shape. In fact, she'd been surprisingly eager ever since I picked her up after the end of classes.

Anyways, I followed her finger and found a particularly large smartphone. Seriously, it was basically a small tablet. It was covered in a garish pink casing and had a big yellow sticker declaring it *The Best Selling Model of 20XX!*

"Buy that," she told me with a subdued passion and accompanied it by another series of tugs on my coat.

"Why that one?" I inquired with just a hint of suspicion.

"It's pink."

"Yes, I can see that." This time, it was no longer just a hint. "What does that have to do with anything?"

She mulled over the question, and then her eyes lit up.

"Real men wear pink."

"Pardon?" I asked, doubting my ears for a moment.

"Real men wear pink," she obediently repeated for a second time. "Pink is considered feminine. Most men feel uncomfortable wearing it because they fear others would think they are effeminate, but by taking it for your-self and using it proudly, you tell the world that you are so manly you are above such concerns."

By this point, my suspicion already morphed into skepticism, and after a long beat, I directly asked her, "What does that have to do with how sturdy it is?"

She pondered the question, and then answered with a not-exactly-confident, "It makes people think you are really manly, so they won't try to break it?"

"That... ugh..." I rubbed my face to stifle a groan. "Admit it. You just like the colour."

My assistant blinked in what felt like shock and conspicuously averted her eyes.

"What gave you that idea?"

"Your notebook?"

She clicked her tongue, which sounded really weird when done with a poker face.

"I've been foiled."

I decided to ignore her for the moment, and I was about to turn back to the display case when I noticed Josh wasn't nearby anymore. He'd slipped away to talk with the clerk while I was with Judy, so I walked up to them, and my friend beamed at me the moment I arrived at his side.

"Guess what, Leo? I found the perfect phone for you!"

"Did you?" I asked, trying to ignore the chill of apprehension running down my spine.

"Indeed, my good sir!" the young salesman grinned at me with un-bridled enthusiasm, which only raised more alarms. "Dear customer, I am honoured to introduce you to the Megatel Twenty-XX, the latest in high-quality telecommunications technology!" The clerk continued beam-ing as he set a large box on the counter.

"Am I the only one who's hearing infomercial music?" I muttered.

"The Megatel Twenty-XX is the latest and greatest on the market, an integrated telecommunication and entertainment nexus for the whole fam-ily, in your pocket!"

"I can hear it too," Judy suddenly declared, making me whip my head around to look at her so hard I was afraid I might have strained a muscle.

"Wait, you mean the infomercial tune? I thought I was joking!"

My assistant gave me an odd look, and then stated, "In that case, I'm joking too."

I locked eyes with her for a couple of seconds, and at last I raised a hand to my forehead while simultaneously telling her, "Judy, your sense of humour is weird."

"Thank you, I learned it from the best," she responded without missing a beat.

"That wasn't a compliment and... You know what? Never mind."

"What are you talking about?" Josh looked at us like we were talking nonsense. In all fairness, we kind of were.

Meanwhile, the clerk continued to bombard us with his pitch, completely unfazed by our lack of attention.

"Sixty-four gigabytes of ram! Thirty-two processor cores! The latest mobile operating system with free apps! A solid synth-diamond screen! No more scratches! Solid eighteen-carat gold casing! Diamond-encrusted buttons and—"

"Whoa, hold on a minute!" I raised my hand and finally got the salesman to stop before I turned back to Joshua. "Is trying to get me to waste my money that much fun?"

"Why?" he smiled with the innocence of a newborn weasel. "You have enough to spare, and you might as well spend it on something awesome."

"Sorry, but 'diamond-encrusted buttons' don't really fit my definition of awesome. It's more along the lines of 'gaudy' and 'wasteful.'"

"Do you have it in pink?" Judy suddenly asked on my left.

I rolled my eyes and cut the clerk off before he could even begin.

"Don't you have something more... traditional? Something tough and practical, preferably with a long battery life?"

The young man looked at me with the disconcerting vacancy of a placeholder before he smiled again and got another box from under the counter.

"We just received this new model yesterday and it should be right up your alley!" He took a relatively normal-looking phone out of the box and showed it off with a flourish. "Water- and shock-resistant casing, elephant-glass screen, and automatic cloud-backup so that you will never lose your data!"

"Elephant glass?" Josh asked, leaning over to take a closer look.

"It's like gorilla-glass, but better."

"What's gorilla-glass then?" I inquired in turn, and the man's smile somehow grew even wider.

"It's like elephant-glass, but weaker."

"That was... the least helpful thing I've ever heard."

The man continued to beam at me, completely disregarding my complaints, and began packing out a series of accessories to the illusory tune of an infomercial.

"But wait! If you buy now, you not only get this state-of-the-art, nigh-indestructible pocket-computer, you will also receive a two-year warranty, a spare battery, a set of spare cases, a mobile keyboard with a stylus, unlimited mobile data for three months, an XXL pack of screen-cleaners, and a chance to win a brand-new sports car, all for the low, low price of eight hundred and ninety-nine Jen, tax included! It's a steal, I tell you!"

Josh let out a jaunty whistle by my side and gave me a thumbs-up, probably to encourage me into buying it. Truth to be told, I could probably buy their entire stock of this phone without even denting my account, but I was still somewhat apprehensive about the price. My hesitation didn't last long, as Josh soon rolled his eyes and elbowed me in the side.

"Come on! If you want quality, you have to pay the price."

To my surprise, I found Judy also nodding at my side.

"He is right. You cannot be stingy with electronics. They get outdated fast."

I held her eyes for a second, then shrugged my shoulders in defeat.

"Fine, fine. I'll take one."

"Marvelous!" the clerk exclaimed with so much enthusiasm, it was unnerving. "We have several loan plans you can choose from, and in case of certain carriers, you can—"

I cut him short by dropping nine hundred Jen bills in front of him.

"Keep the change."

He blinked at me, then stared at the bills in confusion before smiling and scoping them up.

"It is a pleasure doing business with you, sir! Can I interest you in one of our phone plans as well?"

That made me pause for a moment. I had no idea what kind of plan I had at the moment. In fact, I knew nothing about how these things worked. Thankfully, Joshua came to my rescue with a big, colourful brochure in hand.

"Check this out! If you take this plan, then you can designate three numbers from the same carrier that you can call for free for a year, and then renew the contract a year later and get the same benefit!"

"Is that normal?"

"Yeah, most service companies do this kind of thing. It apparently increases loyalty."

"So you say this is a good one?"

"Yup!" Josh grinned at me. "And I use the same carrier, so you can add me right off the bat!"

"Just one question. Why would I want to do that?"

"So you can talk to me for free?"

"Why would I want to do that? I'm already talking to you for free at school. I'm happy I can finally get rid of you after that!"

Josh gave me a flat look, then punched me in the shoulder.

"Ow-ow! Just kidding, I'm kidding!" I exaggeratedly rubbed my shoulders and shook my head. "So violent!"

"Shut up and buy it already," Josh fumed, though from the twinkle in his eyes I could tell he wasn't really mad.

"Fine, fine..." I was just about to turn to the clerk again, but instead I froze mid-motion as I remembered something and faced Judy instead. "Say, what carrier do you use?"

Instead of answering the question, my assistant only blinked at me like I'd just asked which soda brand was her favourite mode of transportation.

"Carrier?"

"Yes, that. Which company does your phone use?"

Instead of answering, Judy fell suspiciously silent. I waited for her to respond, but none was forthcoming, so I cleared my throat.

"Judy, you do have a phone, right?"

She still didn't answer, but for some reason her perma-deadpan seemed to give way to some embarrassment. In a way, that was answer enough.

"Well, that won't do." On a whim, I turned back to the clerk, who was in the middle of packing my new phone into a thick nylon bag. I knocked on the counter to get his attention and then pointed behind me, to the display case not so far from the counter. "I would like that one too, please."

The young man leaned to the side to look behind me and his smile faltered. "The pink one, sir?"

I gave a huge nod and his smile immediately solidified.

"Most certainly, sir! It is a great choice, sir! It was last year's best-selling model, and while it doesn't have the latest operating system upgrade yet, I can assure you it is..."

The salesman continued his pitch even as he began packing up the second phone, but my attention was elsewhere, namely the girl harshly tugging my sleeve.

"You really don't have to."

"Actually, I kinda do," I interjected before she could gather steam. "We need a way to communicate, plus it should be a good alternative for taking notes. Really, you cannot get around in today's world without a phone."

"But it costs a lot."

Now that she mentioned it, I didn't even ask for the price. Unsurprisingly, the clerk was just getting to the end of his spiel as I turned back.

"... and the chance to win a brand-new sports car for the low, low price of five hundred and ninety-nine Jen, tax included!"

Josh whistled again and I rolled my eyes as I placed another set of bills on the counter.

"I'd like it to have the same carrier plan as mine."

"Most certainly!" the clerk answered with unbridled enthusiasm as he began searching for something in a nearby stack of papers. Meanwhile, I took the two wrapped boxes and handed the pink one over to my assistant.

"Here."

"I cannot take this." Her protests were surprisingly feeble. I just smirked at the display of this unusually timid side of hers and pushed her new phone into her hands anyway.

"Sure you can. Consider this an early birthday present." She finally took the package and I was about to smile at her reassuringly when a new thought elbowed its way into my frontal lobe. "Speaking of which, I don't even know when your birthday is."

Judy shuddered and pointedly averted her eyes. Puzzled, I tried to lean in to take a better look at her face and found her blushing. Well, okay, only very slightly flushed, but it was Judy, so it practically meant the same. After a couple more seconds of intense silence, she finally glanced at me and immediately averted her gaze again and uttered a single word.

"Yesterday."

It took me an embarrassingly long time to register that single word, but then an involuntary, "Wait, what?" escaped my lips, followed by a slightly less surprised, "Seriously?"

She nodded, leaving me lost for words, though not for long.

"Happy belated birthday?"

She finally looked up at me and was about to mouth a *Thank you* when Josh cleared his throat.

"Am I a third wheel here?"

I blinked at him in confusion. "Third wheel? No? Why?"

My friend rolled his eyes with a secretive smile and waved his hand dismissively, but then stopped halfway through the motion and snapped his finger instead.

"Hey, I just realized! She just had her birthday, right?"

"Yes, that's what she just said..."

"You know what that means!" He opened his arms and gave us an expectant look, but when neither of us gave him a response, he dropped his shoulders in disappointment. "Come on, guys! Birthday cake! I know an awesome, high-class bakery nearby!"

I sent my friend a critical look and sighed.

"Is that your next plan for emptying my wallet?"

"Hey, don't be paranoid." Josh grinned and patted me on the shoulder, then he turned to Judy. "By the way, I don't have our friend's funds, but please accept this." With that, he handed her a long, pink phone strap matching the colour of her new phone. "Happy birthday."

"Thank you," Judy accepted the gift with weirdly mechanical motions and looked at me like she was asking for help. She probably wasn't used to these kinds of situations, so I smiled at her reassuringly.

It was about this time when the clerk finished gathering his papers and presented two identical stacks to us. After some deliberation, we handed our new acquisitions over to Josh, and after filling out the paperwork (during which I learned for certain that Judy's birthday was indeed yesterday) we received a pair of new SIM-cards and our own copies of the contracts. Normally we would've needed an adult, as we were all minors and thus not allowed to sign these contracts, but I greased the wheel of bureaucracy with a couple of twenty Jen bills and the clerk obligingly turned a blind eye.

Once we made sure everything was in order, and partly due to Joshua's insistence, we left the shop and headed towards a nearby bakery he was familiar with due to Angie dragging him over there the day before. Thinking of Angie, I glanced over my shoulder and, speak of the devil, I saw some girls conspicuously peeking around a corner on the opposite side of the street. I sighed and Judy, by this point back in her usual non-flushed deadpan, gave me a questioning look. I leaned closer to her and whispered right into her ear.

"They are still following us." She was about to glance back, but I stopped her. "Don't."

"Why?"

"I don't want to interrupt them. This kind of thing is fairly normal."

"It is?"

"Yeah, it's date-stalking. Girls do that all the time in harem-comedies. Angie is there to keep an eye on Josh, the princess probably wants to catch Mystery Girl X, while the class rep is just trying to keep those two on a short leash."

"I see." Judy nodded like I'd just said something profound. "Does that mean we are on a date?"

I let her question sail past me, and instead I focused my attention on the three girls I could see skulking from one alley to the next. They stuck out from the crowd like a sore thumb, yet Josh and Judy didn't seem to notice them until just before we entered the phone shop. In fact, Josh was still blissfully unaware of them. Actually, I could go even further: he was showing an absolutely appalling lack of apprehension, and I can say that without holding back because the proto-harem weren't the only people he didn't notice.

I carefully glanced in the other direction, making sure I seemed as natural as possible, and I quickly managed to catch a peek of a comet of silvery-white hair dashing from one alley to the next on our side of the street. Both her and Angie's group seemed so focused on us that they didn't even note the existence of the other, even though all they had to do was to look over to the other side of the road for a moment.

In the meantime, we reached the bakery, and to my surprise, it looked like a fairly normal family restaurant, its only unusual feature being the large neon sign saying *La Sweets Shoppe*. It took me a moment to decide whether that was supposed to be horrible French or horrible Ye Olde English, but in the end, I decided to take the third option and completely disregard the whole thing. Regrettably, there was another issue that was not so easy to ignore.

I glanced back and caught another glimpse of the white-haired girl dashing for cover. What was her angle? Why was she stalking Josh? And more importantly, just what kind of crazy shenanigans would she cause today? Actually, that last question was the true reason behind my current conundrum. We were just about to have an impromptu birthday party for my brand-new assistant, and I wasn't keen on Mystery Girl X potentially crashing it. But then again, what could I do about it? Or rather, what *should* I do?

The plan came together surprisingly fast, and I had a general idea of what I would do and say by the time Josh opened his mouth as he turned back to us in front of the bakery. I cut him short by raising a hand and giving them a regretful frown.

"Crap! I forgot my ID at the phone shop!"

Josh looked at me sideways.

"Seriously?!"

"Yeah, I should go back and get it ASAP. Why don't you guys go inside and pick a cake while I'm away?"

"... You're not trying to bail on us, are you?"

I directed a hurt look at Josh and shook my head.

"Hey, who do you think I am?" Saying so, I turned to my assistant next and handed her my wallet. "Pick whatever you want. My treat."

She looked dubious, but I winked at her and she seemingly understood my intention. Or maybe she just reacted well to winks in general. Either way, I proceeded to shoo the two into the bakery with exaggerated motions. I barely waited long enough for them to close the door behind themselves before I took off down the street. My target was standing behind a signpost by a bus stop and she looked at me like a deer in the headlights as I strode towards her.

She was pretty, though I already expected that much, being a main heroine and all. She was about as tall as Angie, so a little on the short side, and she was wearing a form-hugging black knit sweater, a tiny jacket, a jean miniskirt with black stockings, and a pair of fur-trimmed leather boots. Her only accessory was a thin, silvery choker around her neck that seemed to sparkle almost unnaturally in the daylight, to the point I wondered if it had tiny gems encrusted in it.

Her most striking characteristic was, of course, her white hair—glossy and seemingly glowing with a shade of aquamarine. She wore it in a pair of thick twin-tails held together by ribbons with small red beads attached to them, which only further accentuated her pale white skin and piercing red eyes. An albino? In retrospect, it should have been obvious from Josh's description, but seeing the white-haired girl up close was surprisingly eerie, nevertheless.

At last, I reached her and flashed a toothy smile to take her off guard. It worked so well that for a moment it looked like she was about to run away. It only lasted for a second, though, as after the first shock, her expression turned rigid and melted back into an alluring smile.

"Well, what do we have here?" she purred, her voice deep and confident.

I paused before answering. That was a disturbingly sudden change in attitude. Maybe she was trying to take me off guard in return? Either way, I let out a pointed cough before I renewed my smile.

"So, you are the mysterious girl who has been following Josh around, huh?" I looked her up and down, though it didn't seem to unnerve her any further. "Nice to meet you. I'm Leonard Dunning."

"I know," she purred again, her eyes practically licking me all over. In her case, the unnerving part actually worked, so we were even, I supposed.

"That makes things easier for both of us. You see, I have a request."

"Oh? And just what could little old me do for such a large, imposing guy like you?" She flashed me a sultry smile, and I involuntarily groaned, much to her apparent surprise.

"Okay, I actually have two. Could you please drop the whole vamp-thing?"

"V-vamp?" She sputtered as she took a step back, her voice sounding much more natural. "I'm not!"

"Well, you kind of are. I mean, who else talks like that?"

"I wouldn't know because I am not one!" she protested, her voice getting more and more high-pitched to the point where she started sounding her age, an insulted teenage girl.

"Fine, whatever you say. So, can we get back to my actual request?"

"Of cou—" She abruptly caught the fact that her voice was slipping and lowered it to a purr. "I mean, of course."

I rolled my eyes and decided to ignore her tone for the time being.

"So, you see, I noticed you developed a habit of messing around with my friend, which of course is none of my business. However, we are about to hold a birthday party for my assistant, so could I ask you not to cause any ruckus while we celebrate?"

"Is that all?" She smirked at me and leaned forward, a move that would've revealed some of her fairly modest cleavage if she wasn't wearing a turtleneck. She seemed to notice the problem as well and awkwardly switched the posture into her running her hands over her hips. "I am sure a guy like you has better requests than that."

She theatrically fluttered her long eyelashes at me, and I could only roll my eyes in return.

"Seriously, just stop this whole charade," I told her flatly, freezing her mid-motion. "This whole femme-fatale vamp act is getting really old."

"But I'm not—!" she protested again, her real voice breaking through the façade once more in the process.

"Okay, then putting that aside, could you please go home for today? I'm sure being out in the sun is not good for you anyhow."

As far as my research told me, albinos in harem-comedies often filled a niche called *The Sick Girl*, a character archetype that was considered "moe," another term that was so ill-defined I only had the barest grasp of it even after several hours of research. It had something to do with being attractive and/or cute based on a set of seemingly contradicting criteria, which being ill apparently fell under, somehow. Either way, whether she was actually sickly or not, being an albino meant that she didn't produce melanin, the body's built-in sunscreen, and thus staying outside in the sun was risky for her.

Her face tensed up in an awkward smile.

"W-w-what do you mean by that?"

"Oh please," I swept my hand in front of her to indicate all of her. "It's easy to tell even by first glance. The red eyes, in particular, are very telling." I waited for her to respond, but since she only shuffled her feet, I cut the chase and told her, "So, will you let up your hunt for Joshua for the day if I ask nicely?"

"I am not hunting!"

"Stalking?"

"That's the same thing."

"Then what would you call your behaviour?"

She paused for a second and was about to answer when she once again realized how relaxed her posture and voice had become, so she took up another highly suggestive stance and fluttered her eyelashes in my general direction.

I groaned and cut her off just as she was about to take a breath.

"Seriously, stop that! I just want you to leave this birthday party alone, but how is one supposed to have a conversation when you—?"

I got roughly that far when I noticed that her eyes were widening in shock. I hastily glanced behind me just in time to jump out of the way of the flying tackle that I presumed was supposed to take down both of us. Because of my swift dodge, however, it hit Mystery Girl X with full force and both she and her assailant tumbled to the ground in an undignified sprawl. I didn't even need to look to know who the latter was.

"Princess!" I yelled angrily at the golden-haired girl lying on the ground. She twitched at the word and looked at me with a mixture of thinly veiled indignation and apprehension before she jumped to her feet... only to fall back onto her knees with a hiss. I reflexively reached out to her and caught her before she could topple over. "Let me guess. You hurt your ankle again, didn't you?"

"None of your business!" She glared at me, the look in her eyes more petulant than anything else, before she realized what was going on and her head quickly turned left and right. "Where is she?"

"Where is who?" I looked around with her, and to my surprise, I realized that Mystery Girl X was nowhere to be found.

"Argh! She got away again!" The princess fumed, so infuriated that she didn't even notice that she was clinging to me while I helped her onto her feet.

By this point my disapproval was immeasurable, and since she didn't seem to get the clue, I proceeded to lightly bonk her over the top of her head.

"Ow!" She looked at me wide-eyed, but I didn't let her talk.

"What did I tell you about tackles?" She was about to protest, so I glared at her and asked again, this time with an extra emphasis on each word. "What. Did. I. Tell. You. About. Tackles?"

She only met my eyes for a moment before she sheepishly looked away. "That I shouldn't do it because I'd hurt myself."

"Precisely."

"Sorry?"

I sighed and shook my head.

"Seriously, if you don't want me to worry about you, stop doing things that hurt you. Seriously."

"Sorry..." she repeated in a barely audible voice. I sighed and patted her on the head where I bonked her.

"There, there. So long as you keep it in mind."

"Elly!"

I looked up and found Angie running towards us with the class rep trailing further behind her. The moment the princess noticed her, she began flailing and tried to stand on her own, which only resulted in me having to catch her again.

"That was dangerous," the class rep scolded her as she arrived. "You shouldn't cross the street when the light is still red."

"Sorry," the princess apologized again, this time much more readily than with me. It was also about this time that the two newcomers noticed me and they both smiled awkwardly.

"Oh, look! It's Leo! Fancy meeting you here!" Angie promptly elbowed the class rep in the side, at which point she awkwardly nodded. "What a koinkidink!"

"Sure, let's go with that..." I murmured as I searched for a better hold on the princess. "Can you stand now?"

"I'll try," she told me, but the moment she put any weight on her ankle, she let out a pained hiss.

"Elly, you hurt your leg again!" Angie gasped and fell to her knee to take a closer look. "Aw, it's swollen. Pain, pain, go away. Pain, pain, go away."

She kept chanting as she massaged her ankle and I could only frown in reaction.

"We are not kids anymore," I grumbled, but she didn't seem to care.

"Try now," she beamed at the princess, and after some hesitation, she tried to stand on it again. To everyone's surprise, she didn't cry out this time.

"It's... better?"

The princess was flabbergasted, and she wasn't alone.

"Well, I'll be damned..." I whispered by her side, and I had a feeling my expression wasn't far from hers either.

She took a few tentative steps and looked at Angie with gratitude. She, on the other hand, had her fists on her hips akimbo and grinned like a well-fed cat before she turned to me.

"So, Leo. Whatcha doing?"

I wanted to shout *You know exactly what I was doing!* but I held it down and instead smiled back.

"We were just about to have Judy's birthday party."

"Who?"

"My assistant."

"Sorry, I'm drawing a blank here."

"What's-her-name."

"Oh, her!" She flashed a toothy smile that felt almost too wide on her face. "Why didn't you say that in the first place!"

I had a feeling she was teasing me, so I didn't answer. Instead, I just turned around and was about to leave them behind when I noticed something on the walkway. I crouched down, picked it up, and then put it into my pocket in just one motion.

"What was that?" the class rep asked over my shoulders, once again closing in on me out of the blue and betraying her secret ninja training.

"Just something that fell out of my pocket while I helped the princess up," I told her smoothly and brushed her off with a smile. "Now then, I'd better get going."

"Wait a moment!" Angie stopped me in my tracks by entwining her arm with mine. "You were talking about a birthday party just now, weren't you?"

"Yes?"

"Soooooooo?" She squeezed my arm, which didn't really hurt but was obviously supposed to represent her coercing me.

"You want to be invited?" I guessed, and she immediately let go of me with an ear-to-ear grin.

"Oh Leo, you didn't have to, but I don't want to be rude, so I guess I have no choice!"

"Wait, I didn't invite you yet."

To my tremendous surprise, I suddenly found my other arm seized as well, and by none other than a beet-red princess. She also squeezed my arm, which in her case actually hurt. I was waiting for her to say her piece, but instead she just looked at me, tried to open her mouth, then froze up, turned one shade redder, and squeezed my arm even harder. After she did the cycle the third time, I was ready to cry uncle.

"Fine, fine! I get it, I invite you! Sheesh!"

"Oh Leo, you are so nice!" Angie grinned at me and let me go. The princess, on the other hand, began squeezing me even harder, so I had to manually peel her off me. With that done, we headed for the bakery, arriving just as Josh peeked through the door. He blinked uncomprehendingly at the sight.

"Where did you guys come from?"

"Long story," I told him with a weary breath, and he shrugged in return.

"It's cool, we were just wondering how the three of us were going to eat all that cake."

I could feel the corner of my mouth unconsciously twitch.

"Wait, how much cake are we actually talking about?"

"Well..." My friend faltered. "Have you seen one of those life-size car cakes? You know, the kind that celebrities order for their parties?"

I slowly set my mouth in a thin line, turned to the three girls behind me, and quietly told them over the sound of my popping knuckles, "Girls, could you step back a few paces?"

"Um... Why?" Angie sounded apprehensive but took a step back, nonetheless.

"I don't want your clothes to get splattered with Josh's blood..."

PART 2

"Stop touching me!" the princess hissed into my ear, and my stifled groan of misery barely managed to convey the exasperation I felt.

"I don't have much of a choice, now do I?" I retorted while adjusting the annoying package on my back, making sure to get a firm grip.

"Ow! You did it again!"

"As I said, I don't have much choice. You were strangling me."

"That's no excuse! A real gentleman would put up with it!"

This time I groaned aloud and muttered, "How did it come to this?"

"Mostly your own fault," Judy stated coldly at my side, her otherwise emotionless voice sounding unusually sharp.

"How was that my—?" I halted my outraged question mid-word and raised a single eyebrow. "What are you doing?"

My assistant looked over at me, though her fingers never stopped tapping on the screen of her new phone even as she spoke to me.

"I downloaded a word processor and now I am testing it." Her fingers drummed so fast on the device's touch-screen keyboard that I wondered if it could keep up with her pace. "I am making new observations."

"Such as?" I asked, against my better judgment.

She looked at her digital notes. "You graduated from flirting and now you are a full-blown molester."

"No, I'm not!" I objected loudly, startling the princess on my back and nearly dropping her in the process. I quickly readjusted my grip on her thighs and continued to carry her.

"You are touching me again!" she protested on my back and I lightly shook her in frustration.

"I told you, I am only holding on to you." Judy nodded to herself at my side and began tapping again. I looked at her flatly and repeated, "As I said, I am not molesting anyone, I'm just carrying her! I'm completely innocent! It's not even the first time this happened!"

"A repeat offender then. I'd better make note of that too."

I opened and closed my mouth repeatedly, trying my best to express the depth and profundity of my outrage, but in the end, I could only shake my head in despair and reiterate a previous question: Just how did things turn out like this anyway?

One didn't have to look too far back to answer that query. The ad hoc birthday party, while starting out on the wrong foot, was ultimately a resounding success. Though it took some very amicable and in no shape or form violent persuasion (if you don't believe me, just ask my lawyer), I managed to convince Joshua that a life-size Dodge Viper cake was a bit of an overkill for just six people, not to mention imposing a spoiled-celebrity-level demand on the bakery staff. In the end, I chose a huge, tiered straw-berry cake instead—a bit too sweet for my taste, but otherwise I had no complaints about it.

The rest of the party went off without a hitch, and while I wouldn't have called it a blast, we had a really fun and relaxed afternoon... though I was mostly just listening in the background as I knew nothing about the most common topics, such as local gossip or the new popular TV shows. Josh didn't seem to have such reservations, spending a roughly equal amount of time with all the girls, including Judy. Still, all things considered, it was a nice diversion from our unrelated toils and troubles, and it also served as a perfect opportunity to familiarize the group with my assistant.

Once we finished (and they made me pay the bill, of course), we broke into two groups. Angie, Josh, and the class rep went one way, the rest of us the other, courtesy of the fact that we lived in two different neighbourhoods. As for what led to the current situation... let's just say, the princess decided to once again reinforce my impression of her being a total klutz. In a nut-shell, after I innocently offered to take her home, she once again declared her undying hatred towards me in the company of a series of high-pitched noises, and then she immediately managed to fall over. On flat ground, no less. And thus we reached the present. She was situated on my back in a piggy-back-ride, I was taking her home anyways—and my assistant was picking the worst moment to mess with me.

"Is this your way of getting back at me for the cake?" I asked the girl still immersed in poking her new toy at my side. Judy looked at me blankly and shook her head.

"No."

"Are you sure? You seemed unusually enthusiastic about that car-cake..."

"I wasn't." She paused for a second. "Joshua just made it sound really interesting." She paused again, this time for a bit longer. "I also liked the strawberry cake. And the party. It was... nice of you to indulge me. Thank you." She returned her eyes to the screen in her hand. Needless to say, I couldn't help but smile at her unusually earnest words.

"You are welco—" I started, but my words—and my air supply—were cut off.

"Stop squeezing!" the princess exclaimed on my back while simultaneously putting me in a choke hold.

"You are the one squeezing! Stop trying to strangle me!"

I gave her a shake and she finally calmed down. For the next couple of minutes, neither of us said anything, so I had some time to think as I looked over the evening streets. The sun was so low that there was only a little of its red light left painting the buildings, yet it wasn't dark enough for the streetlamps to light up yet. The dim residential streets felt surprisingly spooky, especially with the monotonous background noises my brain was already filtering out due to sheer repetition. It also didn't help that there were no placeholders on the streets, either. They probably followed their schedules to the letter in the evenings as well as they did in the mornings, I presumed.

I looked up and for the first time noticed the early heralds of the starry sky. It should have been quaint, but all I could think about was whether the flickering pinpricks of light I could see in the darkening skies were artificial. After all, no matter which of my hypotheses I considered as a basis, they couldn't be real giant balls of hydrogen-fusion. There was no way this dream/simulation/whatever would detail something that distant and irrelevant. I was just about to wonder whether I should get a telescope to study them when I was startled by a pair of soft mounds pressing against my back. I stiffened for a moment (no, not like that) and glanced back at the princess. She was resting her head over my shoulder and, contrary to just a few seconds before, she was pressing her entire torso against mine. I raised a questioning eyebrow at her, and she immediately averted her eyes.

"D-don't get the wrong idea!" she sputtered, but instead of separating herself from me, she clung to my back even harder. "It's just cold!"

I raised my brow even farther. "Is it?" It was still early autumn, and while I wasn't planning to grow bananas in this weather, it was still balmy enough that I felt thoroughly baffled by her statement.

"Yes!" she vehemently pouted.

I would have left it at that if not for outside interference.

"Maybe it's just your clothes?" Judy quipped at our side without looking up from her phone, and the girl on my back dangerously narrowed her eyes in response.

"And just what is that supposed to mean?" the girl on my back growled.

"Actually, that is a good question," I interrupted, trying to sound reasonable. "You are both wearing the same school uniforms."

"It's not what you wear, it's how you wear it," came my assistant's ready response.

"And just what is *that* supposed to mean?" the princess repeated, though this time her question sounded more genuine and less confrontational. When she didn't get an answer, she petulantly puffed her cheeks and pointed her customary finger at my assistant. "Why are you even following us around if you only speak to ridicule us?"

"I'm not following you in particular. I'm with the chief. He is going to take me home afterward."

"What?" The princess proceeded to squeeze my neck on purpose, though she tried to make it look like she was just losing her balance. "Are you taking her home with you? Are you in that kind of relationship?!"

I pointedly cleared my throat and frowned at my assistant. "I told you people would misunderstand if you said it like that." Judy only shrugged her shoulders and returned to her phone, apparently making some new notes, so I addressed the princess next. "I am taking her home the same way I'm taking *you* home."

She momentarily stiffened. "W-w-what do you plan to do to me? Is that the kind of man you are, one that takes advantage of injured girls? I should have known! I knew you didn't smell right from the first time I met you!"

I would have facepalmed if my hands weren't occupied, so instead I did the second best thing and groaned so loud it hurt my throat.

"No! I am taking you to *your* home and then I'm taking her to *her* home!"

"Oh."

"Seriously, what the heck is wrong with you two?"

Neither of them answered aloud, though the princess did start squirming on my back.

Thankfully, we were near our destination. I could already see the huge brown roofs of the mansion down the street. It was just as needlessly huge and gaudy as I expected. I set my jaw, readjusted the princess on my back, and thought about relaxing things while trying to ignore the soft girly-parts still squished against my back.

It only took a few subjectively long minutes to get to the mansion gates, but no matter how hard I tried to relax, for some reason the closer we got, the more irritable I felt. Anyways, said gates were overseen by a single black-clad man. He was tall and lean, though not wiry. His hair was pitch-black save for two wide strips of pale grey on the sides, a colour scheme that so closely mirrored his thick goatee, I had to wonder if he had it dyed that way on purpose. The only thing sharper than the pair of dark eyes situated under his bushy (yet inexplicably well-groomed) eyebrows was his suit, a custom-cut ensemble with pure white gloves and shiny black leather shoes. In fact, he was so impeccable, just looking at him made me feel frustrated… for some reason. As I said, I was feeling kinda irritated at the moment. Anyways, I could tell who he was without even having to ask. Sebastian couldn't have looked more like a butler if he tried.

As we got closer, I quickly became aware of the bone-chilling glare he directed at me, though I was so thoroughly inoculated against those by the princess that I didn't even mind. I wanted to return the gesture, but by the time we got into speaking distance, he closed his eyes and shook his head.

"Again, milady?" He spoke as he glanced up at the girl on my back. His voice was impossibly deep and raspy, like he was smoking cigars made of sandpaper or something, and he had a hint of an accent. Maybe German? Anyhow, instead of answering, she only hid behind my shoulders, which made the old servant glare at me even harder. We were off to a rocky start, it seemed.

"Can you stand?" I directed the question to the girl on my back after tearing my eyes away from the man's irritating gaze. She silently nodded, which was surprisingly meek coming from her, and so I let her down. To my further surprise, she was still sticking to my back like she was trying to hide from the scrutinizing glare of the butler.

"This is a different one," he stated dryly.

"If by *a different one,*' you mean the guy carrying her home then yes, it is," I answered in a sour tone, but he was apparently completely ignoring me as he continued addressing the princess.

"Milady, your father might have allowed you this… excursion… but you should not take it as an endorsement of promiscuity."

I rolled my eyes in frustration.

"Seriously now, does everyone in this town have their heads permanently stuck in the gutter today?"

"I did not give you permission to speak," Sebastian growled, finally looking me in the eye.

"Then it's a jolly good thing I don't need it," I answered with fake joviality before I turned around and faced the girl hiding behind my back. She was red as a lobster and at first refused to stop staring at her toes, but after a few pokes, I got her to look up.

"Yes?" she whispered in a very uncharacteristically tame voice.

"Listen, you should stay home tomorrow or your ankle will never heal at this rate."

She looked at me with wide doe eyes and was about to open her mouth when she was cut off by the outraged hiss of a positively fuming butler.

"Insolence!"

I looked at him over my shoulder and gave him a huge nod. "Yeah, interrupting people when they are talking *is* rude. Shame on you."

For a second or ten, the tall servant kept repeatedly opening and closing his mouth like a landed fish, which give me the opportunity to finish my thought.

"I'm serious, princess. At this rate, you might permanently damage yourself. Stay home tomorrow and then rest through the weekend too."

"But... but I have to go to school..." she protested meekly, and I could barely stifle a chuckle. I never thought I'd ever see her as subdued as she was at the moment, though I was a little troubled about why Sebastian's presence led to this kind of reaction. I decided to worry about that later.

"Listen, if you are worried about falling behind in the race for Josh, I will send him over to deliver the homework to you. I might even be able to convince him to come alone so you can have him all for yourself for an entire afternoon. How does that sound?"

She quickly turned a different shade of red (maybe I should put together a colour chart for her one of these days...) but ultimately shook her head.

"What about the girl?"

"What girl?"

"That prowling succubus," she hissed, her usual temperament finally showing through her restrained exterior.

"Oh, *her*? Don't worry, I should be able to do something about her."

The princess's eyebrows shot up and she looked at me incredulously.

"You can?"

"Sure, I already talked to her, remember?" As if just remembering the time she tried to tackle me, her eyes twinkled with recognition, though she still looked doubtful. I sighed and smiled at her reassuringly. "She is no more troublesome than some other girls I know. I should be able to deal with her just fine."

She was still looking at me funny, but before she could say anything more, I could see a dark shape reflected in her eyes. She wilted like a flower in the microwave. I looked over my shoulder and immediately staggered back.

"The hell!" I exclaimed as I barely restrained myself from throwing a decidedly nondiplomatic punch by sheer reflex. "Have you even heard of personal space?"

Sebastian wasn't fazed by my outrage and instead he continued staring at me from a few centimeters away. We were roughly the same height, but somehow his glare made him seem bigger at first glance. Since standing my ground in this situation would have meant standing so close to him I could feel his breath on my face, I decided to be the bigger man and take a half-step back.

"Just who do you think you are?" he growled, exposing all fifty-two of his teeth in the process.

"Leonard Dunning," I answered without missing a beat. "And you are?"

A vein bulged on the old servant's forehead.

"I am Sebastian von Fraenir, steward and headmaster of the Dracis household's servants," he declared between clenched teeth.

"Neat." I forced myself to smile nonchalantly. "Could you please make sure the princess stays home and doesn't exert herself tomorrow? I would be much obliged. It takes a lot of effort to look after her."

Sebastian glared, his eyes as cold as icebergs. He raised a hand and the gate automatically opened, letting through two identically dressed (and identical looking) French maids. I was impressed. Didn't maids like that only exist in fiction these days? But then again, maybe this world *was* fiction, and I shouldn't have been surprised after all.

The two maids, short and thin with tidy bubble-cuts of auburn hair, got the princess between them and headed for the mansion. She could barely say her goodbyes before she was taken through the metal gate towards a third maid, a tall young woman with two long braids of platinum-blonde hair, and it closed behind them, leaving me alone with Sebastian. Well, okay, technically Judy was still there as well, but she had completely removed herself from our circle and spent all her time typing on her phone at a good five paces away, so for practical purposes it was just the two of us.

The aged servant looked me over, his eyes sharp and discerning, even a little interested.

"What did you call milady just now?" he inquired, his voice strangely soft, like the proverbial silk hiding steel underneath.

I blinked in response.

"Crap... I called her princess, didn't I?"

He didn't answer, but the twitching of his brows was enough of a clue to guess.

"Sorry, force of habit."

"So you know."

Honestly, I still didn't know diddly-squat about her, but I wasn't one to let that get in the way of some good verbal sparring, so I shrugged my shoulders and told him, "Well, it wasn't hard to figure out." For the first time, the man's face showed an emotion different from acidic disapproval as he raised a single, curious brow. "I mean, how many blonde-with-ringlets girls living in a mansion with a grumpy old butler do *you* know?"

That seemed enough to satisfy his curiosity for the time being and so the butler's gaze swiftly returned to its normal acidity levels.

"And what exactly do you plan to do with this information?"

"Pardon?"

"What is your angle?" he growled, accentuating each word individually.

Before I knew it, I sighed—much to his confusion.

"Is being paranoid this common in this household?" The question seemed to take him further aback, so I decided to elaborate. "I do not have an angle or agenda or anything. I'm not even particularly interested in the princess beyond finding her amusing from time to time. I am just collecting data."

"Data?"

"It's complicated. No offense, but I doubt someone like you would understand."

Sebastian narrowed his eyes and made his voice drop an octave, which nearly put it into infrasound territory.

"I want this to be clear, boy: You are playing a dangerous game here. If I find out that you pose even a sliver of threat for the Dracis family, *you and I are going to play the most dangerous game.*"

"You mean the one where we play tennis on the wings of a plane with a live grenade while riding on feral grizzly bears?"

"I... No... I mean... NO!" The man took a step back and looked at me with eyes wide open, an expression that looked downright comical after all this time. "Who even comes up with something like that?!"

"Well, as much as I would like to claim credit, I actually saw this on the net," I paused thoughtfully and raised a contemplative finger to my chin. "Also, you do not *play* the most dangerous game. The word *game* in that context refers to *prey*, so you should have said we would be *hunting* the most dangerous game, which I must respectfully decline. I mean, I know that rich people have weird hobbies, but hunting people is still a little iffy, if you ask me."

Sebastian silently waited for my explanation to end.

"You are right, of course. Only I will *hunt* the most dangerous game, and I am more and more tempted to start right away."

"So long as we are clear on that," I commented with a chipper smile. "Oh, but before I go, remember what I said: make sure she stays home. She is pretty reckless, and I wouldn't put it beyond her to try attending classes anyway."

"Just go," the man growled.

"Oh, and before I forget it, you might want to call a doctor. I don't want to sound like a worrywart, but she's hurt that same ankle like five times by now. That can't be healthy."

"Fine, now go!" Sebastian snarled between clenched teeth.

"Okay, bye." I turned around but instead of walking away I did a full 360° turn and smiled at the butler with a raised finger. "Oh, before I forget it, I wanted to tell you that I love what you did with your hair and beard. It looks great. Did you dye the white parts black or the other way around?"

"GO!" he finally bellowed and I did just that.

"Fine, fine. No need to be that loud. See you later." I waved at the seething man and walked away. After about twenty meters Judy joined me, her face as blank as ever.

"Your skills at getting under people's skin are quite impressive."

"What can I say? It's a gift," I answered with fake modesty. "He was also really irritating," I muttered under my breath, but she didn't seem to care. Instead, she was busy flicking at her phone, making small sweeping motions to scroll through her notes. At last, she seemed to find what she was looking for and looked up at me.

"Question: What was that part about the..." She looked at her notes as if to double-check, though I already knew her memory was better than that. "*Prowling succubus?*"

"Oh, that? It was about Mystery Girl X. You know, the white-haired girl Josh was talking about before?"

"I see." She poked the screen a few times in response. "And you have already talked to her?"

"Yeah, before your birthday party."

For some reason, the corners of Judy's mouth seemed to tense up, a small gesture that I would've probably never noticed on someone else's face. I was really getting attuned to her, I concluded, and I might have even considered that a good thing if her next words weren't: "So you have already flirted with her."

"No!" I protested aloud, getting tired of her accusations. "I was most definitely not flirting with her. In fact, if anything, *she* was flirting with *me*!"

"Was she?"

"Yeah!"

"Did it work?"

I gave my assistant a look so flat it was nearly two-dimensional. "No, of course not! She was terrible at it."

"I see. So your extensive experience with flirting reached the point where you can criticize others for their lack of technique."

"No," I stressed the word so hard it nearly devolved into a grunt. "What I meant is that she was really, really clumsy about it. And no, I didn't give her any leads, I only asked her not to cause trouble during your party."

"Oh."

For the next couple of seconds, Judy refused to meet my eyes and instead buried herself into her little screen.

Maybe she's feeling guilty for teasing me? I wondered.

Of course, she soon destroyed the moment by throwing another inappropriate question my way.

"So, are you really not interested in Eleanor?"

I gave her a pointed look and sighed.

"No, I'm not. She is pretty and kinda amusing, but I have only known her for a few days... Though technically the same could be said about everyone else I know, I suppose."

"What about the other girls?"

This time I gave her a downright severe look.

"Are we really doing this?"

"Research." My assistant flashed her phone at me.

The sigh could not be stopped.

"No, I am not particularly interested in anyone."

That comment made her face twitch for a moment, which I had no idea how to interpret. I didn't have the time to ponder its meaning either, as she threw another question at me.

"Could you describe how you feel about them?"

"Didn't I already give you my analysis on them?"

"Yes, but I want to know about your personal opinion." The look she gave me at this point was especially serious, and she stressed, "We are supposed to collect observations separately, and I need a baseline to put mine against."

I clicked my tongue, half irritated and half impressed. So many things happened in rapid succession recently that I almost forgot about the reason why I had Judy along for the ride.

"Yeah, I get it."

She nodded and tapped on her phone, "Angeline?"

"Well... She is pretty cute and a bit of a troublemaker, but it is fun to be around her, so I suppose she's okay."

"I see. Amelia?"

"Who?"

"Ammy."

"Oh, the class rep? She is pretty enough, and I like her hairdo. She is nice and helpful, but she could use some help with her insecurities, and I still cannot figure out how she keeps finding my blind spots to startle me."

"Uh-hm. What about the new girl?"

"Mystery Girl X? She is pretty, I suppose, but I don't really know much about her. For some reason, she was also trying to repeatedly hit on me to change the subject when we talked. I am really curious as to why."

I finished speaking, but Judy didn't say a word. I turned to her and found her looking at me with a small frown, which when extrapolated through her deadpan was effectively a full-fledged glare... but then again, she also had her mouth set in a strange way, so maybe she was... pouting?

"Is there a problem?"

"According to you, you do not flirt."

"Yeah?" I answered hesitantly, not really getting where this came from.

"Then how come the first thing you note about every girl is that they are 'pretty'?"

"Because they are?" I answered with no small amount of bafflement. Judging by my assistant's unchanging expression my explanation was unsatisfactory, so I quickly elaborated. "Listen, *every* girl is pretty in this world. That's just how this place works."

"Does that include me?"

"Of course. Why wouldn't it include you?"

"I see..." She looked away from me to type.

"Speaking of the opposite sex," I grabbed the conversation by the horns before she could change gears again. "What about you and Josh?" To my sincerest surprise, Judy stumbled and nearly fell over before she caught herself. "Whoa! Careful!" I withdrew my extended hand once I was sure she was steady on her feet and shook my head. "Listen, just because you are writing into your phone instead of your notebook, it doesn't mean the *'don't take notes while walking on the street'* rule is suddenly void and null."

She nodded, though it took some more prodding to get her to put away said phone into the same breast pocket where her notebook resided just this morning.

"Good. So?" She looked at me uncertainly, so I repeated the question. "I asked, do you find yourself attracted to Josh?"

"No," she answered with a startling hardness to her voice.

"Really? You seemed pretty receptive when he gave you that phone strap." I pointed at the coloured strip poking out of her pocket, which she unceremoniously tucked away in an instant. "Did you get hit by his harem-protagonist magic?"

"Most definitely not," she answered, and this time I was almost 100 percent sure that her frown was hiding a pout. I made a mental note of that, then I chuckled and waved my hand dismissively.

"Sorry, sorry. I just felt like teasing you. It's not fair that I get all the embarrassing questions." I paused thoughtfully before continuing with, "Though to be fair, I didn't ask you *only* for that reason. I'm actually curious if you started to like Joshua. Maybe he really does have something of a '*harem protagonist aura*' that affects girls."

Judy shook her head a wee bit more vehemently than usual, but I decided not to comment on it.

"Are you sure?"

"Yes. He is handsome, but so are most of the guys in our school, and he is not my type."

"So it's about personal preference. But wait, you say *most* guys are handsome?"

"There are exceptions."

"Really?"

Judy pondered for a second before she answered. "One boy in Three-C. He is obese and wears thick glasses."

"Oh, him? He doesn't count."

"No true Scotsman?"

I wanted to ask "*Where did you even learn that?*" but I refrained from derailing the conversation.

"No, he is just an otaku-archetype."

"Otaku?"

My skeptical brow climbed my forehead without my consent, but she didn't seem to be able to read it, so I told her, "So you know what *No true Scotsman* means, but not *otaku*? I should really give you that list of required reading materials I was talking about this morning. Anyways, an otaku is someone obsessed with a hobby, usually anime, and they are…"

And with that, we successfully sailed past the stormy (and awkward) waters of the *How do you feel about Person X?* line of questions, and instead we fell into the comfortable pace of one of our research discussions, which in this case mostly meant that I was explaining pop-culture- and storytelling-related tropes as she asked about them in quick succession. It was a strangely relaxing experience, and before either of us knew it, we were already at the intersection where we'd met in the morning. Without further prompting, I led her down the road on the left, towards her house. We were almost there when suddenly she asked something peculiar.

"Are you really going to deal with the new girl?"

"Hm?" I probably made an embarrassingly slack face when I got hit by the non sequitur (we were talking about what a *donkan* male lead is just a few seconds before, you see), but I managed to gather my wits. "Oh, you mean Mystery Girl X?"

"You promised it to Eleanor."

"That I did," I answered just a touch coyly as we came to a stop in front of her house. Judy looked curious, no doubt intrigued by the smile on my face as I reached into my coat's inner pocket and took out a phone. It was a different model than mine, and more importantly, it had a big red heart engraved on its back, tribal-tattoo style. "She dropped this when the princess tackled her."

Judy looked at the phone from several angles like it was some sort of artifact she had to study, then looked up at me again.

"What do you plan to do with it?"

"I... honestly don't know yet, but it should be a good enough excuse to ask her out for a talk."

"You only met her once and you already want to ask her out on a date? How bold."

"Why you little—!" I scowled theatrically at the retreating girl. "I thought we were over this!"

"Goodb—"

"Welcome home!"

We both froze in our tracks as Judy's getaway-jab was foiled by a painfully energetic voice following the creaking of the front door. In said doorway stood a tall young woman wearing casual clothes and bunny slippers, though I couldn't see most of the former because of the frilly yellow apron she wore. Without missing a beat, she opened her arms wide and glomped my unprepared assistant in a giant bear hug, her long, curly ponytail whipping around her head in the process like a brown avalanche.

"Mom!" Judy protested, which sounded especially funny in her stoic voice. "Stop embarrassing me!"

"Don't be silly, darling!" Judy's mother smiled as she noticed me. "A friend of yours?"

"Yes. He just took me home."

"Oh, what a gentleman!" I could only blink awkwardly at the woman's perma-smile, which was in polar opposite to her daughter's permanent deadpan. She was one of *those* moms, the kind you would mistake for an older sister. "Please do come in. We are just about to have dinner!"

"Mom, don't be overbearing."

"I must respectfully decline," I wedged myself into the conversation. "I have some important things to do, but I thank you for the invitation."

"Oh, what a nice boy. Maybe some other day, then." I gave her a tentative nod and said my goodbyes. I couldn't even tell if Judy returned the courtesy, as she was completely overshadowed by the woman waving after me... with a ladle in hand.

"Well, that just happened," I muttered to myself while barely managing to suppress a smile.

PART 3

After parting with Judy, I headed right home. First, I ascertained that the ninja maids had once again cleaned up the place and stocked the fridge in my absence. Once I checked everything and made notes of the number of different food items in the fridge and in the cupboards for the sake of future experiments with this restocking phenomenon, I returned to my room for a fresh change of clothes. After a quick shower and a bit of evening snack, I decided I was mentally ready for making the call.

As such, I fished out Mystery Girl X's phone from my bag and sat down on the comfy sofa in the living room. I undid the simple key-lock on the phone (which, since this was a smartphone, was more of a screen-lock, but let's not get bogged down by semantics) and quickly browsed through the contact list. There were only a handful of numbers stored, and only one caught my interest—but that one did so big time. It read *My Esteemed Elder Brother*. Well, that either had to be so tongue-in-cheek that it broke through the skin, or someone was trying to translate an idiom. Either way, after some hesitation I pressed the dial button.

The phone on the other side only rang twice before a snappy male voice picked it up.

"What is it?"

Hearing the flippant tone made my brows furrow in irritation. Just why was I getting so easily irritated today? Or better yet, where did all of these infuriating people come from? Anyways, I cleared my throat and answered, "Well, hello there," with mock joviality.

There was a brief but heavy silence on the line.

"Who is this?" the man said, his voice lowered into a threatening glower.

"Exactly what I wanted to ask, though I suppose it doesn't really matter," I answered in a calm and in no way condescending or purposefully annoying voice. "You see, I had a run-in with your sister today and she lost her phone in the process. She should know who I am. Please tell her to come and talk to me next time she's skulking around."

I could hear some commotion in the background and a moment later the voice in the phone gained a quality that I could only describe as *velvety*, but I couldn't help but feel it was just masking a pool of industrial-strength smugness underneath.

"Speak of the devil. It seems my dear sister has just come home. Do you wish to talk to her?"

"Might as well," I told him with a shrug, though of course he couldn't see that. After a few seconds, a familiar voice wormed its way into my ear.

"Hello, sugar."

It was indeed Mystery Girl X, her voice as husky and suggestive as ever. I took a huge breath and sighed loudly enough so that she could hear it too on the other end of the line.

"I told you to drop the vamp act, didn't I?"

"I'm not...! I mean..." She pointedly cleared her throat and returned to her seductive purr. "I knew you would miss me, but to take my phone just so I would meet you again? What a naughty boy."

"Excuse me? You dropped your phone during the tackle."

"No need to be so defensive, sugar. I understand you perfectly. If you cannot wait, I guess I have no choice but to oblige."

"No, actually I—" I paused and a sudden thought came to me. "Wait, are you perchance putting up a show in front of your brother?"

"In the park, you say? Under the night skies? How naughty!"

I sighed again.

"Okay, just for the record, could you say a total non sequitur just so that I can be sure?"

"Butter? Kinky."

I rubbed my forehead to stifle a chuckle.

"So you *are* putting up a show. Got it. You said something about the park. Does this mean you want to meet me tonight?"

"Calm down, stallion. I need at least an hour to get ready. In the meantime, think about me. It'll make it all the better."

"So, at the park, in an hour? Where exactly in the park?" She didn't answer, so I ventured a suggestion. "How about the large information board by the gates with the rose bushes?"

"Oh, you know I love it when you talk dirty, but everything has its time and place. Very well, though. I think we might try what you suggest anyway. See you soon."

She put the phone down and I finally let the tension escape my shoulders. I was glad she agreed to meet me at the board, as that was the only part of the community park I knew. Speaking of which, since I had an hour to waste and got reminded of geography, I decided I might as well check a map before I forgot about it again.

With that rationale in mind, I briskly walked up the stairs and plopped down in front of my computer. I fired up my browser, clicked in the search bar, and froze.

"I don't even know the name of this place!" I muttered angrily, but then I had a different idea. "What if I search for the school? There cannot be many 'Blue Cherry Highs' out there..."

I did just that, and to my eminent satisfaction, I could find my school on the first page of the search results. After that, it only took a little digging to get an address, and once I put that into the online map...

"The hell...? I'm living on an island?"

According to the map, that was the case indeed. It appeared that Blue Cherry High, and consequently I, was situated on the island of Critias in the middle of the Atlantic Ocean. A small-ish island by any measure, with only a capital city, a couple of small towns around the coast, and a smattering of villages farther inland. By the way, this town's name was apparently *Timaeus*.

"Timaeus and Critias? That sounds familiar..."

I typed those keywords into my search bar, and it turned out my initial hunch was right.

"Two books in Plato's dialogs that talk about the mythical Atlantis... and this is an island in the middle of the Atlantic. Someone thought they were clever. Or at least I hope it's not a prediction."

It was around this time that I noticed that nearly half an hour had passed. I'd spent more time searching than I'd thought. I clicked my tongue and closed my browser. I needed at least twenty minutes to get to the park on foot, so if I wanted to arrive on time, I had to leave soon. I threw on a thicker coat (it was well past seven now and the evening breeze was a little chilly), slid the lost phone into my pocket, and left the house at an unhurried pace.

Since I had nothing better to do on the way, I let my thoughts wander, but they inevitably kept coming back to the same topic: just what exactly was the deal with Judy and the princess? I mean, my current theory was that this world operated on the logic of some kind of romance narrative, so I was already on the lookout for such developments, but I would've had to be blind not to notice the princess's tsundere tendencies getting aimed at me, or Judy's small signs of jealousy and clumsy hints of interest. It was a little troubling, honestly.

On one hand, Judy is, or rather was, a generic placeholder who rapidly developed into something else. I still had no idea about how that happened or worked, and to be frank, the way she went from a background extra to a full-fledged person raised a couple of alarms about the nature of free will in this world. More importantly, she was obviously attached to me, but it was possible she simply imprinted on me as the person who jolted her out of her placeholder routine, and she would lose interest as her personality and relationships got more defined over time. Returning her interest at this point would have been taking advantage of her state of mind, but I certainly didn't dislike her, even if she was a handful at times, so who knew where we could end up down the line?

As for the latter, Elly was supposed to be part of Josh's entourage. Not even that, but by the tropey logic of the genre, she was supposed to be the default winner on the relationship tug-of-war as the new girl shaking up the status quo. My embarrassing misunderstanding apparently derailed her a little, so I had to do my best to correct my mistake, and not showing any interest was the first step in that direction. Trying to play chaperone was the second, though I had to be careful not to overdo it and step on the toes of the other girls.

In short, I figured it was best to take things slow with those two and keep a professional distance. While their attention was flattering, I really didn't have the time to get bogged down in romantic shenanigans when there was still so much to discover about literally everything. Not to mention, there was the teensy-weensy chance that I was horribly misreading their intentions due to my preconceived notions about the world we lived in, and this whole dilemma was moot from the beginning.

Anyhow, while I was pondering about these things, somehow I managed to get to the park a good ten minutes before the time we agreed upon, so I circled the place a few times to familiarize myself with the area. The play of starlight amongst the reddening leaves of the large oaks overhead looked surprisingly pretty, and I spent a few minutes just staring at them by a public fountain. At last, roughly five minutes before the one-hour mark, I headed for the actual meeting point, only to find Mystery Girl X coming from the opposite direction.

By chance, the two of us reached the huge information board at the same time and I nearly grimaced when I took a closer look at her. She was wearing a low-cut, sleeveless red blouse, a dark miniskirt, fishnet stockings, and a pair of high heels. On an even closer look, I could also see a good amount of makeup on her face, as well as a random assortment of necklaces, bangles, and other jewelry. The only two constant things about her apparel were her hair beads and the silver choker around her neck.

"Ooh, punctual. I like that in a man," she spoke in a low voice as she tried her best to walk towards me in a sexy strut, but she either wasn't used to high heels or hadn't mastered the technique yet, as she looked more clumsy than alluring. All in all, I couldn't rein in my frustration any longer and buried my head in my hand, taking her aback to the point where she froze on her tracks.

"Seriously now," I griped between my fingers. "Just how many times do I have to tell you to drop the act?"

"I'm—" she started to speak, but I interrupted her with a scoff.

"And if we are at that, are you serious about those clothes?" She only looked at me sheepishly, so I shook my head in frustration. "It's not summer anymore. At this rate, you're going to catch a cold!" I fumed angrily for a second or two longer before I decided what to do. "Okay, you stay here. Or better yet, there is a row of benches over there. It's under a wall, so it should be protected from the wind. I will be with you shortly."

I didn't wait for her to answer, but instead I took off while blessing my foresight of scouting out the place just a few minutes prior. When I returned a short while later, I found her sitting on one of the benches I indicated, with her legs gathered under herself in a pose that would have looked demure on any other girl, but with her outfit it seemed mismatched as all hell. She looked up at me uncertainly as I got near and I handed her one of the paper cups I held.

"I didn't know how you liked yours, but I figured you were a latte person."

She reached out timidly and took the cup from me, then let out a small hiss as she slackened her fingers around it.

"It's hot!"

"Of course it is. That's why I bought it. Drink it slowly, don't burn your tongue."

She gave me a sheepish nod and took a small sip. In the meantime, I sat beside her and she shuddered, giving me a suspicious sideways glance.

"How is it?"

"It's... tasty." She hesitated, then took a deep breath and added a barely audible, "Thank you."

"You're welcome," I told her with a smile and took a sip from my cup. I wasn't really a coffee person, so mine had even more milk and sugar than hers, yet I still jolted from the slightly bitter aftertaste. "Needs more sugar."

The underdressed girl at my side was still looking at me with an expression that was dancing on the borderline between being apprehensive and curious. She didn't seem like she was about to speak up, so I decided to break the ice.

"Is there something on my face?" I asked her, and she shook her head so hard she almost let some of her drink spill.

"Awawa! Sorry, I didn't mean to stare!"

"Uh... No problem, I suppose."

"It's just that... I... I don't know..."

"What?"

"Um, why are you nice to me?"

The question took me by surprise so much that I even forgot to shudder on my next sip of coffee.

"What do you mean? Do I have a reason not to be?"

"I... wouldn't know?" She gave me a timid look before asking, "Could it be that you... fell madly in love with me on our first meeting?"

I blinked at her and then let out a sigh a Hindu universe-exhaling deity could envy.

"Here we go again. What is wrong with everyone today?"

"I'm sorry..." the girl apologized, and I could only shake my head.

"No need, it's not your fault. It's just that... well, today's been hectic, and I'm a little tired of these kinds of questions." I took a deep breath to clear my head and flashed a smile at her. "Anyways, I don't think we have been properly introduced yet."

"N-no..."

"I am Leonard Dunning, nice to meet you."

She gave me a tentative nod and answered in a mousy voice.

"I'm Neige Liliam Inanna. The... pleasure is mine."

"Neige? Is that French?"

She nodded.

"It means *snow*."

"Really?" I was genuinely interested now. "Because of your hair?"

She nodded.

"I see... Wait, how did they know you would have white hair? Aren't all babies platinum blond anyway?"

Neige only looked at me like she didn't understand what I was getting at, so I waved my hand.

"Doesn't matter, I was just thinking aloud."

For the next few seconds, we quietly sipped our drinks in a surprisingly comfortable silence.

"So... what happens now?" she finally asked me as she reached the bottom of her cup.

"First, this." With a small flourish, I reached into my pocket and handed her the lost-and-found phone. At first she looked at it like she was afraid to touch it, then she tentatively reached for it.

"Thank you."

"You're welcome, again," I smiled at her reassuringly. The more I talked to her, the more it felt like I was trying to befriend a scared bunny. "As for the other thing we needed to talk about..."

"Yes...?" Her posture tensed and she looked at me like she was about to bolt.

"Well, I wanted to ask you to please stop stalking Joshua."

Her shoulders drooped like she'd heard some bad news she really didn't want to face.

"I... cannot do that."

"Why?"

"Because I need to get close to him to—" She cut herself off and shook her head. "No, I cannot talk about it."

"Okay then. But why do you stalk him?" The look on her face told me that she thought I was senile, and she'd already answered my question.

"I told you, I need to—"

"No, I mean why are you *stalking* him? Why don't you just talk to him normally?"

"I can't because... I..." She vacillated for a few seconds before she gave me an almost pleading look. "You think I could?"

"Of course you could! Though first, you would have to explain yourself to him properly. You didn't really start off with the right foot, kissing him out of the blue and then trying to kidnap him and all that."

Neige flushed lightly, a sight that was surprising in its small scale. Considering her complexion, her blushing should've been much more noticeable than the ones I'd seen on the other girls in my social circle.

"But... but... he has guards! They wouldn't let me close to him like that!"

"Guards? You mean the other girls?" She nodded repeatedly in response. "Well, I suppose they would be apprehensive, but then you just have to do it in a way they couldn't object to." She looked at me intently, apparently waiting for me to go into the details. "Well, for example, there is the option to write him a letter. You could even ask him to talk to you at a secluded place where the other girls wouldn't bother you. I can cover for you two, in that case. Or, if you are really dedicated, you could always transfer to our school, even if only for a little while. Just enough for you two to get acquainted so that you can be friends afterward." It was about this time I noticed Neige was looking at me with wide, unblinking eyes. "Is there a problem?"

"Why are you helping me?"

I scratched my chin. The truth of the matter was that she just looked so vulnerable that I couldn't help myself, but I naturally had other reasons. Deep and important reasons that were in no way just hasty rationalizations. No, sir.

"You see... Let's just say I am seeing the big picture, and I want to make these kinds of transitions as painless and hassle-free as possible."

"I... see." She wanted to say something else, but her nose scrunched up, and before I could even blink, she let out a cute little sneeze, something I would have expected from a kitten that drank too heartily from the milk pan. I involuntarily smiled at her and stood up.

"I guess that's as good a sign that we should call it a day. We wouldn't want you to catch a cold."

"I'm fine," she protested with a weak, nasal voice. I handed her a tissue. I always had spare paper tissues on me; they are incredibly useful and versatile. The common man's towels. She blew her nose and quietly thanked me again.

"Do you live far from here? Should I call you a taxi?"

"You don't need to..."

By the time she said that, I was already in the middle of waving to an empty cab conveniently rolling down the street. The car stopped with a screech of burning rubber and backed up to the walkway. I strode up to the vehicle and Neige followed after me as if by reflex. I opened the back door of the cab and ushered her in. It was a fairly new car with clean seats and a thick plastic shield with a series of small holes separating the front seats from the back and a revolving container set in the middle. Probably for safety reasons, I surmised. Once she got seated, I moved to the front to talk to the cabbie. He was a middle-aged guy with a well-trimmed beard and a thick accent that I couldn't identify.

"Where to?"

"Ask the lady."

He turned back and looked over Neige. There were a number of different emotions running through his expression, from surprise to suspicion, with a bit of sleaze in between. In the meantime, she gave him the address, but she spoke so quietly that I could only understand the "eighty-seven" at the end. The cabbie seemed to understand well enough, though, so I gestured to him.

"How much will that be?"

The man looked me over, no doubt paying extra attention to my attire and gauging just how much money I could have.

"Well, at this time of day, I reckon about thirty Jen should be enough."

"Fair enough."

With that, I reached into my wallet and handed him thirty Jen in notes, plus about twenty more in change. The man smiled and leaned closer conspiratorially while he counted the money.

"You had a good time with your lady-friend?"

I managed to keep my face stoic and answered, "She is my sister."

"Oh." The man's fingers froze mid-motion.

"She is going through a rebellious phase, if you know what I mean."

"I can see that..."

"I didn't want her to walk home like this. Who knows what kinds of people roam the streets at this hour? Could you make sure she gets to her place in one piece?"

Just finishing the counting and appearing very satisfied, the cabbie grinned at me widely, revealing a missing eyetooth in the process.

"Most certainly, sir. Thank you for your patronage."

"Godspeed."

I looked over at Neige, who appeared to be eyeing us suspiciously, though I was sure she couldn't actually hear our whispers from the back seat. I moved to her side and knocked on the glass. After some stumbling and ineffectual tugging, she managed to get the manual window crank turning and she looked at me anxiously through the gap.

"Yes?"

"I just wanted to ask you again to think about what I told you. Also, trust me when I say this—the vamp act won't work on Joshua. Don't even try it." To be completely honest, I wasn't completely sure my friend would see through it, but that was one of the complications I wanted to nip in the bud.

"I'm not a vamp!" she riposted, raising her voice for the first time.

"If you say so," I smirked at her and began to wave as the cabbie turned the ignition. "Goodbye, Snowy."

She blinked at me, probably not understanding what I said, but after a bit of a slip she waved back, though by then the car was already moving and she was too far away to say her own goodbyes. I watched the taxi get out of sight around a corner and at last I let my posture slacken. I looked up at the dark sky. By now the night had completely enveloped the town. I put my hands into my pockets and headed home with light steps.

A lot of things happened today, I thought to myself as I walked.

Judy collapsing, buying a phone, throwing a birthday party, making a possible new friend (and a possible new enemy)... I could only hope tomorrow would be slightly less hectic. I could really use a breather episode.

CHAPTER 10

PART 1

It was maybe five or ten minutes after midnight. I was sitting in front of my computer in my room when I first noticed the sound. It was faint and dull, but after a few seconds of listening, I could make out a definite tune. At first I wondered just what it could be at this time of the day, but then the proverbial incandescent bulb lit up over my head and a second later I was already flying down the stairs towards the living room. There, after some fumbling, I managed to get my new phone out of my coat carelessly discarded on the back of a chair and I accepted the call without even looking at the caller ID.

"Yes, it's Leonard... er..." I paused for a moment, but then the momentary brain freeze was over and I exclaimed, "Dunning! I mean, Leonard Dunning speaking."

For a few seconds, there was only faint static in the ether. I wondered if maybe someone called the wrong number, but then at last a familiar voice said, "Good evening, Chief."

I involuntarily frowned.

"Hi, Judy. I think we are a little beyond evening, if you ask me."

"Did I wake you?"

"Nah, I was researching stuff on the net."

"Sorry, I... I should have thought about the time."

That answer threw me for a loop for a moment or two. It wasn't just the apology (though admittedly my assistant didn't strike me as someone who apologized at the drop of a hat), but the tone itself. At first I thought it was just a compression artifact of the connection, but by this point I was sure I'd heard it right: Judy's voice sounded frail, almost mousy. It made me worry.

"Is everything all right?"

"Yes."

I waited for her to elaborate, which didn't happen, so I sighed and ventured a guess.

"You couldn't sleep again?"

There was a faint rustle on the other side, and I frowned.

"Please don't tell me you just nodded."

"Oh..." She sounded genuinely surprised—whether at herself or me, I couldn't tell. "Force of habit."

"It's not a big deal, but be aware that it will be kind of hard to uphold a conversation if you don't talk."

"Sorry."

"You know, you are apologizing an awful lot. Are you sure everything is all right?"

There was a long, tense pause, during which I most certainly didn't nervously walk up and down in the room like an expectant father in a maternity ward. Eventually Judy spoke again, her voice somehow managing to sound even less secure. Speaking of which, it was weird to hear emotions in her voice like that. Maybe she let her guard down while on the phone? Or maybe it was just that I always focused too much on her severe deficit of facial expressions and never noticed the small nuances in her admittedly enchanting voice?

At any rate, she finally answered, "I was just... thinking."

"Oh, that happens even to the best of us. It's nothing to be ashamed of."

There was a stretch of silence between us, and for some reason I felt mother-in-law levels of disapproval emanating from the phone in my hand.

"Sorry, that was... inappropriate?" I grasped for a response. "So, what were you thinking about?"

"Many things... About the world. About me. About everything."

"Oh!" I exclaimed as I plopped onto my comfy sofa with a somewhat awkward smile. "I get it! You are having an existential crisis."

"I... I'm sorry. I shouldn't bother you with—"

"Oh, no, no!" I interrupted her before she could gather steam. "It's all right. Having an existential crisis is a perfectly legitimate reason to call me."

"It is?"

"Yep. It's nothing to be ashamed of. I think anyone would have one in your shoes."

In truth, the only strange thing about it was how early it'd happened. Considering that she was a placeholder, I expected the dread to set in much later.

After a second or two, Judy tentatively asked, "Even you?"

"*Especially* me," I answered with confidence, though I realized how inappropriate that was by the time I said it. Oh well.

"You seem to deal awfully well with it."

"Oh, that's just the surface. I am screaming incoherently on the inside even as we speak." There was another stretch of very loud silence, and before I knew it, I found myself apologizing. "Sorry, I guess it's not the time to joke about this." I waited until I heard a noise from her, which I chose to interpret as a sign of forgiveness, so I proceeded to do the sensible thing and shamelessly changed the topic. "So, I guess that's the reason why you couldn't sleep yesterday."

"Yes."

"Why didn't you tell me?"

"I thought you would ridicule me."

"Wait, do you really think I'm the kind of guy who would do that?" My mouth moved before my brain did, so I hastily added, "Wait, no, don't answer that question. I think we'd both be better off if you didn't."

"Agreed."

After another lengthy period of nail-chewing silence, I finally sighed.

"So, why exactly did you call me? How can I help?"

"I… don't know," she replied in a wispy voice, and I was once again astounded by how different she sounded from her usual level deadpan. "I think I just wanted to hear your voice."

"Is that so?" I hesitated. Then I told her, "I guess I should apologize too."

"You? Why?"

"Well…" I awkwardly scratched the back of my head, though she obviously couldn't see that. "If you look at the root of the issue, we would not be having this conversation if I hadn't gotten you involved, so—"

"Stop." The word cutting me off was icy cold. "If you try to tell me you regret involving me, I will be really, really angry at you."

I smiled awkwardly to myself. I was a little curious what an angry Judy would look like, though I concluded that I really didn't want her to be angry at me in particular.

"No, that's not what I wanted to say. I should have just… done it better. Ease you into things. In fact, that's what I originally wanted to do, but I guess I got impatient. Sorry." She didn't say anything to me, so I cleared my throat aloud and tried to smile. I cannot attest, but apparently doing so makes one sound friendlier too. Anyways, I said, "So, do you want to share your worries? Get them off your chest?"

This time there was only the briefest of pauses.

"I shouldn't. It's silly."

"I don't think it is. Trust me, you'll feel better afterward."

Judy fell silent, probably collecting her thoughts, then spoke up with a slightly firmer voice.

"It is because of our research… I am usually too busy to think about them throughout the day, but when I go to bed, they just overwhelm me. Questions. Is this world really just an imitation? Am I even real, or just a figment of someone's imagination? What about my memories? Are they really mine, or only preprogrammed images someone else put into my head?

What if all I am, or what I think I am, is a lie? What guarantees that if I go to sleep tonight, I won't be reprogrammed into a different person by the time I wake up? Or if the entire world just *ends*... would I even be aware of the moment it happens? And... and..." She let out a pitiful sound that made me wince in sympathy. "I am rambling. Can you even understand what I want to say?"

"Of course I do," I answered confidently. "I have these kinds of thoughts all the time."

"You do?" She sounded genuinely surprised.

"Of course I do. I told you, it's only natural."

"How do you deal with it?" she asked so eagerly I tried to imagine what kind of expression would suit such a tone, and I just couldn't overlay it on her face. The image still made me smile, though, and I leaned forward in my seat.

"We're both dealing with it already." I could sense that she didn't get my meaning, so I hurriedly continued. "Isn't that what our research is all about?"

"Really?"

"Of course! We are collecting data and constructing hypotheses because we are uncertain. Being uncertain is troubling, and being uncertain about heavy topics like your own existence is just plain scary. We are combating this dread by taking the thing that makes us uncertain, observing it, picking it apart, poking its innards, putting it back together, and ultimately attempting to figure out how it works. Then it'll no longer be uncertain, and thus we'll have nothing to fear."

"But what if it *is* something we should fear? Like us not being..." She seemed to struggle for the right word before uttering, "... real."

"It is a possibility, but once we know that, we can move on. It's better to know things like that than not to."

"And in the meantime? What do we do until we get our answers?"

"Live in the present," I answered without a moment of hesitation.

"What is that supposed to mean?"

"Exactly what it sounds like. So what if the world can end at any moment? So what if you cannot ascertain the continuity of your consciousness? It's not like we can do anything about it right now, and obsessing over it will just turn us into nervous wrecks. Personally, I'm not a fan of that. There are so many interesting and fun things out there, new experiences and people to meet, that I find worrying about these things a waste of time and effort better spent elsewhere."

"So, you say we should ignore our existential concerns and engage in escapism?"

I was once again wondering where she got her vocabulary, but asking her at the moment seemed a tad inconsiderate.

"No, I advocate enjoying yourself moment by moment. That's what I'm doing whenever I am not doing my research, and usually even when I do. I hang out with Joshua and company, piss off annoying butlers, and make friends with girls who call me in the middle of the night to spill their hearts to me. Stuff like that."

"This is fun to you?"

"Yeah, I like talking to you."

There was another long pause ending in a quiet *"I see..."* Just then, I had a thought.

"Hey, should we go and see the ocean this weekend?"

There was a silence that decidedly felt more baffled than anything else on the other end of the line.

"Did you just invite me on a date?"

I pointedly fell silent, though I suppose it had little effect since we have been doing that a lot during our conversation anyway. "Just for the record, I am currently rolling my eyes. I just thought you should know."

"So it's not a date?"

"No, it's a research excursion!" I told her with a tired sigh. "I just discovered today that we live on an island and I want to see the shore. Maybe check out a local port and the ships. See if we can find the boundaries of the world. Take your mind off the vast emptiness of existence by doing something fun and productive. Stuff like that."

My assistant gave me a small "Hmph," and at last answered, "Two deluxe cheese sandwiches."

I sighed. "Do I have to pay you separately for everything? Also, that sounds like compensated dating. Makes me feel dirty."

"You said it's not a date, so it's fine. Call it compensated research tripping."

"Might as well... So, should we call it a day for today? We should discuss the details tomorrow and—"

"No!" Judy exclaimed and it almost made me jump out of my seat. "I mean..." She mumbled something I couldn't understand.

"Could you repeat that?"

"I said... please talk to me some more. Until I'm ready to fall asleep."

She sounded surprisingly earnest, like a little kid asking for a bedtime story, but I really didn't want to ruin the moment by poking fun at her.

"Fine, fine. What should I talk about?"

"I don't know..." She hesitated. "What were you researching when I called you?"

"Oh, it was time travel. Time travel in fiction, I mean."

"Ah, that sounds perfect to help me fall asleep."

I involuntarily set my jaw.

"Let me warn you, it will be on the test."

"What test?"

"The one at the end of the semester."

"I'm pretty, so I don't need to worry about my grades."

"Young lady! Your lack of study ethics is appalling! Kids these days just can't appreciate proper education! You have no idea how easy you have it nowadays! Back in my time, we had to mine our own textbooks from the deep, dark crevices of Mount Librarium! You youngsters have everything at your fingertips with your interwebz and social media and... and..."

"And lolcats?"

"*Especially* lolcats! I truly fear for the future of our country and/or species!"

"Oh, the humanity?"

"Oh, the humanity indeed!"

We both paused for a few seconds, and at least on my end I had a hard time stifling my snickers. At the same time, I also felt really, really relieved that Judy seemed to be back to normal... well, as normal as she can be considered, but I might not have been the best yardstick in that regard.

"So, back to the topic: time travel in fiction."

"Do you think it happened in this world?" Judy interjected before I could even gather momentum.

"Hm? Oh, no. Or rather, I have no idea, but probably not. Otherwise, we'd be up to our necks in paradoxes."

"Then why did you look into it?"

"Oh, that's a bit of a tangent. You see, I was originally researching school life comedy stories for common tropes and formulas when I came across this particular galge—"

"Galge?"

"Oh, right, you probably don't know this. Galge are romance-focused games about a single male protagonist wooing one or more love interests, except they are more like virtual books with images, and then there are the ones that are all about raising statistics and stuff, and... that's another tangent. The point is, I was looking into this particular eroge—"

"Eroge?"

"It's a game with... well..." I awkwardly scratched my chin and averted my eyes, but then I realized I had nothing to avert them from and instead I just rolled them and muttered, "... sex."

"So it's porn?" Judy answered dryly, apparently completely unfazed by the subject matter.

"Not always. At least depending on whom you ask. One of my sources told me most eroge are story-heavy and only have about as much sexual content as your average paperback romance novel while another insisted they are all horrible child-porn made by Satan or something... I think I will need to do more research."

"For science."

"Indeed."

"And it has nothing to do with you trying to hone your flirting skills through virtual training."

I smiled ruefully and grunted directly into the phone so she could certainly hear it.

"I'm glad to hear you are completely back to normal. Now stop it."

"Aw. I was scolded."

"A-ny-ways, there was this one particular story that had time travel in it, so I clicked on a link pointing to that topic and was reading through that when you called. It's actually pretty fascinating."

And with that, I began my long, detailed, and in no way dry explanation of fictional time travel over the phone. I didn't get too far, though. I was only beginning to explain how the grandfather paradox worked when I noticed my assistant was suspiciously silent.

"Judy? Are you asleep?" I waited for a few seconds for an answer, and after listening very closely, I thought I could make out the sounds of a soft, even breathing over the white noise of the phone line. I smiled. "Good night."

With that, I ended the call and pocketed my phone before I jumped to my feet and headed to my room, already thinking about the research trip we would have on the weekend. I originally wanted to do it on my own, but now that I'd asked her to accompany me, I had to make sure I got her to relax properly.

"Before anything else, I should check the local maps for docks. Oh, and a nice shoreline. Are beaches still open at this time of the year? Transportation, food, tickets... I wonder if there is a good movie in the theaters we could check out? For science..."

Mumbling so, I entered my room and tried my best to ignore how excited I sounded.

PART 2

"I tell you, this episode was the best since the third season finale!" Angie declared angrily while waving a still intact fried chicken drumstick in the air.

"Are you serious?" Joshua retorted just as animatedly. "How can you even compare the two? The action was nowhere near as great!"

"Hey, it had action too, but this finale was great because it focused on drama and romance!"

"Hah! You just say that because your favourite pairing got to be canon!" Josh snorted derisively while crossing his arms in front of his chest.

"Oh, now you did it! You revealed your true colours!" Angie shook her drumstick at Josh while stomping her feet under the table. "You are like this because Trucy ended up with Elliot instead of Ceraph!"

"Well, she should have!" my friend retorted with a sneer. "He had three seasons' worth of buildup and he was totally sidelined in the finale!"

"He has a point," the class rep quietly interjected while cutting her beef croquettes, not even looking up from her plate.

"Not you too, Ammy!" Angie staggered back theatrically, but a moment later she was pointing the drumstick of accusation at her friend. "And what do you mean *'He has a point'*?! Elliot's been the main male lead since season one! He had way more buildup than Ceraph!"

"Well..." the class rep fidgeted for a moment, then she glanced at Josh, who in turn gave her a reassuring smile, so she stated, "True, but he didn't really *do* anything since season one."

"Right!" Josh continued the assault. "Not to mention, turning Ceraph evil again, after it was established that his love for Trucy fixed that, was just dumb."

"Oh, so you say that *your* precious Ceraph alone should have been able to resist the bloodlust of the Red Moon?!"

"No, but it should definitely *not* have turned him into the chief enforcer of *the Dread Wolf Vladimir* at the end."

"Well, okay, that should have been better explained, but it was totally in character."

"No, it wasn't!" Josh objected a bit too loudly.

"Please don't disturb the other students."

After getting scolded by Ammy, the two of them immediately toned it down a notch.

"Oops, sorry. Anyways, it *wasn't* in character. He just had to be written out of the series because of his own spin-off."

"Wasn't that just a miniseries?"

"It gets a full season next year," the class rep supplied. "It's called *Ceraph: The White Wolf Chronicles*, and it is about..."

And so on and so forth. I let out a tired sigh and popped another french fry into my mouth. This lunch break was noisier than usual, probably because the entire gang ate together in the cafeteria, save for the princess who was on sick leave as per my instructions. Anyways, I was just about to cut a ribbon off my fried pork when my assistant poked me in the shoulder.

"Yes?"

She looked much better than yesterday, though I could still see traces of the black circles under her eyes. She had her pink phone in one hand and a half-eaten ham sandwich in the other, her lone pinky finger extended. She apparently used it to type while eating. Anyways, she leaned closer.

"What are they talking about?"

"Some TV series. *Trucy the Werewolf Huntress*, I think. Seems like it's really popular."

"I see."

I was just about to turn back to my food when the table shook violently as Angie planted her hand on it so that she could lean way forward and hold the drumstick up to my face like a microphone.

"And what do *you* think about the ending?!"

"The what now?"

"The last scene where Elliot shared part of his soul with Trucy so that she could reawaken her disabled huntress-powers and take down the Dread Wolf Vladimir, entwining their souls forever and ever! It was awesome, right? And totally romantic, right?"

I awkwardly glanced at the other two participants of the conversation, but they both avoided my eyes, so I couldn't avoid telling her, "Sorry, I didn't watch last night's episode."

Angie gasped and staggered back in her seat like she was struck by a mortal blow.

"How could you, Leo? I thought you were my ally! My stalwart partner! How could you abandon me like this?!"

I rolled my eyes and proceeded to cut another slice of pork.

"Sorry, I had other things to do."

"What other things? Didn't we leave the party early so we could all catch the finale?"

Well, they most certainly did. In fact, I could vaguely remember them mentioning that the three of them would watch the episode together at Angie's place and that's why we went our separate ways, though I didn't pay it much attention at the time. Either way, all I knew about the show were the snippets I'd gathered when the others were talking about it.

"What do you have to say in your defense?" Angie menaced me with the drumstick of divine retribution, and I could only sigh.

"As I said, I had stuff to do."

Still unsatisfied, Angie turned to my assistant.

"What about you?"

"I don't watch the series," Judy stated matter-of-factly without looking up from her notes.

"What is wrong with you people?" Angie exclaimed, and it looked like she would finally raise her drumstick to her mouth, but she didn't take a bite. As for the question, I really wanted to ask the same, but then she suddenly squinted at me through skeptically furrowed brows. "Suspicious!"

"Pardon?"

"I said, this is suspicious! You say you two didn't watch the last episode even though we have eyewitnesses claiming they saw you two leave early so you could watch it!"

"No, that was you guys. Also, *eyewitnesses?*"

"Yes, all three of us!" She indicated Josh and the class rep.

For the record, they were obviously very busy eating so that they would not have to enter the conversation.

"Not only that, but the only other person who would know what the two of you were doing after we parted is Elly... who is conveniently missing! Super-suspicious!"

"Why, exactly?"

"Thank you for asking!" Angie declared in some kind of fake accent while holding her drumstick like she was smoking a pipe... so I guess it was supposed to be British? Anyways, she began talking, but the mention of the princess reminded me of something, and I gestured for Josh to lean closer to me.

"I just remembered something. I forgot to tell you this morning, but I have a job for you."

I could barely make out Josh's answer over Angie's spiel on the left. It was something about alibis and the *"Howdunnit"* or something. Judy seemed to be paying her attention and was taking notes, so I decided not to bother them.

"I said I have a job for you," I repeated myself while leaning even closer.

"I heard you. I asked what it is."

"I told you the princess wasn't coming to school till Monday, right?"

"Yeah, I noticed. She twisted her ankle again, right?"

"Yup. Listen, I need you to bring today's homework over to her."

Josh raised one of his trademark critical eyebrows and grunted softly.

"Okay, what's the catch?"

"What do you mean?" I guess I might have sounded slightly defensive, for Josh gave me a look saying *I knew something was up!* and leaned forward on his chair.

"Why don't *you* bring her the homework?"

I gave my friend a flat look.

"Listen, do you really need me to give you a reason to ask you to go to a friend's house?"

"Well..." Josh averted his eyes. "To be perfectly honest, I really don't like the place. And the butler really unnerves me."

"Oh, don't worry about that!" I jested with a smile. "Yesterday I pissed him off so badly you are going to look like a prim and proper gentleman in comparison. He is going to love you."

"Is the unrequited love of an old butler supposed to be a selling point for this *job*? Because if it is, you are a terrible salesman."

I rolled my eyes, and while doing so I caught a few snippets of the discussion between Angie and Judy.

"... so there cannot be any hidden passages, nor can there be a chinaman."

"What is a chinaman?"

"Oh, it's one of those clichés that are no longer used, like the 'mystical black guy' in old movies. You know? The wise old man who has all the answers, saunters into the crime scene, and tells the solution. They don't really have to be Chinese, but the name stuck."

"Sounds like a cop-out."

"Yeah, and that's why they are not allowed!"

I had no idea why they were talking about the murder mystery genre, and to my reassurance, I found that I didn't have any urge to learn, either. That said, I returned to my own conversation.

"Listen, Josh, just go there and give her the homework. It's really not that hard."

"But do I have to do it alone? Can I take Ammy along?"

I glanced at the class rep, who subtly perked up at the mention of her name, and covertly shook my head. To my surprise, she didn't seem to need much convincing, as she followed suit and shook her head, as well.

"Sorry, I can't." Her voice sounded surprisingly conflicted, but I didn't think much about it. It was probably about her wanting to spend time with Josh but not finding doing so at the princess's mansion appealing or something. Anyways, I turned back to Joshua and grinned at him.

"Well, that's how it is."

Instead of quietly accepting his fate, Josh seemed to be defiant to the end, crossing his arms in front of his puffed-out chest with an exaggerated sneer.

"Make me, punk!" he grunted, and I rolled my eyes, reached out, and grabbed him by the ear. "Ow-ow-ow! Hey! No violence! I was kidding, kidding!"

I made a disappointed sound and let him go. After some further inter-mezzo (during which the two girls at the side were apparently discussing the efficiency of different poisons... weird...), Joshua finally settled down.

"Fine, man, fine. But you have to make it worth my while."

"Seriously? You want to extort me for this?"

"*Extortion* is such a nasty word..." he said, smiling broadly. "I would rather call this... err... Okay, let's call it extortion after all."

"You couldn't come up with a less malicious word, could you?"

"Oh, shut up! Just go and buy me some truffles."

"Truffles," I repeated blankly. "You want me to buy you more over-priced food."

"Overpriced? I'll let you know that truffles are a true delicacy that is—!"

"Fine, stop!" I raised my hands in surrender and thankfully my friend, the moocher extraordinaire, didn't continue one of his culinary info dumps. I sighed. "What kind of meal here has truffles?"

"It's funny you asked, I just happen to have a handy list on me!"

Completely disregarding my glare, Josh handed me a small piece of paper with a bunch of food items and prices listed on it. For a moment, I almost had to have a double-take at some of the higher-end ones.

"Okay, you are getting the cheapest."

"Awwww! At least consider the dessert first!"

"No! You don't need truffles and edible gold foil with your vanilla ice cream!"

Josh was about to protest again when all of a sudden both Judy and Angie faced me and pointed a pair of accusatory fingers at me that even the princess would have envied. For a second, I could only blink at them.

"What?"

"Ms. White, in the kitchen, with a candlestick!" Angie declared with a haughty grin. "What do you say to that?"

I blinked again and cocked my head to the side. "That you should stop playing imaginary *Cluedo* and finish your lunch before the break is over?" I answered tentatively.

Angie clicked her tongue. "Damn, he is onto us."

"I told you he is sharp," Judy told her with some empathetic, though slightly mechanical, pats on the shoulder.

"I am glad you guys have such a high opinion of me, but didn't you go totally off topic?"

They both perked up with a silent "Ah!" and Angie aimed her still-intact drumstick at my face.

"Right! You still haven't told us the salacious details about what you two were doing instead of watching the season finale of *Trucy*!"

"*Salacious* details? Seriously?" Angie kept looking at me with what I presumed was supposed to be an accusatory scowl, but on her face, it looked more like the look a hurt puppy would give to the person who accidentally stepped on its tail. I couldn't bear it for long, so I gave up with a small sigh. "Listen, because I am only saying this once... After we left the bakery yesterday, we took the princess home, then I took my assistant home, and finally I went home and spent the night on the internet doing research for a paper I'm working on. There is no secret."

"Paper?"

"Extracurricular project."

Still suspicious, Angie raised the drumstick to her mouth again and did an exaggerated smoking motion.

"Do you have any eyewitnesses who would corroborate your alibi?"

"No?" I answered, too puzzled to put up an intellectual front. "I live alone."

"You do?" This time the question came from a surprised Joshua. I looked at him and shrugged.

"Yeah, my parents are... overseas?" If I sounded unsure, that was only because I was. I'd spent some time combing through the house, and the only clues I could find about my presumed family were the names on my legal papers, the account number of my beneficiary, and a single unmarked key that apparently belonged to a safe-deposit box. But since it had no emblem or numbers on it, I couldn't even tell which bank held it. In other words, I still wasn't sure my parents even existed in this world, let alone get them to provide witness testimony about where I was instead of watching a TV show.

"Really?!" Josh exclaimed again. "Why didn't you tell me sooner?"

"Um... Why?"

"We could've held Judy's birthday party there! We could have gone all-out!"

"Yeah, no. I'm not a fan of house parties."

"Aw..."

"More importantly!" Angie demanded our attention by tapping on the table. "The jury finds you guilty of gross negligence of season-finale-watching-duties!"

"What jury?" I asked flatly.

"Me," the girl beamed at me, but then she caught herself and returned to her hurt-puppy-frown. "I hereby sentence you to hanging out with all of us at your place on Sunday and marathoning the entirety of *Trucy the Werewolf Huntress!*"

I gave her a wry look and shook my head.

"I already have plans for Sunday."

"Plans? What plans?"

"You mean our trip to the shore?" Judy asked at my side with the worst timing possible.

"Ooooo?" Angie smiled at me impishly. "So that's how it is!"

"No, that's *not* how it is. It's for research." The smile didn't wash off Angie's face, so I decided to change the course of the discussion. "In any case, I am not entirely against the idea of hanging out over the weekend. Why can't we do it tomorrow instead?"

"Tomorrow?" Angie wondered aloud. "Well, I suppose, though we could only start after my weekend practice is over."

I wanted to ask what kind of practice she was talking about, but then I remembered that she was in the tennis club, and I bit back the obvious question.

"It's fine with me. I don't have a club." Josh smiled contently.

"Because you are a lazy bum." Angie poked his cheeks with her drumstick. Josh tried to take a bite out of it, but she retracted it before he could.

"I'm not lazy; I'm just economical." He grinned before he looked over to the class rep. "What about you, Ammy? Are you free tomorrow afternoon?"

"Hm?" The class rep looked distracted for a moment. She blinked at Josh, and it felt like she was rewinding the last few minutes in her head to figure out what he was talking about. At last her eyes sparkled with recognition and she nodded. "Yes, I can make the time."

"Great!" Josh's contagious smile spread over the table, infecting everyone but my assistant, who was busy poking her phone. "I will ask Elly about it too! We should totally have a second birthday party while we're at it!"

"Nope," I responded as I gave him a totally dishonest toothy smile.

It was about this time I began to wonder if maybe this was a bad idea...

PART 3

"I demand a rematch!" Joshua exclaimed at my side as we were collecting the balls and pads left behind by the other students. Our last lesson for the day was PE, and this time we were playing table tennis inside the school's pointlessly huge gymnasium. Needless to say, I paired up with Josh from the very beginning and we conducted a long and arduous campaign of intertabular ballistic warfare against each other. It was fun, though at least one of us had some gripes about the final tally.

"Are you sure?"

"Yes!" he growled at me, swiping another white ball up from the corner. I shrugged.

"Fine by me, but are we going with a clean slate or carry our current score?" I asked innocently as I used one of the paddles in my hand to try to fish out a stray ball trapped under the wall-bars.

"Clean slate. Definitely clean slate."

"Are you sure?" I teased as I finally managed to overcome the resistance of the stubborn white plastic fugitive and placed it into custody inside its cardboard prison cell. Once I was done, I turned to Josh and grinned. "I mean, a rematch is nice and all, but wouldn't your victory be all the sweeter if you could overcome my initial score advantage? What was it again, fifty-seven to two?"

"That's because you were cheating." He gritted his teeth, and I could only shake my head in response.

"Just how can one even cheat in ping-pong?"

"It's because of your—"

"Are you finished?" Josh's presumably well-reasoned and in no way resentful explanation was cut short by the class rep poking her head through the half-open door of the hall. She'd asked us to help her gather the discarded equipment beforehand and we'd agreed, though I really couldn't tell why we were doing it. Maybe cleanup was part of her duties as the class representative? Or maybe that was just the honour-studenty thing to do? Either way, I faced her and gave her a small wave.

"Yeah, we got all of them," I told her as I raised the filled cardboard box in my other hand.

"Good." She passed through the door with lithe steps and no matter how hard I tried, I couldn't help but feel that her PE uniform was at least one size smaller than it should've been. Though, as I reflected on it, I supposed the same could've been said about the other girls as well. I wondered if that was the thing Josh was hinting at the other day.

Anyways, she walked over to us and took the box of balls from me and the paddles from Josh.

"I'll put these away. Thank you for the help. You can go now."

"You are welcome." Josh smiled at her and gestured for me to follow, his previous saltiness over his abysmal score already filed in the annals of ancient history under "u" for "unimportant."

"On second thought, Leo?" the class rep addressed me just as I was about to take the first step. "Before you go, could you help me with one last thing?"

"Sure, what is it?"

She fidgeted for a second, then sheepishly said, "The balls should be placed on the top shelf."

"Aaaaaah…" I couldn't help but chuckle at her request and nodded hard in response. "Of course, lead the way."

"Should I wait for you?" Josh inquired. I thought about it, but shook my head.

"Nah, you should head for the princess's mansion. Tell her I said hi."

"I'm sure she will be riveted." My friend prodded me with an impish smile that would have been more at home on Angie's face. I rolled my eyes and shooed him away with exaggerated motions. He gave me one last wave from the door before he left, after which I turned to the girl waiting at my side.

"Lead the way."

She nodded hard, and I actually had to quickly (and very inconspicuously) avert my eyes from her jiggling assets. Not that I paid much attention to them, of course. They were just hard to ignore. It was the fault of the gym clothes, I tell you.

Anyways, the important part was that I followed her to the storage room at the back. It was pretty much what I expected: a small room with a surprisingly high ceiling and only a small window about four, maybe five meters above the ground. It was probably just for ventilation, as it barely provided any light and was too high up to serve any other purpose. The room itself was filled to the brim with sports equipment and the storage compartments for said sports equipment. Needless to say, everything was in mint condition. I grimaced to myself and took the box from the class rep, which was kind of silly considering she'd just taken them from me a minute before, but I decided not to complain.

"Where to?" I asked, and she pointed at a tall cabinet at the back under the window. I opened it and found several identical boxes on its top shelf. I reached up and slid the box into place, then heard a noise behind me.

Click.

By the time I turned around, the class rep was already walking back from the closed door, a serious expression on her face.

"Leo, we need to talk."

Uh-oh. That was her class representative voice. I silently gulped and straightened my back with an awkward smile.

"Am I in trouble?"

"Maybe," she answered enigmatically. "I just want to ask you a few questions."

"Oooookay…" I leaned my back on the cabinet behind me and crossed my arms. "Shoot."

She seemed confused for a second, but then the seriousness returned to her eyes.

"Why did you lie to us?"

"Pardon?"

"I asked why did you—"

"No no, I heard the question; I just need you to be more specific."

She looked at me dubiously, her face practically screaming *Is he lying so often he needs me to pinpoint which lie I am talking about?*—which wasn't exactly flattering, but at the same time wasn't entirely untrue. It made me sad.

"During lunch, you said you were home browsing the internet yesterday."

I nodded in response.

"That was a lie."

"Errr... No, not really. That's what I was doing."

"Then why were you outside after dark? In the park?"

"Ahhhh!" I smiled at her in sudden realization. "Now I get it!" A moment later my smile faded though, replaced by an inquisitively raised eyebrow and a curious smirk. "Speaking of which, what were *you* doing outside at that hour?"

"I... I was going home from Angie's place. After the show was over." The mask of the class representative fell away in a flustered scamper as she tried to explain herself.

"And Josh didn't even offer to take you home? Damn, I need to have a talk with that guy about being a gentleman."

"That's beside the point!" Her authoritarian manner reasserted itself, and she scowled at me again. "We are talking about why *you* lied to us about it."

"I didn't lie, I just omitted information. It's not the same," I corrected her, but she didn't seem to care about the nuances. I sighed and uncrossed my arms. "You are making this seem a bigger deal than it actually is. I was outside because I met with an..." I paused thoughtfully. "... Well, I suppose I can call her an acquaintance. Anyways, it doesn't really concern you guys."

"Then why lie about it?"

"I told you, I didn't lie, I just didn't go out of my way to mention her."

The furrows on the class rep's forehead deepened as she took a step towards me.

"Listen, Leo, that girl is dangerous. You shouldn't involve yourself with her."

I blinked in surprise at her harsh words and cocked my head to the side.

"Snowy? Dangerous? Are you sure we're talking about the same person?"

"Snowy?" The creases on her forehead gave way to a surprised look and I almost snickered at the sudden change in her facial expression.

"Right, you probably don't know her name. It's the girl the princess tackled yesterday. And the day before too. Anyways, I was meeting with her in the park. Her name is..." I paused for a moment and scratched the nape of my neck in embarrassment. "Actually, I can't remember her name. I'm kind of bad with those, but I do remember that it means *snow* in French, so I just call her Snowy."

"Neige?"

"Yeah, that one!" I snapped a finger. "I didn't know you spoke French."

"A little." She looked away sheepishly, but then remembered that she was interrogating me and hastily resumed her scowl. Unfortunately for her, by this point I knew it was so paper-thin, it had absolutely no effect. "Why were you meeting her?"

"To return her phone." The answer seemed to take her aback, as she only blinked at me uncomprehendingly, so I elaborated. "Yesterday, when the princess tackled her, she lost her phone. I picked it up, called her brother on it, we set up a meeting time, and I gave it back to her."

"You talked with her brother...?"

"Yeah." I rolled my eyes at the mere mention of the guy. "Sounded like one smug asshole."

The class rep shook herself and looked at me with harsh eyes.

"Leo, you really don't know what you involved yourself in. Those people are bad news."

"Really?" I was doubtful and it really showed in my voice. "I mean, yeah, her brother sounded like a piece of work, but Snowy seemed pretty harmless to me."

"You shouldn't let appearances fool you," the class rep warned me sternly. "She is a seducer."

I blinked at her and then immediately and uncontrollably laughed out loud. The weirded-out look she gave me afterward didn't help my laughing fit either. At last, I managed to get my diaphragm under control and wiped the tears from the corners of my eyes.

"A seducer? Her? Oh please, that girl couldn't seduce a virgin on a prom night if her life depended on it!"

Once again, the class rep looked at me funny and I almost entered into another laughing fit, but I forced it down.

"You mean that?"

"Yeah!" I answered with a grin. "She was absolutely horrible at it. It was like watching a really bad rendition of one of those noir femme fatale characters." I paused again and exhaled sharply. "Though, I suppose if one is really into that kind of thing... I'm not judging anyone, but I personally liked her better after she dropped the act."

"Dropped the act..." It wasn't a question, but instead she seemed to be thinking aloud. "What was she like then?"

"Hm? Fairly normal, I suppose. A little awkward and fidgety, though that might've been just the cold. Otherwise, she seemed like a nice girl. Maybe a little sheltered. Actually, her vamp act could have been just chuunibyou, and..." I trailed off as I noticed that the class rep wasn't even looking at me anymore but staring a hole in the cabinet behind me. I tried to figure out if there was something there, but it seemed like she was just so deep in thought she didn't even notice. I waited for her to ask her next question for a minute or two, but after she didn't react and the silence got uncomfortable, I pointedly cleared my throat. She was startled for a moment and looked at me like a deer in the headlights, but then she remembered where we were and put on her game face again.

"Y-yes?"

"I was just wondering why you keep insisting that Snowy is dangerous. I mean, you obviously know more about her background than I do, and I can't help but feel curious."

She looked me in the eye for a good five seconds, but ultimately she shook her head.

"No. The less you know about her, the better. You shouldn't get involved."

"Well, I already am. Kind of."

"No," she stated firmly, turned around, and headed for the exit. "You really should take better care of—"

However, the class rep's final words were abruptly cut short by the air being squeezed out of her as she smacked headlong into the closed door with a dull, metallic clank. She wobbled for a moment and then fell on her butt.

"Ow-ow-ow!" she cried, cradling her forehead.

I rushed to her side.

"Whoa there! Are you all right?"

"Nooooo," she answered in a long, childish whimper. Thick beads of tears flowed down her cheeks. I gently moved her hands from her forehead, but thankfully there was only a small bump there, nothing serious.

"There, there. It's just a small bruise. It will get better in no time." I patted her head to comfort her before I turned my attention to the big door. It was big, brown and a few knocks affirmed that it was made of surprisingly thick metal plates. Furthermore, it was obviously locked. I rattled the knob a few times and I could only groan and roll my eyes at the result. "Dammit, I should have known. This is so..."

"What?" The class rep looked up at me from the ground, her teary eyes partially obscured by her bangs.

"This is such a stereotypical development. I should've seen it coming." I complained to no one in particular as I tried to force the door open. It didn't budge. "Damn... This is the kind of situation Josh should be involved in, not me!"

"What do you mean?" my fellow storage-room prisoner asked as she got onto her feet. She seemed to have regained her composure. Not only that, but she'd stopped trying to sound like a teacher, so at least that was a plus.

"Nothing. It would take too long to explain, and it wouldn't help the situation."

Though apparently unconvinced, she didn't press any further. Instead, she got next to me and tried the doorknob as well.

"It's locked."

"Yeah, I already figured that out."

"Maybe the latch fell down when I closed the door..." she theorized.

"Okay, does that help us? Can we open the latch from the inside?" She considered our options and shook her head. "Great, so what do we do now?"

"Ours was the last PE class, so..."

It didn't take a genius to connect the dots.

"You want to tell me we'll be trapped here until Monday?"

"No, only until tomorrow morning!" she corrected me hastily. "The sports clubs will need to get their equipment for their weekend practice."

"Well, that isn't much better either," I griped and raised my eyes to the small window. It was high up, but if I tried really hard, I would've probably been able to squeeze through. I looked around the room and after a few seconds of planning, I nodded. "Okay, that should work."

I turned to the expectant-looking girl at my side and pointed at a cluster of containers in the far corner.

"Can you help me move a few things?"

"Why?" she asked, but still started stacking boxes at my side.

"We are going to make a ramp to the window using these equipment boxes and the cabinet. I will climb up, go through the window, circle around the building, and open the door from the outside to let you out."

She glanced up at the window and then back at me. There was an uncertain glint in her eyes.

"Can you fit through?"

"I'll worry about that when I get there," I answered with what I hoped to be a reassuring smile. "Hand me that box, please." She nodded and tried to lift a large cardboard box filled with basketballs, but she couldn't even get it to budge. I smiled ruefully and pointed at a smaller box. "On second thought, I'll get this one. Bring over that instead."

Like that we managed to put together a ramp in less than five minutes. A wobbly and decidedly dangerous-looking ramp, but hey, beggars can't be choosers.

"Well, here goes nothing!" I grinned fearlessly (or at least I hoped that was the impression I gave off) and began scaling our construction.

"Are you sure you want to do this?" Ammy stopped me with a whisper. I looked back at her and awarded her a critical frown.

"I'm already halfway there. Don't you think it's a little too late to ask that question?"

"Oh, right..."

With that, I returned to climbing. Getting to the top of the storage cabinet was fairly easy, but getting onto the unstable boxes we piled onto the top of that? Now that was a different story. I somehow managed to gain a somewhat stable footing and crawled onto the top of the first box. It creaked ominously under my weight, the balls inside bulging out the sides of the box like a balloon that was about to pop, but slow and steady did its magic, and in a minute, I was on the top of the pile with the windowsill roughly in line with my chest.

I reached out for the latch and immediately cursed under my breath. How the hell is it that everything in this bloody world was brand-new except this single rusty latch?! I groaned loudly and got on my tiptoes to get a better view, which unfortunately made the entire ramp wobble under me.

"Whoa!"

"Careful!" the class rep called out, but by then I already regained my balance and let out a sigh.

"I'm fine, don't worry... but on second thought, you might want to take a step back. Just to be on the safe side."

"You are jinxing it," she muttered even as she obediently backed away until her back hit the wall right next to the door.

I tried to reassure her with a smile before I returned to my contest with the rusty latch. Even as I worked on different angles, I let my mind wander about why this bolt in particular was rusty in the first place. Sure, if one only considered its position, maybe it was because moisture in the air tended to condense on windows and it would trickle down, rusting the metal. But then again, the window itself showed no signs of this; it was as brand-new as everything else.

The other, and far more likely, option was that this was a plot device, or at least was supposed to be under different circumstances. As I have alluded to, a boy and a girl getting locked into a storage room (or in the case of outdoor activities, a storage shed) is a bread-and-butter cliché of school-life romance stories. Of course, if I presumed that it applied here, it would've meant that this situation, or at least a similar one, was meant for Josh. In that case, the positioning of the window and the rusty latch made sense, as they were just there to further the romantic development between the people trapped inside by making sure they could not easily leave the room and instead force them to spend quality time together.

Just then I pushed against the window and the latch moved. Unfortunately, it also unbalanced me and for a second or two I teetered on the edge of tumbling down.

"Wait, Leo, I'll help!" Ammy cried out.

I immediately snapped, "No, stay where you are!"

She froze mid-motion. Thankfully I also managed to regain my balance once again and exhaled.

Yeah, we had almost quite literally fallen into the second clichéd development, where I would have tumbled onto her in some kind of compromising position. A lot like the whole *girl falls down the stairs, guy accidentally gropes her* deal, which I wasn't a fan of either. At any rate, I tried the latch again and it indeed moved, though only a little. If only we had some kind of lubricant...

"Oh well..." I mumbled under my breath as I placed one hand against the window and grabbed the bolt with the other. As a wise man had once said, *"When out of options, use brute force."* Well, okay, the original saying was a bit more eloquent, but the point remains the same. "Here goes nothing, again..."

I tried to plant my feet as best as I could on the unsteady boxes and took a deep breath, held it in for a moment, then exhaled sharply as I pushed against the window with all my might while simultaneously pulling on the latch to dislodge it. To my sincerest surprise, it worked. In fact... it worked too well...

"Sonova...!" The curse got trapped in my throat as the bolt gave way and the window swung outwards. Since it happened so unexpectedly, I completely lost my footing and fell forwards, hitting my forehead on the top of the frame. I could distantly hear the class rep gasp in horror, but a moment later I found myself outside, tumbling through the air like a crash test dummy that just got flung out of a speeding car's windshield.

For a very long moment, everything seemed to blur together and I felt nauseous, which I attributed to the weird spinning feeling I experienced at the time, but just as I was about to grasp the gravity of the situation, I found myself landing on my butt with a surprisingly painless thud. For a couple of seconds, all I could do was to blink blankly at my surroundings, but at last my brain caught up and I jumped to my feet like I was sitting on fire.

First, I quickly patted myself down. I didn't seem to be injured. Even the spot where I'd hit my head on the window frame only stung when I poked it, so it didn't seem serious. Once I made sure I still had all my limbs and organs, I focused on my surroundings. I was standing outside by the back wall of the gym, and as I looked up, I couldn't help but whistle. The entire building had an elevated foundation, so from the outside, the window I just fell through was a good five meters above the ground. Sure, the soil I fell on wasn't particularly packed, but damn, getting out of a fall like that with only a sore butt was pretty miraculous.

Just then I remembered why I was climbing out in the first place and raised my hands around my mouth to form a funnel. "Hey, class rep! Are you okay in there?"

"I'm fine!" came the hasty reply. "I should be the one asking that question! Are you okay?!"

"Perfectly fine! I'll let you out in a minute!"

I didn't wait for her to answer but began jogging to the left... only to stop and go the other way around as I remembered that the entrance is on the other side. This small, embarrassing intermezzo aside, I quickly found my way into the gym and rushed up to the door. On closer inspection, it turned out only the tip of the hook of the latch was in its socket, so in retrospect shaking the door a bit more could have possibly dislodged it and let us out. Oh well, spilled milk and all.

After undoing said lock, I opened the door and the class rep all but jumped through.

"How did you do that?!" she leveled the question at me with a strangely intense expression.

"I undid the latch. See, it's—"

"No, not that!" She shook her hand vigorously to halt me. "The window! You fell through the window!"

"Yes, I did that," I answered a tad hesitantly. I really didn't know why she was making such a big deal out of it. Maybe she was just still in shock after my sudden exit?

"How? How did you do that?"

"I really can't follow your questions."

"You fell through the window!" she repeated herself, obviously frustrated with my incomprehension.

"Yes, I opened it, lost my balance, and then fell through the opening. What about it?"

"But you fell through the frame, too!"

Now it was my turn to look at her funny.

"That's just silly."

"I saw what I saw." She stood her ground. I, on the other hand, could only shake my head. She was probably still in a shock of fright over my unintentional stunt, and I couldn't blame her.

"Now, now. I'm not saying you lied, only that you might have seen it wrong. It happened fast and you were probably pretty tense, so you might've mistaken something. For example, I hit my head when I tumbled forwards. Maybe that looked like my head went through the frame from your point of view?"

"Maybe," she answered hesitantly, and I smiled to reassure her.

"It had to be. It's not like people can phase through walls."

"Not unless they are part of the First Earth Battalion."

"The what?"

Suddenly the class rep perked up.

"They were an elite psychic unit of soldiers. They could phase through walls and use ESP and even kill goats by staring at them."

"Uh-huh." I tried to nod politely while also grasping for a quick excuse to change the topic. "I see, so... Oh, wow... Look at that mess!"

I pointed behind her and she fell silent with a frown. The inside of the storage room was a mess indeed. Our makeshift ramp had tumbled over during my escape and the contents of the boxes were strewn all over the floor in a giant heap of balls, rackets, and assorted whatchamacallits. While falling on the outside had me drop from higher, looking at all the sharp edges on some of those things made me think that if I'd fallen down with them, I wouldn't have escaped with just a bruised bottom.

"I guess we'd better clean this up, huh?"

She looked at me funny in return, but after a while she nodded, and so I passed by her and returned to the storage room. I glanced behind me and grinned at her.

"If possible, please leave the door open this time."

She frowned at first, but then she relaxed and sighed as she picked up one of the dented boxes. However, the moment she gave it to me, she blurted, "You see, according to some research, people with psychic powers *can* move through walls, so maybe you did do just that."

I feigned polite interest but rolled my eyes when I turned back to put the box away.

"I don't think I can do something like that."

"But you seem to have great psychic potential! We already saw it!"

I gave her a flat look upon receiving the next box. "I told you, that was just a joke. I'm not psychic."

"I see..." She thoughtfully nodded to herself. "Right, you're definitely not psychic. Don't worry; your secret is safe with me. Anyways, according to the First Earth Battalion Training Manual, one can..."

Mentally facepalming, I just gave up. Might as well let her talk while we work, I decided. She seemed really enthusiastic about it, and I didn't have the heart to stop her.

As such, we kept piling boxes, and I learned more about defunct military psychic operations than I ever wanted to.

CHAPTER 11

PART 1

"The next stop is... Bayview Station," the oddly mechanical female voice of the train's announcement system announced, as per its job description, which happened to coincide with the exact moment my assistant raised her hand to cover up a giant yawn.

"Yesterday was tiresome," she stated at last, probably as an excuse, and I could only nod in agreement.

"Yeah, but it's okay every once in a while."

"I suppose."

I smiled at her thoughtful answer and checked the time. It was a little past 10 a.m. and we were sitting in the jewel of the local public transportation system, first-class seats on a brand-new bullet train. Well, okay, maybe it wasn't exactly a bullet train per se, as it ran on traditional rails instead of magrails, but it was a sleek, white machine that nonetheless ran through the mountainous landscape at scary speeds. Speaking of the landscape, the view outside our tinted windows was truly scenic, with rolling hills, sharp mountain cliffs, dense green forests, and the occasional sparkling white shoreline. I had no idea how all of these geographical features would even begin to make sense on an island of this size, but after a while, I decided to just turn off my brain and enjoy the scenery.

"I still don't think that show was particularly outstanding," Judy opened a conversation only a minute or so later, drawing my attention away from the window.

"I don't know... Sure, it wasn't as great as the guys made it out to be, but it was fun to watch."

"Not for eight hours," my assistant griped with what I was pretty sure I could label as a *sulky voice*, though, as usual, it didn't show on her face.

"Hey, now. We didn't just watch the series for eight hours; we did other things too. It was five hours at most."

As a matter of fact, the previous day's *Trucy the Werewolf Huntress* marathon had less to do with the show than the small, usually random trials and tribulations that kept creeping up on us. We started a little before noon, when Angie got back from her tennis practice. Josh and the class rep arrived a little later, while the princess arrived precisely at noon, delivered by a limo, no less. Judy of course had been around since the morning, as she made me promise during our late-night phone talk that I would pick her up in the morning. It was on its way of becoming a habit. The late-night phone conversations, I mean, not the picking up part.

We originally wanted to order pizza for lunch, but Elly declared that she would cook for us even if she had to use "commoner ingredients." If you asked me, she just really wanted to do something useful for a change but was too embarrassed to do it normally. It also turned out that we faced our first big hurdle right at the beginning, as I didn't actually have a Betamax player. That's right, I said *Betamax* player. Not Blue-ray, not DVD, and not even VHS, but Betamax of all things! The random technological discrepancies of this world were baffling, to say the least.

Anyways, in the end we broke into two groups: Josh and I were in charge of buying the equipment (in the end I actually bought all the seasons on DVD along with a player in the supermarket instead, as it was both a simpler and cheaper solution) while the girls were doing the cooking.

"Speaking of which..." I decided to broach a subject I'd been curious about for a while. "Can you tell me what caused the *Calamity Lunch* incident?"

The name came from Josh, but it was descriptive enough so I started using it too. To put it bluntly, when we returned from our shopping trip, we were welcomed by not one, but four different meals. It was quite shocking considering I wasn't even sure there was enough time to make *one* dish, let alone *four*. Three were complete disasters while the fourth was... well, a plate of ham sandwiches. You can have three guesses about who made those.

"Where should I begin?" Judy pondered before continuing. "Eleanor wanted to make a kind of soufflé. I decided to make some sandwiches in the meantime. She questioned why I was making those and accused me of having no trust in her cooking skills."

"That sounds like her all right. How did you answer?"

"I didn't. I continued preparing your ham sandwiches."

I stopped her with a move of a hand. "Wait, you made those sandwiches for me in particular?"

She nodded.

"Yes. I thought you might want something edible, and I knew you like those."

I looked at her flatly while trying to suppress a frown.

"Doesn't that mean you really didn't trust her cooking skills?"

Judy returned my flat stare with one of her own, but before long she shook her head.

"At this time, I cannot confirm nor deny such accusations. Please consult my lawyer." For a moment I didn't know how to react to that, so I just let it go and gestured for her to continue. "At this point she told me she would challenge me to a cooking contest."

"Yeah, in retrospect I should have warned you about that. That's another of those typical developments in harem comedies, where the girls compete in cooking."

"Is that so? I thought she was simply being competitive, as usual."

"Nah, it's actually a thing." I crossed my legs and rested my chin on my hand. "It has something to do with scoring femininity points."

"What's that?"

Before I noticed it, she already had her phone in her hand, so I let out a small breath and continued.

"It's this thing where girls in harem comedies compete with each other based on different attributes they have. The cook-off is one of those clichéd developments where they all make food for the guy in the middle to see who is the best cook and would make the best housewife."

"I see." My assistant nodded while typing, then she glanced up at me. "I guess I should have put in more effort then."

"Hm?" I tried to imitate Josh's intrigued single-eyebrow-raised expression, but I quickly realized I needed more practice, so instead I told her, "If you wanted to enter the race for Josh, then sure, be my guest."

"No," she retorted with the bluntness of a warhammer and the tiniest of frowns.

"Then there is no problem," I answered with a smile. "Plus, the sandwiches were perfectly fine, anyway."

"I'm glad to hear that." She nodded to herself, like she often did, and then gave me a questioning look. "Does that mean I have scored some femininity points?"

I couldn't help but smile.

"Sure."

"Yay."

I allowed myself a single chuckle at her deadpan delivery and moved on.

"So, back to the Calamity Lunch. What happened next?"

Judy put her phone away and returned to her explanation.

"After Eleanor made a scene, the others came into the kitchen. Then Angeline and Amelia also decided to accept the challenge, and they all tried to make an unusual dish."

"Ah, right. The vegetarian cordon bleu and that seafood pasta thing..."

I didn't even know where they found the ingredients for those. My fridge was pretty mysterious sometimes.

My assistant nodded once more, and added, "The rest is history."

"Indeed."

With that, we both fell silent, and I returned to my window-gazing. There was an announcement about the next stop, but I didn't pay much attention to it. We were only getting off at the last terminal, and that was still a good twenty minutes away. I would've probably continued looking at the scenery until then if not for the sudden tugging on my shoulder. I looked over and found Judy delicately pinching a fold on my coat and pulling on it at regular intervals even after I returned my attention to her.

"Yes?" I asked without even trying to hide the amusement in my voice.

"Chief, I have a question too."

"Really? I'm listening."

Still tugging at my clothes, she leaned closer and murmured, "What were you and Joshua talking about?"

"When, exactly?"

"Before Eleanor arrived," she clarified as she leaned even closer. "You seemed awfully secretive about it."

"Oh, that?" I grinned and carefully pushed her back to get some breathing space. "It wasn't really a secret. We were discussing his experiences at the princess's mansion the day before." Judy looked at me expectantly, so I told her, "Apparently, they were not only under constant supervision, but Sebastian was interrogating him about me."

"You left an impression."

"It seems so."

"Why were you whispering about it?"

"Well... let's just say some of the old guy's questions were pretty weird and they made Josh nervous." Once again my assistant didn't speak aloud, but it was obvious she wanted me to continue, so I did so after a quick sigh. "He was asking after my family, where I lived, what kind of people I hung out with, whether or not I was related to the British royal family..."

"One of those things is not like the others."

"One of these things just doesn't belong," I answered reflexively, but she only gave me a flat look. "Oh... sorry, I thought you were doing a thing." There was an awkward pause hanging in the air for a moment, after which I cleared my throat and proceeded as if nothing happened. "So, Josh wanted to know why he would ask these things."

"Background check?"

"Probably."

"Maybe he wanted to see if you had the pedigree to marry into the family."

"That isn't a funny joke," I responded a bit more flatly than intended, but then paused for a moment to think. The previous day was so hectic I didn't really think about it, but looking back at it with a clear head, those questions *were* odd. I made a mental note of them and decided to ask the butler the next time I had the misfortune to meet him, then I shrugged my shoulders at my assistant. "It's more likely he was checking if anyone would care if I went mysteriously missing."

"I would."

I chuckled at her instantaneous answer.

"Thanks. That's reassuring." Still smiling, I casually glanced over my shoulder and sighed. "By the way, they are still following us."

"Yes." My assistant nodded without looking. "It was probably Eleanor who paid for the tickets."

"Go figure."

As a matter of fact, the rest of the gang had been following us all morning, and they were about as subtle as the last time the girls stalked us at the phone shop. I pretty much expected this since the moment Judy blurted out that we would be going on a trip, but it still surprised me how all four of them trailed behind us, including Joshua. Of course, maybe he was being dragged along by one of the girls. This did sound like one of those wacky episodes you'd get see in a harem comedy after all, which made me all the more determined not to get involved. That's why I bought a prohibitively costly train ticket that took us on a round-trip around half the island. But as you might've gathered, they still followed after us like baying bloodhounds, except less subtly.

I slumped my shoulders and returned my attention to the girl at my side. "So, should we keep trying to get rid of them or should we take them for a ride?"

Her brown eyes seemed as flat and uninterested as usual, but by this point I was well on my way to master reading the tiniest changes in her expressions, and this time they added up to a single word: *mischievous*.

"Why not both?" Her words confirmed my reading, and painted a similar grin onto my face.

"I like the way you are thinking."

"I will take that as a compliment."

"Yes, that's how I meant it."

"Really? Then... yay? I was complimented again."

I sighed and shook my head.

"Let's practice expressing overt joy another time." I rubbed my hands together and cracked my neck as a show of intense preparation. "So, we have about fifteen minutes until we reach our destination. Let's see the ideas."

As if we rehearsed it beforehand, we reached for our phones in unison and began poking at the screens. I hated to admit it, but in the short time since she had hers, Judy had become something of a virtuoso with her machine and worked much faster than I did.

"What are the essential stops?" she asked without looking up, her tone dead serious.

"The Northern Piers, the Critias Museum and Library, the Central Monument Park, and the Black Baron's Multiplex Cinema."

She looked up from her phone on the last one.

"What are we researching there?"

"Nah, they just have a good movie at six o'clock. I thought we should watch that once we're done with our trip. You know, to end on a high note."

"I see." She gave me a small nod and returned to her screen. "I will place that one at the end of the timetable, then. Any other points of interest?"

"A few small ones I thought we could visit if we've got the time. I'm sending you over my initial plan."

"So you had a plan." Judy looked up from her screen while I sent the file over. "Very diligent of you."

"Thanks," I replied, just as the list got through. "It's just a few interesting-sounding curiosity shops and restaurants. Most of these wouldn't pose much of a challenge to the guys, so we should spice things up a little."

"Hmmm..." My assistant pondered that while absently swiping her screen. "How about the amusement park?"

"There is an amusement park out there?" Well, "out there" didn't say much in this case. Technically we were only going to the outskirts of the town, but because of the huge (and, in retrospect, pointless) round trip that took us back practically to the same part of the town where we started, it felt like we were going to the backwoods. Anyways, I used my built-in browser to look up a map, and sure enough, there was an amusement park not far from our primary destinations.

"According to this site, it has numerous attractions, including a roller-coaster, a haunted house, and a lovers' tunnel," Judy informed me with the efficiency of a salesclerk.

"Hmmm... All of those sound like nice places to give the gang a run for their money. I especially like the haunted house idea." I could totally imagine the princess going around and screaming at everything while futilely trying to look brave and dignified. It was in her character.

"I am partial to the lovers' tunnel."

"I don't know," I muttered as I scratched my chin. "I think that's too early for them. It would probably lead to friction in the entourage, and that's not funny."

"True."

For a second or two we both fell silent, so I hastily put my phone away before it could become awkward.

"Okay, is there anything else?"

"I don't think we need more sites."

"Yeah, I suppose the park should keep us busy for the afternoon."

Just then the mechanical voice of the train announced our next stop, and we both stood up in unison.

"Anything else?"

"Act natural, don't look their way, and stick to the plan."

"Got it." Judy nodded solemnly at my side, and we headed for the doors while trying to ignore a totally conspicuous group making a commotion in the other car as they scrambled to their feet.

PART 2

Our first stop at the apparently renowned Critias Museum and Library was one of the more relaxed and at the same time perplexing experiences I had. The exhibits, which mostly dealt with the island's history, were housed in a large baroque building that would have fit right into any old European capital if not for the unsettlingly new state it was in. It didn't even make sense! Why would someone try to emulate an antique building style and then make it look brand-new? Wasn't the patina half the point? But then again, it wasn't like this was even close to making it onto my list of the ten most glaring absurdities this world had thrown my way this far, so I decided not to get too hung up on it, especially since I was just in the process of reading something even more baffling as we spoke.

"So the island's traditional claim to fame and chief source of income is its extensive mining industry?" I scratched my chin in a most cerebral manner while leaning forward to get a better look at the eye-strainingly tiny letters engraved on the bronze plaque. It was fastened onto the stump of a Greek column in front of a series of large pictures depicting gaping mineshafts and eerily happy miners. After some time, I straightened up and shook my head. "That's just silly."

"How come?" Judy inquired while also straightening herself. I hadn't even noticed she was leaning forward the same way I was.

"This is a volcanic island," I stated dryly.

"Really?"

"Yes. What else could a small island in the middle of an ocean be?" I stated confidently. Then after some hesitation, I cleared my throat and added, "Also, that other plaque said so."

"Oh." Judy's voice sounded faintly impressed either way.

"Anyways, the point is that volcanic islands are fairly new geological formations, so there's no time for ore veins to accumulate, let alone fossil fuels like oil or coal. I have no idea what they could be mining that would warrant an industry. Maybe sulfur?"

"It's unobtanium," Judy stated at my side, and the word immediately managed to skyrocket my brows.

"Bullcrap," I caught myself responding flatly and quickly cleared my throat. "Pardon. What I wanted to say was: 'Ha ha, yeah, we just talked about that yesterday, not falling for that.'"

My assistant let out a soft *tch* sound, though as usual, her face didn't show any irritation.

"I was found out."

"It was a good try, though."

"I see." To my relief, she seemed to perk right back up and calmly walked over to the next plaque in line. "Ah!"

Surprised by that unusually excited noise, I quickly made my way over.

"What did you find?"

"The actual answer," she told me as flatly as ever, but in contrast to that, I couldn't help but notice that she puffed out her chest. It wasn't proper to stare, though, so I leaned closer to take a better look at the information tablet in question.

"Well, I'll be damned. It says the island has large deposits of nickel, gold, and... diamonds? Really?"

"It says so."

"Yeah, but..." I scratched my head while trying to keep my mouth from grimacing. "Damn, I should really look into this on the net once we get home." I was about to move on, but my assistant's relentless stare made me stop and raise a curious eyebrow. "Is there a problem?"

"Why did we come here then?"

"Excuse me?"

"I just don't see the point of visiting a museum if you are going to search the internet for information found there. Why did we come here in the first place?"

Somehow she made the otherwise confrontational question sound reasonable. I opened my palms and shrugged.

"It's all about the experience."

"Is it?"

"Yep. Sure, if you are only looking for just the particulars, then the internet is much faster, but doing the legwork like this has its charm too."

"If you say so." She looked around, probably looking for the right words to let me down gently. "I just think it's inefficient. And a little boring."

"Wait, you're bored?" My reaction was, of course, in no way panicked or defensive. "I'm not bored. Are you bored?"

My assistant awarded me another of her long deadpan gazes (which didn't look much different from her usual look, but I was pretty sure that was the intention behind it) before she decided to answer.

"I'm not bored." She nodded to the side. "But they are."

"Oh..." I had to remind myself to only look from the corner of my eye, and it didn't take long to locate the entourage. They were hiding behind one of the large round columns upholding the ceiling of the exhibit hall... except for the class rep, who was out in the open and reading one of the plaques in the back. It said something that she was the least conspicuous member of the entire bunch.

"So?" I returned my attention to my assistant. "No one is forcing them to follow us around."

"But they do, and if we keep loitering around, they will think we are boring people. We should hurry up."

"Oh, come on. Could we not schedule our trip around the whims of our stalkers, please?"

"I just feel sorry for them. It's probably not very interesting to watch us viewing an exhibit."

"I don't know..." I tried to object, but she was actually kind of right. But still, a stubborn streak in me just didn't want to give in like that. "Damn, now you made me wonder what they are thinking about."

"You can ask them tomorrow. We should move on."

I shook my head. "No, I was rather thinking about listening in on them right here and now."

Judy discreetly glanced at the still hiding entourage, and when her eyes returned to me, there was a look in them that I figured must have been skeptical in nature.

"They are pretty far from us. Do you plan to sneak up on them?"

"Depends," I told her as I looked around the hall. I could practically count the people around me on one hand, and they were all silent. In fact, the place was eerily quiet, though in this case it was a good thing. "Let's act like we are wandering around and get a little closer to them. We might be able to hear something if we focus really hard."

"If you say so."

Ignoring the unbeliever at my side, I closed my eyes and tuned my ears in the direction of Josh and company. Figuratively, of course. To my surprise, I managed to pick up something right away. At first there were only small snippets, word-fragments masked by minor environmental noises I didn't even notice before, yet slowly but surely I was able to make out more and more. I held my breath to reduce the background noise even farther and, with the suddenness of a popping soap bubble, everything came into perfect focus at once. So much so, in fact, that I involuntarily gasped—it felt like the princess was right beside me. I opened my eyes, but only Judy was at my side, and she was looking at me with her usual deadpan expression coloured by a tinge of incredulity.

"So?"

"I can totally hear them," I whispered while trying my best to reign in my shocked excitement. "I can hear them loud and clear."

"Really?"

She still didn't sound convinced, so I instructed her to focus as I did. After a few seconds, she shook her head.

"I can't hear anything."

"Maybe it's the acoustics," I hypothesized. "Try standing over here."

My assistant followed my instructions without any complaints, but she didn't seem to hear anything. I decided to try to show her the ropes.

"Listen closely. Right now Angie is complaining that I didn't buy you any snacks at the kiosk. And now Josh is talking about how said kiosk wasn't nearly expensive enough and that I should have brought along some kind of dish I can't pronounce."

"That sounds like something they would say," she tentatively agreed. "But I still can't hear them."

"Seriously? They are completely audible. Try closing your eyes."

My assistant obediently did as I instructed, scrunching up her eyes in concentration.

"What are they talking about now?"

"Right now? Give me a second... The princess is saying that I must have tricked you into closing your eyes so I can molest you."

Judy opened one of her eyes at me.

"Did you?"

"No, and one of these days I really have to sit down and talk with that girl before things get out of hand."

The answer seemed to satisfy her, for she closed her eyes and began concentrating again. It was apparent Judy tried her best to listen, but in the end, she just shook her head.

"Sorry, couldn't hear anything legible."

"Seriously? But they are talking so loud, and—" I paused as a disappointed frown settled onto my face. "Oh, you looked their way."

"I did?"

"Yeah, Josh just pulled the princess back. He has his hand clapped on her mouth and... Wow, that's so typical."

"Did something happen?"

"Hm?" I grunted groggily as I glanced at her, then shook my head. "Nah, it's just that the princess apparently got a nosebleed. It's one of those trope things. It's supposed to signal arousal or something."

"How did you know that?"

"It's on the site I showed you last time. Just search for nosebleed. It has something to do with an old wives' tale."

Judy shook her head so abruptly her hair whipped around her face. She quickly straightened her hairdo and continued without missing a beat.

"No, I meant how'd you know she has a nosebleed?"

"I told you, I'm listening to them. It's not that hard."

"Chief, they are behind the column. Literally out of sight. How can you tell something like that?"

"I..." The words got caught in my throat and instead turned into a confused grunt. "That's... actually a very good question. How the hell can I tell that?"

As a matter of fact, I had a crisp picture of exactly what was going on behind that column, in glorious HD resolution no less. I was just about to ponder whether I was seeing the actual events or I was just hallucinating, when my arm got hijacked by my assistant, pulling me along and instantly bursting whatever *vision* I had like the aforementioned soap bubble.

"Let's move on, we need to have them think we didn't notice them."

"Fine, fine! I'm coming, no need to pull! Geez..." I agreed automatically, but after a few steps, the gears in my head finally caught up and made me knit my brows in puzzlement while simultaneously planting my feet and stopping the girl dragging me with a sudden jerk. "Wait, why do we need to make them believe that? The cat's out of the bag. I think we could just ignore them pointedly until they leave."

"No. If we do that, it will make the rest of our destinations pointless," my assistant argued while still trying to pull me along. I noticed that there was something wrong with that argument, but at the moment I found myself strangely preoccupied with the sight of Judy tugging at my arm. She didn't actually put her back into it. In fact, she was only pulling on my sleeve with two slender fingers pinched on a crease, ineffectually tugging at it at regular intervals while staring holes into my face.

"So...?" I asked her, and she gave me a strange look in return, so I clarified my question with, "So what if our plans are torpedoed? We still have my original timetable."

"No," she emphatically stated between two tugs. But then she seemed to be thinking, and added, "It would be wasteful."

"I really don't see what you are getting at," I admitted, and it turned out my mouth was one step ahead of my brain once again, as a second later the realization hit me like a sack of bricks. "Oh. Ooooh... I get it now." I flashed a toothy smile and she visibly twitched. "You were looking forward to going to the amusement park, weren't you?"

Judy didn't answer, but instead she tried to show no reaction whatsoever. I say *tried*, since at this point, I was so used to her natural poker face that her efforts to appear level and stoic manifested as the most overt reaction I have ever seen on her face. It was pretty ironic.

"You know you could've just said so? This entire trip is for your sake in the first place."

"And the research?"

"That's just a side-benefit," I told her while gently unclenching her still absentmindedly tugging fingers. "In fact, I guess we can skip the memorial park too. Let's go to the amusement park."

"Are you sure? I don't want to go there that much."

Completely disregarding her protests, I clasped her hand and began dragging her along in a mirror opposite of the situation just a minute before, all the while trying to ignore the strange snippets of excited conversation from the other side of a certain column.

PART 3

"I love it!" I exclaimed with a grin that threatened to split my face.

"It's not funny," my assistant smoldered, pointedly avoiding the piece of polaroid wonder in my hand.

"No, of course it's not. I never said that."

"Then why do you sound so happy about it?" she continued to fume with a pout thoroughly ruined by the cotton candy stuck to her face.

"Because it's amazing! Look." I showed her the picture, and she was just a split second too slow to look away. She twitched and quickly turned her back to me, though I was sure I saw some blood rush to her cheeks.

"I told you I don't want to look at it," she stated coldly, another expression ruined by the mountain of sweets she was burying her face into.

"But you look really good in it! I didn't even think you could make that kind of face."

Instead of an answer, my assistant lightly kicked my shin and turned away from me. It didn't really hurt, but I let out an obligatory *ouch* anyways before I returned to gazing at the picture in question.

Speaking of which, the previous conversation requires some context, doesn't it? At this moment, we were sitting on a bench near the huge central fountain of the amusement park, its finely choreographed water jets vigorously sparkling in the midday sunlight.

Since we'd arrived at this fine establishment, we'd been on a nonstop campaign to conquer all the rides in the park before closing time. The picture in my hand was a trophy of one such conquest, belonging to the world's sixth tallest rollercoaster, which sounds less impressive than the actual ride was, but that's beside the point.

It was everything one could have expected from a coaster, and one thing I didn't. As it turned out, there were cameras set up around the track that, upon reaching the hairiest turns and dips, engraved the image of every customer's expressions into the annals of history, or at the very least onto photographs of various framing-compliant sizes, all for the low-low price of five Jens, tax included. Normally I wouldn't have been interested in souvenirs like that, but when the clerk presented us with this particular picture, I knew I had to get multiple copies of it.

The scene itself was normal enough. It was of the front car of the coaster as it was in the process of plummeting down the rails of the world's sixth tallest... whatever they call those peaks. They must have a name for that too, like *reverse sidewinder Immelmann butterfly inversion* or something. Either way, the point is that there were two people in the focus of the picture—one ruggedly handsome, intelligent, charming, and criminally humble young man and a girl whose pretty face was in the process of displaying a terrified grimace so profound that cartoon characters would stand in line to get performance advice on replicating it.

I must have spent more time admiring my assistant's photographic likeness than strictly necessary, as she found it appropriate to remind me of her presence by delivering another feeble kick at my shin. Needless to say, this one was more like a small tap than an actual kick, which momentarily made me wonder about the various other peculiar means she employed in the not-so-distant past to get my attention. I didn't have much time to ponder though, as she demonstrated yet another of them by poking my cheek with the end of her empty cotton candy cane. It wasn't particularly sticky, so I presumed she used the clean end. She was thoughtful like that.

Anyways, I turned to the still quietly fuming girl at my side with an awkward smile. "Please stop that. It hurts." Of course it didn't *actually* hurt, but it was only appropriate to display the proper reaction in situations like this.

My assistant puffed her cheeks imperceptibly, which still had that piece of cotton candy on them, by the way, and stared daggers at me for a good five seconds. Though, on second thought, she might've just been squinting against the sun. What can I say? My Judy Facial Expression Translation suite was still under development, so it was only to be expected.

"I will stop when you stop looking at that picture," she stated, and kept relentlessly poking my face even as she spoke.

"Oh, fine." I sighed in defeat and pocketed the day's treasure. "I am totally going to frame it and hang it in my living room, though."

"If you do that, I will start hating you."

"Ouch, the lady drives a harsh bargain." I grinned as I pinched the end of her stick and yanked it out of her hands with an effortless motion. I then used the still sticky end to skillfully pick off the loose piece of cotton candy sitting contently on her cheek and presented it to her with an apologetic smile. "Will you take this as a peace offering?"

She glanced down at the piece of sweet fluff offered, and then, without any warning, she leaned forward and snapped her jaws around the end of the stick so hard I thought she'd bite the entire thing off. Thankfully, she just scooped off the digestible part at the end and then proceeded to lick the fingers she'd used to hold said stick, kind of like a well-fed cat.

"That offer was suggestive in nature and could have been easily misunderstood as intentional innuendo for fellatio," she told me in the same tone one would report on the weather. Now that she mentioned it, she kind of had a point.

"Why did you take it then?"

She gave me one of those looks that people reserve for really obvious questions.

"You never turn down food for silly reasons like that. Also, I was reasonably certain it wasn't intentional."

"Thanks for the vote of confidence." I chuckled and pointed at a nearby kiosk. "Wanna grab one of those chocolate-covered banana treats? With extra cream?" She didn't even bother to answer, instead she kicked me again. I didn't even mind. "Yeah, yeah. Sorry, I had to do it." She still seemed peevish, so I decided to change tactics. "By the way, did I mention I had other pictures too?"

"I really am going to start hating you. Just you watch."

"No, no. Not pictures of your reactions, the one I just showed you is all I need." Since I subscribed to the *one picture > thousand words* school of thought, I reached into my breast pocket and presented her with a set of pictures I'd pilfered from the booth after our ride, though getting these required a bit more convincing, as they didn't actually depict us.

"They followed us onto the ride?"

I couldn't tell if she was impressed or annoyed, so I decided it must have been both. Or as I like to call it, *improyed*.

And... yeah... after this, I'm totally going to get arrested by the grammar police for word abuse.

Anyways, I waved the pictures like a fan and answered with a pleased grin.

"Yup. We have dedicated stalkers."

The first picture naturally depicted the first half of our less-than-sneaky shadows in the form of Josh and Angie huddled together in the small cart about halfway down the train. My dear friend was in the process of clutching the safety belts, white-faced, while his childhood friend was having the time of her life at his side, her smile so wide it threatened to split her face.

The second picture, on the other hand, was of the princess and the class rep in the car behind them, and it was arguably the more interesting of the two. On the left, the class rep had the excited, if slightly guarded expression I expected, while the blonde girl on her side... Actually, her expression was almost a mirror image of Judy's.

I was about to voice my observation to the girl in question, but she beat me to the punch by pointing at the picture and stating, "That is hilarious. I love it."

For a moment or five, I could only blink at her suspiciously, unsure whether her comment was genuine or another of her sudden sarcastic outbursts, but she seemed too preoccupied with gazing at the picture to care.

"Let me guess. You want to frame it and put it on the living room wall too, right?"

"If you let me," she answered without missing a beat.

"Well. You *are* aware that she's making the exact same face you did, right?"

She glanced up with another of those *I have no idea what the hell you are talking about* looks she was so good at dispensing and shook her head.

"Now you did it. Now I hate you."

"Really?"

"A little."

I shrugged.

"Well, I suppose that decided who will not be getting this month's Employee of the Month bonus."

Judy hesitated.

"And if I didn't hate you, I would get it?"

"Probably. I have no other employees to give it to."

"I see." Judy nodded sagely before pointing at me. "You are trying to make me like you by threatening to withdraw benefits. That is psychological abuse, Chief. We have an abusive relationship."

"Really?"

"Yes."

"Oh, the horror."

"Oh, the humanity?"

"That too."

Done with our customary bouncing of the random-ball between the two of us, we both leaned back on the bench and basked in the sun for a good five minutes. I was just about to get up and try to move on to the next ride when I found my assistant still looking at the picture in her hand, which, I just realized, she'd snatched away from me during our highly abusive argument.

"If you really want to put it on your wall, you can keep it. I have back-ups," I teased her, but she shook her head in response.

"No, I was just wondering what they're doing right now."

"Right now?" I asked suggestively, but she raised a hand to stop me.

"Wait a moment." I did so, during which she pocketed the picture (which didn't make me confident of her denial about framing and hanging it later) and retrieved her phone from its customary nest in her breast pocket. She turned on the machine and gave me the go. When I didn't start right away, she flashed the screen towards me and said, "I'm documenting what you say so I can cross-reference it with the others later."

"Diligent as always," I commented with a smile, which she returned, much to my shock and surprise. Loud surprise. "Whoa! Did you just smile?!"

Her lips straightened and she gave me a look so flat, you could've built an airport on it.

"I am not even allowed to smile now. Truly, our abusive relationship has reached a new low, Chief."

"No-no-no! You can smile all you want! In fact, you should smile more."

"Then you should praise me more often."

I hid my smirk behind a polite nod and gave her a composed, "Duly noted," before I returned to the task of locating our beloved stalkers, our main source of amusement throughout the day. It didn't take long. Not that it ever did; these guys were so bad at shadowing us, I wondered if they were acting clumsy on purpose. Anyways, I found them idling near a food kiosk selling an assortment of traditional amusement-park sweets and other related calorie bombs.

I took a deep breath, closed my eyes, and extended my senses towards them. It was the best way to explain the experience, as it definitely wasn't just listening very hard. Repeated attempts and experimentation had proven that I could do it anywhere, be it in a quiet museum, on a crowded train, or in the noisy amusement park. I still called it *listening in*, though, mostly so that I didn't have to try to explain it to Judy again. Either way, I did so for a few seconds and then turned to my expectant assistant.

"Right now they are talking about the roller coaster. The princess and Angie are arguing because she said it was boring."

"Which one?" Judy interrupted.

"The princess. According to her, it was, and I quote, 'just not fast enough.'"

"She is full of it."

"The proper term is *boasting to save face*. As for the others, Josh is eating an ear of corn. The class rep... she's buying something from the kiosk. A hot dog, I think? It's shaped weird."

"Anything else?"

"Nothing in particular. Let me try for a little longer." I did so, and after a few short minutes, a smile crept onto my face. "Now the princess and Angie made up over their hopes that we won't want to head for the haunted house next. Because we absolutely won't want to do exactly that, right?"

By the time I opened my eyes, Judy had put her phone away and was on the move. I followed suit. Neither of us had to say anything at all.

The aforementioned haunted house was tucked away in one of the quieter corners of the park. It was easy to locate, as from the outside it looked like a giant warehouse made of uniformly painted grey shipping containers. The actual haunted house was inside said building, and after a surprisingly short wait in line, we entered with our stalkers following close behind us. Apparently, they thought that we wouldn't recognize them if they put on huge, reflective mirrored sunglasses. If anything, they just looked like four inept undercover cops from a cheesy eighties TV show, and about as conspicuous.

The most amusing thing was, however, that despite all their efforts, they still couldn't follow us directly. As it turned out, unbeknownst to us, the attraction was holding a special event. Normally, people would go through the house, which looked like a dilapidated family home from the outside, though it was hard to make out the fine details due to the mood lighting, in groups of five to ten. However, when we got to the front of the line, the young female clerk looked at us, flashed a snow-white smile, and simply asked, "Couple's promotion?"

I had no idea what she was talking about, so I glanced at Judy. She only shrugged her shoulders, or at least that's what I thought at the time, though in retrospect it's possible she was just tense. Anyways, I took that as her silent agreement and nodded to the attendant. She smiled again, displaying more teeth than I thought a human mouth could possess (which incidentally made me wonder if she was already part of the attraction as some sort of humanoid teeth monster) and pressed a button on her panel. Following that, the turning bars in front of us unlocked with a loud clang.

"Please follow the green line and have fun," she told us with robotic enthusiasm.

"Thanks, I think..."

We stepped through and, to my momentary surprise, the bars locked back down behind us, meaning it was only the two of us. Judy stayed unusually close to me, so I smiled at her reassuringly.

"Come on, let's get going. They cannot let in the next group until we're at the first checkpoint."

My assistant nodded, and we walked up to the creaky door of the home inside the pitch-black warehouse with only a fluorescent green line on the floor telling us which way to go. I was surprised by the lack of tour guides, but I supposed they were keeping an eye on us with IR cameras or something. We entered the house, passed by the first few, admittedly cheesy-looking, jump-scares, and I was just about to turn to my assistant and grumble about the lack of creativity when I was interrupted by an ear-piercing shriek coming from behind us.

For a moment I was almost impressed, as this one really did startle me, but at the same time I also found it strangely familiar. I glanced at Judy, and her expression told me she had the same idea. We stepped back to see what was going on and carefully glanced around a corner covered in what I really hoped was artificial slime, and we found the princess standing over the decapitated body of a decidedly cheap-looking vampire-animatronic right by the entrance.

Upon noticing our gazes she let out another yelp, this time one of her overly cutesy noises instead of a shriek, and dashed out of the haunted house with the rest of the mirror-glasses brigade in tow, pushing people aside and jumping over the bars like wanted fugitives. A moment later the lights came back on, momentarily blinding me as the hidden lamps flared to life, and from some unseen loudspeaker a pleasant female voice announced, "We are experiencing some technical difficulties. Please stay where you are until an employee can come and get you. We are terribly sorry for the inconvenience."

I looked at Judy, then at the decapitated vampire robot, and all I could do was laugh and laugh.

PART 4

It was around four in the afternoon when the cabin of the Ferris wheel carried us to the top of its never-ending circular journey for a truly scenic view of the area. On my left I could see the long white ribbon of the sandy shoreline of the island, its outline made even sharper by the dark waters of the ocean beyond it. On my right, there was a city that should've been bustling with the after-work rush of an army of workers... except I wasn't sure there were any placeholder workers out there in the first place. A good excuse for another research trip down the line, I supposed.

Anyways, neither of those thoughts was important, nor did I pay much attention to them, as I was still hard-pressed to hold back my chuckles.

"I still can't believe she did that," Judy responded to my snickers. She sat in front of me, as it wasn't comfortable to sit side-by-side in the small cabin, and while she looked as deadpan as ever, I liked to imagine she was just as amused as I was.

"Yeah, it was insane," I agreed heartily. "I didn't even know those things' heads come off."

"I don't think they are supposed to," she mused thoughtfully. "Do you think they can be repaired?"

"I'm sure they have a few spares lying around in case people want to punch Dracula," I answered, which reminded me of the scene once again and I nearly burst out laughing.

"I can't understand why she reacted like that." Judy shook me out of my reminiscence with these words and I raised an eyebrow to urge her to continue. "That vampire wasn't particularly scary."

"Wasn't it?" I grinned playfully while leaning forward. "I can distinctly remember a certain person jumping behind me when it popped up as we passed by it."

"I wasn't scared, just startled," she retorted.

"Suuure, let's go with that."

As I said that, my assistant began swinging her legs. For the next few seconds, I watched her with an expression I could only hope wasn't too dopey before she exhaled sharply and looked me in the eye again.

"Come over here. You are too far. I can't kick you."

I won't lie, her saying that with a dead serious face while framed by the distant horizon in the window behind her was pretty dang cute. Of course, I'd never say that to her face—

"Aw, you are so gosh darn cute."

—except my mouth was once again working ahead of my brain. I should fix that one of these days. Nevertheless, she continued kicking at the air without stumbling for even a moment.

"Don't try to sweet-talk me. I still hate you a little, remember?"

"You do?"

She tried to give me a nod, but she was also swinging her leg, so she almost fell forwards. I decided that allowing her to keep doing this was dangerous, so I raised a hand to stop her.

"Okay, I can join you, but it'll be cramped."

She only stared at me, so after a few silent moments, I awkwardly shuffled over next to her. As I predicted, it was cramped. For some ungodly reason, the designers of this particular Ferris wheel decided that the closed gondolas should be too wide for one person but too narrow for two, and our efforts to take a seat on a single bench resulted in a lot of fidgeting, squeezing, and ultimately Judy sitting on my lap sideways. Yeah, I didn't know how it happened, either.

For the next minute or so there was complete silence. At last, after some awkward "ums" and "ahs," I finally remembered the reason why I came over to this bench in the first place.

"Weren't you supposed to kick me?" I asked innocently.

She just glanced back over her shoulder and shrugged.

"I don't feel like it anymore."

"Really? Don't you hate me a little?" In lieu of an answer, she actually kicked my leg this time. "Ow. You see, I knew you had it in you."

"That was different. It was for failing to read the mood."

I laughed awkwardly and automatically scratched my cheek.

"Yeah, sorry. I'm not good with these kinds of situations."

What followed was another bout of slightly awkward silence only punctuated by the creaking of the Ferris wheel. All things considered, it wasn't a particularly unpleasant experience.

"What's next?"

"Hm?" It took me a long second to get out of my stupor and process the question. I looked out the window and said, "We should get back to ground-level in about ten minutes. I guess we should have dinner and then head to the cinema right after that."

"I see." After such a noncommittal answer, I was ready for another walk down awkward silence lane, but instead Judy steered the conversation right into non sequitur avenue by uttering a soft, "Thank you."

"You are welcome? Wait, why are you thanking me again? I am a little confused here."

"For the entire day. You didn't actually have to take me out on a date like this to get my mind off certain things, but I really appreciate it."

"Nuh-uh." I wagged an insistent finger in front of her. "Not a date, research trip."

"We didn't do much research, though."

"True, but we did *some*. Also, that doesn't automatically make it a date, either."

"We spent the entire day fooling around in an amusement park while followed by our very own comedic date-stalkers, ate in suggestive contexts, got a couple's discount, and capped it all with a scenic ride on a Ferris wheel."

"That's... I mean..." I tried to protest, but after ineffectually opening and closing my mouth for a while, I just buried my face in my hand. "Dear spaghetti monster in the sky! That *is* a date!"

"I thought you realized that a while ago."

"I should've. I'm normally smarter than this!" I paused while looking for a plausible-sounding excuse and found one really quickly. "I was just too preoccupied with my newfound ability to see and hear people through walls. That must be it."

"Your *alleged* ability," she corrected me with a poke.

Speaking of which, I was curious what the others were doing during all this. I didn't even know if I could listen in on them when I had no idea where they were, but I tried it anyway, and to my surprise, it worked as well as before. My elation over the fact that I apparently had a potent peeking ability swiftly turned to disbelief as the image solidified in my head.

"Wow. That's a bit too much."

"What are you talking about?" Judy inquired while looking over her shoulder.

"Josh and company are currently spying on us with one of those coin-operated telescopes they put near landscape views."

"That goes beyond dedicated."

"Yeah, it's a bit creepy, isn't it?"

Judy nodded. There was a brief pause, then she asked, "What are they talking about this time?"

I tried to listen closer, and I could only shake my head.

"You don't want to know."

"It's not nice to tease people. Now I only want to hear it even more."

"Oh fine," I relented with a sigh. "They are betting on whether there's going to be a kiss before the ride ends."

"I see. How much?"

I didn't see how that mattered, but I answered anyway. "Ten Jens."

"I see. And who's betting on what?" she continued her interrogation while taking out her phone.

I gave the girl sitting on my lap a sideways look, but I figured it was probably another of the questions she'd use to see if my ability was for real, so I answered, "Josh and Angie for yay, the princess is for nay, the class rep doesn't play."

"I see. Give me a minute." With that, she began poking her phone, and while at first I thought she was typing, she subsequently raised it to her ear. I could hear a phone ring on the other end, which was weird, and saw the class rep pick up her mobile. "Vote for yes." That was all Judy spoke into her phone before she put it down, pocketed it again, and then faced me. I wanted to ask her what she meant by that, but before I could say anything, she gave me a single peck on the cheek.

For a second or two I could only blink at the sudden development, but then I finally figured it out.

"You know, I don't think it counts as a kiss unless it's on the mouth."

The look Judy gave me was somewhat troubled, but in the end she shrugged and turned her head around.

"I'm not doing that for ten Jens. I have standards."

I stared at the back of her head for a while, trying to figure out what made her tick, but in the end, I just rolled my eyes and leaned back on the bench. Judy soon followed my example, which in her case meant that she laid her back against my chest. When we sat like that, the top of her head was roughly in line with my chin, her hair tickling my lips. We stayed like that for a while, during which I was trying my best to stay calm and gentlemanly, but at some point, I couldn't bear it any longer and gently blew at her hair. She turned her face to me in response, and for a couple of seconds we were just staring at each other from a few centimeters away.

Things were just about to get awkward, but before I could think of something snappy to ease the mood, Judy softly asked, "What kind of movie are we watching after this?"

It was a transparent ploy for changing the topic, and I grasped it all the same.

"It's a sci-fi action-comedy. It's about a group of misfit space-adventurers trying to find the space-holy-grail before the evil space-pirate with the space-galleons catches up to them. It looks hilarious."

"I see." She nodded again, though didn't seem particularly enthusiastic about it. I tried to think of something else to say, and there was one other thing that came to mind.

"Do you think they'll follow us to the cinema, too?"

"Probably."

"In that case, do you want to watch a horror movie instead?" Her eyes narrowed momentarily, but a second later they returned to their usual shape except with a mischievous spark in them. I liked that, so I added, "It has vampire mimes."

"Then it is not a question. It's an imperative."

With that, we both nodded, which once again threatened to end with both of us receiving cranial trauma due to the way we were seated. For the time being, though, I decided to lean back again and enjoy the ride while it lasted.

CHAPTER 12

PART 1

I slammed my front door shut in a hurry that morning, though not because I slept in. Not at all. In fact, since technically I didn't sleep, even semantics agreed with me. Anyways, the reason behind my hurried departure was quite prosaic: I forgot to set my alarm clock, and I was so busy writing scathing critiques on the internet about a certain B-movie adaptation of a certain famous mystery/horror novel that I was almost ten minutes late with my morning routine. Maybe that didn't sound so bad until one realized that said meticulously planned sequence of day-starting rituals only had an error bar of about thirty seconds. Because of this, my entire day started off on the wrong foot, compounding in my current predicament.

Once I made sure the door was locked, I rushed down the street. I didn't run, though. Doing that would've been as good as admitting that I'd messed up. Instead I just... rapidly marched, but in a calm and casual manner that in no way looked weird or forced. No sir. That aside, I rounded the corner leading to the street with Judy's house, and all of a sudden, the air was shoved out of my lungs by a bony impact.

I staggered back (while still maintaining a casual and in no way frantically rushing appearance) and scanned the area for the source of said impact. It wasn't particularly hard to find the culprit, as Judy was sitting on the sidewalk right in front of me. Let's just say one didn't need to have Sherlock Holmes's intellect to connect those two dots.

"Soffy..." she mumbled while rubbing her forehead with one hand.

"I told you to pay attention when you are walking on the street," I chided her half-heartedly and offered her a hand.

"Fhanfs," she mumbled again after I helped her onto her feet, and when she lowered her hand and I could take a better look at her face, I was tempted to get something to drink just so that I could have a spit take.

"Correct me if I'm wrong," I started after quickly clearing my throat, "but is that a piece of toast in your mouth?"

My assistant nodded, the brown slice of bread animatedly dangling by its corner in front of her chin like a bell on a string.

"I faf ifn a fhuffy. I fheft ifn."

"Don't talk when your mouth's full."

She nodded again and then a moment later the toast began disappearing into her mouth like a classified document into the shredder, filling her cheeks to the point where she looked like a particularly well-fed hamster. It was about this point that even the last shred of my poise left me and got replaced by an amused grin.

Anyways, once my assistant was done devouring her late breakfast, she repeated, "I was in a hurry. I slept in."

"Only a little," I replied while checking my phone for the time. "We can still get to school at our usual pace if we start moving now." She nodded and wordlessly fell in line beside me as I started walking. I glanced over to her, and after some hesitation I told her, "By the way, that was really clichéd."

"What was?"

"The whole *running into someone with toast in your mouth* thing."

"Was it?" Before I could answer she'd already whipped out her phone and her fingers began dancing on the touch screen like a five-legged ballerina. I would've warned her about doing that while walking, but I'd long since given up trying and resigned myself to paying attention for two so that she wouldn't get herself injured. For example, by falling into an uncovered manhole. Like the one right in front of us.

I exhaled a soft groan and gently pulled her to the side. She wasn't exactly in danger of falling in even if I didn't do that, but better safe than sorry, right? By the way, who leaves an uncovered manhole on a walkway? That's just gross negligence. If someone falls into that, they could get hurt really badly.

I was about to stop and start looking for some sort of warning sign I could place in front of the hole when Judy tugged on my sleeve. I faced her, and she had an unusually serious look in her eyes.

"I looked up the toast thing. It definitely wasn't on purpose," she stated quite emphatically.

"Are you sure?"

She nodded. And then she nodded again. I figured that meant she was extra-sure. I smiled and waved my hand to dismiss her worries and we began to walk once more.

"Relax, I knew that already. I just thought it was amusing." She was a little puzzled by my comment, so I added, "I mean, I didn't think *you* would be the one invoking the trope."

"Who?"

"Hm?" I grunted, thrown off by the non sequitur.

"Who did you think would do it?"

"Well, all things considered, the most likely candidate was—" I got exactly that far when the gods of comedic timing decided they were out for my blood, and I was once again assaulted by a hard impact on my chest just as we were rounding a corner. This time I instinctively braced myself, and the person who collided with me only bounced off and hit the ground with a thud. I shook myself and groaned aloud.

"That makes it—" I paused, recognizing the girl sitting on the asphalt, and my hand lashed out to point at her. "That makes it *twice* today! What the hell!?"

"Faftf mfy fine!" The blonde girl glared at me from the ground while cradling her head in her hands, a neatly fried French toast defiantly hanging from the corner of her mouth like a particularly clumsy trapeze artist.

"Don't speak with your mouth full," Judy parroted my earlier line at her. The princess flushed red and proceeded to devour the toast in about three bites. It was a little scary to watch. She didn't even chew!

Once she finished, she jumped to her feet and returned my pointed finger with a scowl that was half offended and half embarrassed.

"I said, that's my line! Pay attention to where you are going!"

"I was!" I answered, deeply hurt, but before I could continue, my assistant tugged at my sleeve.

"You were right about the toast."

"I suppose..." I answered vaguely. I actually wanted to say I thought it was Angie who was most likely to do the cliché with Josh, but hey, I'm not above taking credit when it's freely handed out. It's not like I have high standards.

"So, did you sleep in?" I asked as I turned back to the girl in front of me with an amicable smile.

"I most certainly didn't!" She sounded about as peevish as I expected.

"If you say so... But then why were you in such a hurry?"

"I was—" she started, but then suddenly clamped her own mouth shut and glared at me as if I'd asked her a trick question. "It's none of your business."

"She was going the wrong way, too," my assistant noted, earning a glare of her own. It was somewhat reassuring that I wasn't the only one in the crosshairs for a change. Refreshing, even. But then again, Judy's question was a good one. While we lived in the same neighbourhood, the princess lived closer to the school than we did. Not only that, we generally used different streets to get there, so the three of us running into each other was unlikely to begin with, but she was also going the opposite way when she bumped into me. I had a few ideas about her reasons, but I decided voicing my suspicions in front of her would've been counterproductive. As such, I simply shrugged my shoulders and nodded towards the street.

"Doesn't really matter. We should get going, though, or we'll be marked late."

I started walking, and before I knew it the two girls both walked beside me. I was about to resign myself to an awkwardly silent commute for the rest of the way, but to my sincerest surprise, the princess cleared her throat and gave us a smile that was only about 80 percent fake.

"So... what did you do yesterday?"

I raised a single brow at the unexpectedly direct question, but quickly regained my composure and let out an awkward laugh.

"Nothing in particular. I spent most of the day reading this webcomic I was interested in for a while. It's about these space cowboys with a kickass ship that—"

"Wait! What are you talking about?! You were in town! I-I mean, weren't you in town? You said you two would go somewhere, didn't you?"

"Oh, that?" I smiled and glanced at my assistant.

"I had a family emergency," she spoke up right away without missing a beat.

"Oh, speaking of which. How is your uncle?"

"He is recovering well. He should be out of the hospital in a week."

"He got lucky. Why was he in the sewer in the first place?"

"Something about *'everything floating,'*" Judy continued without even the slightest bit of hesitation. "He hit his head pretty badly."

"Yeah, something about alien spiders masquerading as mimes, right?"

"No, that was from before he hit his head. He said the mime has been following him since he was a kid."

"Tough."

"He should get better, though. He says he defeated it by hitting its glowing underbelly with a silver slingshot bullet."

"Really? Isn't that only supposed to work on werewolves?"

"I'm not an expert, but he said it worked. He threw it into a big hole and it no longer follows him."

"Well, that's one way to get over paranoid delusions, I suppose..."

"All right, I get it!" the princess burst out (and between us). "Stop making fun of me! I know you are talking about that movie!"

"What movie?" I asked innocently.

"We didn't see any movie," Judy doubled down with a denial of her own.

"Yes, you did! Yesterday, in the cinema!"

"Really?" I smiled wickedly as I leaned closer. "And just how would you know that?"

"I..." She paused, fell silent, then slowly built pressure like a volcano, an analogy which she dutifully followed up on by exploding all over us. "Shut uuuuup!"

With that, she turned on her heels and dashed away at breakneck speeds. I rolled my eyes and made my hands into a funnel.

"Slow down, princess, you're going to hurt your ankle again!"

She came to a screeching halt, right at the end of the street. She whirled around, pointed at me, and yelled so hard I could hear it clearly even from that distance.

"Shut up! I hate you! Both of you! And your stupid mime movie!"

With that, she turned away from us and ran away, though at a much less dangerous pace. Let's call that a small victory. I turned to Judy with a small smirk and gave her an appreciative nod.

"Good improvisation there."

She blinked at me (or maybe she just blinked in general, it was hard to tell), but then she faced forwards and gazed at the slowly disappearing form of the princess.

"Do you think she really hates me?"

I grunted dismissively.

"Nah, it's probably quite the opposite. She is contrary because she is shy."

Judy continued gazing after her for a few more seconds before she muttered, "She is complicated, isn't she?"

"A little, but who isn't? Come on, we should get going too."

Judy nodded, but we could only take a couple of steps before we were once again halted by some fresh faces entering the picture in the form of Josh and Angie rounding the corner in front of us. They were looking in the direction where the princess left, so they didn't notice us until we were almost right on top of them. I hesitated a bit, but at last I just shrugged and called out to them, though maybe a bit louder than strictly necessary.

"Morning!"

The two of them didn't really twitch so much as jump out of their skins. Angie recovered first and she flashed me an upbeat smile that barely had any visible traces of embarrassment.

"Morning, Leo! Fancy meeting you here!"

"What a coincidence," Josh added with much less success at trying to hide his guilty conscience.

"Not really," Judy interjected. "We take the same streets to school."

"Yeah, we only met up a little earlier than usual."

Josh chuckled awkwardly at my comment for a while, at least until he remembered that the ball was in his court, and he quickly used the opportunity to change the subject.

"So, was that Elly?"

"Yeah," I answered nonchalantly as I began walking, pulling the rest of the group with me. "She slept in and was in such a hurry she went the wrong way."

"Really? And why did she yell she hated you?" Angie inquired with her head poking over Judy's shoulder.

"Just the usual."

It must say something about our daily interactions that this explanation was deemed 100 percent satisfactory by everyone present. We walked in silence for a while, until Josh couldn't hold back his curiosity any longer.

"So... what did you guys do yesterday?"

I glanced over in my assistant's direction and found her doing the same. There was something decidedly mischievous in her eyes, though in retrospect it might have just been my reflection.

"Nothing in particular. I was mostly reading this webcomic about these awesome space cowboys, and..."

PART 2

The school's rooftop was somewhat windy but otherwise pleasantly warm for the season. It was the kind of weather that was just begging for everyone to get together and have a giant ad hoc picnic under the bright blue skies. Sadly the others didn't share my enthusiasm, so it was only Judy and I sitting on our customary bench and eating our typical lunches.

"They refused to talk to you, too? How cold."

"Indeed," my assistant agreed with me between two bites of her usual sandwich. "Amelia did ask me a few questions, though."

"Really? About what?"

"About how I knew they were betting yesterday."

"Oh, right. You called her up," I mused while trying to figure out if I should eat my fish sticks with mayonnaise or ketchup. In the end, I decided on both, though not at once. "What did you tell her?"

"That you used your newly developed psychic powers to spy on them and told me about it."

"Hey!" I protested aloud as I took a page from Angie's book and pointed a piece of deep-fried sea-life at her in a decidedly accusing manner. "I told you that was a secret."

In light of this new information, though, all those times the class rep was bothering me with her First Earth Battalion Standardized Test

Papers (patent pending) between the morning classes started to make a lot more sense.

"It's refuge in audacity," she replied between bites. "Because it's her, the others would be less inclined to believe her and would think that I was joking."

"That's..." I paused and tried not to frown. I failed. "Did you just steal my modus operandi?"

"I did my homework," she answered with her casual monotone, but then she capped it off with a wink while somehow keeping the rest of her facial muscles completely motionless. It was so sudden and unexpected that I involuntarily laughed out.

"Ha! Clever girl! If you continue like this, I might even promote you to chief assistant. For now, you can have a bonus." I sarcastically offered her my molded fish-meat product, and she bit down on it without blinking an eye. She bit, chewed, and swallowed it in less than three seconds, after which she looked at me with eyes even more deadpan than usual.

"What am I, a dog?"

"You took the treat."

"Because turning down food is rude."

"Sure," I smiled and held out the other half of the fish stick. She looked at it for a moment, uncertain about what to do, but then a blink of an eye later she snatched it out of my fingers and plopped it into her mouth.

"You are lucky these are tasty. Otherwise I would consider this teasing. And then I would sulk."

"No, you wouldn't." I chuckled and lightly shook the box in my hands. "By the way, you can have more if you'd like. I've got plenty."

She glanced at the premade lunch box in my lap and nodded.

"Don't mind if I do."

She reached out for the box and picked another piece, but as she was about to raise it to her mouth, there was a sudden, loud bang on the rooftop. It startled her and the fish stick slipped from her grasp, landing with a thump accompanied by a soft "Ah!" from her mouth. She gazed longingly at the deep-fried aquameat bar on the concrete before she glanced up at me.

"Five-second rule?"

"No! We are outside. Take another one. I'll throw that out later."

"Aw."

Before she could reach for the new piece though, the source of the previous loud noise began making its way towards us. Well, fine—technically it was the rooftop access door that made the noise, but let's not get bogged down in semantics. Anyways, once he found us, which wasn't that hard considering that the two of us were the only students on the roof then, Josh briskly walked over and stood in front of me with a difficult expression.

"Man, I need your help."

"What was that?" I turned to Judy with faked puzzlement plastered all over my face. "Did you hear that? I could have sworn I heard Mister Cold Shoulder a moment ago... but there's no one here."

My friend curtly rolled his eyes and flashed an almost growling grimace in the process.

"Ha-ha. Very funny. Listen, I'm sorry for ignoring you, which you brought upon yourself, by the way—"

"It really is strange." My assistant nodded with her cheeks full of fish fillet. "You're right. Eerie."

Josh slumped his shoulders in defeat and let out a pained noise.

"Fine, I get it! I already apologized. What else do you want?"

I sighed and finally looked him in the eyes.

"All right, what's the problem? Did you have another fight with Angie?"

"No, it's the transfer student!"

That raised a brow.

"You mean the princess?"

"No!" Josh all but yelled in exasperation. "The other one!"

Now, that raised two eyebrows.

"*Another one?* We didn't get a new transfer student."

"She is not in our class. She is a freshman in One-A."

It was around this time the puzzle pieces fell into place in my head.

"Let me guess. She is your stalker from before."

"Yes, she is the girl who... Wait, how did you know that?"

"He is psychic," my assistant blurted out between bites. I sent her a sharp glance in return.

"No, actually this time it was just simple deduction. Also, stop stealing my food."

"You gave it to me."

"I offered you *some*, not the whole box! I only ate a single one and half the box is gone already!"

"Stingy." She looked down at her own package and offered me one of her sandwiches. "Exchange?"

I tried my hardest to stay mad at her, but in the end I just snorted and took the offer, and before I could say anything, she'd already snatched another fish stick.

"Listen, guys, your little quarrel is cute and everything, but I need help here! Seriously!"

I turned my attention back to Joshua while absentmindedly unwrapping my new acquisition.

"Okay, I'm listening."

"She wants to marry me!"

I was about to bite into my sandwich, but that made me pause and lower it back down.

"Seriously?"

"Yeah! She declared it when she attacked me in the first-floor hallway."

"So?"

He looked at me like I was a particularly dim kid who needed simple concepts explained.

"I'm too young to marry!"

I blinked at him, and after carefully placing the unwrapped sandwich beside my depleting seafood reserves, I facepalmed so hard it might have even left a mark.

"You know, just because she wants to marry you, it doesn't mean you automatically have to."

"Dude, you don't get it." Josh's cheeks flushed red and he sheepishly averted his eyes. "She is very... persistent."

"Uh-huh." I must have sounded even more skeptical than I intended, for Joshua gave me a look so severe I momentarily entertained the idea of taking a picture of it and selling it as bear-repellant. I sighed once again and crossed my arms. "So, how exactly am I supposed to help you?"

"I dunno... You are the one who is good with girls; I figured you can give me some advice or something..."

"Wait, hold on. Me? Good with girls? Didn't we already establish this was an unfounded rumor?"

Instead of answering, Josh only glanced at my assistant, who happened to be in the middle of simultaneously taking another fish stick while sneaking another of her sandwiches into my lunch box without me noticing. I raised a questioning eyebrow at her, and to her credit, she had the decency of reddening a little.

"Equivalent exchange?"

I finally gave up and just took the whole box and put it into her lap.

"There, you can have it if you really like it."

She looked blankly at the remaining fried fish fractions and promptly returned it into my lap while saying, "It's no fun like that."

So she really *was* doing it for attention! However, before I could properly express my disapproval over her behaviour, my attention was drawn away by a smooth metallic sound as the well-oiled hinges of the door leading to the roof gave way. A moment later a familiar face emerged from the doorway, her long, impossibly white hair gently blowing in the previously established breeze. With each step she swung her otherwise rather petite hips like she was walking down a runway—though to be fair, she managed to make the uniform she was wearing look borderline glamorous. Now that I had a baseline for comparison, I had to say that as far as raw attractiveness was concerned, she was easily on the level of the princess.

"Darling, where are you? I don't mind if you want to play hard-to-get, but there is no reason for you... to..."

The sultry voice of the girl entering our vision slowly faded to a whisper as she noticed me sitting on the bench. I shook my head disapprovingly and sighed.

"Snowy?"

"Y-yes?" she stuttered as her previously seductive strut came to a guarded stumble. She awkwardly held her hands in front of her chest and refused to meet my gaze.

"What did I tell you about the vamp act?" She averted her eyes even farther and mumbled something under her breath. "I can't hear you."

She stepped closer and spoke again, her voice impossibly soft.

"You said I shouldn't try it on Joshua."

"And then what did you do?"

She finally looked at me and her eyes were filled with uncertainty. "I... I couldn't help it."

I shook my head again and sighed, but before I could say anything, my friend raised his voice in disbelief.

"Wait a minute! You two know each other?!"

"Yeah, we ran into each other a few times." I smiled at the motionless girl on the front. "Right, Snowy?"

She nodded meekly, but Josh didn't let up just yet.

"Snowy? Is that her name?"

"Wait, you haven't been formally introduced yet?" She shook her head, so I waved for her to step closer and when she did so I turned to Joshua. "Josh, this is Snowy."

"Actually, her name is Neige Liliam Inanna," my assistant interrupted, prompting a puzzled eyebrow from me.

"Wait, how do *you* know that?"

"You told me on Friday."

As I thought about it, I could faintly remember off-handedly mentioning the name to her at one point or another.

"I keep forgetting about your amazing memory."

"Don't worry, I will remind you."

"Thank you very much," I told her with a smile that was only the slightest bit strained before I returned my attention to the duo in front of me. "Anyways, Snowy, this is Joshua Bernstein, aka the guy you have been stalking."

"You didn't have to put it like that..." she muttered dejectedly, a response which I promptly ignored.

"So!" I abruptly clapped my hands, startling everyone present, and smiled. "Handshake!"

The two of them blinked at me in unison, but nevertheless, their hands moved as if on their own accord. They both stared at their clasped hands like they didn't understand what was happening, but after a few awkward moments, they proceeded to engage in a limp-wristed handshake while simultaneously trying to out-blush the other. I silently groaned and shook my head. They continued with the lifeless handshake for several long and increasingly uncomfortable seconds until they thankfully stopped, took a step back, and began to restlessly gaze at their toes.

At last, Josh sidled up to me and whispered, "Now what?"

"What do you mean *'now what'*? Talk to her."

"But I don't know what to say! She is acting completely..." He paused, apparently looking for the proper words. "... different from before! What did you do to her?"

"Nothing."

"Then why isn't she..." Josh animatedly wiggled his brows in the silent girl's direction. "... you know..."

"It's because she entered into the range of the chief's womanizer aura. It's like when a predator goes into another's territory. It makes them nervous and subdued. Nature in action."

I frowned at the girl sitting at my side, who by the way continued to periodically pilfer my food reserves without the slightest of reservations.

"I told you that I'm not a womanizer. Also, if you don't stop that, I will have to cancel your dental plan."

She looked back at me, fake surprise sparkling in her eyes, but her hand still moved to take the last vestiges of my lunch.

"I have a dental plan?"

"You had."

"And you removed it because I took your food?"

"Yep."

"Are we returning to an abusive relationship?"

I groaned aloud.

"Not now, we have other things to do."

"Spoilsport."

It was around this point when Snowy began slowly backing away with an apologetic smile forced onto her face.

"I'm sorry... I think I better leave."

"Wait," I instructed her, and she obediently stopped in her tracks. I placed my nearly empty lunch box back into Judy's lap and stood up, grabbed Josh by the shoulder, and pushed him towards the still idling girl on the front.

"What are you...?!" my friend protested my rough handling of him, but due to the difference in our bulk, he couldn't really stop me.

"Okay, you two. See that bench over there? Nice, secluded? A perfect place for explaining yourselves and discussing misunderstandings, don't you agree?"

"Wait, don't I have a say in this?"

"You came to me for help. Now don't complain if the medicine is bitter." With that and one last push, I shooed them away. They both looked at me funny, but at last they walked over to the bench I indicated and grudgingly sat down. I sighed in exasperation and took my seat next to Judy again.

"Playing favourites?"

"Hm?" I didn't get what she meant at first, so she nodded towards the two awkward teenagers in the middle of engaging in awkward teenager-ness. "Nah, I'm just leveling the playing field while also trying to get ahead of any annoying developments. The fewer awkward romance-hijinks there are in the long run, the better for everyone."

"I see." My assistant gazed at the two for a few seconds before she returned her attention to me. "What are they talking about?"

"I don't know. Right now they are probably looking for the right words to start a conversation while trying to avoid eye contact."

"Can't you just listen in on them?"

I awarded my assistant a flat look and lightly shook my head.

"No. I'm not going to intrude on their privacy. I'm no voyeur."

Judy was about to open her mouth, no doubt either to voice her admiration of my moral character or to deliver another of her verbal jabs. Sadly, history will never know which it would have been, as instead our conversation was interrupted by Joshua's voice.

"She's doing it again!"

I looked up and found him waving at me. Meanwhile, Snowy looked crestfallen and was looking at me apologetically. I sternly waved a finger at her, and she shrank back like a wilting flower.

"Sorry, it wasn't on purpose…"

I eyed them for a few minutes, and while it was a rough start with no small amount of stuttering, they finally began talking in earnest. It seemed like the previous intermezzo broke the ice, and while they still seemed uncomfortable, at least they were communicating.

"I see." Judy nodded to herself at my side while she plopped the last of my fish bars into her mouth. I wiggled my eyebrow to urge her to explain herself, and after she swallowed, she continued, "She got outside the effective range of your aura and she reverted."

I sighed and offhandedly answered, "Very funny."

"Thank you, I'm trying." Whether she really meant that or not I couldn't fathom, as my attention was drawn to the box on her lap. It was empty.

"Where did you even put all that food?"

She looked at the box as well, and after a second of thinking, she moved her shoulders in what, with a lot of good will, could be called a half-hearted shrug.

"Girls have a second stomach for lunch."

"Isn't that for sweets?"

I got another flat look.

"That's just silly." Saying so, she also reached back into her own bag and handed me another sandwich. "Here. Boys need to eat more."

"And whose fault is it that my lunch is gone?" I complained, but I still accepted the offer graciously. Though, as I thought about it, I didn't get to eat the ones she gave me either, did I? Weren't they in the box too?

I glanced down at the empty container again and Judy, as if reading my mind, averted her eyes with just the barest hints of embarrassment.

"You know, eating too much isn't good for your health, either," I grumbled as I unwrapped the sandwich.

"Don't worry. All the calories go to the most attractive part of my body."

"Your brain?"

She fell silent for a good five seconds before she almost imperceptibly cocked her head to the side.

"I decided to take that as an endearing compliment instead of a backhanded insult about my appearance. You got lucky."

I ended the conversation with a half-hearted *If you say so* and began munching on my newfound sandwich, but after the first bite I stopped. I chewed and swallowed it in record time before I turned back to my assistant with a question.

"Didn't I buy you a couple of chicken sandwiches?"

"You did."

I looked down at the sandwich in my hand and raised the top slice. "Yeah, this is definitely not chicken." Not only that, it had a full set of condiments and a reasonably fresh beef patty. It even had a different wrapping than the rest. "You know, if I didn't know better, I would say this is homemade."

"It is."

"Really?"

My assistant nodded. "I have more if you like it," she replied, her offer accompanied by her presenting me with a couple more similarly wrapped burgers.

"If you had these on you, why did you make me buy you sandwiches?"

"Because those were my wages."

During this whole conversation, Judy was so straightforward and made all my questions sound so oblivious that I could only groan in annoyance.

"Fine, then I will graciously accept your offer." With that, I took another bite and started leisurely chewing... at least until I noticed how fixated Judy was on my face. For the first few bites I tried to ignore her, but at the end of the day I took a deep breath and turned to her.

"Yes?"

"Are they any good?"

I blinked at her a few times, then quickly tried to give her a *that's an obvious question* look. Just to return the favor.

"Of course they are. Do I actually have to say it?"

She stared at me for a few seconds without a word before she looked away and faced forwards.

"You might be good at flirting with girls, but you lack delicacy. At this rate, you'll never find a girlfriend."

I stifled a chuckle and raised the half-eaten burger to my mouth. "I will burn that bridge when I get there," I told her and was about to take a bite when I stopped, frowned, and glanced back at her. "Also, I'm not flirting with anyone."

"Sure, Chief. If you say so."

After this point, I proceeded to categorically ignore my assistant and instead focused on her burgers (and no, there was no innuendo here), which I had to admit were surprisingly tasty. There were only a couple of minutes left of the lunch break and we spent them in comfortable silence. I periodically glanced at Josh and Snowy to see if everything was all right, but to my relief, they seemed to be getting along surprisingly well.

When the first warning bell rang before the end of the break, Snowy visibly twitched. They shared a few more words before they parted, and the girl scampered to the door. She abruptly stopped as if remember-ing something she forgot, turned around, smiled, and gave me a small wave. I returned the gesture and a second later she was running down the stairs. While all this happened, Josh returned to our side with some residual red still colouring his cheeks. Sheesh, the guy could be really hopeless at the weirdest of times. Anyways, he sat by my side and gave me a sidelong glance.

"She is strange, isn't she?"

"Not stranger than some other girls I know." At this point, Judy lightly poked me in the ribs with her elbow and I shooed her away saying, "That wasn't aimed at you. Stop it."

"I wonder if she will keep stalking me," Josh muttered at my side, com-pletely disregarding the minor commotion at his side. I shrugged.

"Probably won't. There is no point now that you are on speaking terms. If she does, just call me and I'll talk some sense into her."

"Speaking of which." My friend changed his posture so he could look me in the eye. "How exactly did you get to know her in the first place?"

It was at this time the second warning bell rang, signaling that there were only five minutes left of the break. I stood up and tilted my head towards the door.

"Let's get going. I'll tell you on the way."

PART 3

I felt unusually tired as I left the classroom a good five minutes after the long bells signaling the end of the day sounded. Mentally, not physically. It might have had something to do with my assistant being more troublesome than usual, or Snowy showing up... Or maybe, just maybe, it was because I had to spend all the breaks between the afternoon classes restraining the princess so that she wouldn't try to drown the newest addition to the entou-rage in a spoonful of water while we weren't looking. The rest of the girls also took the news with minor reservations, but they at least attempted to feign disinterest.

I let out a weary sigh as I finally arrived at the main hall, trailing the rest of the group. We dispersed near the entrance to get our shoes. I headed for mine, only to stop in front of the locker and blink a few times in disbelief.

"Oh, for the love of..." I griped under my breath as I noticed the piece of white paper sticking out from under its door, an exclamation I soon learned to regret.

"What is it? What is it?" Angie rushed up to me with the well-trained nose (or in this case, nosiness) of a bloodhound, her eyes sparkling with equal amounts of curiosity and mischief.

"Nothing," I grumbled while trying to hide the incriminating evidence.

"Oooh..." She suddenly grinned like a Cheshire cat and began waving down the aisle. "Judy, come quick! Leo got another love letter!"

I sighed and began to very, very delicately grind her temples between my knuckles.

"O-ow-ow! Not fair! Violence is bad!"

"So is spreading lies."

She broke out of my hold and glared at me in a fashion that I was pretty sure had to be a secret technique shared only between teenage girls. Meanwhile, Judy also arrived on the scene and looked over us with her subdued brand of reserved interest.

"Sorry, what did you say? I couldn't hear it properly."

Angie looked over at my assistant and was about to open her mouth, so I quickly gained her attention by clearing my throat and making a few covert grinding motions with my fists. She audibly gulped. After a moment of hesitation, she looked at me, then glanced at Judy, and at last she took a deep breath and exclaimed, "Leo just got another love letter! Bye!"

I reached after her, but she slipped under my arms and dashed away.

"I will get you for that!" I yelled while theatrically shaking my fist at her. She only grinned back at me from the entrance, as if to say *You have to catch me first!* and left with a small wave. I let my fist down and sighed in exasperation, which was followed by another as I noted the piece of paper again.

"So, is that the love letter?" Judy asked with subdued curiosity as she stood right next to me.

Despite my best efforts, my face twisted in exasperation. I had a very good idea about the sender of that letter, and I had a feeling reading it was going to be awkward enough without Judy looking over my shoulder. I could honestly do without all the hassle, especially considering the afternoon I had.

Anyways, there was no point in avoiding it. I reached out towards the locker and opened its door. The simple white envelope inside all but flew out of it as I did so, but I was prepared and caught it mid-flight. I glanced left and right before I broke it open and took out the letter.

"What does it say?" My assistant inquired quite insistently, rising to her tiptoes to get a better look. A quick glance showed that the contents weren't particularly embarrassing after all, so I lowered it to her eye level.

"Meet me at the roof. We need to talk," My assistant read the words aloud. She paused for a moment before she glanced up at my face. "Not very romantic."

"No, not really." I pocketed the letter and closed the locker's door again. "I guess I should go and see what this is about."

I headed for the stairwell but stopped after a few steps as I noticed that Judy was following after me in my shadow. I looked at her, and she gave me a *Why did you stop?* look.

"Why did you stop?"

"That was redundant," I told her, much to her apparent puzzlement. She even raised an eyebrow. A little. Anyways, I told her, "You really don't have to come along for this." She only stared at me as if she was trying to bore a hole into my head with pure force of will, so I decided to change approaches. "Why don't you wait for me here? I should be done in a minute."

She honest-to-goodness huffed (though, as usual, her expression remained the same) and turned on her heel.

"You don't have to rush things. I'll go ahead," she said over her shoulder and walked off, leaving me alone in front of the stairs with a mounting sense of exasperation.

I watched her leave without her looking back even once. I took a deep breath, cleared my mind, and headed for the roof again, but this time a bit more sourly than I'd originally planned.

I was still quite morose by the time I finished climbing the stairs, and to my surprise I found the door leading to the roof slightly ajar. That fact alone almost piqued my interest enough to shake me out of my surly mood. I carefully moved up to the exit and pushed it open with one hand.

I momentarily had to shield my eyes, but even through my fingers, I could make out the figure of a girl standing in the middle of the roof with the afternoon sun behind her. The only problem was that... well, it wasn't the girl I was expecting.

"So you've come," the princess stated in a voice that might have been ominous if she could have stopped herself from fidgeting for a second. I blinked as my eyes got used to the glare and took a step forwards. I honestly wasn't expecting her. I figured this would turn into one of those wacky scenes where Snowy would take my advice about writing Josh a letter, but accidentally put it into the wrong shoe locker. I was expecting a lot of hijinks, maybe something of a heart-to-heart discussion, possibly an opportunity to ask Snowy about her vamp act... But to be perfectly honest, I was actually okay with this situation as well. I wanted to have a private talk with the princess anyways, so her letter only switched up the order of events a little.

I gave her a small smile and closed the door behind me. "You got the key this time? Good. That means you're learning."

"Of course," she snapped at me. "Like I would make a fool of myself in front of you again!" For a moment it seemed like she said more than she actually wanted to, and she bit her lips in frustration.

In the meantime, I was slowly making my way over to her, and to my surprise, I found her constantly shifting her posture to face my direction. In fact, her stance kind of reminded me of a fencer's, just without the sword—trying to provide as small a profile as possible while ready to jump at a moment's notice. Hell, maybe it *was* a fencing stance. She was a noble archetype after all. They often did fashionably anachronistic things like fencing and riding and speaking with *thous* a lot... But back to her posture: did that mean she was on guard? Against me? The idea somehow made me strangely frustrated, so I made an effort to move as carefully and nonthreateningly as possible.

"So." I stopped at a few paces away and flashed my winning smile. "You wanted to discuss something, right?"

"R-right!" As if just remembering why we were on the roof in the first place, the princess took a huge breath, paused, and then directed one of her patented soul-piercing glares my way. "I wanted to talk to you one last time before..." She paused again, and I noticed some uncertainty in her expression, but then she steeled herself. "No, I wanted to give you a chance to explain yourself."

"About what?"

"About her," the princess spat the words out with such venomous intensity that it actually caught me off guard.

"You mean Snowy?"

"Of course I mean her!"

"Okay then. What about her?"

At this point the princess began walking, though it could have been better described as slowly circling at a fixed distance around me without breaking her guarded posture.

"I wanted to give you the benefit of the doubt. I wanted to believe you. To hell with it—I actually did believe you!" Her face twisted into a pained grimace. "Only to see you stab me in the back! I saw you revealing your true colours, and I would—!"

"Okay, stop," I stated as forcefully as I could without actually shouting. I raised an open palm in her direction. The princess shuddered and did just that, staring at me with giant doe eyes before she remembered the situation and doubled down on the glare. I sighed and continued, "You are blowing this waaay out of proportion."

"Am I? Am I really?"

"Yes. Yes, you are. Also, please stop strafing around me. It's distracting."

"S-shut up! Don't try to change the subject!"

"I'm not changing the subject, I'm changing the context." Saying so, I took a step forward and began walking toward her at an even, leisurely pace. For a moment I could see her panic, raising her hands in front of her in some kind of fancy self-defense style, but she hesitated just long enough for me to reach her. I clasped my fingers around her extended hand. The moment our fingers made contact, she let out one of her customary strings of allegedly cutesy sounds (well, okay, in this case they really were kinda cute) and tried to pull back, but it was too late. I had a firm grip on her.

Without further ado, I picked the closest bench and began dragging her behind me. She only offered token resistance, but the entire affair was a little embarrassing, so I began to talk to her with a level, serious voice.

"Listen, princess. Under normal circumstances, I would let you do as you please and listen to your woes in whatever fashion you wanted. However, as it happens, you just managed to catch me in a pretty rainy mood, and I really don't have the patience for all the bells and whistles at the moment. So, this is what we are going to do." By pure coincidence, this was the exact moment we reached the bench. Never one to miss an appropriately dramatic moment, I pointed at said bench and continued, "We are going to sit down, face each other, and talk like reasonable people. No tantrums, no circling, no vague accusations. You say what's on your mind, and I will try to relate to and answer anything and everything you throw at me. Deal?"

At first, the princess avoided eye contact and was stiff as a plank, but she eventually glanced over in my direction. For a blink of an eye, I could see her hesitate, but then she suddenly averted her face (probably to unsuccessfully hide her embarrassment) and then dropped her pretty backside onto the bench while still holding my hand.

"I hate you," she muttered, and I could only smile at the amount of sulkiness on display.

"Yes, you sure do." I sat down as well and tried to let go of her hand, but to my surprise I found her fingers holding on to mine like a vice. For a moment I thought about whether I should ask her to let go, but after a bit of brain-wracking, I decided against it. She was obviously still a bundle of nerves, and I didn't want to set her off with something like this.

"So, you wanted to talk about Snowy, right?" The question seemingly took her aback, but then she gave me a tentative nod. "So? What's the problem?"

"The problem..." She began with a level voice, but her hand squeezed mine angrily. "The problem is that you are supporting her."

"I am?"

She stammered for a moment, but then she glared at me.

"Yes, you are! You stopped me from chasing her away!"

"We are in school. Of course I stopped you from starting a fight."

"But she is seducing Joshua!"

I gave her a wry look.

"You know, I can distinctly remember a transfer student who came here with the express purpose of seducing a certain friend of mine not too long ago. Can you guess who I'm thinking about?"

She immediately averted her eyes and flushed crimson.

"S-shut up! That was completely different! I had legitimate reasons for that!"

"Really? Maybe she does as well. Have you tried talking to her?"

"No, she doesn't! It's just in her nature to seduce men, that dirty..." I was afraid she would get into an angry diatribe, but instead her voice slowly trailed off into a quiet mumble as her eyes opened wide as saucers before she abruptly yelled out, "That's it!"

"That's what? Also, careful with the volume settings there."

Suddenly excited, the princess clasped her hands together, seemingly completely oblivious to the fact that she was tugging my arm in the process.

"I figured it all out! I can't believe I didn't think of this sooner! I was such a fool!"

I sighed and gave her a look that roughly translated to *"Enough buildup, please give me the punchline."* She gave me a knowing smile and tried to point at me, but then she paused and raised her other hand instead. So she *was* aware she was holding on to me! She had to be!

"Listen, Leo!" She leaned closer to look into my eyes. "Whatever she might have promised you, whatever feminine charms she might have shown you, you have to understand that she is only using you. You have to—"

I raised an open palm to make her stop and then used the same palm to bury my face in. "Stop. Please stop. I just realized what you were getting at," I grumbled while massaging my temples with one hand. "You think I was seduced by her, didn't you?"

"Erm... You... You weren't?" I gave her a flat look, and she blinked in surprise before she exclaimed in a weird mix of worry and relief. "You weren't!"

I shook my head and let my hand down. "Seriously now, you must have a really weird idea about how seduction works."

"But... why didn't she try to seduce you?"

"Well, technically she tried..." I admitted, if only to ruffle her feathers. "I just told her to cut it out."

"You did? Why?"

"Because it was really awkward? I don't even know why she puts up the vamp act, to be honest, because she is embarrassingly bad at it. It might have something to do with her family. Or, at least, the last time I talked with her brother, she doubled down on the charade in front of him. I didn't want to pry then, but I guess I'll have to the next time I speak with her, especially so she'll stop doing that in front of Josh at the very least. They got along better once I stopped her from doing it, anyway, and... why are you looking at me like that?"

The princess twitched, then proceeded to try (and fail) to casually close her still hanging jaw.

"You told her to stop seducing Joshua?"

"Yeah."

"And she stopped?"

"Mostly. She still relapses into it from time to time, but she is making progress."

"I see... And when... did you talk to her brother?"

"Friday. On the phone."

"Do you... talk to him often?"

"Nah, it was a one-off thing. It's a long story, but suffice to say, I don't plan on talking to him any time soon. He sounded like a dick."

The princess only nodded, and it was around this time I noticed how sweaty her palm was getting. I tried to loosen my grip on her, but instead she just squeezed even harder as she spoke in a low, melancholic voice.

"You know... sometimes I wonder if I should be scared of you."

"Where did that come from?" She looked at me, ready to answer, but in the end, she closed her mouth again and averted her gaze, earning her an amused chuckle at her unusually timid display. "If it's all the same to you, I'd prefer if you weren't."

She didn't react right away, but then she faced me with a determined look in her eyes.

"I would like to, but first you need to tell me whose side you're on."

"Do I really have to? Take a side, I mean?" She only continued to stare into my soul without even twitching a muscle, so I sighed in resignation. "Fine. If you really want to know, I'm on Josh's side."

"You mean... you are neutral?"

"Kind of, but not quite," I replied while thoughtfully scratching my chin. "I have my own situation here, but as far as your little thing over Josh is concerned, I just want to maintain a drama- and annoyance-free environment which, if I may add, is a lot harder than it sounds because of certain people refusing to get a clue."

"Is that so?" the princess mumbled to herself, apparently still not getting said clue. "So you supported her to avoid... um, drama?"

"Naturally." She still seemed skeptical, so I gave her a reassuring smile. "She is actually a really nice girl once you get to know her. You should give her a chance."

"Impossible."

"Are you sure?"

"Completely."

"Even if I ask really, really nicely? I can be really persuasive." After saying that I promptly proceeded to give her the puppy-eyes treatment. Her eyes opened wide for a second, but then she swiftly turned away from me.

"Awawa! Fine, fine, just stop doing that!"

"See, I told you," I chuckled heartily for a while. "Is there anything else?"

"Just..." She hesitated before turning back to me, her eyes once again serious. "What if she still tries something?"

I sighed, partly to hide my mounting frustration, and answered, "I will do something about it."

"Do I have your word on it?"

"Yes."

"Pinky swear."

I awarded her a flat stare in place of a flat no and stood up, pulling her with me.

"You know what? We should get going. I'll take you home. I think we are done with the most pressing points. We can discuss the fine print on the way."

"Wait, you didn't promise! Also, don't I even have a say in this?"

I pointedly glanced at our still clasped hands and told her, "I figured you wanted to go home together."

Her eyes followed mine and then they opened, wide as saucers, in a show of slow-motion bewilderment. Or at the very least I really hoped it was just a show, otherwise I would've had to conclude that the princess really wasn't aware she'd been gripping my hand for a good ten minutes by this point. I mean, she had to be... The alternative was just way too silly, even for her.

Anyways, she let out a string of cutesy yelps long enough to constitute its own language and let go of my hand like it was red-hot iron.

"I-i-it wasn't on purpose!"

"I figured."

"It was an accident!"

"I know."

"I was just caught up in the heat of the moment! It meant nothing."

"Obviously. You don't need to explain yourself." She finally fell silent, though if the way she was biting her lip was any indication, it took her a lot of effort. I picked up my bag from under the bench where I deposited it when we sat down, and seeing me doing that prompted the princess to scamper off and get her own bag. She returned just as I was reaching the door, and by then she even managed to get her complexion under control and returned to a less-crimson flesh tone.

We walked down the stairs, changed our shoes, and left the school building without sharing a single word. In fact, if it weren't for the fact that the princess was sticking to me uncomfortably close, we could have passed for complete strangers. She positively refused to look my way. We were already halfway to her mansion by the time I got fed up with the silence and decided to break the ice. All I needed was a nice topic.

"You know, I'm kind of under the weather." She finally looked at me, though her reaction was still a bit slow. I smiled at her and added, "Hey, is Sebastian around? I could use a good verbal sparring match to liven up my day."

"Don't do that!" she burst out so suddenly that I almost missed a step, going from meek to her usual tone in about one nanosecond. "Do you have any idea how long he lectured me about not associating with rude people like you the last time you two spoke?"

"Really? That's nice. It means I made an impression."

"A bad impression. Don't make it even worse."

"What about Josh?" She tilted her head questioningly, so I rushed to clarify. "Did he say anything about him? Especially in comparison to me?"

"No. Not particularly."

"Really?" I clicked my tongue. "Damn, I hoped it would help."

She silently stared at me for several seconds, the gears so obviously turning in her head that I could hear their creaking in my mind's ear until she suddenly pointed at me with a drawn-out "Ah!"

"Hm?"

"You made him angry so Joshua would look better in comparison!"

"Well, no. I pissed him off because I found it hilarious, but it was a side benefit, yes. Too bad it didn't work."

Her fingertip suddenly closed the distance and poked me in the chest. "Don't ever do that again!"

"Which part?"

"All of it! It's unfair!"

"The magic word?"

She gave me a truly blank look, almost as if I'd spoken in a completely different language.

"What do you mean?"

"Please?"

"Please what?"

It took all my willpower not to bury my face in my hands. "The magic word is *please*. It's a common idiom. Don't tell me you never heard it."

She started shaking her head, but halfway through she stopped, took a deep breath, and said, "Please don't do that again."

"Oh fine. But only because you asked so nicely." I hesitated. "Still, can I annoy the old guy if we meet anyway? Just a little? For old times' sake?"

"Absolutely not."

I would have probably kept teasing her about the topic until we arrived at her home, if not for our conversation being suddenly (and rudely) interrupted by a deep and all-too-familiar voice.

"Now look at that, boys! It seems like it's our lucky day!"

"Right, boss, very lucky!"

I didn't even need to turn around to recognize the three delinquents sauntering out of a nearby alley, hands in their pockets and stepping at a rhythm like they were extras in a particularly low-budget Broadway rendition of *Grease*.

"Well, if it isn't our resident goldfish poop gang," I exclaimed with fake joviality flavoured by a spoonful of sarcasm and about a metric ton of *shit-I-am-too-tired-for-this-itude*. Sadly, our language has no adequate word to properly describe the exact emotion, but I'm working on it.

"Fancy meeting you here," the behemoth with the pompadour-to-end-all-pompadours exclaimed as he walked up to us, his two flunkies right on his heels like loyal hunting dogs. "And look at that! He has a new girlfriend this time!"

"Yeah, another pretty one, too."

"Friends of yours?" the princess inquired. Her posture straightened the moment she heard the guy's voice and now every pore of her being was emanating the same regal superiority she'd had when she first showed up at the school. It made me realize just how used I got to her dropping her guard around me as of late, but I didn't have time to ponder that.

"Acquaintances. Long story. Let me do the talking."

Once I finished whispering to her, I straightened myself, forced a neighbourly smile onto my lips, and took a long step forward.

"Wow, what a coincidence. I haven't seen you guys in a while." I rubbed my hands together and let my smile gain a bit of a wolfish edge. "Let me guess. After your last humiliation, you spent all your time preparing for our next encounter, and now you are here to show me what you've got."

"Not all our time..." the short flunky protested, albeit weakly.

The big guy—Tony, if I remembered correctly—flared his nostrils and crossed his arms in front of his chest as he thunderously replied, "We are!"

"Though it's not like we were looking for you in particular or anything..." the tall guy with the nasal voice added in a quiet voice, eliciting a snapping glare from his boss.

"Shut up, Jones! You are ruining the moment."

"Sorry, boss."

"So, what is it this time? Are we still going with literature?"

The big guy let out a short but resounding belly laugh and grinned at me provocatively.

"Nah, we are not doing that anymore!"

"I still think we should have gone with the Potter books..." the tall one mumbled, but not quietly enough to escape the notice of mister pompadour.

"I told you, Jones, we are not theme-naming ourselves after children's books characters, and that's final!"

"Actually, technically the books were written to grow up with the audience, so the last few books are considered young adult fiction," came the counterpoint from the short guy, his high-pitched voice sounding unusually dignified.

"Nuh-uh-uh! I don't give a flying crap about your literary theory, Honey Badger! We are not doing it, and that's final!"

"What was that?" I interrupted. "Honey Badger?"

"Yah!" the small guy flashed a shit-eating grin that revealed a chipped incisor. "Because they are small but tough and mean."

"I see... So you are going for an animal motif. What about you?"

"Me?" The tall guy twitched as he noticed I was looking at him and instinctively straightened his back. "I'm Giraffe Jones."

"Hmm. A bit of alliteration there. That's good. But, why *giraffe* in particular? They aren't particularly fierce."

"Oh, but they do have a mean kick! And they can run surprisingly fast. Plus they have no natural predators that regularly hunt them because they are so imposing. And they're cool."

"I see, fair enough. And you, big guy?"

Tony in the middle puffed his chest, though I was pretty sure it was just for show. As far as his eyes were concerned, they were about one-third as self-assured as the rest of his body language was insisting on. He cleared his throat like he was preparing for a big speech in front of an audience before he spoke up at a volume that suggested he had little confidence in our hearing.

"I am Tony the Elephant!"

"I see." I nodded thoughtfully, crossing my arms like an art-house critic. "African or Indian elephant?"

"I... what?"

"I said," I repeated with a raised voice, "African or Indian elephant?"

"I... I dunno. African, I guess? Does it make a difference?"

"Oh, I see." I nodded twice for emphasis. "So it's an elephant because you are big, your hairdo is the trunk, and it's African because of your ears. Clever."

"What? What is your problem with my ears? There is nothing weird about my ears—right, Honey Badger?"

"No, boss, yer ears are perfectly fine!" the little guy whined like a battered housewife, which was actually a little disturbing, but not enough to break my act.

Tony turned back to me and gave me a hurt glare. "You see, there is nothing wrong with my ears!"

"Hmmm..." I leaned closer as if I was examining an art piece and periodically nodded to myself, my insights most profound. At last, I straightened up and nodded. "Right. On closer look, your ears seem to fall into the range of the national average. I suppose your new name just predisposed me to associate big ears with you."

"Well, you were wrong! My ears are perfectly fine, right, Jones?"

"Yeah, boss. Maybe they are a bit on the meaty side, but they are nice ears. Really nice ears. No one would think they are too big."

"Unless you bring attention to them," I quipped with a smirk. The culturally ambiguous pachyderm gave me a piercing look before he threw his hands into the air with a loud "Bah!"

"Fine, then I am an Indian elephant! Are you happy now?"

"I don't know." I raised my hand to my chin again and began to scratch it. "Wouldn't that throw off your theme? The rest are African animals, so if you are Indian, then it'll look like you are separate from the rest."

"He is right, boss," the tall guy agreed with me, quite unexpectedly. "Indian elephants are also domesticated."

"Not all of them! And they are still big and mean!"

"The name doesn't fit, either," I proceeded with the coup de grâce in a purposefully absentminded voice. "If you just call yourself elephant, people will still think of African ones, and if you qualify it by saying you are an

Indian one, it'll just sound too long and convoluted. I think it would be best if you scrapped the whole elephant idea and picked something else."

"Like what, genius?" he sneered at me.

I shrugged.

"Don't ask me, it's your nickname."

"How 'bout a hippo?" the short guy proposed with a smile. "They are big and mean and they live in Africa."

"I won't be no stinking hippo!" Tony bellowed. "They are fat and they slap their crap all over the place with their tails. It's disgusting!"

"You know what?" I gave the guys a broad smile and took a step to the side. "It was nice talking to you, but we are in a bit of a hurry. How about you get back to me once you've finalized your nicknames?"

"Yeah, whatever, move along," the boss grunted at me and then returned to the discussion. "How about a rhino?"

"I don't know, boss... Won't that draw attention to your nose?"

"What's your problem with my nose?"

"Nothing, boss. It's a perfectly serviceable nose, boss, but what if other people..."

That was the last sliver of the discussion I caught before we rounded a corner and the trio was out of earshot, at which point I relaxed my posture and limbered up my shoulders with a small sigh.

"Well, that filled my people-annoying quota for the day. Now I won't even have to bother your butler. A win for everyone, I'd say."

The princess glanced over her shoulder with an uncertain expression.

"Does this happen often?"

"At this point, it's pretty regular, yes."

"You need to find better friends."

"I have. I'm taking one of them home as we speak."

I punctuated the statement in a no way cocky smile, and she predictably averted her eyes and, less predictably, punched me in the shoulder. Unlike Judy's love-taps, this one stung.

"Stop teasing me. I hate you."

"Yeah, you sure do..."

PART 4

It was a little after 10 p.m. when my phone rang, almost on schedule. I was in the middle of looking up just what character archetype fit Snowy the best. Stepford-smiler? The Pretender? The Vamp? The Vamp Pretender? More research was needed in that direction.

Anyways, I reached over my desk, right where I put my phone when I came home after I dropped the princess off in front of her gates earlier that afternoon. I didn't even look at the caller ID before I accepted the call.

"You know, I love these evening talks, but we should really get them started an hour earlier. You are not getting any quality sleep like this." There was only silence on the other end of the line, so I added a tentative "Hello?"

"Um... H-hello? It's me, Neige."

"Oh?" I reflexively sat a little straighter. "Sorry, I thought it was someone else. Hi."

"Uh, hi."

There was another round of silence, though I could have sworn I have heard fidgeting from the other side.

"Are you the one making this noise or the line?"

"What noise?"

"Rustling, mostly."

"It's me, I think. I am hiding under the blankets."

"Okay, thanks for clarifying that."

And yes, she did sound a bit strained, like she was trying to whisper loud enough for me to hear, but not too loudly. I ventured an educated guess and asked, "So your brother won't notice?"

"Yes."

"I see..." Her single-word answer was so melancholic that it momentarily threw off my train of thoughts, but then I remembered the situation and asked the obvious question I should have in the first place. "So, to what do I owe the honour of this late call?"

"Honour?"

"It... it's a figure of speech."

"Oh." Another momentary silence later, Snowy took a breath so deep it was audible on my side as well and continued in a whisper, "I wanted to thank you."

"You're welcome," I answered by reflex. "But... about what in particular?"

"For helping me. For giving me a chance. It's more than I ever deserved."

"Now, now. Don't put yourself down like that."

"You don't understand... I... I was eavesdropping on you when you talked to the blonde girl. On the roof."

"You mean the princess?"

"Princess?"

"Ah, right. Her name is Eleanor. I just call her that out of habit."

"Like you call me Snowy?"

"Yeah. Is there a problem with that?"

"N-no. I like it."

"I'm glad to hear that. Anyways, you said you were eavesdropping?"

"Sorry. I just... I wanted to thank you in person, so I waited at the entrance, but then I saw you head back, and I got curious. I followed after you." I tried to say some filler words to maintain my side of the conversation, but she abruptly continued and cut me off. "I saw you confront her. You stood up for me. And the things you said... It was the nicest thing anyone has ever done for me."

"Now you're just exaggerating."

"No, I mean it. Thank you."

I couldn't keep myself from chuckling awkwardly.

"Gosh, you're making me blush." She didn't reply to that, so I tried to take the initiative, but something caught my attention. "Wait... are you crying?"

"I'm sorry," she replied in a nasal voice. "I'm just... We barely know each other, and you are so nice to me. Too nice. I don't know what to say."

I sighed and switched the phone to my other hand.

"Listen, Snowy. I don't know your entire history, true. I don't even know that much about you as a person. What I do know is that you are nice and you deserve a chance as much as anyone else, whatever your family situation might be."

"You mean that?"

"Of course I do." I heard her sniffing on the other side and waited for her to finish. "Speaking of which, I was thinking about introducing you to the other girls around Josh."

There was another pause, this time more surprised than awkward.

"Are you sure that is a good idea?"

"Well, no, not a hundred percent sure, but it's the most prudent thing to do. If you want to talk to Josh properly instead of just stalking him, you need to be able to interact with them as well. You started off on the wrong foot, but I have already taken care of the princess and the rest should follow suit. Just act like yourself, be nice, and don't lapse into your vamping thing, and they will be your friends before you know it."

"Are you serious?"

"Sure I am."

"Thank you."

"You are once again welcome." I was about to change the topic when there was some extra rustle coming from the other side and Snowy's voice died down to a barely audible whisper.

"I have to hang up. There's someone in the hallway. I'll see you tomorrow."

By the time I could utter a feeble "Bye," she'd already hung up. I took the phone from my ear and looked at the caller ID. I didn't remember giving her my number, but now at least I had hers. I was in the middle of saving it into my contacts list when the phone rang again, startling me to the point I almost let it slip out of my hand. I grabbed hold of it mid-flight with a stifled curse and took a look at the screen, this time making sure to check the ID.

I raised it to my ear and said, "You know, I love these evening talks, but we should really move them forward by an hour. You are not getting any quality sleep like this."

"Sure," my assistant answered. "I tried calling you before. Who were you talking to?"

"Straight to the point, aren't you? Snowy called."

"Did she forget to say something on the roof?"

"So you thought the letter was from her too?" I let out a purposefully loud relieved sigh. "Thank goodness, I thought it was just me."

"So she wasn't the one who wrote the letter?"

"Nope. It was the princess." I could hear her clicking her tongue. "What?"

"Nothing," she answered even more flatly than usual. "What did she want?"

At this point I told her everything that happened after she left, in the most extensive and accurate manner possible. Well, fine, I might have changed a few things when I talked about our encounter with the goldfish poop gang, mainly to further emphasize my stellar wit and disarming charm, but I stayed true to the original spirit of the events, so it was all good in the end. Telling the entire story took about ten minutes.

"... and then I told Sebastian that he should really get a handlebar mustache to complete the look."

"What did he say to that?"

"I don't know, I was running by then."

"Why must you antagonize people at random?"

"Because it's hilarious."

Judy didn't respond to that, but instead she took a sharp left turn in the conversation and said, "Are you still saying you are not playing favourites?"

"With the princess?"

"Not her. With the stalker girl."

"Her name is... well, her name is not actually Snowy, but that's beside the point. Also, I am not playing favourites. I thought I made that clear during lunch break."

"Then you need to reevaluate your definition of *playing favourites*, because it sure looks like that from where I'm standing."

"Oh please. I'm just being helpful."

"Are you sure?"

I let out a sharp breath and leaned back in my chair. "Listen, if you want to say something, just say it."

"I think you are getting too involved."

Her answer was instantaneous. I was expecting at least some hesitation. I had to conclude that she had to be waiting for me to give her the go all along.

"Fine, fine. I might have involved myself more than strictly necessary, but it was mostly for my own peace of mind. Did *you* want to keep watching Snowy ineffectually stalk Josh until something stupidly dramatic happened? Or stupidly comedic? Or just stupid in general?"

"Even if that happens, it's their business. Weren't we supposed to only observe?"

"Well, yeah, but..."

"You specifically hid your amnesia and theories from others to keep our observations unbiased. By meddling like this, you are—"

"Fine, fine. I get it. Geez... When did you become such a stick-in-the-mud?"

"It's my job to keep you straight. I get paid for it."

"True enough." I paused to take a big breath and clear my head. "Fine, no more meddling. I will introduce Snowy to the gang tomorrow because I already promised, but I won't interfere after that."

"No more chaperoning."

"Right."

"And definitely no more flirting."

"I still have no idea why you have this weird idea about me."

"The fact that you can't perceive the problem is a problem in and of itself."

"But I don't flirt."

"Tell that to—" It seemed like Judy finally noticed that her voice was getting heated, so she quickly toned it down to her usual monotone. It still sounded a little strained, though. "Never mind. It's getting late."

"Hey! Don't just end your sentence like that and leave me hanging!"

"Good night, Chief. I am going to get some quality sleep now."

"Haaah... Good night, sleep well."

There was an affirmatory grunt and then she cut the line. I sighed and put the phone down back onto the desk.

She was right. Not the flirting part—that was still dead wrong and a misunderstanding of epic proportions—but she was right about my involvement. I'd let myself get carried away and got myself involved with

Snowy's and Josh's issues too closely. I had to agree; I really should take a step back.

With that in mind, I returned to my computer screen with renewed determination and opened my browser again. Where was I again? Oh, right...

"Maybe she is a variation of the *femme fatale*...?"

CHAPTER 13

PART 1

The date: Tuesday. The time: lunch break o'clock. The mission: introducing Snowy to the entire group. The problem:

"Are you sure this is a good idea? Maybe we should do it another time..."

I let a shallow sigh escape my mouth and turned to the girl fidgeting behind my back. We were standing just outside the cafeteria entrance. It was only a few minutes after the lunch break started, but the place was already packed with placeholders. The rest of the gang was already inside as planned, courtesy of my assistant's efforts.

After a short (and in no way heated) discussion during our morning commute, we came up with a simple plan. No bells, no whistles, no elaborate Rube Goldberg machines that would've dropped Snowy into the midst of the group (which, by the way, would have totally worked if we could only find a mouse to power a conveyor belt).

As it stood, the plan was deceptively simple: introduce Snowy in a controlled environment and make sure everyone gets along before we return to a hands-free approach and stop interfering with the group dynamics. Of course, the last part was easier said than done, but Judy was very adamant about it, so I grudgingly agreed. It didn't mean I'd stop hanging out with the guys, just that I'd stop shepherding them. In theory, at least.

Anyways, I took Snowy by the shoulder and pulled her to the front. She stepped there without any resistance; though getting her to actually move forward took a bit more effort.

"Listen, Snowy, the sooner we get this over, the easier it'll be for everyone. Think of it like removing a band-aid in one pull. It might sting a little, but once it's over, the net pain will be much lower than if you tried to pry it off slowly."

"I don't like doing it either way," she protested as I kept pushing her toward the cafeteria entrance. "I still don't think this is a good idea."

I silently groaned, took hold of her shoulders, and turned her around. I looked her in the eye. "Snowy."

"Y-yes?"

Correction: I tried to look her in the eye, but she steadfastly refused to meet my gaze. She kept silently staring at her shoes like they were the most interesting thing ever.

"Snowy. They are nice guys. I wouldn't be friends with them if they weren't. Just talk to them."

"But.... what if they—"

I help up a finger before she could continue. "Don't worry. I'll be right behind you. Just make sure you act naturally, and everything will be fine."

She nodded hesitantly, and after some further urging, we finally got past the door. The dining hall was about as busy as it tended to be around this time; its air was filled to the brim with inane placeholder-chatter, the kind that blended together into an indistinct buzz of white noise.

I scanned the premises and quickly found the gang sitting at a table in the corner, not too far from the premade foods counter. I gave the girl at my side one last reassuring smile and began walking... only to stop, turn back, and start dragging her along.

We successfully reached the table without causing too much of a commotion (hey, at this point I took that as a small victory). I would be lying if I said I wasn't at least a little worried about the girls' reactions, but I hoped for the best and prepared for the worst, as usual.

Let's count the reactions from right to left, shall we? First off was my loyal (if slightly overbearing) assistant. Her reaction was pretty much as expected, meaning exactly zilch. Then there was Angie at her side, who looked surprisingly uninterested in the newcomer, preferring to instead stuff herself like she'd been starving all morning. Josh smiled awkwardly, though probably more due to surprise than disliking the development, while the princess on his left was also trying to smile, though it never reached her eyes. Last but not least, there was the class rep, and to my disappointment, she was pretty hostile by the looks of it, though not so overtly that one would notice without looking closely enough.

Well, four out of five was still a good ratio, right? Anyways, once we were close enough, I dusted off my charmingest smile and waved at them in the most casual and friendly manner I could muster.

"Hey guys, guess who I ran into!" Saying so I stepped aside and presented Snowy with a small flourish. When she didn't move, I firmly patted her on the back to get her to do something.

She looked at the people at the table like a deer in the headlights of an oncoming truck. For several seconds she kept glancing back and forth between the faces, never lingering on one for more than a split second until she at last locked eyes with Joshua. After some hesitation her eyes softened, her lips curled up, and with a husky voice she uttered, "Hi darling, I missed y—"

She got that far before my knuckle made contact with the crown of her head. She twitched in surprise and then crouched down while protectively grasping her head. That surprised me. I didn't actually hit her. I only placed my fist on top of her head. Hell, I barely even touched her!

Anyways, when she looked up at me, I extended the same hand towards her, palm out and fingers spread.

"Five seconds. You lasted less than five seconds before you lapsed into your vamp act. Were you even trying?"

"S-sorry...!" she answered, still clutching her head like she thought I would hit her. That made me feel bad. Maybe I accidentally touched on some kind of trauma? She must have taken my silence as further proof of my disapproval, as she continued, "I... I just didn't know what else to say. I... sorry, it won't happen again."

I let out a sharp breath and shook my head while extending my hand again, this time in order to help her onto her feet.

"You don't have to be *that* sorry. Just make sure you keep it in mind."

I helped her up, and it was around this time I realized we were still being watched by the gang. I sighed and propped Snowy up, absently straightening her sleeves in order to gain a few seconds of thinking space. Ultimately, I turned to the table with a smile I hoped wasn't too forced and cleared my throat.

"We started off on the wrong foot. Let's try this again." I patted Snowy on the back, in a mirror image of the first introduction, but this time I did the speaking. "You are probably all aware of it, but this is Neige, the new transfer student, and Josh's ex-stalker."

"Ex-stalker?" the class rep interrupted, with her stern expression indicating that she was already in her authority mode.

"We... worked things out." Unexpectedly enough, it was Josh who came to my rescue.

"Really? When?"

"Yesterday, on the roof," I answered and swiftly continued before she could interrupt again. "Anyways, as you can see, she's a little awkward around strangers, so I thought I should help her out a bit as a favor from one transfer student to another."

"You never helped *me*." This time the princess was the one doing the interrupting, though if her tone was any indication, she was more sulky than confrontational.

"Really? Didn't I help you make your first friend in school?" She gave me a puzzled look, so I pointed at myself. "Me?"

She blinked and averted her eyes while muttering something about it *still* being unfair.

"Angeline, say something," the class rep pleaded to her last possible ally, who was in the process of stuffing her face with chicken wings.

"Hrmf?" She quickly swallowed and tried again. "I'm okay with her. Josh already explained what happened."

"He did?" The class rep sounded downright betrayed.

So I nudged Snowy forwards. I wiggled my eyebrows to tell her to capitalize on the situation and say what we agreed on beforehand, preferably before the class rep could come up with some other objection. She somehow seemed to understand the gist of it. She stepped forwards and bowed her head to the table.

"I... I'm sorry about the trouble I caused you. I'm really sorry. I just... I want... I'd like to be friends with you, if it's not too much of a bother to ask..."

Her voice trailed into a mumbled whisper, but it seemed the recipients of the apology got the intention nevertheless. I smiled at Snowy reassuringly as we both awaited the judgment of the jury. To my sincerest surprise, it was not Josh or even Angie that offered the first olive branch, but the princess of all people.

"Oh, fine..." she grumbled. "I accept your apology. And I'm sorry for tackling you. It might have been something of a minor overreaction on my part."

I wanted to point out that her apology sounded a bit insincere when she was glaring like that, but I decided it was better to keep quiet for the moment. The class rep gave the princess a classic *Et tu, Brute?* look, followed by a *we are going to talk about this later, prepare yourself* frown aimed at yours truly, but in the end, she sighed and dropped her shoulders in resignation.

"Have a seat."

Snowy's face lit up, though her eyes were still cautious, like a scared bunny offered a carrot. Should she take it or not?

I gave her another gentle push and she finally walked over to the empty seat next to Judy. My assistant, completely passive until this point, shook her head and pointed at the other empty seat next to the class rep.

"This one is reserved for the chief."

"Chief...?"

Judy nodded and pointed at me.

Snowy mouthed a small "Oh..." and obediently took the other chair. I followed suit, taking my *reserved* seat with a small frown, but the moment I got my backside into position, I slapped my forehead.

"I forgot to buy lunch!"

"Yes," my assistant stated at my side while she unpacked a small lunch box and placed it in front of me. "I have you covered."

"Thanks?" I replied by reflex and raised the lid, revealing three sandwiches wrapped in floral-print napkins. In retrospect, I don't know what else I was expecting. I was ready to dig in, but then something occurred to me and I looked at the white-haired girl fidgeting near me. "Snowy doesn't have anything, either."

"I got her covered too," Judy interjected and subsequently produced another, slightly smaller, box.

She handed it to me and I forwarded the package to its intended recipient while I whispered, "You are the best."

Judy nodded and simply whispered, "I know."

"T-thank you very much for your kindness."

We both looked over and found Snowy staring at Judy with teary eyes. I smiled at her encouragingly in place of my stoic assistant, but before I could say anything, the princess reached over and deposited a croissant into my lunch box. When I looked up at her, she promptly glanced away.

"I bought too much, so I thought I would share." She peeked over at me, flushed red, and averted her eyes again. "Don't get the wrong idea! We are going to have PE this afternoon, and you will need the energy."

"I see." I nodded with a smile. She was such a tsundere. "Thank you very much."

"You are welcome."

"Do you like croissants, Lili?" The question came from Josh, and it piqued my interest three ways at once.

"I... don't dislike them?" Snowy answered uncertainly, her eyes jumping between Joshua and me.

"I figured." Josh crossed his arms and nodded to himself like he'd made a major discovery. "You were looking at them so intensely."

"I wasn't really..."

"Here." To my surprise, the princess actually gave her one. "D-don't take it the wrong way, though. It's just part of my apology. For the tackling."

"I understand..." Snowy replied, though if her tone was any indication, she actually didn't. The better question was, why was the princess periodically glancing at me while she was doing this? Maybe it was her way of showing she was making an effort? I gave her a thumbs up, but she only glared at me in return, so maybe not?

"Can I have one too?" Judy interrupted, stealing another croissant from the princess's plate before she could answer.

"Hey!"

"You said you bought too much. I'm just helping."

"Oh really? Then I suppose with that extra food you don't need this sandwich!"

Saying so, the princess reached over the table and snatched away one of Judy's sandwiches. My assistant let out a crestfallen "Oh," and looked at me with the eyes of a hurt puppy.

"Chief, she stole my wages."

I wanted to point out to her that she started it, but then one of *my* sandwiches was suddenly exchanged with a chicken drumstick. I looked up and found Angie grinning at me with said sandwich in her hands, and when I raised a brow, she simply declared, "Smorgasbord!"

"That's not how a smorgasbord works," I protested dryly before turning to the class rep, who was quietly playing with her food across the table in a rare display of abject sourness. "Could you talk to her before things get out of hand?" To my sincere astonishment, she huffed and shook her head. "Oh come on!"

"It doesn't matter to me."

"You say that now, but it's only a matter of time before your food will be in danger too."

She gave me a critical look and poked her plate with her fork. "I have spaghetti. You can't exchange that."

"Ooooooh! That sounds like a challenge to me!" Angie exclaimed with a grin as she began rummaging through her bag and fished out a small plastic fork.

"Wait, no!" Suddenly drawn into the commotion, the class rep brandished her own fork with an unspoken *You shall not pass!* Initially Angie tried to circumvent her defenses, but the class rep proved to be a formidable opponent. There was no getting near that spaghetti.

"Don't be so stubborn! Just a little taste!"

"Stop it! You are being childish!"

"That's it!" Angie suddenly declared with a fork raised high like a royal scepter. "I request reinforcements!"

"You what?"

"Quick, Neige! Grab a meatball while she isn't looking!"

"O-okay..."

Snowy automatically reached out and plucked a meatball from the side of the class rep's plate with her bare fingers, but then she froze with a difficult expression.

"Um... What do I do now?"

"Eat it!" For a moment Angie sounded like a general giving absolute orders, but Snowy only shook her head.

"But... I have nothing to give in return. I received all my food as gifts. It would be rude to give them away... but it would also be rude to take this meatball without giving anything in return... Uh... I don't know what to do...!"

I smiled and was about to help her out when Josh came to the rescue once again, placing a slice of beef onto the class rep's plate.

"Here, I will cover for you."

"Beef? With spaghetti?" the recipient spoke while poking the slice of meat with her fork.

"Sorry, I don't have anything else."

"I... I'm sorry for imposing on you." Snowy practically bowed to Josh, but then turned to the class rep. "I'm sorry for the inconvenience."

The class rep seemed conflicted, but her frown softened and she lightly shook her head.

"No need to apologize. It wasn't really your—" she started, but then her attention was momentarily drawn away by having to fend off Angie's latest sneak attack on her plate. "Stop that! You are making a commotion!"

After a few stern words and glares, she actually got Angie to stop, though not before she stole her last meatball and replaced it with three chicken nuggets.

I wanted to point out that she should've done that when I first asked her, but at that particular moment, my mouth was too full of croissants to talk. By the way, they were actually quite delicious. I wondered if they were from the unreasonably fancy menu of the cafeteria or the princess bought them somewhere else?

Anyways, once the class rep finished reprimanding Angie, she turned back to Snowy, this time with a small smile on her lips.

"You should eat that."

"Oh..." Snowy looked uncertainly at the meatball in her hand, and she reluctantly bit it in half. "Hm? It's delicious."

This was the perfect opportunity to encourage her to interact with the others a bit more, so I promptly gave her a push.

"Yeah, the standard menus are pretty meh, but the cafeteria makes some nice stuff like that, too. You should ask for recommendations."

"Oh, me!" Josh raised his hand with an ear-to-ear grin. "I have some recommendations!"

"Except from him," I corrected myself while pointing at my friend with my thumb. "He would bankrupt you in a week."

"That's harsh! I didn't bankrupt you, did I?"

"You tried."

"That's a baseless accusation! Slander, even!"

"Very well, we shall settle this in court. My lawyer will soon contact yours."

"Errr... Could we just settle it as part of a friendly basketball game during PE?"

"That works too," I answered while preparing to take a bite from one of my sandwiches, but I stopped halfway. "Wait, now that you mention it... It's Tuesday. Do we even *have* PE today?"

PART 2

As it turned out, yes, we did. Apparently it was Monday's PE switched with our last history class for some reason. It might have had something to do with my previous afternoon being spent restraining the princess, but I honestly didn't notice the switch. Some observer I am, right?

With a self-derisive grunt, I hurled the javelin in my hand a little angrier than before. It flew in a beautiful arc, staying straight and true until the moment it hit the ground with a loud *thunk*, embedding its tip into the grassy ground a good five meters ahead of the second-best throw, which also happened to be mine.

"Wow..." Joshua let out an awed whistle and patted me on the back. "You broke the school record. Again."

"You are a natural!" Angie agreed, though I still didn't know what she was doing hanging around on our side of the field while the girls also had their own evaluations going on in parallel. It was about throwing these small, yellow balls made of rubber as far as they could. I didn't really see the point of it aside from providing a simple number they could pin a grade upon, but I was no PE teacher, so who knew? Maybe it did build the arm muscles. Or failing that, character.

Meanwhile, Angie continued to buzz around me, even going as far as to poke the biceps of my throwing arm.

"Maybe you were a hoplite in your previous life?"

"Hoplites didn't throw their spears," came the instant rebuttal from the class rep on my left, and no, I didn't know what she was doing over on our side either. She still seemed to give me the evil eye from time to time, but otherwise she was back to normal, which was a relief. Anyways, it was Josh's turn on the field, so he grabbed one of the brand-new red-and-white striped javelins from the pile at our side and winked at us.

"Just you watch! I think I've got the basics of your technique down!"

With that said, he raised his javelin, took a running start, and threw it with all his might. The moment it left his hand, it began wobbling in the air, and while it certainly flew a respectable distance, it still fell short, and to the right, of my second-best throw by about two meters. He clicked his tongue in frustration but still smiled.

"It's progress!"

"Yeah." I nodded and picked up another javelin even though it wasn't my turn. I waved Josh over and showed it to him. "You need to hold it a bit closer to the head, like this. Also, you need to focus on where you want to throw it and adjust your strength accordingly. If you just toss it with all your might without giving it a clear direction, you are never going to hit anything."

"But this is about distance, not accuracy."

"You know what I mean."

"Yeah, yeah..." Joshua waved his hand and then grabbed hold of the javelin in mine. "Like this?"

"No, not that close. A little lower, closer to the middle... yeah, that's about right."

"Are you giving free lessons?" This time it was the princess who came over. Her bangs were pulled into a loosely hanging ponytail, probably so that they wouldn't interfere with her activities. It actually suited her. "Where did you even learn to throw like that?"

"The Chief is a man of many talents," came the needlessly mysterious explanation from my assistant. "Throwing things to great distances is merely one of them."

"Now that you mention it," Josh spoke while hefting the javelin in his hand, "you suddenly became ridiculously good at sports. You're a menace on the basketball court too."

"And table tennis. Don't forget table tennis."

"I'm trying to, but you keep reminding me!" he grumbled as he stuck the javelin into the ground next to his feet and faced the girls. "By the way, how is the evaluation going on your side? Are you going to finish soon?"

Judy shook her head and pointed at the princess at her side. "Eleanor lost the balls, so we are on break until they find them."

"I didn't lose them! They are right over there on the field! Er... Somewhere..."

"That was a little vague," I mused as I looked over the girls' side, and they indeed seemed to be in the process of combing the field. "How did you even lose them?"

"Her throws were all over the place," Angie told me while waving in the direction of the field. "Aaaaaall over."

"That much?"

She nodded, earning a contemplative *"Huh"* from me, and after a moment of thinking, I shrugged.

"I thought she would be good with balls, being a tennis player and all, but I can certainly imagine it. She is pretty clumsy."

"Hey! I'm standing right here!" the subject of our conversation protested aloud while stomping her feet. "I can hear you! Also, I'm not clumsy!"

"You kind of are, but don't worry. It's one of your charms. Right, Josh?"

"Um... Sure?" he responded a tad uncertainly, probably because he wasn't even following our conversation.

"See, the male population is in agreement. A little clumsiness from time to time is totally all right."

The princess stared at us for a while, but in the end she turned around with a small huff.

"I'll go and help look for the balls!"

Just like that, she left our side of the field, and Angie and the class rep closely followed after her.

"Well, there she goes," I muttered to no one in particular, but then I noticed my assistant's piercing stare. I raised a questioning brow at her. "What? Did I say something wrong?"

"No."

Following that curt answer, she turned around and left as well, leaving me scratching my head.

"You know," Josh remarked while gathering up some discarded javelins, "it's because of moments like these that I can't decide whether you are good or horrible with girls."

I gave him a flat frown. I thought we were over this already. However, before I could raise the point, Josh switched gears and let out a heavy sigh, stopping me in my tracks.

"How are we going to have our basketball duel like this?"

"You were serious about that?" He gave me a look that could be roughly translated as *Duh?* and *a*fter a moment of consideration, I turned to him again. "How about after school?"

"Not today. I already have plans with Angie." Noticing the subtle signs of curiosity I was giving off, Josh took a deep breath and continued, "There's this new gyro place that opened up in the neighbourhood recently, and she's been pestering me about it for ages. I gave in this morning, so we are going there after school."

"Date?"

"Obviously not."

I chuckled to myself and waved a dismissive hand as we got into the line for the next throw.

"Fine, fine. You were the one who wanted to play. I can wait until you have a free afternoon."

My friend stopped in his tracks for a moment, and after a few seconds of thinking, his mood brightened.

"Actually, we really should do that soon. It's been ages since we hung out, just the two of us."

"All the more—" I got that far before the words froze in my throat. There was a small yellow blur in the corner of my vision, and at once my body reflexively twisted itself to the side with little input from any conscious thought. In fact, I did it so abruptly that I nearly lost my balance and fell on my butt. I managed to catch myself at the very last moment and shook my head with a frown.

"What the hell?!" Josh exclaimed at my side while holding his forehead, and I could already see a circular red bump forming on it. His question mirrored mine perfectly.

"Sorry!" the princess cried out in panic as she rushed up to us. "Are you all right?"

"I'm fine, but that came out of nowhere!"

"Sorry..." she apologized again, and by this time the initial surprise subsided enough for the little wheels in my head to start spinning again and connecting the dots. I dodged something yellow. The girls were throwing balls over there. The princess came running over. Q.E.D....

"Excuse me, but weren't you supposed to throw balls in *that* direction?"

The princess shuddered and gave me a glare that somehow also looked hurt. Don't ask me how that worked; she was a virtuoso when it came to glares, after all.

"I-indeed. It just... slipped out of my hand."

She kept glaring at me as if she was daring me to say anything else. I decided that there was no point in teasing her over an accident like this, so I shrugged and grabbed hold of Josh instead.

"Fair enough. I don't think there was any harm done. Hey, Josh, how many fingers am I showing?"

"Two?"

"See. No concussion. I bet you were more surprised than actually hurt."

"Of course I was surprised! That ball flew through your head!"

"Through my head?" I repeated after him, and Josh responded with an enormous nod.

"Not literally," he grumbled while still rubbing his forehead. "One second we are talking, the next you sway to the right and then I get hit by a ball! Dick move, pal!"

"Wait, what was I supposed to do?"

"Warn me! Or failing that, take the hit! Friends are supposed to take some hits for one another!"

I smiled and patted him on the shoulder. "Well, I guess this time you took one for me, buddy." He only frowned, so I rolled my eyes and patted his shoulder a bit harder. "Oh come on! Stop with the long face. I'll treat you to something later."

"It was a nice dodge, though," the class rep declared, appearing out of nowhere like usual. By now I wasn't even surprised. "I honestly thought it would hit you in the back of the head."

"Back of the head?"

I looked over in the direction of the field and my brows knit themselves before I even knew it. Indeed, considering that Josh was hit squarely on the forehead, and that I was facing him at the time, it meant that the ball was literally coming at me from the back... But I could distinctly remember seeing the ball coming. Well, a blur coming.

I looked at the class rep and, after a moment of hesitation, I ventured a guess.

"ESP?"

She blinked at me, but then she put her hands on her hips and frowned with the ferocity of a wounded... well, maybe not a tiger. Housecat? No, that's too mild. Let's go with *feline of unusual size*. It should cover all the bases. Anyways, she set her mouth in a line and said: "Very funny. I'm not falling for that again."

"Ack. Look at me, Josh! I've become the boy who cried wolf one too many times!"

Everyone ignored me, which hurt a little. In the meantime, Angie rushed over to Josh's side and took a look at his forehead.

"Wow, that left a mark! Are you all right? Do you feel nauseous? Should we go to the infirmary?"

"I'm fine," he protested, but his childhood friend already got herself riled up too much. Resistance was futile.

"Elly, grab him! I am going to tell Mrs. Applebottom where we are going! I'll be back in a moment!"

The princess followed her instructions, and after a little while the group, including Mrs. Applebottom, left the field to take the still objecting Joshua to the nurse's office. Since the teacher wasn't around to give them instructions anymore, the placeholders began doing placeholder things in the background, such as talking about the weather or playing around with the equipment without any rhyme or reason.

As for me, I spent most of the empty time sitting under a tree by the side of the field, near the ball-catching fence of the tennis courts, preoccupied with the possibility of me being actually psychic. That was another notch in my notes under the *Ideas I Never Thought I Would Take Seriously* header. Well, it was already obvious I could do some impossible things. Being able to view people from afar was already ESP territory, but now that I had a second *"power"* under my belt, it opened the idea up for further investigation.

"Chief?"

I looked up and found Judy looking down at me. I smiled at her and patted the ground beside me.

"Perfect timing."

She didn't say anything; she just sat down by my side and waited for me to elaborate.

"Remember my ability?"

"To flirt?"

I rolled my eyes.

"No, I mean my ability to listen and see people at a distance."

"Oh. You mean your alleged ability."

"I thought we pretty conclusively decided it was a *thing*."

"It's still not conclusive, and you haven't been using it since Sunday."

"Well, yeah…" I scratched my chin and tried not to grimace. "I just don't like to invade other people's privacy unless they invade mine first. Also, it's a little disorienting." She nodded but at the same time continued to look at me expectantly, apparently waiting for the reason why I brought it up. "Okay, here's the thing. When Josh got hit with that ball that I dodged? I could see it coming even when I shouldn't have been able to."

"New power?"

"Possibly. Or just an extension of the first one. It's the first time this happened, so I have no idea."

There was silence for a few seconds.

"Testing?" she finally asked in the most excited voice I have ever heard coming out of her.

"Testing," I affirmed with a sharp nod. "We haven't done any experiments yet, so it's about time."

"I'll go and get some tools." After saying so, she stood up and scampered away. In the meantime I moved to an out-of-view corner and prepared the area. After a minute or so Judy returned with a couple of the yellow rubber balls and two cans of soda. She promptly handed one over to me.

"Thanks?" I looked inquisitively at the drink in my hand.

"The vending machine was on the way."

"I see."

After that short exchange we both opened our cans and drank their contents in more-or-less one go.

"All right!" I told her as I rubbed my palms together. "Here's what we're going to do. You will throw a ball at me, and I will try to dodge it."

"Okay."

Without waiting for any signal, Judy threw her ball at me.

Thunk.

"Ow." I flatly declared, more out of obligation than actually being hurt, and picked up the ball at my feet. "You were supposed to wait until I closed my eyes."

"You never specified that."

"I would've, if you'd let me." I paused for a moment, only just noticing the slightly petulant edge her voice had. Normally I might not have noticed, but since our traditional nightly phone conversations started, I'd begun to focus more on her tone and less on her barely existent facial expressions. "Or... did you just want to hit me with a ball?"

"Baseless accusation," she stated and threw another ball at me. This time I avoided it, though not because of any special ability but simply by good-ol'-fashioned reflexes.

"Actually, you have been giving me mixed signals for a while. Did I make you angry without noticing?"

"Not really."

She might have said that, but she was already preparing another ball to throw at me. In fact, she would've thrown it anyways if not for a new voice entering the conversation.

"What are you doing?"

We looked in the direction of the voice and found the class rep there, her hands crossed in front of her chest.

"We are testing the chief's reflexes by throwing balls at him," my assistant supplied the information. It made the class rep visibly ponder for a moment, and then she uncrossed her arms and stepped closer.

"Can I help?"

She didn't even wait for an answer; she picked up a ball and began practicing some over-the-shoulder throwing motions.

"Not just yet," I told her with my hands raised. "Also, what are you even doing here? I thought you would go with the others to the nurse's."

Amelia stopped swinging her arms and shook her head.

"We wouldn't all fit in the room, and as the *prefect*," she stressed the word and gave me a meaningful look before continuing with, "it's my duty to stay here and supervise the class."

I nearly pointed out that she wasn't doing that at the moment, but on second thought I decided to ask, "So, you aren't worried about Josh?"

"Not really. He has a thick head."

"In more ways than one," I mumbled under my breath in a voice I thought no one could hear. Judy might have anyways, though I couldn't understand what she mumbled in reaction. Something about "pots and kettles."

I wanted to ask her to repeat herself at first, but I already had a good idea what it was about, and I didn't want to poke the hornet's nest just yet. The PE class was almost over, so if we wanted to do any testing, we had to do it quickly and without any more distractions. As such, I quickly gave the girls some basic instructions and took my place in front of the fence. I faced them, readied myself, and then paused for a moment.

"Is it just me, or do you two look unusually eager?" I asked them while following the balls Judy was trying to juggle between her hands.

She snatched them out of the air and answered in a voice about 150 percent more deadpan than usual: "It's just your imagination."

PART 3

"Remind me not to get on your bad sides ever again," I complained aloud as we walked down the stairs. "It was a complete dud, too."

The switched PE was our last class, so we changed, got our bags, and were on our way to pick up Josh and the rest of the gang from the infirmary.

"Don't worry, Chief. Next time I'm sure you will do better."

"Next time? I know you guys had fun throwing things at me, but I personally think we don't need any more testing."

Neither Judy nor the class rep answered, but they exchanged some very telling glances that somehow made me afraid of becoming a human target dummy at any moment. In the meantime, we reached the ground floor and headed for the nurse's office. Once we got there, I knocked hard on the door, and it instantly opened.

"O-ho-ho! We were expecting you."

I rolled my eyes at the overly enthusiastic greeting and entered the already crowded infirmary. Josh was sitting on the bed with Angie by his side, the girl poking his steadily growing bump like it was a candy-dispenser button. I couldn't see the princess, but before I could ask about her whereabouts, the nurse hopped before me with expectant eyes. I grimaced in annoyance, but I humoured him nevertheless.

"What's up, doc?"

"O-ho-ho! Now that you ask, I've been looking into your amnesia question. Sadly, your friend didn't provide any new revelations, as he doesn't seem to be missing any memories, but fear not! I still have new ideas that might be of use. For example—"

"Marvelous!" I answered in mock enthusiasm while simultaneously grabbing hold of Judy by the shoulder and placing her in front of the old man. "I would love to listen, but I have to check on Joshua. Please speak with my assistant."

She gave me a deadpan glare, but I just smiled back at her. After pelting me over and over again even after I called off the experiment, this was the least she could do.

With that, I slipped past them and made my way over to Josh's bedside. Somehow the class rep managed to get there already, probably by slipping behind my back while I was focusing on the nurse.

"Hey there," I greeted him with a smile. "Where's the princess?"

"Elly went ahead to get Josh's bag. She should be waiting for us by the entrance," Angie answered while still poking Josh.

"Really? We didn't meet her on the way. Oh well." Saying so, I leaned forwards, placing my hand on my chin, and looked Josh over like I was an art critic assessing the quality of a post-modern statuette. Then, nodding, I straightened up.

"Yup, you seem all right."

"Of course. I tried telling them, but no one would listen." He gestured for me to lean closer again and added in a whisper, "I worry for Mr. Peabody, though. He tried to *treat* me with a hammer."

"Oh, that?" I glanced over at the nurse, who was still in the middle of animatedly explaining something to my increasingly restless assistant. I returned my attention to Joshua and shrugged. "Yeah, he does that sometimes. Also, the proper term is *mallet*."

"Stop whispering and let's get going."

The instruction came from the class rep, who was still unusually cranky. I gave her a placating "Sure," and offered a helping hand to Josh. He obviously didn't need it, but I did so all the same.

Once we gathered everyone's stuff and I managed to peel the still very eager nurse away from my exasperated assistant, we finally left the premises and headed for the lockers. When we got there though, we were welcomed by a bizarre sight.

The princess, already in her outdoor shoes, was hugging the wall next to the entrance and peeking through the glass doors like she'd just walked out of a cheesy spy story. I didn't pay her much attention at first, but then I followed her gaze and found her looking at a large black limo parked right in front of the school gates. Angie and the class rep were still playing mother hens around Josh even as he was insisting that he was perfectly fine, and Judy was on the other end of the hall changing her shoes, so I figured I might as well check on her. I jumped into my sneakers and (please excuse the incredibly lame pun) sneaked up on the girl still staring through the door and poked her in the back.

She let out an amusing little yelp, which was expected. What I didn't see coming was the relief on her face when she turned around and realized it was me, though it only lasted for a moment.

"What are you doing?!" she hissed at me, and since saying, *"Your back was wide open and I thought it would be fun to pester you a little,"* would've made me sound childish, which I most certainly wasn't, I pretended she'd asked a rhetorical question and looked through the glass door instead.

"What are you looking at?"

She gestured towards the limousine with her chin.

"Him."

"Who?" I looked closer, and I finally realized there was a man standing by the school gate, and he was talking to... "Snowy? Ah, then that must be her brother."

"Yes." She looked up at me, her eyes uncharacteristically uncertain. "What do we do now?"

"What do you mean? We go and say hi."

"Are you crazy?" she hissed again, and tried to hold me back even though I hadn't shown any intent to actually go outside yet.

"Oh please. We are in front of a school. What's the worst thing that could happen?"

"That's called *tempting fate,*" my assistant butted in from left field, her bag already thrown over her shoulder and ready to go.

"Don't you get started with it too," I warned her wryly as, against the protest of the princess, we walked through the automatic door.

As we got closer, I was hit by a strange wave of irritation, and the longer I looked at the man, the stronger it became. It was a strangely familiar feeling, like when I first met Sebastian. Anyways, the guy in front of me was pretty big, about as tall as me, though on the lean side. He wore an expensive-looking black suit that probably had some kind of fancy-sounding Italian designer's name attached to it. It was complemented by a pair of black leather shoes and matching leather gloves.

On an even closer look, I could make out his face as well. He was moderately handsome in a slightly gaunt, angular way. It wasn't surprising considering that the same could be said about literally everyone (though his mug somehow seemed eminently punchable), and while it was hard to guess his age at first glance, I would've put it somewhere in the late-twenties range. His hair was long and lustrous like his sister's, reaching almost to his collarbone, and he wore it swept back. In his case it was pitch-black, which made Snowy's white even more striking as they stood next to each other.

Speaking of her, she seemed relaxed, but her body language said *vamp* mode again. Something about how she swayed her hips and held her arms under her chest. By the time we got into earshot, they also noticed us and fell silent, so I couldn't catch what they were talking about. In retrospect, I realized I could've listened in on them with my newfound ability, but it didn't occur to me at the time. When they faced me, I could see Snowy's façade waver, but then she eased her face into a sultry smile that didn't fit her at all.

"Hey," I greeted them both with a light wave.

"Hello there, handsome," Snowy answered with the expected purr, though I could have sworn she nearly stuttered in the middle.

Her brother looked me over like he was sizing me up (and as far as I knew, he was doing just that) until he smiled at me with that broad, eyes-half-closed, so-full-of-himself-he-is-about-to-spill-over-the-edge smile that is a characteristic of cheap bad guys who think they are smarter than everyone else in the room combined.

If that didn't make it abundantly clear, let me spell it out: I really, *really* didn't like his mug.

"Well, well, well. If I'm not mistaken, you are the boy who's been assisting my sister as of late." He paused and his smile faltered for a moment as he looked at something behind me. I only spared a glance, but it still told me that the rest of the gang had caught up with us in record time, with the princess stopping right beside me. For some reason she was breathing hard, so I figured she might've actually run the distance. Nevertheless, she stood tall and gave the man one of her patented glares. Still smiling, he looked over our group one by one, glancing over each face before his gaze returned to me, this time with a dangerous twinkle in his eyes. "It seems like you keep a... colourful company."

"Indeed I do," I answered, employing a fake smile of my own. "And you are the *Esteemed Elder Brother* of Snowy, if I'm not mistaken."

"Indeed." He took a step towards me and removed his thick black leather glove from his right hand before offering it to me. "Noire Irdu Inanna."

I was about to raise my hand in return when the princess at my side hissed a sharp "Wait, don't!" at me... which I promptly ignored and proceeded to clasp the guy's hand anyways. Even though it wasn't particularly cold outside and he was wearing a glove, his hand was surprisingly chilly.

His smile widened for a moment as he began to squeeze, but then as I began to squeeze back, it immediately got overlaid by a surprised frown, which then abruptly boiled into a death-glare before the smile returned once again. It all took less than a second, but it was enough for me to cement my initial impression of this guy. He truly was a pompous asshole of astronomical proportions.

"I'm Leonard Dunning. It's a pleasure to make your acquaintance."

"The pleasure is mine," he answered in a deceptively pleasant voice, and I flashed another toothy smile at him.

"Are you perchance about to take Snowy home?"

"Indeed."

"Oh, that's a pity. We were just about to invite her to hang out with us. You see, there's this new gyro place nearby that we are just dying to try out. Right, Josh?"

"Y-yeah..." my friend muttered uncertainly, which was understandable under the circumstances. He probably had no idea why we even got into this situation.

The big brother (whom I was not going to call Noire, because it sounded pretentious as all hell, and I have standards) gave my friend a good, long look, and after a few seconds, his smile crept back on his face.

"I see. I think it would be inappropriate for an older brother to interfere with his beloved sister's social life." He faced Snowy next. "Very well. You may go out, but I expect you to be home before curfew." Not even bothering to wait for her response, he turned to Josh again and grinned. "Please let my sister take good care of you."

"Um... sure?" Josh mumbled, even more confused than before.

"That sounded really corny."

"What?" His eyes suddenly snapped at me, the murderous sparks once again twinkling like tiny firecrackers.

"I said, that sounded dumb. I'm sure it sounded way cooler in your head, but it really wasn't. It had something of a creepy uncle vibe to it."

The guy's smile hardened and his voice dropped into a dangerously low rumble.

"Are you trying to pick a fight with me, boy?"

"Naaaaah. Me, picking a fight with you? What could have given you such a strange idea?"

We stared daggers at each other without blinking, each trying to out-fake-smile the other. In the end, big bro let out a wheezy chuckle and shook his head.

"And here I thought we could be friends."

"No, you didn't."

"You are right. I didn't." After our short exchange, he paused for a long beat and looked over me with something of a slasher smile. "Here's a bit of friendly advice. I suggest you be careful on your way home, young man."

Now it was my turn to let out a derisive chuckle.

"Oh please. That's the second thinly veiled death threat I've received from an unnecessarily well-dressed man in the past week, and yours is by far the less impressive one."

For a moment the guy's smile threatened to dissolve into a full-blown glare, but then he stopped and for some reason spent several seconds staring at his still ungloved right hand. At last, he put on the missing glove and turned back to me with a surprisingly neutral expression.

"Then let me put it this way: I might be a nice man, but some of my friends are a *lot* less amicable than I. You had better make sure you watch your mouth, or they just might take offense in my stead and... well, let's just say you wouldn't want to meet them in a dark alley."

With that, he gave us a shallow nod and turned around in a way that was most likely meant to be dashing.

"You see, Crowey? I knew you had it in you."

He twitched a little at the mention of his brand-new, off-the-cuff nickname, but didn't turn around. He walked up to the limo and tapped its door with his finger. It opened seemingly by itself, though I figured it was someone hiding behind the darkened windows that did it. He got inside after sending me one last death glare. I grinned in return, though he probably didn't see it as the car lurched forwards the moment he closed the door behind himself and disappeared down the street.

Everyone was silent for a few seconds, then the girls seemed to let out their breath in unison. I looked over with a flat "What?"

"Why did you have to do that?" the princess burst out.

"Do what?"

"All that!"

"The Chief is a man of many talents," my assistant stated dryly. "Pointlessly infuriating people is merely one of them."

"Yeah, yeah. How about we get going?" I gestured for Snowy to come over, and she did so without a word. Needless to say, the moment her brother left, she dropped the vamp act and returned to the awkward girl we all knew and loved.

"That was foolish," she blandly said, though if her eyes were any indication, she was much more rattled than her voice had indicated. "You shouldn't have angered my brother."

"Nah, this would have happened sooner or later anyways. I told you, I already knew we wouldn't get along when I first talked to him."

In the meantime, I began walking and the group grudgingly followed after me.

"What did you call him at the end?" Angie posed the question after she elbowed her way to the front. "Crowey?"

"Yeah." Her eyes—and everyone else's—urged me to explain. "His name means black, but calling him a raven would have made him sound too cool, so I went with a crow instead. It also rhymes with Snowy."

"I was meaning to ask," Josh interrupted before I could fully explain the profound thought processes that led to this nickname. "Why are you calling Lili *Snowy*?"

Now it was the class rep's turn to butt in.

"The better question is, why are you calling Neige *Lili*?"

"Huh? I thought that was her name?" He glanced at Snowy. "Was I wrong?"

"No. I don't mind."

"Oh, that's a relief. For a moment I thought I messed up."

"No, it's fine..."

"Excuse me?" Now it was the princess's turn to interrupt. By now they might as well have passed a baton around and made it official. Anyways, she pointed at me and said, "You said you already received a threat this week. Who was it?"

"Hm? Sebastian, of course. Who else?" I thought my comment about the person also being sharply dressed would have made that clear, but apparently it didn't.

"How come this is the first time I've heard about this?!"

"Oh come on, it's not like he actually meant it. Well, at least I don't *think* he meant it. Or did he?"

"I have a better question," Judy declared, grabbing the proverbial baton for herself. "Are we even going the right way?"

We stopped in our tracks, and everyone was looking at me.

"What? How should I know?"

"I see," Angie declared as she came to the front and puffed her chest out. "It is time for me to take over this expedition! Follow me!"

With that, she began walking in the exact same direction we were walking in before. We all looked at each other, gave a shrug, and followed suit. In retrospect, this was the very first time all of us had hung out at once, yet at the time it felt nothing special. As they say, though, sometimes it's the simplest things that create the best memories.

INTERLUDE

"Good night, Chief."

"Sleep well. I'll see you tomorrow."

There was a sleepy grunt of agreement on the other side and my assistant ended the call. I removed the phone from my ear and checked the call time. We'd talked for nearly two hours. It was almost midnight. I exhaled in a shallow sigh before I put my phone down. I still didn't need any sleep, so it didn't really matter to me how long we talked, but one of these days I needed to learn how to send her to sleep a bit earlier. Staying up so late couldn't be good for her health.

The fact that it was midnight also reminded me of something else as I walked over to the calendar hanging on the living room wall. I gazed at it a little before I reached out and tore off the front leaf.

"It's already October," I whispered to no one in particular. Hungry for my customary midnight snack, I headed for the fridge. It was stocked with fresh essentials, a testament to the dedication of the invisible ninja maids who maintained my household when I wasn't around. Well, at least I liked to imagine they were ninja maids, for lack of a better explanation.

Anyways, when I opened the fridge door, my eyes were caught by a small lunch box on the bottom tray. It took me a second to recognize it, but then I remembered that the last time Judy was over for one of our brainstorming sessions, she made a couple of sandwiches for us. By the way, I still didn't understand why she was so fixated on sandwiches. I'd seen her in the kitchen and I knew she could cook (well, she could certainly cook better than me at the very least), but whenever I asked about it, she changed the subject.

But back to the point: I took out the lunch box and opened it up. While the bread of the three sandwiches inside was slightly stale, I decided to eat them anyways. With that decided, I returned to my room and sat down in front of my sparkling new computer.

I'd bought it a few days before, and while it was a bit of an overkill specs-wise, especially considering that I only used it to browse the web and edit text files, I decided that if I had the money, I might as well use it. I grabbed the mouse and dismissed the classic hyperspace screensaver. I cracked my fingers, wiggled them over the keyboard, and got ready to write up my latest observations and theories, but then stopped. The reason for that was painfully prosaic: I had nothing. For a few minutes I tried wracking my brain, trying to remember something peculiar or interesting, but I came up blank.

Ever since Snowy joined the group almost exactly three weeks ago, nothing had happened. Well, okay, that might have been overstating things a little, but it was still true. While there were tons of small adventures, wacky situations, and amusing group activities almost every day, nothing particularly extraordinary happened. No new member for the entourage, no sudden drama from left field, even Snowy's prick of a brother didn't make good on his threats. Not that I was really complaining about that last bit, but still.

While our days were far from dull, they also became a bit of a routine. Gone were the exciting and dread-filled days of the first week, when everything was new and exciting and scary and ripe for observation and experimentation. What we had instead were fun but ultimately unsubstantial days, just like... well, just like normal life.

It wasn't just my life, though. Things had quieted down around Josh, as well. After the first day, the entourage incorporated Snowy surprisingly easily. While at first there were some sideways glances when she was around, by this point she was as integral a part of the group as any of the other girls, hanging out with us both at school and outside. Just last weekend she even came around for the second *What's-her-face the Werewolf Huntress* marathon (season 2 and some of 3). She was spending most of her time either at my side or at Joshua's when I was looking, though according to Judy she was getting along with the others whenever I wasn't around.

The princess was also making strides to accommodate her, though on the other hand she still seemed overly cautious and tried to stick around with me whenever I was talking to Snowy in what she probably considered a casual and no way suspicious manner. Needless to say, it was neither. Oh, and since we're talking about the princess, by this point there was a full-blown cold war between her and my dear assistant, though when I confronted them, they both denied the accusation. It was pretty obvious that I was the source of the friction, but for the time being, I decided to play things safe and let sleeping lionesses lie.

So, just to reiterate: my past three weeks weren't particularly eventful, and while I didn't really mind it overall, a small part of me at the back of my mind found the situation awfully dull and disappointing.

Regrettably, that wasn't something worth noting in my research, so I quietly closed the document, cracked my fingers again, and decided to spend my time in a less productive but infinitely more fun way: watching children's cartoons and then overanalyzing their themes on forums to the point where even the fans of the series would wish me to hell.

Hey, don't look at me like that! Everyone needs a hobby.

CHAPTER 14

PART 1

"Good morning, Chief," Judy greeted me at our usual meeting spot.

"Morning," I answered offhandedly before leaning closer to her face. She didn't flinch, though she seemed a little confused by my behaviour. I squinted. "Just as expected. You have circles under your eyes."

"It's your fault," she replied with the tiniest of pouts as she started walking, urging me to catch up with her. "You talk too much and it gets late by the time we finish."

"Excuse me? Aren't you the one who keeps calling me in the middle of the night even though I keep telling you to make it earlier?"

"I told you I can't make it earlier. My parents would notice."

"And why is that a bad thing?"

For a moment it seemed like she would answer right away, but then she closed her mouth and made me wait for a few seconds. "It would be awkward."

"I don't see what you are getting at," I told her, but before I could ask her to clarify, we both noticed Joshua down the street waving at us, and thus the conversation quickly got forgotten.

"Hey guys," he greeted us with a toothy smile before falling in line on my other side. "What were you arguing about?"

"We weren't arguing," Judy answered flatly while retrieving her phone, an action I have long since identified as her way of jumping out of a conversation she didn't want to take part in.

"Really? It looked like one from where I was standing." Josh paused, then said with a knowing smile, "Oooh, I get it. It's one of *those* quarrels."

"What are you talking about?"

"Oh, you know." His smile gained an impish quality that would've been more at home on Angie's face. The girl was a bad influence on him. However, before I could form an eloquent answer, we rounded a corner and the sight in front of us once again derailed the conversation.

It was a rare sight, the princess and Snowy together, all by themselves. Less surprisingly, the two girls seemed to be staring daggers at each other, and even at a distance, I could tell that Snowy was in her vamp mode. It was all in the body language. Anyways, Josh and I looked at each other, then hurried our steps. Trouble was coming.

Once we got close enough, I could make out snippets of their conversation, though their growling made it somewhat hard to understand.

"I'm just saying, you have to make up your mind!" Snowy hissed with a glare that looked wholly alien on her face.

"It is none of your business!" the princess answered, her glare obviously being much more natural.

"It is! I care about both of them!"

"Oh really? Then who needs to make up her mind? You or—"

It was at this point that the princess noticed us, and she paled as she frantically tried to bite back her words.

"Morning," I greeted them both with an innocent smile. The princess nodded in response, though her eyes were still wide open and she seemed to be mortified.

Meanwhile Snowy was flushing red. She cleared her throat and kept sheepishly glancing between us.

"Um... Hi. I didn't notice you coming."

"Right..." Josh muttered before flashing an awkward smile. "I guess we should've called out to you earlier, huh?"

"Hindsight, it's twenty-twenty," I said with a shrug before turning to the still pale princess. "Is everything all right?"

"Yes," she squeaked, and before I could say anything else, she turned on her heel and rushed down the street with what I presumed was one of her muffled cutesy squeals.

"Well, I haven't seen *that* reaction in a while," I whispered, then turned to Snowy. "What were you two arguing about?"

"Um... I can't... I mean... It's girl stuff. "

"Oh... I see."

"You can tell me then," Judy suddenly declared while pocketing her phone.

Snowy looked at her and her mouth seemed like it was about to say *no*, but then she paused, obviously thinking hard, and then nodded.

"Good girl," my assistant cooed, which sounded quite weird with her usual flat tone, and patted Snowy on the head. When she noticed my slightly surprised expression, she gave me a questioning look and stopped rubbing her head with a final motion that managed to give the white-haired girl the mother of all cowlicks. "Is there a problem?"

"No, I was just surprised how familiar you two were acting, that's all."

"I'm just doting on my cute junior."

"I see."

In the meantime, Snowy straightened her hair and the four of us fell in line and continued our morning commute. For some reason, my assistant was really adamant about voicing her opinion on how I couldn't stop her from being friendly with Snowy even if I tried. I had a feeling there might've been some hidden subtext there, but for the love of me, I couldn't figure out what it was.

We arrived at school with about ten minutes to spare. I nodded at the armband guy by the gate, as usual, and he coldly returned the gesture as though he disapproved of my presence, whether I was on time or not. Our group broke apart, switched shoes, and banded together again with the perfect timing of a well-oiled machine. We were already walking up the stairs by the time I noticed something that should have been blindingly obvious already.

"By the way, where's Angie?"

Josh shrugged his shoulders. "Early morning tennis practice. They're going to have a tournament soon."

"Really? She never mentioned it..." I responded, but as far as I knew she might have. She had a bit of a motormouth, so keeping track of everything she said could be a little challenging from time to time.

Once we reached our floor, we said goodbye to Snowy, and the rest of us headed for the classroom. I made a special note of Angie, who was sprawled over her desk and all but snoring. She wasn't a morning person to begin with, so I figured the early practice knocked her out cold. I couldn't see the class rep at her desk, so I scanned the room and found her standing over by the princess. Josh and I made our way over to them, and Judy wordlessly followed.

"Morning," I greeted the two with a reserved smile.

"Good morning, Leo," Ammy answered reflexively, but then she frowned at me, earning a raised eyebrow in turn. "Is this your doing?" she asked, gesturing to the princess.

I followed her motion and took a closer look at the girl in question. She was sitting by her desk as usual, and while she had her head down and buried in her arms, said pose wasn't unusual enough (at least for her, considering her previous outbursts) to justify the class rep's question. I looked over to Josh, and he looked just as confused as I felt.

"Hey, Elly? Is everything all right?" he asked tentatively while reaching out a hand. The princess twitched and shook her head while it was still buried in her arms.

"Shut up! I don't want to talk to you!"

"Ouch, princess. That's harsh," I remarked, at which she shook her head even harder.

"Shut up! I don't want to talk to you, either! Leave me alone!"

We all looked at each other and the class rep gestured for us to move to her desk. We all did so before she asked, "What happened?"

"We don't honestly know," I told her. "She had a fight with Snowy this morning, but it didn't seem that serious."

"About what?"

"No idea. They stopped when we got close," Josh supplied the answer this time around.

The class rep didn't say anything and glanced over to the princess, concern clearly showing on her face. After a little consideration, I dusted off my best reassuring smile and tapped her shoulder to get her attention.

"Don't worry about it. I'm sure they will make up in no time."

"I don't know. Telling you off is one thing, but she chased Joshua away. That's not normal."

For a moment I debated whether I should get offended by her jab, but I decided it wasn't too far off from the truth, so I changed the subject instead.

"Judy said she would get the reason out of Snowy, right?" I nodded towards my assistant and she awkwardly nodded back. "Until then, let's give the princess a little personal space. Don't stress over it."

The class rep didn't seem 100 percent satisfied with my suggestion, but she relented, and everyone returned to their seats without bothering the princess. Of course, since she was sitting right in front of me, it was a little harder for me to ignore her, but somehow I managed to restrain my nosiness.

It was almost time for the lesson to start when my phone vibrated in my breast pocket. I sneakily took it out and took a peek at the sender. Judy. I shot her an inquisitive glance. She shook her phone in her hand, which probably indicated I should read her text message. I rolled my eyes and opened said message, and before I knew it, my eyebrows were already climbing my forehead in surprise.

Somehow, my assistant managed to write about five hundred words in the span of the few minutes since she'd sat down. Not only that, it was an extremely dry message that sounded more like a formal letter than something a teenage girl would write... except that it was also full of emoji and other emoticons, half of which I'd never even seen before. In retrospect, I suppose her writing style reflected her personality surprisingly well, but it was still a little jarring at the time.

Anyways, to sum her message up: it said she'd exchanged texts with Snowy and promised she would tell me what the two were arguing about in private. She also warned me not to get too involved in what was happening and to just observe. I sighed and sent her back a quick reply of grudging agreement.

To put it bluntly, I wanted to get involved, even against Judy's wishes. While this fight in the morning did shake up the ennui I was falling into, it also smelled like drama, and I really, really didn't want to have that. Either way, our textual conversation ended when Mrs. Applebottom showed up and we began another perfectly average school day.

PART 2

At the end of the following break, Judy and I went outside to talk, hunkering down near the stairwell out of earshot from the placeholders.

"You can't tell me?" I exclaimed in a bout of incredulity-induced carelessness. My assistant looked at me disapprovingly and shook her head, so I toned my voice down a little and asked, "Why?"

"Neige made me promise I wouldn't tell you."

"Me in particular?" She nodded. "Okay, so how about you tell it to Angie and I ask her?"

"Chief, please don't try to rules lawyer me."

"Yeah, right. Sorry."

She might've taken pity on me, as Judy soon leaned closer and whispered, "It concerns your social life. She didn't want me to tell you because she didn't want to cause complications for you."

Well, that was a hint. Snowy was a good girl, so it was something I could imagine her saying, but it didn't make me any less curious (or worried) about exactly what their fight was about.

"All right then, time for Plan B."

"Plan B?" Judy repeated after me with a quizzical slant on her face.

"Lunch break on the roof. We are going to gather the entire gang and force Snowy and the princess to interact and make up."

Judy's eyes ever so slightly narrowed at my proclamation.

"That sounds like interfering to me."

I set my jaw and frowned at her comment. "Yes. Yes, it is."

"I thought we agreed we wouldn't interfere."

"So you would rather see our friends going at each other's throats?"

Judy's expression darkened and she returned my frown.

"That's a dirty question."

"Your answer?" I pressed, and after staring daggers at each other for a few seconds, she let out an indignant huff.

"Fine."

"You see, I knew you would come around."

"Don't stretch your luck. I will start to hate you if you keep doing that."

"Sure, sure," I placated her with a smile. "Okay, I'll take care of the princess, you get the others."

I wanted to make some plans, but then the bell rang and we had to hurry back to the classroom.

Once lunch break rolled around (meaning two boring lessons later), I gave Judy the sign to start gathering the others. We didn't agree on a sign beforehand, but I hoped my thumbs up and winning smile gave her the right idea anyways. At least she did leave the classroom in the direction of the stairwell, probably going to get Snowy, so that was a start. As for me, I had the much more difficult task of convincing the still lethargic princess to come along with me. I waited for Josh and the rest of the group to leave before I limbered up my shoulders and proceeded to tap the princess between the shoulder blades.

She automatically glanced back, but when she remembered that she should be sulking, she quickly hid her face again.

"Leave me alone. I told you I don't want to talk to you."

"Yes, but that was in the morning. Now it's lunchtime."

"Shut up. I told you to leave me alone."

"Oh please..." I stood up and circled around her desk. "Listen, despite my best efforts, I still don't know why you are sulking like that, but you can't just skip lunch. It's bad for your health." She didn't answer, so I leaned closer and whispered in a low voice, "If you don't come to eat with us, I might be forced to do something really embarrassing."

She visibly shuddered and, after a few seconds of tense silence, she peeked up.

"Such as...?"

"Well, for starters, I might have to pick you up and carry you to the roof." I could see her eyes widen behind her bangs. "In fact, I will do it in a princess carry. It would be fitting."

"You wouldn't..."

"Wouldn't I?"

"I-I will scream and call you a pervert!"

"You do that anyways. People are used to it by now."

"I-I-I will bite you then! I will bite you really hard!"

"A small price," I told her as I leaned even closer. I wanted to tease her a little more, but instead when I got closer, she jumped out of her chair with an especially long and loud squeak and nearly headbutted me in the process. It seemed like she was about to dart away, so I instinctively reached after her and grabbed her by the hand. The moment I did so her voice abruptly cut out and she gave me one of those rare doe-in-the-headlights stares. I shook my head and flared my nostrils.

"Why does everything have to be so complicated with you? Come on, let's go." I started to drag her along, but she held on to her desk.

"W-w-wait!"

"What now?" I asked as I faced her again. "Do you want me to carry you after all?"

"No! Absolutely not! It's... I need to get my wallet and..."

"Don't worry about it, it's my treat." Saying so, I continued dragging the beet-red girl after me, and thankfully she stopped protesting by the time we exited through the door.

Even though we stopped by the cafeteria to get a pair of lunch boxes (which were tricky to carry since I had to keep holding on to the princess, lest she run away), we managed to get to the roof with at least forty minutes left of the lunch break. Once I opened the door and the princess looked through, she spoke up for the first time since we left the classroom.

"I thought it would be just the two of us."

"I don't remember ever saying that," I answered coyly. "Come on, let's not leave the others waiting."

I walked up to the gang sitting on the benches near the far corner of the roof and raised my hand still clasped on the princess's as we got close.

"Sorry for being late. I was weighed down a little." I looked over to the girl at my side and smiled at her, and even though it seemed like she was fighting against the urge, she returned the gesture in a fashion.

I took that as a fairly good indication that she wouldn't try to run away once I let go of her hand, so I did just that and focused my attention on Snowy instead. To my surprise, she wore a disapproving frown that was directed as much at me as it was at the blonde girl.

The princess seemed to share the sentiment, as she made it a point to sit as far from the white-haired girl as possible. We weren't off to a good start. I needed an icebreaker.

"The weather is getting chilly, isn't it?" I opened the conversation.

"Yeah," Angie nodded with an exaggerated shiver. "Winter is coming."

She gave me a meaningful look like I was supposed to react to that.

"Was that a reference?"

Angie set her lips in a thin line of disapproval and casually snatched away a croquette from my lunch box.

"Hey! What was that for!"

"It's punishment for being an uncultured swine," she stated before throwing the croquette into her mouth. More importantly, though, she was derailing the conversation, so I subtly signaled to Josh for support.

"That may be," he started uncertainly, "but I think Leo has a point. Soon we won't be able to have lunch breaks up here. Should we move to the cafeteria?"

"I don't know," I spoke while theatrically rubbing my chin. "What do you guys think?"

I purposefully asked the question while glancing over at the princess. She obviously received my intention, as she immediately shuddered.

"I... I don't know."

To my surprise (and dread), Snowy scoffed.

"What was that?" the princess responded eagerly, with one of her customary glares.

"Nothing," she said brazenly while opening her own lunch box. "I don't think any of us were expecting you to come to a decision in the first place."

The princess dangerously narrowed her eyes at the comment, and I had a feeling this was about to erupt into a full-fledged catfight, so I extended my arm between the two.

"Whoa there, guys. Calm down."

"I am calm," Snowy answered with a small pout.

"No, you are not," I countered. "Why are you picking a fight? It's not like you."

This time it was the princess's turn to snort, which then shortly turned into a derisive chuckle.

"Right, like you would actually know what she's like."

Contrary to my best efforts, it seemed like the situation was only getting worse by the second. Worse still, Snowy suddenly stood and slipped into her vamp persona with a throaty, "What was that?!"

Not giving an inch, the princess also sprang to her feet with a glower.

"Blood is thicker than water. You might try to act like the good girl, and I played along because Leo asked me to, but I am not going to—!"

I was about to stand up as well to cut between the two, but before I could do that another voice cut off the princess's words.

"Stop it! Stop fighting!" Josh yelled out, startling everyone present, including me. There was a moment of silence, but then the princess let out a harsh "Hmpf!" and strode towards the roof exit before I could grab her. Though, to be honest, I didn't even try. This plan of mine had turned into an unmitigated disaster, and keeping the princess around against her will would have only made things worse.

Once she left, Snowy let out a pent-up breath and slowly slouched back onto the bench next to Josh without a word and began eating with morose movements. For a minute or two, the rest of the group kept sharing uncertain glances with each other, but began eating in silence too. Needless to say, it was probably the most unpleasant group lunch we ever had.

It didn't mean I stopped thinking, though. In fact, the situation was driving me crazy. I wanted them to get along. I wanted *everyone* to get along. I hated to see them at each other's throats like that, and the possibility that my meddling made it worse left me with a pang of guilt I was unfamiliar with.

I was so immersed in these thoughts that I barely noticed as, one by one, everybody left the roof. In the end there were only two people left, Judy and me. She moved to my side and whispered, "It didn't work out."

"No, it didn't," I answered bitterly. "I don't know what to do now."

"Nothing?" she proposed. "We should stop getting involved and get back to research."

I finally snapped. "But there is nothing to research anymore!" I yelled, and immediately regretted the outburst. I hid my face in my palm with a groan. "Sorry. I didn't mean to shout."

Judy didn't answer, but I could see her nodding from the corner of my eye. By that point I was too dispirited by my own words to care, though. It was an unspoken truth I'd been chewing on for the better part of a week. Sure, there had been a few additions every now and then, but as far as figuring out the nature of this place was concerned, we'd hit a roadblock the size of a mountain.

We had quite firmly established that this world was running on the logic of a school life harem series, and we described and tested most of the elements related to that, but by now we'd run out of even those. Worst of all, said research brought us no closer to the answers to the *How?* and *Why?* questions, arguably the most important ones we had to solve.

I was broken out of my momentary lapse into depression by a soft hand tapping on my shoulder. I glanced up and found Judy holding on to me with a pained expression beneath her poker face.

"You need to relax, Chief. You're getting unhinged."

I chuckled in self-derision and, looking up at the sky, took a deep breath.

"Yeah, I think stress is finally catching up with me." I didn't want to tell her, but I figured it didn't help that, due to my lack of need for sleep, I had an extra eight hours per day to ponder over these things. It wasn't healthy in the long run.

"You could use a date then." My gaze snapped back at her, and this time, the laugh forcing its way through my teeth was genuine. She looked at me funny for a moment before she added, with just the barest hint of pouting in her voice: "Well, it worked for me."

"I know, I know," I replied while trying to rein in my chuckles. "Maybe you are right. Are you volunteering?" She nodded sharply. "Very well. I'll think about it. For now, we should get going. The break is almost over." I stood up and Judy followed suit. We were almost at the door when I stopped and turned to her. "By the way... thank you."

She hesitated for a moment, but then a small smile took hold of her lips and she answered, "Don't even mention it, Chief. This is what I'm here for."

PART 3

Needless to say, I couldn't really focus on the afternoon classes. Although to be perfectly honest, I never paid that much attention to them to begin with. My sleepless condition left me with plenty of free time to study whenever I wanted to take my mind off of certain things, which often happened these days. There was only one problem this time: I was *trying* to study, but I couldn't. I had no idea why, but I had a sense of foreboding rising in the pit of my stomach, and it always broke my concentration. It must have been the stress, I concluded.

At long last the final bell rang, and I couldn't help but sigh in a mixture of relief and exhaustion. The princess in front of me sprung to her feet before the chime even finished, which would have been rude to the teacher if she didn't immediately cut herself off as usual. I almost smiled about it. I got so used to her cutting the lessons short that I didn't even take note of it under normal circumstances.

Anyways, as I was saying, the princess stood up and glanced back at me. When our eyes met, she gave me an indignant "Hmpf!" and stormed out of the classroom. It reminded me of her behaviour when she transferred, but after all the time I spent with her, her cold shoulder felt especially chilly and even a bit distressing.

I tried not to dwell too much on it, and instead I waved to Judy, signaling for her to wait for me. The others left while I was packing my bag, probably expecting to meet us by the lockers, but I had other plans. I waited for my assistant to come over before I stood up.

"Are you available this afternoon?"

She gave me a quizzical look in turn.

"Date?"

"No," I said, while trying to keep the exasperation from showing in my voice. "I'm still thinking about that."

"You see, Chief, this is your problem. You are indecisive."

I sent a critical look in her direction and followed it up with a mocking little nod.

"Maybe I am. But back to the actual reason why I wanted to talk to you: I wanted you to tell me what the princess and Snowy were fighting about so that we can figure out a way to defuse the situation."

Judy shook her head. "I told you, I promised—"

"I know," I interrupted with a hand raised to stop her. "I know, but I cannot deal with this situation without knowing why it happened. If you cannot tell me outright, at least give me a clue."

Judy looked around, probably to see if any placeholders could overhear us talking, though I couldn't fathom why. Those guys were still as flaky as ever, and letting them hear anything wouldn't have meant much. After a while she gestured for me to move over to the windows, out of earshot. Once we were there, she hesitated, but at last she took a deep breath and spoke in a hushed but deadpan voice.

"You are aware that Eleanor likes you, right?"

I nodded. "Yeah, she is tsundere about it, but it makes it all the more obvious. What of it?"

My assistant looked at me like I just said something incredibly dumb, so I wiggled my eyebrows to urge her to continue.

"If you know that much, how can you not figure out the problem? Chief, you are supposed to be smart."

I grimaced and rubbed my face before I spoke again.

"Fine, let's just presume I'm an idiot. How is she liking me and her fight with Snowy related?"

"It's *because* she likes you, and you are stringing her along," my assistant finally spilled the beans in exasperation.

"No, I'm not," I denied. "I'm just being friendly."

"No, Chief, you are flirting with her. Constantly."

"I'm definitely not."

She shook her head and leaned even closer.

"Even if you don't think you do, that's what it looks like, and she certainly takes it that way."

"But... even if what you say is true, it shouldn't matter. She loves Josh."

Judy stayed silent for several seconds after this. Soon she took out her phone and began tapping on it. I waited patiently for her to finish, and at last she turned the screen in my direction. It was a page from her notes, one about the tropes related to romance stories, with *Love Triangle* highlighted. I let out a scoffing laugh and shook my head.

"Come on, Judy. I admit that I might've muddled the waters a little with the princess, but she is the closest thing a harem narrative would have to a main heroine! Even if she did develop a sweet spot for me, there is absolutely no chance she would favor me over Josh. This whole conversation is—"

"Chief," Judy cut me off with the utmost seriousness as she crossed her arms under her chest. "You have already caused bigger changes to the standard template, and it is blindingly obvious to everyone that Eleanor has a crush on you. This includes Joshua as well. Please stop trying to pick this hill to die on and face reality."

"Seriously?"

She nodded at my question, and I couldn't stifle the groan escaping my mouth.

"I knew things were brewing in the background, but a love triangle? With me in it? Really?"

As if waiting for the moment to deliver the coup de grace, Judy suddenly declared, "If you are still unsure, I can tell you, with one hundred percent certainty, that you are in a love triangle. There is no question about it."

Oh, great. And now she was giving me a roundabout confession, too? I mean, I already knew that Judy was interested, but even if I wasn't, I would've had to be both blind, deaf, and stupid not to recognize the subtext in that declaration.

However, this was not the time to get bogged down in *that* discussion, when I already had so much on my plate, so for the moment I shelved it for a more opportune time and returned to the topic at hand.

"So, that means that I am the one who caused this whole mess? Marvelous." I exhaled sharply and shook my head to clear it. "But how am I supposed to fix *that*? And how is that related to Snowy? Don't tell me she—"

And then, right in the middle of that question, my entire world turned literally upside down. Well, maybe not *literally* literally, but close. There was a flash of nausea washing over me that went away as fast as it came, and when I blinked, the world before my eyes appeared inverse, kind of like I was staring at an old photo negative. I barely had time to process the sight, though, as there was another short flash and the scenery returned to normal.

"What the hell?!" I exclaimed as I took a step back and blinked repeatedly. On second thought, things weren't normal after all. As my eyes adjusted, I quickly realized that suddenly all the colours around me had been muted and gained a purplish hue. Not only that, but the walls, the desks, even the people were covered in eerie, glowing hairline cracks that covered them in spiderweb patterns. Speaking of people—all of them were abruptly replaced with generic, faceless mannequins frozen in place. They were grey, completely bald, and featureless.

"Judy?" I looked at my assistant, and to my shock and horror, she was also missing, replaced with a mannequin with its hands crossed in a mirror image of hers. I reached out and touched its shoulder. It felt hard but strangely warm to the touch, and as I moved my hand, I could feel small jolts of electricity when it came in contact with the glowing cracks.

"Okay," I whispered as I took a deep breath. "I either went crazy, or something is really, really *wrong* here..."

I leaned closer and tried to peek at the mannequin's face, and to my shock, I found Judy looking at me... but then her face was gone and I was looking at a featureless ball again. It was as if the two images were overlaid on each other, fading in and out as I was looking at it. I reached out again, grabbed hold of my assistant/mannequin's shoulder, and gave it a good shake.

"Judy!"

There was another flash of light and the two images abruptly snapped together in front of my mind's eye. I blinked in surprise, and when I opened my eyes again, I was face-to-face with my assistant. Her eyes were wide open, and it looked like she was frozen in the middle of crying out in surprise. Instead of that, she closed her mouth and very slowly looked around the room.

"Chief... what just happened?"

"I'll be damned if I know," I answered honestly as I let go of her. "One moment we were talking and in the next..." I gestured vaguely towards the classroom. "... this happened."

We didn't have much time to think about the absurdity of the situation, as suddenly the entire building was shaken.

"Earthquake?" I exclaimed in surprise.

Judy stumbled forwards, but I managed to catch her. As I did so, however, something in the edge of my vision caught my attention and drew it to the field outside the window. I had to double-check to make sure I wasn't seeing things, but once I was certain, I tapped Judy on the shoulder and pointed at the sight.

"Please tell me you can see that too."

She followed my pointing hand and after a few moments of hesitation, she nodded in the affirmative.

"If you mean Eleanor and Neige, then yes, I can see them."

"And...?" I urged her with a question while trying to keep the confusion-infused panic from buckling my voice.

"They have horns."

I let out a sigh. Good. I wasn't going crazy, then. The entire world was going crazy. That was soooo much better!

I unconsciously began taking slow and measured breaths.

Right, I needed to keep calm.

Calm people live, hysterical people die. Panicking wouldn't solve anything. Learning about what's going on solves things, not panicking. Calm, good. Panic, bad.

Following that line of thought, I leaned on the windowsill and squinted to take a better look. Snowy and the princess were facing each other on the grassy field near the footpath leading to the sports field. They were still wearing their school uniforms, but even from this distance, I could see that they had changed.

The princess was standing in what looked like a martial arts stance and her hands were covered in something dark red. At first glance I might have rationalized that it was some kind of glove, but then she also sported several horns. From the place I was standing at, I could see a pair of long, ridged red horns in a flat S shape arching over her head at a slight angle, while between those there were three smaller, flat horns ending in points—two smaller ones and one big one in the middle. Looking at them together reminded me of a crown, or at the very least an oversized diadem.

I couldn't take as good a look at Snowy, as she was slightly farther away, but she seemed to have a pair of horns as well. Hers were shorter and curled downwards, framing her face instead of arching over her head. Then, right as I was looking at her, her uniform exploded off her body as a pair of large, leathery wings emerged from her back. Once even the last vestiges of her clothes had disintegrated into something resembling blue fire, I could finally take a better look at her. Now she was dressed in something that I could only call a black leather fetish outfit that left most of her skin uncovered. She also had long black boots that reached up to her thighs, and if her posture was any indication, they ended in stiletto heels.

Most importantly though, now she sported organic-looking wings that fanned out behind her before they began slowly flapping and taking her to the air. A small corner of my mind tried its hardest to inform me that wings of that size would never be able to lift a person. Another, much louder part of my brain, however, was way too occupied with the fact that *she had bloody wings* to care about such details. I mean... holy mother of cheesecakes, how was one supposed to think straight after seeing something like that?!

Well, as it happened, the pair on the field gave me a perfect reason to do so, as suddenly the princess lunged forwards and raised her right hand in a clawing motion, swiping at the white-haired girl before she could take to the air. Snowy responded by pointing her hand at the other girl, and in a split second, a pillar of ice materialized in front of her, which the princess promptly tore apart like it was made of Styrofoam. The sight made the blood run cold in my veins and all the confused, intrigued, and terrified thoughts vying for the attention of my frontal lobe were silenced by one overwhelming impulse that seared through my mind like a blazing star.

"I have to stop this!" I exclaimed as I turned around and dashed out of the classroom in an adrenaline-fueled frenzy. I burst through the half-closed door, tearing the flimsy sliding apparatus off its buckles, and darted towards the stairwell. I somehow managed to cover each turn of the stairs in less than three steps even while weaving between the frozen mannequins, and reached the ground floor faster than I thought was humanly possible. I dashed down the alley between the shoe lockers and, to my momentary horror, I found that the automatic doors of the main entrance weren't working. I had no time to look for another exit. In retrospect, what I was about to do was incredibly foolish, but in my defense, I was pretty out of it.

So, I ran back, got down into a runner's start, and sprinted towards the still closed entrance. I figured that the doors must've been made with safety glass to avoid accidents, so I planned on using my shoulder to ram right through it. Since there was a set of stairs on the other side, I even prepared a plan for jumping off towards the left side where I had a better chance of landing on the grass instead of the paved walkway in case I couldn't stop my momentum. Well, *plan* might be too strong of a word for my hastily cobbled together ideas, but hey, at least I was trying.

Nevertheless, I was still woefully unprepared for what was about to happen. On my last step, I braced myself and rammed the glass... only to pass right through it. The unexpected lack of resistance made me stumble for a moment, which I tried to salvage by jumping forwards and rolling like I "planned." My hang-time was actually much shorter than I expected, but I hit the ground fairly well, though I was certain I got some light bruises out of the affair. I got onto my feet in a moment, but when I looked back, I froze. I was on the grass a good three meters from the edge of the walkway, way further than I even hoped I could jump. Under other circumstances I would've been shocked and wondered what just happened, but then a low, rumbling noise from the direction of the field erased any such stray thoughts and I broke into a sprint once again.

I rounded the main building at a pace where a single missed step could've introduced my face to the ground before I could even blink. I didn't care, though—my adrenaline-fueled heart was beating in my ear like a war drum and tuned out any thoughts not related to getting me to the girls even faster. I reached the field under the classroom window and came to a stumbling halt. They weren't there.

All around were signs of some outrageous battle, including what appeared to be several-centimeters-deep claw marks on a tree and a giant icicle stuck in the ground with moisture condensing around it in a fine mist. I looked left and right, trying to figure out where they had gone, when another low rumble shook the ground under me. It was soon accompanied by a loud, pained scream.

I could practically feel the blood escaping my face, and my legs took off in the direction of the noise before I could even consciously note that it was coming from the track field. It made sense in retrospect, I suppose. Where else would they find a large open field for their battling needs?

Once I got closer, I caught a glimpse of them. Snowy was flying low while chucking spear-like double-ended icicles at the princess, who in turn was circling around her in a mad dash while periodically dodging any projectiles that came too close. For those she couldn't dodge, she swatted them out of the air with her forearm, which also caused her to stumble momentarily before she resumed her sprinting.

After one such occasion, she threw her hands back and opened her mouth wide. The low growl coming out of her throat made it obvious that she was the source of the periodical rumbling I experienced. However, it wasn't just a roar that came out of her mouth, as it was immediately followed by, for lack of a better description, a searing bright red laser beam. It wasn't an actual laser, though, as it moved slower than the speed of light (not to mention it was visible), but it was wicked fast.

Snowy spun in the air and avoided the brunt of the beam, but she lost a lot of altitude in the process. She came to an abrupt stop just a couple of meters over the ground and raised both of her hands over her head. As she did so, a number of those long icicle spears started forming over her hands, floating and rotating around their axis as they grew to the point where the middle one was thicker than her thigh.

Seeing that, the princess dug her feet into the ground of the field and opened her mouth again. This time, there was no immediate roar. Instead the ground itself began pulsing as a steadily growing pinpoint of crimson light appeared in front of her mouth.

Just then I jumped over the railing separating the track field from the rest of the grounds, and I forced my aching legs into one last, desperate dash. My entire vision shrank into a tunnel as I pushed my adrenaline-addled body to its limits. I covered the thirty or so meters at Olympic speeds and came to a screeching halt between the two of them, planting my feet so hard I wouldn't have been surprised if I'd left skid marks behind me. I flung my arms wide, pointing one open palm at Snowy and the other at the princess, and yelled so hard it made my own ears ring.

"WHAT THE BLOODY HELL DO YOU THINK YOU ARE DOING?"

There was a moment of silence, only broken when the ball of light in front of the princess's face popped out of existence with, fittingly enough, a quiet *pop* reminiscent of a bursting bubble. The face it revealed was priceless, and I might have even found it amusing if I wasn't in the grip of a fury so cold it could freeze stars. Snowy's expression wasn't any better either, and she visibly shuddered as I looked at her.

"Snowy, get down from there this instant! And put those away—you are going to poke someone's eyes out!"

"Y-y-yes!" she squeaked as she all but fell to the ground. Her hands made some sort of gesture and the icicles floating over her head began sublimating out of existence.

Once I was certain they were gone, I turned to the princess.

"And what do *you* think you were doing?" I growled at her with a mixture of outrage and disappointment. "You could have killed her!"

"I..." She shrank back like a frightened kitten even though, if their fight was any indication, she could've probably broken me in half like a twig. She averted her eyes and mumbled, "It wasn't real dragon fire. It wouldn't have killed her. Probably."

"Probably?!"

She twitched and lowered her head in shame.

I groaned aloud and waved both my hands. "Come here, both of you."

The two looked at me, and then each other, before they both lowered their faces again and shuffled over to me. Now that blood finally began to return to my adrenaline stream, I calmed down a little and took the opportunity to look at them a bit closer.

They were both bruised, and Snowy had what appeared to be a shallow scratch on her leg that had already stopped bleeding, but otherwise they didn't seem to be seriously hurt. That was good. A closer look also shone a light on a few uncertain things from before. What from a distance looked like red gloves on the princess turned out to be her hands. They were now covered up to her elbows in small red scales that had a pearlescent shine to them, and her fingers ended in short but vicious-looking claws instead of nails. A quick glance at her legs revealed that she had scales on them, too, reaching up to her mid-thighs just under the hem of her uniform's skirt. Speaking of skirts, there was also something unusual on her butt, or rather protruding from above her butt: a thick, somewhat prehensile lizard tail. I could also see a little bit of her belly peeking through her disheveled clothes, and it was covered in larger, flesh-toned scales, yet her face seemed completely normal aside from the horns above her forehead which, I had to admit, gave her a regal appearance.

A glance at Snowy also revealed a number of new insights. The fetish gear I saw on her from a distance appeared to be a lusterless, leathery-looking black material that was sticking to her skin like it was fused with it. It didn't change the fact that it barely covered her body though, as it was hardly more than a thong, a pair of long boots, an X-shaped set of straps covering her breasts, and long-sleeved gloves that reached up almost to her armpits. All she needed was a whip and she could've been mistaken for a dominatrix, if not for the large black wings on her back, currently folded in a way that made them look deceptively small, and the thin black tail ending in a spade.

I stayed silent for several seconds on purpose before I channeled my best "disapproving parent" impression and slowly shook my head.

"I am disappointed." They lowered their heads again, and I used the opportunity to bonk them over the head (careful to avoid the horns) before I continued with, "Also, I'm angry."

"Sorry..." Snowy apologized reflexively.

"Sorry," the princess parroted her half-heartedly before adding, "but it was your fault, anyway..."

"Excuse me? I couldn't hear that," I raised my voice, and the princess fell silent with a shudder. I let out a ragged breath and raised her face by putting a finger under her chin. She looked at me sheepishly for a moment before she tried to avert her eyes. I pulled her head in the opposite direction so she had to look at me, and once she finally stopped trying to avoid my gaze, I told her, "Listen, Elly. I am aware of the reason why you two were fighting. I know this whole mess is, at least partially... *mostly* my fault. One of these days we both have to sit down and come clean, but this is neither the time nor the place. Can I ask you to be patient a little longer?"

She nodded, albeit feebly. Once I was done with her, I turned to the white-haired girl fidgeting by her side.

"As for you, Snowy, I can understand the princess starting a fight. She has a bit of a temper," I paused and set a frowning glance at the person in question. She stifled an embarrassed yelp and lowered her head again so hard, for a moment I was afraid she wanted to ram me with her horns.

Once it became clear she was just embarrassed, I turned back to Snowy and continued. "However, I thought you knew better than that."

"Sorry... I... I just wanted to help."

"How is fighting your friends helping anyone?" She stayed silent for a few seconds, so I extended my hand and rubbed her head where I'd thumped her before. "I know you were meaning well. I'm not really mad at you for that, but I really don't want to see my friends hurting each other." I paused and gave her a stern look. "Also, what is with this getup?"

"Is that really your biggest concern?" my assistant inquired while walking up to us. She tried to appear prim and proper, but from her heavy breathing, I could tell that she was running at least part of the way.

"Of course? Who goes into battle in a thong and high heels? It's completely impractical!" Meanwhile, Judy reached me and began to pat me. "What are you doing?"

"You have grass on you," she told me flatly as she continued to dust me and straighten my clothes.

"Judy?" the princess finally spoke up after several seconds of hesitation. "What are you doing here?"

"I followed the Chief," she replied without taking her eyes off me.

"Speaking of which, what are *you* doing here?" the draconic girl exclaimed like she'd just noticed something extremely unusual.

"What do you mean *what are you doing here*? I followed after the sounds to stop you from hurting each other."

"Yes, but how did you enter the Restricted Space?"

"The what?"

"She probably means this place," my assistant whispered as she reached up to dust my hair. "It seems to be a copy of the real world."

"Oh, so what you actually wanted to ask was how I entered the creepy purple zone of convenient battlefields?" I paused meaningfully before I smiled and confidently stated, "It's a secret."

"What do you mean it's a—"

"Stop right there!" A new voice suddenly startled all of us as a large crack opened in the middle of the track field. Although to be precise, that crack wasn't actually on the ground, but in midair. A split second later, the shimmering purple fissure snapped open into a circular portal and a short figure burst through it, landing in a pose straight from an action manga. She was dressed in a long, frilly green dress with detached sleeves and more bows and ribbons than I could shake a cane at. At first her head was hidden under a wide-brimmed witch's hat, but then she raised her silver staff high into the air.

"In the name of the Critias School and the authority of the Assembly, I command you to stop this foolishness!"

There was a flash of green light in the large emerald set into the tip of said staff, and with a loud rumble, the earth erupted behind her as a huge stone hand rose out of the soil, soon followed by the rest of a large statue with giant hands and an almost comically small head.

Once the stone creature was out in the open and towering over her, the girl twirled her staff and tried to strike a menacing pose... only to notice our deadpan looks halfway through and nearly drop her rod in surprise. At this point, all I could do was rub my face in exasperation.

"Class rep... what are you doing?"

She blinked at me from under the brim of her hat and leaned on her staff, probably more for the sake of appearances than for actual support.

"I thought you were..." she began while pointing at the two transformed girls before she pointed at me instead. "And you! What are you doing here?"

I let out a groan and rubbed my face even harder. By now the last of the adrenaline left my system and I suddenly felt really tired and nauseous. In other words, I was rapidly losing my patience, and thus I answered, "I'm a super-duper mega psychic savant demigod who can pierce the veil of time and space so long as he is fueled with homemade sandwiches."

She looked at me wide-eyed for a second.

"Really?"

"No!" I exclaimed with righteous indignation and hid my face behind my hands before I shook myself and set my jaw. "I am too tired for this. Could you please get a change of clothes for the girls and let me think for a few minutes? In fact..." I turned to Snowy and the princess, both of whom were still standing in the exact same spot. "You guys should go with her. By the next time we meet, I expect you to be fully clothed, hornless, and completely friendly. Got it?"

They tentatively nodded, and after some further shooing, the three girls left through the hole the class rep opened in the air. I waited for a while after they were gone before I turned on my heel, marched up to the closest bench by the field, and promptly dropped my backside upon it with a pained groan. Right now my legs were shaking, and I was covered in cold sweat.

"Bloody... hell..."

"Are you all right?" Judy came to my side with an alarmed expression that looked even more unusual in the strange lighting conditions. I shook my head.

"No, I am not all right." I rubbed my eyes with one hand, and by the time I was about to speak up again, I found myself wrapped in a pair of soft arms. I looked up and found myself face-to-face with my assistant.

"You looked like you could use a hug."

I stared at her for a while and then let out a chuckle, patting her hand that rested on my shoulder.

"Thanks. I suppose I do."

We stayed like that for a minute while countless recent memories and terrifying revelations kept swirling in my head and threatened to overwhelm me. Hell, if I was a little slower getting between them, I could have died! Or even worse, one of them could have died! The mere idea made my stomach churn. At last, I gestured for her to let go of me.

After a few minutes of molar-grinding and breathing exercises, I finally managed to get my thoughts in order and prune off every irrelevant one in favor of focusing on the one that was most important and useful at the moment.

"Judy?" I spoke softly as I stood up. My assistant perked up and looked at me with what passed for being really excited for her. I took a deliberately slow breath and exhaled the same way before I spoke again. "Get your notes."

She did so without further ado. I waited for her to finish poking at her phone and only continued once she gave me the go.

"All right. Here we go. This is what we know for sure. This is not just a harem comedy narrative. It also has supernatural and, if what we saw just now was indicative, battle shounen elements."

"Battle shounen?"

"It's... it's a pretty varied genre, but if I had to sum it up, I would say it's a genre of fiction that focuses on personal combat with various flavours of superpowers. Think of people shooting beams from their hands while shouting the names of their attacks, highly visible ninjas, and silly spiky hairstyles."

"I see. I think I got it."

"So, as I was saying, the more important thing is that we also have supernatural elements. That means magic, which means we can pretty much throw all our previous notes about the world out the window."

"Literally?"

"Feel free to do that, but you cannot expect another phone from me until your next birthday."

"How about Christmas?"

I awarded my assistant a critical look that roughly translated to *Do I look like I'm in the mood for this?* She didn't seem to read faces very fluently though, forcing me to voice my exasperation.

"Do you *really* want to throw out your phone that much?"

"No, I'm just exploring all possibilities."

I sighed and continued, "So, the point is this: all the inconsistencies and weirdness we have seen in the world can now be dismissed as 'it's magic.'"

"Including your *Far Sight*?"

"Far Sight?"

"Your alleged ability to watch people from afar."

I snorted and began pacing in a circle in front of Judy. Right, that ability was "alleged" because I didn't want to use it. I guess I was in a bit of denial. I didn't want magic to be a thing in this world because I was afraid of how much of our research it would invalidate. That said, at this point there was no point in crying over spilled milk.

"I don't know if my *Far Sight* is magic or something unrelated. We don't even know exactly what constitutes 'magic' in this world." I glanced at my assistant with a small smile. "By the way, I like the term."

"I found it on the internet. I'm glad you like it," she answered without looking up from her phone. In the meantime, I continued pacing up and down, as I found it helped me think.

"Anyways, since everything weird we've seen thus far *could* be magic, we have to completely change our approach. Instead of cataloging everything strange, we should figure out what can and cannot be done with magic in this world, and only focus on the things that are *still* weird by this place's logic."

"Should we go through the list now?"

I thought about it but shook my head.

"No, we can do that later. For now, we should note the new things we learned first. Such as this." I waved my hand around to indicate the entire field. "What did the princess call it, again?"

"Restricted Space."

"Right, thanks. This is probably some kind of phantom zone. It's not uncommon to have these in battle shounen stories—copies of the real world without any noncombatants, where people can fight without worrying about collateral damage."

"Convenient."

"Indeed. It might also have some kind of time-dilation effect."

Judy raised her hand to stop me for a moment.

"It's sixteen seventeen now. We entered just after the last lesson was over, so... around fifteen fifty?"

"Let's go with that. Please check the time once we get out in case I forgot."

"Understood."

"Now, where were we?" I looked around and made note of one of the broken icicles lying in the middle of the field. "Right, the girls. By the looks of it the princess, Snowy, and even the class rep are all involved with this Restricted Space phenomenon. Not only that, they are..." I paused, unable to find the right word.

"Magical?"

I shrugged my shoulders at the suggestion.

"A little broad, but I've got nothing better. As for individually, I'm fairly sure the princess is a dragon girl, and the class rep was obviously a witch or wizard or whatever."

"Chief, you are getting sloppy with your terminology."

"Well, excuse me. I'm only guessing based on what I can see. Can *you* tell what she was?"

Judy lowered her phone in order to place a thoughtful finger over her lower lip in a show of pondering before she answered, "Magical girl?"

"That is a completely different genre."

"I'm only guessing based on what I can see."

"Oh, ha ha. Less snarking, more constructive input please."

"What about Neige?"

"What about her?"

"You didn't say what she was."

"That's because I don't know. Considering the wings, I would say she might be a dragon girl too, but she didn't have scales and the way she was dressed was more like a demon girl."

"That sounds accurate to me."

"Maybe, but calling her a demon of all things sounds a little silly."

"Maybe a succubus?"

"That's... hm. That's actually a distinct possibility. Write it down."

"Way ahead of you."

"Good." I nodded and let my eyes wander for a little while, only to be inevitably drawn to the ice spears again. As I did so, a new idea reared its head in my mind, and I frowned to myself.

"She was using ice."

"Yes."

"And her name means snow."

Judy looked up from her notes and cocked her head to the side.

"Coincidence?"

"I doubt it. We also have a 'Dracis' who is a dragon. We might have a case of meaningful names on our hands. I think we should look into the names of everyone we know. There might be some sneaky references hidden there."

"Roger. Is there anything else?"

I fell silent for a minute or so in order to get my thoughts in order again before I continued speaking.

"All right. Here is a rudimentary action plan for the near future: First and foremost, we need more information. If there really is a masquerade going on, I doubt we can find anything in the public domain. That leaves us with investigating what we come across and interrogating the entourage."

"Interrogation. Understood. I'll go get my pillows and comfy chair."

I blinked at her and after taking a second to process the image, I promptly rolled my eyes.

"Was that a random Monty Python reference just now?"

"Yes. Is there a problem with that?"

"No... I just wasn't expecting it."

"Of course. No one expects the Spanish Inquisition reference."

I palmed my face with a cynical chuckle.

"Damn, I walked straight into that one. I'm getting tired."

"Should we call it a day?"

I looked around and shook my head.

"No, the purple zone doesn't seem to go anywhere just yet, and there are still some things to discuss. Such as the interrogations," I paused and pointed at Judy. "I was actually thinking about leaving it up to you."

"Really?"

I nodded firmly and began pacing again.

"Yes. Thinking back on some choice discussions with the princess and the class rep, I think they are convinced I already know about the masquerade. Asking them to explain the basics would mean I would have to reveal my amnesia, and already too many people know about it for my liking."

"So you want me to approach them as a newcomer and ask them for the basics?"

"In a nutshell, yes."

Judy gave me a firm nod.

"I can do that."

"All right. The second issue is that I unwittingly made some enemies in the past few weeks that might be more dangerous than I expected. I need more info on Sebastian and Crowey. If this really is a battle shounen, it might come to some kind of supernatural slugfest I am woefully unprepared for, so I need any advantage I can get. I will take care of that part once you give me the basics of the supernatural world so that I won't raise too much suspicion."

My assistant absentmindedly nodded and looked up from her notes.

"Understood. Anything else?"

"Too many things to count, but these are the most pressing ones." I stopped pacing for a moment and frowned at my surroundings. "I wonder how much longer it will take for this purple zone to end."

"Maybe it doesn't? It could be that it has to be dismissed by the one who made it?"

"Hm. Could be, though we don't even know whether the princess and Snowy made this or if it's a natural phenomenon. Also—"

Just then, as per the unwritten laws of conventional timing, the world around us began to wave as a low buzz filled the air. A moment later there was a flash of blinding light, and by the time I stopped rubbing my eyes, things were back to normal. I looked at my assistant, still sitting on the bench, and she muttered, "Speak of the devil."

"Yeah. Time?"

"A moment... It's sixteen twenty-nine."

I looked up at the sky and clicked my tongue.

"The sun is roughly in the right spot, and it seems most of the students have left. There was probably no time-dilation, but check your clock anyways. It's better to be safe than sorry."

"Very well. What should we do after that?"

"Go home?" I answered with a shrug. "You need some rest and I have a full night of research ahead of me."

"You need some rest too."

"Nah. Research is how I take it easy."

Judy was obviously unsatisfied with my answer, yet didn't press the issue. As we were heading for the main building, I noticed three figures coming from the opposite direction. It didn't take a genius to figure out who they were.

"There you are!" Amelia exclaimed once she got within earshot. She had changed her clothes and was back to her school uniform. I was a little disappointed about that, as I really wanted to take a closer look at her dress under better lighting conditions. Oh well, maybe next time.

"Is everything all right?" Snowy followed up on her heel with a worried question. She was back to normal, and wearing a spare uniform that was about two sizes too large. "We were worried when you didn't come back."

"Well, we're here now. Let's go home."

"Wait," the princess interrupted. "Weren't we supposed to... um... talk?"

I slowly shook my head.

"Sorry, but not today. We are both high-strung and tired. It's not the best time to discuss relationship topics."

"You're right."

"Aren't I always? Let's sit down sometime, once we are both in better shape. Oh, and Snowy?" I gestured for the other girl to come forward. "This is an order for the both of you: No. More. Fighting. By tomorrow morning, I expect you two to be the bestest friends again, understood?"

"Tomorrow?" the class rep interrupted with a hand on her glasses. "Where are you going?"

"Home? This has been a long day."

"No, you won't," she declared, now definitely in her authority mode, and she folded her arms in front of her chest. "We need to talk."

"Class rep... I just told the princess I'm not in the right shape to talk. What makes you think I would turn around and have a talk with you?" She tried to answer but I silenced her with a raised palm. "Don't even bother arguing. We are going home and we'll talk tomorrow. Agreed?"

She scowled at me for a while, but at the end of the day she relented with a small huff.

"Fine."

"Thank you for your understanding," I told her with a smile and gave a small wave to the three of them. "See you all tomorrow. Stay safe."

Judy mirrored my goodbyes at my side and we headed back to the classroom to get our bags. On the way, I couldn't help but sigh in exhaustion. This day was bad. All things considered, this was the first time I wished I was able to sleep at night. As things stood, I would've given an arm and a leg for a couple of hours devoid of thinking.

CHAPTER 15

PART 1

I started the day with an enormous yawn. I would've liked to say it was only because of habit, but frankly, I was completely out of it. Spending the entire night frantically scouring the web for information does that to people, I supposed.

It was worth it, though. Or so I hoped, at the very least. My deep dive into symbolism and interpreting names and certain terms the entourage used the day before bore some fruit, though the results were mixed at best. Still, it was a step forward. Not to mention getting lost in research let me cool off a bit, which was a good thing. While my shock was quite palpable this time, it was nowhere near as bad as my first brush with existential crisis way back when I first figured out the nature of the world, and the same medicine worked just as well this time.

Anyways, back to the fruits of my research: a good portion of the information I gathered was public domain knowledge about mythology and the supernatural, but there were some juicier nuggets hidden between the lines whenever the island of Timaeus got mentioned. I didn't feel prepared to jump into the supernatural side of this world just yet, but at least I wasn't completely in the dark anymore, and that counted for something.

That said, I limbered up my shoulders as another yawn escaped my lungs and I headed for the shower. It was a bit ahead of my usual schedule, but during our unusually short phone conversation last night, my assistant and I agreed to head to school a little earlier so that we'd be able to have a tactical discussion. With that in mind, I washed up in a hurry and capped my morning ritual with a simple but filling breakfast.

I left the house a good half an hour earlier than normal and headed for the usual intersection. Judy wasn't there yet, and while under normal circumstances I would have waited for her, this morning I decided to head straight for her house. When I got close to her place, I had to stop and scratch my head. It had been quite a while since I'd last taken her home, and I honestly couldn't remember which of the identical family houses was hers.

I thought for a moment and closed my eyes with a wry smile.

"Far Sight, was it?"

I took a deep breath and tried to remember the feeling. It had been quite a while since I last used this ability of mine, but I supposed it was time

I stopped turning a blind eye to it and started exploiting it to its fullest. To my surprise, it came to me naturally. Like riding a bicycle. The first few seconds were a little dicey, but then it all came back to me, and in a second, I could tell exactly where Judy was in relation to my location.

I opened my eyes and glanced at the second house to the left. As if on cue, the front door opened and the familiar form of my assistant stepped through, followed by her awfully youthful mother. I walked up to the gate on their picket fence and waited for Judy to notice me. Instead, it was her mother who smiled at me and waved in my direction with a familiar-looking ladle.

"Look, dormouse, your friend came over to pick you up! Isn't that nice?"

"Mom, not in front of him," Judy protested half-heartedly while her mother kept rubbing her head.

"Ahhh... Looking at you makes me wish I was young again..."

"You are quite young yourself, ma'am," I told her as they got to the gate. I wasn't lying. From up close, she only looked a couple of years older than Judy, and she had a figure that would have turned heads even in her frilly apron and bunny slippers.

"Oh, you flatterer!" she answered with a demure smile as she absent-mindedly straightened her daughter's uniform.

"Let's go," my assistant huffed while grabbing hold of my sleeve.

"Goodbye, ma'am," I said with a small wave as I was being dragged away.

"Have fun!" she replied with a bright smile as she watched us leave.

Once we were out of earshot, Judy glanced up at me and murmured, "I would appreciate it if you stopped flirting with my mother."

"I wasn't flirting. I just told the truth. She *is* surprisingly young."

"Whatever," she huffed again as we rounded the corner. As we did so, we both slowed our pace, which was a good thing since I was too preoccupied with gazing at my assistant to look forward.

"Are you sulking?"

"No."

"Okay, just checking," I told her with a small smile before I recalled something and it turned into a big smile. "By the way... dormouse?"

My assistant's cheeks flushed red in an uncharacteristic gesture of awkwardness and she refused to look me in the eye.

"She likes to give me pet names."

"But why dormouse? Does it have some special meaning?"

She thought for a moment, then just shook her head.

"It's probably because I am unremarkable and my ears are big."

I stumbled and nearly fell flat on my face on the sidewalk. She turned to me with an expression saying *What?*

"That's really your first interpretation?" I exclaimed as I recovered from my absurdity-induced near-faceplant.

"What else could it be?"

"Well..." It took me a few moments to find the right words. "Dormice are... small and cute, aren't they?"

My assistant gave me a flat look and pointedly cleared her throat.

"Chief, I have a new hypothesis."

"Oh? Let's hear it."

"I believe you use flirting as a coping mechanism."

"I'm not flirting, I'm just being honest! Speaking of which, I should let you know that you don't have big ears, either. They are perfectly normal."

She nodded to herself and muttered, "Two data points." I decided to ignore her and closed my eyes again, focusing on my Far Sight instead.

"What are you doing?" she interrupted me before I could even get started.

"Just checking where the others are," I told her without opening my eyes and pictured the gang in my mind's eye. Maybe it was because I was trying to keep all of them in mind at once, but I only got brief flashes of their locations and what they were doing at the moment, so I slowed down and focused on one at a time.

First Joshua. He was... well, being literally dragged out of bed by Angie. Josh was sporting some crazy bed hair, while Angie was still in her pajamas. As for how she got into his bedroom, I figured it probably had something to do with the open window and the ladder poking over the sills. I frowned. This was one of those things that always bothered me. If it was a guy who used a ladder to break into a girl's bedroom and dragged her out of the bed, he would end up on a list that would force him to introduce himself as a registered sex offender to his neighbours for the rest of his life, but if a girl did it, it's apparently funny.

I decided not to dwell on the double standards of slapstick comedy and instead moved on to the princess. To my surprise, I found her in a spacious, modern kitchen that looked like it belonged to a high-class restaurant. However, instead of an army of chefs with those funny hats, it was only occupied by the princess and a maid with long blonde braids. She was vaguely familiar, and as I thought about it, I could faintly recall seeing her from a distance a while back. She was talking with the princess as they were packing a lunch box, and while I couldn't understand the specifics, it had something to do with cayenne pepper. It was hard to tell, and their voices sounded weirdly distorted. It might have had something to do with the distance. I made a mental note to try to figure out the range of my Far Sight soon.

A mere thought later, I saw Snowy. She was in the middle of peeling herself out of her underwear and about to take a shower. She was still wearing her choker, though. Weird. I *obviously* didn't linger, but instead I moved on to the class rep in a calm and very mature manner befitting a gentleman like myself.

I found her talking to a creepy, white-bearded old man in a creased black robe. Not only that, they were standing in a room that looked superficially like the school library, except its walls were lit by large, glowing blue crystals in cast-iron sockets. I was just about to try to catch the topic of their discussion when I was pulled out of my experiment by a small hand clutched on my forearm.

My eyes snapped open as I nearly stumbled forwards and found myself staring at a crossroad with a red light shining in my face. I blinked and glanced at Judy. She wore an obviously disapproving expression, though in retrospect I suppose *obviously* might've been too strong of a word. I was fairly certain I was the only person on this planet who could tell that apart from her usual neutral face.

"What are you doing, Chief?"

"Ah... Sorry, I lose track of the outside world when I really focus on Far Sight."

She gave me a dubious look but didn't press the issue, and we both crossed the road as the traffic light switched.

"What is the plan for today?"

It took me several seconds to switch my brain over to the new track, but once I did, I nodded to myself maybe a bit too eagerly.

"Right. Plan." I paused as I tried to remember exactly what we agreed on the previous night and what had changed since then. "All right, here are the basics: You ask the class rep. She should be the most knowledgeable about these things. She is the mage after all; she should have a high Lore skill."

"You are stereotyping her."

"Maybe a little, but if I'm right, then you would get the most info out of her, and if I'm wrong, it's just a brand-new data point for future considerations."

"I see. I still don't know how I should ask, though."

"Hmmm..." I'd thought about that a fair bit the night before and decided to share the idea I'd come up with. "Make me the bad guy."

"You... need to elaborate on that."

"Nothing too terrible. Tell the class rep that I'm keeping you in the dark. Tell her you want to know more, and I've refused to give you information. If she still refuses, elaborate on how you want to help me, but I don't want to get you involved for your own protection, but you want to help anyways, et cetera. Be creative and tug at her heartstrings."

"I'm not really good at that."

"Would you still try it? Please?" I gave her a puppy look, and she rolled her eyes in turn.

"Yes, I will."

"Good!" I clapped my hands and proceeded to rub them sinisterly. "The second stage of the plan depends on the success of the first stage."

"I see. Anything in particular I should ask about?"

"Funny you should ask..." I muttered as I stopped rubbing my hands and took out my phone. A few pokes later, hers vibrated in her pocket. She took it out without looking away from me as I told her, "This is a short list of the keywords I gathered that might produce a reaction."

Judy opened the attached file in my mail and scrolled through it with record speed.

"I see. It's a lot, though. Anything in particular I should focus on?"

"Let's see... " I thought about the question for a few seconds and managed to narrow things down a little bit. "I think the three most important terms should be *Celestials*, *Abyssals*, and *the Assembly*."

I scoured those from an obscure live-chat log. I got linked to it on a similarly obscure image sharing site, and while it was filled with some hard-core conspiracy nutters (the *NASA put mind-control chips in my genitals so that bigfoot can monitor my thoughts for the space-jew overlords* type), yet some throwaway posts there seemed surprisingly legit. Judy read the list again, probably to commit it to her photographic memory, and she put away her phone.

"What about you?"

"What about me?" I asked back reflexively.

"What are you going to do while I interrogate Amelia?"

"Well... uh..." I proceeded to scratch the back of my neck, but it didn't help the awkwardness at all. "I'm going to talk to the princess and come clean. After what happened yesterday, I really want to resolve this love triangle business before it really gets out of hand."

"That's good," she muttered, accompanied with a small nod. "And? How are you going to answer?"

"You know, it's not like I was confessed to. You don't have to put it so directly..." She gave me an impatient huff, so I sighed and told her, "I'll try to let her down gently."

"Good," Judy spoke before I even finished, and gave an even bigger nod.

"I mean, it's not like I don't like her, but by conventional logic, she should be the main heroine. She should focus her full attention on Joshua. I mean—"

Judy cut me off by placing a hand on my arm and shook her head.

"You don't have to excuse yourself in front of me, Chief. I know you don't want to hurt her, but being too nice can cause just as much pain in the long run."

"That was... unusually eloquent."

My assistant narrowed her eyes a bit, the equivalent of an angry glare on anyone else's face.

"What do you mean *unusually*?"

"No hidden meaning," I told her with a smile and simultaneously started taking longer strides. "Come on, Dormouse, we should hurry up."

She opened her mouth for a quick retort, but then she paused and her eyes narrowed even farther, which was probably meant to be an angry scowl, but was made hilarious by the way she was scampering to catch up with me at the same time.

"Did you just call me what I think you just called me?"

"That depends. Did you hear 'Dormouse'?"

She gave me an *I knew I should've stayed in bed this morning* look, which I answered by flashing a 200 percent innocent smile at her.

"Oh, don't look so down. Weren't you the one who wanted to have a nickname on the second day we met?"

"But why Dormouse?"

"I told you. Because they are small and cute. It really fits you."

She was obviously incredulous at first, but then she looked away with what I hoped was fake displeasure and mumbled, "Fine, whatever."

I couldn't help but chuckle.

"Don't worry, I promise I'll only use it when we are alone or when it would be really amusing."

She didn't even bother to answer that one; she just kicked my shin. I barely felt it as usual, but I still gave her a small "Ow," as courtesy dictated.

We were now within spitting distance of the school gate, and I couldn't help but smile. This morning was definitely miles better than the last. I could only hope the rest of the day would follow suit.

PART 2

The classroom was unusually lifeless this morning, probably due to the placeholders sticking to their schedules like they were superglued together, and thus there were only two of them in the room. On closer look, they seemed to be both the academically hyperactive type, so that at least explained their early arrivals. As for how I knew that? They wore glasses. A stereotype, I know, but this was that kind of place after all.

Judy and I headed for our respective desks, and while I was planning on walking over to hers after I put down my bag, my plans were torpedoed by the appearance of the class rep. She had a suspicious look in her eyes when she noticed the two of us, and after depositing her own bag, she walked over.

"Good morning, Leo."

"Morning," I returned the greeting with a lazy wave.

"We need to talk."

"I figured."

She glanced around for a moment before she leaned in for a conspiratorial huddle.

"Listen, about what happened yesterday..." She glanced around again and leaned even closer. "How did you break into the Restricted Space?"

I sighed. Wonderful. The day had barely even started, and I was already facing questions I couldn't answer. After a bit of high-speed thinking, I decided to stick to my previous story.

"I didn't. I just tagged along with the princess and Snowy."

"And Judy?"

"Her? She tagged along with me."

The class rep nodded, though the look in her eyes said she thought I wasn't telling her the truth. She wasn't really off the mark, to be honest, but then again, how was I supposed to tell her something I didn't know?

"Very well," she finally told me with a small sigh of her own. "I told the school it was only a minor incident and that your involvement was accidental. They might still want to talk to you soon, so don't do anything stupid."

Now *that* perked my interest. "The school, eh?" I mused as the implications started to line up in my mind. So we had an organization that was aware of the supernatural elements in this school and, according to the class rep's words, regulated them. I made a mental note of telling Judy to get some more info about them, but for the moment I had to keep up my side of the conversation. "Before you go, please define *something stupid*."

"Things like jumping into a Restricted Field to stop a fight."

I frowned and shook my head.

"Sorry, but that's not happening. You cannot ask me to stand around while my friends are fighting each other." I paused for a second as I remembered something, and I couldn't stop a smirk creeping onto my face. "Also,

I can distinctly remember someone *actually* jumping in and trying to stop a fight yesterday."

The class rep reeled back like I'd just hit on a sore spot.

"That's different. I was there as an official representative of the school and the Assembly."

Ah-ha! There was one of my keywords! I tried not to show my satisfaction as I forcefully wiped the smile from my face and looked the girl in front of me in the eye.

"Listen, Ammy. I know you just want to keep me safe, but I will not be standing idly by while my friends are in danger. Period."

"You are going to get hurt."

I shrugged.

"I could. Or maybe things work out well like they did yesterday. Either way, I would rather try and fail than not try at all."

The class rep silently held my gaze for several seconds longer before she closed her eyes and her shoulders slumped in resignation.

"I never thought you were the hot-blooded type."

Her words took me aback. Me? Hot blooded? Nah. If anything, I was too calculating for my own good.

Since I didn't respond right away, the class rep straightened herself and took a step back from my desk. "Very well. But remember, I have warned you."

"Yes, and I am grateful for that, even if I am going to completely ignore it."

Her lips curved upwards a little, though the smile barely touched her eyes.

"All right. Just so we are clear." She paused for a second or five before her expression turned stony once again. "Before I go, there is one last thing I wanted to ask you. How did you get into the Restricted Space without triggering any of the mana sensors around campus?"

Ooooh... *Mana sensors?* Look at those juicy tidbits, just falling into my lap, one after the other! After a moment of consideration, I decided to just lean back on my chair and smile mysteriously.

"Would you believe me if I told you my exposure to you guys supercharged my latent psychic abilities into phenomenal cosmic powers?"

"Yes."

I blinked at her. Hard.

"Well, you shouldn't."

"Then how?"

I had a feeling she wouldn't take *I don't have a bloody idea—why don't YOU tell me?* too well, so I decided on a more indirect approach. I quickly relapsed into my mysterious smile and quipped, "I cannot tell you just yet. When I can, you will be the first to know."

"Do you promise?"

I nodded, and she returned the gesture, albeit hesitantly. By this time, students had begun to steadily trickle into the classroom. She was about to leave and attend to her duties when she faltered and turned back to me and whispered, "Are you sure you are not psychic?"

I let the smile drop and gave her a critical stare.

"I was joking."

"I know, but..." She leaned closer again and lowered her voice to the point where I could barely hear her. "I'm writing my thesis on unconventional and spontaneous mystic arts, and I thought you might have... insights into the matter."

All her words needed was a knowing wink and an intriguingly raised eyebrow to complete the classic *I know you know, and now you know that I know you know that I know you know* exchange, but the class rep just wasn't subtle or self-conscious enough for those kinds of things, so I gave her the benefit of the doubt and a meaningful nod in turn.

Although, to be perfectly fair, she was correct. So far, I definitely fell under the "psychic" umbrella, an ESP to be precise, especially if I were to play fast and loose with the traditional definitions, but it was exactly because I had no idea about the proper terminology of this world that I had to be careful about claiming anything. Who knew? Maybe I *was* psychic? Or an alien. Or a genie locked out of his lamp. I had no idea, so I did what I was best at—act like I knew what I was talking about and at the same time be as vague as possible.

"Fine, fine. We'll see about that. If I come across anything that might interest you, I'll call you."

As I said that, the princess arrived in the doorway with perfect timing. The class rep followed the direction of my gaze and promptly left without saying a word. I knew she was only doing so to give us some space, but geez, it was still cold of her.

Anyways, the princess visibly staggered when she noticed that I was already in the classroom and for a moment I thought she would run away (possibly accompanied with a fitting assortment of "*Kyuuun!*"s and "*Awawawa!*"s), but instead she showed admirable self-restraint by shakily walking up to her desk in front of mine and taking a seat.

I waited for her to say something, but after it became obvious she was not going to speak first, I gently cleared my throat, which made her nearly jump out of her chair. Talk about being tense.

However, before I could start a conversation, she whipped her head around so hard that for a moment I was afraid she would pull a tendon in her neck. She stared at me with an expression that hovered somewhere between bone-chilling rage and utter panic... or at the very least that's what it looked like, though I had a hunch it had more to do with embarrassment than either of those emotions. A tsundere, through and through.

Meanwhile, she tried to speak, but no words came out of her mouth. I waited for her to finish her struggle, but in the end she just turned back around and buried her face in her arms on her desk. What a wonderful conversation that was.

I let loose a sneaky sigh under my breath and tapped her on her shoulder. "Do you want to talk?"

She didn't react right away, but then she nodded without looking up.

"So... are you going to talk?"

This time she shook her head.

"Then what?" There was no answer. "How about you write it down?"

She suddenly sat up straight like she was shocked by electricity and began rummaging through her bag. She took out a sheet of paper and some writing utensils and then wrote at a frantic pace. Once finished, she checked the page, nodded, and presented it to me over her back while still avoiding eye contact with extreme prejudice. I reflexively rolled my eyes and took the page.

I found her handwriting very familiar, which honestly shouldn't have been that surprising considering I'd already seen it on her two challenge letters. This one, predictably, also called me to the roof.

"So you want us to eat lunch on the roof so we can talk?" She silently nodded. "Just the two of us?" She nodded again. "All right then," I told her as my lips slowly curved into a sardonic smile. "It was nice talking to you."

She didn't react; she just hid her face in her arms again and refused to look up, no matter how gently I called out to her. With this intermezzo over, I sat back in my chair and tried my best not to think about how troublesome my lunch break was promising to be.

PART 3

I checked the time on my phone and had to take a second look to be certain. It was only a couple of minutes before noon. Just where did my morning go?

That was a rhetorical question, by the way. I knew full well how it went: one half reading my assistant's increasingly elaborate reports after she came back from discussing the supernatural aspects of this world with the class rep, and the other half was spent connecting all of those tidbits together while trying to keep my jaw from hitting the floor.

As it turned out, the magical background of this world was way, way more extensive than I'd ever dreamed possible. There was a mountain of new terminology to learn, politics, factions, et cetera... Even after spending the entire morning studying, I only scratched the surface of the data Judy provided, which itself was only a fraction of the basics. This of course meant that I paid exactly zero attention to the lessons, but in my defense, I would consider that learning about the amazing and dangerously real nature of this world should take priority over symbolism in twentieth-century poetry.

Anyways, I was fairly confident that I now knew enough to avoid making a fool out of myself if I tried to bring up the subject, but as they say, a little knowledge can sometimes be more dangerous than ignorance. As such, I decided to keep to my strategy of speaking very vaguely so that instead of flaunting what I knew, I'd get the others to talk about things I didn't.

However, as overwhelming as all the new information was, I could feel my brain being bogged down and unable to think properly. I couldn't help but groan in silence. No matter how hard I tried to suppress it, that strange mixture of guilt and anxiety kept bubbling up between the gaps and kept reminding me of my upcoming discussion with the princess. I was once again reminded why I didn't want to get involved in any romantic shenanigans. Even getting myself disentangled from one made me unable to function properly. Stupid hormones. Anyways, I checked the time again and then winced in surprise when Joshua unexpectedly whispered to me, "Are you that hungry?"

"What?"

"You've been checking your phone for the time a lot. Are you looking forward to lunch that much?" Just as he said so, the long chime sounded and he broke into a childish grin. "Speak of the devil. Oh! Speaking of which, do you want any recommendations? They just put a new caviar dish on the menu. You should *definitely* give it a try."

I awarded my friend a look so flat its edge could divide atoms.

"Three things. One: No. Two: How is caviar a good recommendation if you think someone is hungry? Three: No."

Josh clicked his tongue and shrugged.

"You are no fun."

"Nor am I made of money."

"But you are! Almost! Nearly! At least thirty percent."

I resisted the urge to roll my eyes and stood up. Josh followed my example immediately and flashed me another kiddy grin.

"All right—then maybe not caviar. There is still a lot of other stuff we haven't tried yet. Are you coming?"

I shook my head as I pointed upwards.

"Sorry, not today. I have plans on the roof."

"With Judy?"

I shook my head again and nodded towards the blonde girl. She was still sprawled out on her desk, but she might have heard that we were talking because she looked up at the exact same moment. She froze when our eyes met, but to her credit, she didn't engage in any of her usual over-the-top antics.

"Really?" Joshua wondered aloud in a tone that was more than a little skeptical. "It's rare for you two to hang out like that, isn't it?"

"Not really," I answered nonchalantly as I put away my books and got my wallet.

"Would you mind if I tagged along?"

"Actually..." the princess spoke up before I could. She stood up and rubbed her face. She had an imprint of her sleeve on her forehead, but I decided it was not the time to bring that up. Once she was upright, she turned to Josh apologetically and said, "Sorry, but Leo and I... we have something to discuss."

"Just the two of you?" My friend eyed both of us suspiciously, but I couldn't really care less, as I was too taken aback by the sudden change in the princess's behaviour. She was, for lack of a better word, regal. I had seen her relapse into a more formal attitude in the past, but I couldn't recall her being *this* formal since the day she transferred. It was a little uncanny, to be honest.

"Yes," she stated in no uncertain terms.

"Um... Okay?" Josh looked at me, apparently just as weirded out by her behaviour as I was. I made some covert shooing motions, and after a little more nudging, he left the scene with a huff. I watched him go before I returned my attention to the princess.

"Sooooo... should I go and grab something from the cafeteria?"

"Not necessary." She stopped me and dove into her bag to retrieve a familiar-looking tiered lunch box. "I brought enough for both of us."

"Is that so?" I flashed her a reserved smile and added, "Very thoughtful of you."

To my utter bafflement, she returned my smile, without any cutesy noises or flailing. For a moment, I wanted to yell *Who are you, and what have you done to the princess!?* but I managed to subdue the urge and instead led her out of the classroom.

I don't know how it worked. Maybe it was the regal aura surrounding her, but the placeholder hordes rushing to besiege the cafeteria parted around us like the Red Sea, and we managed to reach the roof in a little under a minute. That was pretty much a personal record. Not only that, but when I opened the access door, I found the roof practically empty. I already noticed that placeholders tended to conveniently vacate the area whenever I was about to have a special discussion with someone, but right now I would've really preferred at least a few idlers in the background, if only for my peace of mind.

We wordlessly headed over to our usual seats on the benches in the far corner of the roof and sat down without much fanfare. By this point I had already steeled my nerves and come up with the exact words I wanted to tell her, so I got ready to speak up the moment my butt touched the seat... yet somehow the princess was still faster than me.

"Leo," she slowly turned towards me with a serious expression. I involuntarily gulped. There was a silent pressure in her eyes, and I couldn't help but recall the battle from the day before. Right, I'd kind of forgotten about it, but she was an actual dragon-hybrid-something-or-the-other that could turn me into a bloodstain on the floor with a single swipe. That was definitely not good for my peace of mind.

"Yes?" I responded with a smile I hoped wasn't too strained.

"Leo, please tell me something."

There was a slight tremble in her voice, which made me finally tear my gaze away from her eyes. It was only then that I noticed that she was red as a lobster. That made me feel a little better for some reason, so I responded without thinking.

"Sure."

"Are you in a relationship with Judy?"

The question was a bit of a curveball, so I involuntarily frowned.

"Why do you ask this now?"

"J-just answer me!" she demanded while her voice rose an octave. Now that I calmed down a bit, it became obvious she was trying her hardest to appear calm and dignified. For the most part it worked, but thankfully she was still clumsy enough to let some of her nervousness slip, and thank God for that, or I might've become a nervous wreck before the end of our talk.

I took a deep breath and was about to tell her the truth, but then I paused. Couldn't I use this to let her down gently? If I told her I was dating Judy, she would probably stop being confused about me and could focus all her efforts on Joshua. That sounded nice on paper, and I was almost tempted to use it, but then what? Wouldn't that mean that I would be forced to pretend to be going out with Judy, at least for the time being? That wasn't something I could impose on her without her consent (even if I was certain she would agree without a moment of hesitation). These kinds of pretending plots never resolved any conflict, anyway.

As such, after a long hesitation, I shook my head.

"No, we are not in a *romantic* relationship at the moment."

"Good." She nodded and I could see her clench her fists. She caught the gesture, and hastily relaxed her hands while clearing her throat. "I mean, it is good that we could ascertain the current state of affairs. It is important that w... w... Awawawawa! What are you doing?"

"Nothing, please continue," I told her as I poked her cheek again.

"S-stop doing that! Why are you poking me?"

"Because you're acting weird."

"I am not acting weird!" she screamed and slapped my hand away before she hung her head. "You ruined it! I was preparing myself for this moment all morning and you ruined it!"

For a second, I didn't know what to do. I tried to crack a joke to get her attention, but then a soft sob escaped the princess's throat and it made me freeze. Oh crap. I made her cry...

"Um... I'm sorry. I didn't think you... I mean, I just wanted you to relax a little. You weren't acting like yourself." I put my hand on her shoulder and lightly patted it. She didn't throw me off, so I continued, "The princess I know would turn red at the mere mention of dating and would have made cute little noises if I poked her." Since she still didn't react, I let out a defeated sigh and pleaded, "Please don't cry. I'm sorry for teasing you when you were trying your hardest. What do you want me to do to cheer you up?"

At last, she glanced up at me.

"Are you going to hear me out?"

"Sure."

She looked me in the eye for a couple of seconds before she straightened herself and rubbed her eyes. It wasn't perfect, but it seemed she managed to regain at least a sliver of the dignity she was projecting before.

"You are not allowed to make fun of me or tease me until we are finished here."

"Understood."

She gave me a nod and then fell silent. I waited for her, but she didn't say a word even after several seconds. I was just about to reach the end of my rope when she suddenly inhaled.

"I assume you know why I had a fight with Neige yesterday." I wanted to tell her I had a good idea, but before I could say anything, she continued with the same breath. "She said that I was being indecisive, and that I was stringing you along. I... was angry at the time, but last night I reflected on what she said, and I think she was right. So... after thinking about it a lot, I decided to come clean."

"Really?"

She nodded sharply.

"Yes." There was a meaningful pause after this point, during which she flushed so hard even the tip of her ears turned red, then she forcefully exhaled and quickly said, "Leo, I think I like you."

Shameful as it sounds, I totally froze up for a moment. I never in a million years expected that she would outright confess to me like that, and I had no idea how to answer, so I proceeded to do what I always did when I was feeling awkward and changed the subject posthaste.

"Wait a minute! Weren't you in love with Josh?"

She averted her eyes for a moment, but then forced herself to look at me again before she answered.

"I do like him, but... I don't think I like him the same way I like you."

"But why do you even like me? That makes no sense."

"I don't know, either."

"We've only known each other for a month, right? How can you just casually pick me over Josh?"

"I am not doing this *casually*!" she burst out before reining in her temper again. "I mean... I only really knew Josh for a month too."

"But you knew each other as kids!"

"For a week."

"But you promised to marry him!"

"And he still doesn't remember me, let alone the promise."

"But... but... he's *Josh*!"

"I don't know what that means but... when I look at him, I just don't feel the same way as when I look at you. I don't know how else to explain this."

"That's messed up," I whispered in a groan.

"Sh-shut up! I can't help it, okay?!"

I hastily raised my hands in surrender to her rapidly disintegrating regal façade and vigorously shook my head.

"I didn't mean it that way. It's just that... you had a connection with Josh before. I just don't see how you would pick me in a competition between the two of us."

"I told you, that's not how this works! I just... I asked a friend with a little more experience, and she told me I shouldn't divide my attention, or I might end up empty-handed. She told me not to force myself and just follow my heart... and I just did."

There was a short beat, then I muttered, "That sounded really corny, but kinda sweet."

"Shut up!" she exploded again and punched me in the shoulder. It hurt a little, but I couldn't help but laugh. "You promised you wouldn't tease me until we finished! You are incorrigible."

"I got it, I got it!" I repeated between chuckles. "I'm sorry, but seeing you saying stuff like that so bashfully just tickles my teasing instincts."

After my non-apology, she finally calmed down a little. She inhaled and exhaled a couple of times before she looked me in the eye with a stern expression.

"I already told you how I feel, but what... about you?"

"Well, I do like you," I answered absentmindedly. "Though I don't know if—"

"Yes!" she exclaimed, flexing her fists again.

"As I was saying," I raised my voice to get her attention, "I am not sure it is the kind of 'like' you are looking for."

"I don't mind," she stated, to my utter bafflement.

"You don't?"

She flashed a determined smile at me that somehow managed to be both dazzling and childishly cute at the same time, and then declared, "It means I have a chance! This is a war I am definitely going to win!"

"What? War? What? I'm sorry but I am getting a little confused about your analogies here..."

"Never mind that! We have already built up a familiarity over the last month. With a little more time, I can totally..."

While the princess slowly descended into excited mumbles, I threw my head back and let out a tired groan. I was caught up in the conversation, but didn't this become the exact opposite of my original plan? I wanted to gently reject her so that she would focus on Josh alone, and instead somehow she decided to focus on me alone. Just why? Had Josh lost his harem protagonist aura or something?

Realistically, this was my last chance to cut her off before things got even more complicated. If I didn't, then Judy would probably kill me... yet when push came to shove, I was still reluctant. I mean, I didn't want to hurt her, but if I didn't reject her, that would hurt Judy, and I didn't want to do that, either.

Damn.

Was this what being an indecisive harem protagonist in a love triangle felt like? Just what kind of heinous crime did I commit in my previous life to end up with an experience like this?

Anyhow, I shook my head and took a deep breath. I had to make a choice now, or I would...

"Wait a minute..." I blurted the words out before I could catch them, and Elly immediately perked up. Well, crap. I needed something to hold her attention for a moment while I ruminated on this new idea that popped into my head, so I quickly grasped for the first topic that came to me. "So... how exactly did you even develop a crush on me?"

"What do you mean?" she asked with her head cocked to the side, so I quickly elaborated.

"Weren't you always going on about how much you hated me and how I smelled bad? How did that turn into 'I like you'?"

The curious expression on the princess's face was quickly replaced by an awkward frown and she soon began fidgeting.

"I-I didn't really mean that. I never really hated you, you know? I just don't like being teased! And, um... you actually don't smell bad. It's just a little weird. But I... I don't dislike it."

"Did I just awaken a fetish in you?"

The princess's eyes opened wide. Then she punched me in the shoulder again. This time she didn't hold back, and I could feel my bones creak in response.

"Ow! Hey!"

"You are such a blockhead! Why do you have to keep ruining the moment!?"

"Sorry, sorry." I apologized for what felt like the hundredth time that day while rubbing my shoulder. "I am just bad with these kinds of topics. I can't take the pressure, so I tease you to release it."

"I see." To my surprise, the princess actually accepted my hastily cobbled together excuse with a serious expression. "S-so you are bad with... um... this. I see... But it is still no excuse!"

"Yeah, I got it."

What followed after this point was a solid minute of much-appreciated silence, which let me get my bearings and think things through. No matter how I looked at it, my idea would never fly under normal circumstances, but these were not normal circumstances by any means, now were they? We had dragons and demons and mages and possibly psykers running around and battles and a weird-ass world with placeholders and technology all over the map and, most importantly, we had a *harem battle* setting. That last part could not be stressed enough.

In other words, so long as I played my cards right, I might be able to engineer a scenario where I wouldn't have to trample on anyone's feelings.

I just needed to lay some groundwork. No, scratch that. A *metric ton* of groundwork. However, it could work. In theory, at least. I really wished I could ask Judy for advice, but considering this concerned her as well, I figured I'd have to wing it myself. No biggie. What is the worst thing that could happen? I mean, aside from lethally embarrassing myself and completely destroying my social life?

"So, Leo?" Elly spoke up in a soft voice that nevertheless made me shudder in surprise.

"Yes?" I answered reflexively.

"You might not like me the way I like you right now, but I will do my best to change that in the future. Please take care of me."

"Um... okay?" I responded as my brain finally caught up with the conversation. "That sounded a bit too formal, didn't it?"

Her face turned sour for a moment, and she shook her head.

"You are still horrible at reading the mood."

"Guilty as charged," I answered with forced cheerfulness and a toothy grin before I reached for the box between the two of us and took off the lid. I'd been saving it for a moment like this. Few things worked as well for cutting difficult conversations short as good food. "Now that we are done with that, we should get started on the food. I'm curious about what you made this time."

"All right, let's—" She didn't finish her sentence, and instead she narrowed her eyes into a suspicious squint. "Wait, how did you know that I made it?"

I couldn't really tell her I *Far Saw* her making it in the morning, so I decided to play it coy and only smile at her knowingly.

"Oh please, princess! I've seen your cooking before."

I removed the top tray containing the utensils and small bottles of condiments that came with the tiered box and took a look at the second layer. It contained fries, fried strips of chicken breast, and a few triangular sandwiches in the side compartment. It was a very safe and simple menu, and it also looked eerily familiar.

"Ah! This is just like your first lunch box I ate!"

"You mean the first one you stole," she pointed out.

I decided to ignore the barb and shrugged. "I still ate it, so my statement stands." While I said so, I picked up a fry and popped it into my mouth. It was still warm, a testament to the quality of the insulation. Or it was magic. One or the other.

The princess was giving me an intent look that, to my surprise, I found weirdly familiar. I swallowed and told her, in no uncertain terms, "It's good."

"O-of course it is!" she exclaimed with hints of that fake irritation she sometimes projected whenever she was embarrassed, but not so much that she would resort to the cutesy noises. Was it weird that I was at the point where I could recognize the degrees of her embarrassment? Anyways, she seemed pleased enough. She was like Judy in that regard; apparently girls really liked it when someone complimented their cooking. But then again, so did I, though people rarely found my fried bacon or instant noodles praiseworthy.

I took another bite, this time from the surprisingly spicy chicken, and remembered the scene I saw in the morning. I let curiosity take the better of me and asked, "Did you get some help with this one?"

"W-what is that supposed to mean? Are you saying I cannot cook something like this?"

"No, I meant the flavouring is different. It's cayenne pepper, isn't it?"

She seemed to be torn for a moment, but she soon confessed. "Yes. It was Melinda's idea."

"Melinda…" I mused while chewing on another piece of fried chicken. "The tall maid with the long braids, right?"

"Yes, it's—" She stopped again and her previously apprehensive gaze suddenly went downright damning. "How do you know her name?"

"I've met her, remember? She was there when I took you home the first time."

"I'm quite sure I didn't tell you her name."

"I'm quite sure you did," I retorted while picking another french fry from the box. "Otherwise how would I know?" I popped it into my mouth and started chewing, but she still looked at me suspiciously, so once I swallowed, I decided to change the subject. "By any chance, was she the friend you talked about? The one you asked for advice?"

"Yes. I trust her. She's been my chambermaid since I was nine years old."

"Chambermaid, huh?" I swallowed another fry before continuing. "Is she draconic too?" The princess twitched and looked around in a hurry, prompting me to roll my eyes. "Oh come on. There is no one else here, we can talk about it."

She kept checking the perimeter for a little longer before she turned back to me with a sour expression. She was apparently not keen on this discussion, but she still told me, "She is a distant relative from one of the European branch families."

"A branch family? Really?" Now that she mentioned it, they did look similar. More importantly though, it meant that they shared blood, which in turn meant… "So she *is* a Draconian, huh?"

Elly nodded while I picked up another chicken breast and munched on it, partially to use the chewing as an excuse to think, but mostly because I was hungry and it was delicious. But back to the topic: Draconians. I tried to recall as much as I could about them, which wasn't much considering the vast majority of my knowledge was extremely recent and came from Judy's reports.

According to those, they were considered to be one of the Three Old-blooded Clans, which sounded both ominous and like a really clumsy literal translation of something, but I decided not to dwell on it. They were apparently descendants of actual dragons, or at least of whatever constituted as "dragons" around these parts. They must've still been reptilian fire-breathers, though. I could glean that much from the princess's appearance on the day before. Speaking of which, I finished chewing and decided to probe for extra information.

"So, can she transform too?"

"I don't think so. Her blood is too thin to awaken it."

"Which means yours isn't?"

"Of course it isn't!" she retorted angrily and puffed out her chest. "I am the proud scion of the Dracis family! Ours is the strongest draconic bloodline still in existence."

"Of course you are," I nodded sagely while making mental notes. So, that meant there were multiple bloodlines. Not only that, but there was some sort of hierarchy based on how thick their blood was, as shown by a branch family member serving as a maid. In the meantime, the princess's face began to twist in displeasure. She must have taken my previous words the wrong way, as she puffed her cheeks and turned her face to the side in an image that I was tempted to take a snapshot of and upload as an example of *tsundere* on my favourite site.

"I know that my draconic form might not be very impressive yet, and I don't have wings, and I can't breathe true dragon fire, and my tail is too short and thick but..." Her voice slowly trailed into a mumble the longer she went on, only to flare up at the end. "But I am still the scion of House Dracis! Give me a few years, and you will see!"

I raised my hand apologetically and shook my head.

"No, no. I wasn't being sarcastic. Not to mention, I think your transformation looked impressive."

She suddenly twitched and began awkwardly fidgeting at my side.

"You... really think so?"

"Yes. Though... your tail *did* look a little stubby."

To my sincerest bafflement, the princess let out an ear-piercing squeak that startled me to the point I nearly dropped the fry in my hand.

"I-i-idiot! Pervert!"

"What?"

"H-h-how can you say things like that so casually?!"

"Well... it's just a tail. And it *is* kind of short."

She let out another muffled scream and hid her steadily reddening face behind her forearms.

"Idiot! Dunderhead! Pervert!"

"There, there..." I patted her on the shoulder to calm her down, but instead she just began flailing at me.

"How can you say that to a girl? I'm really self-conscious about that!"

"Whoa, calm down! I didn't mean it in a bad way!" By this point, I recognized the innuendo in our exchange, which meant I just walked into a ridiculously awkward conversation by accident. Marvelous. I took a deep breath and tried to salvage the situation the best I could. "It's still a very nice tail. And I'm sure it will grow."

At long last, the princess stopped flailing and began sulking instead.

"But what if it doesn't?"

"Well, then you are still going to have a very nice tail. Long tails are overrated anyways. Short ones are cute."

"I-I don't want to be cute!"

"I'm sorry to say, but that boat has already sailed." Her eyes opened wide, and she hid her face behind her palms with a series of her customary "hauhau" noises, but I ignored them and continued with, "Why don't you focus on your better aspects in the meantime?"

She peeked through her fingers and tentatively asked, "Such as?"

"Erm..." I wracked my brain for a moment, trying to come up with something that hopefully wouldn't make the situation any worse. "I... like your horns?"

"You do?"

"Yes. They are very regal."

"You really think so? Aren't they a little on the small side?"

"No. If they were any bigger, they would throw your profile off-balance. They look really great as they are right now."

"I see..." She calmed down and even started smiling, at which point I sneakily exhaled a relieved breath. I had no idea what I was talking about by the end, but it apparently worked. Anyways, it was time to change the topic once again before she would want to discuss the precise curvature of her horns or something.

"Say," I started, startling her out of her smile. "You mentioned you cannot spit dragon fire." She cautiously nodded, so I continued, "If so, then what was that beam that you fired yesterday?"

She looked away as if recalling an embarrassing memory (for her it might have been... for me it was just scary as hell) and once more began to clumsily fidget.

"It... wasn't real Dragonfire." She must have mistaken my curious expression for something else, as she became flustered and began sputtering. "I-I mean, I wouldn't use Dragonfire on a friend! True Dragonfire eats through wards and enchantments like tissue paper—it could easily kill someone. I'm not that reckless!" She paused and in a mumble added, "Not that I can use it, anyway..."

"I got it. I was just curious," I told her with a reassuring smile and knocked on the side of the lunch box. "Aren't you going to eat? At this rate, I'll finish it all up by myself."

As if only waiting for my prompting, she reached out for the utensils and picked up a fry with a fork. She dipped it in the sauce held in the small compartment in the corner and took it to her lips, but instead of biting down on it, she gave me a puzzled look.

"Is there a problem?"

"Hm? No, why would there be a problem?"

"You were staring."

I chuckled and pointed at her fork.

"Ah, nothing. It's just that I suddenly got reminded that you really are a princess."

She looked at her utensil and her cheeks reddened.

"W-what do you mean? This is how you are supposed to eat properly!"

"Yes, yes," I replied with a smile while taking another fry with my fingers and popping it into my mouth. She gave me an indignant huff and ate her own piece with extra dignity. I couldn't help but smile at the display, but then I noticed the pout on her lips. "Is there something else?"

She glanced at me while playing with a piece of fry in the box. At last, she grimaced and uttered, "Why do you keep calling me that?"

"What? Princess?"

"Yes! We just got a little closer, so..." As if she just realized the meaning of her words, her face once again flushed red (at this point I was really tempted to only mention when she *wasn't* beet red) and added, "Um... why don't you address me less... formally?"

"I don't think I was ever being formal with you."

"But you keep calling me that! You never call me by name!"

"Because that's your pet name," I told her matter-of-factly while dipping a piece of meat in the spicy sauce.

"A pet name?"

"Yep. You know, the thing people give to people they like."

"I know what a pet name is!" She huffed indignantly, but at the same time, she also gave me a sheepish look. "So you call me that because... you like me?"

I only nodded, since I was afraid that if I spoke, I might've accidentally revealed that I only started calling her that because her reactions to the word were hilarious. Because of that, the princess's lips widened into a dopey smile and she honest-to-goodness giggled.

"In that case, it's okay. I'll allow you to call me that."

It wasn't like I needed her approval, but I flashed her an appreciative smile, anyway. There was something else that the whole "princess business" reminded me of, and this was as good a time as any to bring it up.

"Say... I know this might sound a bit abrupt, but is your family okay with what you are doing?" She raised a single puzzled eyebrow, so I hastily continued. "I mean the whole *coming to school to be with your childhood crush* thing."

To my sincerest surprise, her face turned solemn and even a little hesitant. She apparently didn't appreciate the sudden return to the topic of relationships.

"It's complicated."

"You don't want to talk about it?"

"I'm... It's not that. I'm not sure I should."

"Oh, so it's a secret? Or something embarrassing?"

"No, it's..." She paused, visibly wavering, but at last she gave me a firm nod. "Very well. I think I owe you this much."

I wanted to ask *You do?* but I bit my tongue and waited for her to continue.

"Have you heard of the prophecy?"

It took inhuman willpower on my part to keep myself from giving myself a concussion via high-velocity face-palming.

I mean, sure. *Of course* there would be a bloody prophecy! Because why wouldn't there be one!? Bah!

My outrage didn't show on my face, though (or at the very least I hoped it didn't), and I decided to keep fishing for details.

"That depends on which prophecy you are talking about."

The princess gave me a priceless look of surprise that nevertheless sent shivers down my spine.

"There's more than one?"

Dammit, I overexerted myself! A brief yet subjectively endless moment of manic later I managed to regain my composure and flashed a knowing smile. "Of course there are. So, which one is yours?"

Albeit a little dubious, the princess proceeded to explain herself. "You know how the old dragons are gone, right?" I nodded even though I naturally had no idea, but revealing that right now would've been really counterintuitive. "According to the prophecy, a human in our generation will help us resurrect the old bloodlines."

"And that is Josh."

"Probably."

"Probably?" I echoed her. "So you are not sure."

"He could be," she said in a disheartened tone. "I mean, he should be the one. There aren't many candidates."

"And you convinced your family to let you get close to him to make sure?" I completed her sentence.

"That is... oversimplifying things a lot, but yes."

I couldn't help but rub my face in irritation after hearing all that.

"Just for the record—if he is so monumentally important, wouldn't it make more sense to cling to him instead of trying to pursue little old me?"

"I told you, that's not how it works!" she protested a little half-heartedly, only to then pause and hastily add, "And just because I like you more than Josh doesn't mean that I cannot be with him. As a friend. Not *with* him in that sense, but, like, around him. *As a friend.*"

"All right, all right. I got it the first time," I told her with both palms raised.

We remained silent for a while, and I couldn't help but notice that Elly was giving me a conflicted look, so I prompted her with a curious "Hm?" She was hesitant, but she gathered up her courage and asked, "Do you think he is the one?"

I was tempted to answer with a loud *How the hell should I know?* but I restrained myself. She was very forthcoming with me, so it was only fair I share some of my insights with her.

"Most likely."

She was obviously taken aback by my answer, and her eyes urged me to continue, so I obliged.

"You probably already noticed this, but Josh is in the focus here. We have you and Snowy and the class rep and Angie all buzzing around him like flies. I think that's telling enough."

"I'm not buzzing around him," she protested in a deeply offended voice. "And what does Angie have to do with this. She is just..." Her words trailed off into silence and she gave me a startled look. "You don't mean—"

"I'm not implying anything," I interrupted before she could drag me deeper into a discussion I knew nothing about. "I'm just stating the facts."

"And what about you? You are, um, *buzzing* around him, too."

I stared at her through critically narrowed eyelids for a few seconds before I let out a groan of exasperation.

"First off, I do not swing that way. Second of all, I have my own business unrelated to him. Finally, he is my friend first and foremost, and any supernatural whatchamacallit comes second."

"Oh. I understand. I think."

I grunted in approval and popped the last fry into my mouth. The lunch break was almost over, so I stretched my arms, much to Elly's confusion.

"Well, this discussion went in an entirely different direction than I originally planned, but it wasn't that bad. We should do this more often."

"Y-yes!" She repeatedly nodded, and then hastily repacked the empty lunch box. Thinking about it, she barely ate. I felt a little guilty about hogging all the food, so I made a mental note to repay her. Maybe I should invite her for a crêpe or something. Girls liked crêpes.

"I would also like to learn a bit more about your family. Could you introduce me one of these days?" I told her offhandedly as I stood up. I could hear a clatter behind me and I saw her grasping the box as it nearly fell out of her hand.

"W-w-what do you mean by that?" While it was obvious she was trying to act calm, her voice still came out as a high-pitched squeak. "Why would you want to meet with my family so soon? Did you change your mind? But isn't that too sudden? I mean, I would be happy to, but wouldn't it be..." I shook my head with an amused smirk and turned around to help her with the box.

"Calm down, princess. It's simple. If your little fight yesterday proved anything, it was that I wasn't taking things seriously enough. I think it's about time I step up my game and try to get to know the big boys on the playground."

"Big boys? Playground?"

"It's... ugh, it's a euphemism. It means I want to learn about the more important people involved with the masquerade."

"Masquerade?"

I sighed and dropped my shoulders in resignation as the bell sounded.

"I will explain what I mean to you next time, okay?"

She gave me a curt nod and we both left the roof.

On the way back to the classroom, the princess needed a restroom break, and since I didn't want to loiter around the girls' toilet all by myself, we decided I should go ahead. Because of that, I returned to the classroom all alone, with only the empty lunch box in my hands.

I put it onto the princess's desk, and by the time I turned around, Judy was already there looking me in the face.

"I presume she didn't take it well."

It took me a moment to remember our morning conversation, and I promptly shook my head.

"Actually, things... well, they didn't go as planned."

Judy's already stoic expression froze over with disapproval in an instant.

"In what way?"

"Well, let me put it this way: the love triangle kind of got resolved, just not in the way I expected."

"So she confessed."

"Yes."

"And you didn't turn her down."

"Well, to be honest, I didn't." My dear assistant was giving me a look that told me she was about to carve my spleen out with a grapefruit spoon, so I hastily raised my hands and told her, "She confessed, and then things were awkward, and then I got this new idea, after which we talked about some supernatural odds and ends, and so I kind of forgot about the whole thing."

"How can you forget about something so important?"

"Sorry. You know how I am when I get caught up in collecting data."

I flashed my most innocent smile at Judy, and after a fairly long stalemate she let out a long, very deadpan, and somewhat disappointed sigh.

"Chief, you messed up."

"Yeah, guilty as charged," I confessed right away. In fact, I might've done so too readily, as she kept eyeing for a while, forcing me to redouble my efforts to look innocent.

Finally she let out another noise, something halfway between a sigh and a huff, and she raised her hand to her face in a clumsy facsimile of a face-palm and told me, "Please excuse me. Now I have to rethink my whole strategy."

"Erm... okay. You do that."

"See you later."

Saying so, she turned on her heel and walked away from my desk, allowing me to slump over and let the tension drain out of my shoulders.

While everyone around me seemed to be swimming in a hormone-rush-induced fixation on romance, no doubt due to Joshua's harem protagonist aura, I always thought of myself to be above it all. However, in retrospect, I've been getting into almost as many weird and stereotypical romance developments as him. I even had a love triangle on my hands, which was in dire need of resolving... but not yet. I needed to lay some foundations, come up with some convincing arguments, and then when I felt confident, I had to drop the bombshell on the girls when the time was ripe. All things considered, I would probably take a while, but it was worth a try, if nothing else.

I was still thinking when Josh returned to the classroom and sat down next to me. At first he wore a provocative smirk, no doubt planning to start some kind of silly shenanigans regarding my lunch with the princess, but after observing me for a while, he leaned over with concern written all over him.

"Hey, pal? Are you all right?"

"It's nothing." I waved a dismissive hand at him and slumped even deeper into my chair. "I'm just thinking about stuff."

"Stuff?" he repeated after me a tad dubiously.

"Yeah. You know? Like our future, or dragons, or secret societies, or our country's legal stance on polygamy? Those kinds of stuff."

"You're weird."

I gave my friend a flat glance, and simply answered, "I know."

CHAPTER 16

PART 1

The relief was palpable in my sigh when the last bell of the day sounded. Normally I was all over PE classes, but on this particular day I was way too out of it to perform at my best, and the exercise only served as a distraction, interrupting my concentration and preventing me from thinking clearly.

Once the teacher gave us the go, I followed my placeholder classmates and headed towards the changing rooms. The weather had turned for the worse since noon; the sky was covered in thick grey clouds, and I really wanted to get inside and change into something warmer than the gym clothes on my back.

"Why the long face?" Angie sidled up to me after only a couple of steps, torpedoing my plans with nigh-precognitive timing. Not only that, but if the impish smile plastered on her face was any indication, her opening question was only a foot in the door.

"Nothing," I grunted as I stopped beside her and started looking for my assistant. She was still in the middle of a group of girls leaving the tennis courts, and I almost waved to her, but I changed my mind at the last second. The girl at my side, completely unaware of my considerations, let her smile creep even wider.

"Oh, don't be a sore loser!" She chuckled like she'd just said something funny. "You can let him win every once in a blue moon, you know?"

I blinked at her, and it took me a few seconds to realize what she was talking about, but when I did, I could barely stop myself from letting out a snort. Yeah, because losing to Josh at basketball was obviously the biggest of my problems right now.

No, the reason why I was in my current sour mood was due to Judy running out of information to give me. After their last conversation, the class rep told her that she should know enough to confront me and ask me about the rest. Trying to squeeze more out of her after that would've been way too suspicious, so my assistant wisely went along with her "advice" and abandoned direct questions, but it ultimately meant that the class rep was no longer a free fountain of info to us.

That was, frankly, annoying. We were still only beginning to find our sea legs, and losing our crutch was a big blow. Still, there were other sources...

I looked down at the short girl still grinning expectantly at me, and after a brief moment of vacillation, I made up my mind.

"Are you free this afternoon?"

The mischievous smirk on Angie's face withered in slow motion, but then she caught herself and it was replaced by an awkward grimace.

"Wow, that was... a little sudden, don't you think?"

"Yes, but we need to talk."

"About what exactly? I'm a little busy right now, and while I would love to hang out, I already have some plans and—"

My hesitation lasted only a moment. It was a stab in the dark, but it was a necessary one. I needed more info, and she was the next on my list, anyway. I took a deep breath and leaned closer for a whisper.

"Is it Celestial business?"

Her eyes opened wide as saucers, and she glanced left and right like she was expecting a candid camera crew to jump out of a nearby bush. After a few long seconds, her eyes snapped back to me and her hand lashed out. I twitched, almost expecting a slap to the face, but instead she covered up my mouth with an uncharacteristic frown and whispered, "Not here."

This time I actually snorted, half in amusement and half in irritation, before I proceeded to remove her hand.

"That's why I asked if you were free this afternoon. Are you still busy?"

She was visibly torn over the question, but she nodded with a thin-lipped smile. "I will make time for you."

"Thanks."

There was a threat of an awkward silence hanging in the air around us, but before it could materialize, it was dispelled by a jaunty whistle. It seemed somewhat familiar, but I couldn't recall where I've heard it before.

"What's with the long face?" Josh asked playfully as he came up to us.

"Was that the victory tune from 'Final Fantasy'?" Angie inquired back without bothering to answer his question.

"Indeed it was," my friend answered with a shit-eating grin.

"Nice!" she exclaimed and the two high-fived without further prompting. It might've been a childhood friend thing or whatever.

"So?" I addressed Josh with well-veiled irritation. "Did you just come over to brag?"

"Mostly," he admitted with the same grin. "Hey, if you are allowed to rub your victories in my face, so am I!"

"When did I ever do that?"

"All the time?"

"I can't remember."

"You're getting old then."

"Or maybe he is amnesiac?" Angie chimed in with the perfect timing of the completely oblivious. "Did you hit your head?"

Josh fidgeted suspiciously, so I punched him in the shoulder with an exaggerated groan.

"Yeah, like that would happen."

"Uh, yeah," Josh agreed with a nod.

"So, if that was what you were *mostly* here for, what's the other reason?"

He looked at me blankly for a moment, but then he finally remembered our previous conversation and the smile crept back onto his face.

"Ah, right! Since you refused my invitation during lunch break, I thought I would ask you if you wanted to hang out after school. It's been a while since we did that, just the two of us."

I drew in an awkward breath through my teeth and shook my head.

"Sorry, I already have plans."

"Again?" He slumped his shoulders in disappointment. "Is it with Elly or Judy? Or are you two-timing?"

"No and no." I pointed at the girl out our side. "I need to discuss some things with Angie."

His eyes opened wide as he stared at Angie.

"You are three-timing? Man, you are crazy!"

I glanced at Angie and there was an unspoken unison between the two of us as we both raised our hands and punched the guy in the opposite shoulders. He staggered back with a surprised yelp and rubbed his upper arms.

"Ow-ow-ow! Hey, I'm joking!"

"It wasn't funny," Angie pouted with an exaggerated sulk.

"Fine, I get it," he grumbled in defeat, but only to change gears a moment later. "So, can I tag along?"

"Nope," I told him bluntly.

"Oh come on! We barely hang out lately! If this keeps going on, I'm going to become a total shut-in!"

"So you want to go into town just for that?"

"Is keeping my social life alive not a good enough reason for you?"

I shrugged. If that's all he wanted, I could help him. I looked around the field, and once I found her, I waved for the princess. She looked at me questioningly as she stepped out of her ring of followers (the placeholder girls really took a liking to her as of late), and after some more urgent waving on my end, she apologized to them and strode over to us. She had her hair done up as usual and she was a little disheveled after the class, but she somehow made even that look good.

Anyways, she stopped just outside of arm's reach and looked over each one of us in turn before finally settling on me.

"Yes? Is there a problem?"

"Nah, nothing of the sort," I said and pushed my friend to the front. "Josh was just feeling down because we couldn't hang out with him today. Could you stand in for us and spend some time with him? As friends?"

Her eyes immediately narrowed. I guessed she didn't like my meddling so soon after we both agreed to be vague on our relationship status, but at least she didn't say no right away.

"Don't I have a say in this?" Josh protested more out of habit than actual displeasure.

"Oh shut up." I patted him on the back and quipped, "Stop acting like hanging out with pretty girls is new to you."

After the obligatory blush from the two pretty girls at our side (to her credit, the princess only flushed slightly harder than Angie, probably due to my extensive immunization efforts), Josh relented.

"Fine, fine... Geez." He turned to the princess and tried to smile, though it didn't quite reach his eyes. "So, Elly... are you free this afternoon?"

"I don't have any plans, if that's what you are asking."

I left the two awkward teenagers to their devices and covertly pulled Angie to the side with a few short gestures.

"Let's get changed and meet at the lockers."

"Where are we going to talk? The roof?"

I shook my head. I'd had way too many serious conversations on the roof already. I could do with a change of scenery.

"I was thinking more along the lines of..." I frowned. Just what other places did I even know where we could discuss things? Should I invite her over to my place? Nah, that would've been a bit too forward. But then, what else was there? "... the park?"

She nodded as if my awkward suggestion was just what she was thinking of. I also couldn't help but notice the disapproval in her eyes. She probably didn't like me setting Josh up with the princess, but then again, sometimes we had to make compromises. Not to mention, things between the princess and I were somewhat troublesome at the moment, and I needed some time apart from her to impartially coalesce my long-term plans.

Anyways, we patiently waited for the two to agree on their afternoon activities. It included karaoke, which made me really conflicted. I would've absolutely loved to be there when the princess sang. It was guaranteed to be absolutely hilarious. Oh well, maybe next time.

Either way, we headed for the changing rooms. By the time I got into my uniform, Judy was already outside, waiting for me with a pair of soda cans. I smiled at her and accepted one of them.

"Thanks."

She didn't say anything, only nodded once before we headed for the classroom to get our bags, and I shared my plans for the afternoon with her on the way. She listened while emptying her can and then asked, "Isn't this too early?"

I shrugged noncommittally.

"We'll see. We need to get info out of them, and she is the only one who doesn't already think I know everything." That gave me an idea. "Say, do you want to come along?"

She slowly shook her head.

"No. If I were to do that, she might get suspicious. Not to mention, I have other plans."

"You do?" I might've sounded a little too surprised, as she gave me a hurt look. Maybe she thought I considered her unable to have plans of her own? However, before I could correct the misconception, she beat me to the punch.

"Yes. I wanted to talk to Neige."

"Oh…" It made sense in retrospect. If I talked to Angie, and the class rep was out of the question, it naturally only left her. Though again, there was always the princess, but the two of them didn't really get along at the moment, so I doubted she could've gotten any extra info out of her by asking nicely.

We reached the first floor, and after a single glance, I gestured for Judy to slow down. She obediently halted and then followed the direction of my gaze, which led to Neige.

"Speak of the devil," I whispered jovially, though I was actually more curious than anything. It was rare to see her around these parts. First years had their classrooms on the ground floor. She sometimes came up to the second floor, where our classrooms were, but unless she was looking for someone else around here, she should've had no business on the first floor. It didn't look like she did though. In fact, she was leaning out an open window (a safety hazard if I'd ever seen one) and tapping her fingers against the windowsill with a difficult expression. For a moment I entertained the thought of sneaking up on her and scaring her a little, but I discarded it and called out to her from afar. While she wasn't as clumsy as the princess, I didn't want to risk her falling out the window by accident.

"Snowy!"

She twitched as she looked up with a panicked expression, but when she realized it was only us two, she calmed down. She'd been especially jumpy as of late. I wondered why that was, but I decided to leave the question for a later date.

We walked up to her, and she smiled at us. It seemed somewhat strained, though.

"What were you looking at?" Judy asked, poking her head through the open window.

"N-nothing in particular," she answered just a tad nervously. There was something fishy about her behaviour, and while normally I would've drilled her until I found out what bothered her, right now I had an appointment to catch. Still, there was just something weird going on.

I stared at Snowy and then I looked out the open window as well. As I did, my eyes caught something peculiar and my brows began to furrow without my consent. I caught it early, though, and turned to the girl with what I hoped was a natural-looking smile.

"You know, we were just talking about you," I told her as I ushered her towards the stairwell.

"You were?" she asked dubiously, as if she was expecting a trick.

"Yeah. Judy wanted to talk to you. Speaking of which..." I turned to my assistant and said, "Could you two get my bag too? I have to go to the washroom."

My assistant wanted to object, but I wiggled my eyebrows at her and she got the message. She nodded and grabbed Snowy by the elbow, gently pulling her towards the classroom without a word. To my surprise, she didn't even protest.

I waited until they reached the stairs before I walked over to the window and poked my head through one more time. There was nothing strange going on outside. Most of the placeholders were already on their way home, with only a few slowpokes still idling around. All things considered, the scenery looked perfectly normal.

What wasn't normal, however, was the weird purple glow coming from the outside of the windowsill. I leaned closer to take a better look, but it looked like nothing more than an indistinct blotch of luminescence stuck to the wooden frame. If I strained my eyes, I could make out a few faint lines in the middle of it, but they were rapidly dissolving by the time I started observing them. Seconds later, they had completely disappeared, together with the glow.

"Well, that was strange," I mused as I headed for the stairs. I had no idea what that was, so I decided to ask Snowy the next time the opportunity presented itself. It probably wasn't anything important, but one could never know.

I met up with the girls just as they were leaving our classroom, and Judy handed me my bag. We left the second floor and greeted Angie, Josh, and the princess as we passed by each other on the way down. Once we reached the ground floor, Snowy left to get her bag, and by the time she returned, the aforementioned trio also caught up with us.

We went through the usual routine: our group separated at the shoe lockers and regrouped at the entrance once everyone retrieved their outdoor footwear. I finished first, as usual, since I had a pair of really comfy sneakers I could simply jump into without messing around with shoelaces, so I had time to think about a weird sensation I was getting. There was a person missing from the picture. It didn't take a genius to figure out who it was.

The last time I saw her, the class rep was heading towards the changing rooms behind the rest of us, yet we hadn't seen her since then. I wondered how we could've missed her on our way back, and before long I found myself slipping into Far Sight. It was a little disturbing how naturally it came to me, but I shooed such concerns away and concentrated on finding her.

In my previous experiments, I already determined that I could sense the general direction of the people I was observing, at least in relation to me, so I was a little confused when this internal compass told me the class rep was under our feet by at least several floors. The confusion quickly faded as my vision snapped into place and I found her standing in a familiar room talking to an equally familiar old man.

"... cannot trace them. At first I thought they were just fluctuations, but they happen only during school hours," came the class rep's voice as if through a badly tuned radio. By the time the other person started talking, the sound became crystal clear.

It was the same white-bearded old man I saw in the morning, and in the same room, too. He looked to be at least eighty, if not more, and his voice sounded exactly what you would expect from an old wizard, if a little dull and monotonous.

"So you say someone is using magic under our very noses? How fascinating. We should—"

"Hey, Leo!" I was pulled out of my Far Seeing by a hand shaking me by the shoulder. I opened my eyes and blinked at the girl at my side. Angie gave me an apprehensive look and stood back. "You were zoning out."

"Uh, sorry," I apologized hastily while looking for a plausible excuse. "I... didn't sleep much last night."

"Really? You should. Sleep deprivation is bad for your health."

"I know."

Well, considering I hadn't slept for over a month, I was holding up pretty well. It wasn't something I could tell her, though, so instead I just agreed with whatever she said. However, as I was nodding away, I noticed that it was just us by the entrance.

"Where are the others?" I let the innocent question slip, and Angie's usually carefree eyes were immediately set into suspicious squints again.

"Did you really fall asleep? They left just a few moments ago."

As she said that, I looked up and I could just catch Snowy's unmistakable white ponytails disappearing behind the school gates.

"Sorry, I'm a little out of it," I continued with the excuses while I threw my bag over my shoulders and began striding. "A stroll in the park should get me fresh and awake in no time."

"If you say so..." the girl at my side answered while still eyeing me skeptically, but she followed after me all the same.

PART 2

During our walk to the park, the atmosphere was unusually tense. I was tempted to break the silence several times, but I didn't have any good topics. Or rather, I had a few, but they all concerned either the supernatural or my love life, neither of which was exactly the right material for a lighthearted chat. Yet, just as I was about to give up and tried coming up with a good lead-in into my questions once we arrived, I noticed something peculiar.

Angie was humming at my side. It wasn't a complex tune, more like a nursery rhyme. What really freaked me out for a moment, though, was that she was glowing in the rhythm of her humming.

"What are you doing?" I asked her in a whisper that seemed to jolt her out of it, and the glow surrounding her dispersed like a thin fog.

She blinked at me in surprise and told me, "I'm humming because I'm bored."

With that, she averted her face with an exaggerated "Hmpf" and returned to her humming. I paid closer attention to her this time, and as the glowing started, I noticed a couple of thin lines extending from her. They looked like strands of spider silk in the wind, but they were way too weird to be anything so ordinary. My first instinct was to try to find out what they were connected to, but they were instead passing through objects. In fact, they seemed completely intangible.

After some further observations, I noticed something even more troubling: I couldn't see it at first because we were standing so close together, but there was a string pointed right at my chest. Not only that, it was much thicker than the ones randomly floating around her and it seemed to glow in unison with her weird aura. Speaking of which, how come no one found it strange that she was lighting up like she was bitten by a radioactive fluorescent light bulb? Was it something only I could see?

Those were questions for later, as I was more interested in the line connected to me at the moment. Angie's humming was getting a little erratic, as if she couldn't quite remember the exact tune of a song, and it also made the strand wiggle like it was alive. It was pretty squicky, to be honest.

I reached out a finger and plucked at the string. It was insubstantial, and when I touched it, it felt like there was a mild electric current running through my skin. It wasn't painful, but it was decidedly unpleasant. It was about this point I got really fed up with the entire situation, and I pinched Angie in the side. She literally jumped with a high-pitched yelp and sent me a look of injured pride that only she could manage. I stopped and faced her head-on.

"What are you doing!?" she exclaimed with a scowl that made me realize why Josh was so afraid of her wrath. In this case though, I matched her scowl with one of my own and pointed at the still attached strand between us.

"A better question is this: what are *you* doing?"

She gave me a puzzled look, and my further gestures only made her look even more incredulous, so I just rolled my eyes, crooked my finger into a hook, and slashed at the line in irritation. I only intended that as a vague gesture, but somehow my finger actually caught the line, stretched it out, and then it snapped like a rubber band. Angie's eyes opened wide in surprise, completely wiping away her previous frown. To be honest, I would've probably had a similar expression, but I managed to stay in character and simply shook my head.

"Seriously, I have no idea what that was, but stop it."

"I... Uh... Okay?" She nodded several times in a daze, but when I tried to start walking again, she called out to me in a borderline panicky voice. "Wait! How did you do that?"

"Which part?"

"How did you..." She paused for a moment to make sure no one was in earshot. "How did you dispel my probe spell? Was that a somatic counterspell? But you are not an Abyssal, so that can't be it..."

I let her mumble to herself for a while. My brain, on the other hand, was already switching to a higher gear.

She said *somatic* just now, didn't she? That reminded me of a particular byline in one of Judy's first reports. It said there were three kinds of magic in practice: vocal, somatic, and harmonic. According to the info collected from the class rep, magi like her were using vocal magic. Chants and the like. Somatic magic, at least by the dictionary definition, probably had something to do with the body. I figured it was movement, and according to what Angie just said, it had something to do with Abyssals. More on that later.

However, there was a third one, which made me furrow my brows: harmonics. I didn't really know what to think of it until a few minutes ago, but in retrospect, it seemed pretty obvious it had to do with music. Angie was humming, and there was weird glowy magicky stuff happening. Q.E.D., she was using harmonic magic.

It also raised an intriguing question: were these magic types unique to specific supernatural entities? Magi were vocal, Abyssals somatic, and Celestials harmonic? It made a certain sense from a constructional stand-point, but at this point it was just a stab in the dark, so I filed it under *things to figure out later* and returned to the conversation.

I had no answer to Angie's question, and since I had no idea what happened either, bullshitting my way out of answering was too risky. That left only one avenue open for me: a blatant and shameless change of topic.

"What exactly *were* you probing for, if I may ask?"

Credit where credit's due, the girl had the decency to act properly self-conscious when faced with the question. She chuckled awkwardly, but when my stare made it obvious that I wasn't giving up on the question, she let out a defeated breath and told me, "Nothing intrusive, just checking if you are under the influence."

"I'm not drinking."

"Not that kind of influence, silly!" she exclaimed while she playfully swatted at me. She was obviously trying to lower my guard a little, and to be honest, I wasn't entirely against a less formal conversation, so I smiled at her as encouragement. She grinned back and continued, "It's to see if you were bewitched."

"Bewitched?"

"Charmed, controlled, having your free will ripped from you and stuffed in a tiny cage where you can only scream endlessly on the inside as your body is being controlled by malevolent magicks... That kind of thing."

"Well. That was needlessly graphic."

"Sorry," she said, but according to her grin, she really wasn't.

"Whatever. But why would you think that in the first place? Isn't that a bit of a logical leap to make?"

Angie shrugged, which incidentally corresponded with the exact moment we arrived at the park. It was still in the early afternoon, but the skies were overcast and so it was a little darker than usual, and when you combined that with the autumn trees surrounding us, it created a somewhat eerie atmosphere. It didn't seem to get to my companion, though, as she continued discussing the matter with her usual gusto.

"It wouldn't be the first time. For some reason, the higher-ups have this creepy obsession with sending random mind-controlled dudes for correspondence. Once they even sent a nine-year-old girl just to tell me they had nothing new to say, can you believe that? After I undid the spell on her, I had to spend the entire day looking for the poor thing's parents." She paused, then gave me another puzzled look. "Speaking of dispelling, you still haven't told me how you did that."

I suppressed a twitch and turned it into a tired sigh instead. It was mostly just to gain a moment to think, but it didn't actually help, so I put on my best mysterious smile and answered, "We all have our little secrets, don't we?"

Angie nodded to herself like I'd just said something really profound, but then her brows knit again.

"Actually, now that you mention it... if it wasn't the higher-ups that sent you, then how did you know that I—?" Her face suddenly tensed and she looked around again, quickly spotting a deserted bench by a side path. "Let's continue this conversation over there. We are in the open."

I wanted to point out that we would be in the open even if we went there, but I wasn't entirely against the idea of sitting down, so I curtly nodded and we walked over to the bench without further ado.

Angie dusted the bench seat and sat down. I was about to do the same, but a small gust of wind made me reconsider. It wasn't too cold, but it *was* October already, and considering she only wore her school uniform with its short skirt, I was fairly certain she was feeling its bite more than I did. So I held up a hand.

"Hold my seat. I'm going to go and grab some warm drinks. I'll be right back."

I left in a hurry, though not before flashing her a reassuring smile. It had been a while, but I knew there was a vending machine not too far from where we stood. It wasn't the same one I used when I met up with Snowy, but this one was closer. Or so I thought. But then it turned out I couldn't get to it, as part of the park was closed down. According to the sign next to the cordon, the police were searching for some kind of large goat or ram, and once I finished reading it, I had to shake my head in disapproval. Just how dangerous could a goat be that it would warrant locking up half the place? Maybe if it was a mountain lion or a cassowary, I could understand that. But a goat of all things?

Anyways, I still managed to get the hot cocoa, even if I had to go the long way for it. On the plus side, at least I got some extra time to think, so it wasn't all bad. It didn't take a genius to figure out that my approach with Angie was the wrong one. I did get her to talk to me, but she was extremely on guard, and while I already learned some tidbits just from observation, I managed to accidentally get her to think I was involved with their magic masquerade as much as the others. That didn't bode well for my plan of asking about the basics, but all I could do was to grit my teeth and carry on for now.

I was so lost in my thoughts that at first I didn't even notice the light-show down the path, but by the time I got within a stone's throw to the place where I'd left Angie, I had to squint my eyes or risk going blind. The glow surrounding her was way more intense than when we walked, so much so that it took my eyes a while to adjust enough to make out her shape under the bright, if oddly colourless, light.

The first thing that struck me was how many of those translucent strands surrounded her. They weren't attached to anything, but instead slowly undulated around her like the tendrils of a giant jellyfish, slithering around (and sometimes through) trees and other obstacles as if licking them. It was a little creepy, to be honest.

Some of those strands were waving in my direction, and for obvious reasons that needed no stating, I didn't really want them to touch me. So I carefully wove around the tendrils while making sure I wouldn't spill our drinks, which was getting harder and harder the closer I got to her, but I was always up for a little challenge.

I was practically next to Angie by the time I realized that she was humming again, though at such a low volume I could barely make out the tune. I was more interested in the glow surrounding her.

To my surprise (though to be perfectly honest, at this point I shouldn't have been surprised by something like this), I found that the main source of the light was a ring floating over her head. It was as insubstantial as the strings, and it was slowly rotating in a horizontal plane parallel with the crown of her head. No matter how I looked at it, it was a halo, and not the medieval artwork kind that looked like someone had a stage light behind their head. No, it was a stereotypical, ring-shaped halo you would find floating over the head of a chubby cherub on a Valentine's card. Speaking of cherubs, she also had a set of similarly insubstantial wings on her back, clipping through the backrest of the bench even in their folded state. It looked weird and yet strangely fitting at the same time, which was also weird. In other words, it was double-weird.

For the next five seconds or so, I silently waited for her to realize I was beside her, but all I got for my trouble was nearly spilling my drink as I had to continually dodge the tendrils. I soon lost my patience and loudly cleared my throat. Her reaction was several magnitudes more extreme than I expected, as she jumped onto her feet with a loud shriek and waved her hands around like she had an entire swarm of bees surrounding her. It took her a couple of seconds before she realized it was only me, and she gaped at me in shock.

The silence between us seemed to last for hours, and it was positively deafening.

"Leo..." she uttered, her legs still shaking. "You're freaking me out right now."

"Why? You don't like cocoa? I can get you an espresso, if you want." Her eyes told me, in no uncertain terms, that I should stop joking, so I dropped my shoulders in resignation. "Okay, okay. You are not in the mood. I get it. Sorry for startling you."

"It's not about that!" she denied, but I could still see her legs trembling a little, so I gestured towards the bench with my chin and she promptly sat down. I followed suit, but I could barely rest my backside before she spoke again. "How did you do that?"

"What exactly do you mean by *that*?" I asked innocently while sipping from my cup. "Ah, it's hot!"

"Leo, stop messing around and answer me seriously."

"If you mean how I got close to you without you noticing, it wasn't that hard. You were really caught up in your humming magic or whatever."

"The entire point of that *humming magic* was to alert me if someone comes close!"

"Oh," I blurted out as realization dawned on me. So those strands were like tripwires, huh? I let out a thoughtful little grunt and turned to her with a small smile. "So *that's* what it was! You should work on it a bit more. They were pretty easy to dodge."

By the looks of it, she still thought I wasn't serious, for she let out an indignant huff and crossed her arms in front of her chest. She also gave me one of those glares of hers, the one that was probably supposed to look withering, but it rather reminded me of a sulky puppy missing its chew toy.

"Whatever. You obviously don't want to answer me."

"I do, you are just being too tense. Here, have a drink and unwind a little."

She gave a doubtful glance at the second cup in my hand, but she accepted it all the same. She took a cautious sip and the scowl on her face slowly faded as the warmth spread through her. I waited for her to finish drinking before I got ready to clear things up, but I was beaten to the punch yet again.

"Leo," she spoke up in a soft voice that somehow made her words sound even more meaningful. "We are friends, aren't we?"

"I was led to believe so, yes."

She looked at me flatly and then proceeded to pinch my forearm. I was expecting it, and it didn't really hurt, so I only smiled at her in return.

"You can be such a jerk," she continued, pouting. "Please take this seriously."

"I do, I do. Sorry."

She took a deep breath and her voice became soft again.

"I want to believe we are friends, so please tell me... Whose side are you on?"

Now it was my turn to give her a flat look before I buried my forehead in my hand.

"Really? Is this really a stock question around these parts?"

"Stock question?"

"Yeah. Literally *everyone* asked me this! Some even verbatim! As in, *literally* literally, word for word!"

She fell silent for a second, thinking.

"By everyone, you mean... um, everyone?"

"You are being redundant, but yes."

"So... they thought you were associated with someone else?"

"Yep."

"But you are not?"

"Nope."

"And you weren't sent by the Celestial Intelligence Network, either?"

"Obviously not."

"But the... who told you about me?"

"I figured it out on my own," I told her off-the-cuff, and she instantly paled and leaned closer for a whisper.

"How?!"

For a moment I was tempted to tell her, *You know your name literally means "divine angel," right?* But it seemed people in this world were unaware of the meaningful names floating around the same way they were ignoring any weird behaviour from the placeholders, and I didn't want to break the illusion by pointing it out. Who knew what I could break by spreading meta-knowledge around?

I still had to give her an answer, though, so I said, "Honestly, just a hunch. You only confirmed it a few minutes ago."

She looked me in the eye as if searching it for traces of deceit. I really hoped she didn't have the ability to detect half-truths. My worries were proven unfounded soon, though, as she let out a relieved sigh so over-the-top, I was afraid she'd fall off the bench. But then she pummeled my shoulder with her fists. It was only for show, so it didn't actually hurt or anything, but it was sudden enough to make me instinctively reel back.

"Leo, you jerk! Do you have any idea how scared I was? I thought my cover was compromised!"

"Calm down, calm down..." I gently grabbed hold of her wrists and made her stop hitting me. "It's not my fault you were jumping to conclusions."

"Maybe..." she relented with a sideways glance before she returned her gaze to me. "But you still nearly blew my cover, so it's your fault all the same."

"Yet nothing happened, and you even got a free hot cocoa out of it."

"That's a good point." She nodded like I'd just said something insightful. I wanted to point out that it was a joke, but thought twice about it and let the topic drop.

"Whatever." I raised my cup to my mouth to finish it up, though the real reason was to gain a second to think.

The situation had successfully defused, and Angie was back to normal. That was good. On the other hand, now she was completely convinced I was neck-deep in their little masquerade, so my original plans were out the window. Still, I could try gathering some info from her all the same.

"So, how long have you been undercover?"

"Undercover?"

"Yeah. You've known Josh since childhood, right? That means you were placed pretty early."

She laughed awkwardly and avoided eye contact.

"That... was actually just a happy coincidence."

"Really?"

"Yeah! It's not like everything we do is part of some long-running nefarious plan, you know? Coincidences happen."

By *we,* I presumed she meant Celestials as a whole.

"So you just accidentally happened to be the childhood friend of the guy around whom the entire universe revolves. That's some coincidence all right."

She avoided my eyes again and muttered, "I don't like it, either."

"Yeah, I figured."

"It can't be helped, though. The others must have caught wind of the prophecy."

I tried, I really did, but I still couldn't stifle the groan. She gave me a funny look, so I cleared my throat and said in my most diplomatic voice, "Which one?"

"There's more than one?"

"Apparently. What is yours?"

She looked dubious, but nevertheless, she told me, "Well, it's actually pretty simple. You know how the Deus sacrificed himself to seal away the Abyssals in the... well, Abyss?"

Naturally, I had no idea, but I nodded anyway.

"I always wondered if they were also called Abyssals before that... Anyways, that happened a long time ago. After that, we had this prophecy saying that the Deus would be reborn as a human and they would return to us one day."

"And that would be Josh?"

"Uh, maybe?" she said cautiously, but then added, "I mean, there are a couple other candidates, but Josh does seem to be in the center of attention. Maybe they know something we don't?"

I thought that was a rhetorical question, but the way she looked at me made me realize it was aimed at me. I pondered that, then answered with a diplomatic, "I think it's a little more complicated than that."

I wasn't lying about that. Anyone with half a brain could see that Josh's position at the center of the attention was a contrived one. He was not only a harem-protagonist pursued by four girls, all of whom belonged to different supernatural races to boot, but he was also the focal point of at least two prophecies, and nothing said *contrived significance* like a prophecy trope. In fact, I wouldn't have been surprised if the other two girls and their people also had their own brand of prophecies. It was a little depressing, to be honest. I really wasn't a fan of anything that involved "prophecies" and "destinies" or any other plot devices that clobbered free will over its head, but I wasn't exactly in a position where I could do anything about it.

"Complicated, you say? So you do know something about it."

"Only a little," I responded while projecting false modesty. I had an image to keep up at this point, and if she was convinced I knew more than I did, then I had to act the part. "I'm gathering information for unrelated reasons, and sometimes I just stumble upon interesting things."

"You are brokering secrets?"

If her tone was any indication, she seemed totally flabbergasted by the idea. I didn't know whether that was a good thing or not (though I had a feeling it was the latter), so I took a deep breath and engaged in the traditional practice of free-form discussion derailment.

"I cannot confirm or deny such accusations... But now that you brought it up, just how long do you plan to keep *your* secret from the others? Wait, scratch that. The better question is, *why* do you keep it a secret in the first place?"

If her deadpan gaze was any indication, she might've been onto me, but she didn't call me out and only shook her head.

"Leo, you *are* aware of our reputation, right?" I probably hesitated too long (though to be fair, I really didn't know whether I should nod or shake my head at that), so she continued, "They would probably think I'm here as part of some centuries-old master plan or something. It would be... really awkward. Not to mention it could strain our friendship. I don't want either of those to happen."

"Are you actually here as a part of a centuries-old master plan?" I asked her point-blank, and she froze up for a second.

"Um... no?"

"Then I don't see the problem. They are going to figure it out anyway, sooner or later."

She twitched and glanced at me with a concerned expression.

"What do you mean by that?"

"Well..." I hesitated again, but I figured I might as well just run with it. "First off, it probably wouldn't take them long to realize that Celestials are missing from the picture. We already have a Draconian, a Magi, and an Abyssal in the group, after all. Once they realize that, it won't take long to put two and two together."

"That doesn't mean anything. There are no knights or nerds in our group, either."

"Knights and nerds...?" I echoed her, but I quickly put the question aside. "That's beside the point. Listen, what I'm trying to say is that it's not a secret you could, or indeed *should*, keep for long under the current circumstances."

"What circumstances are we talking about?"

"You've heard about the battle yesterday, right?"

To my surprise, Angie tensed up like a piano wire and exclaimed, "Battle? When? Where?"

"You really don't know?" She shook her head, so I elaborated. "Okay, here's what happened in a nutshell: The princess and Snowy had a disagreement that may or may not have been related to me. It escalated, and they took it into the purple zone."

"Purple what?"

"Restricted space, but don't sweat the small details. Anyhow, the important part is that they tried to duke it out between each other after getting all horny."

"That sounded really dirty."

"Yeah," I said while scratching my cheek. "I realized it after I said it. Anyways, I managed to stop them, but they could've gotten really hurt if I hadn't intervened in time."

"That's good to hear, but how does that relate to me?"

I paused to collect my thoughts and purposefully lowered my voice.

"Listen, Angie. Tensions are high right now. Whether it comes to light during another crisis or whether you reveal it yourself under controlled conditions could make all the difference between another fight and a peaceful reconciliation. I don't think it needs saying, but I would prefer the latter, thank you very much."

"Wait, I don't follow. Why would there be a crisis in the future?" She frowned. "Do you know something the rest of us don't?"

I raised an accusative eyebrow at the blatant change in topic, but her eyes seemed earnest enough, so I let it slide. She let me get away with my topic switches, so this was only fair. Either way, I looked up and took a deep breath. How was I supposed to answer that?

"Put simply, the situation surrounding Josh has been developing at a ridiculous pace lately. As much as I'd hate it to happen, I think we reached the point where the current status quo is going to be shaken up. Hard."

That was a very diplomatic and non-meta way of saying that we reached the end of the preambles and it was time for the main act. And if my research into supernatural harem stories had convinced me of anything (aside from them being a lot less entertaining when you were inside one of them), it was that the first act inevitably ended with a bad guy showing up and threatening people. I already had a couple of candidates for the role, and I planned to keep tabs on them, but who exactly the Big Baddie was remained to be seen.

Something was about to happen, and that something would involve Josh, the girls, and, by proxy, me. This reminded me of my current goal: I wasn't just collecting data on the supernatural out of intellectual curiosity, nor just to help me answer the big questions about the world. It all had a much, much more practical benefit. I needed to know so that I could effectively look after my friends when push came to shove, which would inevitably happen, and rather sooner than later, most likely.

But back to the current conversation in progress. Angie once again looked me in the eye like she was looking for the truth in my retina.

"So... it's a hunch?"

"You could say that, yes."

"And you expect it would cause a conflict in our group?"

"With all of these prophecies and other friction points? If nobody does anything about it, I can practically guarantee it."

She paused, genuinely surprised by my direct answer.

"And you want to be the one to do something about it?"

"That's the plan," I told her with an expression I hoped was suitably solemn. "I don't have anything to do with your prophecies and whatnot, so I can act as a neutral party. I'm going to try my best to make sure nobody gets hurt and everyone stays friends, even if I have to work overtime."

"That's..." she began, only to falter, pause, and then started sniffing and rubbing her eyes. I was just about to ask her if everything was all right, but before I could open my mouth, she suddenly exclaimed, "That's so admirable!"

Her teary-eyed response was so unexpected, I couldn't help but shoot her a skeptical glance.

"Are you making fun of me right now?"

"No!" she protested while rummaging through her bag to get a tissue. "I mean it! I knew you were a good guy, but I never realized you were so..." She blew her nose, and by the time she continued, the end of her sentence got lost.

"I'm really not," I protested, though I had to admit it felt nice to be praised every once in a while, even if the praise was wholly undeserved.

"Can I help?" The question took me aback, in part because of its sudden ferocity. "I want everyone to keep getting along too! Please?"

I honestly didn't know how to answer that. Considering that a few minutes ago she was borderline paranoid about me, her sudden enthusiasm was downright jarring. That said, I had no real reason to doubt her sincerity, so after a little thinking, I gave her a tentative nod.

"Fine by me. First things first, you really need to tell them you are a Celestial."

Her enthusiasm wilted in fast-forward.

"Do I have to?"

"Yes. I told you, I want to get rid of anything extraneous that could cause friction in the group."

Of course, there was always the main source of said friction, namely Josh, but I couldn't really do anything about him, now could I?

"But it would compromise my cover..."

"And I told you that you don't really need it, but if you really insist, we can make them swear to keep it a secret. We can trust them with that much, can't we?"

"I suppose..."

She didn't sound entirely convinced, so I cleared my throat and moved on before she would lose whatever passion she still had for the idea.

"More importantly, though, I could really use some information."

"What kind?" She immediately perked up, probably happy about leaving the topic of her *cover* behind. "Financial? Political?"

"I was... actually thinking about the basics first."

"The basics? How basic are we talking about?"

"Very basic." She looked at me doubtfully, but by then I had a perfectly reasonable explanation in store. "I am in a unique position where I can ask for info from all of you. I want to be able to cross-reference what you can tell me, and I don't want to leave any stone unturned."

I admit, it was a pretty flimsy explanation, but I only came up with it a few minutes beforehand, so I decided to cut myself some slack. Angie seemed to be perfectly satisfied with it, though, so maybe it wasn't as bad as I feared.

"That's pretty smart. For you."

"Hey!"

"Just kidding!" She snickered while she rummaged through her belongings, then handed me a small, dog-eared booklet. I must have looked at it funny, for she rolled her eyes in exaggeration and shook it in front of me. "This is my old field manual. I got it when I was ten, so it's a little worn out, but it has most of the basics in it."

"That's... convenient."

"Yeah, I suppose." She shrugged as she deposited the booklet in my hand. "Not as convenient as the website, though."

I originally wanted to ask her why she was carrying around such blatantly incriminating evidence if she cared so much about her cover, but then her words finally registered with me, and I could barely keep my voice down.

"Wait, there is a site for that?!"

"Yeah."

"On the internet?"

"Technically it's in the 'deep web.' I don't know what that is, but you access it with a browser, so I suppose it's there." She stared at me for a moment before a familiar, impish smile crept onto her face. "Why are you so shocked, Leo? It's the twenty-first century, you know."

I wasn't paying her much attention. I hurriedly took my phone out and fired up the built-in browser.

"Can you send me a URL?" I blurted out, only to belatedly realize that Angie also had an old brick phone, so she couldn't have even if she wanted to. She didn't point out my gaffe, though—just flashed me a toothy smile instead.

"Sure! It's kinda long and weird and full of numbers, but..." She turned around again and descended elbow-deep into her bag. "I haven't been up there for years. It has articles about all the basics a newly initiated Celestial should know, but it is written so dryly and it's so convoluted that I only looked at it once and never bothered after that. It's kind of like that sex ed site we had to check out when we were freshmen... Oh, right, you weren't with us back then. Did you have to go to a site like that?"

"I don't think we did," I answered without much thinking. "I can't even really remember the details."

Angie giggled with a knowing expression, probably reading something wholly unintended into my words, then she abruptly grinned at me and brandished a torn page from a textbook.

"I knew I still had it on me! Here!"

The page she handed to me contained only a single web address, and she wasn't kidding when she said it was long and full of numbers. It took me nearly a minute to manually enter it, and once I did, it took several seconds for the page to load.

And there it was. A very simple, white main page with Comic Sans lettering and a whole throng of male enhancement ads filling the sidebars. I gave the girl at my side a wry glance. She shrugged apologetically.

"Hey, you know we're not involved with human society on principle. We have to pay the server bills somehow."

I only shook my head at her excuses and returned to the screen. On the top of the site, there were a few buttons with text so tiny they were barely readable, and the layout was so horrible any semi-competent web designer would've gotten a heart attack just from a glance, but it was functional enough. I tried poking at *News*, but when I did so, the site gave me a pop-up window asking for log-in information.

"Ah! I completely forgot about that!" Angie exclaimed as she theatrically hit her forehead with the heel of her palm. "You can only access the actual articles if they give you an account. Sorry, my bad."

"Don't worry about it," I told her reflexively, though I'd be lying if I said I wasn't a little disappointed. "Is there no way to circumvent it?"

"I don't think so." Then she reluctantly said, "I can lend you my account, if you really need it. It was..."

She started mumbling at my side, probably trying to remember her password. I felt conflicted about that. I really didn't want to borrow something like that, since it could get her into trouble, but at the same time, access to this site could make things sooo much easier for me. I glanced back at the screen and stared long and hard at the log-in prompt.

"Oh well, here goes nothing..." I whispered under my breath as I poked at the screen and entered *admin* for username and *password* for password, and... it didn't work.

Oh well, I thought. I was about to abandon the attempt as a pointless whim, but then I decided that one more try wouldn't hurt anyone, so I put in *admin* and *12345*, and...

"You've got to be shitting me."

"What?" Angie looked startled by my language. I quickly put my phone away and flashed my innocentest innocent smile.

"Nothing. Just talking to myself."

"Oh..." My smile probably wasn't as perfect as I hoped, for she looked at least a little suspicious, but she didn't pursue the topic, and instead she told me, "I can't remember my password, but my username is—"

"Wait!" I stopped her before she could say anything else. "I really don't want to impose on you any more than I already have."

"Are you sure?"

"Yes, I'm perfectly, one hundred percent fine with what I already have."

"If you say so..."

She sounded surprisingly dejected, and I needed a quick way to change the direction of the conversation, lest she realize I'd accidentally hacked their secret webpage.

"Say, all these heavy topics made me hungry... Do you know any places nearby with good crêpes?"

"Crêpes?"

To say that *she perked up at the mention of sweets* was an understatement bordering on "*the ocean is wet*" level.

"Yeah, I'm in the mood for some," I said with a wink. "Are you?"

"Does the sun rise in the east?"

"I guess that's a yes."

"Of course it's a yes!" With that, she jumped to her feet, all of our previous seriousness evaporating, and gestured for me to follow. "I know the perfect place! It's only a couple of minutes on foot from here."

I stood up and followed after her, suddenly feeling like the owner of a really energetic puppy. I supposed I could indulge her for the rest of the day. Making my life infinitely easier with a single URL deserved at least that much in return.

CHAPTER 17

PART 1

"I still can't believe this…" I whispered for the umpteenth time between two sips from my giant *I <3 Coffee* mug. I reread the section in question to make sure I interpreted it properly before I jotted down a few questions into my notebook, crossed out a previous one, and then dropped it all onto the desk with exasperation and stood up from my computer with a low groan.

A quick glance at the clock told me it was well past midnight, and while it wasn't late per se (the word kind of lost its meaning because of my sleepless lifestyle, anyways), it still meant I spent close to seven hours hunched over in front of my monitor. I was fairly certain that was unhealthy, but after a quick bathroom break and grabbing some snacks from the fridge downstairs, I continued right where I left off.

I stared at the site still open in front of me. Should I feel incredibly lucky or absolutely terrified? I wondered. I couldn't decide. Angie probably had no idea about it (or at least I hoped she didn't), but its main purpose wasn't to educate newly initiated Celestials. By the way, yes, Celestials living in human society had to be initiated at a young age, and before that, they didn't even know they were magical. It had something to do with protocols and hierarchy and something that sounded suspiciously like a caste system, but it was beside the point.

Wait, what was the point again? Ah, right: the Celestial Hub. In short, it wasn't just a crappy site designed to show the ropes for the newbies. It was actually a crappy site designed to show the ropes for the newbies… that also happened to be the hub of the entire Celestial Intelligence Network. In other words, I'd just hacked into the Pentagon of the supernatural by complete accident.

I mean, what the actual hell? I knew mundane governments had lots of problems with cybersecurity, but being able to guess an administrator-level password of an allegedly elite branch of a secret supernatural superpower was a failure of such epic proportions that I was still half-expecting it to be a trap.

Yet, the rewards were simply too great to ignore, and what originally began as cautious browsing of the more innocent-looking items soon turned into a deep dive into the secrets of one of the supernatural giants of this world.

Most of the data contained within the databases and reports, which had to be accessed through a separate interface that reminded me of the DOS era, were obviously about Celestials and their sneaky business. Looking at it made me realize just what Angie meant when she said her people *"had a reputation"* and that everyone would think she was a mole in the group. Hell, after what I saw here, even I wasn't 100 percent certain she wasn't.

But I'm getting ahead of myself. According to what I gathered, Celestials were defined by three things: their frantic search for this previously mentioned "Deus" fellow (who, contrary to his name, wasn't a god, just a very powerful not-angel and a bit of a cult leader), their rigid adherence to a stratified society, and using third parties and counterintelligence to keep the other factions at bay.

All three of those defining traits were related to said Deus fellow, so I might as well explain his deal. A couple centuries before, the Celestials and Abyssals were at war. I can't say I was particularly surprised by that. Angels and demons obviously wouldn't get along, even if they were roses by any other name. Anyways, the Abyssals were actually winning, so Deus, the dear leader of all Celestials, hallowed be his holy socks, sacrificed himself in order to create an impenetrable barrier to seal the Abyssals into the Abyss—and just to answer Angie's offhanded question, yes, apparently they were called that even before they were sealed away.

What's that? You wonder how Snowy and her big bro are running around if there is a totally-impenetrable-and-in-no-way-contrived barrier locking all Abyssals into their underground realm of slight unpleasantness? Well, okay, technically it wasn't all that unpleasant. As one informant in a thread shared, they have great vacation destinations. More on that later. Anyhow, the reason for the Abyssals' presence on the island was...

... entirely unclear to me.

Since Judy didn't know about all this when she talked with Snowy, she naturally couldn't inquire about it, so I supposed it was left to me to ask the girl later. By the way, my dear assistant also sent me another report with all the info she drilled out of the white-haired Seducer (that was the technical name of her kind; I suppose "succubus" wasn't on the nose enough), but I was so deep in my site-crawling that I only skimmed it before I returned to my PC. I didn't want to devalue her efforts, but damn, this site was a treasure-trove that was hard to compete with.

According to the long mourning discourses on the site's Tutorial (and I do mean long; there was even a three-hour-long eulogy included), the Celestials were devastated by the death of their most noble, courageous, and charismatic leader, and dedicated themselves to upholding *"the perfect society he created.*" Did I mention he was a bit of a creepy cult leader? Because he totally was.

By the way, this is where the Celestial prophecy comes into the picture. According to it, this Deus fellow's soul would be reborn as a human and usher in a new golden age for the Celestials. However, they had absolutely no idea exactly when or where he would return, and they were afraid that if they interbred with humans (which, for your interest, they apparently could do) it would make finding the needle in the haystack even harder. So they not only completely removed themselves from human affairs, but even proceeded to work in the shadows to limit the influence of the other factions, as well.

What were these other factions? Well, I was already well-acquainted with the Draconians and the Abyssals. The former were descendants of an ancient race of shape-shifting dragons that had interbred with humans and become the dominant force in human society until a few hundred years ago. Then they were hunted down by knights. Whether those knights were also rescuing princesses from tall towers in the process, I had no idea.

Seriously, though, there were a couple of references to something called *the Knightly Brotherhood of the Most Heroic Bloodlines*—a mouthful of a name if I'd ever heard one. More relevantly, they appeared to be a sort of secret society that existed for nearly a thousand years and had been fighting the supernatural races in general and dragons in particular. The Celestials had a pretty bad opinion of them, calling them a "*failed experiment*" and whatnot, but they were apparently responsible for the extinction of the real dragons and the Draconians' decline in power.

Now, silly as it sounded, I actually wasn't kidding about them rescuing princesses, though I was still entirely unsure about the tower part. As my research revealed, Draconians seemed to have a strange obsession with kidnapping royalty. Or rather, Sebastian in particular had a strange obsession with it. If those records were to be believed, a dapper gentleman with white stripes in his hair had been running around Europe and occasionally kidnapping people in power since the freakin' fifth century. Well, I had to give it to him, he was dedicated to his craft. Or maybe he just had a fetish for princesses. Or their ransom money. One or the other.

Speaking of fetishes, while the Celestials didn't like the knights, they must've found the dragons incredibly sexy, as Abyssals are actually a race that was born from a mixed Celestial/Dragon lineage. The articles on these guys were also all over the place. About half of them described them as crazy, war-mongering madmen leading armies of Fauns (some kind of animal-human-hybrid monsters or something... The authors never went into great detail about them) constantly fighting each other over something called "*Mana Wells*" in the Abyss, while the other half described them as creepy, manipulative assholes that would sell their own mothers for power. Granted, the two depictions weren't mutually exclusive, but then there was a very small minority that said that the Abyssals were perfectly normal people who were just being driven to extremes because of their exile.

Now, the faction I didn't actually know much about was the Magi. Or Wizards. Or Mages. Or Sorcerers. Or whatever.

That wasn't a joke. It seemed that no one could make up their mind about what these guys were called. I've already referred to them as Magi, since according to Judy, that's what the class rep called her *people*, so I decided to stick to that.

Thankfully, *what* they *were* was a little bit easier to figure out than their official name. Magi were, according to the introductory articles, another secret society focused on researching magic and "*piercing the veil of creation*," whatever the hell that meant. They had a central governmental body called the Assembly, but they otherwise lived and worked in "*Schools*" dedicated to certain pursuits. While I figured this was a reference to the different schools of magic one would see in an RPG, I had a hunch it might have been fairly literal in our case. In fact, I was pretty sure the local School was right under our actual school.

More importantly, Magi were something of a grudging ally of the Celestials, or rather, their goals were fairly similar. The Magi wanted to preserve the status quo to be able to research magic and do whatever else they wanted in peace, which was pretty much in line with the Celestials' noninvolvement policy. The grudging part came from the fact that the Magi viewed the Celestials as just as much of a nuisance as the other factions, and thus their relationship was less about cooperation and more about turning a blind eye to their activities so long as it didn't involve Magi business. So yeah, petty power-politics were very much alive in the supernatural world.

There were also some footnotes about another minor faction in the articles, something called *the Non-causative Science Research Society*, an off-shoot branch of the Magi that had broken off a couple decades before. There wasn't much known about them, and they didn't seem to be a major player, so I also relegated them to my own footnotes.

Speaking of which, my notebook was getting messy again. I looked over the questions I'd written down and decided to start doing pinpoint searches. My first target was the word *prophecy*, but when I looked up at the screen, I noticed a red exclamation mark on the button just above the search bar. It said *Chat*.

I hovered my mouse over it for a moment, uncertain about how safe it would be to make direct contact like this, but curiosity took the better of me. I thought I was being fairly safe. I was using a proxy and was accessing the site with a browser designed to be hard to track, so unless I made some mistake with the settings, my identity was fairly secure.

I took a deep breath to steel myself and clicked the button. After the site reloaded, I was treated to a blank white chat window. It didn't stay that way for long.

"MoroseMoose: Hello Admin."

"MoroseMoose: Where have you been?"

"MoroseMoose: We haven't heard from you for months."

I gulped as my fingers hovered over the keyboard, albeit not for long.

"Admin: I was busy with work."

"MoroseMoose: I figured."

"MoroseMoose: Are you back for good?"

"MoroseMoose: It was a pain in the ass to manage the site in your absence, you know? T_T"

"W1NG3D N1NJ4: ADMIN IS BACK?!?!?!?!???1?!!?one (*°▽°*)"

"MoroseMoose: Yes. I just noticed it too."

"W1NG3D N1NJ4: FINALLY!!! (≧▽≦)/"

"W1NG3D N1NJ4: DUDE WE REALLY NEED YOU TO GET RID OF THESE F****G SPAMBOTS!!! (ノಠ益ಠ)ノ彡┻━┻"

"W1NG3D N1NJ4: WHERE DID YOU DISAPPEAR TO ANYWAYS?!?!?!"

"W1NG3D N1NJ4: HELLO, ARE YOU STILL THERE?!?!?!!!!?!? (•̀ω•́)"

"Admin: Yeah. Stop yelling."

"W1NG3D N1NJ4: oops.sorry. /(//•/ω/•//)/"

I paused for a moment. I recognized the names from the forums attached to the main site. These guys were some of the regulars, and while they were "agents," they seemed fairly typical as far as internet denizens were concerned. Then again, most Celestials living in the human world only knew this site as a crappy PSA page dedicated to helping newcomers catch up. Because of this, we had a lot of fairly normal people who used the forums to ask questions from more *experienced* Celestials, while the actual spies and field agents only used the site to deposit their reports into the main database.

These guys were the middle ground—users who were serious members of the Celestial intelligence network but at the same time used the forums and chat to socialize, too... and I had no idea how to interact with them. In retrospect, maybe entering into this chatroom was not one of my brighter ideas, but I had no choice but to run with it and improvise as best as I could.

"Admin: I was underground."

"MoroseMoose: You were in the Abyss?"

"Admin: Not literally."

"Admin: Also, the Abyss isn't actually under the ground."

I paused again and suddenly recalled a fairly recent report I skimmed through a few hours before.

"Admin: I had to move because of the fallout after the Cardhouse incident."

"W1NG3D N1NJ4: THAT S**T AGAIN?!?! F***K, WAS THERE ANYONE WHO WASN'T F*****D OVER BY THAT S**T?!?!?!!!?!?!?? (≧Д≦)"

"W1NG3D N1NJ4: ARE YOU ALL RIGHT?!!?!?!?! (6‿ඞ。)"

"Admin: Mostly. I have to lie low for a while."

"MoroseMoose: Good to hear."

"MoroseMoose: Are you going to keep managing the site?"

"Admin: Yes, I will try to clean things up a little."

"W1NG3D N1NJ4: GOOD. START WITH THE M**********G SPAMBOTS!!!!"

"MoroseMoose: I have to agree with my eloquent colleague."

"MoroseMoose: I'm not joking. It's been a huge problem since you left."

I massaged my brows to help them unknot as I looked at the chat window. So now that I'd taken the identity of the administrator, I had to keep pretending until I finished getting as much info out of the site as I could. Though, on second thought, having the hub of the Celestial Intelligence Network at my beck and call had potential. Oh, and danger. Blood-curling, run-for-your-life, the-entire-might-of-the-Celestial-people-crashing-onto-your-head kind of danger. Any sane person would've pulled the plug at this point. I suppose it says a lot about me that I just snorted and limbered up my fingers before I continued.

"Admin: Fine. We are going to do a full reset."

"MoroseMoose: What? :\"

"Admin: We reset all the passwords. I'm also going to get rid of the ads, they are a security risk."

"W1NG3D N1NJ4: AND HOW ARE WE GOING TO PAY FOR THE SERVER?!!!!?!?!"

"Admin: Let me worry about that one. You guys spread the word, I will take care of the new security measures. We need better password security too. I might also hire someone to redesign the main page while I'm at it."

"Admin: If everything works as planned, we should get the site working as intended in a few days."

"MoroseMoose: We? Since when are we working on the site?"

"Admin: Since about ten seconds ago. Congratulations on your promotion."

"W1NG3D N1NJ4: WOW!1!!one! O(≧∇≦)O"

"W1NG3D N1NJ4: ADMIN TOOK A LEVEL IN AWESOME!!! I APPROVE!! (●♡∀♡)"

"MoroseMoose: Whatevs. I'll do my part."

"Admin: Good."

I stretched my fingers and began to enact my plans with enthusiasm that surprised even me.

PART 2

It was 6:30 a.m. when I hit the *Confirm* button on the designer app and the new site went online. I knew practically nothing about programming, but as it turned out, the original site was made with one of those handy template designer programs, and after reading the documentation and some tutorials on the net, I was able to fix the most glaring problems with just a little trial and error.

The reappearance of "Admin" also ran through the community like wildfire, and I was bombarded with questions in the chat about my where-abouts. My cover story was that I was involved in the *Cardhouse incident*, where several Celestial operatives were busted by the Magi while they tried to infiltrate a School. Since operatives were only briefed on a need-to-know basis, I actually had more info than most of them, and thus I was able to uphold my fake identity pretty well. Or so I hoped.

As I thought about these things, the site finally finished updating. A brand-new main page welcomed me. It was nothing special, but it was miles better than the original mess. It hadn't been up for more than a few seconds when the chat button flashed.

"KittYkaTT101: wow great job admin"

"19891224: Where did all the ads go?! How will I get my male en-hancement pills now?!"

"MoroseMoose: You talk like you actually need those."

"19891224: Hey, you can never know when a few extra inches could be useful. "

"W1NG3D N1NJ4: WHAT ARE YOU TALKING ABOUT?!?!!!? YOU ARE A GIRL!!!1! δ('д';)"

"KittYkaTT101: you are confusing him with his sister 19891223"

"19891224: Common mistake."

"Admin: Settle down, kids."

"MoroseMoose: Look, the man of the day is back!"

"Rock998: Hey man! Great to have you back!"

"19891224: Gimme back my ads! :3"

I chuckled to myself. I never thought top-secret supernatural operatives would be this lively, but I was honestly starting to like these guys.

"Admin: Behave yourself and you might get to keep one in your sidebar, but only if you promise to take care of it."

"19891224: Sure daddy, I promise I'll take it on walks and everything."

"MoroseMoose: You sure this won't cause a problem with the servers?"

"Admin: No, they are already paid for."

In fact, the servers didn't even cost that much. They were on a shady Eastern European server-farm, though, and since I didn't trust those guys as far as I could throw them, I had to jump through a couple of annoying hoops to pay them, which included setting up fake accounts, buying fake credit cards to make it harder to track me, losing a thousand Jens in a scam (it happens), and then finally paying them. Still, if they held their end of the bargain, we were in the green for a couple of months.

"W1NG3D N1NJ4: ADMIN IS SUPER-AWESOME!!! one!! (♥ω♥) ~♪"

"Admin: I am."

"Admin: Moose, are you up for what we discussed?"

"MoroseMoose: You mean the database? Sure, I can reorganize it, but it'll be hard with just the filenames."

"Admin: Just do what you can. I plan on getting some help with that from a friend of mine."

"19891224: A new friend? Do we know him?"

"Admin: It's a she, and no you don't. I vouch for her, so be nice."

"W1NG3D N1NJ4: ARE YOU BRINGING YOUR GIRLFRIEND INTO THE BUSINESS?!?!?!!!?!"

"W1NG3D N1NJ4: ARE YOU EVEN ALLOWED TO DO THAT?!?!?!1!?!"

"W1NG3D N1NJ4: AND HOW COME THIS IS THE FIRST TIME I HEAR ABOUT YOU HAVING A GIRLFRIEND?!?!!!?!?????"

"W1NG3D N1NJ4: YOU ARE TEARING ME APART, ADMIN!!!!!!!! (》Ω《)"

"Admin: To answer your questions in order:"

"Admin: No, no, see answer number one, and please settle down."

"W1NG3D N1NJ4: SOWWY /(//•/ω/•//)/"

I was about to continue when I glanced at the clock again and gasped. It was past seven already, and I hadn't even packed my bag! In fact, I was usually eating breakfast by this time and getting ready to pick up Judy. I cursed under my breath and returned to the browser one last time.

"Admin: I have to go now."

"Admin: I have a meeting to attend."

"Admin: Spread the word about the security reset."

I didn't wait for them to answer. I closed my browser and rushed out of my room posthaste. My first destination was the kitchen, where I grabbed some snacks I could eat with one hand while I returned to pack my bag. I only washed myself in the sink before I threw my clothes on and dashed down the stairs for a second time. I locked the entrance behind me and headed for the usual intersection with a light jog. I wasn't late yet, but I still didn't want to leave Judy waiting if I could help it. I made it there in under a minute, and my timing couldn't have been more perfect, as she was just arriving there herself.

"Good morning, Chief," she greeted me, her usual deadpan voice already coloured by some curious undertones. It was probably my disheveled appearance that threw her off.

"Morning," I replied, trying to straighten my shirt.

"Did you sleep in?"

"Not really, I just lost track of time."

She nodded and stepped closer. She fussed over my clothes before she stood on her tiptoes and reached for my head.

"Lean forwards, please."

"Er... Sure," I complied in a mildly embarrassed daze while she arranged my hair into something I hoped was a bit more presentable. She also muttered something about me being too tall, but that was neither here nor there.

At last, she stepped back and looked me over from head to toe before she let out a satisfied grunt.

"It will have to do."

"Thanks."

"You are welcome," she answered with a barely visible bend in her lips, and she began walking. I automatically followed her. "What's the plan for today?"

I thought for a few seconds as we proceeded down another street.

"I think I will go and talk with Snowy. You got a lot out of her, but I have some specific things I'm curious about."

"I see. What should I do in the meantime?"

"Actually, there is a site I would like you to get familiar with."

I quickly explained to her the Celestial Hub and how I stumbled upon it, including the password, the reports, the other users, and I even outlined the mountain of information I had gathered in such a short time.

"I see. That was quite a find."

I almost nodded, but then I stopped midway. While she might've sounded perfectly dry and deadpan, I could detect some disappointment and even irritation in her voice, and this time I was fairly certain it wasn't just my imagination. The concern might've shown on my face, as she turned away with a tiny little pout on her lips.

If anyone else did that, I might've felt irritated it, but since Judy was normally so reserved with her emotions, noticing new ones felt like a brand-new discovery that always managed to cheer me up.

"Oh, please," I chuckled while gently poking her in the side with my elbow. "Don't be like that. I appreciate the work you've done."

"Even though it became redundant?"

Yep, that question sealed it. She *was* sulking. I half sighed and half chuckled as I let out a deep breath and smiled at her.

"Oh come on, Dormouse. It's not like I can replace you with a silly website."

She blinked at me, her cheeks flushed with just a hint of red, and then she pointedly averted her eyes again.

"I know. I'm not stupid."

"Of course you're not. You are the smartest person I know."

With a harrumph, she turned her face even farther away from me.

"Now you are trying to butter me up and change the subject."

"Guilty as charged," I answered, then hooked a finger under her chin and made her look forwards. "You should still pay attention to where you are going, though. You're about to hit a streetlamp."

She didn't give me any over-the-top reaction like the princess would have, instead she let out a soft grunt and circled around said streetlamp before she got back beside me. It was probably just my imagination, but she may have even walked a little closer than before. Not that I really minded.

"So, what should I do with that site?"

Even though it wasn't a real change in topics, the question still caught me off guard, and I had to think for a bit.

"Make a throwaway email address and use it to register. I will approve you and give you moderation rights."

"You can do that?"

"I told you, I got administration access."

If I was reiterating that, I took the opportunity to tell her all the other things I had done with the site during the night, as well. She listened attentively as I explained my changes to the user interface and the database's structure and how I asked some of the regulars to take care of the everyday operation of the site, periodically nodding to herself whenever I went into important details.

"A moment, Chief," she stopped me just as I was about to get into the gritty details of the cross-referencing between reports. "Correct me if I'm wrong, but did you just take over a spy ring, spend your own money hosting it, and plan to run it without telling the people reporting there they are no longer under whatever Celestial bureau they used to be working for?"

"In a nutshell, yes."

"Doesn't that strike you as incredibly risky?"

"I'd say it's more of an unbelievably, jaw-droppingly risky thing, but worth it. Speaking of which, I will show you how to bounce your IP and hide your online signature when we have the time."

"Why?"

"To mitigate some of the risks? I do the same. It makes us harder to find online. I don't think they have people competent enough to track us anyways, but it's better to be on the safe side."

She nodded, more to herself than in approval of my reasoning, and after a while she said, "How about this afternoon then?"

Her sudden request made me pause.

"Sure, why not."

"Good," she uttered absentmindedly as she whipped out her phone and typed out a message.

"What's that about?" I inquired while I was trying to get a look at her screen.

"I'm telling Mother that we should have you over for dinner." She looked up from her phone and gave me a tiny little smirk. "You will come over to set up my computer, right?"

I nodded.

"Then you should stay until dinner. Mother has been asking me to introduce you to my father."

"I don't like the sound of that."

"Why?"

"Because it sounds like a setup in a sitcom designed to lead to embarrassing misunderstandings that will inevitably lead to your father chasing me out with a shotgun in hand."

"Why would you have a shotgun in hand?" she asked innocently. I gave my dear assistant a wry look and she once again averted her eyes. "What I meant to say was that you are just paranoid. Everything will be fine."

"If you say so..."

I still wasn't convinced, but I didn't want to start a fight over something silly like that, so I wisely shut up and looked ahead... and by complete accident, my gaze met a pair of sapphire eyes peeking around the corner. Their owner immediately disappeared behind the building, but the high-pitched "Awawaaaa!" coming from that direction made her identity so obvious she might as well not bother.

I glanced at my assistant and we shared a tired sigh as we walked up to the girl hiding behind the corner. When we rounded it, she was standing in front of us with a transparently fake surprised expression.

"Oh, hi, Leo! Judy." The princess nodded at each of us in turn with a strained smile. "Fancy meeting you here. Quite the coincidence, isn't it?"

"Why are you here?" Judy spoke before I could, and she was about as blunt as a sledgehammer.

"W-what do you mean?"

"What she means," I interjected as I stepped between the two of them, "is that your mansion is in the opposite direction. We literally couldn't meet up by accident."

"Y-yeah... I suppose you are right..." She hung her head and took a step back. "I... I guess I'll just move along then."

She tried to bolt away, but I quickly reached out and grabbed her shoulder.

"Whoa, easy there, princess. Was there an actual reason why you came here to meet with us?"

She glared at me from behind her bangs but at last she stopped trying to get away and instead turned on her heel again and faced me.

"Why do you think there has to be a reason?! Why can't I spend time with you..." She stuttered for a second and glanced at my assistant and added, "... two," before she regained her composure and finished with, "just because I felt like it?"

"Wait." I held up an open palm to calm her down a little. "So you just wanted to go to school together? That's all?"

"Yeah?" She crossed her arms with a pout. "Do you have a problem with that?"

"No. Quite the opposite, actually."

The pout fell away and was replaced with a suspicious squint.

"Really?"

"Yeah. Why didn't you just say that in the first place?"

"But... I thought..."

She looked at my assistant questioningly. They might have engaged in some sort of female-only telepathy, as they wordlessly went through a series of nods, grimaces, and eyebrow-wiggling (mostly on Elly's side), culminating in a shrug on the part of Judy.

"We should get going or we will be late," she spoke in her usual tone as she walked past us. I followed after her by reflex and the princess quickly fell in line with us on my other side.

We walked without uttering a single word for a while, and since I wasn't a big fan of awkward silences, I cleared my throat and turned to the blonde girl.

"So, how did yesterday's date go?"

"Wha...?!" The princess stumbled and glared at me once she regained her balance. "What are you talking about?"

"Yesterday? Didn't you spend the afternoon with Joshua?"

"Arg! You are teasing me again! I told you to stop that!" she protested so loudly I had to gesture for her to tone it down a little.

"But it's fun."

"For you, maybe."

"Come on, don't sulk." I waved my hand in front of her to get her to look at me and I flashed a toothy smile to lower her guard. It must have worked, as she promptly cleared her throat.

"A-as I was saying... It wasn't really a date. We just spent time together. Friends do that all the time." Suddenly she squinted her eyes as if she just remembered something and then she lightly poked me with her finger. "Speaking of which. Spend some time with Josh!"

"Uh, where did that come from?"

She threw her hands into the air with an exasperated huff.

"I had to spend the entire afternoon listening to Josh complaining about how you don't hang out with him anymore and that all you care about is girls and that he has no one to talk about 'guy stuff,' whatever that is, and that—"

"So, you're saying it wasn't fun?" I interjected, and she looked really unsure for a moment.

"It was, but..." She dropped her shoulders and groaned. "But it was like, *We used to come to this place with Leo all the time, but not anymore,* and *I couldn't talk about things with Leo for ages!* or *I wonder what Leo is doing right now, he is always spending time with you girls* and—"

"All right, all right! I got the gist of it, no need to continue... though I do admit, your imitation of Josh is spot-on."

"Thanks, I think."

"So, which was the fun part?" Judy took the question right out of my mouth.

The princess pointed a wry look at her, but then she raised a finger to her mouth, probably to accentuate her thinking.

"That place where you have to sing was nice."

"The karaoke?"

"Yes, that one! I got a bunch of perfect scores."

"Really? That's... pretty amazing."

The princess giggled with a broad grin that would've been more at home on Angie's face. Not that it didn't suit her. In fact, she looked positively radiant for a moment.

"I *have* been taking singing lessons since I was little, you know?"

"Really?" I whistled in surprise, even though it shouldn't have been one. She *was* a princess after all; high culture must come with the package. "Now I really want to hear you sing."

The princess's grin faltered and she sheepishly looked away. For a moment, I thought I might have said something weird, but then she let out a sharp breath and faced me, red as a lobster and one finger absentmindedly curling and uncurling her left ringlet.

"Maybe... maybe next time? I mean..." she paused, during which time I could barely hold myself back from rolling my eyes. I had a very good guess about where this was going. She let out another sharp breath and pointedly looked me in the eye. "S-so, since I spent time with Joshua, I think we need to balance the scales."

"What scales?"

"S-shut up! Don't interrupt me now!"

"Fine, fine. Geez..."

"So... Um... Would you like to go to the karaoke with me?"

"Well..." She kept staring at me expectantly, so I stopped stalling and told her, "It's fine by me."

"Really?" She began grinning again, but then she quickly stopped herself for some reason and fidgeted. "S-say, are you free today?"

I really wished she would decide whether she was forthcoming or shy and stick to it, but then again, being a little weird like that was one of her charms. I was about to answer when Judy, whom I shamefully forgot was even there, interjected again.

"He is not. I've already reserved him."

The princess nearly stumbled and her shy smile disappeared into a scowl directed at my assistant.

"What is that supposed to mean?"

"It means," Judy answered while tucking away her phone, "that I already asked him to come over to my place."

"She did?" The princess looked at me with a betrayed shock.

"Yes. He is going to stay over for dinner."

The princess's eyes widened.

"Is that true?"

"Yes, but—"

"He is coming over to introduce himself to my parents," my assistant cut me off again without giving me a moment of break.

"I-introducing to... but I thought..."

"And then we are going to discuss our plans for the future."

"Your plans? What plans?"

Instead of answering her, I sent a disapproving frown my assistant's way and asked, "You are doing this on purpose, aren't you?"

She didn't react to my question, but instead she continued where she left off.

"And then, once we get my parents' approval, we will head up to my room, and then..." she continued even though the princess obviously wasn't listening anymore, since she was too busy trying to punch me, which I deftly avoided by a hair's breadth.

"Leo, you idiot! You told me you two are not in that kind of relationship!" she burst out and stomped her feet.

"Because we aren't. Judy's just—"

"I hate you!" she interrupted me and twirled around, ready to dash away. Before I knew it, my hand reached out after her on its own and I managed to hook my fingers into the back of her collar, so when she leaped forwards she got yanked back. I quickly reached out with my other hand and caught her before she could completely fall over. Once I was certain of her safety, I scowled at my assistant.

"Judy! Why did you do that?"

She shrugged.

"Because it's fun to tease her."

"Agreed, but this is going a little too far."

"Umm... Leo?"

The question came from under my chin, and as I looked down, I found the princess straining to look up and stare me in the face.

"Yes?"

"Y-you don't need to hold me so hard..." she told me in an uncharacteristically meek mumble. "It's embarrassing."

It was only at this point that I realized I had my arm around her and was squashing her against my chest. She was a lot firmer than girls were rumored to be, but on the other hand, she was surprisingly warm and pleasant to the touch. I quickly chastised my monkey-brain for suddenly flooding my imagination with R-rated images and took a breath to get my voice steady.

"I'll let you go if you promise you won't try to run away." She nodded, so I unhanded her, and she staggered a little as she stepped back. I saw that Judy was about to say something, so I quickly raised a finger to stop her and focused on the princess again. "Just to set the record straight: I'm going over to set up Judy's PC, and I was invited to eat with her parents. That's all."

"Oh?" she lowered her head, probably because of embarrassment over her previous reaction, but then a second later, she was up and staring at me again with a new dose of luminescent blush on her cheeks. "So today is no good?"

"Yes, I just said that."

She nodded once, twice, and then a third time before she spoke again.

"In that case... how about the weekend...?"

"I already have him reserved," Judy butted in again, much to my eternal exasperation.

"And what is *that* supposed to mean?!" Elly exclaimed in a high-pitched voice. Again.

"Here we go again," I muttered, but the two girls on my sides didn't seem to notice or care.

"We agreed that the Chief would go on a date with me."

"You did *what*?! When did this happen?"

"After your fight with Neige. He was tired of your antics, so we decided to go on a date to help him relax."

"I don't remember us specifying the reason. Or that it was a date, for that matter," I whispered, but I was once again summarily ignored. It seemed like my entire role in this conversation was demoted to being a barrier between the two of them.

"Then you just exploited a moment of weakness! That's incredibly underhanded!"

"That is only your opinion. He is quite happy with the state of affairs."

"Does it even matter what I have to say?" I asked no one in particular, and true to form, no one in particular cared.

"Stop hogging him!" Elly exclaimed, prompting me to mutter a tired, *"I didn't think so..."*

"Why?"

"Because it's unfair!" Suddenly the princess stepped closer, grabbed my arm, and entwined it with hers. I shot her with a *Really? Are we really doing this?* look.

"Unfair to whom?" Judy countered as she stepped closer and grabbed hold of my other arm.

"Et tu, Dormouse?" I whispered in a state of utter trepidation.

The exchange between the two continued for a good minute. I imagine the situation probably looked hilarious from the outside, but when caught in the crossfire, it wasn't half as amusing. Then, all of a sudden, the princess let go of me and rummaged through her pockets.

"Fine, let's do that then!"

I had to blink and rewind the last few seconds of the conversation in my head. Judy said something about chance being fair and a coin flip and... No way...

I glanced at the blonde girl by my side, and she was already brandishing a coin in her hand. So, yes way. This situation wasn't silly enough, I supposed.

"Heads or tails?"

My assistant thought for a moment before she released me. "Tails."

"Fine!"

The princess placed the coin on her thumb and grinned fiercely as she flipped it through the air. It flew high and completely straight up. I let out an annoyed grunt as it reached its peak, and then, on its way down, I snatched it out of the air.

"Hey!" the princess protested and reached for my clenched fist, but I pocketed the coin and faced her with a frown.

"Would you please stop ignoring me and behave yourselves?"

"But the coin..."

"Listen, girls. You either stop bickering, or I won't go anywhere with anyone."

The two of them looked at each other, more confused than ashamed by my scolding. For a while I didn't know what else I could say, but just as the silence was about to get uncomfortable, a sudden idea came to me like a lightning bolt out of the blue.

I quickly cleared my throat and proclaimed, "It's a Schrödinger's coin now."

"A what?" Judy blurted out in surprise, and I doubled down.

"It's a coin that is in a superposition of both heads and tails," I explained with a knowing smirk. "That means you both won and lost at the same time."

"Um... I'm not following." The princess turned and asked, "Judy, what is he talking about?"

Before my dear assistant could open her mouth, I hurriedly added, "What I'm trying to say is that we cannot be certain who won until we collapse the wave function."

"A coin has no wave function to collapse," Judy pointed out with an extra-deadpan voice. "A coin is not a fundamental particle."

"It's a minor technical detail, barely even worth mentioning," I dismissed her with a leisurely wave of my hand, but then I used that same hand to point at her and say, "However, since we cannot determine the result, I propose a compromise."

"In what way?" Judy continued to eye me with the kind of suspicion usually reserved for used car salesmen, but I was in too deep to quit, so I took a deep breath and flashed my most convincing smile.

"Let us presume that you both won."

"But that would mean... we *both* go on a date with you?"

I answered Elly's question with a nod.

"At the same time?"

I nodded again.

"It's the best possible outcome," I told her. "It's like the solution to the prisoner's dilemma."

"Prisoner's what?"

"Exactly," Judy agreed with the princess, and by this point I had a feeling she was onto me. "This is nothing like the prisoner's dilemma."

"It is," I stressed. "You guys have two choices: you either assume it was heads or tails. If you both assume it was one or the other, one of you loses. If you both presume the other won, you both lose. Therefore the best available choice is to presume that you *both* won. Quite elementary."

"So... both of us to win at the same time?" Elly whispered as she tried to wrap her head around my words.

Silence descended once again, and the way Judy was squinting at me didn't make it any less awkward. I was just about to spill the beans, but she beat me to the punch with a sudden suggestion.

"I have a better idea," Judy said. She reached into her pocket and took out another, identical coin. "We'll just flip again."

"No!" the princess cried, startling us both just long enough for her to pry the coin out of Judy's fingers. She cradled it close to her chest and declared, "No take-backs! It was decided already!"

"It would be more accurate to say that the Chief made it up," my assistant stated. "With a coin flip that didn't actually happen."

"Oh please, Dormouse! Just a few seconds ago you were completely okay with flipping the coin to decide. Don't argue with quantum physics just because the results aren't intuitive."

"That's right," Elly agreed with me on the spot, much to Judy's chagrin. That said, Judy's resistance only lasted for a second before she switched gears and let out a really long sigh.

"So it's going to be a double date, then," she relented and stepped up to Elly, followed by the question of, "Where should we go?"

"The karaoke is a must!" the princess exclaimed with a mixture of excitement and determination, and I couldn't help but sigh in relief, though I would be lying if I said there wasn't a hint of exhaustion in there too.

The rest of our commute to the school was spent with the girls discussing their plans for the "date." The way the two of them suddenly got along, at least as far as this discussion was concerned, was a wholly unexpected but pleasant surprise. Now I only had to keep encouraging this kind of cooperation. Maybe we'd actually end up with something workable in the long run.

Long-term plans aside, we were late. The familiar armband guy was just getting ready to close the gates by the time we crossed them. Once we reached the classroom, my assistant and the princess huddled together at the former's desk and continued their somewhat heated planning.

As for me, I practically fell into my chair and buried my head in my hands. I stayed like that for a few minutes, right until I was tapped on the shoulder, prompting me to glance up groggily.

"Morning," Josh greeted me with a grin. "Women problems?"

I am the first to admit that my friend had many good qualities. Tact wasn't one of them.

"You could say that," I answered while straightening myself and nodding at him instead of a proper greeting.

"Serves you right for playing around," he quipped with a toothy grin. He obviously wasn't serious. Well, probably. Hopefully. "So, what is it this time?" He inquired while nodding towards the two girls.

"They are planning our trip this weekend."

"You are going on a date? With which one?"

"Both." Josh whistled, but I continued before he could say anything else. "By the way, I think we should stop calling it a 'date' whenever we hang out with one of the girls. It completely dilutes the real meaning of the word."

He looked unusually thoughtful for a moment and nodded in agreement. "Right, we do that a lot, don't we? How about we just call them outings unless it involves a goodbye kiss?"

"That sounds reasonable. Speaking of which, how did your *outing* with the princess go?"

To my surprise, my friend averted his eyes, followed by an awkward cough.

"Didn't she tell you already?"

"I'm curious about your impression."

He shrugged, leaned closer for a conspiratorial huddle, and whispered, "Honestly? It was fun, but she couldn't stop talking about you."

"Really?"

"Yeah. She was bringing you into all kinds of conversations. When we were in the karaoke, she asked about what kind of music you like. Then at the fast food place, she asked about your favourite meal..." He leaned closer to me, his voice falling even lower. "Seriously, I'm sure you have noticed already, but she seems to like you. A lot. Do you get what I'm saying?"

I awarded him a flat look and sighed.

"Thank you, Captain Obvious."

"You're welcome," he flashed one of those childish, toothy grins of his before he leaned even closer. In fact, he was leaning forwards so much I was afraid he would fall out of his chair. I grudgingly leaned in so he wouldn't have to. He nodded in appreciation and whispered, "Listen, I don't want to stick my nose into your personal life or anything, but do you really think playing around with both of them is a good idea?"

"What are you talking about? I am not 'playing around' with them."

"Fine, so you're just enabling them. Either way, I think you should sit down with them and clear things up before things turn nasty. You know what I'm saying?"

I wish someone had taken a picture of me at that exact moment. I figured my expression was so flat its edge could be used to split photons, and that didn't even make any sense!

"Dude... did you just say what I think you just said?"

"Uh... Depends. What did you hear?"

"Zero self-awareness, for a start," I grumbled, but seeing that he still didn't get it, I gave up and threw my hands into the air. "Fine, I get your point."

I certainly did. While the previous day's sudden confession complicated things a little, the whole situation with Judy and Elly had been brewing for a while, so I had plenty of time to think about it.

There was only one small problem: the whole concept of teen romance drama made my skin crawl. I know, I know. It's a little weird to say that while being trapped in a harem narrative. But it was the truth. I was really, really bad with this stuff, to the point where I would've fought tooth and nail against getting entangled in such drama if I wasn't already neck-deep in it. Heck, a small part of me still kept whispering about how I should just stonewall the girls and focus on more important things, but doing so would have made me a monumental jerk, so I'd long since given up on that idea.

Not that purposefully "keeping my options open" was much better.

In my defense, I had a plan. Or at least half a plan. ... Well, okay, maybe it was just a rudimentary idea that may or may not royally bite me in the ass later, but if it worked, it was my best chance for resolving this annoying love triangle thing without any metaphorical bloodshed. It was at least worth a try. If only others would let me work it out without meddling.

... Nah, I'm kidding. I wasn't mad at Josh. He'd only tried to help, as clumsy and oblivious as he was, so I had no reason to blow him off. I took a deep breath and returned to the conversation with a slightly cooler head.

"Let's just say I'm going to make sure not to make anyone cry. Is that good enough?"

"I suppose," my friend acknowledged, though he didn't sound entirely convinced.

Our conversation would've probably gone on for a little longer if not for the appearance of Mrs. Applebottom. The classroom fell silent as everyone scurried to their seats, including the princess, who sat down in front of me with a satisfied smile. I honestly didn't know whether I should feel relieved or afraid.

PART 3

"No!" Josh yelled while he stood in front of me with his arms spread out, as if guarding the girl behind his back from a vicious predator. "We just talked about this kind of thing this morning! First you do it with Judy, then with Elly, then with Angie, and now Lili? I am drawing the line right here and now!"

I suppose the situation probably requires some explanation. It all started with the ringing of the lunchtime bell. As per my morning plans (before they were derailed by the girls), I was planning to probe Snowy, since now I had enough knowledge about the supernatural world to go beyond the basics.

The problems started right away. First off, when I tried to ask Judy to come with me and take notes, she declined, saying she already had plans with the princess. The last time I saw them, they were heading to the cafeteria while arguing about whether we should go to the zoo or ice-skating. I was secretly a little happy about that and left them to their own devices, but then when I tried to leave for the ground floor classrooms, I was hijacked by Angie, who pulled me aside (quite literally, if I may add; my shoulder was still a little sore from all the tugging) to inform me in code-words that the Celestial Hub was resetting everyone's passwords and that it was a great chance for me to get an account.

According to her, I could get one without any problems as long as she vouched for me. Sure, it would've been a basic account like hers, but it would still be something. By the way, I checked last night, and she really wasn't part of any spy rings or centuries-old conspiracies, so she only had access to the site's basic functions. I pretended to be really interested and thanked her for the opportunity, and made a mental note about the whole "vouching" thing. That was an obvious security risk.

Anyways, after she let me go, I continued on my way to Snowy's classroom, but by the time I got there, Joshua was already talking with the girl. The rest speaks for itself.

"You're just being irrational," I told Josh as I tried to take a step towards the confused girl, but he stood his ground and drew a half-circle in front of him with his foot. It was probably supposed to be the proverbial line in the sand, but taken that we were in a hallway, it was more than a little silly.

"I am serious. I am not letting you past this line until you promise to—"

"Snowy, would you come here for a moment?"

"Huh? Sure."

The still puzzled girl walked right past Josh and over his imaginary line without a moment of hesitation. He looked betrayed, but for the moment I couldn't care less. I turned to Snowy instead.

"Would you mind if I asked you a few questions?"

"You too?"

I chuckled and smiled at her in reassurance.

"Yeah, me too. There are a few things about your... *family situation* I'm curious about."

She agreed, if a little hesitantly, and I was just about to grab her hand and lead her to a quieter area when Josh inserted himself between the two of us again.

"Dude, I'm serious! You really need to stop hitting on the girls and..."

He continued with what suspiciously sounded like a heartfelt intervention. I summarily ignored him and instead checked out who was the closest scapegoat with my Far Sight. Once I found one, I raised an open palm to halt his tirade and turned on my heel without a word. I rushed down the corridor and grabbed hold of the class rep's hand as she was about to reach the bottom of the stairs. She let out a surprised yelp, but by then I was already towing her back to the others. It was only once we got there that she wormed her hand out of my grasp and glared at me in a manner that was about 70 percent petulant and 40 percent curious. Yes, that added up to 110 percent, but I feel that expressed her over-the-top reaction perfectly.

Anyways, she set her feet, planted her arms on her hips, and leaned into her disapproving class representative persona before she spoke.

"Leo, what do you think you are doing?"

"Getting Josh a replacement lunch partner. He feels terribly lonely lately. Please remedy that," I told her smoothly as I sidestepped her burning gaze, grabbed hold of Snowy's shoulder, and pulled her over to my side. "Now, if you excuse me, we have things to discuss. Right, Snowy?"

"Y-yes?"

"That is not an excuse to... hey, where are you going? I haven't finished with—!"

It was at this point we got out of earshot and rounded the corner leading to the back exit. Thankfully, neither the class rep nor Joshua tried to follow after us. We were almost at the courtyard by the time Snowy finally spoke out.

"Uh... Y-you can let go of my hand. I'm not running away."

"Oh, right. Sorry. Not that I ever considered you would," I answered and let go of her. She rubbed her fingers with her other hand. Maybe I was squeezing too hard? Oops. I tried not to get too hung up on that and smiled at her again. "Let's head to the cafeteria and find a quiet corner, shall we?"

She nodded curtly and we headed for the hall. Once we got in line, I turned to her and asked, "What would you like?"

"I... don't have much pocket money, so I think I will go with the 'A' menu."

"No, you don't get it. I am paying, so what would you *actually* like?"

"You mean... you are treating me?"

"Of course. I dragged you away, so this is the least I could do," I told her, but then I paused, thinking. "Just for the record, though, no matter what Josh says, don't ask for caviar. It's not bad, but it isn't filling at all."

"I see..." She nodded solemnly like I'd just said something really profound and looked over the menu as we inched forwards. "Um..."

"Yes?"

She looked up at me and was about to say something, but then shook her head. "Never mind."

"Never mind what? I thought there was something you liked."

"Yes, but..." She raised a hand to her mouth, which meant that for some reason she was regretting blurting that out. I gave her a wry look and tried to find what she was looking at, but it was hard to tell on the crowded menu. At last, she let her hand down and gave me an upturned look. "Promise me you won't laugh."

"Is it something I would laugh at?"

"I... don't know?"

"Was that a question?"

She shook her head so vigorously the tips of her twin-tails nearly hit her in the face. For a moment I wondered what kind of conditioner she used that kept her hair flowing together like that, but then I remembered my "hairdo theory of importance," and it seemed obvious why it would act like that.

Anyways, she looked up with a little pout and said, "Do you promise?"

"Fine, I promise. What would you like?"

She leaned closer, balled up her fists in front of her chest, and declared, "Apple pie!"

"Apple pie?"

"Apple pie," she repeated with an enthusiastic nod. To be perfectly honest, I very nearly broke my promise. Not because of what she asked for, but because of how excited and innocent she sounded while doing so. I tempered the laughter trying to escape my lungs into a broad smile and nodded.

"Very well. Apple pie, it is."

Before I knew it, we already had reached the counter and I swiftly placed my orders. I bought a fairly boring fried chicken dish and, amidst the frantic (but wholly unconvincing) protests of my current companion, an entire pie fresh out of the oven. I had to wonder where those ovens actually were, though. In fact, I had to wonder just how big the kitchens had to be to supply the entire school with freshly made dishes, but I digress.

I turned around and scouted an empty table in the far corner of the hall. It was fairly deserted, and I figured it was a good enough place to have our conversation in something approaching privacy. Snowy didn't seem to care, though, as she was completely mesmerized by the still steaming pie in her hands. She was all wide-eyed and sparkly, like a little kid holding her unwrapped Christmas present. I couldn't help but smile at her as we made our way over to our seats and sat down.

"You didn't have to..." She started again as she put down the tray in her hands, but I gestured for her to stop talking and start eating. She immediately complied... or would have, but she didn't know how to cut the pie. I sighed and helped her out, all the while feeling like a single father spending quality time with his daughter. It was a weird but not necessarily unpleasant experience.

She took out the first slice and dug in, naturally burning her tongue even though I warned her. After a little blowing and excited waiting, it finally reached an edible temperature and she took a large bite. Her face was so blissful, I wanted to take a photo and use it as the background on my phone, but I refrained. It was just the kind of thing the girls would misunderstand and would lead to all kinds of annoying hijinks.

"Is it really that good?" I asked, a little dubious about the objective quality of the mass-produced pastry, but she only nodded at me, her cheeks still bathed in bliss.

"Yes, it's great!"

"You act like you've never eaten one before."

"Um..." She paused, looking embarrassed for some reason. "I really haven't. I just saw Joshua eat one the other day, and I wanted to try it."

"Really? Don't tell me there are no apple trees in the Abyss."

She twitched a little, automatically checking if anyone was listening, and put down the slice in her hand.

"There are. It's just that..." Her voice trailed off before she took a sharp breath and continued. "You see, my brother says it's commoner food, so we never eat it at home, and I never have enough pocket money to buy it myself."

"Oh come on, it's not 'that' expensive." She fell into a depressed silence, which told me I'd said something I shouldn't have, so I backpedaled and pointed at her tray with a smile. "Let's eat before it gets cold. I haven't even touched my plate yet."

"Yes, let's!" She nodded resolutely (what she was resolute about, I had no idea) and picked up her pie again, and as she started eating, her face once more mellowed out into an expression of pure bliss. I couldn't help but grin as I began raiding my own plate. I've always been a fan of multitasking, though, so I kept thinking while I did.

I joked about the apple trees, but as far as the pictures in the reports I read were concerned, the Abyss actually looked remarkably similar to the island we inhabited at the moment. There were even some notes about it being a mirror image with corresponding landscape and all, but I didn't know how far that went. Either way, for something called "the Abyss," a supernatural prison for the entire Abyssal race, it seemed practically cozy.

Speaking of which, I glanced up from my food and nearly choked as I laid my eyes upon our resident Abyssal. Her eyes were still lost in a sea of happiness, her face stuffed like a desperate hamster's. Was this really one of the famous Seducers of the Inanna family? Though again, this was probably the most "seductive" act I'd ever seen from her, but all it made me want to do was take her home and adopt her as a little sister.

I'd looked into her family background a little. The Inannas were one of the seven dynasties of the Abyss, clamoring for dominance like warring noble houses often do. That made me wonder: just what would cause both her and her brother to leave that kind of backstabbing-prone situation behind, even temporarily? Disappearing to the sidelines was usually bad for a political career. Oh, and there was still the question of *how*. I still didn't know how they got through the not-at-all-contrived impenetrable barrier of utter impenetrableness. Though again, I supposed the more one insisted on something being impossible to do in a world like this, the more likely it would happen sooner or later.

Then something quite obvious occurred to me.

Why don't I just ask her? That's what we were here for, weren't we? I waited for her to finish her current slice before I drew her attention with a deliberate clatter of utensils.

"So... if I may be so bold, may I ask what you are doing here?"

She seemed more than a little conflicted. Then she put her own fork down and absentmindedly tugged at her choker.

"If you mean… why we are in the outside world... it has to do with our prophecy."

Wow, I thought. That was... refreshingly direct. I smiled at her and pressed on.

"Prophecy, you say? That word seems to come up a lot lately."

"Really?"

"Yeah, annoyingly so." I put my hands onto the table and linked my fingers. "What is yours about?"

"Uh…" She continued to awkwardly tug at her neckwear. "I suppose I can tell you. It's about the Emperor of the Abyss."

"The Emperor?" I interrupted before I suddenly recalled a footnote I'd read the night before. "Wait, wasn't that supposed to be your version of that Deus fellow?"

Snowy twitched before she smiled at me awkwardly. "You could say that. The prophecy says there will be a human capable of absorbing the power of the Abyss and using this power to usher in the Emperor."

"So, he's not supposed to be the Emperor himself?"

Snowy shook her head.

"And you say he 'absorbs' the power of the Abyss? You mean the mana wells?"

She shook her head again.

"No, it's rather…" She fell silent for a long time, only her finger tugging, before she continued. "It's more like he has a lot of power and it can be swayed towards the Abyss by... um...." I waited for her to continue, and once it was obvious I was doing so, she hunched over a little and told me in a low voice, "He can be revealed by injecting a little power into him and then looking for a reaction."

"Injecting power? That sounds a little vague. How would you even do that?"

Snowy fell completely silent and her cheeks flushed slightly. The confusion must have been visible on my face, for she looked up at me and after a few seconds she mouthed, "E-exchanging of essences?"

"Essences? What exactly are we talking about here?"

"S-s-saliva…" she muttered before she lowered her burning-red face. I was just about to ask her how one would do that, but then the question got caught in my throat as my brain began to assemble the pieces.

"Okay, let me see if I got this straight. To reveal this Emperor fellow, or rather the one who would reveal the Emperor…" I muttered "convoluted crap" under my breath, "… you need to give him some essence?"

She nodded.

"And to do that, you need to share… fluids."

She nodded again.

"Was the reason why you kissed Josh the first time you met? To look for a reaction?"

There was a longer pause this time, but she nodded once again.

"But how? You didn't know it was Josh until you kissed him, and there was no reason for you to kiss him unless you knew it already, so…"

She lowered her face in shame, so I ventured an educated guess.

"Don't tell me you were going around kissing random guys on the street and just stumbled on Josh?"

"Girls, too…" she told me feebly, and I felt a pang of guilt for bringing the topic up in the first place. She must've taken my momentary silence as a sign of disapproval, for she lowered her head even farther, to the point her forehead nearly touched the table, and in a mutter added, "My brother said it was the only way."

I looked at her trembling shoulders and once again got reminded that, while she might've been an Abyssal and a Seducer and whatnot, at the end of the day, she was still a fragile teenage girl. I reached out a hand and rustled the top of her head. She twitched as I touched her, but stopped trembling and looked up at me, her wet eyes open wide and a little incredulous. I smiled at her reassuringly and patted her head.

"You're a good kid. It's not your fault your brother's a prick."

She didn't answer, so I continued patting her until she calmed down. Doing so also made me realize why Judy got into the habit. Rubbing her head was strangely relaxing. Anyways, I finally stopped and waited for her to get her bearings before I hit her with my next inquiry.

"Staying on the topic of your quest for this usherer of emperors or whatnot, just what kind of reaction were you looking for?"

Snowy looked at me thoughtfully as she began tugging at her choker again. "It's mostly magic. He just... absorbs magic and tunes his own to it. It's hard to explain."

"So he turns into an Abyssal?"

"Kind of?" She answered with a question, obviously unsure. "I only saw it once, and it only happened very briefly." She flushed again and shyly averted her eyes. "I-it was only a peck... on the lips."

"So, you're saying that if you two, say, French kissed, the effect would be more pronounced?"

She turned a shade of crimson that, for some reason, reminded me of the princess, and nodded several times.

"Interesting. Do you think it would work with the other girls too?"

"I... don't want to kiss any of them."

I snorted and shook my head.

"No, I don't mean you. I mean, you said this usherer of yours should be able to tune his own power to the one that was 'injected' into him. Would the same reaction happen if he was kissed by another kind of magical folk?"

Snowy thought hard for several long seconds, but finally shook her head.

"I don't know. I didn't even think it would work until it happened."

"Just checking."

Hmm, there were so many implications to all of this. For one, Josh could theoretically become an Abyssal with a kiss, and since no one else mentioned anything about this the first time around, the transformation was only temporary. Furthermore, the same thing might work with others, too. The latter was just my conjecture, but it made sense from a narrative standpoint.

I didn't know if this trope had a name or not (though it probably did, I just had to look it up later), but this sounded suspiciously like a convenient power-up coming to light at a suitably dramatic moment. I decided to file this information under "important stuff to keep track of" and returned to the conversation, only to find Snowy still tugging at her choker.

"Is it too tight?"

She was puzzled by my question, so I reached out to point at her neck. Her eyes opened wide and she reeled back so hard I feared she'd fall over with her chair in tow. She didn't, but the resounding "No!" she yelled out made me lurch back just as hard. For a couple of seconds we only stared at each other in silence until I threw out a feeler question.

"Is there a reason why you don't want me to touch it?"

Snowy hesitated, then nodded.

"Does it have some sort of sentimental value?"

This time she didn't hesitate before she shook her head.

"So it's not sentimental. Dangerous?"

This time she actually thought about her nonverbal answer for a while before giving another tentative nod.

"I see..." I muttered as I linked my fingers again in thought.

So it was something that was dangerous to remove. Or maybe something dangerous to me in particular? Either way, it was probably enchanted or somesuch. Truthfully, when I looked closer, I could swear I could see a dim glow surrounding it. It was hard to notice at a glance due to the background light, but after seeing Angie's light show the day before, I was fairly certain it was magic... which of course meant it was high time I admitted that *Holy crap, I can see invisible magic stuff!* But I still hadn't done any controlled tests, so I only considered it a strong possibility and filed it under my ever-growing "stuff to look into later" corner of my poor, overexerted brain.

But back to the choker. I couldn't help but wonder what it was about. If I had to guess, I would've guessed it was a power-limiter, or something to that effect. Those things were fairly common in supernatural harem narratives like this, only existing to be released at an opportune moment to provide a sudden boost in power and save the day. Cheap but effective, I supposed. Although, on second thought, it might've been a safety power-limiter instead. For example, Snowy could be unconsciously drinking the souls of everyone around her without it. Or worse yet, it might hold back a cruel and vicious split personality that would take over Snowy and destroy the world. So yeah, there were lots of weird possibilities there, ranging from silly to outright scary, but that's how these things usually worked.

Anyways, I slowly exhaled before I addressed Snowy again.

"Let's forget about your choker for now. Your pie is getting cold."

She suddenly perked up at the mention of her treat and quickly put a hand over the pastry. The relief was clearly visible on her face when it turned out it was still warm. I cut her another slice as a symbol of leaving the previous topic behind and allowed both of us a little breather before we returned to the heavy topics.

PART 4

By the time I returned to the classroom I was well-fed both in terms of food (Snowy gave me the last slice she couldn't eat) and information. Once I got her talking, she turned out to be quite knowledgeable about Abyssal politics and metaphysics. Most of it was fairly boring technical stuff, but it was still new and probably useful, so it was all good.

But back to the classroom. First off, I noticed that Judy and the princess were still huddled over my assistant's desk and animatedly discussing something. I didn't need to peek in with my Far Sight to realize it was still about their date plans. I would've sighed and wondered just how much time one needed to plan these things out, but then I remembered how I had spent half a night looking up areas of interest before my first outing with Judy. Though that was originally supposed to be a research trip, so I didn't know how much that applied to the current situation.

Either way, I headed for my desk. Or tried to. The class rep flagged me down after a single step.

"Leo, we need to talk," she announced in place of a greeting, already in her authority mode. "Are you free after school?"

I thought about it for a moment. While technically I was only invited to Judy's place for dinner, we had a lot of things to discuss, and I had a feeling she wouldn't have taken it well if I told her to go ahead while I talked with the class rep, so I shook my head.

"Sorry, I already have plans for today. Is it urgent?"

"Yes."

"Oooookay...How about the next break, then?"

"It will have to do."

I nodded to her and, and since she didn't add anything else, I continued on my way to my desk. I found Joshua slumped over the neighbouring one. He only looked up once he heard the creak of my chair as I sat down.

"Welcome back, Casanova," he greeted me with an uncharacteristically acidic tone.

"Would you please stop with that?" I answered in kind, with a pinch of exasperation sprinkled on top. "Just how many times do I have to tell you that just because I discuss things with the girls one on one, it doesn't automatically mean I'm flirting with them?"

"No matter how many times you say it, it doesn't matter if you keep doing it." He huffed, but the jab probably allowed him to let out some of the steam, as he continued in a more casual voice. "So, how was your lunch break?"

"It was nice enough. I learned a bunch of new things."

"Oh? Such as?"

"Snowy's family situation, amongst other things," I told him, carefully omitting all the other crazy stuff.

"Her family, huh?" My friend slumped over his desk again and muttered, "She never told me anything about them."

It took me several seconds to recognize the, in retrospect quite obvious, expression on his face. I raised a hand to my temple to rub it.

"Are you seriously sulking right now?"

"No, I'm not!" Josh bit back, but then he averted his eyes and added, "I'm just a little disappointed, that's all."

With my temple-rubbing steadily intensifying, I leaned back in my chair and dropped my shoulder. I couldn't believe we were having this conversation.

"I'm sure she will tell you in time. It's not like it's going to stay a secret forever... I hope."

"A secret? What secret?"

"One that wouldn't be a secret if I told you," I responded with a roll of my eyes. The grimace he gave me in return was just too pitiful to bear, so I threw him a bone. "Fine, here's another secret I can actually tell you."

"What is it?"

I leaned closer and whispered to him, "She loves apple pies."

"She likes apple pies?"

"No, she *loves* them." I paused for a meaningful beat before I winked and added, "Use that information how you will."

"Um... thanks?"

"You are welcome."

It was a good thing that the teacher showed up at this point, as I had no idea where to take the conversation from there. The lesson itself (biology, FYI) was the same as always, and the forty-five minutes passed by in a blink, especially since I had so many things on my mind.

First and foremost, I'd be lying if I said I wasn't curious about what the class rep wanted to talk about. She sounded really serious, so maybe it was something related to the fight a couple of days ago? Or maybe it was because of Judy's questions? Or the Magi organization in general? Either way, I was about to find out when the chime finally sounded. Maybe it was because of dumb luck, but Mrs. Applebottom just finished talking about taxonomy, so this time she didn't leave her sentence half-finished. Yay for progress?

Our last class was PE again, so all the placeholders sprung to their feet and began trickling out of the classroom with gym bags in hand. I was about to get up and head towards the class rep, but she beat me to the punch. She gestured for me to follow, so I did so after grabbing my own gym bag. We exited the classroom posthaste and headed in the opposite direction from the others, towards a short dead end leading to the computer room and the emergency fire escape. We didn't go that far, only a couple of meters to put us out of earshot.

"We need to talk," she told me grimly once she stopped and faced me, and I almost gulped in reaction. This had to be big if she was this serious.

"Yes, you already told me that. I'm listening."

She eyed me suspiciously, as if looking for traces of sarcasm in my words. For the record, there weren't any. Then she took a deep breath, looked me in the eye, and said, "Leo, you have to stop leading Judy and Eleanor on."

I blinked at her, opened my mouth to respond, but then I closed it again and instead facepalmed so hard the sound of the impact must've been audible on the frickin' moon.

"Are you serious? Are? You? Serious!" I hissed through gritted teeth. She was taken aback by my reaction, so I let out most of my pent-up frustration in a breathy groan and threw my hands into the air. "We just had a battle two days ago and the supernatural exploded into the forefront yesterday, but all you guys can talk about is my love life? Really!"

"Leo, I—"

"Don't 'Leo' me right now! Do you have any idea how annoying it is to keep explaining this to every single one of you? I have way too much on my plate already. I do not have the *time* for this!"

"Then why are you flirting with them?"

"I am not flirting!" I hissed a little louder this time, turning a few placeholder heads, but I didn't care. At all. Not one bit. I still lowered my voice a little, though. Just because I felt like it. "Why do all of you immediately assume that if I am friendly with a girl I must be automatically flirting?"

"You are doing more than being friendly."

"That is entirely your subjective opinion."

She furrowed her brows. "It's not. Do you think they would like you so much if only I thought you were flirting with them? ... You *are* aware that they like you and aren't just being *friendly*, right?"

I scoffed and rolled my eyes.

"Of course I am. I'm not Josh."

"But if you are, then why don't you tell them?"

"Tell them what? That I'm aware of the blindingly obvious?"

"No. You should tell them whether you reciprocate their feelings or not." She paused here to narrow her eyes, and even tweaked her glasses a little before she added, "Do you actually like them?"

Her question threw me for a loop for a moment. Without noticing it, my voice also became a bit more subdued.

"It's more complicated than that. I mean, I do like them, just not necessarily in the face-sucking, cuddling, date-going way."

"Aren't you going on a date?"

"It's more of a group outing, and you are also purposefully misrepresenting my point. Stop it."

Her brows furrowed even deeper as she looked me in the eye again and then subsequently emphasized, "Listen, Leo. You need to tell them how you feel about them. Otherwise, everyone will get hurt."

"Okay, time out. The truth of the matter is, I'm doing a *thing* right now precisely to avoid that. It's complicated, it could backfire, and I would probably have a much better chance at getting it right if you guys stopped meddling." I stopped here to catch my breath, and then continued with, "Also, this whole 'you must tell them your feelings' thing would sound a lot more convincing if you practiced what you preach."

Ammy twitched like I'd sucker-punched her and hastily excused herself with, "My situation is different from yours."

"If you say so. It looks similar in principle."

"It doesn't matter," she burst out and simultaneously poked me in the chest. "We are talking about you."

"And I would prefer if we weren't."

"But we have to. Especially if you keep playing with the others, too."

I had a snappy response on the tip of my tongue, but then her words sank in and it turned into a dumbfounded, "Wait, what?"

"I've heard from Joshua. You've been spending a lot of time with Neige and Angie, too."

"If by 'a lot' you mean one lunch break and a short afternoon then yes, though I would like to see your dictionary first, because that is the loosest damn definition I've ever heard." I paused to take a breath, and then let out a soft "oh" as realization dawned on me. "Wait a minute... I get it now! Josh set you up for this!"

"He didn't *set me up*," Ammy denied, just a touch defensively. "He just shared his worries with me."

"All the same," I grumbled as I made a new mental note about whacking the guy over the head for creating even more misunderstandings. "Listen, this is just a case of miscommunication. I was talking to them about supernatural politics, and I didn't want Josh to stick around when we did that, so he is sulking about it. There is nothing more going on."

"With Angie, too?"

I mouthed a silent *oh crap*. Right, Angie being a Celestial was supposed to be a secret. I had to salvage this ASAP, though I had no idea how.

"Um... Yeah?" I nearly hit myself in the head for saying that. Stupid brain! That was the *opposite* of salvaging the situation! "I mean... could you pretend you didn't hear that? It's supposed to be a secret for the moment.

Not a dangerous kind of secret, mind you, but I would prefer if Angie was the one to tell you, so could you please let it go?"

She gave me a dubious look, but eventually shrugged and answered, "Fine, but only if you promise me that you sit down with the others and discuss your..." She pointedly cleared her throat at this point and finished with, "... this *thing* of yours with them."

I tried to object, but I was too mentally drained to come up with a witty response (not to mention, at this rate I was only going to dig myself even deeper), so I grabbed hold of the opportunity to end the conversation and gave her a nod.

"I'll think about it. We should get going, though. We still have to change."

With that, we began walking. She made me promise several times that I would have that pointless discussion with the girls, but I managed to get her to stop hounding me by the time we reached the changing rooms. When I got there, there was only one thing left to do.

"Hey, Josh?"

My friend turned to me. He was already wearing his gym clothes and he looked at me skeptically as I walked over to him.

"What?"

I smiled at him and promptly whacked him over the head. He let out a loud "ow!" and gave me a look that was equally hurt and confused.

"What the hell was that for?"

I shrugged, saying, "Think about it," and left him to do just that while I changed.

PART 5

"Are you sure this is safe?" Judy asked me as she peeked over my shoulder.

"As safe as I can make it," I told her while finalizing the last few settings on her new, secure, and completely 100 percent untraceable browser. Well, so far as I knew. I'd gone out of my way to hide her identity behind as many proxies and false accounts as I could, but even then, 100 percent is a bit of a hyperbole.

"Should that make me relieved?"

She was still unconvinced, so I gave her an emphatic "Yes."

After a beat, she nodded and walked over to her bed and sat down. If the previous conversation didn't make it abundantly clear, we were in Judy's room. It was a sparsely decorated place dominated by earth tones, beige and ocher in particular, including the drapes and the furniture. It wasn't exactly girly, but it was neat and had a lived-in feel that my own room severely lacked, probably due to me belonging to the sleepless persuasion. In fact, her entire home felt like that, but I didn't bother to tell her. Not that I had any chance to do so.

When I arrived, I was immediately besieged by her distractingly youthful mother. We had to sit down with her for a while when she invited me for a cup of tea, and while she said she wanted to talk to me, I didn't think she meant that literally. For about half an hour, she chattered nonstop and about so many different things I lost track of the conversation five minutes in.

Judy gave up as well after several failed attempts at interrupting her and only fidgeted awkwardly beside me. It was fun to see this side of her, but I started feeling sorry for her after a while and decided to politely tell her mother that we had things to do. She finally let us go, much to my assistant's relief. She apparently was really bad at dealing with her hyperactive mother, which I found absolutely hilarious (though only in private, as Judy's sour disposition made me consider expressing my feelings a teensy bit dangerous).

I was later also introduced to her father, a stocky fellow with a bushy mustache and a fashion sense right out of the 1950s. Thankfully, I didn't have to interact with him much, but when I did so during dinner, all his lines were just thinly veiled threats about "making his little angel cry." Judy seemed to be embarrassed by him too, so that was yet another topic I decided to steer clear of.

That left me with nothing to focus on but the actual thing that brought me here: the website.

"Come back for a moment please," I gestured for Judy, and she got up from the bed and walked over to me. "We need a username for your account."

She thought for a couple of seconds before she leaned over me and began typing with one hand while supporting herself with the other. She was kind of pushing her chest against my shoulder in the process, but I decided it wasn't polite to mention it, so I bore with it until she finished.

"Just 'Assistant'?" I asked while peering at the screen.

She nodded.

"I guess it's fine, but it's a little plain."

"You are called Admin on the site. I think it's fitting."

"Touché."

I asked her to come up with a password, which she did while still brushing her chest against me, but by this point I didn't particularly mind anymore. Once she was satisfied, I clicked the OK button and leaned back, which finally broke our contact.

"I will approve your application once I get home and I'll introduce you to the regulars. You should be able to access most of the site. For now, we should limit ourselves to browsing it on our PCs. I'll look into whether I can get a safe browsing interface on our phones later."

"Understood. What do you want me to look into first?"

"To be honest, I don't know. There are thousands of reports there, and even more in the repository. I only skimmed the most recent ones, but the site has been running for a couple of years and the database is a mess. First, we should get that organized a little."

"And after that?"

"It should take us a while, but after that, we should focus on our immediate area. The articles are a good primer, but the actual reports are more focused on local and political issues. We should only concentrate on the ones that are related to the island in general and Josh and company in particular."

"Sounds logical."

"The next step should be—" I started, but then I was interrupted as the door opened without a single knock and Judy's father stuck his head through the opening.

"Hello!" he greeted us with a strained smile. He'd changed out of the business suit he was wearing during dinner, instead sporting jeans and a plaid shirt that was unbuttoned at the top, possibly on purpose to show some chest hair. He looked me in the eye and his smile, barely visible under his mustache, became even more strained. "Good. Good."

"Father, what are you doing?" Judy asked, and he turned his eyes to her.

"Just checking to see if everything is all right," he said with fake pleasantry before he looked at me again. "And delivering a friendly reminder: I have a shotgun."

"Duly noted?" I said with no small amount of puzzlement.

"Take care!" he quipped, and closed the door behind him… only to immediately open it again and look us over once more like he was expecting that we would move in the half-second he was gone. After he did so, he let out a satisfied grunt and closed the door again, this time very, very slowly.

Once we heard him leave, I turned to my assistant and flatly told her, "Your parents are weird."

"I know," she agreed, and we left it at that.

By then, it was getting late. Well, it was only 6:30, but the sky was already pretty dark. It was autumn, after all. I said my goodbyes to the family and told Judy I'd call her later when I approved her account. Her father gave me the evil eye at that and once again reminded me that he was allowed to legally carry firearms, which obviously made me a little uneasy, but aside from that little intermission, I managed to leave without any drama.

Once I was already on my way home, I let out an unconscious sigh. The day had been way, way too hectic for my taste. The thing that bothered me the most was this "love life" business, though. Just where did I go wrong? I was 100 percent sincere when I said I didn't want to get involved in any kind of dumb romantic drama while I had so many other things to worry about, yet somehow it only led to even more problems. Why can't anything be simple for once?

I was lucky that even with all my internal grumbling I heard the noise. It was a scraping sound, like shifting gravel reverberating in an empty drum. I instinctively stopped and faced the source of the sound. I had to strain my eyes for a moment, but then I noticed *it*.

A large shape barely visible in the dark. It was just outside a streetlamp's light cone, it was vaguely humanoid, but far too large. Just from a glance, I put it in the ballpark of about two and a half meters, but unlike actual Guinness Record holders, it was also as wide as a car.

Not only that, even a cursory look revealed that there was something wrong with its head. It looked like it had large, ridged horns that curled around its skull, and while I couldn't see the face, its eyes were glowing with a dull orange light. For a moment I thought it was like a cat's eye, reflecting light, but the longer I looked at them, the less certain I was about that.

And then it happened. I kept staring into its eyes, and without any warning, our gazes linked, like two magnets dangling on strings snapping together and refusing to let go. It was a weird and more than a little scary experience, as for a moment I thought I could feel emotions pressing against my forehead. Not literally, of course, but then again, there really isn't a good way to express how it feels to experience another being's emotions projected onto you.

I expected something alarming, like anger or an intent to kill, but instead the first emotion that swirled against my consciousness was surprise. Not only that, it was a pleasant surprise, followed by confusion and then, at last, curiosity. There was an undercurrent of hostility deep below these emotions, but for the most part, it was just honest-to-goodness interest.

He let out a low grunt, but even that didn't sound particularly aggressive. Bolstered by this, I was just about to call out to him when something even weirder happened. As if this wasn't weird enough already, eh?

His outline abruptly flashed with the same incandescent orange light as his eyes, accompanied by what looked like a swirl of embers in the air, and he lunged at me. Except he didn't. Only his outline. I almost let out a panicked scream, but it got trapped in my throat as another amber outline appeared. This one came from me—and it ran towards the incoming outline of the creature at an angle. The spectral copy of the huge thing raised its fist, which was about as big as my head, and swung it towards my own outline. It rolled under the strike and sprung to its feet in a single motion and the two constructs of light squared off against each other.

Then, just as I thought the orange silhouette of the creature was about to lunge again, I was hit with another wave of emotion. It was astonishment and... respect? Was respect even an emotion? Either way, "he" let out a noise that sounded like a content chuckle coming from the throat of a whale, and turned away. As our eye contact broke, the orange specters rapidly faded. By the time I recovered my wits, the creature was already gone, his footsteps soft despite his enormous size.

I took a deep breath and hurried to my place. I got there in record time, opened the door, closed and locked it behind me, and headed for the sofa, trying to ignore the cold sweat covering my body. I fell into the seat, held my head in my arms, and asked one very basic question.

"What... the bloody hell... was *that?*"

CHAPTER 18

PART 1

"Another perfect score," Judy flatly stated at the end of the last song by some lesser-known pop band. I emerged from my thoughts and looked at the other girl grinning broadly in front of me. After a second or two I returned the gesture, albeit weakly. My reaction must not have been satisfying enough, since the princess's smile withered and got replaced by the apex predator of all pouts.

"Don't you have anything to say?" she asked me as her brows twitched dangerously.

"Good job. You are a great singer," I answered in a machinelike fashion, which only made her pout harder.

"You didn't mean that at all!"

"I did," I told her with a sigh. "You cannot expect the same enthusiasm after the... what was it? The sixth time?"

"Eighth," Judy corrected me and poked at the karaoke touchscreen.

The princess turned up her nose with a huff and sat down beside me, letting Judy onto the center stage of the small karaoke booth. I did feel a little sorry for her, so I tried to come up with some minor praise, but I never had the chance to say it as Judy began singing, and I once again felt myself slip into a tired stupor.

It was more about mental exhaustion than physical, though the latter also played a role in my sour disposition. After my encounter with the creature on Friday, I'd spent all my time knee-deep in research. I didn't know how other survivors of near-death encounters coped with the experience, but in my case, it manifested as a compulsion to find out as much as I could about my assailant lest I be found flat-footed again.

Unfortunately, I couldn't turn up much. It was a Faun, one of the demi-human foot soldiers of the Abyssals. Of that, I was fairly certain. However, I could not find any reference to the outline light show that we engaged in. Not only that, but according to the Celestial Hub, Fauns were supposed to be these inarticulate monstrosities that only cared about fighting and destruction, another bit that didn't fit my attacker's modus operandi. I was getting so desperate I even tried to call Snowy, but she had her phone turned off all weekend for some reason.

It was more than a little infuriating. I had the entire Celestial Intelligence Network at my disposal, combined with having an actual Abyssal in my phonebook, and yet I still came up blank. And then there was the date—or rather, the *outing*. I was tempted to pull the plug on it, or at the very least postpone it indefinitely, but both Judy and Elly kept bombarding me with text messages about their plans, and I just didn't have the heart to rain on their parade. Not to mention, while that Faun was probably really, really dangerous, he didn't actually *attack* me per se. Or maybe he did? No, in hindsight I can say that whatever that special effects show was back there, it didn't *feel* like an attack. Not to mention that I was reasonably certain that if he wanted me dead, I wouldn't have been sitting in this karaoke booth. I couldn't even attribute the uninterrupted continuation of this old habit of mine called *breathing* to just staying indoors all Saturday. My wooden front door probably wasn't going to stop him if he really wanted to come in.

In retrospect, my dat—*outing* turned out to be fairly uneventful. That didn't mean it wasn't hectic, tiring, and positively exhausting, but at least there was no sign of the Faun anywhere.

Now, I'm not saying it was all bad. When we started out, it was actually fairly exciting, as seeing the two girls in their casual clothes was a refreshing experience... though I suppose I'd already seen Judy like that, but this time she put extra effort into her appearance. She was wearing a knit sweater under a light coat with jeans and a pair of ankle boots, which fit the season pretty well, and she looked pretty good in it. The real surprise was the princess, who showed up in a low-cut blouse with a short skirt and stockings with a pair of long boots. I couldn't help but ask if she was cold like that, but she insisted that she was fine. Draconic physiology, I supposed. Needless to say, I felt a little under-dressed, as I was only wearing my uniform's trousers and shirt with one of my black, double-breasted woolen long coats, of which I had about twenty in my wardrobe for some reason. The girls insisted it suited me, but I still regretted not wearing a different pair of shoes at the very least.

Not that these silly apparel issues held my attention for long, as it was hard to keep my mind off the Faun and our encounter, and the girls quickly noticed that I didn't have my whole heart in the activities. Speaking of activities, the two of them couldn't agree on exactly where to go and what to do, so we went everywhere and did everything.

The morning started out with us heading to the zoo, followed by a snack at a bakery at the other end of the town, after which we had a brief window-shopping session ending with a short lunch at a fancy restaurant. After that, we visited an aquarium, watched a god-awful romantic comedy in the cinema, and finally ended up in the karaoke bar tucked away in a corner of the shopping district.

"Your turn."

I twitched and blinked with what I hoped wasn't a particularly stupid expression before the words properly registered, and I took the microphone from the hand extended towards me. I stood up and walked to the song picker.

But back to the topic of the outing: While I wouldn't say we had a bad time, there was something of a tension in the air between the three of us.

By all intents and purposes, this little outing should've been a blast. I was spending time with two people I liked, we were going around to places traditionally associated with fun, and even without that, just hanging out with my friends like this should've been enjoyable in and of itself... and yet it wasn't. Not really. It felt more like we were eyeing each other the whole time, waiting for someone else to break the ice and address the elephant in the room, but neither of them did it. Though again, nor did I. Stones and glass houses, eh?

And so we were here, trapped in this non-relationship where no one really dared to make the first move in fear of ruining it for everyone. I was seriously tempted to just break the status quo and get it over with, sink or swim, but at the same time I knew it was too early to do so. I was damned if I made a move, damned if I didn't. God, I hated these stupid social Gordian knots.

"Are you okay?"

"Hm?" I was a little startled as I looked up and met the princess's eyes. "Yes, why?"

"You've been cycling through the songs for two minutes," my assistant supplied the answer. I frowned and glanced down at my hand, which was still absentmindedly poking at the screen. I stopped and stifled a groan.

"I'm fine, I just... I was just lost in thought."

My two companions shared a skeptical look between each other at my expense.

"Chief... if you don't feel well, we can always end the day early."

"Nah." I shook my head as I began cycling through the songs again. "I'm fine. Just give me a moment."

I sighed inwardly. Great. Now I'd made them worried. This was steadily shaping up to be the best worst double non-date in the history of ever.

PART 2

"Say whatever you want, I definitely won," the princess declared, smiling ear to ear.

"That is quite the achievement, considering it wasn't a competition," my assistant responded in a deadpan grumble.

"You're just saying that because you lost."

"Once again, and I cannot stress this enough, I couldn't have lost since it wasn't a competition."

"You wouldn't say that if you were the one who won."

My assistant sent her a scathing glare (read: she slightly furrowed her brows) before she turned to me and said, "Chief, please say something."

"Huh? Sorry, what were you talking about?"

This time she turned said scathing glare on me, but then she shook her head and said, "Nothing."

To be perfectly honest, I *was* listening, I just refused to get involved in their bickering. Not that I wouldn't have stepped in if the situation evolved into a full-fledged argument, but as things stood, I needed my attention elsewhere.

We were already on our way home after the last stop of our outing, a dinner at an extra-fancy restaurant (a different one from where we'd eaten our lunch). The sky became overcast while we were at the karaoke bar, so dusk settled a little earlier than usual. Because of that, I was paying extra attention to our environment, scanning every alleyway and crossroad for signs of the mysterious Faun.

I even went as far as to try to use my Far Sight to find him, but no matter how hard I tried to picture him in my mind, I couldn't see anything. Maybe I needed to have prolonged contact with people to be able to look for them? Or maybe it could be as simple as knowing their actual name (which in this case I didn't)? Damn, I was always putting off learning more about my Far Sight in favor of more pressing issues, but at this moment I would've given an arm and a leg to know what made it tick.

I obviously didn't make any headway on that front during the couple of minutes it took to take the princess home. It didn't mean I stopped trying until we got there, though.

When we arrived at the gates of the mansion, I was once again hit by how it looked both majestic and utterly ridiculous in the suburban neighbourhood. One would think I'd get used to it after a couple of visits, but no, it was just as jarring as the first time. But back to the gates: upon our arrival, we were greeted by a familiar-looking maid. She was young, tall, and wore her long blonde hair in two tidy braids on the back of her head under that white frilly headwear-thing that all stereotypical maids sported all the time. Her name was... ugh... something starting with M... Melissa, maybe?

She clapped her hands and the gates opened by themselves, though the soft whirring noise coming from the nearby bushes told me it was probably just some mundane machinery that did the heavy lifting. She lowered her head and curtsied to us as we came closer.

"Welcome back, milady. Shall I tell the staff to prepare the parlor?"

"The parlor?" the princess muttered uncertainly. The maid looked over each of us in turn and lowered her head apologetically.

"My apologies. I presumed we were having guests."

"Oh no, they are just—" the princess began, but it was at this moment that a sudden idea kicked down the back doors of my frontal lobe screaming, urging me to step forwards and raise my hand.

"Actually!" I interjected loudly, baffling everyone present for a moment, including myself. I cleared my throat and smiled awkwardly before I lowered my voice and continued. "Actually, I don't think we've seen your mansion from the inside, have we?"

"No, we haven't," Judy answered, apparently deciding to follow my lead even though I gave her no reason to do so. My assistant was at the top of her game, as always. I sent her an appreciative glance and faced the other two again.

"Isn't this a good opportunity to do that? It would be a better way to end the day than to just separate here."

"True," Judy nodded, and we both looked at the princess expectantly. She was taken aback by our proposal at first, but she quickly collected herself and grinned at us in full nobility mode.

"I agree. I don't think there's any harm in doing so." She turned on her heel and addressed the maid next. "Please tell the twins we have guests after all. Could you prepare us some tea and biscuits?"

"Most certainly," the young servant woman answered with another curtsy.

I let the princess cross the gate first and urged Judy with my eyes to follow. I trailed after them a few steps behind, but as I entered the courtyard, I gestured for the maid to come closer. She was confused at first but still walked over.

"Yes? May I help you?"

"I really hope so," I told her while glancing back at the girls. They stopped only a couple of meters ahead of us, where the princess was in the middle of animatedly showing Judy around a small pond. I turned my attention back to the maid and, after pondering on her name for a few seconds longer, took a stab in the dark.

"Melinda, right?" If she was surprised, it didn't show on her face, but instead she just nodded sharply. She was a professional. "Is Sebastian around?"

"Yes, von Fraenir is in the mansion. Do you wish to keep your presence hidden from him?" I raised a single brow at her inquiry, so she added, "I was under the impression you are not on the best of terms."

"That is a very polite way to say that we hate each other's guts, but you are correct. However, I'd actually like to ask for the opposite. Could you tell him I wish to speak with him?" She blinked at me like she didn't understand the request, so I added, "It's about Draconian business."

Her eyes narrowed and she nodded sharply. I returned the gesture and swiftly followed after the others, who were in the process of discussing the architectural style of the mansion's veranda. I wasn't particularly well-versed in the field of architecture, so I pretended to understand what Elly was talking about and periodically nodded in agreement to whatever she said.

One thing was clear, though. The place was fancy as hell on the outside, but it held no candle to the interior. The foyer had an enormous crystal chandelier that would've looked gaudy anywhere else, but since everything was so gaudy to begin with, it fit right in. I admittedly knew even less about interior design than architecture, but looking at the décor made me think of the word *Victorian*. It was all about showing off the household wealth, though the amount of gold and rare wood in the hallways was maybe a bit of an overkill.

The parlor itself wasn't half shabby either. It was huge, dominated by a gently burning hearth surrounded by a set of old, leather-bound red sofas arranged around a coffee table. It had a thick glass top sitting on four cast-metal legs in the shape of, surprise-surprise, dragons. The walls were also covered with a series of fancy (not to mention expensive) looking paintings depicting aged patriarchs with stern brows, unexpectedly outnumbered by the matriarchs trying to out-glare the men. I guess it ran in the family.

"That one is Great-Grandfather Antonio. He was a duke in Italy," the princess chattered as she pointed at the next painting in turn. We were going backward in chronological order, and I could see the change in the art style of each painting, but even the latest one seemed quite old. It was a little disappointing, as I was actually hoping to see if they had a cubist portrait. It would've looked hilarious in this environment, but alas, I had no such luck.

"Are all of them your ancestors?" I asked as I arrived at their side.

"Yes." Elly nodded with a proud smile. "These are the members of the main family from the past five hundred years!"

That made me remember a question I'd wanted to ask for quite some time, so I raised my hand like in the classroom and waited for the princess to notice me.

"Yes?"

"I have a question."

"By all means, ask."

I pointedly looked over the paintings one more time before I turned back to her.

"Looking at the age of these portraits makes me curious. Just how long do you Draconians live?"

Our host raised a contemplative finger to her lips.

"It depends. Those with thinner blood only age a little slower than humans, so... about one hundred and twenty. Give or take a decade."

"And the ones with thicker blood?" Judy followed up while inconspicuously poking at her phone. She must've been taking notes for a while now. Elly cocked her head to the side in reaction, with her finger still on her lower lip.

"I... actually, I don't know. Being a Draconian is very dangerous, so few of us die of old age. I think Father once mentioned that my great-grandpa lived for over three hundred years and he was the oldest living Draconian at the time." She paused, and seeing the completely unrelated expression of interest on my face, she continued with renewed vigor. "I don't know how old one of us *could* get, but dragons were rumored to be so long-lived they were practically immortal, so I don't see why we couldn't be like that once—" She suddenly winced, apparently remembering something unpleasant that momentarily scrunched up her face. She shook her head and forced a smile onto her lips a moment later. "B-but that's beside the point. Let's talk about something more interesting."

"No, no. This was *very* interesting. Thank you very much."

"You are... welcome?" the princess answered with a somewhat confused expression, probably completely unaware of the fact that she just handed me the last puzzle piece I needed to make my upcoming discussion with the annoying butler a hundred times more profitable.

I was ready to move on, but no matter how hard I tried to ignore it, the skewed gender-ratio was bothering me, so I asked, "By the way, is your family more likely to have daughters? Is it a Draconian thing?"

Elly didn't understand my question at first, but then she followed my gaze, and once she saw that I was still looking at the paintings, she quickly shook her head.

"Oh, that's not it. Those are the wives of the past patriarchs."

"That doesn't add up," Judy noted at my side, and I agreed. My ballpark estimate said that for every male portrait, there was an average of two and a half females.

"It's because the patriarchs of the past had more than one wife," Elly informed me like it was common knowledge. "It was necessary to keep up the bloodline. Dad doesn't practice it, but one of my uncles has three wives, and my grandpa…"

The princess continued to explain her family's peculiar traditions, but I couldn't really pay attention, as the word *precedent* was ringing in my head like a naval cannon. Nudging Elly to invite us in was rapidly turning into one of the best decisions I'd ever made. I couldn't help but wonder if I could keep up the track record during my meeting with the butler, as well.

By chance (or maybe not, as I could totally imagine her waiting until we finished talking), the blonde maid showed up in the doorway and gestured to me. I smiled back at her and said to the girls, "Uh… I think I drank one too many cans of Coke today. I need to use the toilet." The princess let out a soft giggle and was ready to show me the way, but I raised my hands apologetically and subsequently pointed at the maid. "You really don't need to. I'll ask her. You two stay here and have your tea. I'll be back before you know it."

As if they were waiting for my words as well, a pair of thin maids with bob-cuts entered the parlor pushing two small serving carts, one with an elaborate porcelain tea set and another with a veritable mountain of biscuits and other sweets. I smiled at them appreciatively, though they didn't return the gesture. They were also a little familiar, and after racking my brain, I recalled them from the time I first took the princess home. They didn't seem particularly friendly back then either, so I just shrugged them off.

Following this, I headed towards the blonde servant still standing by the doorway and she immediately turned around to lead the way. I followed half a step behind her as we ventured into the depths of the estate. That might sound overly dramatic, but trust me, the place was massive.

After navigating the hallways and stairwells of the mansion for several minutes, we arrived in front of a heavy mahogany door with *Sebastian von Fraenir* engraved on a thick, golden plaque. So the guy had his own office with his name on it. Neat. I was ready to knock and enter, since I was in a bit of a hurry, as I'd told the girls I was only leaving for a couple of minutes, but I was stopped by a polite cough at my side. I faced the young maid with a curious "Yes?"

"Before you enter, may I ask you something?"

"Of course."

"Considering that this might be the last time we have the fortune to speak—"

"Well, that's not ominous at all!" I grumbled with a roll of my eyes. I could swear I saw the corners of her lips twitch, but she continued like I didn't interrupt her.

"—I was somewhat curious about one thing. How did you know my name?"

"It's because the princess told me." I wanted to add a soft *Duh!* but I refrained.

"She did?"

"Yes, just a couple of days ago, actually. During lunch break, to be exact." I paused and flashed a smile. "By the way, I appreciated your help with the lunch box. It was delicious."

"The lunch box was milady's creation in its entirety. Neither I nor any other servant took part in its making." She corrected me in a slightly mechanical voice, like her line was rehearsed or something.

"Except for suggesting the pepper," I corrected her playfully.

"She told you about that, too?"

"Of course she did. Why, is that strange?"

She paused again while she collected her thoughts and finally shook her head.

"No, it isn't." After a moment, she dipped a curtsy. "Please continue to support milady in the future."

I was taken aback for a moment, but I let out an awkward chuckle and answered with, "That was what I wanted to ask you to do too."

She nodded with a level of solemnity that was completely unbefitting the situation and excused herself. She pattered away in a dignified strut, her large skirts all but billowing as she walked. I waited for her to disappear before I turned to the door and knocked.

"Come in," came the familiar voice of the old butler from inside. He didn't have to say it twice, as I already had my fingers on the doorknob.

The inside of the large office, or whatever it was called, somehow managed to be even posher than the rest of the mansion. It also had a gently burning fireplace like the parlor, but instead of the unified look of that room, this place seemed more like a giant, elaborate trophy room filled to the brim with objects from vastly different cultures. The floor was covered by Persian rugs; the furniture looked vaguely Chinese; the walls were covered in a wide variety of wild game trophies, plaques with various weapons and other items mounted on them; and there stood a full set of gilded plate armour in the corner, holding a plain spear that nevertheless shone with that ethereal glow I'd already associated with magic.

Combine that with the red lighting of the room, provided by the open fireplace and the last rays of the sunset, and add in that weird smell of history that permeated every really old place, and it truly felt like I stepped into a different world altogether. I didn't wonder for long, as the old butler cleared his throat. He was standing by a large, curtained window and staring into the distance. Or maybe he was just refusing to look at me as some sort of silly power-play. Sure, we could still see each other in the eye through his reflection on the glass, but it was still rude.

"So it is true." He let out a decidedly sinister chuckle. "To think you would willingly come to my lair to have counsel with—" His eyes suddenly opened wide and a second later he turned on his heel and shouted, "Put that down!"

"What, this?" I waved the statuette I'd picked up from the drawer next to the door. It looked similar to one of those Neolithic fertility idols, except obviously more recent. "I was just curious. What does it do?"

The butler rushed up to my side and snatched the statuette out of my hand.

"That is none of your business. Who gave you permission to touch anything?"

"Sorry, but it's just hard to contain myself with all of these interesting things around me. Like that creepy Japanese doll over there, or that lion head on the wall, or that spear. *Especially* the spear."

The old man's face tensed up as he looked me over again. He placed the statuette back onto the drawer and faced me with a measured voice.

"What do you find interesting about that spear?"

"Eh, it's just enchanted or something," I told him offhandedly while I walked over to one of the old sofas and gestured for my host to join me. "Anyways, I came to talk business, so we should get started."

Sebastian glared at me before he sharply exhaled through his flared nostrils and walked over to the sofa in front of mine.

"And here I was hoping milady has finally convinced you to apologize for your insolence. How foolish of me."

"Foolish indeed," I nodded sagely, completely ignoring his thundering eyes. "I am looking for information."

"Are you now?" He swept back his monochrome hair as he sat down and looked me in the eye. "According to what I've heard, you wanted to discuss," he raised his hands and continued, in air quotes, "*Draconian business.*"

"Well, kind of. It would be more accurate to say that what I want to discuss might interest you as the steward of the Dracis family. It might even concern the estate's security."

The change in my tone made him falter. He let down his hands.

"Speak, then."

I took a deep breath. "First and foremost, I wondered if you knew about any out-of-place characters wandering in the neighbourhood."

He eyed me for a few seconds, but then he said, "Only a trio of children of your age. They have been wandering around the streets as if looking for something, but they hardly seem to be a threat to us."

"I think I know the guys you are talking about, and I agree. Those guys couldn't threaten their way out of a wet paper bag if their lives depended on it."

"That doesn't make any sense."

"I know. It sounded better in my head," I told him with a sigh before I continued. "Let me try this from another angle. What can you tell me about Fauns?"

The word resulted in a surprised look that slowly eased back into a scowl.

"And why do you think I could tell you anything about Fauns? They are creatures of the Abyss, not of our kin."

"True, but considering you have been around for, what, fifteen centuries? I figured you might have picked up a few bits and pieces along the way."

The old man's demeanor changed again, this time hovering between caution and open hostility.

"I have to say, I have no idea what you are talking about."

"Oh come on," I exclaimed with a wave of my hand. "There are records of your escapades going back as far as the early Middle Ages. True, they are fragmentary and vague, but there aren't exactly a lot of people related to dragons with white stripes in their hair running around kidnapping royalty for ransom. I'm surprised no one else made the connection yet." At this point he looked like he was ready to snap my neck and bury me in the backyard, so I sighed and waved again. "Don't get so worked up, I just told you no one else made the connection that you are not just a Draconian in service of the Dracis but an actual—" I was suddenly interrupted when the old man's body started making actual, literal cracking noises as he grew a good head taller in a matter of seconds. I raised my open palms in surrender and hastily added, "I figure you already know what I'm talking about, so I won't spell it out."

The now oversized butler steadied himself, and after a couple of seconds, he somehow deflated to his original size while he still glared at me with glowing eyes.

"Give me one good reason why I shouldn't fry you where you are," he hissed through clenched teeth.

"I can give you three," I answered with a smile while ignoring the cold sweat on my back. "One, it would damage the sofa, and that would be a shame. Two, it would make the princess sad, which is an even bigger shame. Three... you can't."

His eyes still burning with a strange red glow (which was probably not just the ethereal magic light I had been seeing recently, as it was casting shadows around me), Sebastian slowly cocked his head to the side.

"And pray tell, just why can't I erase you right here and now?"

"Remember those records I told you about?" I asked, and he nodded. "They are not exactly public, but if I stumbled upon them, so can someone else. Even if something happens to me, they are still out there. Sooner or later others will find out, and they will use it as a bargaining chip, as blackmail, and sell it to a third party that may or may not be hunting your kind."

"You are doing that already."

"No, I'm not blackmailing you yet. Quite the opposite, actually. I'm offering you an opportunity to get rid of some stray evidence pointing at you being more than just an old Draconian."

"And you want information in exchange."

"Indeed. You are catching on quickly despite being so old."

Sebastian snorted and his eyes finally stopped glowing. He fixed his tie and sat down again.

"Not that it seems to matter to you. Back in my days, the young actually respected their elders."

"I see." I smiled at his slightly less murderous tone and clapped my hands in a gesture to dispel the previous tension. "Now that we have all that behind us, let's talk business. So, about Fauns. What can you tell me?"

The old butler leaned back in his seat and crossed his legs before leaning forwards again and resting his chin on his knuckle.

"Would you mind telling me why you want to know about them? Does it have something to do with your first question?"

I hesitated for a moment, but I decided to be honest about it.

"It does. I ran into one this week." The old man's face became stern again, but this time it was not aimed at me. His eyes hurried me to continue, so I did. "It was after dark, only a couple of streets from here. I couldn't make him out properly, but I'm fairly sure it was a Faun."

"This is the first time I've heard of this. It is indeed a security risk," Sebastian stated in a surprisingly soft voice. "Boy, if you would have told me this from the beginning, your whole charade would have been unnecessary."

I wanted to ask what kind of *charade* he was talking about, but I refrained. I shrugged and continued by saying, "So, what can you tell me about Fauns?"

My host gave me a wry look before he let out a soft grunt and answered with, "They are the loyal lapdogs of the Abyssal Lords. The older they get, the larger and more dangerous they become, but they are not a threat." I imitated Josh's signature skeptical eyebrow, and seeing it made Sebastian clear his throat. "To us. They are no threat to us. To you, however..." There was another long pause as the butler's brows furrowed. "Tell me, boy, how did you meet this Faun? Was it after the young lady?"

"It was probably hunting me," I answered him honestly, earning another skeptical look from the man.

"Would you mind telling me why you would think a Faun would hunt you?"

I let out a self-derisive chuckle and awkwardly scratched the base of my neck as I told him, "You see, I might've ever so slightly antagonized the current head of House Inanna."

"How so?"

I let out another awkward laugh while trying to find a way to change the topic, but the butler's eyes looked so uncharacteristically curious I gave in and told him, "Well, I told him he sounded like a creepy uncle in public, then I called his death threats lame, and in the end, I gave him an embarrassing nickname. Oh, and might have called him a dick a couple times. That's all I can think of right now."

Sebastian gave me a measuring look before he simply stated, "Exactly the kind of insolence I expected from you."

"Hey!" I protested, albeit feebly, before I shook my head and said, "Anyways, we were talking about the Faun, right? Have you heard anything about looking one in the eye?"

By this point most of the old man's hostility had disappeared in favor of curiosity.

"Looking them in the eye..." He stroked his beard, perhaps stalling for time just to piss me off, and then shook his head. "It has been ages since I have last seen one of those brutish creatures in person, and I never had any problem looking them in the eye. I have, however, heard tales about how a single look from a powerful Faun could paralyze even the bravest warrior. I always considered that merely a poetic way of saying that they were quite frightening."

"So you have heard nothing about afterimages? Or glowing orange specters?"

"No, I can't say I have."

I clicked my tongue in frustration. "Damn, I thought if there was anyone who knew about this, it would be a—" I swallowed back the end of my sentence upon seeing the hostility returning to the old man's eyes, and hastily replaced it with, "—a steward of the Dracis family."

"Life can be disappointing like that," Sebastian murmured while crossing his fingers on his lap. "So, about those *bits of information* you spoke of..."

I mirrored his pose and shook my head. "So far your secrets and what we just discussed are not even in the same ballpark. You are going to have to give me more. A lot more."

"You are testing my patience, boy."

"That's strange. I've heard the elderly were supposed to be quite patient." I shook my head with a smile and looked the man in the eye. "I want an exchange of equal value."

The old man exhaled in exhaustion.

"Fine. Name your price."

"More information," I answered. "I would like to have access to any records you might have. History of Draconians, biographies, past involvements, any info you have on the other Old Blooded, et cetera."

Sebastian lapsed back into glaring at me.

"You are getting greedy, boy."

"I know." I grinned. "But I thought of another bargaining chip that I could throw in gratis."

"Oh? And what would that be?"

I let the smile creep even wider on my face.

"I heard you are not exactly on good terms with the knights with the ridiculously long name?"

The old man's demeanor took a sudden turn to the grim at the mere mention of knights. It wasn't the kind of anger he showed whenever I messed around with him, but a genuine, coldly burning hate.

"You are a master of understatement," he spat the words at me. I felt a chill run down my spine, so I retreated behind my fake smile.

"Why, thank you." I leaned closer and softly said, "So, what would you say if I told you I could give you detailed information on their activities over the past couple of months?"

The old man's eyes flared up with a mixture of surprise and suspicion.

"And how would you even have such information?"

"Does it really matter? I have it, and while they are as good at covering their tracks as you are, there's still much you could mine out of it. Who knows what kind of disasters you could avert by having all that at your fingertips?"

Sebastian gritted his teeth in frustration, yet it didn't take long for him to relent.

"So let me see if I understand your proposal. You wish to trade my identity and information on the movements of the accursed knights, information that you refuse to source, in exchange for access to the Dracis library."

"If by *library* you mean the archives the family accumulated over the centuries, then yes."

"And what if the information you provide proves to be useless?"

I shrugged.

"Hey, the same could be said about your library. It might be completely useless to me." I leaned forward even more and linked my fingers for emphasis. "But what if it isn't? Can you afford the chance?"

The old butler followed my example and said, "In other words, we are both gambling. At worst neither of us gets what they want, at best we both walk away content." He narrowed his eyes and added, "The only problem is that I'm not going to gamble on our household's security."

"You don't need to. You can exclude any information that would pose a direct threat to the Dracis family or yourself."

"How generous of you."

"I know," I answered with a self-conscious grin.

We sat in silence while Sebastian mulled over my offer. It also gave me a little time to think about what I was doing, and it made me want to hit myself. Talking with the butler was a spur-of-the-moment idea, but it somehow spiraled into something far more dangerous. But then again, I was looking for information of any kind, and having a different source aside from the Celestial Hub would be very helpful.

At last, Sebastian harrumphed, drawing my attention back to him.

"Very well, boy. I naturally have to discuss this with the patriarch, but if he agrees with your terms, then I shall grant you access to our library." He paused meaningfully before he added, "I hope you will live up to your end of the bargain, or I might have to hunt you." He paused again, this time more spontaneously, and for the first time, I saw him smile. It was unnerving, to say the least. "Though, on second thought, at least I can look forward to that in case you fail to deliver."

"Good for you," I told him with a fake smile and stood up. "How long do you think the process will take?"

"I will have our answer by tomorrow night."

"I can work with that," I told him before clapping my hands. "Now then, if you excuse me, I have to get back before the girls start missing me."

I offered him a hand to shake and he grudgingly accepted it, though he made a point out of crushing my poor fingers. It wasn't that bad, though; it only took about ten minutes for the feeling to return to my hand. Anyways,

I left after he made some more thinly veiled threats and headed back to the parlor... or I would have if I had any idea about where to go.

As I mentioned beforehand, the mansion was pretty big and uniformly posh, and I really couldn't remember the way I came from. For a moment I entertained the thought of turning around and asking the old butler for directions, but then I remembered that I had some alternatives, so I just used my Far Sight to figure out which direction to go in... which actually provided me with a new surprise.

I'd already discovered that if I was only using my Far Sight in general, without any person in mind, I could tell where certain people were in relation to me. This is how I figured out that there was a secret underground mage school dungeon thing underneath Blue Cherry High even before I actually learned about it. As I did just that and slipped into a shallow daze, I quickly picked out the princess and Judy, but there was another presence very close to me. I focused on it, and suddenly I (or at least my vision) was back in Sebastian's *office*, where he was in the middle of a heated conversation on an old-school rotary phone.

The door was probably soundproofed, I figured, but more importantly, this meant that I could use my Far Sight on Sebastian, as well. I was fairly sure I couldn't do that before, and the only thing that changed was...

"Physical contact, huh?" I mused as I continued rubbing my still aching right hand. That was nice to know.

That said, I didn't actually listen into the man's conversation, as I was in a hurry. I focused my attention on the girls, and after some trial and error, I managed to bumble my way back to the parlor. I was prepared for some apologizing about my tardiness, but maybe exactly because of that, I was woefully unprepared for the sight as I entered the room.

I only left for about twenty minutes yet the entire place changed, courtesy of the mountain of clothes strewn on the sofas and tables. They looked like gowns of various levels of fanciness, draped over the furniture like work clothes a tired guy had tossed after a long day. My two companions, on the other hand, were nowhere to be seen. I was just about to use Far Sight again when I noticed movement near the back door at the other end of the parlor, which itself was a new find I hadn't noticed before.

"Oh, you are back," Melinda noted dispassionately as she walked in. "And with all limbs attached. Impressive."

"Thank you, I guess," I answered and waved towards the clothes. "What is all this about?"

"Milady wanted to ask Miss Judy's opinion on some of her formal wear."

"Just on a whim?"

"Yes. Is there a problem with that?"

"No, it's just unexpected," I told her while I looked over the mess again. "I also don't know where to sit."

"There is no reason for you to sit down. They should be back at any moment."

"If you say so..." I responded half-heartedly as my eyes lingered on the gowns. Some of them were surprisingly risqué, but before I could study them any further, I noticed that the blonde maid was staring at me expectantly. "Yes? Is there something else?"

"I was just wondering, if I may be so bold, how well your counsel with Meister von Fraenir went."

"Oh, that?" I shrugged as I ran my eyes over a red dress that looked like it was made to be held on with double-sided tape. I momentarily tried to imagine the princess in it, then Judy, then finally I returned my attention to the conversation before I started blushing. "It was less *counsel* and more *mutually advantageous agreement*, but yes, it went well."

"I am glad to hear that. That means I—"

Whatever she wanted to say was cut short by the back door opening again and the princess backing out of it while dragging something.

"Come on! Stop being so obstinate!"

"I'm not," came the slightly petulant answer from the other side. The words barely registered, though, as my attention was caught by the princess's attire. It was a shiny, silken one-piece red dress with a narrow neckline that plunged nearly down to her belly button and an open-sided skirt that revealed her bare feet. As Judy was dragged into the parlor, I saw that she was also wearing a dress. Hers was infinitely more modest, dark-blue, and something like a Chinese qipao, but it also had detached sleeves with those weird fingerless evening gloves that ended with a ring one had to put on their middle finger.

They weren't wearing any makeup or had their hair done up (not that they needed to, considering the way hairdos worked around these parts), yet they looked so different that if I saw them on the street, it might've taken me a while to recognize them. They were really pretty. Or rather, prettier than usual.

"Come on, we need to take up our places before he comes back!" Elly insisted while dragging my assistant, and I found this to be a good opportunity to interject.

"Actually, I'm already back."

The princess froze and glanced over her shoulder.

"Oh... H-hi, Leo..."

"Hi," I answered her awkward greeting as she straightened herself and gave me an embarrassed smile.

"You... um... you were late, so we thought..."

While the princess shared her excuses, I walked over and took a better look at her from up close.

"Hm. This dress really suits you."

"You... think so?"

"Yes. It might be a little bold, but it brings out your... personality."

"He is talking about your br—" my assistant offered her deadpan contribution to the conversation from the side, but I cut her off.

"Yep, red fits your personality perfectly. And the cut really emphasizes your... eyes."

"He still means your bre—" Judy interjected again, but I cut her off once more.

"Yes, the blue of your eyes really comes to the forefront like that." I looked at Judy to see if she had anything else to add, but she only gave me *a we both know what you really mean, and you'd only cut me off, anyway, so why should I bother?* look (admittedly, her eyes were a little verbose every once in a while). As I looked over, though, I found myself paying extra attention to my assistant as I slowly circled her. "Speaking of blue, this dress looks great too."

"If you say so," she feigned disinterest, but the slight flush on her cheeks betrayed her.

"Yeah, it suits you surprisingly well."

The blush disappeared as quickly as it came. She narrowed her eyes. "*Surprisingly?*"

"Oh come on, stop complaining and just take the compliment," I told her and poked the crease between her brows. "By the way, while I'd be lying if I said it wasn't fun to see you girls in a different outfit, I still can't help but wonder what this is all about."

"It was Eleanor's idea," Judy told me as she removed my finger from her de-scowlified forehead.

"I-it wasn't just to show them off to you!" the princess exclaimed. "It's for the ball!"

"What ball?"

"The Christmas ball!"

"Oh, that..." I nodded knowingly even though this was the first time I'd ever heard of it. "But it's only October."

"You can never start preparing for these things early enough," she told me with a puffed chest that threatened to spill out of her outfit.

"Gowns like these have to be fitted before the event, so we have to pick them in advance."

"I see..." I agreed noncommittally as I turned to Judy. "And you?"

"I had no choice."

I was about to ask what they were planning to do with the rest of the outfits scattered in the parlor when the princess inserted herself between us.

"Actually, now that you are here, you can help us choose!"

"Us?"

Judy sounded a little startled, and I shared some of her sentiment... but then again, this was an opportunity to look at pretty girls wearing tastefully skimpy clothes, and while I was trying not to get myself bogged down on the relationship end of things yet, it didn't mean I didn't appreciate the female form. Not to mention, if playing around like this helped them bond, it was an absolute win for me.

"Fine by me," I told them with a smile, and much to my surprise, my assistant didn't even protest any further.

PART 3

"I'm not going to lie," I struck up a conversation as we were walking towards our neighbourhood, "that last dress was unexpected, but not in a bad way."

The impromptu fashion show lasted well after dark, and it was a little after eight by the time we waved our goodbyes at the mansion gates. Judy lowered her face and muttered, "Please refrain from mentioning it again. Ever."

I chuckled mirthfully as I recalled the borderline stripperific dress Judy wore for last. It was just like the red gown I thought only double-sided tape could hold on to the wearer, except somehow it had even less covering. Heck, on second thought, it might've been slightly transparent. I couldn't take a good look, but I swear I clearly saw the outlines of her underwear.

Recalling that image might have put a peculiar expression on my face, because Judy averted her face again. "I'm never going to live this one down."

"Oh come on, Dormouse!" I encouraged her with a pat on the shoulder. "You were just caught up in the heat of the moment. And it was only the three of us. Not to mention, even though I only saw it for a few seconds before you ran away, it looked great on you."

"You just say that because you are trying to be nice."

"No, I'm not. I *am* nice. Jokes aside, it really looked good on you. You should have more confidence in your figure."

"It's hard to do with this competition." I looked at her questioningly, at which point she casually cupped her own breasts and pushed them up a little so that a bit of her cleavage showed through the neckline of her sweater. "Mother Nature has betrayed me."

I would have chuckled, but at the same time her words piqued my interest, so I stifled it and instead I asked, "Wait, girls actually do compare each other like that? I thought that was a stereotype."

"It's hard not to do that when you are changing in the same room. I was under the impression boys did the same with..." In a rare (and surprisingly adorable) show of embarrassment, she averted her eyes and finished in a mumble with the words, "... other parts of their anatomy."

"I think that's a stereotype too. At least, I've never done that." She nodded, but still seemed awkward (not to mention she still had her hands cupped under her chest, which was distracting), so I began looking for alternative topics that did not involve secondary sexual characteristics. It didn't take long to find one. "By the way, I have a new source of data."

"You do?" She faced me again, finally lowering her hands. "I presume that was the reason behind your long absence."

"It wasn't *that* long, but yes. I was having a talk with the butler."

"That sounds very uncharacteristic of you. Are you ill, by any chance?"

"Ha. Ha. You are very funny."

"Thank you, I'm trying."

"You sure are. Anyways, I traded some intel, and if everything works out well, we should get access to the Dracis family's records."

"I presume that is good news."

"Hey, having more sources is always good. Although, it's apparently a library, so accessing it would take more effort than the Celestial Hub. On the other hand, it might have different and older texts that could help us in unexpected ways."

"It's a library?" My assistant squinted at me suspiciously. "That means you will have an excuse to spend time at Eleanor's mansion."

I gave her a flat look in return and shook my head.

"That is a very peculiar way to say it. Do you think I want to hang out there that much?"

"I don't know. Do you?"

I stifled a groan and told her, "If you are so worried about that, why don't you do it?"

Judy paused for a moment and then gave me a huge nod.

"Challenge accepted. You already have your hands full with the website; I should pull my weight there, at the library."

"Are you sure? I don't even know how much data we are talking about. It might take a while to comb through all of it."

"Don't worry about me, Chief. It will be better this way. You are good at deductions, but you are horrible at organizing data. Let's work with our strong suits and share the work."

I really couldn't object to that, and even if I could, I had no time as we were almost in front of Judy's home.

"All right, then. We will discuss the details once the old guy tells me his answer. Until then, let's focus on the Celestial Hub and whip it into a semblance of efficiency."

She shook her head with a difficult-to-read expression and abruptly sighed.

"Why do you have to bring our work to our dates?"

The question took me by surprise, and I cocked my head to the side in reaction.

"*Outings*, and are you saying this was still part of it?"

"Of course. A date doesn't end until the goodbye kiss. Speaking of which..." Before I could react, she stood on her tiptoes and gave me a peck on my cheek. "I know this date was for your sake, but I still had fun. Thanks."

"You are welc—wait, what?" The question broke through my reflexive words, but by then my assistant was already at her door. She gave me one last glance, which may or may not have been very bashful and incredibly cute, and then closed the door behind her. For a moment I couldn't decide whether I was pleased or irritated over the latest blow on my anti-romance armour, but I decided that I might as well let the day end on a positive note, and I headed homewards with a little smile.

There might have even been a slight spring in my steps, which sadly didn't last long, as after rounding the corner, I noticed a slight movement in the darkness stretching beyond the light of the streetlamps. I stopped and, straining my eyes, made out a familiar silhouette.

I was ready to bolt at a moment's notice, but the longer I looked, the less afraid I became. The Faun, still as large and imposing as before, was standing still in what I presumed to be a relaxed stance. After a few more seconds, I became able to make out some of his features.

He had a wide, flat nose that didn't seem to have any nostrils, a pair of thick, pointy ears, and large eyes that looked incredibly dark on his spotty white face. I didn't have time to figure out why his eyes felt strange, as my attention was drawn to his mouth when his lips parted in a surprisingly harmless smile. It was still looking weird on his large, flat face, but it didn't unnerve me. Then the Faun locked eyes with me again and I could once again see flashes of orange lights swirling around his form as a single feeling hit me: curiosity. It only lasted for a moment, but when I blinked, both the emotion and the Faun were gone.

I wondered if it was because of my eyes adjusting slowly after the sudden light or if it was some sort of magic. I knew so little about Fauns that both seemed like a distinct possibility. Either way, whatever that Faun was here for, it wasn't to paint the neighbourhood red with my blood. I was both relieved and puzzled by that, so I shelved it in my *things to worry about later* folder, which was admittedly about to burst at this point. What can I say? It wasn't my fault the world kept throwing flies into my salad every five minutes.

That said, after I was sure he was really gone, I continued on my way with considerably less spring in my steps. This time I didn't bother to raid the kitchen once I got home, as I had already eaten enough tea biscuits to last me a lifetime, and instead I headed for my room. I fired up my PC, logged into the Celestial Hub, and cracked my fingers before I simply wrote in: "Admin: Guys, I have a request for you."

CHAPTER 19

PART 1

I looked over the search results on the monitor and nodded in satisfaction. With this, all traces of Sebastian's past should be shrouded well beyond recovery. Well, at least as far as the Celestials were concerned, and not counting the backup I had safely tucked away on a USB drive, but that was beside the point. I'd also already printed out a set of the offending database entries. I planned to hand those over to the stuck-up bastard later, just so that he couldn't claim I was lying. He always struck me as an analog person, hence the tree-carcass-based information carrier.

Now granted, we were talking about the repository of the biggest, most well-organized information network of the world here (according to them, at the very least), so if the Celestials couldn't figure out the man's real identity with all this data at their fingertips already, Sebastian's secret was probably fairly safe. Until a suitably dramatic moment demanded its reveal, that is—but that was just my speculation based on the setting, so it was neither here nor there.

Of course, there was another way to quickly figure out his identity, considering his name was literally a variation of *Fafnir* from the Nibelungenlied. However, taken that other people here didn't seem to be aware of the significance of their names, be they placeholders or *main characters*, the chance of someone connecting the dots just like I did was vanishingly low.

Anyways, I spent the extra time I had after editing the database trying to figure out if the Hub offered me any way to deal with my newfound supernatural stalker, but the best advice my roundabout inquiries got me, both as "Admin" and under a different alias (I'd started using several sock-puppets for editing and questions, by the way), was that I should talk to the local Magi representative. It was apparently one of those unspoken rule things; any such disturbances were supposed to be run by them first, as they didn't take kindly when other factions operated in the open inside their territory.

I sat back in my chair and thought about that for a second. I'd have to talk to the class rep and her ilk sooner or later, as they were the logical next step in my exploration of this world. The Celestial Hub provided me with recent and relevant information. The Dracis library should, hopefully, provide me with cross-references and a less *dear leader*-centric history of the world. Those were both very important in terms of helping me pass as an informed player in the local secret societies, but neither of them helped my ultimate goal of figuring out the actual nature of the world.

My biggest obstacle in that regard was magic. The very existence of it. So long as I didn't know the exact nature or limitations of it, I could never be sure if something was an actual indication towards how this universe worked or just plain old, run-of-the-mill magic, silly as that might've sounded. On top of all that, I still had my Far Sight to experiment with, plus there were all those other times I did inexplicable things. For example, during the time when the princess and Snowy were fighting, I remember jumping through a glass door without actually hitting it. Which reminded me of my very first day when I'd fallen down the stairs and somehow landed on the locked roof. That couldn't have been normal.

So yeah, I supposed I might have other superpowers, though I had no idea how to test them. Maybe by running into walls to see if I passed through? That could cause some headaches, quite literally.

Oh, right, and on top of *all that* I was also embroiled in Josh's harem with my own love triangle, because why would I ever catch a break? Well, okay, that last one I could solve fairly quickly, but I was still waiting for the right opportunity to do so. It wasn't like I was indecisive or anything; I was just doing a *thing*.

After a while, I simply let out an exasperated groan. Sometimes I wished that there were more hours in a day. Not having to sleep, a minor superpower in and of itself, already made me unnaturally efficient, but it just wasn't enough.

I stretched my arms and looked at the clock. It was a little after six. I still had a good hour before I had to set out for school, and I already had my fill with the Celestial Hub. I didn't want to think about my relationship hardships either, so instead I decided to focus on my powers.

As I mentioned before, walking into walls wasn't my idea of fun, so I tried to concentrate on Far Sight, and I already had a target in mind. I emptied my mug and put it on the desk before I closed my eyes and focused on the image of Sebastian.

There was a moment of mild nausea, as usual, before my consciousness expanded towards my target. If I had to visualize it, I'd say it felt like I extended a very thin and long tendril towards a dot on the edge of my sight, and once the two connected, I was suddenly seeing everything like I was actually there. It was eerie, but I already got used to it.

After the first second of disorientation passed, I quickly recognized the place as the stuffy old trophy room in which I'd met Sebastian just a couple of hours before. He was sitting in his large armchair behind the big desk opposite the door and was in the middle of gingerly polishing the detached front plate of the gilded armour from the corner. I glanced over there, and I involuntarily raised a brow as I noticed three large tears running in parallel on the exposed back plate. They frankly looked like claw-marks, and as far as I knew, they were just that.

The butler raised the piece of mirror-shined metal in front of him and grinned with a childish glee that was incredibly weird on his face. He stood up and carried the plate over to the rest of the armour and, with a satisfied chuckle, skillfully buckled it into place. Then, and I swear to God I'm not lying, he put on a pair of large, floral-print oven mittens and picked up the worn spear from the floor and positioned it in the hands of the suit until it looked exactly like it was when I first came to the room.

He spent the next couple of minutes moving around in his lair and arranging his belongings, which wasn't particularly riveting to watch. I was about to leave and take a look at my next target when his antique rotary phone rang. He walked over to the desk and picked it up.

"Yes?"

Someone was talking on the other side, obviously, and he sat down and stroked his beard while he listened.

"Of course. It appears the boy took a fancy to your daughter. ... Yes, as much as it pains me to admit it, the attraction seems to be mutual. ... No, you do not need to worry. I believe he is only doing all this to try to impress us. It's typical courtship behaviour, I believe. Yes? No, I don't think there is any harm in giving him access to the library, though he might require over-sight. Yes. Yes, I will do that. No, I shall only tell him about your decision in a couple of days. It will do the newt good to learn that not everything falls into his lap. ... Thank you, I wish the same to you."

With a smug smile, he put down the receiver and returned to fiddling with his collection. I took a deep breath to stop myself from trying to whack him over the head with my nonexistent limbs and put my simmering irritation aside. I purposefully averted my attention and began slipping out of the Far Sight. I was just about to return to my room when I stopped mid-transit and pondered for a second.

I'd already determined that I could observe people with whom I've been in physical contact. Because of this, I couldn't detect the Faun... but maybe I could detect his boss. I tried picturing Crowey, though I had a slightly harder time, considering I'd only seen the guy in person once, yet I could still make out a fuzzy dot I could reach towards. I did so, and while the nausea was a little stronger than usual, I still found myself in the presence of my target all the same.

Not only that, I somehow managed to show up in my incorporeal form at the best possible moment. How's that? Well, I just happened to barge in on a meeting between the bastard and my stalker.

"I believe," the Faun spoke in a deep, rumbling, yet surprisingly articulate voice, "we must observe him further."

"You are testing my patience!" Crowey snapped at him from the dining table. Speaking of which, they were in what I presumed to be a fancy hotel room, and the guy was in the process of stuffing an entire turducken into his spindly frame for breakfast. The Faun stood at a respectful distance, and to my surprise, I found his silhouette hard to make out. It was as if he was covered in a kind of dark haze. However, once I focused my attention on him, I also realized that he was subtly glowing with the colourless magical light that probably only I could see. As I thought about it, maybe there was something similar going on during our nightly encounters, and I just attributed his low visibility to the darkness of the late evening. Now that I knew that I should be on the lookout for telltale signs of magic instead, I suddenly felt much more confident about noticing him first.

That said, the Faun bowed his head subserviently.

"It is my sincere opinion that the young man is more than meets the eye."

"No, he isn't!" Crowey exclaimed, brandishing his fork. "I touched that boy and tried to set the Mana in his veins aflame. He is so powerless, he didn't even notice!"

"My liege, I believe there are many qualities of power not predicated on one's command of the mystic arts."

"No, there aren't! And stop growling already and talk like a normal person! You are taking away my appetite."

I swear I saw the Faun's brows twitch, and I couldn't help but feel sympathy for the poor bastard. I mean, I didn't like him stalking and ambushing me, but having that prick for a boss must've been tiresome.

"Yes, lord," he answered with an abrupt change in his tone, suddenly sounding like the stereotypical brute his appearance suggested.

"I want you to shadow that boy, and if an opportunity presents itself, off him. Make it look like an accident. You are good at that."

"Will do. Throw in front of car?"

"That should do."

"If there is car, I will do," the Faun rumbled, and while Crowey was apparently satisfied with his answer, I couldn't help but laugh. He didn't see it, but the Faun was definitely rolling his eyes in exasperation.

"Go wake my sister and tell her to continue her task. I want the area prepared by the end of the week."

"Will tell."

"Of course you will. Once you are done with that, make sure the Chimera is well fed. I don't want another accident. You are dismissed."

The Faun bowed deeply to his irritating master and walked out of the room with quiet steps, though I couldn't help but notice that he seemed to favor one of his legs. I stayed around for a few more minutes to see if there would be any further developments, but all I got to see was Crowey stuffing his trap, which got old quick. As such, I returned to my room and made a note about not going anywhere near traffic for the foreseeable future.

Checking the time, I proceeded to engage in a slightly more elaborate morning routine than usual to help all the new info sink in, including a full bath, some extra time fixing my eternally unruly hair, and I even had a full meal for breakfast, or at least as far as instant noodles plus a plateful of warmed-up spaghetti could be considered a full meal.

Still, I was a little early when I left my house and headed for Judy's place. She'd just finished her breakfast when I arrived, and soon we were both headed to the princess's mansion. On the way, I gave her a quick outline of the data I'd gathered from the Hub and the extra tidbits I gained from observing Sebastian and Crowley. I naturally left out the part about how there was a big ram-man after my blood. Didn't want to worry her too much.

"I think I can recall a certain person saying he would not use his powers to spy on people."

"Who was this person?"

"You, Chief."

I waved a hand dismissively.

"Pics or it didn't happen."

"I have an eidetic memory and I can vouch for it."

"Objection!" I exclaimed as I pointed a finger at her. "I would like to forward a motion to dismiss the testimony of the lovely young lady on the witness stand, as she is obviously biased."

"Objection overruled," she answered as she brought down her fist on her palm. "The jury finds no problem with her testimony."

"What jury?"

She pointed at herself. "Me."

"Ack! So you are both judge, jury, and executioner?"

"Indeed." She nodded emphatically. "I am the law!"

I forced myself to stop snickering and nodded in approval.

"So I guess you watched the movie we talked about?"

"I did," she answered with a nod of her own. "It was funny."

"I'm glad to hear that."

My last words punctuated our arrival at the gates of the mansion. Once again proving that my timing was absolutely impeccable, the princess exited the front door mere seconds after we showed up. She was followed by Melinda, and I waved for both of them to come over.

"Hi, Leo," she greeted me with a surprising lack of embarrassment. "Judy too."

"I was relegated to an afterthought," my dear assistant stated in a whisper, but she still returned the greeting in the form of a nod.

"Morning, princess. I figured we should pick you up for a change so that we wouldn't need to run into each other by accident."

Now that I finally got a blush out of her (not that I was looking forward to it or anything), I switched my attention to the maid dutifully standing by at her side and told her, "Could you please ask Sebastian to come out for a moment? I wish to speak with him."

Melinda twitched in surprise and shook her head apologetically.

"I'm sorry, but von Fraenir has left on a business trip this morning."

I raised a skeptical brow at her, and then I peeked a little with my Far Sight and shook my head.

"Melinda, please. I know he probably told you to lie to me, and I'm not going to hold it against you, so could we cut to the chase and just pretend you didn't say that? Please go in and tell him to stop arranging his creepy Japanese dolls and step out for a moment."

She opened her mouth to argue, but then she closed it without a word and left after a short curtsy. I shook my head and turned to the curious pair at my side.

"This won't take long, but you can go ahead if you'd like. I'll catch up."

"Are you sure?"

"Yeah, I have long legs."

The princess gave me a flat look and turned on her heel with a small grimace. Judy followed suit, leaving me alone in front of the mansion's gates for a good minute until the disgruntled steward appeared.

"What is it, boy?" he asked with thundering eyes under low-set brows. I smiled at him in turn and reached into my bag.

"Good morning to you too. Here, my part of the bargain." I handed over the documents and swiftly explained what they were about, including the original sources he should look into if he wanted to make sure others wouldn't make the connections in the future. He looked fairly surprised at first, but then he rapidly forced himself back into his angry butler persona. I shrugged off his scowl and told him, "I'm going to come over with my assistant later this evening to see your library. I will hand over my intel on the knights then."

"Now, hold it right there, boy. As I told you yesterday, I still need to contact the head of the household to—"

I cut him off by raising a hand. I took a deep breath and straightened myself, which I followed up with deepening my voice and adopting a British accent (which came quite naturally) just for the heck of it.

"Von Fraenir, I would prefer if you didn't take me for a fool. You have already contacted your patriarch, and he allowed me to browse your library just this morning, a little after six a.m., to be precise." At this point I leaned a little closer and tried to plaster a *very friendly smile* on my face. "Also, just to be clear, I do not like being called a newt."

I was ready to leave it at this point and let the old man boil in his own confusion awhile, but as I tried to turn around, I was stopped by a hand clasped around my upper arm. I glanced back and found Sebastian looking me in the eye with literally glowing pupils.

"Explain yourself."

That was all he said, and against my better judgment, I tried to brush his hand off... which I magnificently failed to do, so I pretended I was only fixing the creases on my uniform around his hand and said:

"Who knows? Maybe I have all your phones bugged. Or I am listening to all telecommunications everywhere. Or it could be that I have informants everywhere. Or I am just reading your mind. Hell, I might even be an omniscient physical god incarnate pulling your leg for shits and giggles! The possibilities are endless."

"That wasn't an answer."

"No, it wasn't, but we all have our secrets, don't we?" I told him with a strained grin.

A short yet subjectively very, very long stalemate followed, but at last the annoying butler hissed a sigh between his clenched teeth.

"Whatever method you used, stop it. I will not tolerate anyone compromising the security of my household," he told me sternly. Then he leaned in closer. "Are we clear?"

"I'll think about it," I told him noncommittally, earning me another glare. Maybe the princess picked up the habit from him?

"You better do," he growled and gestured for me to leave.

"What, no death threats this time?" I joked, but to my surprise, the old butler shook his head.

"They seem to be ineffective, so I won't even bother."

"Look at that! Someone's learning!" I exclaimed with an expression that was most certainly not a shit-eating grin.

"Indeed. Now I'm looking into ways to make your personal life with Lady Eleanor difficult."

The not-shit-eating-grin disappeared from my face, and I flatly told him, "Don't."

"I will think about it," he answered with a small smile that was somehow a hundred times scarier than all of his glowy-eyed glares, so I changed the topic.

"Speaking of death threats," I began while poking at the hand still clasped around my upper arm, "Do you have anything on the Faun?"

"Nothing substantial," he told me while he squeezed a little harder, but I endured it without flinching.

"That's too bad," I answered. I finally forced a smile on my face and asked, "Could you let me go already? I don't want to make the princess wait for me."

We stared daggers at each other for a few seconds, then he relaxed his grasp so that I could slip out of it. I ignored the impulse the massage my stinging arm and gave the old man a small nod, which he surprisingly returned without a glare, and hurried after the girls. As I have noted before, I had long legs (or they were moving really slowly to make sure they wouldn't leave me behind, one or the other), so I managed to catch up with them fast. But not quickly enough, it seemed.

"What is this about a goodbye kiss?" came the question from the princess, accompanied with an accusing finger shoved in my face as I arrived.

"Pardon?"

"I said," she repeated while punctuating her words with a poke at my chest, "What is this *goodbye kiss* she is talking about?"

I gave my assistant a critical look before I returned my attention to the princess.

"I have absolutely no idea what you are talking about. Why do you keep letting her push your buttons like that?"

"Your accusations are completely baseless," my assistant retorted as I got in line between the two of them as usual. "Also, your denial hurts my fragile feelings."

"Oh the humanity," I mumbled flatly.

"So... no kiss?"

I sighed and pointed at my face. "Only a peck on the cheek. It's perfectly normal."

"No, it isn't!" the princess objected loudly.

I spent the rest of my commute trying to convince her that it was nothing particularly damning, but in the end, I had to surrender myself and let her give me a supremely embarrassed peck on the other cheek in the name of her weird sense of *fairness*.

The things I had to put up with sometimes...

PART 2

Once our small group arrived at school, I tried to avoid the prying eyes of the others, to no avail, and it still led to some headaches in the form of Josh complaining about my horrid womanizing ways. At this point I couldn't care less, so I shrugged him (and his insistent challenges to a gentlemanly duel) off. He was getting lonely, I surmised, so I might or might not have given him some vague and in no way specific promises to whoop his ass so bad, he'd need half of the Arctic ice pack to treat the burn. Or something like that.

Nothing particularly noteworthy happened until lunch break, when I finally managed to pull the class rep aside. She looked a little haggard, so I felt a bad about troubling her with my problems as well, but since the guys at the Celestial Hub told me I should ask a Magi about my Faun situation, and she was the only Magi I knew, I more or less had to go to her.

"I'm listening," she told me after we arrived at a fairly deserted part of the courtyard. Once again, the placeholders seemed to have a sixth sense that told them to avoid places where we were talking about meaningful stuff, like the supernatural or my relationship tribulations. Since this was the former, the number of idlers seemed even lower than usual, which was a good thing, as it meant we wouldn't have to keep our voices down.

"I have a problem."

"With Judy or with Elly?" she asked back with a stern look.

"Neither!" I retorted. "I mean a real problem, the supernatural kind."

"Oh," she crossed her arms in front of her chest before glancing around, then gestured for me to continue.

"I'm being stalked by a Faun," I told her straight up.

This time her eyebrows shot up, drawing even more attention to the circles under her eyes, and she hurriedly asked, "Are you all right? Did you get attacked?"

"I'm fine, and no, I didn't get attacked... Or at least I don't think so."

"Please tell me exactly what happened," she requested, and I complied. After my quick description of the two times I met with my would-be-assassin (speaking of which, I naturally didn't tell her about me witnessing Crowey ordering the hit on me, as then I would've had to explain my Far Sight, and that would've drawn things out even more), she let out a pent-up breath and shook her head. "So there was no actual attack?" I nodded in response and she clicked her tongue. "That's a problem."

"How so? I thought it would be a good thing."

"That's not what I mean," she explained in a hurry. "If you were attacked, I could report that to the School, and we could get some seniors to investigate, but since the Faun only spooked you in the dark, we can't do anything."

"So you need them to actually do something before you can kick down Crowey's door?"

"Yes."

"That's..." I wanted to say *surprisingly rational, almost like real law enforcement*, but then the class rep told me:

"Sorry, our rules can tie us up sometimes." She paused, then tapped her chin and added, "Though if you can provoke him to attack you, and then survive, we could actually start an investigation."

"Wouldn't that be entrapment?"

Instead of answering, she just shrugged. I never knew she had a side like this to her, but I was too disappointed about her answer to try to argue about *due process* and stuff.

"Well, at least I know my options. Or lack thereof. I'll try to do something about him myself."

She gave me a strange look and then said, "Why don't you just talk to Neige?" There was a short pause, during which her brows furrowed into a frown. "Speaking of which, do you know what she is doing?"

The question honestly took me aback for a moment.

"You mean right now or in general?"

"Yes."

I scratched my chin to hide the fact that I was peeking with my Far Sight, and I found Snowy on the sports field. She was still in her gym clothes, so I figured they had PE class, and she was dourly walking around the field. There was a bit of a glow about her, but that happened to everyone nowadays, and the only immediate thing I got out of the observation was that I wanted to pat her on the head and cheer her up.

I returned my attention to the class rep and shrugged.

"Sorry, I know you were doing a *thing* there, but I still don't get it."

She momentarily deflated, but then she crossed her arms in front of her chest again and told me, "She's been acting strange lately. Aloof, distant, secretive... does that ring any bells?"

I thought about it for a moment and shrugged again.

"Maybe. I don't think it's particularly unusual."

"It is. She barely talks with any of us and she looks like she isn't getting enough sleep. Then we have this whole Faun business. It is way too suspicious for my liking." She paused here, as if trying to get her feelings to coalesce into words, and finally muttered, "I am not saying I am suspicious of her, I'm just... worried about her. A little."

I almost chuckled, but I held it down and nodded instead. It was a little funny seeing the person with the greatest reservations about Snowy reaching a 180 turn so quickly, but her sentiment rang true, and laughing at her because of it would've been wrong. I took a deep breath and nodded in agreement.

"So you want me to go and talk to her?"

"Yes. You are her patron."

"That is a needlessly fancy way to say it."

"But it's true. She should also be able to help you with the Faun where I couldn't."

Once again, since I saw Crowey give the order, and knowing their relationship, I was fairly sure Snowy couldn't really tell me anything new about my ram-headed shadow, but the rest of the class rep's concerns sounded legitimate enough for me to say, "All right. I'll go and see what this is all about."

As such, I turned down any pending lunch invitations and headed for the sports field. I didn't expect her to still be there, yet there she was, walking around the perimeter of the field with the same dejected look on her face while softly glowing. I was reaching the point where I was unconsciously tuning out such ambient glows, but hers was prominent enough to see even under direct sunlight.

By the time I reached her, she was in the far corner of the field and tapping her feet as if she was getting impatient over something. She was so immersed in her thoughts that she didn't notice me, even though I was standing only a couple of steps away from her. I waited for her for a while, but I ran out of patience fairly soon, and so I cleared my throat to get her attention.

She visibly shuddered and glanced around like she was being caught doing a prank, and even then it took her several seconds to notice me. We stared each other in the eye, during which she gave me a classic deer-in-the-headlights expression, right until I completely lost my patience and called out to her.

"So, what are you doing?"

She twitched again and looked around as if she was expecting that I was talking to someone else. When it became clear there was no one hiding behind her back, she sheepishly raised her hand and pointed a questioning finger at herself.

"Yes, I mean you. Do you see anyone else loafing around all alone out here?" She honest-to-goodness thought about that entirely rhetorical question for a second before she pointed at me. I smiled and shook my head. "That doesn't work. I am not alone here, now, am I?"

"No, you are not..." she muttered uncertainly as she did a weird, complicated motion with her fingers and the glow suffusing the air around her dissipated. "What... are you doing here?"

I pondered whether I should tell her I was sent by the class rep to check up on her, but I figured there must've been a reason why she didn't want her to know she was worried about her (otherwise she could've done this herself), so I only smiled and told her, "I saw you wandering around with a long face and I decided to check up on you."

"I... see..." she mumbled with a nod.

I waited a few seconds for her to continue, but when she remained silent, I decided to simply walk up to her and pat her on the head. She twitched a little, but then she gave me another confused deer-in-headlights stare that made me wonder if I have overstepped my boundaries. Well, she didn't reel back and run away, so I figured I probably hadn't offended her that much, so I finished rubbing her head and pointed at a nearby bench. She followed after me meekly and we sat down next to each other.

I was already prepared for this part of the conversation, so I reached into my pockets and pulled out two soda cans I'd picked up on my way there. I handed one over to her and she accepted it without a word. We sat in silence for a few minutes as we emptied our cans and I waited for her to get calm and comfortable enough to finally open up and tell me what was bothering her. It apparently didn't work, for she stayed silent for several minutes after we both finished drinking. As such, I once again had to be the one to speak up.

"So," I turned to her with a jovial smile. "What's eating you?"

She swiftly averted her eyes, but then she took a deep breath and faced me again.

"Leo... I would like to thank you for all you have done for me."

Now *that* came out of left field.

"You're welcome, I guess? What's this about?"

"I..." She glanced away yet again before she absentmindedly tugged at her choker and said, "We are moving."

"By *we*, you mean you and your brother?"

She nodded.

"And by *moving*, do you mean another town or back to the Abyss?"

She hesitated a bit before she answered this one.

"The political situation at home is… difficult. We are needed back there."

"When?"

"Soon."

"I see." I nodded solemnly. "I suppose you didn't let anyone else know?"

She shook her head surprisingly hard.

"I can't. It's supposed to be a secret. My brother says it's important I don't tell anyone."

"But you are telling me."

Unexpectedly enough, she smiled a little and told me, "You are a special case."

"Thanks, I guess."

We sat in silence for a few minutes more as I digested the news. I would certainly miss her; there was no question about that. I was fairly sure she would be back sooner rather than later. She was a main heroine, so I doubted she'd be gone for good, but still. I was starting to think of her as something of an awkward little sister, and I was sad to see her go even if only for a while.

I was just about to share the sentiment with her when she reached out and took my hand.

"Leo." She spoke softly, but with an unusual conviction in her voice as her fingers squeezed mine for emphasis. "Promise me you'll look after yourself. Don't go out after dark and make sure that Amelia or Eleanor is around you even during the day. Promise me that."

"Sure, I promise, but…" I agreed by reflex, but then I realized what she was referring to and couldn't help but grin. "Ah, I get it! You're warning me about that Faun guy!"

She was genuinely shocked by my words, and it took her a second or five to ask, "You know?"

"Yeah, I met the guy already. Big, hairy fellow with ram's horns? We ran into each other twice already, and he was a good enough sport not to try to bash my head in when he had the chance. Please tell him I appreciated that the next time he wakes you up in the morning."

Snowy studied me for a while, no doubt trying to figure out whether I was serious or not, and in the end, she surprised me again when she began to giggle, then chuckle, and finally outright laugh as the tension visibly drained from her shoulders. I let her get it all out of her system, though I would be lying if I said I wasn't mildly perplexed by her behaviour. At last, she returned to a demure smile and told me, in an impossibly soft voice, "Sorry, I was getting worked up over nothing. I keep forgetting that you are amazing."

"Oh, come on now," I chided her awkwardly as I reflexively patted her on the head. "Don't flatter me like that, or I might just get embarrassed." It was then that I remembered her previous reaction to my patting, so I gave her a questioning look to seek her approval. Instead of words, she leaned against my hand, so I smiled and continued rubbing the crown of her head. I honestly wouldn't have been surprised if she'd started purring. She didn't, but it would've been funny.

We stayed like that for a short while, but then my growling stomach reminded me that it was lunch break and I still hadn't eaten anything. I removed my hand and used my thumb to point at the dining hall.

"I think we should get going, or we won't have time to eat. You have to change, too."

She looked over herself and nodded, and I noted with relief that colour had finally returned to her face. We stood up and headed for the cafeteria, but after a few steps, she tugged on my sleeve to get my attention.

"Yes?"

"Um... please don't tell anyone I'm moving."

"Sure. It'll be our secret." I was getting ready to wink like the rapscallion I was, but instead I paused and added, "Actually, I think you should tell Josh. At least the day before you leave. He will miss you too." After some hesitation Snowy gave in and nodded, her cheeks flushed with just a hint of red. I had a feeling she would get depressed again if I ended our discussion on that note, so I grinned at her and said, "All right, let's go and get lunch. What would you like? My treat."

As expected, her eyes sparked up, and I didn't even have to hear it to know her answer.

"Apple pie," we said in unison. She gave me a surprised look and then giggled as she dashed ahead to change out of her gym clothes.

Yeah, that was much better. Smiling suited her way more than moping, and I was dedicated to keeping her smiling until the day she left. I guess it was my duty as her "patron."

CHAPTER 20

PART 1

"Booyah! A thirteen-hit combo with a Super-Finisher! Who's whopping whose ass now, big guy?"

Josh continued pumping his fist while I rolled my eyes with an annoyed smirk. I'm not going to lie, Josh's face looked eminently punchable just then.

"Would you stop bragging? You're just picking cheap characters," I grumbled out a retort with thinly veiled exasperation.

"Wrong. You just suck at playing zoner characters. You just need to strategize better."

"Says the button-masher."

"I am not a button smasher; I just use burst characters."

I let out a sigh and put down the controller in my hands.

"One of these days, you really have to explain to me how these different types of fighting game characters work."

Instead of answering, Josh only eyed the controller on the table, then he faced me with a shit-eating grin.

"Haha! No rematch this time?"

"Nah."

"So you admit defeat?"

"Yah."

Josh raised his hand without the grin wavering even for a moment.

"Awesome! High five?"

"Why would I give you a high five for beating me in *Street Kombat*?"

"Because there's no one else in the house to give me one?"

I looked at his outstretched arm and rolled my eyes once again. It didn't stop me from complying with the gesture, it was just so he knew I wasn't doing so happily. Not that he cared. He let out a decidedly childish laugh before he put his controller down and stood up to stretch his back.

"I think I have some leftover pizza in the fridge. Do you want some?"

"I'd rather have something to drink."

"Iced tea?"

"Good enough."

My friend gave me an enthusiastic nod and left, leaving me alone in the living room of the Bernstein household. I stared at the open doorway for a few seconds before I let out a pent-up breath and sank into the comfy couch in front of the television.

To be honest, I didn't really have my heart in the game. My last week was uneventful, but tiring nonetheless. Between the optimization of the Celestial Hub, Judy's constant stream of reports about the contents of the Dracis library, and the continued tribulations of my personal life, I had my hands full all the time. On the bright side, my triangular relationship with the girls finally stopped interfering with my work. My groundwork was also proceeding fairly well, and by this point Judy and Elly could be mistaken for friends if I wasn't around to rile them up, which also helped with reducing the drama levels at school.

Unfortunately, while I'd gathered a lot of data in a short time thanks to having access to two vast treasure troves of information, there were some things I couldn't achieve. First and foremost, even after employing every trick of persuasion in the book, I still couldn't get Angie to share her background with the others. Though to be fair, I was fairly certain the princess and the class rep both had their suspicions about her due to a few unfortunate word choices on my part in the past. I also tried and failed to draw any information related to magic theory out of Ammy, though this one was more due to the fact that I didn't want to pester her too much. The past couple of days, she'd clearly been stressed. What I could glean from some of our frustratingly short conversations said it had something to do with the school's security being compromised.

Now, if you ask me, I had no idea whether that was the school in the *place where mandatory education is taking place* or the *local Magi headquarters* sense of the word, but it ultimately didn't matter, as neither of those should've been the responsibility of a seventeen-year-old girl. I wanted to lend her a hand, but she categorically refused the first time I offered, and I never really had the chance to pester her afterward.

I was still lost in my thoughts when Josh came back from the kitchen with a tray loaded with snacks and two drinks. He put it down in front of me, and after thanking him, I grabbed hold of my glass and emptied it in pretty much one gulp. By the time I put it down back onto the tray, Josh had already sat down beside me with a controller in hand.

"What?" I asked while gesturing towards his hands. "Haven't you beaten me enough times yet?"

"No," he answered with a grin, but then added, "You wanted me to tell you about the different character types, didn't you?"

"So you want to explain them while you beat me a few more times?"

"That's the plan," he declared with smiling eyes.

I dropped my shoulders in resignation and retrieved the second controller.

"Fair enough," I told him, and we entered into the character selection screen.

I suppose this was as good an opportunity as any to explain what I was doing, right? To put it bluntly, after several days of constant pestering and being exposed to the guy's sulking, I freed up a weekend afternoon in my busy schedule to accommodate his need for recreational activities.

He came over to pick me up after lunchtime with his moped (and forced me to dust off my own bike, which I didn't even know I could ride until he told me about it), and our program included visiting the local retro arcade, hanging out in the shopping district, visiting "guy stores" (whatever the hell he meant by that was lost on me, as we did the same kind of window-shopping as always), and finally watching a brand-new and absolutely terrible horror movie in a small cinema specializing in independent flicks before we headed to his place.

It wasn't a particularly bad way to spend a day, but I just couldn't get it off my mind that if I was doing the same with a girl instead of a guy, it would have been a date. I tried to refer to it as an outing then, but then *that* started to feel weird because I only associated the word with dates before. In conclusion, I decided that I positively hated language drift and left it at that.

"Come on, Leo! Stop stalling!"

I gave my friend a quizzical look, then realized that I was so lost in thought I'd forgotten to attack. My character was just dashing around the screen.

"Sorry, just give me a second to prepare myself," I told him with an apologetic smirk.

"How much more time could you need? Just do a low-sweep, combo it into a mid-uppercut, and then combo that into a super. It's easy."

"I literally have no idea what you just said."

"Argh, that's it! Practice is the best way to learn this. I will teach you through actual combat!"

"Don't you mean simulated virtual combat?"

"Shut up and try to dodge this!"

PART 2

"Stop dodging my throws!" my friend exclaimed angrily while gripping his controller.

"Would you make up your mind?" I grumbled while barely avoiding another blue fireball thrown at my fighter. I did a double-jump and landed in the exact right position to start a combo, so I did a low-sweep, then a mid-uppercut, and then comboed it into a super that helicopter-kicked Josh's character across the screen.

"K.O.," the announcer declared in a needlessly epic voice.

"That's cheating! You were not supposed to master that move so fast!" my friend griped through a mouthful of chips.

"Fast? You've been drilling me on this one character for the last two hours. I am pretty sure at this point I could do half her combos with my eyes closed."

"Yes, but you are not supposed to use what I taught you against me! That's ungrateful towards your sensei!"

"Since when are you my sensei?"

"Since I taught you the basics, my young padawan."

I chuckled at that.

"You are mixing the lingo, but whatever. Next round?"

I was sure he would take me up on the offer, but instead he only glanced at the clock. I followed his gaze. It was a little after six in the evening, and since the sky was cloudy, it was already starting to get dark outside.

"Hm... maybe later."

I turned my gaze back to him and found him with his brows furrowed. I knew that look. I'd already seen it on his face a couple of times that day. I steeled myself accordingly and waited for him to breach whatever heavy topic he'd been chewing on all day. I didn't have to wait that long, as he turned to me only a second or two later.

"Hey, Leo?"

"Yeah?" I answered with fake nonchalance, pretending that I wasn't expecting the coming tonal shift.

"I know this might sound weird, but... are you keeping any secrets from me?"

We exchanged solemn looks, and I soon shrugged my shoulders with a self-deprecating smile. I might as well be honest about not being honest.

"Yeah. I keep lots of secrets. So many I wouldn't even know where to begin telling you what I cannot tell you about, except I wouldn't, because I cannot tell you what I cannot tell you about either." At this point I let out a rueful sigh and shook my head. "Oh come on! Don't look at me like that! Secrets wouldn't be *secret* if people were telling them to their friends all the time."

"So you say."

"Actually, that's kind of the definition of a secret, but yeah, so I say."

He let out a thoughtful "hmm," and then asked, "Then let me be more precise. Is there one about Lili?"

"Snowy? Sure, a few, yes."

"Will you share them if I ask directly?"

"Again, that is not how secrets work..." I began, but then shut my mouth once more. There was something about the way he was looking at me that made me consider my words very carefully. "You know what? Tell me why you are asking, and if nothing else I will tell you whether I could, theoretically, answer them. Deal?"

Josh gave me a skeptical look, no doubt aware of the way I steered the conversation into a more vague territory, but in the end he spoke up in a quiet voice.

"I'm worried because she is acting strange."

"Is she? I didn't notice."

Frankly, I wasn't interacting with Snowy all that much during the past week, but after our talk on the track field, she seemed to be back to normal as far as I was concerned.

"Because you are the only one she talks to anymore," my friend stated bluntly, and I was shocked to detect resentment in his voice. Or maybe it was just frustration? Either way, he sounded particularly bitter. "Whenever I try to talk to her, she makes up some excuse to go away. It's not just me, either. Angie says the same thing happened to her multiple times."

"Really?"

I closed my eyes for a moment. It made sense. A twisted, socially awkward kind of sense, but it did all the same. She was going away for who knew how long and she wasn't the most socially adept person I knew. I could easily imagine her hiding away and trying to distance herself from her friends to make the separation hurt less. I was the exception since I already knew about it. It was a childish thing to do, but then again, Snowy was the youngest of us, and she always struck me as someone who was extremely inexperienced when it came to dealing with interpersonal relationships. It might've had something to do with her upbringing in the Abyss which, in retrospect, also explained her adoption of the vamp persona, though I could only guess about that part.

Unfortunately, my thoughtful silence probably lasted a wee bit too long, as by the time I turned back to Josh to answer, he was already speaking again.

"Leo, we are really worried. Not just me, but Angie and Ammy and even Elly and Judy. Are you sure it's a secret worth keeping?"

"Well, I'm not the one who decides that, really," I told him with a shrug. "If you really want me to, I could ask her to talk to you about it, but that's the best I can do."

"Good enough."

"I make no promises, though. I already told her once that she should talk to you, so maybe she's just waiting for the right moment. You might as well wait and see a little longer."

"How much longer?"

"Actually... I don't know."

There was a short pause, then Josh let out a long breath.

"Why does everything in my life have to be so complicated?" he muttered with a frown, and I couldn't help but burst out laughing at the comment. He frowned at me and uttered a confused "What?"

"S-sorry," I stuttered between two bouts of self-derisive laughter. "Dude, you think your life is complicated? Then what about mine?"

"Maybe you should stop double-dating. That might help."

"Dude..." My laughter instantly stopped. "I know you think my interpersonal situation is hilarious, but would you please stop hammering on it? It's annoying and it is far from the biggest of my problems."

"Wanna talk about it?"

I gave him a long, hard look, and dismissed him with a wave of my hand.

"I can't. It's a secret."

"There you go again. I think I figured out what your biggest problem is." He paused, waiting for a reaction on my part, so I handed him a quizzically raised eyebrow as a prompt and he continued. "You are keeping too many secrets. Especially for a guy with no memory."

"Well, to be fair, the former problem kind of grew from the latter."

"I see..." He nodded like I'd just said something deep. "Are you one hundred percent sure you don't want to talk about it?"

"Listen, Josh," I spoke softly but with as much gravity as I could muster under the circumstances. "You should be glad you are not wrapped up in this mess yet."

"Yet? You expect I'll join your harem too? Dude, I don't swing that w—OW!"

I restrained the urge to shout *You're one to talk!* and instead I only flicked his forehead again, this time without even looking. I took a deep breath and told him, "To be honest, I think it's only a matter of time before you get roped in, anyways. Maybe soon, too, I'm afraid. If it makes you feel any better, once that happens, you can come to me and I'll explain things as well as I possibly can."

My friend was still rubbing his forehead when he looked away, obviously deep in thought. Neither of us spoke for a while, but then he abruptly turned back to me with an awkward grimace.

"Could you bear with me for a moment?"

I cocked my head to the side.

"Sure."

"You see... since we're already talking about secrets and everything, I think that I probably won't find a better moment to ask this question, but before I do that, I want you to remember that we are friends and that I am not judging you either way."

"Okay, you are starting to weird me out right now."

Josh only smiled awkwardly, then took a deep breath and asked, "Are you involved with organized crime?"

This time I couldn't help but cock my head in the other direction before answering with a question on my own.

"Where the hell did *that* come from?"

He fell silent for several seconds before he spoke again.

"Hear me out, because this might sound like a bit of a stretch. Things began changing when Elly came along, right? Her family is obviously very rich, but when I tried to ask if they owned a corporation or something, the butler warned me not to dig too deep or he would have to hunt me down."

"He says that to everyone."

"If you say so." He shrugged, but his expression said he didn't appreciate the interruption, so I shut it for the time being. "Then there's Lili and her brother. From the moment she showed up, everyone was wary of her for some reason, and her brother was giving me the chills even though I only met him once."

"The chills?"

"He looks like a mafioso, doesn't he? He had a limousine, too, and wore a suit and leather gloves. That's not normal."

"I suppose..." I mumbled and nodded noncommittally.

"Okay, so here is my theory. Hear me out, and tell me if I am wrong... Both Elly's and Lili's families are connected to organized crime. That's why they have all that money and why no one wants to talk about them. You're connected to both of them, and you have a lot of money too, so I figure you might've worked with them, or for them, before your amnesia, and that's why you are hanging out with them all the time now. I don't know how Judy fits into the picture, but I'll figure out something. Am I right this far?"

"Nope," I answered cheerfully. "You are waaaaay off the mark."

"Awww..." He slumped down with a disappointed groan. "And for a while, I thought I might've actually been on to something. I guess I should be relieved. It would've been too weird anyway, right?"

I was tempted to say *No, you're not thinking weird enough,* but I refrained from voicing my opinion. Instead I stood up with an exaggerated yawn and pointed my chin towards the clock on the wall.

"Sure. By the way, I think I should be heading home soon."

Josh glanced up at the clock as well and gave it a quizzical look.

"Isn't it still early? I have the entire house to myself until tomorrow. You could stay until dark."

"Nah, I've got stuff to do."

He gave me a strange look, but after a while he just shrugged. He sluggishly rose to his feet and began packing away the remaining snacks and empty glasses. I watched over him for a while and at last decided to throw him a bone.

"You know, your reasoning actually wasn't bad."

"It wasn't?"

Seeing how he immediately perked up, I continued with, "Yeah. You came up with an answer that made internal sense based on the information you had. It's not your fault you didn't have all the details."

"Is this the point where you explain those details?"

"I'm afraid not."

"Tch. Fine then. Forget I even asked."

"Will do."

He rolled his eyes and we left the living room. I helped him by opening the trash can so he could throw in the empty chips bags and then we headed for the main entrance. The basic layout of the Bernsteins' home was the same as mine, so I didn't need a tour guide, but I suppose it was only common courtesy to see me out.

"So, what are you going to do after this?" Josh attempted some small talk while I put on my shoes.

"Internet stuff. I have to finish up designing a site."

"You do web design?"

"Not really. I'm still learning."

"That's neat. I always wanted to try my hand at that, but I don't have the patience to learn to code."

"It's not that hard. You can get started with some templates and then..."

With that discussion in the background, I let him see me off. In retrospect, I might've saved myself some headaches if I'd stayed over. Or I might've died. I couldn't know, but either way, hindsight is a bitch.

CHAPTER 21

I got home a little after six that afternoon, and nothing noteworthy happened until just after nine. I did my usual things in the meantime; I checked the Celestial Hub for anything urgent, then I read Judy's latest report from the library while I worked out. I've always been a fan of multitasking. It contained a lot of new and interesting things about the underground politics and treaties defining the areas of influence of the different factions. Nothing caught my interest in particular, so once I finished reading, I took a quick shower and had dinner.

I was getting ready for another uneventful evening filled with research and maybe just a bit of leisure time when my phone rang. To my surprise, I found it to be a call from Snowy. Now *that* was unusual. She seldom called me, and her doing so right after Josh and I talked about her hit me as just a smidgen too convenient for my taste. Nevertheless, I picked it up with a smile.

"Good evening, Snowy."

"Leo!" The urgency in the whisper coming from the other end of the line made my expression wither. "I don't know how long we have to talk. Listen."

"Is there a prob—"

"Whatever happens," she interrupted me. Her voice sounded more and more frantic by the word. "You have to promise me that whatever happens, you stay indoors! Did you hear me? Stay indoors and stay away from the school, no matter what!"

"I don't—"

"Just promise me. Please..."

I hesitated only for a moment.

"Sure, I promise, but only if you tell me what's going on."

"I can't. I'm sorry, Leo, but I can't. If I told you—"

There was a sound in the background, some kind of commotion, and before I could say anything else, the line was abruptly cut. I stared at the phone in my hand for several long seconds, my mind desperately running through the possible scenarios.

The stupor only lasted for a moment. Whatever the hell was happening, Snowy was in trouble. Her final words said it all. While she couldn't finish her sentence, I was fairly certain I could.

If I told you, you wouldn't promise me to stay away...

I pocketed my phone, my legs already carrying me towards the entrance. I hastily slipped into the long black coat I left on the hanger by the door and left the house as fast as humanly possible through the chilly darkness of the early night.

I closed my eyes and concentrated on her image. I didn't have time for a full Far Sight gaze, as it would've interfered with my running, so I only used it to ascertain what I was already certain of. Snowy and her brother were in the school for some reason. Also, there was another "dot" in their company, which signified someone else I knew. It only took me a second to figure out who that was, and I almost stumbled and fell over in my rush as the realization hit me. They had Josh with them.

I dispelled the Far Sight, and once the disorientation died down, I gathered my wits and continued running, only to slow down a few seconds later when the phone began ringing in my pocket. I took it out and checked the caller ID. I hoped it was Snowy and this was all just a misunderstanding, but the call was coming from Angie instead. I accepted it and raised it to my ear as I began moving again.

"Leo, there's trouble!"

"Tell me about it," I answered flatly. She probably didn't notice the sarcasm, as she did just that.

"There was a commotion next door! I went over and Josh is missing! Someone kidnapped him through the first-floor window! I tried to follow after them, but I lost their trail!"

"They are at the school," I told her in a calm, level voice. Well, calm and level considering the circumstances. I've read somewhere that the best way to keep people from panicking is to talk to them in a firm tone, and while I wasn't happy about the opportunity to try the advice in practice, I didn't have much to lose.

"The school? How do you...?"

"Yeah. He is there with Snowy and her brother."

"What? Why?"

"I have no idea, but I'm already on my way. Call the others, I'll meet you there when—"

The words got trapped in my throat as I was hit by a sudden premonition of danger. Maybe it was a flicker of a movement I caught in the corner of my eye or a scent or I don't know what, but it clearly told me running ahead was a bad idea, so I came to a stumbling halt a couple of blocks away from the school.

Whatever that forewarning was, it was proven correct a second later when a huge body fell seemingly from the sky and landed a couple of meters ahead of me. With a distinct chill running down my spine I noted that, if I hadn't stopped, I would have been standing well within his arm's reach.

The hazy form of the now-familiar Faun rose to his feet with a deep, primal grunt. A moment later the indistinct black miasma surrounding him dissipated, allowing me to look at him without any obstructions. Maybe it was the adrenaline, but he looked even bigger than before, and he was carrying a large spear as tall as he was, with a flat, rhomboid head and a strange crisscross pattern running down its black shaft. He wore only a pitch-black metallic breastplate for protection, and no other armour, showing off his muscular arms and legs for all to see.

"Oh, crap..."

My mind locked up for a moment as Snowy's warning about staying indoors finally hit home, but I was just as quickly shaken out of my shock when I remembered I was still on the phone with Angie. The Faun didn't seem to be attacking just yet, but a single look at his softly smoldering orange eyes told me he was looking at me intently, probably searching for an opening. While a part of me said this was a perfectly good time to scream like a little girl and run away, another, more insistent part told me that the best course of action was to stay calm and appear confident. I'd already met with this Faun before, and he did not attack me. It was unwise to give him an excuse to do so now.

As such, I raised the phone back to my ear and tried to sound as composed as I could manage.

"Sorry, I ran into a bit of an obstacle. I might be a little late. You can start without me."

"What? What obstacle? Leo, what are you—?"

I ended the call and casually slid the phone back into my pocket before facing the huge humanoid creature in front of me with a neutral expression. I kicked my brain into overdrive to remember everything I could about Fauns.

They were big and strong. Well, duh, I could tell that just by looking.

They were brutish and barely sentient. Well, that was bullshit. I'd already seen this one talking with Crowey, and he seemed intelligent enough to appreciate irony, which already made him smarter than some people I knew.

They attacked in packs. That was a bit of info I had gotten from the Dracis library, and one that could've been useful... except this guy was obviously alone now, just as he had been every single time we'd met before. Or so I believed. Not that knowing there might be multiple extras hiding in the bushes would've made my chances any better.

So, in conclusion, I apparently knew less than nothing. I took a deep breath, and after a half-second of hesitation, I decided to do what I was best at and wing it, sink or swim.

"[I wish you an evening most auspicious,]" I called out to him genially, though I might've raised my voice a bit too much, as it made my throat tingle.

I knew that he could understand what I said, which made his reaction to my greeting even more unexpected. He lowered his head a little, his ears twitching, and his lips parted in a wide smile that revealed two rows of surprisingly white ivory. Even more surprising was his voice, which sounded just like a series of low, throaty grunts yet it also sounded like perfectly intelligible English at the same time.

"[You speak our language, and thine command of it is respectable indeed. A truly pleasant surprise.]"

I cocked my head to the side and answered, "[I have yet to commune with one of your kin in person, so please exonerate any inadvertent mistakes.]"

Well, that's what I said, but only because that was all that came to mind as my brain was frantically trying to reconcile with the fact that *I wasn't speaking English*. In fact, I was speaking the same language as the Faun, whatever the hell that was, without even noticing it. What came out of my throat was a series of low grunts that weren't even in the same ballpark as English syntax, yet somehow my brain interpreted them before I even had the chance to think about the sounds. Did that mean I was a native in Faun-ish? Maybe I was, before my amnesia, and it only came to light now because I was talking to one of them? What other languages was I fluent in? Was I even speaking English with the others all this time? What if the official language of the island was pig Latin and I hadn't even realized it? There were a lot of things I really wanted to test, but this was obviously not the time, considering I was still engaged in conversation with a creature that could probably bench press a truck and snap me like a twig at the same time.

Speaking of him, the Faun's smile widened even farther at my previous comment.

"[Thine person never fails to surprise me, young one. This only one truly wishes we could have met under different stars.]"

"[How so? Would you be so generous as to enlighten me regarding our current circumstances?]"

The smile vanished from his peculiarly shaped face and was replaced with a grim scowl.

"[I am under direct orders from my liege to...]" He paused, his brows twisting like he'd just tasted something sour. "[... *end* you.]"

That was bad. Like, ridiculously, soul-crushingly bad. I mean, I knew he had those orders, but I hoped against hope that he was on his day off and we only met by accident while he was on his way back from grocery shopping or something. I slowed my breathing and kept my voice calm as I returned to the conversation.

"[An assassin then.]"

The light in his eyes flared up like two tiny furnaces as his lips parted again, this time in an angry snarl.

"[You stand before Brang Shadowfeet, scion of Malrog Silvereyes, scout-general of the Faun Inanna! I am no lowly knife in the dark.]"

Even though I tried to stay calm and wear a neutral face, I flinched at his outburst. That was an unexpectedly angry reaction, exactly the thing I'd wanted to avoid. That was bad. However, he wasn't mad at me per se. So... less bad.

Hey, I'll take my silver linings where I can find them, thank you very much.

More importantly, did I just detect a touch of wounded pride in there? What did that tell me? That he didn't want to act like a killer. He showed himself to me even though he could have landed right on top of me and pulverized me into the sidewalk. Yet he didn't. Why? Maybe because... it wouldn't have been fair? That revelation opened a floodgate of ideas.

The Faun were warriors in the service of the Abyssals. Even if everything else I learned about them was hogwash, of this I was certain. An entire *race* of warriors. That was the key. There was a character type I stumbled upon during my research called the *Proud Warrior Race Guy*. As the name suggests, it refers to a character who is culturally conditioned to be a warrior. Pursuit of glory, honour, epic battles, and all that crap were the things that made these guys tick.

Now, while simply stereotyping the Faun in front of me like that might not have been nice, if I took a step back and focused on the idea that this narrative certainly used these tropes, his behaviour started to make a modicum of sense.

So. Could I use this tenuous deduction to my advantage?

Only one way to find out.

I took a deep breath while I casually pocketed my hands and took up a relaxed stance. I was hoping he would consider this a sign of nonaggression. It must have worked, as the Faun's expression softened. He swiveled his short, horse-like ears with evident curiosity.

I let out the air in my lungs in a slow stream as I decided on my approach. First, I had to find out whether my hunch was correct. I had to establish whether he was indeed an honourable warrior. As such, my first target was his pride.

"[You are the scout-general?]" I spoke with a series of grunts that I subconsciously recognized as a more casual dialect. "[Isn't pursuing unarmed prey below one such as you?]"

I had no idea if it was or not, but I had to give it a try. Brang let out a low grunt. I couldn't really decide whether that was a good thing or not at first, but then he leaned on his spear and spoke in a softer voice.

"[Aye, it is. But I have no choice. I delayed the inevitable, but alas, I can delay no more.]"

I could see him shift his weight on his spear, which could have meant many things. Just on the off chance that it was in preparation for lunging at me and impaling my spleen, I blurted out the first thing that came to mind, just to keep the conversation rolling.

"[But a scout-general? Truly? I find it hard to determine whether I should feel honoured or affronted.]" That made him pause and raise an eyebrow, a very human gesture that looked subtly wrong on his face. I gulped very, very quietly before I continued. "[I presumed—]" I paused for a moment as I struggled to get the word "Crowey" across, but in the end, I had to settle for, "[... the crow-haired one would face me on his own. I must assume his cowardice overshadows even the wildest of my imaginations.]"

That was another calculated gamble. Insulting his *liege* or whatever could have easily goaded him into attacking, but at the same time, I knew that there was no love lost between the two. If I could play his own sense of honour and/or pride against the Faun, I figured (or rather hoped) it would take me one step closer to getting away from this encounter with my skin still draped over my everything. I kind of preferred it that way.

There was a tense couple of seconds there, but my bet ultimately paid off.

"[It is not my place to speak ill of my liege...]"

I couldn't keep the smile off my face. With this, I already had my foot in the door. I just needed to wedge it open a bit more.

"[Even though you cannot deny my words ring with truth.]"

"[Thou art...]" Brang paused meaningfully. "[... not entirely wrong, that much is certain.]"

"[So we are in agreement that he is a sniveling coward who can't even make an effort to fulfill his own obligations.]"

"[Perhaps not in so many words.]"

"[Please, general,]" I shook my head. "[It's only the two of us. There is no need to still your tongue.]"

Brang let out a throaty chuckle ending in a sort of snort, another human gesture that felt subtly wrong when performed by a more than two-meter-tall mountain of muscle with a ram's head.

"[Aye, you are very much correct, but I don't see how that changes what we both know must happen.]"

"[I fail to see the inevitability in our situation. Following your orders would tarnish your honour.]"

"[Aye, but shirking my duty would do so, as well.]"

I opened my mouth to retort but then closed it as my brain caught up with his train of logic, and I raised a finger to stall.

"[Please allow me to ponder whether I understand this situation,]" I spoke, partially just to keep the chills from running down my spine. "[You do not wish to fight me. I do not wish to fight you. Not only that, but I cannot afford to fight you either, as my comrade is in danger and may be in dire need of my assistance. However, you cannot afford *not* to fight me, as it would damage your honour. But fighting me would *also* damage your honour.]" I paused and gave Brang a questioning look. He nodded, apparently satisfied with my brief summary of the situation. "[Thus... maybe it is only my incomplete understanding, so correct me if I am wrong, but no matter what we do, we both lose.]"

Not to mention that at least one of the outcomes would lead to me losing something much more concrete than *honour*. It seemed neither the place nor the time to discuss the relative worth of my life stacked against the gigantic ram-man's principles though.

Brang canted his head and let out a short puff of breath through his nose, a gesture which I presumed was a stifled chuckle of some sort.

"[Indeed. A major predicament, I must say.]"

"[It is. So... this might be just a stray idea, but would it be possible for us to pretend we never saw each other? You could hardly lose honour over a fight that never happened, and I...]" I paused as Brang frowned disapprovingly. I quickly shook my head. "[On second thought, please forget I said that. Such deception isn't very honourable, either.]"

The frown melted away, replaced with yet another of those unnervingly wide smiles of his.

Backpedaling: successful.

It was a little silly, in retrospect. I should've already figured that whatever these guys considered to be honourable was internalized enough that it no longer needed public scrutiny to work. So long as it would go against his code, he would refuse it, even if no one else would ever know about the transgression.

I clicked my tongue in irritation. Normally I would have considered my opponent's adhering to a code of honour as an advantage. It makes them predictable. Sadly, not knowing the actual tenets of the code turned that advantage upside down, as I had no idea what he would consider acceptable or not.

I pondered for a moment, which Brang patiently observed.

"[I am drawing a blank,]" I told him, though the actual wording was a little different in Faun-ish. Something about white rabbits. Slang didn't seem to translate particularly well. Anyways, I decided upon another gamble. "[I don't see a way we can walk away from this without a confrontation.]"

"[Indeed,]" he nodded, but didn't change his relaxed stance. He obviously expected me to continue, so I dusted off my best smile.

"[I have but one question. Must our confrontation necessarily have to be physical?]"

Brang's eyes opened wide as a mirthful laugh escaped his lips, taking me completely aback for a moment.

"[Hah! I was afraid you might never ask! But let me ask thou before we begin, as it is tradition…]" It was his turn to clear his throat, after which his voice somehow managed to become even deeper and more booming. It was like listening to a landslide in motion. "[Tell me, whelp, are you ready to test yourself against your better in the Rites of Dominance?]"

I froze up. I had been thinking of something more along the lines of a contest, like rock-paper-scissors or riddling. Instead, I found myself being challenged to... well, *something* I had no idea about. My hesitation only lasted a second. I didn't have the luxury to refuse the challenge, so I promptly nodded.

Sink or swim.

"[Aye?]"

My opponent let out a bellowing belly laugh that shook his armour and sent the short braids of his mane tumbling around his massive shoulders.

"[Very well, young one!]" he declared as he lowered his stance, sparking a moment of apprehension in me.

I hastily threw my hands into the air and made him stop.

"[Er... I must beg your pardon, but before we begin, I am afraid my knowledge in regard to such traditions is very limited. Would you please enlighten me to the rules of our contest?]"

Brang's ears swiveled ambiguously for a moment before he relaxed and nodded.

"[I was under the impression thou wert already experienced in the ways of Dominance. If I was mistaken, thou must forgive my presumption.]"

"[Such apologies are unwarranted. I might have been well versed at one time, but I am sadly unable to recall such a time. It is complicated and its explanation is best suited for another time.]"

Brang nodded.

"[I understand, young one. We all have our secrets and circumstances.]"

My imminent opponent cleared his throat at this point and rested his weight on his spear again. For a moment his image reminded me of a grandfather leaning on his cane while preparing to share an old tale with his grandchildren, but then I remembered that he was a scary-huge warrior creature sent here to murder me, and that killed off the sentiment pretty quickly.

Anyways, in a slow, deliberate voice, he said, "[The Rites of Dominance is our way of fighting without fighting. It requires the participants to lock gazes, project their spirits at their opponent, and defeat them in the future. Once one side establishes their supremacy, the loser has to forfeit their stance. It is our way of settling disputes without drawing blood.]" He looked me over curiously. "[Thou art the first of thine kind I have heard of who could engage in Dominance with one of my kin. I have been looking forward to thine performance since the day I witnessed it firsthand.]"

"[I see. That's... fascinating.]"

This time it wasn't just the excessively polite way the Faun language translated into English that made me say that. I was truly fascinated by this system and its practical elegance. Such *mind-battles* would not only help establish a clear and unquestionable hierarchy between fighters, but it would ingeniously do so without the threat of death or injury that could impact the fighting efficiency of the Faun race. Quite the contrary! What other system could so easily simplify recruit training and keep veterans in practice without risking their lives? Whatever Abyssal created the first Faun, they knew what they were doing.

As for why I was able to engage in this Dominance thing... I hadn't the foggiest idea. The obvious (if stupid) first option was that I was a Faun in disguise. That was, of course, silly. More likely it was related to the way I was able to see magic and interact with it in weird and unforeseen ways. Or maybe it was a completely fresh pile of what-the-hell-pie right out of the oven and waiting to hit me in the face when I was least expecting it. As things stood, I couldn't even hazard a guess, though I intended to find out more later... well, presuming I survived the night, that is.

"[Thou art in earnest,]" Brang stated with a puzzled tilt in his head, harkening back to my previous statement.

"[Indeed, and why should I not? I know far too little of you and your kin, and I am one who wishes to know everything.]"

"[An impractical sentiment, yet an honourable one. It is a sad affair that our roads had to cross like this, for I would have liked to share the tale of my people with one such as thou. Finding an eager audience is an opportunity that is a sin to waste...]" Brang fell silent and his expression darkened as he shifted his weight off his spear and began limbering his massive shoulders. "[But alas, one cannot always choose their road. Art thou ready, young one?]"

"[Ready enough,]" I answered with a regretful smile, which I used to hide my nervousness.

Brang closed his eyes and took a breath so deep that for a moment I thought his lungs were replaced by a pair of industrial-sized bellows. Then, his eyelids rose again, revealing a familiar orange light.

"[Tell me, whelp, are you ready to test yourself against your better in the Rites of Dominance?]"

The question must have been ceremonial, as while the translation suite in my head might have rendered it into perfectly legible English, it somehow sounded (or rather, as silly as it might sound, *tasted*) archaic. I stood tall, set my shoulders, and answered with a firm "[Aye.]" and locked my gaze with his.

The moment our eyes met, the world faded away into an indistinct haze. The experience was similar to the first time, but magnitudes more intense. For a moment I felt myself brushing against Brang's mind. Only the surface, but it still imparted a few impressions on me like it had the last time. Determination. Excitement and bloodlust restrained by an iron will. A sense of curiosity and respect. Regret.

The experience only lasted for a second, though it felt longer. I was back in my head and Brang in his, like two vast oceans whose shores briefly overlapped, yet no matter how much of their waters mixed, it would never change their bulk.

I wondered for a moment why I was thinking in terms of water, but my attention was required elsewhere, so I discarded the question. By now Brang's figure was enveloped in a thick golden-orange aura that sharpened by the second. A moment later he lunged, even though he was standing still. He brandished his spear even though his hands were unmoving. He bellowed even though his lips never parted.

It only took me a split second to divorce the image of the real Faun from the golden phantom charging my way, but once I did, my own doppelganger rushed forwards without me even being consciously aware of it. Except... I kind of was. I saw through its eyes, yet at the same time, I didn't. Being in two places at once should've been a very disorienting experience, but it strangely felt natural.

I calmly observed my copy dodge and weave around Brang's image with a deft and deliberate agility I didn't think I was capable of, its long coat billowing behind it as it sidestepped, jumped, and was generally awesomely nimble. How? I wondered. During Dominance, could it do things my real body couldn't? With a thought-nudge, my doppelganger halted and tried to float in the air. It got punched in the face for its trouble.

So no, apparently I couldn't do things I wasn't capable of, or at the very least flight was out of the question. I would've really loved to experiment, but then again, I felt it was a small miracle my copy survived its mistake and could continue dodging—no mean feat. Brang's phantom was like a whirlwind, his spear dancing with seemingly impossible grace in his large, meaty hands. A part of me wanted to point out how all of those twirls and brandishes he did between stabs and swings were completely superfluous, but then again, my doppelganger could never find an opening to attack him, so it somehow still worked. Not to mention, it looked amazing.

That, however, also reminded me of my conundrum: while my mental copy was able to dodge Brang's attacks, it had absolutely no way to strike back at him, and that consequently meant I had no hope of winning either. Maybe this was the wrong approach? I thought about this with a strange, absentminded detachment while my copy fought for its life, and I probably wouldn't have come up with anything if not for Brang making an unexpected move. The real one's body flared up with golden light again and I was assaulted by a second golden phantom. For a long moment I thought it would be a two-on-one fight, but then I realized that the second wraith was coming right at me.

"Oh, I see now..." I muttered as my own second doppelganger rolled backward. Brang's copy passed right through me, the real me, spear point first, and the two began fighting behind my back. Common sense told me that fighting two Brangs with two of myself should've been mind-bogglingly, brain-meltingly hard... except it wasn't. I was even a little disappointed about that, but only for a moment before my brain finally decided to stop lazing around and kick into a higher gear.

So, fighting with multiple copies was possible. It also didn't seem to be particularly taxing for the participant. That... opened up lots of new opportunities.

I furrowed my brows, careful not to blink and break the eye contact in the process, and tried to recall the feeling of a new phantom springing forth from me. For the first time, I ran into a setback. While I could picture my doppelganger, and I felt like I was on the verge of creating one, the last step somehow eluded me. In the meantime, my copies kept dueling their respective opponents, much to my annoyance. It made thinking harder than it should've been. The one in the front was particularly annoying, as it was injured, and keeping it dodging took more and more effort from whatever subconscious process was governing its actions.

At last, it got too slow to dodge one of Brang's swings and the shaft of the spear caught him under its armpit. My subconscious informed me that this was a blow that broke at least two of its ribs and fighting on in that condition was impossible. I groaned in frustration and dismissed the doppelganger, only to stop and wonder how I just did that. My copy brightened for a moment and then it faded out abruptly like a broken lightbulb. To my considerable surprise, Brang's copy did the same almost exactly at the same time.

I didn't have much time to wonder, though, as the Faun's body shone as he unleashed another golden copy of himself. I answered in kind, this time paying extra attention to *how* I did it. As it turned out, the answer was frustrating in its simplicity: I didn't just have to imagine the shape, I also had to assign Brang as an opponent to it. I let the new copy settle into the familiar dodging routine while I collected my thoughts. I had a lot of possibilities to explore, and I barely knew where to begin. But then again, with this system in place, I didn't really *have* to pick and choose. I wanted to close my eyes for a second to think, but that would have broken the line of sight, so instead I zoned out and tried to imagine as many extra copies as I could. I could comfortably go as high as nine. Anything above that was beginning to strain whatever part of my brain was responsible for moving them. I wanted to stay on the safe side, so I decided to stick to eight. That meant that, together with the two copies already in action, I had ten phantoms ready to try out every possible variation of actions I could've taken.

I smiled wolfishly. This was fun. No, better. Exhilarating.

I focused for a second and with the snap of an imaginary finger I ordered all my copies to enter the fray. There was a moment of intense light as all eight of them shone around me, answered by an equally bright light from Brang's direction as his phantoms also entered the fight. As they dispersed, the Faun once again became visible, and I took a bit of satisfaction from the astonished look on his face. It only lasted for a moment, though, before I quickly switched my attention to my phantoms and their individual tactics.

Phantoms one and two were still engaged in their duels on the sidewalk, neither of which seemed to have progressed at all. While they continued to dodge the Brang-copies' strikes with impeccable swiftness and precision, they had no way of counterattacking. Brang had the longer reach thanks to his spear, and even if my copies could have gotten close enough, he was so physically dominating, I doubted they could have done any damage at all. As such, these copies' job was to observe his movements. Even in these short minutes, I have learned many things, though the memories and rudimentary thoughts streamed from the phantoms were so fragmentary, they took effort to assemble.

So far, I knew that Brang was big, fast, smelled like wet hay, was left-handed, liked to wave his spear tip in an "8" pattern before he stabbed, and was nursing his left leg. His strikes were always a little slower and weaker whenever he was using it as his lunging leg.

That was all for preliminary tactical assessment. The rest of my phantoms had very different tasks, however. Phantoms three through five were tasked with finding makeshift weapons in the environment. Phantoms six through nine rushed down the streets in various directions, trying to avoid fighting and heading for the school using different routes. Phantom ten was on offensive duty.

Neither of them achieved much. The scavenging phantoms couldn't find anything even remotely useful and thus were repurposed to runners as well. The ones that were running to begin with found themselves relentlessly pursued by Brang's copies, who were remarkably fast and nimble despite their size, being able to scale walls and leap fences with practiced ease.

The offensive one lasted only a couple of seconds before it got turned into a shish kebab, but I didn't really mind. The beauty of this Dominance thing was that, as long as I had ideas and I was determined enough to try them, I had unlimited extra lives. As such, I sent out another one. And another. Copy after copy rushed Brang and got skewered or their head bashed in, but I had reserves, and each one of them lasted a little longer, incorporating every new experience of the previous assaulters, the dodgers, and even the runners into their repertoire. It was fascinating, if a little disturbing, to watch. It was technically me who was getting beaten and injured repeatedly after all, and while it was a little squicky, it was still enthralling overall.

Some of the moves my copies pulled off made me wonder if I could replicate them in real life, though. The runners managed to scale walls I wouldn't have tried under normal circumstances, and the dodgers were getting downright acrobatic with their act. If I presumed that my idea about them only being able to do things I in the flesh could do, it would've logically meant everything they did was possible for me as well. But... what about things I wasn't sure whether I could do?

I zoned out for a second once again, my phantoms continuing to fight, dodge, and run without my oversight, and I retreated into the recesses of my mind to think. My Far Sight was incredibly useful as a utility power, but not so much in a fight. However, there was another ability I theorized I might've had, and it seemed likely I was inadvertently using it in this Rite of Dominance: dodging. Not just the garden variety, but one that bordered on precognition. Heck, now that I thought about it, it *was* precognition. It made my body react to dangers before they happened and let me dodge attacks from Brang with ridiculous ease. I almost felt bad for the guy. Aside from the first one (which was a fluke) and the assault phantom, he didn't manage to land a single clean hit on my copies. He still wanted to kill me, so I didn't feel *that* bad, but still.

That left one last ability I theorized about, one which I was never too keen on experimenting with as it would've resulted in a lot of head trauma. I refocused my eyes and flashed an evil grin at my opponent. He didn't react, but I kept on grinning because stopping would have been awkward. Anyways, I concentrated hard on my runners.

Honestly, while Brang might have been unable to land a hit, he was really good at kiting my copies. None of my runners were able to get closer to the school, as their cat-and-mouse chase around the streets was somehow always steered back into the same neighbourhood by the Brang copies. They were good. But then again, he was a *scout-general*, so I figured he had more experience running around and herding opponents than I did.

Actually, my previous statement was not entirely true. One of my copies wasn't in the neighbourhood anymore. It was running down a highway in the exact opposite direction, dodging indifferent cars, trucks, and motorcycles in a reckless rush. My original plan with this one was to lure the Faun's copy into a dangerous environment and use an opportunity to shove it under a vehicle, but instead it provided me with a perfect opportunity to test my idea. I paid extra attention to the phantom in question, waited for the right circumstances to present themselves, and in just a couple of seconds, I found what I was looking for.

My phantom threw itself into the traffic once again, closely followed by its chaser, and they headed right towards a large truck thundering down the middle lane. I crossed my fingers (quite literally) and made my specter dash towards the oncoming vehicle without stopping, focusing all my attention on what the phantom felt and did. The truck closed in at an alarming rate. It wouldn't hit the brakes, of course. The phantoms were invisible to other people.

I could feel the cold sweat on my back as I got so in sync with my copy that I could almost smell the exhaust fumes on the highway. The truck was only a couple of meters away, but I kept running towards it nonetheless. Finally, I leaped forwards, my heart beating like a war-drum in my throat, and... my bet paid off.

There was a moment of dizziness as the world blurred and streaked by my phantom. It wasn't from an impact, though. Instead, he landed right behind the truck and continued running, much to the apparent astonishment of my opponent.

Well, he might've been baffled by what I'd just done, but that couldn't come close to how I felt. First and foremost, I was surprised. Partially that it worked, but more importantly about how simple it felt. The actual act of... whatever just happened was suddenly as clearly in my mind as my Far Sight was. It felt downright silly that I couldn't do it before. In fact, that was the source of the second part of the overwhelming feelings churning in my head: uncertainty. It felt so easy, but I knew it was not supposed to be.

It wasn't magic. I knew that even from the cursory knowledge of magic theory I managed to gather. It was something else, but that something felt as natural as riding a bicycle. Was this something I could always do, and I'd forgotten about along with everything else? And if it was, just how many other powers were sleeping inside my head?

However, all of those misapprehensions were dwarfed by the sheer fist-pumping, yell-from-the-depths-of-your-lungs elation that filled my mind with cheers and my blood with dopamine.

"So I can teleport now," I said with a giddy grin.

Like that, as if a dam had broken, all my phantoms began to use this new power like it was part of their repertoire all along. The runners used it to hop onto ledges and roofs, bringing the chase to the rooftops. The dodgers incorporated it into their acrobatics, making their avoidance of Brang's attacks absolutely trivial, while the assaulter used it to find new and even more innovative ways to get skewered by the Faun's spear. And it was all amazing. Yes even, the skewering part.

I'm not going to lie, I felt pretty good about myself. For several minutes I absently observed my phantoms and marveled at the kinds of things they were doing. However, as the seconds kept ticking down, I started to become more and more uncomfortable (and not just because my eyes were itching from the lack of blinking). The ability to teleport short distances gave my runners an immense advantage, yet they were still herded around by their respective opponents. For the dodgers, it just made what they were already doing slightly less physically taxing, but aside from that, it didn't change much, while the assaulter still lacked a way to actually damage the Faun.

That's when it hit me: I was losing. I was way better at dodging and evading strikes (in fact it seemed I was downright specialized in that), but this entire game or ceremony or whatever was about asserting *dominance*. It existed to show that one side would be able to defeat the other without question if it came to actual combat, and thus the combatants should avoid it altogether. I was losing in that regard. Big time.

I furrowed my brows and recalled my runners one by one. While they helped establish that I could avoid combat, possibly indefinitely, they didn't help with the actual Dominance. So I set up something new: four dodgers, five assaulters, and one whose purpose was to establish whether or not I could use the teleportation offensively.

It turned out I couldn't. When it tried to blink into his respective copy of Brang, it just didn't happen. I hoped there would be a displacement effect of some kind (after all, teleporting like that had to displace the air at the target location), but then I realized that I had no idea how this new power worked.

But let's look on the bright side: now I knew one thing it *couldn't* do. That's progress, right?

Either way, I made little to no *actual* progress. I was like the wind; so long as I was moving, he had no way of catching me. However, he was a rock; no matter how hard I came at him, he remained steadfast and repelled me without any difficulty. Sure, I suppose I had the advantage in the grand scheme of things. Wind will wear down any stone, if given enough time. But time was the thing I didn't have. The best I could do right now was grind the Dominance to a standstill and force a tie, but I didn't know how long that would take or if it was even possible.

The clock was ticking, and I had no idea how much time I had. In fact, I had no idea how much trouble Snowy and Joshua were in. My hunch said it was a whole honking lot, but to know that for sure, I had to get there, and I had wasted too much time already.

I took several evenly paced deep breaths and discarded any stray thoughts, such as about the way my newfound teleportation worked (or why I even had it in the first place), and I focused on the task at hand.

Question one: *What was my goal?* The first answer that came to mind said, *To beat Brang,* but I discarded it. That wasn't enough. He had beaten my phantoms many times, but hadn't automatically won. No, my goal was *to dominate the fight.* I not only had to beat him in this mock battle, but I also had to do it in a way it was clear he would lose if we fought in the flesh, period.

Question two: *How do I do dominate?* Well... that was a very good question. As I said, I could theoretically make him give up, or at least make him declare a tie if I stopped trying to fight him and just dodged him until he got bored, but that wasn't a viable option. I had to find a way to beat him solidly and consistently.

Question three: *What was stopping me from doing so?* I mulled over that one for a while. It wasn't just that he was bigger and stronger than me (though it most certainly wasn't a trivial detail). The real problem was that he was armed and had a better range. Even if he was a normal guy and not a magical half-animal humanoid bred for the express purpose of warfare, that spear would've made him a tough nut to crack. Combine the two factors and he was unassailable.

Question four: *How do I solve the problem?* I had to level the playing field. I needed a weapon. There was only one problem, though. I'd already established that there was nothing I could turn into a makeshift weapon in the vicinity. I could theoretically send my runners out again to look for something outside this neighbourhood, but that would've cost me time, and I was uncertain I could find anything that could match up to the reach and heft of that spear.

And then, just like that, I had an idea. It was an unthinkably crazy idea, but that just meant that, if anything, it was more likely to work in this world. I had to make certain of one thing first, though. I took a deep breath and took a step forwards without breaking eye contact. Brang didn't react. As a matter of fact, the Faun's eyes seemed to be glazed over. Maybe this was more taxing on him than on me? Either way, he didn't react even after I smiled and waved to him.

Okay, that part of the plan could have worked. That was one step. I had to make sure, though. After a moment of hesitation, I focused inwards and exhaled hard. There was a blaze of light surrounding me for a moment and then four more phantoms joined the fray, getting their numbers up to a mind-straining fourteen. That was my limit, and the suddenly appearing creases on the Faun's large forehead told me it was close to his, as well.

"Good," I muttered. "Focus on those."

I steeled myself for a second and took a step forwards, then another. They were slow, deliberate steps, and after just a couple of them, I was standing right in front of Brang. From this close, he somehow managed to look even bigger than before which, if you asked me beforehand, I would have said was impossible. Even his smell, a not-unpleasant earthy musk, was thick and overwhelming from up close.

Steadying my breathing and my nerves, I made sure one last time that he was too busy with the Dominance. I was reassured by how he still seemed to be looking through me instead of at me. I knew I had only one chance at this, so I limbered up my fingers, counted to three, inhaled sharply, and then acted without any further hesitation.

"[Wha...?!]" The Faun gasped as my hands lashed out and grabbed hold of his spear. Even though our eye contact broke, the phantoms lingered for several seconds, during which I pulled on the spear with all my might. He obviously wasn't expecting that, so by the time he had the chance to get his grip, I'd already torn it from his grasp. Brang staggered back in shock, his eyes blinking in confusion. It was an opportunity I couldn't miss, so I used the momentum I had to swipe his left leg with the butt of my new weapon.

The Faun let out a downright pitiful yelp as the strike connected and his stagger turned into a full-fledged tumble. He landed on his back with a loud thud that shook the ground under my feet. I wasn't sitting on my laurels just yet, as I followed after him with a half-step. I held the spear in both hands and pointed its head right at my fallen opponent's neck, stopping the tip just a few centimeters from his oversized Adam's apple.

It was at this point that I looked him in the eye again, reestablishing the Rite of Dominance. All the vaguely lingering phantoms around us disappeared in a blink of an eye to be replaced by fourteen copies of myself overlapping me pointing fourteen spears at fourteen fallen Fauns. Neither of us said or did anything for several seconds. The only sound that registered in my ears was the heavy drumming of my heart threatening to burst from my chest.

Then, to my complete and utter bafflement, Brang closed his eyes and laughed. At first it was just a chuckle, then it blossomed into a throaty chortle that reverberated through my entire body. More surprisingly, it was genuine. I couldn't detect a shred of distaste or bitterness in him, even though I was afraid he would be outraged by the way I'd rearranged the power levels in our contest.

At last, his laughter died down and he raised his gaze at me with a smile in his eyes.

"[Splendid,]" he said in a slightly croaky voice. He cleared his throat and tried again. "[It has been decades since my last defeat in the Rites of Dominance, yet to think thou wouldst overcome me the same way Warmaster Whlor Redmane did... Truly remarkable.]"

"[I see...]" I muttered, still more than a little uncertain. "[I welcome your praise.]"

He tried to nod, which was fairly hard considering he was on his back and already straining his neck to look at me. At last, he let his head back down and stared at the starless sky.

"[You are the victor, young one. Do as you must.]"

There was a strange finality in his words, and I realized with a chill what he meant. He was defeated and ready to be killed. It should've been obvious, but for some reason it only dawned on me in this second, and it made my stomach roil. I imagined stabbing him in the neck and moving on, and just the mental image was enough to make me look away in shame.

I steadied my breathing and lowered my weapon. Brang twitched when he heard the butt of the spear hitting the pavement and looked up at me again with a dumbfounded expression. I let the corners of my mouth twitch upwards a little and, after a brief moment of hesitation, I offered him a hand.

"[What are thou doing, young one?]" he asked, looking at my face and my outstretched hand.

"[Not what I must, but what I want,]" I said. I was trying to stay cool, but my shaky voice probably ruined the image. If it did, Brang didn't mention it but, hesitating, reached out and grasped me by the forearm. It took considerable effort, but I managed to get him onto his feet. Strangely enough, once he was no longer armed and staring me in the eye, the Faun stopped being humongous. Now he was just plain huge. Funny how perception works.

Brang awkwardly dusted himself off and looked at me with a face that said, *Now what?* It was a question I wanted to ask as well, but since I was the victor, it was obvious I had to come up with the answer. I quirked a smile and leaned on the spear as I'd seen him do, though considering that it was longer than I was tall, it took some effort to get the balance right.

"[I have never slain a worthy foe before, and I am not about to form a habit now,]" I told him with the conviction of a technical truth.

"[So I see.]" Brang nodded agreement. "[It appears we have also answered thine question. 'Twas an insult.]"

It took me a second to recall what he was referring to, and I shook my head.

"[Do not value yourself so lowly. It was your liege who did not realize his mistake, so the shame falls on his head, not yours.]"

"[Kind words, if undeserved,]" he answered with a ceremonial bow. "[I fear thou might face my liege as well this night. It might not be my place to say so, yet I hope it never comes to that.]"

"[We shall see,]" I said with a small grin before I hefted the spear in my hand. It was a little long for a human, but it was surprisingly light and well-balanced. I frowned at the weapon thoughtfully before I turned back to Brang. "[Would you mind if I borrowed your weapon for the night?]"

The Faun's expression became fierce for a moment before it mellowed out again.

"[The spear is the symbol of my rank and place in the Faun Inanna. It was what I am,]" he told me flatly. Then he let out a defeated sigh. "[But thou art the victor, and thus it is thine to take.]"

I rolled my eyes and hefted my new spear again. "[I shall take your spear, rank, and honour with me, then.]" The Faun's ears drooped at my declaration, so I quickly continued, "[I shall return them to you once this night is over. You may have my word of honour on that promise.]"

That made Brang's ears and expression make a complete turn. He bowed again, almost reverently, and answered, "[So be it. I cannot aid thee in thine quest, as it would put me at odds with my liege, yet I wish thee the best of luck, Leonard Blackcloak.]"

That last part felt oddly significant, but I had no time to ponder on it. I'd already spent precious minutes nursing the feelings of the guy who was to be my assassin, time I should've been spending on the road. I gave him an appreciative nod and took a couple of steps before I was halted by Brang's voice one last time.

"[Beware of the Chimera,]" he said before his shape blurred in a familiar black haze and he turned around, walked over to a nearby lamppost, and sat down beneath it. I gave him one last look, then I tightened my grip on my newfound weapon and picked up the pace again, wondering if I'd just escaped the frying pan only to fall in the fire.

CHAPTER 22

My burning lungs threatened to initiate a strike as I ran up the hilly road leading to the school campus. I considered myself a decent enough runner, but there was a hell of a big difference between the track field and the city streets, not to mention I was lugging around a large spear that threw off my balance and made sprinting tricky.

Speaking of the spear, I'd turned a couple of placeholder heads as I dashed past them. Was it just me, or were the streets getting more alive over time? Not to mention the old placeholders would've continued to carry on with their conversation about the weather or the local sports team or whatever even if a giant radioactive fire-breathing lizard stomped right next to them. A guy with a spear shouldn't have even registered.

But I digress. I had more important things to worry about than place-holders. I took a huge breath, much to the continued protest of my lungs, and got ready to dash again. I came to a stumbling halt after just one step. There was a familiar, wispy tendril of silver light waving back and forth not too far ahead of me. I turned my stumble into a brisk walk and headed towards it. Once I got close enough, I grew certain about what it was. The last time I'd seen something like this, it was Angie's magic. I used the op-portunity to catch my breath and reached out towards the gently undulating misty something-or-the-other and tugged on it three times like it was one of those old-timey doorbells.

After a brief moment, the thread trembled and was hastily retracted. Now all I had to do was to be patient. But I was really bad at that. So instead I used the momentary lull to close my eyes and utilized my Far Sight to see the others' locations.. The dots of Josh, Snowy, and Crowey were still in the direction of the school, though they were strangely fuzzy. I could sense the others in the area as well. The princess and the class rep were only a couple of blocks from me while Angie was... above?

I opened my eyes and looked up just in time to see the girl falling towards me, her form drenched in a thick layer of silver light. I tensed, my brain caught between the impulse to try to catch her and questioning just what the hell she was doing in the sky. Thankfully both of those issues were solved at once as she opened a pair of large, slightly translucent angel wings on her back that broke her fall and let her land as softly as if she'd just stepped off a curb. The logical part of my brain wanted to inform me that, while large, those wings didn't have the surface area necessary to break the fall of a human at terminal velocity, let alone raise one into the air, not to mention how a sudden deceleration like that should've pulverized her bones like they were made of cookie dough. A more accepting part of my brain, which was already acclimatized to this world, countered by pointing out it was obviously magic, and there was probably some kind of spell or enchantment that let her fly and negate G-forces like that. The third part of my brain then told both of them to shut up because we didn't have time for this. They graciously obliged.

Where was I? Ah, right. Angie.

She was in the middle of fixing her ruffled, slightly damp hair. Maybe she'd been taking a shower when Josh was taken? More importantly, she was wearing a fairly unusual garb consisting of a pair of white boots with metal greaves, a white tabard with a blue circle pattern on the stomach that showed off her legs (to the point where I was sure a small gust of wind would have revealed her panties), a small chest plate that only covered her right breast, and a pair of large bracelets just above her wrists. I would've questioned what the hell she was thinking, going outside dressed like that, but then I recalled Snowy and how she had a weird outfit when she transformed, and I wisely shut up. It still made me grind my teeth, though. I made a mental note that if I survived this night, I'd do something about those outfits. It was getting bloody cold lately, and fighting in those stripperific clothes just wouldn't do.

But speaking of transformations, Angie now also sported a pair of fashionable wings and a pointy halo that kind of looked like a very stylized compass rose. The look fit her, and I already knew she was a Celestial, but I had to admit she looked quite mesmerizing in the dark all the same. Her outfit was still stupid, but even that couldn't ruin the image. No, what did it were the streams of tears and the trail of snot running down her face.

"Leooooo!" she bawled and threw her arms around me and squeezed hard enough to give a Siberian bear a run for its money.

"There, there..." I patted her on the back while she wiped her nose on my jacket. I didn't dare to tell her to stop, so I quietly waited for her to finish sobbing. It happened sooner than I expected, as only a few seconds later she separated from me.

"I can't find him, Leo," she said in a mousey voice. "I looked everywhere, but I can't find him. He disappeared. I tried, but I—"

I raised a finger to her mouth. "Shhh..." I tried to soothe her and closed my eyes. No matter how I looked at it, the three of them were still in the school building, though their dots were hazy. Since I was standing, anyways, I decided to use my Far Sight properly, and after a second of concentration,

I was staring at Crowey standing in the middle of a dark area that I vaguely recognized as the school's track field.

Just as I was wondering why Angie couldn't see him from up above, I noticed something that should've been blindingly obvious from the beginning: a small, slowly swirling circular cloud of some kind. It was right next to Crowey, hanging in the air like a large bathroom mirror, except it looked like a miniature whirlpool of stars and emanated a soft violet light. Then, just like that, I connected the dots, and it shook me out of my Far Sight.

"That son of a bicycle merchant!" I exclaimed angrily as I began walking, practically dragging Angie along.

"What? What happened?"

"I figured out what they're trying to do!"

"What?"

"They are—" I began, but then I noticed someone running on an adjacent street and I shook my head. "I'll tell you when everyone gets here. I don't want to explain it to all of you individually."

She obviously wasn't entirely satisfied with my answer, but at the very least she didn't protest and just followed after me without a word. We got to the school gates just a few seconds before the class rep showed up from the aforementioned other direction. She was panting heavily from the exertion, even more so than we were, and she was already in her frilly green mage clothes with the big witch hat.

"Leo! And... Angie?" She looked over the girl at my side in her obviously Celestial attire and furrowed her brows above her glasses.

I waved to her and said:

"Evening, class rep. Yes, it is Angie. Yes, she is a Celestial. No, we don't have the time to explain."

Now she frowned at me. She had the good sense not to start a fight, though, and only nodded.

"Where are the others?"

"They should be here momentarily," I answered and, as if on cue, a car's headlights illuminated us as it rounded a corner. I expected it to be a large luxury car, but instead it was a dark-brown family sedan that stopped by our side. I glanced at the two girls stepping out of it and could only shake my head.

From the back seat came the person I was expecting. The princess was wearing a red summer dress and a pair of sneakers, a weird combination that told me she'd dressed in a hurry. The other person exiting from the front, on the other hand, was as prim and proper as ever, even in her casual clothes.

"What are you doing here?" I asked my assistant in a tone that might've been a little too disapproving. In my defense, it was probably the stress speaking.

Judy gave me a flat look and pointed at Angie.

"She said there was trouble at school, so I came."

I looked at the girl at my side and she shrank back with a sniff.

"I panicked, okay? You told me to call the others, so I called everyone."

I sighed and looked at the other girl exiting the car after exchanging a few pleasantries with the woman in the driver's seat. Judy followed my gaze and said, "She was on foot, so we picked her up on the way."

"I see," I said, though I was honestly a little disappointed. I expected that at least some of the Dracis muscle would be with her.

I wanted to greet Judy's mother too, but then the car honked and leisurely rolled away, interrupting the flow of the conversation. Speaking of interruptions...

"That reminds me," Judy spoke again. "My father wanted me to tell you that he still has a shotgun, so no funny business under the night skies."

I blinked at her in astonishment before I buried my face in my palm.

"Typical," I muttered before I shook myself and looked over everyone present, one by one. "Is everyone here?"

"I called Sebastian," the princess informed us a tad dejectedly, "but he wasn't available. Father is coming back from China, and they are at the docks. It will take time for them to get here, and he said they might not be able to act before they get a permit because it's Magi territory."

"Speaking of which," I turned to the class rep next. "What about you guys?"

She shook her head sharply.

"There is a Gathering in Glasgow. All the Schools were required to attend, so there was only a token staff present, and I can't contact them."

"So this is all we have?" I clicked my tongue. I feared this might be the case, but it still made my heart sink. As far as I could tell, this was something of a climax in narrative terms. As silly as it might have sounded, it would've been anticlimactic if the authorities swooped in and dealt with the problem instead of us, so they were all conveniently tied up elsewhere.

That made me wonder—was there some sort of overarching intelligence guiding this world, like a writer or director who set up all of these coincidences? Or was it something that arose naturally through a chain of causes and effects just by having the right people placed in the right place at the right time? These were questions I'd been battling with for a while, every time a contemplative mood struck me late at night, but this was the first time such things directly impacted my life. I didn't like it, but I had to work with what I had.

That said, I had more important things to worry about at the moment, and I could always discuss this with Judy later. I had to focus on getting Josh and Snowy back first.

"Can I address the elephant in the room?" Ammy spoke up with a hand raised like she was in the classroom.

"Which one?" Judy asked back.

The class rep frowned at her for a change and pointed at Angie.

"Since when are you a Celestial?"

The girl, who was conspicuously hiding behind me, cocked her head to the side.

"I don't know..." she answered a little uncertainly. "Since I was born, I think. Why?"

"No, I mean..." The class rep let out a frustrated groan and turned to the others. "Don't you have anything to say about this?"

"I knew already," Judy said nonchalantly.

"You did?" Ammy and Angie exclaimed in perfect unison.

"The Chief told me."

Angie glared up at me and pinched my arm.

"Didn't we agree this was a secret?"

"Ow! Hey, stop that! I told her because she's my assistant. She has to know these things."

"I already figured it out," Elly stated next with just a hint of smugness.

"You did?" Angie gaped at the news. "So only Ammy didn't know?"

"I had my suspicions," the class rep stated hesitantly. "Considering that we had representatives from all other factions, I thought you had to be either a Celestial or a Knight, and no offense, but you are really not the knightly type."

"Precisely." The princess nodded in agreement, now with more than a hint of smugness. "My same train of thought."

I wanted to point out that I was pretty sure I was the one who gave them that idea, but I decided to refrain from objecting in fear of further antagonizing Angie. Speaking of which, the Celestial girl slumped her shoulders and let out a disappointed whine.

"Aww... I am the worst secret agent ever."

"Technically you are not an agent yet, only an asset," I pointed out by reflex, conditioned by the long hours I've spent restructuring the classification structure of the Celestial Hub. I realized what I was doing on the spot, though, so I quickly shook my head to clear it. "Not that it matters. Don't you think we have more important things to worry about?"

"You're right," the class rep turned to me with a nod. "What is the situation?"

I took a deep breath and checked the time. It was a little after 10 p.m.

"Here is what's going on in a nutshell. About forty minutes ago, Joshua was kidnapped from his home by Crowey and his minions."

"Crowey?" Angie interjected with a puzzled expression.

"Neige's older brother," Judy explained in my stead, so I continued like I wasn't interrupted.

"He was taken to the school where they are planning to open a gate to the Abyss and take Josh with them. We cannot have that, but since the authorities are apparently busy, we must rescue him on our own. Any questions thus far?"

"How do you know all this?" came the first suspicious inquiry from the resident mage.

"I have my ways," I answered with a wink. She probably would've pressed me more if not for the princess and her question.

"What about Neige?"

"She is with them, but she is on our side. She was the one who warned me."

I didn't want to mention that technically she didn't warn me about the kidnapping, but that I should not interfere. Nevertheless, the subtext told me that she wasn't cooperating with her brother willingly, and explaining her situation to the others would've taken too long, anyways.

"You said they are going to open a gate to the Abyss," Ammy grabbed the proverbial mic again. "Where?"

"On the school grounds, somewhere on the track field."

"There was no one there," Angie chimed in. "I flew over the field a couple of times and I saw no one."

"Of course you didn't. They are in a purple zone."

"A what?"

"Restricted Field," my assistant came to the rescue once again.

"And just how do you know that?" the class rep protested while holding on to her glasses so that her scowl wouldn't misplace them.

"Because that is the only place where they can open a gate?" I stated what I thought was obvious, but since they only looked at me blankly, I was forced to elaborate. "The barrier sealing in the Abyss is impenetrable from any direction, right?" They all nodded. "The purple zone is closer to the Abyss somehow. Don't ask how, I have no idea, I am only relaying what I was told. It's just closer, okay? So, the trick is that from there you can tunnel into the barrier. Another group tunnels at the exact same location from the Abyss using the mana-whatchamacallits that each big family has, and once the two tunnels meet, they create a way through. It stays open for only a couple of minutes before it collapses. During that time, people can move back and forth, but the stronger the person going through, the wider the tunnel has to be and the longer it takes to dig it out. That's why Faun and weak Abyssals can move back and forth using tiny tunnels that can be formed quickly, but Crowey and Snowy would need a big tunnel that requires a long time and a lot of effort to make, and.... and why are you looking at me like that?"

It took a moment for the class rep to get shaken out of whatever state she was in and close her hanging mouth.

"And just how do you know THAT?" she practically shrieked at me, baffling me for a moment.

"I... asked?" I told her, not knowing exactly what kind of answer she was expecting.

"You asked?"

"Yes. From Snowy. I asked her nicely and she told me."

"Seriously?"

"Yeah," I nodded, getting increasingly more baffled by her outrage. "You want to tell me this isn't common knowledge?"

I was honestly surprised by her reaction, but to be fair, the others were giving me weird looks as well. Okay, all except my loyal assistant. She was too busy taking notes.

"No!" Ammy exclaimed in borderline anguish. "We've been trying to figure out how they do it for centuries!"

"Why didn't you just ask one of them?"

"I think you are underestimating the weirdness of your situation," the princess enlightened me, earning a curiously raised eyebrow in the process. "Normal people don't make friends with Abyssals."

"You are friends with her too," I countered, only to get shot down.

"That's because you introduced her. Decent people don't associate with Abyssals unless absolutely necessary."

"Some Schools even have a kill on sight policy," the class rep added.

"That's harsh. Also, we are really losing our track here."

"You... are right," she reluctantly agreed. She was still giving me a perplexed stare, which I didn't like, so I smiled at her to throw her off guard.

"Of course I am. I'm always right," I told her jokingly, and the nod she gave me in return had me worried for a moment that she took me seriously. Either way, it didn't really matter. "So, any other questions before we rush into dangers of epic proportions to rescue our friends?"

"I have one." Judy raised her hand without looking up from her notes. "Where did you find that spear?"

"Yeah!" Angie exclaimed like she was waiting for the opportunity for ages. "It's been bothering me since forever, but no one else seemed to care!"

"I was curious," Elly added a touch hesitantly, "but as you said, no one mentioned it so I thought it would be awkward to ask."

"So? What's the story behind it?" Ammy rounded the circle with her own inquiry.

"Long story short," I began, and trimmed my story real quick before I continued. "On my way here, I ran into a Faun sent to kill me."

"You did what?" The princess paled, and I sent her a sharp glance to convey my disapproval of her interruption.

"As I was saying, I ran into this Faun that Crowey sent to kill me. We had a bit of a chat about honour and mutual respect before we dueled."

"You did what?!" came the echo of the first question, this time from Angie.

"Well, technically it was a ritual of dominance we fought..." I paused and raised my left hand to my forehead and wiggled my fingers, "... in our *minds*. It is hard to explain, but I won and so he let me borrow his spear." I looked over the aghast faces surrounding me and decided that I'd stretch my luck just a little further. "By the way, did you know that Faun talk in Shakespearean English? It's freaky."

"Okay, that's it," the class rep objected with an annoyed slant on her lips. "You're just messing with us at this point."

"I'm not," I protested, but it fell on deaf ears.

"If you don't want to tell us why you have that spear, you could've just said so."

"But I already told you how I got it. I'm one hundred percent serious."

"Sure," Ammy muttered dismissively before she turned to the others. "That aside, if what Leo says is true, then we have to enter into an already existing Restricted Field. I can do that, but it will take a while to open a gateway. Watch my back."

I gave her an affirmative nod and we headed to the track field in a tight cluster. Once there, the class rep pulled out a familiar magic staff from thin air. She probably had some sort of hammer-space where she stored it until she needed it. I wondered if she could lend me one once this was all over. It would make carrying stuff around so much more convenient.

Jokes aside, we stood guard around the class rep while she chanted in a language that sounded like gibberish, yet my newly minted language awareness told me she was pretty much arguing with the universe about breaking down the rules of physics for a moment so she could do her stuff.

It was weirdly fascinating, though not particularly fun to listen to. In fact, I was getting dangerously relaxed and had to repeatedly remind myself that we were about to enter a battlefield at any moment. It was just that, well, I didn't feel like I was in danger. Not yet. Maybe it was because my expectations were very much betrayed by the lack of resistance. Not that I was about to complain, but still, I thought there would have been at least some token trouble by this point.

"Leo. Trouble," Angie chirped at my side in a hushed tone, making me roll my eyes and swear never to ask for problems in the future lest the universe would think it was a challenge.

"What is it?" I answered in a whisper for some reason.

"I cannot open the gateway," the class rep said in a normal voice.

"Me neither." We all looked at the princess questioningly and she sheepishly averted her gaze. "I thought I'd try my own way. I cannot open a gate for others to go through, but I thought I could jump in ahead of you and draw attention away from the gate... or something."

"Please don't do that," I told her firmly. She was getting ready to glare at me, but I cut her off with one of my own. "I'm serious. Going in alone is dangerous, and the last thing I need is for you to get hurt."

I expected her to keep protesting, but she resigned herself unexpectedly fast.

"Fine, I won't do it."

"Good." I clapped my hands. "Still, you helped us learn something important."

"I did?" She perked up immediately. I nodded.

"Yes. You established that the problem isn't just with the class rep's spell."

"Definitely not," spoke the subject of my statement. "It feels like there is something stopping my gate from opening on the other end."

I would've liked to sit down and ask her how her spell worked and maybe figure out a way to overcome the problem, but I doubted we had the time for that. I turned to Angie next.

"What about you?"

"Huh? Me?" She pointed to herself and I nodded. "Er... this is the first time I've done something like this, so I have no idea."

"I understand," I told her reassuringly before I turned to Judy. "Your opinion?"

"Railroad," she stated dryly, and I nodded in agreement.

"Yeah, I don't think we were supposed to just jump in there. It would lack proper build up."

"This is the final boss we are talking about here. It is only natural."

"Well, he's more of an introductory villain in my opinion, but your point still stands."

"Of course it does," she told me with a barely perceptible smirk that didn't touch her eyes. "I think if we presume that we were not supposed to enter this way, it means there should be another way we are supposed to use."

"So you suggest a different approach?"

My assistant nodded.

"Yes. Not to mention, opening a glowing portal in the middle of the hostiles' operation would have exposed us to crossfire."

"I... didn't actually think of that. Very well, we should do this the more conventional way." I turned on my heel to address the others, but when I did so, I found them staring at me like I was a strange, exotic animal. "What?"

"What were you talking about?" Ammy voiced the question reflected on all their faces.

"It's... complicated and we don't have the time to explain. Let's just get going."

I turned around again and began walking at a brisk pace towards the edge of the track field while ignoring the protests of the class rep. Once she realized I wasn't going to tell her anything, she gave up (though she swore she'd pester me later) and we repeated our attempt to crash the party via portal a couple more times, each time a little farther from the field, until we finally made progress.

"I can do it!" Elly yelled, then she toned her voice back and repeated. "I can do it, I mean. We can enter the Restricted Field here!"

"That's neat..." I told her, careful not to let too much irritation show in my voice. We were in front of the school's main entrance by then, meaning we were practically back to where we'd started. In other words, we'd wasted a lot of time for nothing. I clicked my tongue in frustration and gestured at the class rep. "Open the gate here, please."

"I'm already doing it," she responded, waving her staff.

Since the process took some time, I used the opportunity to sneak a quick peek at Josh and company. To my relief, they were still in the middle of the purple-tinted field. Something bothered me, though. I couldn't see the portal to the Abyss anywhere. I hoped this meant they'd run into technical difficulties like we had, giving us some time, but I knew better than to pin my hopes on something like that.

On the other hand, by the time my perception returned to my body, the class rep's gate was all but open already. I didn't know how I actually knew that, but just looking at that swirling magical mist in front of her was like looking at an hourglass. I didn't know how soon it would be finished to the second, but I felt I could give a fairly accurate guess. I still had no idea how I did that—perceiving magic, I mean—but I resolved myself to figure it out as soon as possible once the present crisis was averted.

It took only a few more seconds for the class rep's gate to finally open, and it did so with the sound of a longing sigh. Its edges shimmered into existence. Did that mean that the ball of magic I was looking at before was entirely invisible until this point? Again, I really, really needed to experiment on this one.

"I'm done. We should get going," Ammy stated while straightening her wide-brimmed hat.

"Yes, we should," I agreed with an uncertain nod. I couldn't get rid of this nagging feeling that there was something I was forgetting, but I obviously couldn't remember what it was. We stepped through the portal one by one (even the princess, who insisted that she could totally do it on her own if she wanted to), and in a few short moments we all stood in front of the same school building tinted in an eerie shade of purple.

"Everything's clear," the class rep stated in crisp words, and I had to agree. There was nothing out of the ordinary in sight.

"Let's go," Angie urged us and we complied.

We circled around the main building and were just about to round the corner leading to the track field when an unexpected chill ran down my back.

"Stop!" I yelled, startling the girls around me.

"What? What?" The princess glanced left and right frantically as she scanned the area for enemies. I gestured for her to stop and pointed in the direction of the track field.

"There is some kind of barrier here," I told them flatly. It took me a moment to make it out in the dark, and they probably had an even harder time doing so. It wasn't exactly a wall per se, more like a row of thin pillars of magical light reaching about ten meters high with a barely visible, shimmering field of glowing mist stretching between them.

The class rep deliberately inched forwards beside me, with one hand stretched out. She slowly reached for the barrier. When her fingertips brushed against it, there was a sudden sizzling noise and she jerked her hand away with a hiss.

"Good catch," she told me with attempted gravity ruined by her sucking on her burned finger. "If we'd walked into that, we could've been seriously hurt."

"What kind of barrier is it?" Elly asked, straining her eyes. "I can't see anything."

"It's like…" Angie spoke between two hums, her form once again bathed in the white tendrils that cautiously tapped against the invisible force-fence. "It seems like a specialized barrier. It is coming from many distinct points around the school, like fence posts with a wire stretched between them." She cocked her head to the side like she was listening to a distant sound. "I think it's tuned to only let certain people through. If you are not on the list, you get zapped."

"But how?" The class rep glowered at the barrier. "How did they erect this on the school grounds, right on top of our school!?"

"Does it really matter?" Judy piped in with the same question I had on my mind.

"She's right." I agreed on the spot. "You guys can figure out how they did it later. We should focus on our rescue operation for now."

"But we are walled out," Angie piped in with an obvious point.

"Right," I muttered, looking over the barrier. It seemed to circle the entire track field. It was unlikely that there would be any holes in it we could exploit. "Can we break through somehow?" I asked no one in particular.

"What about dragonfire?" Judy proposed, and all eyes focused on the princess.

"That's right!" Ammy exclaimed. "Dragonfire can break magical enchantments and barriers."

"I… I…" the princess stuttered for a moment before I came to her rescue.

"Hers can't. She cannot use true dragonfire yet."

"True dragonfire?" our mage inquired while tweaking the edge of her hat. "Is there any other kind?"

"It's complicated, right?" I said, gesturing towards the princess. She nodded. "See, she agrees. Anyways, we have to think of something el… se…" My voice trailed off as I raised my eyes high and stared. "Holy crap."

"What is it?" Angie asked while she tried to follow my gaze.

They probably couldn't see it; light in the purple zone behaved differently from the outside, and in the dark of the night, anything non-magical disappeared into the black void after just a couple dozen meters. The portal didn't. It was swirly and sparkly and, most importantly, huge. I didn't notice it when I was looking at it through my Far Sight because it was so big its edge got outside of my field of vision.

Even more troubling was that I could see the timer on it. It was kind of like the way I could judge how close the class rep's gate was to completion, except way fuzzier. Even still, I could clearly see one thing:

"Damn, we have no time!" I exclaimed. "We need to get through this barrier ASAP!"

"But how?" Elly voiced the obvious question.

"I have no idea. Not yet." I inhaled deeply to calm myself. "Come on, brain, think...!" I muttered under my breath as I looked for some lead, anything I could use to get across this damned force field. I squeezed my eyes shut for a moment and then opened them wide to look over the entire area once again.

The barrier ran around the outer edge of the school's backyard, circling the track field, tennis courts, and basketball court. It didn't stretch as far as the pools. Still, it covered a large area, which meant there must've been some weak spots we could exploit, but we didn't have the time find them.

I took another very deep breath, sucking in the evening air through my nose until I felt my lungs ready to burst, and then I slowly exhaled. It helped me focus, just a little. I knew I was missing something. I closed my eyes again and left the game board for a moment to look at the instructional booklet. I just had to think narratively and figure out how I was supposed to use the tools already present. I gestured for my assistant to come over, and we distanced ourselves from the rest of the group.

"Yes, Chief?" she whispered, obviously noticing my efforts to be covert about this.

"I want to bounce a few ideas off you. Do you mind?"

"No. Please go ahead."

I nodded.

"Let's presume that the world follows narrative tropes when it comes to events, not just people and metaphysics."

Judy's eyes flashed with sudden interest, and she took out her phone without a word. I gestured for her to put it away, as we didn't have the time for notes, and she complied.

"Let's also presume that this is something of a climax at the end of a story arc. We are the heroes. Crowey is the antagonist. Josh and Snowy are the damsels in distress. According to the traditional formula—"

"You mean cliché?"

"*The traditional formula*," I stressed again, "at this point, the heroes face off against the antagonist and save the damsel. Are we clear on that?"

Judy nodded.

"Do you see the problem yet?"

"The barrier," she answered without a second of thought. "We cannot face the antagonist because there is a barrier in the way."

"And what does that tell us?"

This time she did think for a second before she said, "That there must be a way we can overcome this barrier as we are right now. Otherwise, there would be no confrontation, no climax, and no narrative."

"Precisely. I hoped you would come to the same conclusion."

"But to reach it, we had to make two big assumptions," my assistant objected dryly, prompting an uneasy glance from me. "While the assumption that the narrative affects the way events unfold has some prior evidence, nothing tells us that this would be a climax. It is entirely possible that Joshua was supposed to be kidnapped and the climax is his rescue from the Abyss. Or that we are not supposed to save him and instead he would have to save himself. We have already established that, in all likelihood, he is the hero. It is likely he doesn't even need our rescue."

That was... as well-reasoned and as much of a buzzkill as I expected from my assistant. But then again, that's why I kept her around, not to be a yes-woman. I still had to shake my head, though.

"If we follow that logic, we must presume that the narrative is beneficial and that not interfering and letting the act play out on its own is an option."

"I was under the impression we already wanted to interfere as little as possible."

"Not when our friends are in danger."

"But how do you know that your actions are not putting them at more risk than your inaction?"

"I..." I exhaled sharply and rubbed my forehead in frustration. She was right. If I presumed that this narrative followed a traditional heroes-beat-the-bad-guys formula, any interference from us could potentially derail it and put them at risk. However, what if we had a role to play in the first place, and us *not* participating was also a form of interference?

I groaned and massaged my temples. This was the problem with being inside a narrative. Being able to see the strings that tugged at the events was useful, but without being able to see everything at once, it was impossible to tell if I made the right decisions. That thought gave me a pause, though.

So what if I couldn't perfectly predict the outcomes of my actions? Isn't that just how life works in general? I just had to take a step back, rebalance myself, and make the best choices I could, based on the available information. Knowing the events were influenced by a narrative was one such bit of information, a crutch to help those decisions.

With that in mind, I got ready to take another stab at my options... Or at least I would've, if only I wasn't startled out of my skin by a loud bang followed by a sickening, sizzling sound. I spun on my heel and faced the source of the noise which was, to my relief, not an incoming attack. What I found instead was a giant slab of slowly disintegrating rock. I vaguely recognized it as the remains of the golem-thing the class rep summoned during her dynamic entry at the time of the masquerade-breaking incident between the princess and Snowy.

At this point, one of its bulky arms was in the process of melting off without actually giving off any light or heat, soon followed by the rest of its body as it crumbled to fine dust.

"What are you doing?" I inquired with more than a hint of disapproval...

The class rep set her mouth in a thin line and frowned at me in return.

"I was trying to break through. What did it look like?"

"Something foolish that I wasn't expecting from you of all people," I snapped back, and she averted her eyes. To my surprise, Angie and the princess did the same beside her.

So it was a group effort, huh?

I was just about to chew them out for rushing and not thinking things through, but then I was once again interrupted by a noise. This was not a bang, but more... organic, for lack of a better word. A growl sounding like the combination of an elephant, a whale, and a roaring lion with the volume slider set high enough to make my bones vibrate.

"What was that?" Judy asked with no small amount of apprehension as she practically clung to my back. "Some kind of animal?"

As usual, it was at this very moment that I remembered the thing that I couldn't recall and had been bothering me for a while. After a silent gulp, I turned to the other girls (who were also trying to hide behind my back, but that was beside the point) and asked, "It might be a little late to ask this now, but could you tell me what a *Chimera* is? In two sentences or fewer, if possible."

The class rep's eyes widened in shock. "It's... a creature from the Abyss. It is a monster that is resistant to magic and can change its shape in a fight depending on its opponent."

"No one has seen them for centuries," the princess added in a whisper. "They are supposed to be extinct."

Technically their combined explanations were longer than two sentences, but I didn't complain. Instead, I tried to force a smile and said, "Well, I'm afraid they are not."

The class rep and the princess visibly paled. Angie and Judy, on the other hand, were apparently unaware of the danger, so they only looked at me uncertainly.

"We need to get out of the open," the princess hissed, mirroring my sentiment.

I looked over the area, and then an idea hit me like a ton of bricks. Evidently my brain only operated at full capacity under stress, since the solution to our problem now seemed blindingly obvious.

"The main building!" I exclaimed as I pointed at the subject of my revelation. "The barrier only covers the wall facing the track field—the back entrance should let us right in. We have to get there before—"

Before the Chimera shows up, I wanted to say. But in that moment, the point became moot.

The Chimera didn't rush at us. It didn't even run. It simply walked over with a slow, deliberate strut that looked incredibly odd and disconcerting. But I was getting ahead of myself. First off, here is what I was actually seeing:

It was big. No, scratch that. Brang was big. This thing was plain huge, at least three meters tall even while hunched over, and its shoulders were so massive it would've put an NFL player to shame, padding included. It was also ugly as sin, an unholy combination of a primate and a crocodile with vivid red skin covered with black scales, fur, and the occasional bone protrusions scattered around its body like pieces of disjointed body armour.

It had a lumbering gait, like a giant gorilla walking on all fours, but it was also dragging a long, serpentine tail and had an elongated head with a large jaw containing long, pointy teeth visible even while its mouth was shut. Its eyes had the same kind of orange-ish glow I saw in Brang's.

It raised its long head in our direction and blinked one set of its eyes. It had three of those, by the way, and they blinked individually in a sequence. Two pairs of different sizes looked forwards like a tiger's while the last pair was staring sideways at an angle more suited for a prey animal. Its massive chest heaved as it let out a puff of smoky breath in a deep hiss that made the hairs on the back of my neck stand on end. It was like I was staring down a hungry grizzly bear that was trying to decide which one of us it should eat first. Except, you know, a dozen times worse.

The stalemate continued just long enough to unnerve me, but not long enough to come up with a coherent idea about how to deal with the situation.

"Leo...?" the princess whispered and sidled closer to me. In retrospect, that was a mistake.

The beast's eyes snapped wide open, their smoldering orange light rising to a flare, and it stood upright on its stumpy hind legs and opened its jaws so wide, it was downright uncanny. And considering that we were talking about a monstrous mishmash of creatures, that was most certainly no mean feat. Then came the roar. It was the same sound we had heard minutes before, except louder and meatier. It shook my insides as if there was a jackhammer trying to escape my chest, and judging by the way the girls flinched back, it affected them too.

For a split second, I wondered if there was magic involved or just our instincts screaming at us about the dangerous predator in front of us that made us dizzy, but I didn't have the luxury of time, as the Chimera crouched down on all fours like a feline before it leaped forwards, its thundering paws shaking the ground. Credit where credit's due, the girls didn't require instructions on how to scatter. In fact, if anything, I was a bit too slow when it came to reacting to the sudden charge.

"Shit!" I exclaimed as I rolled to the side. I still wasn't used to the spear, so I felt really clumsy when I tried to rise to my feet and my legs got tangled in the shaft. By the time I got up, the creature already barreled past me and was chasing after the princess. For a blink of an eye, my brain wondered why it was targeting her. Maybe it was because she made the first noise? Or because it considered her the biggest threat? But then again, she wasn't transformed yet, so maybe it was thinking she was the weakest in the group and tried to get rid of her quickly? Just how intelligent was this thing?

All those questions were soon drowned out by another innards-rumbling battle cry that I found to be coming from—to my considerable surprise—my own throat. I raised the spear as high as my shoulder and leaped forwards, stabbing towards the exposed side of the creature using all my momentum. There was a hard *thunk* as my strike connected and the creature once again roared. This time, though, it was not the aggressive roar from before, but a more high-pitched cry.

I should've felt exhilarated about hurting the creature. Hell, I was fully expecting some caveman-portion of my brain to rejoice at the experience. Instead, I found my mind extremely sharp and clear, like the blade of a well-honed knife, and it told me one thing: it wasn't enough. The cut was too shallow to be fatal. It might not even hinder it much.

As if to agree with my assessment, the Chimera's massive tree-trunk of an arm swung at me and sent me flying through the air. What really surprised me was how little the strike hurt. Maybe it was because I instinctively jumped with the impact, so it didn't as much hit me as it pushed me away. It also had a useful side effect, as it tore the spear's tip out of the creature's side, prompting it to shudder and loose another pained roar. That gave me just enough time to roll a landing and rise to my feet, this time minding the spear and thus doing so in a slightly less bumbling fashion.

"Leo!" at least three of the girls yelled in unison, and I couldn't tell which ones. Not that it mattered. What did was how the princess was right behind the creature now, and the ambient reddish light gathering around her told me she was preparing to transform. I almost felt relieved about getting some backup, but another thought overwrote the emotion, and I yelled at her from the top of my lungs.

"Stop! Don't engage it! Head for the school building!"

Elly hesitated, and it almost proved fatal as the monster twisted around and swung its elongated arm at her. The only reason she wasn't sent flying was because of a meaty impact hitting the creature's side, throwing it off-balance just long enough for the princess to duck to the side and scamper out of its reach. Relief washed over me. I pushed it aside and focused on the source of the previous distraction.

As I looked closer, I saw something sticking out of the Chimera's side. It was slightly translucent, and I quickly recognized its light—an arrow bearing Angie's magic. My deduction was promptly confirmed when the Celestial girl swooped down from the sky and landed beside me. To my surprise, I found that one of her bracelets was unfolded into a sleek bow that, if it was made from regular metal, probably would've collapsed in on itself just from the internal strain. But then again, I couldn't see any bowstring between its arms, so as far as I knew, the entire "bow" might've been just cosmetic.

Angie was smiling defiantly, but even a cursory glance told me she was heaving hard and her legs were shaking. She tried to say something, but her mouth must've been dry, as she only gulped repeatedly without letting out a single sound.

I subtly rolled my eyes and patted her on the shoulder. The creature was busy grasping at the shaft in its side, so I took the opportunity to say, "Good job. Now go to the main building with the others. Try to find a way past the barrier through the back entrance."

"What about you?" she squeezed out the words through her clenching throat.

"I'll keep this thing's attention and follow after you once you are inside."

In the meantime, the rest of the girls also circled around and got into earshot, so I pointed at them one by one.

"Class rep, you're in charge. Princess, take point. Angie, you are ranged support. Judy, you're in charge of communications. Everyone clear?"

They looked at me funny, but then their faces turned pale as the Chimera stopped messing with its wound and lunged towards us without warning. I let my instincts take control of my body the way I practiced with Brang's shades and, to my immense satisfaction, it worked surprisingly well. I sidestepped the incoming charge and whacked the thing on the side of the head with the blade of my spear. It let out an ear-piercing shriek as it turned mid-run and swung at me. I nimbly ducked under it and poked it with the spear once again. I wasn't doing much damage, but I was fairly certain I'd be able to wear it down with time.

I looked up and found the four girls still gawping at me. This time I didn't bother to be subtle with my eye-rolling and yelled, "Go!"

They took a few hesitant steps towards the main building, but then the princess turned on her heel and yelled at me, "Leo! I want you to know that I—!"

She got that far before Judy and Angie grabbed hold of her arms and dragged her along, much to her protests. I didn't mind, though. Anguished declarations of love were red flags that set either the confessor or the receiver up for dying a poignant death, a prospect I didn't mind avoiding if at all possible. So I hefted my spear and glowered at the creature... who promptly ignored me and went after the girls.

"Oh no, you don't!" I screamed in frustration at the obnoxious monster and stabbed it in the back. It roared and spun on its heel again, finally focusing on me.

Sheesh, just how many times does a guy have to stab someone to be taken seriously?

The Chimera howled and leaped at me. I ducked to the left and let my hands slide down on the spear so that I was holding it more like a pike. I took a couple of lithe steps backward and poked the creature a few more times as it tried to regain its balance. While it was big and had claws the size of my fingers, that meant little when I had the longer reach. For the time being, I was satisfied with only keeping it at spear's length and stopping it from going after the rest of the group.

After a few more useless rushes, the Chimera finally stopped its rampage and we circled each other. I was actually really pleased with myself. Maybe it was because of my protracted mind-battle with the Faun not too long ago, but I found the terror one would've anticipated from facing a giant monster made of teeth and claws and radiating bloodlust curiously absent. I was fine. Too fine, even.

But then again, maybe it was just my way of dealing with the incongruity of the situation. I was fighting against a huge monster that looked like the progeny of an especially wild drunken party between some gorillas and a bunch of crocodiles, and all I had was a spear I'd snagged from an honourable goat-guy warrior while under the eerie pale-purple light of a distant moon in a pocket-dimension made of violet ambiance and eye-strain. Maybe all of it was just too unreal for my brain to take it seriously enough to freak out, so instead my thoughts bounced on a cushion of complacency even as I faced a horror that should've ended an entire Call of Hastur campaign with sanity damage alone.

The cold, analytical part of my mind was still as alert as ever, though, as were my strange, supernatural dodging instincts. The creature threw itself against me time and time again, and each time it did so, I rebuked it with a solid poke in the abdomen or the chest and a light sidestep. I was even a little disappointed. From the girls' description, and even more so from their reaction, I expected something truly brutal. While the creature in front of me looked menacing all right, it wasn't particularly dangerous to me.

Then, about five seconds later, I had to remind myself to never, ever complain about not having enough troubles, as the Chimera abruptly lashed out with a growling grunt and my instincts told me to dive aside immediately. My legs followed the advice even as my hands were trying to stab back to keep it at bay, only for me to realize that the main bulk of the creature didn't move. Yet there was something swinging over my head when I got out of the way.

The Chimera didn't give me time to think. It struck again. This time I paid attention to where the strike was coming from, and to my astonishment, I found that it didn't actually take a step towards me. Instead, it made its arm grow longer than my spear.

Well, that's one way to level the playing field, I supposed.

A really, really unfair way, but I wasn't one to talk.

I dodged to the side again, thankful that we were engaged on the grass instead of the pavement, otherwise, I would have probably gotten myself bruised into oblivion with all the rolling and skidding left and right.

But back to the Chimera: its arm didn't just grow or elongate, but melted into a large tentacle tipped with a clawed wrist. It was also still growing, to the point where I was the one getting squarely outmatched in the reach department. For the moment, all I could do was to run around it in circles and duck whenever it tried to strike me down.

And then there was a guitar solo.

"What the hell?" I muttered, almost forgetting to dodge before I recognized my ringtone. I let out a nondescript curse aimed at no one in particular and let go of my spear with one hand so that I could reach into my pocket. My opponent wasn't particularly considerate, and it kept up its barrage of swings.

"Oh, screw it!" I yelled, my patience reached its boiling point, and even though I wanted to do it under controlled circumstances first, I did my best to recall the way to use my newly discovered teleportation power. A moment later, I disappeared from my previous location and reappeared a couple of meters to the right, though not exactly at the point I'd planned. The whole process felt really odd and a little nauseating, but I didn't have time to dwell on it, as I had to use this opportunity to answer the phone.

"Hi, Chief," my assistant greeted me under layers and layers of static, like this was just an impulse call on a slow weekend evening.

"Hi," I answered, only to let out a pained hiss a second later when the Chimera rediscovered me and I tried to redirect an incoming lash with just one hand on the spear. The impact nearly twisted the weapon out of my hand and sent a sharp tinge of pain running up my forearm. I stepped back to avoid the follow-up strike and flexed my fingers. It didn't hurt anymore, so I hoped nothing was broken.

"Is everything all right?" Judy asked. Her voice sounded almost painfully clueless.

"Just a little busy over here!" I answered. "Why'd you call?"

"You said I was in charge of communications."

"Oh, right..." I mumbled. "Wait, how do our phones even work in this place?"

"I have no idea, and I can't ask Amelia. She's busy."

I had a snappy retort to her happy-go-lucky words, but then the creature struck at me again, forcing me to teleport again, and this time the nausea was much worse than the first time around.

"Are you sure everything's all right?"

"No! As I said, I'm kind of busy!" I grumbled as I dashed to the side just in time to avoid a vertical strike that would've probably broken me in half were I still in the vicinity when it hit the ground. I groaned, half in pain and half in exasperation, and told Judy to hold the line.

I pocketed my phone, grabbed hold of my spear with both hands, and surveyed the area. Until then, I'd been sticking to the open grounds next to the main building, as I preferred the extra mobility it allowed for ducking, weaving, and scampering for dear life. It wasn't really conducive for taking a breather, though, so after a moment of thinking, I turned tail and dashed to the closest of the titular cherry trees. The Chimera roared as it flailed its limb at me, but I refrained from further teleports for the time being, as using it in quick succession was really disorienting.

Through agility, luck, and mad skillz, I managed to get behind the tree without any incident. I figured it would buy me only a couple of seconds at most, so I snatched out my phone.

"Status report."

Judy answered, "The back exit is also covered by the barrier. So are the windows on the ground floor."

"Damn," I sighed.

"We need another way in. Any ideas?" came the barely audible question from the class rep. She was probably shouting it into the receiver from a distance.

I took a deep breath and thought hard for a moment. So, if the back entrance wasn't good, what else was there? She said they tried the windows on the ground floor and... and then the realization hit me in that peculiar mixture of elation and embarrassment only the blindingly obvious can manage.

"Get to the roof!" I all but shouted into my phone. "The barrier only reaches up to about ten meters high! You cannot go through it, but you can go over it!"

"How?" Judy asked, and I couldn't decide if she was incredulous or honestly thought I could tell her the answer.

"How the hell should I know? You have the magical people with you—have them come up with something!"

"Will do. Judy out."

With that, she cut the line and I hastily put my own phone away before I grabbed hold of my spear once again. I was honestly a little surprised I wasn't interrupted yet, and I had a hard time deciding if that was a good thing or something to worry about. I'd expected the Chimera to have torn out the tree by its roots by the time I finished, or something equally excessive at least. Instead there was... well, nothing.

I took a cautious peek around the trunk of the old tree, and I actually had to stop myself from laughing out in surprise. The Chimera was, for lack of a better word, hobbling towards me on a pair of ridiculously fat, stumpy legs. Not only that, but its upper body was completely deformed. It still had the same head with the same six glowing eyes, but its face was gaunt and its torso lost most of its musculature on one side while bulging out on the other. In fact, its left arm looked like it was sucked back into its shoulder.

It took me an embarrassingly long time to connect the dots, but when I did, I couldn't help but laugh for real. Yes, the Chimera transformed to be able to negate my reach advantage, but contrary to my expectation, it didn't just do it via magic. Well, fine, I was certain magic was involved in one way or the other, but it looked like its transformation was actually that: a transformation. It only reconfigured its body, creating new tissues and body configurations without adding or subtracting from the starting biomass. I'm not going to lie, the last thing I expected to obey the laws of thermodynamics in this world was the insane shape-shifting monster, though I wouldn't say the revelation was an unpleasant surprise.

After some further observations, I surmised it must've used up the material that made up its left side and chest to create the tendril and then put the rest of its biomass into those elephantine legs in order to make itself bottom-heavy enough to keep from toppling as it swung its arm. I couldn't decide whether that was really a clever or really dumb plan. Either way, did this mean it was intelligent after all? But then again, maybe it just reacted to my actions. That would explain why it took things to the extreme without considering how vulnerable (not to mention stupid-looking) it became in the process. I wondered if I could get it to elongate its arm even farther by kiting it while slowly retreating until the rest of its body couldn't support the limb and would collapse by itself... but that would take too long.

There was another option. As pitiful as the horrible murderous creature looked at the moment, it was likely helpless at close range. If I could charge it and avoid getting hit by its whiplike arm in the process, I could build up enough momentum to pierce its skin and deliver a fatal strike. I only had a few seconds to decide. Should I try?

Bellowing a battle cry, I jumped out from behind the tree and charged the creature. I kept the spearhead low and held the shaft as firmly as I could. My goal was to run straight at the creature and transfer all the kinetic energy I accumulated into the spearpoint. Sounded great in theory, but I barely took a step before I ran into setbacks, namely the fact that by then the Chimera hobbled close enough for its arm to reach me. I ducked under the first swing, jumped over the second, and continued charging while I shouted elaborate curses from the top of my lungs.

By now, the Chimera's jointless right arm was at least six meters long, his entire upper body swinging it like a whip. Even though said arm was fairly lean, especially compared to how oversized and muscular its original limbs were, I was sure a direct hit would shatter my ribcage like jackhammered porcelain. If my theory was correct, then said whip-arm contained about a third of its bulk at this point, so any hit would be a crushing blow indeed. A fearsome weapon at a distance, but at closer ranges, it was clumsy and cumbersome, as I quickly found out to my immense satisfaction.

At last, I got into striking distance. Focusing on the left side of the monster's chest, I pushed forward, putting as much force into my stab as I possibly could. The strike connected beautifully with a visceral, meaty *thunk* followed by a deep, pained howl.

The spearhead entered into the creature's chest cavity, the flat blade sliding between two ribs and disappearing in its flesh. It continued to cry out in pain and shook its torso, no doubt in an attempt to bring its weaponized arm to bear. It couldn't do that, but the thrashing was so violent that my hands slipped and I was thrown off while my spear remained lodged inside its body. I didn't have the opportunity to roll with the fall, so I landed on my back with a painful impact that shoved all the air out of my lungs. Tiny specks of light danced in my vision.

For a long second, I could only blink at the fake starless sky before my instinct told me to dodge again. My weary body followed its instructions before I could even see the danger. It was a good thing it did, as only a moment after I got out of the way, the creature lost its balance and fell forwards, nearly flattening me in the process.

I rose to my feet in a hurry and retreated before I stopped to catch my breath. The Chimera was lying motionlessly on the grass. A whining hiss escaped its body as its lungs deflated. There was a different wheezing sound in the air as well, and it took me a moment to realize it was my own ragged breathing. I tried to control it. Instead my efforts only turned it into a rough chuckle that soon blossomed into a relieved laugh.

"Damn!" I exclaimed as the euphoria of victory washed over me. "Daaaaamn! That was almost too easy!"

I let out another bout of not-at-all crazy laughter before I realized that I wasn't out of the frying pan. I shook my head hard to clear it from stray thoughts and tried to assess my situation.

First and foremost, I had beaten a monster. Normally this was when I'd receive experience points and some random loot, but I'd lost my weapon instead. "That's horrible game design," I muttered under my breath, still a little high on adrenaline as I circled the motionless body of the Chimera.

It was just as I feared—my spear was lodged under the entire bulk of the creature, and I had no means of retrieving it. I sighed in frustration and glanced over at the main building. "I should hurry after the others," I muttered to no one in particular.

Then the guitar solo sounded again, making me jump in surprise. I let out a grunt and reached for my pocket while heading towards the main entrance of the school building.

"Yes?" I asked once I got my nerves under control.

"There's trouble," Judy stated in answer.

"I figured. I'm on my way. What's the situation?"

"We are being chased by three... no, four Fauns." I almost stumbled when I heard the news. I subsequently increased my pace while she continued, "They are in the way, and we cannot get to the roof. Any advice?"

I slowed down as I was about to reach the corner of the building and uttered the first thing that came to mind.

"Tell the others that I said you should not let them herd you up the stairs and corner you on the roof. Do it as loud as you can so that they can hear it too."

"Okay." My assistant obliged on the spot. She must've put her hand over the phone, because I could only hear a muffled string of syllables. A second later she told me, "Amelia says I should stop shouting or they will overhear us." There was a moment of pause and she added, "And Eleanor asked me to tell you to 'make up your mind already.'"

"Disregard the latter. As for the class rep, yell about how it doesn't matter because the Fauns are so incompetent, they wouldn't be able to use the information to their advantage, anyway. Make extra sure they hear that one."

"On it." The noises coming from the other side once again got muffled for a few seconds. "Message delivered. Where should we go now?"

"To the roof, obviously."

There was some commotion in the background. Then Judy said, "Eleanor wants me to tell you, '*You should really, really make up your damn mind.*'"

"Comment noted. Now, I want you to retreat towards the roof. Put up token resistance and make it look like you are really trying to avoid going there. Let the Fauns believe they are actually forcing you. Once up there, you should be able to hold them back at the only exit. That should buy you some time while you figure out how to get over the barrier."

"Okay. We'll try." She paused meaningfully before she suddenly asked, "How will you get there if the Fauns will be in front of the door?"

"I have my ways. I'm on my—"

A chill ran down my spine and I dove to the left. Claws scraped plaster in an ear-piercing shriek. I rolled to the side and laid my eyes on my new attacker. Or rather, the old one.

The Chimera stood in front of me once again, changed. Gone were the stumpy legs, replaced by thick digitigrade limbs. It was walking on three legs now, the previous stump of its left foreleg reasserting itself into a new, fully functional extremity even while I was looking. It was still dragging its long whip-arm behind it as it awkwardly tried to follow after me, but it looked withered. Just under its shoulder, it pulsated as if a second heart was pumping out all the usable biomass from the now pointless limb.

Weirdest of all, the creature still had the spear sticking out of its torso... except from the back. The only way that could've happened is if all of the Chimera's extremities had twisted around to turn its back into its new front— and as implausible as that sounded, the spear-shaft sticking out of its back like a huge quill on an otherwise bald porcupine told me it had to be true.

It shook its body like a wet dog before it let out a deep snarl and tried to lunge at me, but it got tangled by its own whip arm and it fell flat on its belly before the huge, scything claws of its brand-new left arm could even get close to me. It let out a curiously frustrated whine before it rose onto its hind legs once again, grabbed hold of its elongated limb with the other one, and hauled it forward like a thick string of taffy. Then, without even flinching, it opened its giant maw wide, revealing two rows of sharp teeth, and bit down hard on the appendage. There was no blood, only a sort of black ichor that got absorbed right back into the creature's body.

It took several bites for the arm to be severed, and when it did, the Chimera tossed the lifeless limb aside like it was trash. Even as it did so, I could see the new foreleg forming from the stump. I looked over the recovering creature as I slowly backed away. It was then that I remembered the phone in my hand, so I gulped and raised it to my face.

"Judy," I told my assistant as calmly as I could. "I ran into some complications. I might be late. Don't wait for me."

CHAPTER 23

The Chimera was, frankly, pretty damn massive from up close. Not as big as it used to be when it was in its gorilla-guise, but it was still damn big. It lost some of its bulk due to the lost limb (as far as I could tell from a glance, it had about the biomass of an average human in it before it was torn off), but considering how honking huge it was before, the difference in size was only academic.

More importantly though, this was the first time I could observe its transformation happening in real-time. Its hind legs grew both longer and more muscular, its torso elongated, its shoulders moved to allow its head to take a forward-looking position, and the front legs formed into digitigrade limbs with clawed paws right in front of my eyes. In less than fifteen seconds, the creature resembled a giant feline with a misshapen dinosaur head and a thick lizard's tail.

I kept staring at the metamorphosis in a daze until my higher brain functions finally got a handle on the situation and asked a very simple yet profound question: *Why are you standing still and gawking like a slack-jawed idiot instead of running as far as your legs can carry you?*

I... had no good comeback to that, so I roused myself and followed my own advice, dashing around the corner of the building like the devil himself was on my tail. Normally this would've been the time when I came up with something snappy about how *it might not have been the devil, but definitely the next worst thing,* but considering my track record when it came to taunting the narrative, I decided to think of more immediately lifesaving things instead. Not to mention, considering the company I kept, I wasn't entirely certain there wasn't an actual devil in this world, and he might find the irony delicious enough to show up, just for kicks. At this point, it would've only mildly surprised me.

Now, where was I? Oh, right. Running for my life while screaming from the top of my lungs. The latter was something that my lower monkey-brain decided on without asking my higher functions first, so I promptly put an end to it. It was embarrassing and wholly counterproductive, as my lungs could've been put to much better use by pumping delicious oxygen to my leg muscles.

Speaking of which, I winced as my feet slapped painfully against the pavement with every adrenaline-fueled step. I was a good thirty meters from the stairs leading up to the entrance, and while it came from a gut-level instead of a more sophisticated logical response, I had no better idea at the time than to get inside. It carried the threat of being cornered indoors, but I doubted it would have been any worse than trying to wrestle the Chimera in the open and without a weapon.

I dashed towards the doors with all my might, only allowing myself a quick peek over my shoulder. I nearly stumbled when I realized the creature was literally behind my back, and my instincts kicked in, forcing me to dive as the creature's meaty paw sliced through the air above me. It probably wasn't used to its quadrupedal form yet, as the miss threw it off-balance. It stumbled and rolled on its back, the spear making a painful scraping noise as it hit the pavement, but a moment later the Chimera was back on its feet again.

Gasping, I concentrated on running again while trying to ignore how quickly the distance I gained was starting to rapidly decrease once again. I absently noted that the area of the stairs was littered with shards of safety glass. The source of said shards also became obvious as I came a little closer; the main doors of the building were broken into smithereens. At the time I considered that a good thing, as it meant an easier entry. In retrospect, I concluded it was probably caused by the girls. The last time I was in the Purple Zone, the automatic doors wouldn't open on their own, so they must've taken a more direct approach.

Then I glanced back, and my stomach sunk into a dark pit. The Chimera was upon me again, and this time its gait told me it wasn't going to comically stumble on the last leap. Time slowed to a crawl as I scrambled for a way to avoid my steadily approaching and seemingly inevitable fate as monster-chowder. I glanced ahead and saw that the now busted entrance was only about ten meters away from me. It might as well have been on the other side of the moon for all the good it did to me. I wasn't going to reach it on foot either way.

And then it happened. It was another of those head-slapping, self-berating, utterly embarrassing moments when the blatantly obvious hit me like a runaway tow truck. It was the doors that did the trick. Or the lack thereof. It reminded me of the first time I ran into them and how astoundingly stupid I had to be not to remember it until now.

I swiftly recalled the feeling, and it came to me with laughable ease. It started with a moment of violent nausea, my vision dissolving like an oil painting under a torrent of paint thinner. I pictured the hall just on the other side of those broken doors that seemed so far away just a few seconds ago. As a matter of fact, it was still very far, and every nerve in my body violently protested against my attempt to rip through space-time. I nearly stumbled as the backlash hit me. An idle part of my brain noted that I've only done very short teleports even during my mind-battle with Brang, and it was entirely possible the hall was simply out of my range, but the rest of my grey matter silenced it as I focused on doing it anyway, because I had no choice. My only other choice was getting eaten. So I pushed ahead, strained whatever part of my being was responsible for the ability, and all of a sudden my senses were assailed by a prickling sensation all over my skin, followed by a solid tug, like I was falling from a great height, except sideways.

Then, at last, there was a faint *pop* as my surroundings abruptly snapped into place and I was in the hall, just like that. There was already a triumphant cry in my throat that my stupid monkey-brain authorized without my consent, one which abruptly turned into one of panic as I noticed the quickly approaching shoe locker. I had no way to stop, due to a combination of momentum and a sudden spike of violent nausea no doubt caused by my reckless use of my newfound ability, so I twisted my upper body so that I would hit it with my shoulder instead of my head, and hit it I did. So hard in fact, that the large metal cabinet lurched back from the impact, teetered on two legs, then tipped over, and I fell right on top of it.

For a moment, I lay splayed out on top of the locker, trying my best to keep my violently churning stomach under control. I failed, and spewed my dinner all over the floor. That made me feel marginally better. I pushed my body off the cabinet, and once I was back on my feet, I wiped the corner of my mouth.

My hopes for catching my breath were dashed as the Chimera, alerted to my presence by the noise of falling furniture, barreled in through the blasted open entrance with a blood-curdling roar of pure, primal anger... which turned into a surprised whimper as its paws landed on the shattered glass and it just... kind of slid past me like it was on an ice-skating rink. I couldn't tell if it really rolled past on the glass shards (safety glass tends to break into small fragments one could theoretically slip on, after all) or only its pained flailing created the illusion. Either way, I ducked to the side as the large creature tumbled over the other row of shoe lockers and came to a stumbling halt, one of its massive forearms caught in the metal cabinet.

It looked around, its three pairs of eyes scanning the hall with jerky motions until it found me, still sprawled on the floor where I landed after I got out of its way. It let out a low growl that sounded decidedly exasperated, a surprising emotion to detect in a half-ton shape-changing monstrosity. I was getting ready to dash up the stairs when the realization hit me again and I mumbled to myself, "Teleport, you idiot."

I promptly did so, this time aiming at the faculty office by the stairwell, and this time I reached my destination without any more embarrassing hijinks. The nausea was pretty severe, though, so I threw my back against one of the teachers' desks and quieted my ragged breathing. In the meantime, the creature on the other side of the wall let out a frustrated howl and began doing something, which by the sounds of it either involved scraping the lockers or rousing the world's worst string quartet. Not that I cared. I was more interested in the fact that this intermezzo finally allowed me to breathe. And to think, which was arguably more important. I wasn't doing much of that lately, was I?

I took a deep breath.

Okay, let's analyze my situation. I was being chased by a shape-shifting beast. That was well established, I think. It was also much more resilient than I'd originally imagined. Not super-surprising for a shape-shifter, but still, the notion that losing one of its limbs would somehow make it *more* dangerous was completely outside of my calculations.

I decided to imagine the worst-case scenario and presumed that the thing was functionally immune to physical harm due to high-speed regeneration. How was I supposed to deal with something like that?

The first idea that came to mind was simple: ignore it and focus on catching up to the girls instead. With my teleportation ability, I had a definitive mobility advantage over it. In fact, I could probably even move to the other side of the barrier if I wanted to.

The idea had some nice sequence-breaking potential, but I discarded it as quickly as I came up with it. Using this new ability of mine was really taxing. My range maxed out at around five meters, and anything beyond that was like trying to squeeze through the eye of a needle. Not to mention, even if I somehow managed to evade the Chimera and move to the other side of the barrier, then what? I had no weapon, I couldn't take any of the girls with me, and I couldn't teleport out with Josh, either. Or at least I didn't think I could, but this wasn't exactly the right moment to gamble on that.

In other words, if I tried to avoid this monster and regroup with the girls, it would just put us back to square one, no closer to rescuing Josh and Snowy, and it would even expose them to more risk. So, what else could I do? Kill it? Could this thing even be killed?

That wasn't just a rhetorical question, by the way. I needed to come up with something fast, and so I reached for my vast treasure trove of tropes that I collected during my research. How did people in stories deal with creatures with high-speed regeneration?

Fire would be a good start, I supposed. I was a little short on flame-throwers, but maybe the girls could improvise something. The class rep, in particular, was a mage. Sure she had some level-one firebolts or even a fireball in her spellbook. But then again, didn't they say that Chimeras were resistant to magic?

"Okay, so let's relegate magical fire to the backup plan," I whispered while glancing over the desk. The creature was still busy tearing apart the shoe lockers outside. It might've thought I was hiding in one of them, which was good news for me.

So… what options did I have for non-magical fire?

I needed a source of fuel. My first candidate was the home economics classroom, but then I vaguely recalled that the princess once complained about the electric ovens during a lunch break. That didn't mean the classroom had no gas, but I wasn't going to gamble on that.

There was a place I was fairly certain had gas, though—the basement. The school's heating system was using gas boilers, and they were housed there. I learned this tidbit from the class rep, and I had no reason to doubt her. I could most certainly get down there, but I had no idea how I could set up a trap for the creature using the propane landline. Speaking of which, would there even be gas there? Purple Zones had definitive borders as far as I knew, with the inside being a copy of the real world and the outside being just a dark void. Would that mean that the gas lines were connected to nothing? But then again, our phones were still working even when inside a pocket space, so what the hell did I know? That said, even if there was gas there, I was supposed to head for the roof as soon as possible. Going to the basement first would've been a wee bit counterintuitive.

"Okay, let's call that Plan B…" I murmured while rubbing my forehead.

The more I thought about it, the more I had to realize propane wouldn't work, anyways. It would just explode, and while the shockwave would probably pulverize me, it would likely only mildly inconvenience the Chimera.

"Scratch that, let's make it Plan D instead. Now to fill out Plans A to C…"

What other flammable materials were there? I could go outside and look for cars to get gasoline, but I didn't know how big the Purple Zone was, so that was a long shot at best. Still, it should do for Plan C, I concluded. What other flammable materials were out there? Oil, paint thinner, alcohol… Alcohol?

"The burners in the science classroom!" I muttered with a smile.

Yes, that should work, I decided. The chemistry supplies were kept in a secure cabinet at the back of the room, but I was confident I could break it down with some effort, and I'd once seen Mrs. Applebottom refill one of the alcohol burners from a large metal flask. As far as flammable materials were concerned, I was sure that much was enough to immolate the Chimera—so long as I could douse and then light it aflame without setting myself on fire in the process.

I was ready to declare that Plan A when I remembered something else. In roleplaying games, the second-most common way of dealing with trolls and other nasty regenerators was acid. Or rather, any corrosives, as bases could be just as caustic. Chemistry 101 aside, while I doubted I could get something as floor-meltingly potent as most fictional acids were, I could definitely get my hands on some rather nasty stuff nonetheless, and luckily they were kept around the same place as the burner fuel.

Considering that sprinkling acid on something was easier and comparatively safer than lighting it on fire, I decided that it should be Plan A, and I relegated the burner fuel to Plan B. It was about time I started moving, though, as the Chimera stopped making a ruckus outside and I was worried I would get discovered.

I made a mental floor plan of the school in my head. The science classroom was on the first floor. I needed some prep time, so I wanted to get there unnoticed. With my newly christened teleportation ability, that should've been fairly easy. I had already discovered that it had a relatively short range and I didn't need a line of sight to teleport, though it did help when it came to avoiding collisions. I could teleport up to the next floor through the ceiling, at least in theory, grab the stuff from the supply closet, and then return and ruin the day of the creature growling outside the door. It was a decent plan, considering the circumstances. It might have even worked. But then there was a guitar solo...

"Oh, for the love of...!" I exclaimed as my fingers groped for my phone. "What?"

"Chief, we are in trouble..." my assistant began before her voice was drowned out by a deafening roar as the Chimera tore off the faculty office's door.

"So am I!" I roared back while the creature leaped towards me. My mind vaguely noted that its face was deformed by a pair of huge, batlike nostrils, but then I teleported right to the classroom above me, so I had no time to marvel at its weirdness... and then my vision was filled with stars as I materialized high above the floor, fell on the edge of a desk, tumbled down from said desk, hit my shoulder on the way down on the backrest of a chair, and then hit the ground headfirst for good measure.

For the next couple of seconds, I glared at a random point on the ceiling with all my might, just to keep myself from slipping into unconsciousness. After the first wave of sudden exhaustion abated, I untangled myself from the furniture and rose on a pair of shaky feet. I must've given myself a concussion just now, my sluggish brain concluded after the world stopped spinning. I tried to shake my head, but it only made it worse.

It was only then that I remembered the phone. I looked around in the empty classroom dimly lit by only the small violet cracks on the walls. I was vaguely aware of the ruckus coming from downstairs. The Chimera was no doubt in the process of tearing apart the faculty office looking for me. Good riddance. It bought me some time at least.

I felt around the floor near where I landed, and after some fumbling, I found my phone under a desk two rows away. It took way more effort than expected, but I managed to reach it while crawling. For a moment I was a little disoriented by the brightness of the screen, though I noted with some satisfaction that there wasn't even a scratch on the glass. Then I remembered why I picked up the phone in the first place and raised it to my ear.

"Hello?"

"Are you okay?"

"No?" I answered. "But I'm safe for the time being. Why'd you call?"

There was a short pause in the conversation. It could've been caused by my assistant still being worried or them having a discussion on the other end of the line, which I couldn't hear over all the noise the monster was making downstairs.

Either way, in her worried voice, Judy finally spoke up.

"The fence posts are warded."

"What?"

"They are warded. That's what Amelia said."

"Can't you just break them down?"

"They are on the inside. We can't even touch them."

"Marvelous..."

"What should we do? Eleanor and Angeline are holding back the Faun at the door, but they cannot do that forever." There was a commotion in the background loud enough that I could hear it even through the ambient office-destruction noises and the abundant static noise, and Judy added, "Eleanor asks where you are."

"I don't know... Which classroom is right above the faculty office?"

"Two-C."

"Then that's where I am. Why?"

"She says you should stay there and she will get you."

"No, she won't," I stated defiantly. "Tell her to guard the entrance. I'll go up."

"But there is nothing to do up here. I told you the—"

"I heard it the first time. I'll figure something out by the time I get there. See you soon, and please don't call again unless absolutely necessary."

Saying so, I cut the line and hastily put my phone away. There was silence. That meant the Chimera already got bored with trashing the room below and was likely on the prowl again. I had to move quickly. If I was indeed at 2-C, it meant the science classroom was on the diametrically opposite end of the floor.

I checked myself for injuries. Aside from the bump on my head, I had a scratched thigh, a bruised shoulder, and a torn coat. I considered taking off the latter, as its flaps could restrict my movements in close quarters, but in the end, I left it on. As flimsy an excuse as it was for armour, it could potentially still offer some protection, and the padded shoulder had already proved itself useful during my tumbles.

I headed towards the door and opened it... only to jerk back as I found myself staring into three sets of glowing eyes framed by a large, fleshy snout and a pair of huge ears that made the face in front of me look decidedly batlike. My moment of surprise was then shattered by a close-proximity roar that rattled the bones under my skin.

"Motherfucker!" I roared in response and swung my fist in a mixture of surprise, terror, and exasperation.

I hit the Chimera right on the snout. The impact was soft and meaty and made a muffled *plop* that might've been silly under other circumstances, but I wasn't in the right mindset to appreciate the comical nuances of the situation. The creature let out a surprised yelp in response and shrank back from the strike like a dog hit by a rolled-up newspaper. But once the initial shock passed, its eyes opened wide and its guarded stance smoothly shifted into a lunge.

"Shit," I hissed with only a minor tinge of absolute, blood-curling panic as I tried to slam the door on the monster... only to realize I couldn't. "SHIT!"

Sliding doors. I knew they were going to be my death one day. I didn't foresee the circumstances, but still...

Thankfully, my legs were not fans of ironic echoes, as they propelled me to the side even as the Chimera barreled through the half-open door, tearing the flimsy construction off its rails like it was made of paper. It landed with a feline grace only mildly spoiled by the desks sent flying behind its back. It took a sharp, whistling sniff and snapped its head towards me.

That was the moment I was waiting for.

I raised the chair I bumped into during my dive and threw it at its ugly face. It raised one of its enormous paws and contemptuously swept the chair out of the air. Or at least I think that's what it did. I wasn't there to see.

I stood in the corridor just outside the classroom. My previous experiences with teleporting made me cautious enough to refrain from moving any farther than that in one go. I don't think anyone would blame me for it, considering my jumps through space somehow managed to hurt me more than the giant murderous monster I was evading. Speaking of which, the Chimera let out another window-shaking roar of frustration. While I was getting a little tired of its howls, this time I didn't mind, as it gave me a head start.

I rushed down the hallways at full speed. There was no point in trying to be stealthy anymore; I'd already seen how the creature modified itself to track me down, so all I could do was make sure I stayed one step ahead of it. I allowed myself a short teleport to the end of the hallway, which I could actually see, and I found myself practically in front of the science classroom. Since it had a lot of sensitive (not to mention expensive) equipment inside, this room was always locked. It was also a proper door instead of a sliding one, though thankfully it was only secured with a single cylinder lock. I could hear the Chimera overcoming its confusion and already out in the hallways, so I didn't hesitate to teleport right to the other side of the door.

Not a second later, there was a loud *thud* that shook the ground under my feet, followed by the groaning of metal. I fell forwards by surprise but managed to roll onto my feet and promptly faced the doorway, which immediately revealed the reason behind the impact. The Chimera rammed through the closed door and knocked it off its hinges, but its massive shoulders were wedged between the doorframes as its left paw clawed the air in a futile effort to reach me.

For a moment I almost felt safe. Then I remembered that the thing could shapeshift and that it could probably reduce the width of its shoulders to squeeze through, so I ran to the rows of large glass-doored cabinets at the back of the room. As I got there, I met with an unexpected setback: since the only light source in the Purple Zone came from the luminescent cracks and the violet moonlight, it was too dark for me to read the text on the containers. I switched tactics then, focusing on the warning labels instead of the names of the materials.

Once I got a handful of the more dangerous-looking stuff, I turned around and found that the Chimera had already squeezed most of its upper body through the doorway. I raised one of the glass bottles, the one I was fairly sure contained sulfuric acid, and lobbed it at the shrieking monstrosity with an angry growl of my own.

The Chimera saw it coming and swiped at the bottle. Unfortunately (for it) the container broke on impact and sprayed the creature with a loud splash. For a moment it didn't react, but then it began howling in pain and struggling even harder against the door.

I roared as well as I threw another bottle at it. This one had thicker plastic, so even though I hit it right in the middle of its face, it didn't break. "No matter! There is more where that came from!" I roared and continued to pelt the creature with whatever I could get my hands on, each impact accentuated by a new howl of pained rage.

Soon the air was filled with a dangerous mix of chemicals that made my eyes itch. That was supposed to be my cue to leave the area, but the Chimera thought otherwise. With one last heave, it cracked the doorframe and landed inside the classroom with a *thud* that once again shook the floor beneath my feet. It shivered for a moment, its motions clumsy and groggy like it was drunk. Even in the weak lighting (or maybe exactly because of it), I saw that two of its glowing eyes were closed on one side and the skin on its nose was, for lack of a better word, melting. Not literally, but kind of like a wax statue that was exposed to heat, drooping and elongating as gravity pulled on it. After a short while, it leveled its eyes on me and lunged.

I might've gotten a little light-headed from the exposure to the fumes, as I once again completely forgot that I could bloody teleport. Instead, I let out a roar as well and, in a moment of desperation, I grabbed hold of the cabinet next to me and pulled with all my might. The heavy wooden furniture rose onto two of its peg-legs, wobbled for a moment, and then it toppled right on top of the charging Chimera. Maybe it was the missing eyes, but it apparently didn't see it coming, as it let out a surprised squeak as its legs slipped out from under it.

Then something utterly ridiculous happened: the thing burst into flames. I had no idea why. Maybe it was a combination of the chemicals or the fumes or the burner fuel in the cabinet catching a spark, but all of a sudden the dark classroom was filled with warm orange light. Then came the scream. A positively heart-wrenching howl of pain that made me want to cover my ears.

The Chimera rolled out from under the cabinet, trailing flames where it went as it struggled, wiggled, and rolled on the ground while sending the desks and chairs flying in its wake. At last, it let out a final howl and, to my utter bafflement, it bolted right through the large window and into the night outside.

For a solid five seconds, I could only stare after it in a daze, but another whiff of the painful (and burning) air made me remember that I was supposed to get the hell out of there. So I did just that. I jumped over the puddle of burning chemicals in front of the door and out into the hallway, then I teleported down the corridor right next to the stairwell. It was only then that I started breathing again.

My eyes still itched and I sincerely hoped I didn't just poison myself in my mad haste to hurt the Chimera. Overall, I felt all right for the time being. Well, as right as I could be under the circumstances at least. Even the previous nausea from hitting my head was mostly gone.

Now that there was a moment of peace without a monster howling in my ears, I could hear a commotion from upstairs. It must've been the others, I figured.

"Right... I was supposed to go up there..." I murmured between heaving breaths. I absently got my phone out and dialed my assistant.

After only a single ring, she picked up with a surprised, "Chief?"

"I'm done with the Chimera and on my way to you. What's the situation up there?"

"You are *done* with the Chimera?"

"Yes. Why?"

There was a brief pause.

"Eleanor and Amelie insisted that you had no chance. How did you do it?"

"Doused it in acid.".

"I want to hear that story."

"Later. For now, we should meet up. You still haven't told me—"

At this point, several things were happening pretty much at the same time. First off, the unmistakable shattering of glass. Then I was spinning on my heel so hard I nearly strained my neck. Then there was cursing. Lots of colourful, visceral cursing that no ink would bear, so let's just say it was impulsive and leave it at that. It ended the following way:

"Just how bloody tough are you?" I yelled in exasperation as a familiar lump of muscle and burned skin squeezed its way through the window and landed on the floor with a hard *thud*.

The creature shook itself like a wet dog and, predictably, roared in response to my voice. There was something weird about the sound, like there were two roars of different pitches being overlaid. On closer look I quickly realized the reason. The Chimera's head only had two sets of eyes now. The last pair was softly glowing like a pair of dying embers on a brand-new head protruding from its left shoulder. It was smaller than the first, and as far as I could tell in the twilight of the hallway, it was covered in small black scales. If nothing else, it made the monster look more like its namesake.

Unfortunately, my observations were rudely interrupted at this point by the Chimera leaping at me with a low growl. I instinctively teleported behind it and dashed back, though the latter was fairly unnecessary, and I nearly slipped on the sharp remains of the shattered window. I caught myself and whirled around just in time to catch something striking at me diagonally from the left. I ducked and almost rolled by reflex, but I restrained the urge. I was still standing in the middle of a glass-covered corridor after all.

"What was that?" I uttered in disconcerting detachment from the situation. I squinted just as another lash had me jumping back a moment later. I did catch a glimpse of it, though, and once I added two and two together, it was easy to figure out what was trying to hit me.

The Chimera was still in the process of turning a one-eighty in the hallway. Its elongated body was getting in the way, so its front paws were climbing on the wall and raking deep furrows in the plaster in the process. More importantly, its tail was flailing around like... well, a flail, really. It also went through a form of metamorphosis. Gone was the thick lizard-like appendage, instead it was replaced by a comparatively thin tentacle-thing with a large, fleshy bulb the size of my head at its end. I wondered why that was. Maybe it helped the Chimera climb the wall to the second floor, like a monkey's tail? It looked prehensile enough. Or maybe it was a weapon?

"Chief, are you there?"

I was startled for a moment before I realized that the voice was coming from my phone. I forgot to cut the line, and I imagined my assistant was quite vexed with all the roaring coming from this end.

"Yeah, I'm fine," I told her just as the Chimera finished turning around... so I teleported behind it and continued, "It seems like I haven't finished yet, after all."

I ended my sentence in a tired growl and glared at the creature. Just how was I supposed to get rid of this thing? Should I get down to the basement after all? But that would take time. I'd already wasted too much time on this thing. Maybe I could lure it back into the science classroom. I could maybe barricade it inside and let the fire and the chemicals do it in, but it might just escape through the window like the first time, and...

And once again the blindingly obvious hit me in the face. The Chimera escaped through the window. It came back in through a window too. The windows were warded. That meant it came through the barrier. I could recall Angie saying that the barrier was keyed for Abyssals. Now, put all of those details together, and...

"Change of plans!" I all but shouted into my phone, no doubt startling my assistant. "I'm heading up! Make sure you get out of the way when you hear me coming!"

"Chief, I might not have stressed it enough before, but the exit is swarming with angry goat-men."

"Let me worry about that. Also, tell the class rep to summon her golem thingie. Make it big. I need it to throw something for me."

I didn't wait for affirmation, as the Chimera managed to turn around way faster this time and was already preparing to run me down. I looked the creature in the eye (or at least one set of eyes) and shouted, "Come on, you oversized horror-movie reject! Catch me if you can!"

I had no idea if it could understand me, or if it was even sentient to begin with, but the Chimera let out a defiant growl all the same and lunged at me. Of course, by then I wasn't there. In fact, I was running up the stairs with all my might, three steps at a time. Even so, the Chimera was right on my heel, so I abused the hell out of my mobility advantage and teleported away whenever it got close to filleting me. Each move played havoc with my stomach, but it was still the lesser of two evils.

I reached the third floor in record time, and from there I could already see the Faun ineffectually crowding in front of the door leading to the roof, seven or eight of them packed on the stairs like sardines in a box. They were big, though not as big as Brang or the Chimera, and they had the same kind of goat-ish appearance save for one of them. He looked more wolflike than anything, and he was one of the first that noticed my charge up the stairs. He let out a barking growl that roughly translated to "[Attention!]" and a couple of the goat-heads turned towards me. All their faces turned slack when they noticed the Chimera charging behind me.

"[Out of my way, you miserable nincompoops!]" I roared in Faunish, and the unusual sight combined with the command in their own language must've triggered something, as they stumbled all over themselves to comply, even forcing two of their numbers over the stairwell handrails. This opened a gap that was just wide enough for me to slip through, and while normally I would've considered entering into the arm's reach of half a dozen angry human-animal hybrids built like brick houses a bad idea, the angry double-howl behind me reminded me that it was still the better alternative.

I held my head low and dashed through the opening at full speed. I could hear the Faun behind me getting trampled or worse by the Chimera, but by then I was through the door and facing a very surprised pair of blue eyes. The princess blinked at me as I threw my arms open, embraced her, and pulled her onto the ground into a sideways roll just as the monster behind me burst through the narrow doorway and leaped over us, sending the door and a couple of bricks flying as it broke through.

It landed with a screech as its claws found purchase on the concrete and it quivered briefly, disoriented after the impact.

I jumped to my feet, leaving the still shocked princess on the ground, and scanned the rooftop. Judy was standing near the fence with the phone still in her hand. Angie was a few meters to my left aiming her bow at the creature with an uncertain look in her eyes. Finally, I found the class rep, too. She was crouching by the wrecked roof access, her hat missing and in the process of rubbing something out of her eyes. More importantly, though, there was something big and made of stone missing from her side.

"Where's the golem?" I frantically yelled.

She only looked at me blankly for a second. Then the light of under-standing returned to her eyes, and she said, "I... I was just summoning it when you got here. I think I hit my head when—"

"Sorry about that," I interrupted, "but we need it ASAP. I'm going to get the attention of the Chimera and lure it to the edge of the roof. I want you to use your golem to break the fence with it."

"But... how?" the class rep said as she rose to her feet in a mild daze.

"Ram it, grab it, and throw it—I don't care, just do it quickly!" In the meantime, the princess had also gotten up, so I quickly said to her, "Keep the Fauns out just a little longer if you can," and then turned around and dashed after the monster I was trying to run away from all this time.

While we were talking, Angie kept the creature busy with some stra-tegically placed arrows. They only seemed to annoy it, but that was more than enough for now. I circled the flailing Chimera and came to a stop by the Celestial girl's side.

"Good job," I told her with a smile she weakly returned. "We need to lure it towards the fence. Can you help?"

"Sure," she said after firing another arrow just as the Chimera was about to find its footing and charge us. I'm not going to lie, her nonchalance was kind of cool. "What do you want me to do?"

"I need you to keep hitting it from afar while I keep it busy. Try to pin it when it's swiping at me to keep it off-balance."

"I can do that."

"Good." I nodded and turned to my assistant still standing by the fence. "Judy, get to the class rep! See if you can help with anything. If you can't, lie low!"

"Affirmative," she answered and then scampered away.

With that last obstacle out of the way, I turned to the Chimera with a bold grin and yelled, "Hey! Over here, you oversized mutt!"

I must stress again that I had absolutely no idea whether the creature could even understand human speech. It did seem to find my voice annoying, though (or maybe it just got reminded of all the pain I'd caused it), and both of its heads turned towards me at once. I waved my hands just to make sure I got its full attention.

A second later, it bounded at me and I deftly rolled out of the way, making sure I was moving towards the fence facing the track field.

"Come on, you have to do better than that!" I yelled again as I picked up a piece of broken brick and threw it at the creature's head. *Thunk*. It staggered, then roared at me and got ready for another charge.

While my inexplicable dodging instincts took care of most of the fight, if you could even call it that, I had ample time to take a better look at the Chimera under the light of the violet moon in the sky. I was too busy being terrified of it before to notice, but my little jaunt at the science classroom must've hurt it more than I first thought. Its muscles were noticeably less bulky, probably due to the biomass being redirected to fix its injuries, and two of its eyes were hidden under a flap of melted flesh. Not only that, it didn't bother to regrow its burned and melted skin, leaving large patches of its neck and arms covered in a thin layer of dark mucus with the muscles clearly outlined underneath. If this was a normal animal, I would've been shocked it was still alive. Since it wasn't, I could already see it healing. I was sure that in a couple of minutes, it was going to be back in shape again. We had to end it before that happened.

"Class rep!" I yelled during a slightly less frantic moment when the creature was distracted by an arrow to the knee. "We could sure use a golem right about now!"

"I'm working on it!" she yelled back. I noted in relief that her voice was no longer shaky. My relief then quickly turned to alarm as I looked back and saw Angie flying over the Chimera with her bow drawn.

"Don't get so close!" I yelled frantically, but it was already too late. The Chimera's long tail lashed out and the bulb at the end hit her on the hip, throwing her careening to the ground. She landed gracelessly on her butt and rolled, which probably lessened the impact a bit. Either way, it must have hurt. Not only that, but the Chimera was already about to pounce at her prone form.

"Oh no, you don't!" I yelled from the top of my lungs as I sprinted at the creature and, to my own horror, jumped onto its back. After suppressing a silent *Why do I keep doing this?* I grabbed hold of the spear still protruding from the thing's back and twisted it with all my might. The Chimera let out an ear-piercing shriek and tried to shake me off, but its front legs couldn't reach me, and its wriggling only made the spear in its back mess around its insides even more.

Then it stopped. For a moment I thought it realized it wouldn't get me off that way and was about to roll on its back and crush me. Instead, it wobbled. Then it let out a surprised whine, and as I peeked down, I found a sight for sore eyes.

"Finally!" I yelled as the dark-grey stone familiar raised the creature—with me on its back—into the air, as easy as a weightlifter hoisting a barbell.

"Leo! Get off!" Ammy yelled while frantically waving a staff she summoned out of thin air.

"Don't worry about me! Just throw this thing!"

She didn't hesitate for long before she forcefully pointed her staff at the fence. The golem underneath us let out a low rumbling sound and heaved the Chimera. I figured that was my cue to jump, so I let go of the spear and kicked off the creature's back, just as the golem tossed it in the opposite direction. Because of that, my footing was bad and I spun as I fell, giving me a prime view of the lump of charred flesh hitting the fence.

There was a cacophony of sounds, the beast's roar mixing with the golem's rumbling and the shriek of a twisting, bending fencepost. All of that was promptly overpowered by a loud crackle reminiscent of distant thunder as the barrier's wards fell apart and the field popped like a giant, murderous soap bubble.

I was about to loose a triumphant "Wooo-hoo!" at the sight of the Chimera crashing through and plummeting to the ground below like a rag doll... but it quickly turned into a loud **"FUCK!"** as I felt a powerful pull on my left leg and found myself looking at the ruined fence from the wrong side.

Time, as it tended to do lately, slowed to a crawl as my brain tried to make sense of the situation. I concluded, with a defeatist's detachment, that I was plummeting to my doom. To my own surprise, I found that sad fact unable to dampen my curiosity. Why was I falling from the roof? I glanced at my leg and it took me an infinitely long moment to recognize the fleshy bulb clamped down on it. No one could've blamed me, as at this point it had a glowing eye and a mouth on it. A mouth that was biting down on my leg.

Right. Chimeras were supposed to have a snake for a tail, I mused as my body tumbled towards the cold, hard ground. I supposed this was the time when my life would've flashed before my eyes, but considering I couldn't remember anything past the last two months, it would've been a very short movie. Instead, the Chimera came into view, sprawled out and most of its limbs bent in unnatural angles, its snake-head still spitefully clamped onto my leg. It made me a little pissed off, to be honest.

Here I was, trying to rescue my friends, and this bloody shape-shifting thing that had nothing to do with me until now just kept getting in my way. It made me angry. Angry enough to shake me out of my stupor. Angry enough to turn me totally irrational as I decided to teleport one more time. Not towards the roof. Not towards the building. Not even towards the ground, but right at the Chimera so that I could punch him right in its huge, smug monster-dog-crocodile-bat-gorilla face.

As I said, irrational.

After the now-familiar moment of nauseous twist of space, I suddenly found myself on top of the creature again. Maybe it was the smell of charred meat or the sudden return of the plummeting feeling, but my higher brain functions caught hold of the reins again, and after a brief moment of *What the hell am I doing?!* I grabbed the first thing in sight, which happened to be the spear-shaft inexplicably still sticking out of the Chimera's back. I pulled myself closer to the creature and braced against the centrifugal force created by the two of us spinning through the air.

One revolution. Two revolutions. By the third revolution, I had my leg set against the Chimera's back. I was sure I would throw up again by the fourth revolution. I never got around to finding out, as the world momentarily got dyed in black and the colours of the rainbow at the same time as the G-forces on impact threatened to squeeze my lungs into my abdomen.

Surprisingly enough, I was still thinking at this point. That was a good sign, my recovering brain surmised. That meant that I wasn't dead. Possibly broken beyond repair, but not dead. Silver linings!

I couldn't see anything, though. For a long instant, I was afraid I'd gone blind, then I realized I just had my eyelids down. I carefully opened one eye, then the other. I was on the ground, standing—don't ask me how. My legs hurt like hell and my palms clasping the spear-shaft felt sore, but otherwise, I was surprisingly un-pulverized. I glanced down and I found that the Chimera was less fortunate, much to my relief. In fact, I was standing on its broken back, its body flattened like a clay figurine under my feet. Maybe it was some kind of defense mechanism? Either way, it probably saved my life.

I could feel the defiant smile creep onto my face again. Finally! The Chimera was out of the way, the barrier was down, the Fauns on the stairs were scattered... things seemed to be looking up for us.

And then there was a blinding white light in front of me.

My eyes stung as I looked at it, but I strained to do so anyway. It was huge, swirling, and...

"Shit, the gate…" I muttered and got ready to step off the back of the pulverized monstrosity. My legs froze a moment later as my eyes adjusted to the light and my brain noted how large the portal was. I squinted to see better and the realization slowly dawned on me. It wasn't that the portal was huge. It was an oval-shaped hole, only about four meters tall and two meters wide.

How did I know that? Well, I had a couple of handy measuring sticks close to it in the form of Snowy and company. Oh, and before I forget: I was only a couple of steps away from them.

"You…" came a low, burning hiss from the tallest of the three silhouettes I'd only begun to make out as my eyes adapted. For a moment I was frozen in place, unsure what to do. Then I remembered my mantra. I closed my eyes, took a deep breath, and when I opened them, I had already forced the previously withered daring smile onto my lips. The words *refuge in audacity* echoed in my ears.

"Hello there, Crowey. It's been a while."

CHAPTER 24

PART 1

How did the saying go? Out of the frying pan, into the fire? Times like this made me think we needed a more severe version of that. Like, *"Out of the burning airplane without a parachute and into the blast of a nuclear bomb."* The only problem with it was that, with my luck, I would end up in an even bigger mess afterward. Then I'd need an even more severe expression, and then another, and another, ad infinitum.

I took a sharp breath through my nostrils and tried to forget linguistic escalation issues and focus on the more tangible problem at hand. So, I was standing in the slowly dissolving remains of a shape-shifting monster in front of the portal leading to this universe's equivalent of the underworld. That was the neutral news.

As for the bad news... First off, I was separated from the girls. I was also face-to-face with Crowey, an Abyssal noble of considerable power whom I had already antagonized in the past without knowing a thing about him. What was new?

I quickly scanned the area around the gate, and to my sincere surprise, I only found three people there. Crowey, Snowy in her disturbingly skimpy succubus attire, and Josh. Oddly enough, Snowy was the one showing less skin out of the two of them, as my friend was only dressed in his underpants. Was that how he slept or was he taken after showering? Also, was it just me, or was the guy surprisingly ripped?

Not that it mattered. Also, I've got to insert another correction here: the briefs weren't the only thing on him, as both his arms and legs were tied up with thin, semi-transparent glowing chains. Some kind of spell, I surmised.

When he finally noticed me, he tried to yell something, but his mouth was also tied shut by a series of similar chains around his head and jaws, so I could only hear a series of muffled noises coming from him.

"I must say, I am surprised."

I blinked at the words and almost uttered a baffled *"What?"* before I regained my wits and swallowed it down before it left my mouth. Right, I was talking to Crowey, wasn't I? Time once again escaped me while I was analyzing my desperate situation, and while it subjectively felt like ages had passed since I'd landed on a cushion of goo-ified Chimera remains, it had only happened seconds before.

What was my plan again? Oh, right. I didn't actually have one, did I? I supposed that meant it was time to return to my fallback plan and continue playing charades. I forced a terribly amicable grin onto my face and looked Crowey right in the eye.

He stood at ease, his hands hidden in the pockets of his expensive grey suit and his eyes looking down on me with the distant haughtiness of nobility. Actually, that was the right word. All he needed was a lacquered walking staff and a top hat and he would have passed for a turn-of-the-century dandy in a period piece talking to a stable boy. I could've sworn he looked way more startled and openly hostile when I arrived, so I probably wasn't the only one playing mind-games.

Speaking of which, I wondered which angle would buy me the most time. Mock politeness? I was past that. Groveling? Fat chance. A display of confidence? ... Let's go with that.

"You are surprised?" I asked with a mincing smile as I tried to pull the spear out. It was stuck, and I didn't want him to see me struggle with it, so instead I leaned on it to maintain my laid-back image and told him, "Imagine how surprised I was when I learned that you sent your underling to deal with me instead of doing it yourself. I was quite disappointed."

"I see..." Crowey mused with an inscrutable expression. "So, sending the scout-general was insufficient." Suddenly his face twisted in a facsimile of a haughty smile. "I suppose I shouldn't be surprised."

"Well, duh." I shrugged and stepped off the Chimera's steadily melting remains. As I did so, there was a sudden stabbing pain in my left leg. I didn't dare to look, or even twitch, but I was pretty sure I'd at least sprained that ankle, if not outright dislocated it. I hid my pained gasp in a tired-sounding groan. Well, there went my plan for somberly pacing while delivering a filibuster to buy time. I shook my head and continued with, "He put up a good fight, but as the saying goes, you do not send a Faun to do an Abyssal's job."

The smile slowly evaporated from the sharply dressed man's face and got replaced with a scowl.

"It is the way of the Abyss to have our minions act in our stead. Don't presume to lecture me, cur."

"Really now? From where I am standing, all I can see is a bad boss sending his subordinate on a mission they had no chance in succeeding at, who's now trying to cover his own ass. In your case, I suppose that would also mean your face."

Crowey twitched.

"Are these crass insults all you have?"

"Depends. But do I really need anything else when faced with such incompetence?"

"Incompetence? You call this incompetence?" At this point, Crowey removed his gloved hands from his pockets and theatrically opened his arms. "I found the Herald of the Emperor. I drafted the plans for the impenetrable barrier surrounding this field, and I have opened a gate to the Abyss in the heart of the power of the Magi! You call *this* incompetent?"

"Yes, yes. Very impressive," I spoke with a mocking smile in the corner of my mouth. "Except for the part where it was your sister who found him, she made the barrier, and you only managed to open your gate because none of the Magi are home at the moment. If I were you, I wouldn't brag about it like that."

"What do you know? I timed my departure on the day of the Wingless One's Gathering on purpose! My plan was foolproof!"

"Was," I pointed out with a single finger raised. "It *was* foolproof until you sent your scout-general after me. Think about it. If you were content with just leaving me alone, then I would've never heard about your kidnapping plot and would have no reason to come here to ruin your plans." He didn't need to know I got wind of this situation from his sister, so I kept it out of my story. I still sent a knowing glance at the girl, then added, "In short, you ruined your own plans because your wounded pride just couldn't let you leave me alone. But don't worry about it. Please, keep monologuing to your heart's content about how great your plans are. You still have about... say... fifteen minutes before your portal closes."

I wasn't just taunting him, I was really hoping he'd continue talking. I also hoped that the girls were already on their way, and while I could always check with Far Sight, doing so was distracting, and Crowey could try to attack me at any moment. I also couldn't run, so I had my teleportation ability primed in case of an emergency, but considering how battered I was both physically and mentally, I wasn't entirely sure I could escape on my own even by using it. If only it had some long-range applications...

A long beat of silence stretched between us. I had a sneaking suspicion that Crowey had already realized that I was trying to buy time by taunting him, which was made more evident by the way he was scanning the perimeter of the portal. A few more nerve-wracking seconds later, and Crowey's lips stretched into a thin, wolfish smile, followed by a soft chuckle.

"I see... I see... You are right. I really shouldn't have sent a Faun to do an Abyssal's job."

The words sent a cold shiver down my spine. *I might have gone too far with the taunting*, I noted with the familiar detachment that at this point felt like a prelude of imminent danger, and I mentally screamed at my companions to drag their shapely behinds over to my side already. I focused all my attention on Crowey, waiting for his attack.

Contrary to my expectations, the guy slowly, deliberately slid his hands into his pockets again, his dark eyes still glaring at me with an intensity that would've made water boil faster. Then he tilted his head to the side and ordered, "Sister. Kill him."

I silently gulped as my eyes darted over to Snowy. Up until this moment, she was guarding the incapacitated Josh, but upon being called, she visibly shuddered and straightened her back. There was a flash of light coming off her neck and she took a tentative step forward. The second one was a bit steadier, and by the time she took the third, her gait became an exaggerated, hip-swinging strut. I wanted to roll my eyes at the display, but I didn't dare to take my eyes off her even for a split second. As she drew closer, a pair of long claws made of crystalline ice condensed out of thin air and attached themselves to her thin right forearm. They were about forty centimeters long and reminded me of a raptor's talons. Beautiful, and lethal.

"I'm sorry, darling," she whispered with a voice that was phasing in and out of her vamp persona. "I told you not to get involved. I told you to stay home." Her voice cracked and she repeated, "I'm sorry," in a near sob.

I had a feeling this was the moment when I was supposed to say something meaningful. Something about it not being her fault, or that she didn't have to do this, or something even sappier. I never got the chance.

"Uwooooooh!"

With that strange battle cry, a dark shape dashed in from the left and tackled Snowy off her feet. She let out a surprised yelp, followed by a similarly surprised grunt coming from Crowey as a series of glowing arrows impacted on a honeycomb-patterned purple barrier around him. He still stumbled back, more from the suddenness of the attack than from the impacts, and hastily threw out his hands. The barrier flared brightly, its surface covered in an intricate series of magic circles. It was weird looking at it. I'd seen magic before as tendrils and an indistinct glow, but this was the first time I saw something this complex.

Then the light faded once again as a large silhouette I vaguely recognized as the class rep's golem rushed in and tackled him, pushing him away even as the barrier held the stone familiar from actually touching him. In the meantime, Snowy kicked off her assailant and the princess landed on her back right beside me. A moment later she was on her feet again, tail whipping and eyes glinting dangerously in the twilight.

It was at this point that my brain caught up with the situation. I pointed and yelled, "Angie! Get Josh while they're incapacitated!"

"On it!" came a strained voice from above. I glanced up and saw a pair of glowing wings in the darkness descending upon Josh, who was standing rigid as if he were tied to a pole. Angie swooped down like a giant bird of prey. The wings covered him, and then with a loud *whoosh*, they both rose into the air. Their not-so-majestic flight lasted but briefly, as they rapidly lost altitude and the two of them more-or-less crashed into the ground a few meters behind me.

"Joshua! Angie!" The panicked voice of the class rep reassured me that she was nearby as well, though I still couldn't see her. Bonfire-blindness, I surmised. We were all standing around the portal long enough for our eyes to adjust to it, and thus be blind to the area outside its glow. The girls used it to their advantage, positioning themselves around us for an ambush. Clever. I made a mental note to give a high-five to whoever came up with that tactic.

But back to the rapidly unfolding events: I tried to take a step towards the sprawled-out Celestial girl and my still tied-up friend, but I stumbled and might've fallen down if my assistant hadn't rushed to my side and supported me with her shoulder. Then the princess grabbed hold of my other arm and pulled me up.

"Are you all right?" Judy asked with the kind of frantic worry I would've never expected to hear in her voice.

"I'm fine, it's just my—" I glanced down at my unruly leg and the sight had the words trapped in my throat. It wasn't sprained as I thought; my jeans from the knee down were covered in a thick black liquid that I recognized as coagulating blood.

Oh right, I realized, alarmed. *I was bitten by the Chimera's tail.*

Maybe I didn't feel it because of some kind of venom? Its tail was supposed to be a snake, wasn't it? Questions and observations whirled in my head, but I pushed them all aside for the time being and only uttered a flat "Huh."

"What?" Elly asked with a hint of anxiety in her voice as she followed my gaze and promptly paled.

"Nothing," I stressed with a smile I hoped was at least a little reassuring as I put some weight on my feet again, ignoring the pain. "We should check on Josh before—"

Right at this moment, my insides were shaken by a deafening rumble, disorienting me for a moment. When I got my bearings again, I figured that the new layer of gravel covering the ground in front of the portal meant that the golem couldn't hold back Crowey for too long.

Speaking of the man, everyone's favourite Abyssal asshole let out a frustrated groan and bellowed, "That's enough! Where are the minions?" He looked around, but there was no one else coming. At last, his eyes found me and, with a continued flair for the dramatic, the guy raised a hand and pointed at me with all fingers spread. "Enough with the games! Sister, kill them all!"

From the corner of my eyes, I saw another flare of magical light, but as I wanted to glance over, the hairs on the back of my neck abruptly stood on end. It was the familiar feeling of incoming danger, and my body was instinctively trying to get out of the way... except I couldn't, as both the princess and Judy were holding on to me.

With the sense of mortal danger growing even greater by the moment, a corner of my mind screamed at me to drop onto the ground lest I die... but an even louder part reminded me that I wasn't alone, and while I could let go of the two girls, it would put them into harm's way instead. So I did something stupid. Truly shocking, I know.

Instead of getting out of the way, I went right against whatever instinct told my body to move and did the exact opposite, moving towards danger instead of away from it. Mind you, I still couldn't see the danger we were talking about, but that didn't stop me from acting.

Then there was a soft thud that shook my entire body, followed by a searing pain that raced through my nerves so hard it felt like my whole world was ablaze for a moment. Then there was only white, and nothing else.

PART 2

Two seconds. That's how long I was unconscious after receiving an ice-spike in my abdomen. It punctured my skin, the muscles underneath, passed through my abdominal wall, and wedged between the curves of my small intestines, its sharp end poking out through my back. I grunted with amusement as I noted that it passed through me without hitting any vital organs or veins. I don't know why I found that amusing. It wasn't. It hurt like hell.

I put my irrational thoughts aside and looked around. Time was once again running in slow motion. How peculiar, I thought. I could see the princess roaring at my side as she faced off against Snowy. I could see the young Abyssal girl stare at me with wide-open eyes, the corners of her mouth slowly trembling. I saw my dear assistant's wild eyes as she looked at the spear of ice sticking out of my side with abject horror. I saw all of them. They felt so close yet so far away. I feared that if I reached out and touched them, they would dissolve like mirages in the summer air.

I distantly noted how my thought patterns felt weird. Weirder than usual, at any rate. Was that because I was dying? Was I dying? I didn't know. It didn't feel like I was about to die, but then again, I had a large piece of glassy ice stuck in my stomach, as thick as my index and middle fingers put together. People tended to die from things like that.

I could feel my mouth twist in a sardonic smile. I figured this was the moment when I had to reflect on my past. Was I supposed to do that? It felt natural, so I thought I might as well give it a shot.

So, where to begin? Mistakes were made. I do not mean this whole "being skewered" business. That was a good thing. Well, for a certain measure of good. If I hadn't gotten in its way, it would have hit Judy in the chest instead, and if I'd have dragged her out of the way, it would have hit Josh on the ground behind us. I didn't know how I actually knew this, but I sounded convincing, so I decided to believe my words.

So yeah, getting impaled was the good choice I made. Everything else, though? Just one giant, unmitigated chain of disasters barely avoided by the skin of my teeth.

Why does hindsight always make me feel so dumb?

I glanced around again to take my mind off the steadily intensifying self-loathing when I noticed something peculiar. Snowy's choker, the one I'd often noted, was shining. That light was strangely familiar. I sifted through my memories and made the connection: it was the same kind of light I'd seen just before the attack that led to my currently punctured state. It was easy to recognize. It wasn't the colour per se, it was more like a... texture, for lack of a better word. I had seen it another time, when Snowy first tried to attack me. What common denominator united those two situations?

She was ordered to do so by her brother.

I squinted to take a better look, and my vision blurred before coming back into focus. It was only for a moment, but I felt like I glimpsed the true form of the light surrounding Snowy's neck. It was... a spell? Magic? I didn't know the right word for it. "Enchantment" would do for the time being. The glimpse I saw told me a lot of things about it. It looked a bit like programming code, but at the same time not. It was more... organic. It wasn't binary or based on mathematics, more like... I don't know. I had nothing else to compare it to but itself.

What was it then? I followed its trigger, which was represented by a thin, almost invisible string attached to the angrily shouting black-haired man on the side. I stared at him, and the longer I did so, the more I could feel anger building up inside my chest. It was a black, sticky kind of anger, pure unadulterated loathing so strong it made me feel physically ill.

Right, I thought. I can't die yet. Someone has to take care of this mess and get rid of this prick.

So I took a deep breath, my chest no longer restrained by the lazy ebb of time, gritted my teeth, and focused all my will into a single exhalation.

PART 3

There was a moment of nausea when I came to my senses as time resumed its normal flow. I found myself supported by Judy, her still horrified face dressed in a crimson light. The source of said light was coming from the princess, or rather the growing ball of eldritch power swirling in front of her mouth.

I only had a split second to act. I ignored the searing pain and my assistant's distant protests as I lurched forwards to stand tall on my feet. I drew in a heavy breath between clenched teeth and let it all out in a bellow that shook my insides.

"Elly!"

The princess stumbled when she heard my voice and for a moment the ball of power was about to blink out of existence, so I hastily continued, "Don't stop! Aim for the asshole! He's the one in control!"

Credit where credit's due, the princess didn't as much as bat an eye at my order. There were no whats or whys—she just grunted, faced the Abyssal lord, and let out a booming roar that had no business coming out of a teenage girl's throat. Even though it happened in an instant, I swear I caught a glimpse of Crowey's face slackening in shock before he raised both his hands and the magical barrier sprang to life once again.

The beam of crimson light streaming forth from the princess's attack hit Crowey's barriers like a jet of water blasting a rock, spraying ground-melting droplets of dragonfire around the area with dangerous abandon. It was pretty to look at, but it didn't penetrate, and that was a problem.

"Don't hold back!" I shouted as loud as I could to overcome the sound of the princess's wave motion dragon breath. "I know you can do it! Roar!"

I had no idea whether she could even hear me, but the lion-esque rumble accompanying the attack dropped an octave and the stream of power abruptly changed colour, from an angry crimson to a brilliant golden light so bright and intense it hurt my eyes. I looked anyways, without blinking. I wanted to see it, and my expectations were met with flying colours.

The moment the golden stream hit Crowey's barrier, it shattered like an egg under a hammer. There was a second layer, but it didn't fare any better. The princess's dragon fire peeled layer after layer like a jackhammer peeling an onion, and even though I couldn't hear it over the deafening noise, I was sure the man was howling in anguish. The whole process only lasted a second at best until the last vestige of the purple light around Crowey exploded with a pitiful pop, and a torrent of raw magical force washed over him, sending his prone body flying through the air like a rag doll engulfed in a flaming tornado. Just like that, he disappeared from sight as he got outside of the glow of the portal.

It only lasted a few seconds, but I was sure I'd just witnessed something I'd remember for the rest of my life. I was about to praise the draconic girl at my side, but the alarm bells in my head started ringing the moment I laid my eyes on her.

"Judy, grab Elly."

"But you—"

"Don't argue," I stated forcefully. "Prop her up, quick."

My assistant might've been rattled by the events, but she was as efficient as ever. She got around me and grabbed hold of the heaving girl's shoulders. It was just in time, as the princess's trembling legs gave out and she nearly dragged both of them to the ground. Thanks to Judy's support, they remained standing, albeit barely.

"Are you all right?" I asked.

The princess looked up. Her brows tensed in pain and blood trickled from the corner of her mouth, but she forced a smile onto her face.

"Heh... I must look really bad if the guy with the icicle in his stomach is worried about me."

Her voice was hoarse, but considering that she had the energy to sass me, I figured she was fine. Her words, however, reminded me of another problem. I glanced down and found that the ice spear was still snugly lodged inside my abdomen. Curiously enough, it didn't really hurt. Or rather there was an unpleasant throbbing sensation in my stomach where I could see it sticking out of me, and when I looked down, I could see that I was standing in a pool of dark liquid that I figured had to be blood, but it didn't really *hurt*. I wasn't sure whether to be relieved or worried about it, especially since my head felt surprisingly clear despite the apparent blood loss. Or maybe *because* of the blood loss? Either way, I had to do something about it before Crowey got back up.

I looked over my shoulder and quickly found the rest of the group. Josh was still lying on the ground with his limbs bound by glowing chains, his eyes frantically darting between the two girls leaning over him. They both seemed to be in the process of spell-casting, and while I recognized that getting Josh out of his bondage was high-priority, delaying it a little for my own continued survival seemed like a fair trade.

"Angie, come over here for a second!"

The Celestial looked up from Josh, and her eyes widened in shock. A moment later she pretty much scampered over to my side and fell onto her knees before me.

"Oh no... No-no-no-no-no..." She reached out towards the ice spike with trembling fingers but pulled her hand away before they got close, like she was touching a hot stove. "I... I thought she missed! I didn't see!"

"Angie, look at me." I waited for her to raise her face and looked her in the eye before I continued. "I need you to calm down. Panicking won't help."

For a second, she struggled with her nerves. She forcefully calmed her breathing and gave me a slight nod.

"All right. You can use healing magic. Do you have anything potent enough to fix this?"

"I... I don't know. I never healed a wound like that, only scratches and sprains."

"Could you try? Just patch me up enough so I can move around. I don't care about scarring, just stop the bleeding."

"I can try, but... if I mess up, you could die."

"Same goes if you don't try. I'll take my chances."

Angie's face twisted in anguish like she was the one with perforated guts.

"A-all right... First, we have to remove the object. Slowly. Then..."

"NOOOOOOOOO!!!"

All of us shuddered at the sudden wail of anguish and everyone stared at the Abyssal girl on the ground. I mentally kicked myself in the head for forgetting about her even for a second, and the sight made it even worse. She sat on the ground like a marionette with its strings cut and wailed with a vacant look in her eyes.

And that's when it started.

First, it was just a light breeze, then a squall, then all of a sudden, we were in the middle of a snowstorm. It all happened so fast my body didn't even register the temperature drop until a few seconds later. I shuddered as the cold wind cut to my bones.

I didn't pay it much heed, though, as my attention was firmly held by the veritable geyser of light emanating from the girl. Even with my nonexistent magical knowledge, I could tell that wasn't normal.

"What the hell is happening?" I yelled over my shoulder to the person I hoped knew the answer.

"She's..." Ammy began to answer, but then she stopped to shield Josh from the worst of the sudden blizzard before she continued. "She is burning her soul!"

"I'm not an expert, but that sounds bad!" I yelled over the howling wind.

"If she continues, she is going to die!" she answered, and though I couldn't hear it properly, I was fairly certain she muttered, "And so are we."

"Okay, Angie, change of plans. Just make sure I don't bleed out for the time being."

The Celestial girl gave me a huge nod, then began frantically humming something that sounded like a jazz tune with her bloodstained hands covering my wound. I raised a single brow at the sight.

So that's what one's tissues knitting back together felt like? Painful and yet tickly, like a thousand fire ants laying down brickwork in your guts. I let the Celestial girl do her job and focused my attention on the rest. The princess was out of commission for the moment, too exhausted to move, and Judy had her hands full keeping her upright. The class rep was still frantically trying to shield Josh, who lay motionless on the ground. As for Snowy, she was in the process of being surrounded by pillars of jagged ice. I figured that in a minute she would be completely engulfed. In other words, another ticking clock. Just what I needed.

I momentarily considered trying to teleport over to her side, but considering how battered I was, getting closer to the epicenter of an arctic blizzard was probably a bad idea. I had to get Snowy out of there, but everyone was exhausted, injured, or otherwise down for the count. Well, everyone save for one person...

It didn't take long to make up my mind. Not that I had time for doubts to begin with. Angie just finished humming a long, jazzy tune, and she was just about to start one another one when I grabbed her bloodied hand.

"Wait, I'm not done!" Angie cried in a voice close to sobbing, but I held on to her hand firmly and raised her to her feet. "We need to get the ice out!"

"Will I die in the next five minutes if you leave it in?" I asked, and after a long moment of hesitation, she shook her head. "Then we need to do something about this damn blizzard first, because if we don't, we are *all* going to die. I need you to get out your bow now."

"But..."

"Angie, we don't have time. I want you to shoot the ice around Snowy. You should be able to break it. Stop it from closing in on her or we will never get her out of there."

"But she stabbed you..."

"She was forced to stab me. I'll explain later." She still looked hesitant, and we had no time to waste, so I dusted off my most severe glare and looked her in the eye. "We came here to rescue both Josh *and* her, and we are not leaving until we have both of them back. That is the whole reason we are in this mess, and there's no time for second-guessing. If I tell you to shoot something, I expect you to shoot it. No questions asked. Are we clear?"

I don't know which part of my words was the trigger, but all of a sudden there was a defiant light in Angie's eyes, and she nodded with surprising firmness.

"Yes... You are right. Understood!" Her bow sprang out of her bracelet, and she fired an arrow more brilliant than anything she'd ever released before. It hit an ice pillar and not only broke it, but evaporated its top half outright. "I can do this!"

"Yes you can," I encouraged her with a pat on the back that left a bloody handprint on her white dress. I hoped she wouldn't mind it later.

With that said, I turned to Judy and the princess and beckoned for them to follow me over to the rest of the group. Time was of the essence, so I shuffled as quickly as I could, and we all arrived at Josh's side at the same time.

I pointed at the class rep. "The Faun should get down at any moment now. I want you to summon your golem again and have it sit on the exit. Be quick about it—Snowy's bastard brother is still on the loose."

"Understood."

I thought she might protest, but the class rep nodded and dashed towards the school building. I figured she was either used to obeying orders if they were given forcefully enough, or she understood just how dire the situation was and hoped I knew what I was doing. So did I, but she didn't need to know that.

Next, I turned my attention to the guy lying on the ground making simultaneously outraged and horrified noises through a jaw clenched shut by a set of ethereal chains. I started by getting rid of those. Under the princess's close scrutiny, I stuck two bloody fingers under the chain running down his cheek, curled them, and tugged sharply. Just as they had with Angie's tendrils of misty light, my fingers cut through the ethereal restraints, and they snapped like old rubber bands. It must've been one single spell that kept my friend restrained, as the moment the chain on his face broke, the rest slacked as well. Then all of it burst into heatless blue flames that burned away the magical bonds.

Josh gasped aloud as the pressure on his body abated. His eyes darted back and forth between the three of us, panicked, before he sat up and hugged his knees.

"What's going on!? Lili is a demon! Angie has wings! Elly has horns! What... what the actual fuck is going on?"

While his confusion was completely understandable, I had no time for theatrics, so I promptly slapped him in the face, trailing another bloodstain on his cheek.

"Ow! Wha-what the fuck, man!"

"Have you calmed down?"

He probably thought that I'd slap him again if he answered otherwise, so my friend gave me a curt nod.

"Good. Stay calm, do exactly as I say, and with some luck, we might all live long enough to reminisce about just how crazy this night was. Got it? Good."

This time I turned to the girls at my side. I opened my mouth, but hesitated. I was about to ask something that would be outrageous under other circumstances. Then another despairing wail followed by the crack of breaking ice reminded me of that ticking clock, so I shook off any uncertainty and said, "Princess, I need you to kiss Josh."

Normally at this point, there would have been a beat of silence, but I was over it.

"Yes, I am serious."

"B-b-but... W-w-what? Why?" the draconic girl protested with a face that was redder than her scales. "This is not the time to—!"

"Listen, guys. In case you haven't noticed, I have a chunk of ice sticking out of my stomach, so I'm not going to say this more than once: I need you to exchange fluids so that Josh can power up and save Snowy before she dies," I explained as calmly yet forcefully as I could under the circumstances.

"Die?" The word shook Joshua harder than my previous slap and he looked at me slack-jawed. "But... she was the one who—"

"She was forced to do that by her asshole brother. She is under some kind of mind-control or slave contract or what have you. She was the one who called me for help."

"She was...?" Josh muttered between two confused blinks.

"Yes. Listen, we need to get her choker off her neck. I don't know the details, but we need to get it off her and calm her down before she kills herself, and you guys fussing over a silly little kiss is not helping!"

That made them shut up. They glanced at each other awkwardly for a moment, yet neither of them made a move.

"Do we... really have to kiss right now?"

It was at this point that my assistant rolled her eyes and gently tapped my shoulder like she thought I would fall over if she poked me too hard.

"Chief, you said they need to 'exchange' bodily fluids, right?"

"Yeah," I answered in exasperation. "If I'm right, doing so would trigger some kind of transformation, and then Josh should be—"

Without waiting for me to finish, Judy extended a finger, wiped off some of the previously mentioned trickle of blood on the corner of the princess's mouth, and then promptly stuck the same finger into Josh's still open hanging mouth.

She looked at me with an inscrutable expression, and all I could do was shrug my shoulder and say, "Yeah, maybe that could work too—"

As soon as the last word left my mouth, I was nearly blinded by a sharp red light coming from right in front of me. I shielded my eyes with my forearm, and even though I could not see what was happening, Josh's alarmed grunts and the weird popping and cracking sounds confirmed that it had indeed worked.

When the light subsided and I could lower my hand, I could barely recognize my already standing friend. Considering the panic in his eyes as he looked at his own hands, he had a hard time as well. His body was now covered in rough, pearly white scales with platelike protrusions on his forearms and shins. His fingers and toes ended in sharp, slightly curved claws and he had the characteristically curved horns and long lizard tail of a Draconian.

"H-how? What did you do to me?" he yelled in a weirdly echoing voice while the princess mouthed a silent *How?*

I ignored them both as I stood up as well and pointed at the source of the still raging blizzard behind me.

"Listen, Josh, I need you to—"

"NO!" he roared, clawing at his own forearms. "I don't want to do this! I want out! I can't do this!"

I glared at the still panicking guy for a long second, then stood up, reached out, grabbed hold of his horn, and roughly yanked on it with all my remaining might. Josh nearly fell over with a surprised yelp, but I held on to his shiny new horn and kept him upright. I pointed behind me again and forced him to follow my finger. As if just to accentuate my point, Snowy let out another wail.

"Do you hear that? That is Snowy! She is suffering because you cannot stop feeling sorry for yourself for one goddamn minute and help her!"

"But... but I can't! I can't!"

"Yes, you can!" I let out a groan and let go of him. "Listen, Josh, I know this is crazy and you don't understand what's going on. I get. It is perfectly fine to be scared and confused. However, there is someone in there who needs your help! I can't help her. The girls can't help her. Only you can help her. You are the hero of this story—start acting like one!"

"I..."

I let go of his horn and Josh staggered back. His eyes were unsure and his movements sluggish, but he was no longer panicking. There was another wail and he shuddered and closed his eyes, and when he opened them again, there was no hint of hesitation in them.

"I get it. What do you want me to do?"

Uhh... Right, just what exactly did I want him to do? A moment ago, I was sure I had a plan, a logical one, but after being sidetracked, I could no longer recall it. I grasped for the bits and pieces swirling in my mind and decided to wing it.

"You... We are all down for the count. You are the only one who can get close to Snowy without freezing to death. Try to calm her down and then get the choker off her. It's what her brother uses to control her." I almost added an uncertain *I think* at the end of the sentence, but I swallowed it down. I had to maintain the illusion that I was still in control. Wait, was I ever in control? I couldn't decide. It was hard to focus and my head felt heavy like it was made of lead. Maybe it had something to do with the blood loss.

"I'll try." Josh nodded.

"Do or do not, insert famous Yoda line here, whatever... Just get going already," I muttered while exerting extra effort to keep my head upright.

"Right," my friend answered with a thin smile before he flexed his muscles.

By the way, I think I should mention that while his draconic form was a sight to behold, the picture was somewhat ruined by the fact he was still only wearing his tighty-whities.

He shook himself and dashed past both us and Angie towards the ever-growing fortress of ice pillars surrounding Snowy. He didn't slow down, but instead he threw himself at the ice and began tearing the obstacles apart with his new claws like he was born with them. A part of me wondered if the transformation bestowed basic combat abilities on the guy as well, but a rush of nausea made me halt that line of thought. I raised my hand in the air.

"Medic!"

There was a moment of pause before a voice rang out saying, "Ah, that's me!" and Angie dashed over to us.

"I think the ice melted a little, and I'm losing blood," I told her while gesturing towards my abdomen.

"Okay, this time we really need to get it out of you. First, lay down, and then..." Angie spoke uncertainly as she kneeled down beside me, then she hesitated for a moment before asking, "By the way, was that Josh just now?"

"Yeah. Long story."

She didn't respond, and instead she began humming and waving one hand around my stomach, with her other hand gingerly clasped around the icicle in me.

This time the pain didn't bounce off me; it struck my very core like an arrow and made me shudder as my vision was swallowed up by the white-hot agony. I let out a soft grunt while my brain frantically looked for something to take my mind off the sensation of my flesh knitting, and it quickly found an outlet through my Far Sight. It triggered without my consent, and for the next couple of moments, I saw flashes of images that stayed too short for my brain to register. After a while, it settled on one specific image that held my attention.

It was Snowy. Her exposed skin was turning blue inside the ring of ice monoliths surrounding her... or was it just the white light of the portal filtering through the ice playing tricks with my eyes? It didn't matter. She wasn't crying anymore but only because her tears were already frozen onto her face like two tiny glaciers. Her eyes were vacant, her body limp and motionless, and her mouth half-open like she was screaming. It was painful to look at her like that.

As I was thinking about that, there was a rumble as one of the large ice pillars was uprooted. Josh raised it over his head with an expression that seemed to wonder if it was normal for these things to be so light, but when he finally noticed the girl, his eyes grew panicky and he tossed the ice pillar aside like an empty cardboard box.

"Lili! Hey, Lili! Are you all right?" he called out to the Abyssal girl as he toppled another pillar and kneeled beside her. He reached out a hand but stopped, hesitating like he feared she might crack like the ice when he touched her. He balled his fingers into a fist and then opened his palm again before he touched her shoulders, gently and delicately like he was handling porcelain.

Snowy shuddered at his touch and her eyes blinked in a flutter, breaking the glacier of tears in the process. She looked at the boy in front of her uncomprehendingly for a moment.

"Joshua...?"

"Yes, it's me," Josh answered and rubbed her shoulder. She must have felt so cold. "Everything is going to be all right."

She just gazed at him, her eyes wide. Then her mouth twitched and her face was overcome by despair as tears began to flow down her cheeks again.

"No... No, it won't... I killed him, Josh, I..."

"What are—?"

"I killed him!" Snowy screamed and threw off Joshua's hand, covering her face and shaking uncontrollably. "I didn't want to! I told him not to come! I didn't want to!"

"Are you talking about Leo?" The girl didn't answer, so Joshua reached out, his scale-covered hands taking the girl's into his own, and smiled. "He's all right."

Snowy looked at him like he'd just told her the sky was green.

"But... but I saw it. I hit him. I..."

"He. Is. Fine," he repeated for emphasis, trying to act calm and reassuring even though he was obviously just as upset. "He was the one who told me to come here for you."

"He... he did?"

Josh smiled.

"Yeah. He even slapped me to get the point across. It hurt like hell, too. So don't worry, he's as lively as ever."

Snowy appeared to be looking for deception in his face, but when she finally accepted his expression, her face scrunched up again and her tears flowed like rivers.

"He is... Thank the... I thought..."

"Shh, it's okay..." Josh opened his arms and embraced the shivering girl. "Everything is going to be all right. Come on, let's go back to the others."

Snowy stopped shivering. It was so abrupt Josh had to pull back and look at her to see if she lost consciousness. She didn't. She was just staring at the ground and avoiding eye contact.

"I can't. I have to go home with my brother."

Josh's eyes hardened and he put a hand under Snowy's chin to raise her face.

"Right, now that you mention it, Leo said something about your brother controlling you with that thing." He pointed at the choker on the surprised girl's neck. "Is that true?"

She tried to look away, seemingly out of reflex, but she realized Josh still had her chin in his fingers, so she reluctantly nodded.

"Y-yes."

"I don't know the details…" *he said, then added in a mutter* he thought no one could hear, *"In fact, I don't know shit…"* Then, "But can't you just remove that?"

"I can't… Not without help, but…"

Without waiting for her to finish, Joshua let go of her face and moved his hands around her neck. He tried to get his fingers under the choker, but he couldn't. It looked like a simple strip of leather at first glance, but it stuck to the girl's skin incredibly tightly, and he didn't want to exert too much force on her neck in fear of his talons puncturing her fine white skin.

"That's not how you…" She reached for the choker, but then her fingers froze the moment she realized what she was about to do. She looked into Josh's urging eyes and the two silently communicated with that one glance, as a moment later her own eyes turned resolute, and she grabbed hold of her thin yoke.

Unlike Josh, she could easily fit her fingers under the choker and it stretched to accommodate her. Josh followed her example without a moment's hesitation, and soon they both had two pairs of index and middle fingers under it. Joshua inhaled sharply and tried to smile. It was genuine, though it couldn't hide all his nervousness.

"Together?" he asked with a faint voice.

"Together," Snowy answered resolutely.

They both heaved a big breath and…

This was the moment the pain ended (or at the very least subsided), which surprised me so much it pulled me out of the Far Sight and I found myself gasping for air like a fish out of water.

"Dammit… It was just getting to the best part…" I muttered and noted with some relief that my head no longer felt heavy. When I looked down at my stomach, the icicle was nowhere to be found, and even though I couldn't see the wound due to my bloody clothes, I figured Angie must have already finished giving me her first aid.

"What was?" Judy asked, offering me a hand.

"Nothing," I answered with a shrug and accepted her gesture. "Josh and Snowy should be done soon."

As if my words were all they waited for, a pair of spirited yells rang out on the track field, followed by a noise reminiscent of crackling glass. It gradually grew louder until, at its peak, it got drowned out by an earth-shaking thunderclap that reverberated in my bones.

Then there was silence.

Well, okay, maybe not proper silence, but compared to the cacophony from before, the way the remaining ice pillars fell apart was positively soothing. Even the blizzard's winds had abated, and now that the snowstorm didn't block my vision, I was surprised to see that the ground was covered in a thick cushion of fluffy snow sparkling in the portal's light like a million tiny mirrors.

Once my eyes adjusted, I could finally recognize the forms of Josh and Snowy sitting in the middle of their own little Stonehenge (or should I call it Ice-henge?) in disrepair similar to the original's. The way Josh was propping her up told me that Snowy had lost consciousness. I was about to let out a relieved sigh and relax... when a cold voice said, "Nobody moves."

Crowey entered into the light of the portal magnified by the snow. He was no longer wearing his well-tailored suit. In fact, I couldn't tell if he was wearing any clothes at all. His legs, now digitigrade and sporting talons, were covered in a layer of thick, coarse black fur that crept up to his navel. There was no sign of his genitals, though I didn't know if it was because of the fur, or if they disappeared as part of the transformation. His forearms and hands were also covered in fur of the same colour, though not as thickly as on the legs, and he had pointed black nails on his long fingers. Rounding the look was a pair of curved goatlike horns protruding from his forehead with glowing red patterns that looked like veins on their surface. A similarly coloured tail hung behind him.

Most importantly though, he wasn't alone. One of his arms was firmly secured around the neck of the girl he was holding in front of him like a shield while the other hand was pointing its long fingers towards her temple.

"Ammy!" Angie yelled as she nocked an arrow on her nonexistent bowstring and made a drawing motion.

"Stand down, or the girl dies!" the Abyssal hissed with a fearsome intensity. Angie hesitated, but didn't let her bow down. I wondered why, but then I noticed that she was looking at me with a question in her eyes.

I clicked my tongue in frustration. It was my fault we were here. I'd told the class rep to look out for Crowey. Evidently I had tempted fate by doing so. I'd hoped he would stay out of commission a little longer after being hit by the princess's flame head-on, but that was a naïve hope.

I scowled and let go of the self-condemnation for the moment. I needed to focus. Ammy was still alive. I just had to make sure she stayed that way. I needed to get his attention.

"Hey there, Crowey!" I exclaimed jovially. The hairy demon-man locked onto me. "I don't want to alarm you or anything, but there is something on your face right around...” I told him while absentmindedly scratching my right cheek, then I feigned surprise and smiled. “Oh, right. That *is* your face.”

I could practically taste the animosity he radiated. The right side of his face was red and swollen, and the hair on the same side was burned off. It wasn't pretty, and I figured with time it was only going to get worse. Those were second- if not third-degree burns.

I raised my fingers to my mouth and uttered, “Ouch. Sorry. Too soon?”

“You insufferable cur! I will have you turned into mincemeat while you are still alive for this!” At this point he remembered where he was and he continued between clenched teeth, “But that is for later. I propose an exchange of hostages.”

“Oh, so that's what this is about...” I said with an exaggerated nod. “Sorry, but we are not handing Snowy over to you. That would defeat the whole point of this excursion.”

“I see...” The Abyssal shrugged. I wondered if he really gave up so fast or if it was a ruse. “Then I suppose I will have to make do with this girl.” He tightened his grasp on the class rep. Unable to speak, she reached up to grab hold of Crowey's arm and try to keep herself from suffocating. “I'm sure I will be able to find some use for her.”

I blinked. “You didn't just say what I think you just said, did you?”

The Abyssal only grinned at me maliciously like his threat was an amusing joke.

I sighed. I knew he was trying to rile me up, and I knew I shouldn't act based on emotional impulses. But still...

“So the negotiations have broken down. Very well. I have only four words for you.”

“Four words?”

“Arrow to the knee.”

There was absolutely no delay. Angie already had her bow drawn, and the targeting only took a split second before the arrow was already in the air. Crowey let out a surprised grunt and jumped to the side by reflex, but the arrow grazed his leg and he almost fell over.

“How dare you!” he roared as he raised a hand with a complex gesture. From the outstretched hand grew an oily black shadow that rose into the air and then streaked toward Angie like a whip.

She didn't react. Maybe she couldn't even see it.

I cursed under my breath, and before I knew it, my legs were already carrying me. Unfortunately, Angie was on my left, so I had to leap from my bad leg to reach the incoming attack. The black shadow stretched even farther and was about to reach the girl when my hand made contact with it. My fingers cut through the blackness like it was fine mist and the shadow beyond the point of contact diffused into a thick mist that disappeared in a second. There was no shockwave traveling back on the other side, yet Crowey staggered back like I'd just hit him on the head.

"Bite!" I roared the command at the girl in his arms. She stopped struggling, and then, finally understanding what I meant, sank her teeth into the Abyssal's biceps.

He let out a surprised cry and his grip on her weakened for an instant.

"Josh!" came the next roar from my mouth. Regrettably, it also came with an undignified display as my leg gave out and I fell onto the ground with a painful crash. Still, even as I fell, I could see the silver-scaled Draconian zoom in from the side like an express train and tackle the Abyssal with the force of one as well, taking them both outside the illuminated area.

"You opened your wounds again, didn't you?" my assistant asked as she tried to help me to my feet.

"Maybe, but I'll manage. Look after the class rep instead. She tumbled somewhere over there when Josh hit the bastard."

"Is he going to be all right?" This time the question came from the princess. She was trying to catch a glance at whatever battle was unfolding, but I doubted her eyes could make out anything in the darkness beyond the light of the gateway.

To be honest, I was wondering too. Josh got a sudden power-up, but he still had no idea what he was up against, and he was not formally trained. I think he mentioned he'd taken judo classes, but I doubted they applied to a fight between a dragon-hybrid and a demon. But then again...

"He's going to be fine," I said as I rose to my feet.

"Are you sure?"

"Yeah." I flashed a reassuring smile, and the princess calmed a little. I couldn't tell her the reason for my confidence, mostly because it was just something that felt right. The hero was facing off against a villain, after all his allies had exhausted themselves. This was a typical storybook ending. And if we followed that logic...

I tried to peer into the darkness, but I couldn't see a thing. I thought about moving to the edge of the illuminated area or using my Far Sight to watch, but both of those options would have left me exposed and vulnerable in case Crowey wanted to get a piece of me. Based on the sounds of it, the battle was intense. The two of them showered each other with thinly veiled insults. Though I couldn't make out anything in particular, the Abyssal was better at it. I made a mental note that if we somehow managed to survive tonight, I'd try to give Josh "combat banter" lessons so that he wouldn't embarrass himself next time.

As I thought about that, a body crashed into the snow in front of the portal. A moment later it rose into the air on a pair of batlike wings, just before the silvery shape following it could deliver a clumsy axe kick to its head. Crowey flew higher, to the point the light barely illuminated him, and he positioned himself right above the portal before he roared in frustration.

"Insolent maggots! I will kill you all!"

There was a sudden surge of magic around his body, enough to tell me he meant it. I looked over my friends and back at the flying Abyssal. While it might have sounded like an idle threat born of fury, considering the state our team was in, I could not ignore it.

I turned to the recovering class rep and hissed, "Please tell me he can't just explode us all."

She gave me a flat look and said, "I'm surprised he hasn't done so already. It must be because he wanted to avoid his sister getting caught up in the blast."

"Crap."

That changed things a bit. I straightened my back even though it hurt like hell, then raised my voice towards the flying figure.

"Are you sure you want to do that?" I tried to infuse my words with nonchalant confidence. It made him pause, so I pressed on. "You have about three minutes before your gate closes, you know?"

"Time enough!" he bellowed defiantly, and I could feel an invisible pressure weighing down on me. I slowly shook my head to dispel it and defiantly crossed my arms in front of my chest.

"Really? So you think you can kill us all before the time's up, huh? Let me propose a hypothetical scenario to you: what if you can't?" Crowey only glared at me (or I presumed he did so; it was hard to make out his face), so I continued, "Imagine that you fail. Let's say you kill us all, get rid of all the witnesses, but we struggle long enough so that the gate closes. Opening one of these takes time and effort. You can't just willy-nilly make a new one. It'll take days or even longer to arrange." I paused for effect and smiled. Of course, I had no idea if it really took that long, but I had to pretend I knew everything. "Time is key. Soon the mages will recognize how you barged in on their territory. I'm sure they aren't going to be happy about that. And it's not just them. After all, I don't think any of the powers that be would miss a chance to get their hands on a weakened Lord of the Abyss. Imagine the shame of being held hostage like that!" I theatrically scratched my chin. "But then again, being captured might not be that bad compared to what some would do to you if they learned you hurt their charges. Speaking of which…" At this point, I turned to the princess with feigned absentmindedness and asked, "What did you say about how long until your father and von Fraenir would get here?"

She gave me a blank stare, so I winked at her to get my point across. Since she still didn't answer, I pretended that she'd whispered something and exclaimed, "Thirty minutes, you say? And you called him roughly thirty minutes ago? That's great!"

"You are bluffing," the Abyssal hissed, but I could definitely hear a trace of apprehension under his anger. I'd touched a nerve.

"Maybe. But can you be sure? He could easily get here at any moment if he flew. In fact, he's a little late already." I glanced at the confused princess and flashed an amused smile. "Oh boy, imagine how mad that old guy would be if he got here and found you dead with an injured Abyssal over your corpse." I made sure I was talking loud enough so that Crowey could hear me, but for good measure, I also added, "I wouldn't want to be in the shoes of *that* guy!" in a shout.

I glanced back up and tried to look where I hoped the guy's eyes were. He wasn't moving, so I decided to push him, just a little.

"Furthermore…" I began, and that was how far I got before my instinct kicked in. Surprisingly though, it didn't make my body dodge reflexively, but instead my right hand lashed out in what felt like a cutting motion. I could feel my fingertips touch something, but I could not identify what it was. It was soft, cold, and viscous. Probably another of those black shadow whips hidden by the darkness of the sky.

Crowey roared a high-pitched scream, a mixture of anger, weariness, and despair, then he shouted, "I will remember this! You will rue the day you made an enemy of House Inanna!"

With that, his wings abruptly folded and he fell toward the ground like a rock, only for them to open at the last moment with a low whoosh and carry him through the portal. There was no effect on the gateway, no rippling or wavering. He just passed through like he'd entered a tunnel, and was gone.

"Did… did we just win?" Josh asked uncertainly.

I couldn't blame him. The way Crowey got away was really a bit anticlimactic, but no one was going to hear me complain about that.

"It seems so," the princess replied uncertainly.

I counted down from five, and once I reached zero and was sure he would not poke his head back out, I let the tension escape my shoulders.

And the strength drain from my legs, though that one wasn't on purpose. It took considerable effort, but I gritted my teeth and kept standing. I couldn't show just how weak I was yet. Not while there were onlookers around.

A quick dip into Far Sight told me that there was a small group of red dots coming our way. One of the dots I felt was certainly Brang, and he was surrounded by a couple of others. I figured those were the Fauns I bumped into when I raced past them towards the roof. They were in a cluster on my left, and my Sight told me they were standing just outside the illuminated area. I glanced over, and at first I couldn't see anything, but when I strained my eyes, I recognized a familiar haze in the not too far distance. I faced that direction and wondered whether I should call out to them.

My dilemma was solved when the haze began to move and the person at the front came into view. I long suspected that the cloud surrounding him served as some sort of magical camouflage, a theory which gained strong evidence when Brang decloaked. My companions all noticed him and scurried closer to each other in a hurry.

I looked over the imposing Faun and let out a relieved sigh. Maybe it was part of my weird affinity with language, but his posture told me he wasn't hostile, just as clearly as if he'd said so with words. I forced a weak smile and walked towards him and his men as steadily as I could manage.

"Blackcloak. Greetings," Brang spoke with a rumble. He was using English, probably for the sake of the others present.

"The same to you, general," I answered with a firm voice before I turned to the still cloaked figures behind him and nodded to them. They must have found it rude not to return the gesture, as they decloaked one by one and nodded in turn, each appearing figure drawing confused hisses from my friends in the back.

"Battle. Over?"

I cleared my throat before I answered, "[May we proceed speaking in your people's tongue?]"

My question launched another series of confused whispers, this time from both sides.

"[Aye, it would indeed make things easier for both of us,]" the Faun answered with a grin.

"[Indeed. If I may ask, how is your leg?]"

Brang's ears made a swiveling motion like he couldn't believe them, and a moment later he let out a hearty laugh.

"[To appear in such a state yet still care about the wounded pride of an old warrior speaks long volumes of thine character, young one.]"

I glanced over myself. My clothes were now encrusted with blood, and even though I tried to stand tall, my stance was unmistakably tired. I looked back up and nodded.

"[Your praise is unwarranted. I may have indeed somewhat overexerted myself, yet my injuries appear worse than they are in truth.]" Brang's lips curved in a thin smile, obviously calling my bluff, so I gestured towards the portal. "[More importantly, you might wish to consider leaving at your earliest convenience. The gate shall close soon.]"

"[Indeed.]" The Faun solemnly nodded as he looked over the gate. His eyes lingered on a point before they returned to me. "[What of the young heiress?]"

"[She-whose-name-is-Snow?]" I muttered, briefly forgetting how bad the Faun language was with nicknames. I cleared my throat and started over. "[Neige? No harm has befallen her, though I believe she is exhausted. We shall see to her recovery.]"

"[I see]." Brang nodded. "[While I do not wish to doubt thine honour, may I still ask thee to swear that she will come to no harm? It would take a great weight off this old one's heart.]"

"[Certainly. I swear with solemnity that she shall be under my protection, and that no harm or ill shall descend upon her.]"

Brang gave a satisfied grunt.

"[That shall suffice. We shall follow after our master now.]"

I was about to step out of his way, but then I remembered something and gestured for him to halt.

"[Just a moment, if you please.]"

Brang inclined his head in the affirmative, so I hurriedly (or as least as hurriedly as my injuries allowed) went over the large black carcass at the edge of the track field. The whole trip back and forth took only seconds, but I still kept an eye on the portal just to make sure I had the time.

"[Here,]" I exclaimed once I returned. "[I promised I would return this spear to you. It served me well. I wish it will continue to do so for you.]"

The Faun gingerly took the weapon out of my outstretched hand. He checked it in the light of the portal before he gave a satisfied nod. Then he planted it on the ground and leaned on his spear in a now-familiar manner while he clenched his other hand into a fist and placed it on his chest. After a moment of hesitation, the other Fauns behind him followed suit. I didn't know what the gesture precisely meant, but I figured it was something like a sign of respect.

I wasn't sure if I was supposed to return the gesture or not, and by the time I balled my fist, Brang had already let down his own. I still felt a little uncomfortable about that, but we had a time limit to think about, so I stood aside and gestured towards the portal.

Without a word, the Fauns formed an orderly line and walked towards the gateway with unhurried steps. Then, just as Brang was about to enter, he looked over his shoulder one last time and said, "[Goodbye, Leonard Blackcloak. I wish we had more time to talk.]"

"[As do I,]" I answered.

There was something strangely melancholic in his words, but by the time I mustered the strength to ask, the Fauns had marched through the portal and were gone.

PART 4

"Why do I have to carry her?" the princess complained as she stepped out of the portal connecting the Restricted Space with reality. We were still standing right in the middle of the track field, yet the sight was completely different. No scattered ice pillars, no snow, no purple moon... it was a little scary how surreal it felt for a moment, like I was so used to the extraordinary that the mundane felt strange instead.

I heaved a sigh and glanced at my companions.

"Because you are the only one who can," my assistant answered her flatly. "The others are all too tired."

"I'm tired too!" Elly cried in response, yet carried Snowy on her back all the same. Beside her, Angie was supporting Josh, who was back to normal. After the transformation wore off, he was hit by a mild case of hypothermia, so Angie was using some sort of magic on him to keep him warm. The guy was totally out of it. It made me smile sardonically, and I mentally prepared myself for a night spent explaining everything to him.

Suddenly my world began to tilt to the side, and it took me a long second to realize I was swaying, so I forcefully corrected my posture. After the crisis was over, so was the adrenaline surge, and it made me acutely aware of just how messed up I was. Everything hurt. Even parts of my body I didn't know *could* hurt were in pain. I closed my eyes and took several deep breaths to get the world to stop disappearing into a black tunnel, and when I opened them again, I found the class rep standing by my side with a solemn expression. She looked worn and ragged, her stockings torn at the knees and her face bruised, but she was as composed as ever. She'd just finished closing the gate and gestured for me to stand a couple of steps away from the rest of the group. I obliged.

"We did something outrageous today..." she whispered in a low voice.

"We sure did."

"I... For a moment I thought I was going to die. I thought we were all going to die."

"But we didn't."

"Yeah... But we could have."

"*But we didn't*," I stressed again. "We pulled through, got Snowy and Josh back, and everyone is alive. That's all that matters."

"And what about next time?" She gestured towards the unconscious form of the Abyssal girl. "They are going to try to get her back. Others will try to do it too. What are we going to do then?"

"We'll figure out something when the time comes. Let's not try to cross the bridge before we get there."

She fell silent for a moment and then muttered, "I'm not sure I will be able to think of anything."

I sighed.

"Fine, then *I* will think of something. Are you happy now?"

She looked at me like she was appraising me before her thin lips curved in a small smile.

"If it's you, I think we might be all right."

I groaned.

"Ugh... Please don't put pressure on me like that. I have enough problems already."

"And yet you keep taking more burdens upon yourself without even thinking. I wonder if—"

"Sorry for interrupting," I spoke while raising a hand, "but may I make a request?"

"Certainly. What is it?"

"Please catch me."

She gave me a weird look and was probably going to ask me something silly, like if I meant it *"right now."* By that time, my face was already approaching the ground at an alarming speed. There was a weird "Nyeh," sound that probably came from my mouth upon impact, and I could hear a series of alarmed exclamations of *"Chief!"* and *"Leo!"*

But I didn't care. I was too tired.

So I took one last breath, and for the first time in two months... I slept.

EPILOGUE

It was a dark room. Except it wasn't dark. Nor was it really a room. I had no words for *what* it was, though, so for now, it was a dark room.

In the dark room, there were four presences. They were familiar. The Boy, The Man, The Woman, and The Girl.

"It was an unexpected ending," The Boy spoke, his reserved voice soft and melodious.

"I didn't see it coming, either," The Man agreed reluctantly, as if holding the same opinion was somehow distasteful for him.

"Isn't that why this is so much fun?" The Girl chimed in with a voice reminiscent of birdsong. "Since they are free to act, you can never predict what they will do for sure!"

"True," The Boy agreed. "What was the original plan, again? The demon girl was supposed to die, wasn't she?"

"That was the first draft," The Man grunted. "And she is not a demon, she is an Abyssal."

"Insistent on terminology as always," came the playful rebuke from the soft voice of The Woman. "Nice work, ladies and gentlemen."

I stared at The Woman. She was... was it even a "she"? I presumed she was female because of the voice, but when I looked at her, I saw nothing. Well, no. It wasn't nothing. It was vast oceans of ruby under olive skies. She was immeasurable and inscrutable... but at the same time, she felt small and feminine and... familiar? Did I know her? Had I ever made acquaintances with ruby oceans?

"I must say," she spoke again, her voice full of mirth after a job well done, "I must say that it never occurred to me to have more than one free actor at the same time. Whose idea was that, anyway? It was brilliant."

The other three exchanged confused glances, or what equaled as glances between timeless black barren moons and deserts stirred by glowing sulfuric winds under eternally dark skies.

"Wasn't that your doing?" The Boy asked a touch uncertainly.

"No, I thought it was one of you. Specifically, I thought it was you, *******"

There were words spoken, except they weren't words. They were images, dreams of endless clouds raining molten silicon while majestic orbital rings turned and turned without end above them. Trying to "listen" too closely made my... something hurt. I wanted to say "head," but I wasn't sure where that was.

In the meantime, The Girl shook her head. Strange. She had one. Shouldn't I have one too?

"So it really wasn't any of you?"

"No! I tell you, we didn't add another free actor!" The Man exclaimed.

After his voice died down, there was a brief moment of deafeningly loud silence before the dark room exploded into activity.

"It's him!" The Woman yelled. "It has to be him! Quick, check the records!"

"But how? We didn't pick up anything!" The Boy complained, his voice on the edge of tears.

"It's not his style, either," The Girl mused. "He was never the type that would go around all subtle and sneaky."

"That's right," The Boy agreed. "I was looking out for burning pigs falling from the skies, so I never thought about—"

"Less talking, more working!" The Woman snapped at the others, and they reluctantly began doing... something.

I had a feeling I shouldn't linger, so I left the dark room... except I didn't. It's hard to explain, but the inside of the dark room was infinite and the outside was infinite too, and moving between one infinite and the other was... complicated.

I was moving for a while. Don't really know how long. I was in another dark room now. Or maybe it was the same one. Or maybe I was somewhere else. Or some other time. Either way, this new dark room, which was neither new, nor dark, nor a room, felt strangely comforting. I decided to stay there for the time being. Somehow I felt I deserved a break.

Why did I deserve a break again? Oh, right... I was injured. Suddenly the memories rushed back into my head, and they came with confusion, regret, and self-derision. Hindsight made all my stupid decisions show up on the canvas of my memories like they were highlighted with fluorescent markers.

First and foremost, the barrier. I came to the conclusion that I could circumvent it using the roof, and I never looked for alternatives even after it became obvious it was not a viable option.

Amelia was a geomancer. She could have easily tunneled under the barrier and let us through without a problem. Her magic could have also shifted the ground on which the glyphs were placed and disturbed the barrier that way. It was really easy to do once I pinpointed the anchors.

Then there was Angeline. She could fly. I could've sent her in to scout out the area and she could've immediately discovered the fact that the roof was warded. Furthermore, she could've carried us over the barrier one by one by flying over it. It would've taken a while and she would've been exhausted by it, but that way we could've had the element of surprise.

Moreover, while the windows were indeed warded, the walls weren't. The golem or Eleanor could've easily broken through one and created a new opening in the barrier for us. Or on the roof, they could've destroyed part of the building itself to crumble the fence posts and break the wards that way.

Speaking of the fence posts, technically they didn't even need to wait for me to get the Chimera there. They could've grabbed a Faun and used him as a battering ram. Speaking of which, why did I even bother with trying to kill the Chimera? It was a threat, but my goal was to rescue Josh and Snowy. I could've just teleported to the roof one floor at a time, and the Chimera wouldn't have been the wiser. Maybe I would've even recognized some of the aforementioned mistakes and rectified them. But no. It was more important to douse the monster in acid, and so now I was... now I was...

What happened to me? Why was I here again? I couldn't remember. Did I die? I didn't think so. I would've remembered dying. I tried to close my eyes to think, but then I wondered why I couldn't find them. I found something else, though. A red dot. A familiar red dot. I slowly reached out towards it, and before I knew it, I was sucked through another infinite space.

I was looking down from the ceiling of a room. It was a familiar room. It was my room. It had familiar people in it. There was Judy, sitting on a chair by the window, and there was Eleanor, sitting on the floor by the bed, and on the bed... I was on the bed. I was sleeping. Ah. So that's where my head was.

Still, sleeping. That sounded nice. I tried closing my eyes again, and this time it worked. Or maybe it didn't. I was back in the not-new, not-dark not-room. Then I slept. Not for long, though. Just a little. A nap, if you will. I would soon become me again—the me in that bed—but for now, I was tired. I deserved some sleep every once in a while.

So I dreamed. I dreamed of oceans of ruby. I dreamed of barren moons. I dreamed of glowing winds. I dreamed of molten rain. And finally, I dreamed of vast, immortal red suns.

And then I woke up.

But that is another story altogether.

ABOUT THE AUTHOR

Gábor Horváth is a Hungarian social worker employed in a nursery home for the elderly. He studied archaeology but, due to a financial crisis in the family, was obliged to withdraw from university and enter the workforce. Also known as Egathentale, Horváth has been writing for his own amusement ever since high school and started publishing his work online at the encouragement of friends.

Podium

DISCOVER STORIES UNBOUND

PodiumAudio.com